The NIRVANA BLUES

Also by John Nichols

Published by Ballantine Books:
THE MILAGRO BEANFIELD WAR
THE MAGIC JOURNEY
THE NIRVANA BLUES
AMERICAN BLOOD
CONJUGAL BLISS*

Other Fiction:
THE STERILE CUCKOO
THE WIZARD OF LONELINESS
A GHOST IN THE MUSIC

Nonfiction:
IF MOUNTAINS DIE (with William Davis)
THE LAST BEAUTIFUL DAYS OF AUTUMN
ON THE MESA
A FRAGILE BEAUTY
THE SKY'S THE LIMIT

*To be published by Ballantine Books in February 1995

The NIRVANA BLUES

JOHN NICHOLS

BALLANTINE BOOKS • NEW YORK

Copyright © 1981 by John Treadwell Nichols

All rights reserved under International and Pan-American Copyright Conventions, including the right to reproduce this book or portions thereof in any form. Published in the United States of America by Ballantine Books, a division of Random House, Inc., New York, and simultaneously in Canada by Random House of Canada Limited, Toronto.

Portions of this work have appeared in *TriQuarterly* (Spring, 1980), in *Taos Magazine* (Summer, 1980), and in *Voices from the Rio Grande* in slightly different form.

Grateful acknowledgment is made to Princeton University Press for permission to quote excerpts from *The I Ching or Book of Changes*, the Richard Wilhelm translation rendered into English by Cary F. Baynes. Bollingen Series XIX. Copyright 1950, © 1967 by Princeton University Press. Copyright © renewed 1977 by Princeton University Press. Reprinted by permission of Princeton University Press.

Library of Congress Catalog Card Number: 80-22376

ISBN 0-345-30465-9

This edition published by arrangement with Holt, Rinehart and Winston

Manufactured in the United States of America

First Ballantine Books Edition: May 1983

21 20 19 18 17 16 15 14 13 12

Author's Note

When I sat down to begin *The Milagro Beanfield War* in 1972, I had no idea the story would grow into a trio of books. But I soon realized I had more to say about the vision of life essayed in *Milagro*, and so I wrote *The Magic Journey*. It was a different, and very difficult, book for me: I had an ambitious, even grandiose plan at the start, but wound up, as I usually do, desperately trying to salvage a novel.

Even before *The Magic Journey* came out in 1978, I knew I would be saddled with another Chamisa County novel. I felt bad, realizing this, because I had wanted to incorporate *The Nirvana Blues'* themes, mood, and message in one, or both, of the preceding and above-mentioned books.

But my stories often sprint away from their original intentions like delinquent children, gallumph blindly into all sorts of unforeseen pitfalls, and finally, with luck, stagger to the finish line as total strangers to the original schemes that launched them.

All three novels are set in mythical Chamisa County, where the folks, the situations, and the landscapes resemble parts of northern New Mexico and southern Colorado. Should they survive, I suppose future interested persons might refer to these books as "his New Mexico Trilogy," even though the name of New Mexico never appears in any of the texts.

But that's okay by me. All I truly care about is that people realize the novels are spiritually linked: together, I believe they complete an overall picture.

An aside, here, addressed largely to my "regional" constituency, and especially to all my friends and enemies in the Taos area. Like most novelists, I often borrow physical traits or quirks or adventures of real people as the embryonic starting points for my characters and tales. Then I proceed to invent people and situations that exist solely within my works and nowhere else, hoping that these imaginary creations, by representing universal truths, will seem familiar to the reader. I have been perhaps too successful doing this, for I find that wherever I travel in northern New Mexico or southern Colorado, people are always telling me who my imaginary people are drawn from in real life. Hence I have learned that in actuality a certain character from *Milagro* was born and raised exclusively in San Luis . . . and in El Rito . . . and in Alamosa . . . and in Santa Fe . . . and in La Madera!

But I abhor the roman-à-clef and work hard to avoid that naming game. Patiently, I explain to the curious that if I get locked into dealing with an actual person I usually blow the writing, because it's very difficult for me to invent stories and adventures and dialogue when in my mind I'm dealing with a real-life human being.

So anybody who happens to pick up this book should realize that *The Nirvana Blues* is a make-believe story with invented people in it. All the usual disclaimers apply: any relationship of characters in the book to real people is absolutely unintentional. Put less officially: Please, give me a break and accept these fictional personalities as figments of my own imagination!

A final note. Occasionally I, and my editor, Marian Wood, have differences of political opinion. More than once, in fits of pique, she has angrily denounced me as a "Stalinoid!" and a "four-foot dwarf!" Nevertheless, we have managed to work together now for more than a handful of years. Marian not only salvaged my floundering career by publishing *Milagro* in 1974, but she has also been an enormously careful and encouraging arbiter of my talent ever since. She was aided and abetted, during a time in the latter seventies, by her fine former assistant, Sally MacNichol, to whom I am ever grateful for having had the courage to believe strongly in *The Magic Journey* long before it was launched.

My editor's sanity, humor, and no-nonsense approach have kept me afloat on the chaotic literary seas. I love, depend on, and am very grateful for the friendship, and the working relationship, that I share with Marian Wood.

J. N.
Taos, New Mexico
August 6, 1980

Prologue

(Our story so far)

====================

Clouds and Thunder:
The image of DIFFICULTY AT THE BEGINNING.
Thus the superior man
Brings order out of confusion.

====================

The Vietnam War was "over." Richard Nixon, ex-President of the United States, had been gently ostracized for making a mockery of his high office. All other archcriminals of the Watergate scandal had spent a few months in prison and then become millionaires from publishing their bad novels and self-seeking memoirs. Mao Tse-tung, Chou En-lai, and Ho Chi Minh were dead. Chile's experiment in democratically formulated socialism had long since gone down in Salvador Allende's fiery death and the emotional funeral of the Nobel poet, Pablo Neruda. New York Yankee owner George Steinbrenner had purchased two World Series for mucho bucks, but the Reggie Bar would never replace the beloved Baby Ruth. In Iran, the shah was beleaguered and tottering. But Israeli Zionists had no plans, as yet, for a "defensive" invasion of Russia and the United Kingdom. Notre Dame had won a national football championship. Pulp novelist Sidney Sheldon had raked in oodles of shekels. The noted evangelist Billy Graham was alive and flogging hellfire and damnation comme d'habitude. The current president's brother, Billy, was using a flagrant beerbelly and his White House connection to build on his initial million. Uganda's Idi Amin, impervious to assassination, was alive and well and hiding in Argentina, but poet John Berryman, a more effete personality, had jumped long ago, entering the legend books as one more precious aesthete down the pathetic self-destructive drain pioneered by the likes of Scott Fitzgerald, Sylvia Plath, Janis Joplin, and Elvis Presley. Alan Bakke had won his reverse discrimination case, but the Wilmington 10 had lost, of course, proving that all the regular prejudices were doing business as usual in the USA. The Ku Klux Klan was on the rise, and the Nazis had been granted a marching permit in Illinois, thanks to the American Civil Liberties Union. Heavyweight Champion Muhammad Ali was eternally young...but J. Edgar Hoover had proved to be mortal after all. California's Proposition 13 turned out to be just another

3

tax-break scam that would ultimately pass on the hurt, as always, to the marginal consumer. GM profits were up, as was inflation. Horizontal cities continued to expand outwardly, magnifying all waste, while vertical cities collapsed. China was opening up, Russia was closing down. Former LSD experimenter Baba Ram Das was now messing with Hanumans, and the dollar was taking it on the chin from the yen and the mark. The prime lending rate had just leaped over thirteen percent. Harvey Swados, Jack Benny, James Jones, and Walter Lowenfels were dead: dictators Pinochet Uguarte and Tacho Somoza were still rolling merrily along, handsomely shored up by Jimmy Carter's Human Self-Righteousness. Rhodesia was on the brink of bloodbathhood, Angola had gone to the left, Cuban troops had rallied Ethiopians against Somalia, Argentina had won soccer's World Cup, Italy's Red Brigades had executed Aldo Moro, two new popes had been crowned within a month of each other, the Baader-Meinhof leadership had "committed suicide" in their German jail cells, Canadian Prime Minister Pierre Trudeau's estranged wife Margaret was making movies, the first test-tube baby had been born, Broadway Joe Namath had hung up his gridiron cleats, thus ending yet another era, and three out of every five American black girls living in big-city housing projects had been raped at least once by the age of fifteen.

Meanwhile, back at the ranch, Willie and Tammy and Waylon and Loretta and Ronnie and Merle and Crystal continued nasaling about divorce, adultery, alcohol, loneliness, alienation, and anger. Conservationist Barry Commoner was shrill, the ghost of Rachel Carson continued to haunt all ecologists, sociologist Seymour Melman was still laying it out in no uncertain terms, the Sierra Club bewailed, Buckminster Fuller looked drawn and unhappy, Ralph Nader was extended too thinly.

Eight out of ten leading authorities on the subject said that cancer had become the USA's national disease.

America's answer to all of this was more cars, more defense spending, more McDonald's hamburgers, more leach field, open-pit, and strip mining, more highways, more pork-barrel irrigation projects, less welfare, less education, less health care, less ERA, more rape, more crime, more violence, more cops, more smog, more nuclear power, more GNP, more GSA, more

GOP. "Growth for the sake of growth," wrote Edward Abbey, "is the ideology of the cancer cell."

"Go fuck yourself, Abbey," America replied.

As always, it looked like curtains for the world.

Those people tuned in to the situation had a tendency to hit the road, leaving the stink and tension of wherever they were at in search of a Safe Haven where survival could be more than just an abrasive chore. The Land of Milk and Honey, of Amber Waves of Grain, of Purple Mountains Majestic, and of an equal opportunity for one and all had come up dismally short in the Fulfillment Sweepstakes. Instead of a nation of plump, happy, blond, blue-eyed, milk-filled rubes, the boom of post-World War II capitalism had created a nation of paranoid, dissatisfied, shrink-badgered, alienated druggies and alcoholics and Maalox mainliners, befuddled by so much angst in the midst of so much plenty, having been brainwashed all during their early lives to lust for the "American Dream" (and its inherent promise of "Security" and "Happiness"). They were honestly bewildered by the fact that somehow they couldn't grasp it.

Middle-class college-educated folks especially were in search of a guru, an identity, and a meaningful relationship . . . though their working-class counterparts, of course, were only interested in loose shoes, tight pussy, and a warm place to shit.

Hence, millions of broken-down VW buses, crammed full of iridescent pot smokers, had set to plying the nation's ample highways and byways, searching—like the fabled boll weevils of a golden yore (and lore)—for a spiritual (a psychic), an actual (a beautiful, unpolluted, laissez-faire) home.

Thus it was that throughout the seventies they made pilgrimages to Bolinas, Woodstock, Stowe, and Carmel, Kennebunkport, Austin, Mount Shasta, and Bellingham, Taos, Aspen, Sun Valley, and Jackson Hole. And last—though of course not least—they also headed for the diminutive colorful southwestern Rockies' town of Chamisaville, where three cultures—Anglo, Chicano, and Pueblo Indian—existed in "radiant harmony" in the shadow of the glorious, thirteen-thousand-foot-high Midnight Mountains, in the heart of one of the heaviest "Karmic Playgrounds" on this battered and sputtering globe.

❧

Almost a decade had gone by since electricity entered the Chamisaville Pueblo, and, thanks to the efforts of one Joseph Bonatelli, now known as the terrible Tarantula of Chamisaville, a dog-racing track and a resort development with a ninety-nine year lease had been constructed on reservation land. At the completion of this large project, the town's surviving power brokers had redoubled their efforts to exploit every last inch of that once-pastoral burg's picturesque terrain.

Another dozen motels and hotels had been added to the plethora of tourist havens that had inundated the town even before the resort and gambling complex made it onto Indian land. At the famous Cipi García Dynamite Shrine and Hot Baths, several new bathhouses and dining rooms were built to accommodate the added influx of pilgrims, thrill seekers, tourists, religious fanatics, big-game hunters, and Winnebago pilots who had flocked to the town ever since a miraculous explosion on the brink of the Great Depression had unearthed the fabled hot baths, spawned the Dynamite Shrine, and become the foundation of a tourist-oriented development that had eventually dispossessed most of the native, and largely Spanish-speaking people of Chamisaville during the American-style commitment to what amounted to cultural genocide.

In 1970, nearly forty art galleries, most of which sold western shlock, had been scoring a fortune in Chamisaville: eight years later, you could look up almost seventy galleries in the local phone book, as an accelerated middle-class in-migration occurred to completely change the sociological patterns of the once-lovely valley. The water table was down, Chamisaville's GNP was up, and monoculturality was spreading like a white fungus.

Chicanos die hard, and by the mid-seventies a few of them still populated the valley, hanging on to tiny plots and scuffling a living by the skins of their aching teeth, while praying for some kind of revolutionary rain that might bring about salvation in the face of the rapacious juggernaut overwhelming the valley, chewing it up, macadamizing its alfalfa pastures, concretizing its orchards, prefab-housing its galleries of native sunflowers, expanding its ski valley and polluting its creeks, and in general thoroughly pizzafying its ancient and powerful spiritual estate.

The odds were stacked against the locals, however. For yet one more restless, moneyed, and educated generation out there was on the prod, seeking solace in flight, searching for yet one more mecca to explore, exploit, and exhaust, before moving nervously, irritably, on.

In the thirties, Steinbeckian Okies in Guthriesque droves staggered dispiritedly from the Redwood Forests to the Gulfstream Waters. In the fifties, Kerouackian beatniks tugging on cheap Tokay behind the wheels of battered convertibles created lives that were just one endless run-on sentence after another. In the sixties, Tinkertoy revolutionaries long on rhetoric but short on historical perspective played the universities and ghettoes from coast to coast for suckers, and then burnt out early. And now, as the seventies ignominiously wound down, the privileged, ersatz revolutionary darlings of the Great White Wounded Middle Class hit the road in search of a different meaning for their comfortable, meaningless lives.

A vast army of incoherent pilgrims had descended on Chamisaville, outwardly uninterested in the town's evanescent tourist-oriented delights, but intending, rather, to "Settle Down."

Sprung from incongruous though usually middle-class origins, they filtered into diverse and unprecedented careers in their new home. Microbiology PhDs showed up driving Karmann Ghias: two weeks later, wearing bib overalls and sandals, they had become sensational potters who ran Gestalt therapy groups on the side, piloted rattletrap '52 Chevy pickups, and left town twice yearly to attend Bangkok acaleph conferences, or symposiums in Ordway, Michigan, on the life cycle of the cinnamon teal. Joycean scholars, former Ivy League professors, arrived hourly, their families crammed into Volkswagen Beetles: immediately, they invented better hydraulic log-splitters and were soon inhabiting handmade hogans, eating nothing but rose-hip tea and roasted piñon nuts, and selling firewood, mail-order, to citizens in Cleveland and New York City. Stockbrokers, eschewing messy suicides, chose instead to become plumbers and electricians in Chamisaville. High-class Saint Louis sandalmakers became waitresses at the recently constructed Cosmic Banana Café, took ballet lessons from a onetime Boston physical therapist for the mentally retarded, did yoga on the side, and were constantly canvassing town for good yogurt-starter. Migrating by the hundreds, would-be poets and novelists were soon tending bar, dealing dope, buying Safeway lettuce with foodstamps despite bitter memories of the UFWOC boycotts, working for less—in the Dynamite Fetish factory—than even the natives were willing to work for, outmuscling local teachers for Headstart jobs, or applying to CAP for rabbit-breeding project funds. And soldiers of fortune, once Ibiza bar managers or Las Vegas croupiers, who suddenly found themselves hopelessly trapped in a Chamisaville traffic jam, established photographic laboratories, organic food stores, or garages that specialized in renovating old Bugattis.

On Monday, all the fine valley carpenters, schooled in their trade for centuries, either spoke Tiwa or Spanish. Next day, half the valley's carpenters had graduated from Yale Law or Columbia Medical and were married to brilliant psychotherapists who had decided to be pregnant with a genius for nine months: together, they built their own dream houses.

Trapped in a cutthroat cash economy, old-timers, the impoverished sons and daughters and grandchildren of local residents, could no longer afford building with adobe. When finally losing their land to inflated taxes and unscrupulous developers, they moved into cheap Mutual Help–Operation Turnkey deathtraps, or bought second-hand trailers, renting hookups in Irving Newkirk's park, or in the recently established Groovy Bumpus Trailer Heaven, or in Isiah Kittridge's Trailer Towne. The newcomers, refugees from AT&T, MONY, or Merrill Lynch, Pierce, et al., had excess boodle, and immediately began building elaborate adobe houses boasting circular rooms and turrets, cupolas and bell towers, kidney-shaped patios and all-electric heating. Graduates of Exeter and Reed, Miss Hall's and Goddard, they labored night and day, side by side, constructing sixty-thousand-dollar labyrinthine mud mansions. At the halfway mark, women filed in district court to recoup their maiden names; and the couples celebrated the completion of their exotic adobe palaces by bitterly filing for divorce.

Abruptly, Chamisaville was riddled with young, separated, flatbroke couples juggling their three kids back and forth around the valley in a hurricanelike frenzy of guilt-laden activity whose logistics soon defied comprehension. Peyton Placeism reared its ugly head, as affairs between separated couples cranked up. But here again logistics were near-terminal, as ex-hubbies caretaking two kids patronized the drive-in movie with their best friend's ex-wife and her three children, while his ex-wife and her ex-spouse demolished grasshoppers at the La Tortuga Bar, trying to forget that tomorrow morning those five little monsters were slated to pulverize their own infatuation with sledgehammer blows of infantile bickering.

Deliberate instability, of course, was the name of the commercial game. Divorce is good for capitalism, which likes nothing better than an endless slew of two-house single-family arrangements: double the groceries, double the heating bills, double the automobiles, double the lawnmowers. And look at the windfall for the transportation industries—on the bus visits to Papa, on the plane trips to see Mama!

Things went from bad to worse. Unloading their gorgeous Chamisaville houses at tremendous losses, the ex-husbands and ex-wives were then nailed for income-tax evasion, slipped into dark and devious drug and alcohol addictions, got themselves mugged and raped by sullen teenagers after the Friday night boogies at the La Lomita Dance Hall, and finally gave up, leaving town, heading for Israel to commit suicide in a Golan Heights kibbutz, or hitchhiking to Alaska for pipeline jobs as dynamite blasters, earning eleven hundred a week in a forty-percent mortality rate endeavor, getting their heads straight again, cleaning up their acts, Forging a Fresh Start. They left behind, in the Chamisa Valley, a little more confusion, a slightly bigger mess, the transient, unrealized tatters of their dreams composing the flabby garbage of their brief struggle to achieve a sense of self-worth, an identity . . . Fulfillment.

Each year, each month, each week, each day, each *hour*, countless bizarre human beings drifted into Chamisaville. Many of them congregated at the Cosmic Banana, an outdoor café that sold organic alfalfa-sprout-and-avocado sandwiches. While they ate and sipped iced herbal tea at little toadstool-shaped tables, hippie clowns schooled in mime walked a tightrope three feet off the ground between two trees nearby, balancing fluorescent rubber balls on their noses. And a band, containing a sitar, a zither, and a xylophone, played combination hard rock—Elizabethan folk-song music. At night, exotic belly dancers undulated in creamy blue spotlights while diners dreamily harvested mayonnaised cutworm moths from their sandwiches, admired each other's ruby-colored urban gypsy regalia, and talked about building bubble-shaped houses out of pressurized polyurethane. Or they reminisced about peace, love, good and bad karma, yoga, UFOs, Tibet (in the Gold Old Days), Indian jewelry, *Stranger in a Strange Land*, Castaneda's Don Juan chronicles, Charlie Manson, est, far-out sex, soya bread, vitamin C, motorcycles, solar heat, and grow holes.

Somehow, word had gotten out that Chamisaville was the in place to go to for religious, spiritual, sexual, and organic-gardening kicks. And all at once it was projected hysterically—in the *Chamisaville News*, Chamber of Commerce pamphlets, radio talk shows, drunken bar conversations, laundromat bulletin-board notices, and the town council's weekly meetings—that half to three-quarters of America's hopheaded freakdom (howling, bearded, syphilitic, drug- and sex-crazed, dirty, unthrifty, unclean, unbrave, unreverent, uncourteous, unloyal, unawed, unwed, un-pilgrimlike, ungodly, and, worst of all, unrich), having declared Chamisaville "Mecca West," was planning to descend, like a plague of Afro'd and Tattoozied grasshoppers, upon the suffocating irascible burg mired indefinitely in the urine-colored clot of its own rampaging Betterment.

And descend they did in the early and middle seventies: flower children, teeny-Bs, acid heads, burly bikers, road and speed freaks, stone-cold dopers, flatulent gurus, Edgar Cayce disciples, orgone idiots, hang-glider enthusiasts, and other exotic breeds. Appearing almost out of midair, they settled into the preposterous imbroglio already berating Chamisaville's weary denizens. Suddenly, the crowded plaza seemed equally divided between bank examiners from Walla Walla, outfitted in spanking-clean blue or beige jumpsuits, and lanky zonked no-goodniks who only last week had been guzzling egg creams at Gem Spa on Saint Mark's and Second Avenue, Big Apple, USA. The hippies cruised town enfolded in cheap blankets, stars on their foreheads, and Bowie knives strapped to their belts, waiting for some kind of Cosmic Cowboy to materialize and lay a thousand peyote buttons on them. Other newcomers, looking like a cross between Dennis Hopper, Liberace, and an exploding cock pheasant, were corporate executives' sons and daughters fleeing their parents' crass materialistic lives in order to grow horse peas, blue corn, and Nubian goats, and blow their two-hundred-a-week trust-fund allowances on scads of Colombia two-toke, mean Joe greenies, yellow jackets, Lucid Lucys, and whatever else was up for grabs whenever they were up for dropping, copping, snorting, tooting, or popping.

A mimeographed newspaper, brainchild of, and financed by, various bigwigs in the Chamber of Commerce and given away from newsracks in every chamber member business, immediately appeared and hippie-baited in no uncertain terms. It called the influx "unkempt, diseased hordes" whose only reason for living was to pollute Chamisaville's crystalline creeks with their feces, corrupt its children with drugs, co-opt its sacred cultures, tear down its religious institutions, rip off the merchandise in its stores, and make all its virgins, homecoming queens, and choir singers pregnant with children who would be born on the nod and with crippling, narcotic-induced deformities.

Crime leaped: it was all blamed on the newcomers. An odd assortment of anomalies attached themselves to some of the area's less reputable buckets of blood. Bearing names like Fertile Fred, Sam the Man, Garbage Honky, Dunlop Tyres, Indian Louise, and Myrtle the Turtle, these sweat-stained counterculturists stumbled into the bars like a rainbow just released from eighteen years' solitary confinement in a federal slam, immediately ordered beers, and then, outing little tobacco pouches, commenced rolling joints.

Psychedelic communes mushroomed. There was the Bull Frog Farm in the Mota Llano foothills; the Milky Way landed right next door. Buffalo Bill's Ranch sprung up north of Vallecitos; the Purple Piglet Crash Pad materialized on Ranchitos Arriba mesa. Splashed at random across the valley were the Cosmic Consciousness, the Rainbow Village, and Garbage Honky's Castle of Earthly Delights. And the Family of God commune's chief honcho, Bill Dillinger, Esq., arrived in town lounging against the leather upholstery of a chauffeur-driven Rolls, with the intergalactically famous rock groupie, National Velvet, on his tattooed arm.

A queer commune, settled miles up Chamisaville Canyon, called itself the Duke City Streakers. A dozen men and women pitched three off-white tipis in an abandoned ravine, gobbled alfalfa-sprout-and-honey sandwiches, washed that down with kiefer and some Red Zinger tea, stripped to the buff, and started running.

Warming up with a Streak for God, they hit every Sunday service possible, from Bob Condum's evangelical whoopee-do (nailed by a girl with beautiful waist-length strawberry hair who galloped through the noxious tent just as two dozen of Bob's peroxide blond minirobed Saviourettes were garnish-eeing the weekly paychecks of a hundred destitute Pueblo natives), to the Episcopal church, where Father Dagwood Whipple was so flustered by the bearded grasshopper thundering through his service rattling a tambourine that he tripped on his robe, tumbled against the lectern, opening a thirteen-stitch forehead gash, and dropped his twelve-pound Bible into the front pew, squarely atop a wealthy parish benefactor's purple noggin.

Next, they held a Streak for Peace, synchronizing nude dashes through state and county police headquarters, the town cops' pillbox, and the National Guard armory, where several lackluster local doughboys polishing tanks whistled, cheered, clapped, and grabbed for the two buxom lasses wearing cheap Timex wristwatches and powder-pink Adidas track shoes.

The commune's third streak, heavily advertised beforehand by flyers appearing mysteriously under automobile windshield wipers one Thursday afternoon, was a Streak for Mammon. At 10:45 the next morning, little groups of Duke City Streakers, dollar bills taped across their foreheads, took coup on the First State People's Jug, blowing kisses at the electronic-eye cameras as they sped across the granite floors. Tragedy ensued as a streaker leading the demonstration galloped smack into a plate-glass door, slitting his throat from ear to ear. When the mortally wounded streaker staggered backward flapping his arms and wondering which way to aim for heaven, the bloodthirsty security guard, Tom Yard, shot him three times in the chest . . . by accident.

An ugliness settled upon the valley. Whipped up by the letters to, and editorials by, the *Chamisaville News*, disgruntled and unemployed local teen-agers joined forces with sullen high-school football players, Minute Men, Boy Scout gunnery sergeants, old "Free Lt. Calley" buffs looking for a new cause, and other hopelessly irritated and disorientated citizens—and the so-called Chicano-Hippie war began.

It was the old imperial story: a people divided easily conquered themselves. Chamisaville's power brokers settled back in their Barcaloungers, ignited cigars, and awaited a favorable outcome. A general anguish, a state of constant flux and uncertainty and confusion, could release the last remaining plots of agricultural land into the development market, while further breaking down culture, increasing commissions, and making easier the transformation of Chamisaville into just another haven for middle-class angst.

Bridges went up in flames; dynamite sticks vaporized automobiles; nude and pregnant hippie women sunning themselves by peaceful mountain hot springs were brutally raped; rude zooming jalopies ran Sunday bicyclers and joggers off the roads; bullet holes appeared in subculture business windows. Shotgun blasts riddled Chicano automobiles; tires on all sides were slashed, windshields were gratuitously broken, upholstery set on fire. Several dozen houses—commune shacks as well as three-hundred-year-old buildings continuously occupied by the same family since they were built—burned to the ground. Roving guerrilla hippie bands, emulating Clint Eastwood, crept around community outskirts where the poorest local people lived, indiscriminately slaughtering livestock in revenge for every rape, for every dynamited Volkswagen microbus. And a few more defenseless, Spanish-speaking old-timers who had inhabited the valley even before the Dynamite Shrine miracle had occurred almost fifty years ago, awoke broke, with nothing left for taxes, spiritual needs, or their grandchildren's schooling.

Quiet, religious farmers, these old pioneer people faced the Midnight Mountains bitterly asking: "Why is this shit happening to us?"

And then, finally, almost all of these old-timers disappeared. Pushed out, dislocated, replaced, railroaded into impoverished anonymity in monolithic big cities hundreds of miles away.

And with that, their mission accomplished, the hippies hit the road, took a powder, melted off into the American mainstream, trailing behind them a paraphrase of the old Kit Carson logo:

"They led the way."

🍃

By the late seventies, most of the communes had disintegrated; most of the small farms, native pastures, alfalfa fields had been absorbed in the development fold.

Still, things—to put it politely—remained in flux. In fact, during the final consolidation push, Chamisaville was so unbalanced and disoriented, people did not know if they were dreaming or awake. And a host of totally unreal events occurred, indicating that for the moment there was little surface rhyme or reason in the flow of things.

A small sand cloud, piloted by a confused trade wind, floated over the valley, depositing fine layers of grit. On the day it arrived, a galactic seer, Mojo Shir Bud, hit town, and, experimenting with astral projection, immediately went into a trance atop the plaza police pillbox, freed his soul from his body, forgot how to reel it back in on its silver cord, and keeled over dead as a doornail, becoming the first known case of "death by meditation" in the southwestern United States. Eight hours later, the town manager, Kenneth Eagleton, almost lost his own life under equally weird circumstances. Early that morning he had treated his head with a "dry look" hair spray. Around noon, when he lit a cigar after dining in the La Tortuga with a young lawyer, Bob Moose, and the mayor, Mel "Sonny" Christiansen, his hair exploded into flames, and only some fast moves by the mayor, who doused him with a pitcher of dry martinis, saved the town manager's life. Hardly had Kenneth recovered, than insult was added to injury when a lanky freak wearing a red cape and a chartreuse ski mask walked into his office and nailed him in the kisser with a lemon meringue pie.

Immediately, a rash of pie deliveries occurred.

Mayor Christiansen was leaning against a bulldozer drinking a Coors despite the boycott when he almost suffocated inside a gooey pineapple concoction that came out of nowhere. Bob Moose (the elder) was playing tennis in his backyard when a chubby figure wearing a Superman costume waddled clumsily onto the court, and, aiming for the crusty lawyer's startled face, plastered him instead in the chest with a cherry pie. Then this spastic apparition cantered blindly into the net, fell backward, scrambled on all fours off the court, and, tattered cape flapping, disappeared into some shocked hydrangeas blooming beside Bob's mansion. After that the town moneybags, the Tarantula of Chamisaville, Mr. Joseph Bonatelli himself, during a First State People's Jug board meeting, received his just dessert. A small skylight directly overhead popped open, and the old bastard looked up just in time to get hit flush in the face with an enormous banana-cream concoction, whose thick custard, driven on impact down his throat, through his stomach, and into his duodenum, almost choked him to death.

The electric co-op's tottering prexy, octogenarian Randolph Bonney, swore that the mince pie practically shoved up his nose came out of the telephone when he groggily answered it at 3:00 A.M. And the hospital's new surgical whiz, Ed Diebold, got his—blueberry, with a whipped-cream topping—in the Our Lady of the Sorrows' operating room while he had one arm halfway down Rachel Parker's throat looking for her inflamed tonsils that another doctor, by the name of Lamont, had removed twenty-six years ago.

Then, as swiftly as they had arrived, the pie throwers disappeared.

No telling what would happen next, however. Perched atop his backhoe in a traffic jam, the city road crew chief, Robert Needles, noticed a bumper sticker on the car ahead: "Honk If You Love Jesus." Well, why not? Robert honked, and the most gorgeous woman he had ever seen stormed out of the vehicle, withdrew a tiny .25 automatic from her alligator purse, and, screaming *"Who the hell do you think you're honking at?,"* let 'er rip, emptying the clip at him but doing no damage because she was so enraged she couldn't shoot straight.

No sooner had Robert dusted himself off after that queer interaction, than a suspiciously green-eyed one-eared character chugged into town behind the wheel of a 1954 VW bus crammed full of wooden crates holding a dozen naked chickens each. Parking on the plaza, he unloaded the crates, stacking them on the police-department pillbox, set up a big sign—FEATHERLESS CHICKENS, JAYBIRD NAKED, BORN PREPLUCKED, NO MESS, NO FUSS—A BUCK A BIRD—and commenced hawking his wares, explaining to curious onlookers that the birds, produced through artificial insemination, had been genetically altered, not only to eliminate plucking, but also in order that one hundred percent of the feed protein would go into making meat instead of half of it being sidetracked into the manufacturing and maintenance of feathers.

Well, what the hell? Several Spanish-speaking old-timers, who understood intimately that they needed a miracle to survive, decided to give it a shot. They took out short-term loans at the First State People's Jug, and lugged home a bunch of crates. Come time to kill the birds, they chopped off their heads, disemboweled them with quick strokes, and tossed the pre-

plucked fowl to their wives, who gaily smeared their golden
skin with lard, and, humming happily, popped them into their
ovens. In due course the family gathered expectantly for dinner.
Papá sharpened his carving knife up good, and lowered the
blade to cut a first juicy slice of bosom. But the knife skidded
off the skin, clanging against the platter. Papá shrugged, grinned
at his drooling family, and tried again . . . with the same result.
Flustered, he lightly tested the blade . . . and almost cut off a
thumb!

Returning to the table heartily bandaged, and looking a trifle
grim, the patriarch suddenly stabbed at the bird. But his steel
blade bent with a noise like a saw sproinging, failed to penetrate, and twanged away from the carcass, bouncing across the
floor. The old man grabbed the chicken, tore off a wing, and
rabidly snapped at it with his teeth, breaking his top bridge in
six places. Enraged, shaking a fist at the heavens, the old man
carried the chicken outside to the chopping block and went at
it with an ax. But the roast bird jumped away from each blow
as if it were an indestructible toy fabricated from the same
rubber used in hockey pucks.

In the end, an obvious answer presented itself. The only
thing those genetically altered, preplucked chickens were good
for was playing football.

Then the telephones rang, calling in the loans. And another
dozen marginal farmers—"Adiós, Chamisaville . . . Hello,
Denver and Los Angeles!"—bit the dust.

Lest Chamisaville's few surviving farmers grow soft living
in the lap of such industriously invented luxury, the town VISTA
volunteers came up with a plan for saving those few animals
remaining to the few ranchers remaining on the few ranches
remaining in the valley.

The problem to be solved ran as follows: Because the last
existent agricultural land was poor and overgrazed, many
ranchers often tethered animals around their houses, enabling
them to munch on the lawn and on yard weeds. Unfortunately,
numerous metallic scraps were usually scattered over these
areas—little nails, roofing tacks, and beer tab-tops. Failing to
notice the sharp bits, livestock often accidentally ingested them.
And a few animals had been lost when the shards perforated
stomach walls, causing fatal internal bleeding.

A brilliant VISTA volunteer had read somewhere that if you
forced a cow to swallow a powerful thumb-sized magnet, the

magnet would capture and hold small nails and metallic shavings until digestive acids destroyed them, thereby averting disaster.

Having convinced the CAP office that this was an indispensable program, the VISTAs were funded. They ordered five thousand magnets from a Saint Louis firm and plodded around the country convincing vestigial small farmers to shove the magnets down their animals' throats, saving the beasts from the ravages of accidentally ingested metal. Even the valley's most survival-prone old-timer, Eloy Irribarren, convinced by the VISTA lawyer, Bob Sartorisk, that his milk cow might be in danger, was persuaded to shove a magnet down his beloved Daisy's throat. His sick wife, Teresita, begged him not to do it. But Eloy owed thousands of dollars for her hospital bills, his land was threatened, he would grasp at any straw to earn a nickel, or save a cow.

As might have been foreseen, an unforeseen development occurred. The magnets created in the livestock a rabid desire for poptops, nails, thumbtacks, you name it. So that shortly after the program started, entire herds were crazed with an obsession to eat metal. Tethered close to homes, instead of grazing on weeds, lawns, or fallen apples, cows, sheep, and horses wound up browsing through bald areas for nails, drill-bit shavings, or automobile bodywork leavings. The valley's last ranchers looked on apprehensively, thankful that these valuable animals were protected by those thumb-sized magnets keeping the dangerous metals away from fragile stomach walls. Twice, Eloy Irribarren's Daisy broke out of her little corral in order to forage for tin cans, nails, and junk TV sets around the mobile homes in the Irving Newkirk Trailer Park down the road.

Almost in unison, approximately two weeks after the magnets were introduced en masse, nearly all the remaining Chamisa County livestock belonging to desperate old-timers like Telesforo Arrellano, Tuburcio Casados, and the grave-digging Vigil brothers, Anselmo and Roberto, dropped dead. Ruined beyond repair, these impoverished Chicanos sold out and slunk from the valley—dismayed, defeated, destroyed.

Two VISTAs and Chamisaville's last Chicano farmer, Eloy Irribarren, slit open Daisy's belly. They discovered that her stomach was completely engorged with, and perforated by, an enormous metallic ball resembling a porcupine or a medieval mace. Jaws agape, the volunteers stared at this lethal weapon, then apologized profusely. "Win a few, lose a few," they grinned sickly... and began talking about forming cricket-raising co-operatives with an idea toward exporting the little critters to Indonesia, where apparently they were considered a great delicacy.

But before that could happen, the VISTA program was disbanded for want of floundering Chicano farmers to eradicate.

Eloy Irribarren gathered old tires from the dump and burned his beloved cow. "And the greasy smoke, in an inky cloak, went streaking down the sky."

Other unforeseeable complications continued to run rampant. Tipped into insanity by Eloy's unsuccessful investment in the stomach-magnet program, and not wishing to be a further burden on her loving husband, Teresita Irribarren stole the last two hundred dollars from their sugar jug, and ran away from their tiny house, moving into the shabby Dynamite Shrine Motor Court to die. Eloy was frantic. He searched far and wide for Teresita, but never thought to check out so unlikely a haven as the deteriorating motel.

On her first day in exile, Teresita wandered up to the post office where she had received a letter from a famous Texas department store, pushing its Christmas sales, suggesting that she buy his-and-hers airplanes, a six-thousand-dollar mouse ranch, or music lessons with a world-renowned pianist at four grand for each half-hour shot. Unbalanced by these offers, Teresita wandered downtown to the courthouse and threatened to turn Judge Michael Cooper into a toad. Then she trudged back to the motor court and mail-ordered a single pair of pliers to pull her last tooth. Four days later she received a letter from the mail-order house asking why she wanted ten thousand pliers. Timidly approaching a lawyer, Lafe Stryzpk, Teresita asked him to explain that she only needed a single pair, which he did. A week passed, then Teresita received twenty large reinforced cardboard boxes containing ten thousand pliers. Baffled, she explained to the postmaster, Cal Spooner, that there had been a terrible mistake. In no mood for excuses, having severely sprained his back that morning lugging the boxes in off the rear dock, Cal screamed at her, saying the boxes could only go back to the mail-order house if Teresita paid the return postage, a cool three hundred dollars. Weeping, the puzzled old woman limped over to Irving Newkirk's pawnshop and unloaded her wedding ring for the required amount. But on her way back to the post office, a teen-age hoodlum snatched her purse, slugged her in the face with it, knocking out that remaining tooth, and fled. At the post office, Teresita tried to explain that chain of events to Cal Spooner. He growled, dialed the county sheriff, Eddie Semmelweis, and said, "You better come quick, Edward, I got a real lulu on my hands." Eddie started for the post office, but on his way he heard shots ring out in Irving Newkirk's café, home of Chamisaville's 110-Percent Pure-Beef Horsemeatburger. Slamming on the brakes, Eddie swerved into the café parking lot just as two men waving guns sprinted out the door looking backward as they fired at somebody inside. They galloped smack into Eddie's cruiser, which was still going about forty in a braking fishtail. Eddie jumped out, crossed himself, and ran inside, where the cook, Morty Gimbell, who had signed on with Irving during one of the emergency ambulance service's perennial collapses from lack of county funds, was sitting on the floor between the counter and the kitchen, a bullet lodged in his abdomen. "What the hell happened?" Eddie asked.

"They said I gave them lousy cheeseburgers."

Meanwhile, Teresita Irribarren had returned to her room. She lay on her bed, exhausted, listening to a KKCV news program emanating from her small electric heater. After a while, she plugged in the electric blanket and picked up a Texas country-and-western program issuing from the blanket's coils. Then she noticed somebody was selling clothes in Spanish on a program being broadcast from the light switch. Teresita shrugged and went to sleep. She thought she could hear the violin of an aged friend, Espeedie Cisneros, back in the old days, playing a faint Sunday melody, the beautiful "Vals de Entriega." And was that Juan Ortega's accordion?— but he had died three, or was it four? years earlier. His music was related to a time now characterized as "Long Ago."

Across town, Eloy Irribarren sat behind the wheel of his decrepit pickup truck, weeping quietly, exhausted from his fruitless search, and all out of money he needed to buy more gas to travel around the valley, searching for his beloved wife.

Fifteen minutes after Eddie Semmelweis put out an all-points, hoping to identify the fingerprints of the two dead gunmen who'd plugged Morty Gimbell, a Southern Pacific Gas Company odorant machine, used to scent the normally odorless gas so people could tell if their pipes were leaking, dumped fourteen times the normal amount of stink juice into Chamisaville's natural gas lines, causing utter panic. Stores, office buildings, bars, homes, and tourist traps emptied. The streets became clogged with hysterical people convinced the entire town would explode within seconds. To make matters worse, those who dialed Southern Pacific Gas Company headquarters for an explanation found themselves listening, instead, to a tape-recorded dirty joke dealing with three traveling salesmen, a farmer's daughter, and a watermelon patch, apparently the prank of a demented person who had tapped the phone lines and wired in the recording.

Next morning, Teresita Irribarren awoke at dawn, dressed, walked out her front door, and almost toppled into a six-foot-deep hole that had appeared at her cabin's front stoop during the night. She limped unhappily over to the mayor's office, and Sonny Christiansen sent Robert Needles to investigate. By the time Robert arrived, the hole was ten feet in diameter and eight feet deep. Robert contacted Jim Bob Popper, an ex-cop now head of city sanitation, asking him to dump a truckload of refuse into the Dynamite Shrine sinkhole: Jim Bob happily complied. But that first truckload of garbage vanished into the pit like a peanut disappearing into a zoo elephant. Jim Bob blinked, and called for a second dump-truck load: it also vanished. With that, Jim Bob advised Robert that they had a "live one" on their hands. And for the next eight hours the town's two garbage trucks lumbered in and out of the Dynamite Shrine courtyard, feeding that insatiable hole. By dusk it had slowed down a bit, digesting the day's garbage made by thousands of people. But next morning the hole had widened slightly, devouring Teresita's front stoop—once more she summoned the mayor.

Sonny Christiansen, Peter Moose, Ken Eagleton, Robert Needles, and Jim Bob Popper gathered at the edge of the hole, frowning. Then they sent a fleet of town and county trucks to Randolph Bonney's wrecking yard, and proceeded to dump about a hundred old rubber tires into the hole. The tires joggled, settled, and disappeared. Sonny tapped his upper lip thoughtfully with a pencil eraser, wondering, pensively, if the jig were up. Maintaining a calm exterior, however, he marshaled a group of town employees to wrestle over a few car hulks from the Bonney Junke Yarde, and the wrecks were duly toppled into the hole. They settled slowly into a foreign bubbling substance, and disappeared.

Puzzled, the men paced around the hole, squatted, and sniffed its odor, frowned concernedly, thoughtfully pinched their chins between thumb and forefinger, and stamped about on the ground at various distances from the cavity.

Then, at an impasse, and also at the end of a working day, the disaster technicians decided to close up shop and tackle the problem afresh in the morning.

That night, while Teresita Irribarren lay still listening to a babble of radio programs issuing from the light switch, the electric heater, and her electric blanket, the hole widened and her little cabin slid into it. Awake and alert, fully aware of what was happening, the old woman remained alive for several minutes at the heart of an historical darkness as profound and dismaying as that which must have captured many a dinosaur of yore. Then she was mercifully suffocated by the heavy, engulfing environment, joining eternity, becoming fossil; a slight, white memory of a different, more compassionate age.

As the seventies neared extinction, things calmed down in Chamisaville. The transition, so to speak, had completed itself. Only Eloy Irribarren, a stubborn old man, hung on to his tiny farm, which everybody but *everybody* wished to wrest from his grasp.

Beyond that, Chamisaville's agricultural heritage had finally gone the way of the dodo, and a new society reigned, teeming with adventures of a different mettle. Middle-class America ruled the picturesque valley: Progress had triumphed.

1

Saturday
Night

*Six at the top means:
One falls into the pit.*

It was a springtime Saturday night in Chamisaville. The moon over the Pueblo's sacred peak, Hija Negrita, seemed as soft as the color of a newborn colt. Stars hovered like awed fireflies above the nervous little city. Honky-tonk music from dozens of funky bars danced among the valley's myriad security lamps forever frozen at the foot of the mysterious mesa wave that unfurled from the base of the Midnight Mountains and extended its graceful, sage-flecked spume westward to the Rio Grande Gorge. North of town, the brightly lit lime-green bubble over Tennis Heaven's indoor courts glowed silkily. Into the enchanted night faintly echoed a rhythmic *thwock!* caused by rackets leisurely pummeling high-altitude balls inside that rippling diaphanous gem. A tinkle of cocktail ice sounded at the nearby open-air restaurant. The sizzling odor of charcoal-broiled steaks wafted onto the mesa. Candlelight flickered; perfume pulsed; bare and milky white shoulders gleamed. The laughter of young, tanned, and healthy couples evoked reminiscences of a nostalgic yesteryear.

A small executive jet, its green and red lights blinking lazily, landed at the airport. Greyhounds streaked around the Pueblo track: the glare of stadium lights was softened by the apple-blossom- and chamisa-scented air. Echoes from the loudspeaker carried west beyond the Ya-Ta-Hey Hotel (on the shores of man-made Bonatelli Lake): they could be faintly heard west of the North-South Highway at the renovated hot-baths complex, where late-night diners finished off their Alaskan crabs, and several bathers still cavorted in the steaming mineral pools so seductively illuminated by underwater bulbs. And strains of old-fashioned mood music issued from an orchestra plying the geriatric pilgrim crowd shuffling about the mahogany floors of the King Cole Executive Room of the Dynamite Shrine Dining Salon, above which a peculiarly insistent star twinkled like a gem born of some less than radiant, but still highly provocative, foam.

At first, that pearl-sized glow high above the hot springs

25

seemed immobile. But then it moved, casually floating through
the velvet obscurity, growing larger as it leisurely approached
the earth a half-mile west of the Dynamite Shrine complex. A
flying saucer? Chamisavillians certainly had a reputation for
spotting all kinds of distinctive UFOs. Yet nobody down below
remarked on this phenomenon. It shimmered, but not eerily;
the thing seemed almost shy, unwilling to bask in splendor.
Shape- and size-wise, as it neared the sagebrush plain, it seemed
chrysalis oblong and enclosed, and twice as large as a birchbark
canoe. The light emanating from its soft skin was dulcet, pussy-
willow calm. It settled into pungent mauve vegetation and
quivered relaxedly for a moment, then grew very still.

After a while, a human-shaped phantom seeped through the
vehicle's wall, assembled its fluffy molecules into an even
tighter form, and spent some minutes meticulously brushing
off its toga.

An angel, by God! Complete with big wings and a real-life
halo!

And in its hands? A piece of paper, upon which was written
a single name:

JOE MINIVER

On the plaza, when he descended from his dilapidated
VW bus and headed for the Hanuman Follies Benefit Dance
at the Cinema Bar above the Plaza movie theater, Joe Miniver—former ad copywriter and currently an "independent sanitation engineer"—was a nervous wreck. His life, his future,
his well-being, perhaps even his freedom (and no doubt his
sanity, not to mention his incipient stomach ulcer) were on the
line.

Just that afternoon he had committed himself, on paper, and
with three thousand dollars in earnest money, to purchasing the
last piece of virgin land in Upper Ranchitos. Picturesque, relevant, and useful, the 1.7 acres included verdant pastures, two
irrigation ditches, a host of cottonwoods and chinese elms, a few
scraggly fruit trees, a tiny old adobe ruin (inhabited by Eloy Irribarren, a crippled octogenarian), and even a hand-dug well.

Naturally, it would cost Joe an arm and half a leg, if he

managed to raise the balance due (in cash) by the scheduled closing ten days hence. Since Joe's Chamisaville arrival three years ago, land values in that part of the valley, only a mile west of the plaza, had zoomed from around four thousand to twenty thousand an acre.

"If only we had bought land and a house three years ago," Joe had recently moaned to his wife, Heidi.

"If only Santa Claus was Mongolian," she had replied, "reindeer would have it easy."

The problem, of course, was that Joe possessed not nearly enough bread to plunk down at the closing for this lovely parcel of vestigial greenery that had recently fallen, like a plump South American tapir, into the piranha-infested waters of Chamisaville's real-estate scene. And if he did not somehow accumulate the wherewithal by a week from this upcoming Monday, Joe would no doubt suffer a breakdown watching as the other valley hustlers interested in this final piece of Chamisaville's agricultural heritage maneuvered for the right to rape it loyally.

Working against Joe from the start had been his lack of access to financial muscle. In his favor, however, was Eloy Irribarren's determination to sell to the Minivers if at all possible.

Naturally, Joe had a plan. Born out of desperation, it was a long shot that spotlighted his life savings of fifteen thousand dollars, featured a reprobate East Coast pal named Peter Roth (and five pounds of uncut cocaine) due in on tonight's 2:35 A.M. Trailways bus, involved two Chamisaville buddies—Tribby Gordon and Ralph Kapansky—who'd promised to help step on, and then unload, the shit, and was, of course, a highly illegal operation.

For many Americans of Joe's background, education, and aspirations, such a plan would have been a routine adventure. Joe, however, had never done anything illegal. On top of that, he was terrified of drugs, drug people, drug transactions, and drug culture. His wife enjoyed an occasional joint. And Joe had even toked up on occasion. But he absolutely prohibited Heidi from growing the stuff at home in clay pots on their window ledges. And he had always insisted that her household stash never exceed the quantities that could push a conviction out of the misdemeanor into the felony range.

Still, these days, how was a fellow to purchase some land for the benefit and heritage of his family, let alone build a comfortable house to go on it? Inflation of fifteen percent, and interest rates in double figures on home-loan mortgages that were nearly impossible to come by anyway in the tight money market, had made it all but impossible for folks in Joe and Heidi's middle-class income bracket to score a home through hard work and conscientious parsimony.

Never a whiz at figures, or at the economic legerdemain necessary to manipulate capitalism into a benevolent financial overextension guaranteeing all the amenities America had to offer, Joe had, for the past month, been boggled by the complexities involved in finagling for Eloy's pretty acreage. The old man himself had no desire to sell. Cantankerous, clever, and proud, he was an anachronism, a lost soul, the final human being of his race and cultural line afloat in the valley. During the last few years, as he stubbornly held out against the myriad interests grasping for his little piece of property, Eloy had become a legend in his own time:

Eloy Irribarren, irascible old coot and tenacious SOB—the Last Chicano.

Like a fanatical dervish, Eloy had begged, borrowed (and many said stolen) to save his place, pay for his dying wife Teresita's final illness, and hire lawyers to tangle with the banks, loan sharks, realtors, bill collectors, and other assorted thugs interested in his terrain. Only recently, a week after his wife's funeral, had it become clear to Eloy that the jig was up. He had signed too many promissories, itemized fees, and loan agreements to stall any further. The best he could hope for, once the vieja had been interred, was to avoid foreclosure by selling out quickly to someone who might treasure the land in its native state, simple and green and agricultural, the only monument to Eloy's life and beliefs, the only true reflection of his soul.

Joe had never really sorted out the complexities. He knew only that unless Eloy could sell high and fast, the land would be auctioned off among a variety of creditors maneuvering demoniacally to grab it whole, leaving Eloy broke and homeless into the bargain. Ideally, the old man hoped for a rich hippie who might care for the land while providing Eloy with enough cash to pay off his tangled web of debts and survive on until he died. Unfortunately, Eloy owed outright at least forty-five Gs. And he hoped for another twenty grand to see him through his final years. But few who might have had sympathy for his land could command that kind of cash. And cash was what Eloy needed fast, if he were to have even an outside shot at turning the place over to a caretaker with half a soul, instead of to the commercial institutions intent upon its instant pizzafication.

Joe had dreams of being that caretaker with a soul. Sometimes, thinking about owning that land, he had tingled with an excitement that left him almost faint. He had rich fantasies of going out and possessing the land. He would quarter it, walk all over it, smell it, touch the bark of *his* trees, ladle up a cup of water from *his* well, lie in the back field's brown grass soaking up the solar bennies refracting down through *his own* little patch of pristine atmosphere! At three o'clock in the morning after the closing he had plans to tackle Heidi in the exact center of the little back field beneath the pungent nighttime sparkle of high mesa stars and drill her like a mad wildcatter on the oil-rich flatlands of Odessa! Their precious land, their Future, their shot at a Real Start, their commitment to a Time, to a Place, and to a Way of Life. Roots! he would think, tickled crimson by the concept. At last they had decided on *Roots*!

"Shazaam!"

Joe tried to calm his terror by gleefully flexing his biceps as he crossed the street, pretending to feel more athletic, young, and hopeful than he had in ages. Look at me, everybody: life is a bowl of cherries! He even imitated a prance like a high-energy syndicated stud on the old Kentucky Blue eager for action. After all, at thirty-eight he still weighed 170, same as in his college playing days in the late fifties and early sixties, when he had lettered in football, hockey, and track. Granted, a few infirmities had forged irritating toeholds: asthma, varicose veins, impacted wisdom teeth, arthritic knees (ruptured minisca, shorn ligaments), and a collapsing mitral valve which created a systolic click contributing to a fibrillation-prone ticker that often really kayoed him with frightening tachycardia attacks.

But tonight—ah, tonight he would be a pistol in search of a celebration to mark the beginning of Joe and Heidi Miniver's existence as real live grown-ups in the Actual World. After all, he had made the commitment, he had taken the risk to grab their future in the form of Eloy Irribarren's little piece of earthen nirvana. By this time next week, if nothing went wrong, they'd be close to sitting pretty. And the summer would lie before them like a wide, golden welcome mat, gleaming with promise. Badly in need of R&R from a collapsing marriage, Peter Roth had plans (once their dope deal had gone down) to stay on, drinking Wild Turkey bourbon, fly casting for trout, and helping to build the Minivers' spectacular adobe and beer-can solar-heated castle.

If everything went all right. . . .

Joe had a spasm. Apprehension had him gasping faintly, but he couldn't remember if he had just taken an Aminodur for his asthma, or not. Terrified of ODing, he opted against a pill now. Other people popped pills like candy, they had no qualms about swallowing two Valiums, a Percodan, and a handful of aspirin, then tooting a couple of lines while downing a few drinks and smoking a pack of cigarettes. Then they popped a little Sominex to help them drift off. Joe, on the other hand, had never been able to take three aspirin for a bad headache, fearing the third pill might tip the scales, dumping him into insanity, or maybe death.

Back in the Manhattan sixties, Heidi had tried luring him up to Millbrook, where they could have dropped acid under controlled circumstances with Timothy Leary and Richard Alpert. Joe had looked at her aghast until she quit asking. Why, his first *joint* had been a major, and almost fatal, experience! Eventually, of course, he had learned to smoke. But Heidi always scored the grass: Joe had never had a stomach for illegal machinations. If one undercover police agent and ten thousand junkie freaks pushing weed had been patrolling Saint Mark's Place looking to unload their wares, inevitably Joe would have propositioned the narc for a lid of Colombian two-toke. Hence, he was in the curious position, in modern America, of never having scored anything heavier than a bottle of five-hundred-milligram penicillin pills—for an abscessed tooth three years ago!

But tonight Peter Roth was arriving in town accompanied by five pounds of pure cocaine he had somehow materialized thanks to Joe's twelve thousand clams. And Joe's share of the potential loot, providing he did not die of some myocardial infarction triggered by his shot-nerves arrhythmia in the interim, would be close to $60,000—the asking price of Eloy Irribarren's land!

Joe gulped, shivered, and inhaled deeply. Forging exuberance to prove he was not scared stiff, he took the stairs leading up to the bar two at a time, wanting to call out hysterically as he did so:

Look, Ma—no hands!

&

　　Behind a desk at the top of the stairs sat Nancy Ryan. She accepted Joe's five dollars and stamped his wrist with fluorescent ink. "Hi ho, Nancy," Joe piped a trifle too nonchalantly. "How they hangin'?" For over a year, now, he had harbored enough of a low-key secret letch for her to make him self-conscious in her presence.

　　"Hi ho yourself." Nancy gave him a lazy glance—she always seemed stoned—and smiled. Her teeth flashed ultrawhite, and her eyes—her entire face—lit up as if by magic. Her black hair, cut short, shone iridescently—the metaphor that applied was "like raven feathers." Her glowing eyes were dark, large, hypnotizing. When happy, they conveyed an inordinate luster. A nose like any other nose, lips like any other lips, and a chin like any other chin completed her features. Yet the radiance that face could project had always intrigued Joe. If tired, or merely disinterested, Nancy lost it all, becoming just another everyday, middle-American once-upon-a-prom-girl in her mid-thirties. Joe had never understood how somebody so outwardly ordinary could be that provocative.

　　In response to Joe's somewhat manic grin, she added, "What kind of a canary did you just swallow?"

　　"Big one. Maybe—" Joe pantomimed patting a full belly. But the pat reminded his stomach that it was queasy. "I made an offer on that land today. If nothing goes wrong with the deal, I hope I can entice you and, if you're still on speaking terms, Randall over with all the beer you can drink to help us build the palatial manse this summer. Do leave Sasha at home, though."

　　Sasha was the nasty little monkey perched on Nancy's shoulder, no doubt an added tout for the Hanuman Follies. Whenever Joe's eight-year-old daughter, Heather, happened to be at Nancy's house playing with her son, Bradley, the monkey attacked her. Joe's eleven-year-old, Michael, had threatened to murder Sasha with his BB gun ever since the bald little gnome (Sasha) had pissed in some Kool-Aid Michael had been drinking, and then stolen his (Michael's) baseball mitt and hung it way out of reach in the highest branch of an enormous cottonwood tree, where it remained to this day, two and a half years later, a perpetual reminder of simian perfidy to Michael whenever he biked past the Ryan house in the Perry Kahn Subdivision #4.

Joe and Heidi had emphatically nixed their son's drastic solution to Sasha's delinquencies. After all, Nancy Ryan and Randall Tucker (from whom she had recently split) were members of the Simian Foundation, the group sponsoring this evening's shindig: that is, they worshiped a monkey god.

Nancy fluttered her sexy eyes. "What will it cost you, eventually? The land."

"Oh come on," Joe joshed uncomfortably. "You're the secretary of the SF, and you know as well as I do that Nikita Smatterling has repeatedly approached Eloy Irribarren about buying his land for the foundation's mini-ashram and monkey temple."

Dropping her head back, Nancy viewed Joe bemusedly. "I was just curious," she murmured. "What brings you to the Hanuman Follies, by the way? I never knew you had a spiritual bent."

"Oh, you know . . ." Joe's eyes wandered past Nancy to tables where monkey gizmos—Hanuman T-shirts, rubber monkey masks, Curious George children's books, cheerful little stuffed animals, records of the soundtrack from *King Kong*, and other assorted simianalia—were on sale. "It always pays to know what the opposition is up to," he joked lamely.

Actually, he had come to rendezvous with Tribby Gordon and Ralph Kapansky, his cohorts in crime. They had planned, officially, a Sunday meeting up in Tribby's airplane to test and cut and package the coke, but Joe feared no one had taken that plan seriously. Everybody except himself was so blasé: they acted as if the adventure were a routine transaction—aboveboard, boring, even trite. Joe, on the other hand, had staggered through the last two weeks almost paralyzed by visions of holocaust. In prison for life, he saw himself raped nightly by burly ex-Hell's Angels covered with grotesque tattoos who poked homemade switchblades into his buttocks as they cornholed him. Meanwhile, outside the impregnable slammer, Heidi abandoned the kids and ran away with a Princetonian geek who feathered his hair and wore white turtleneck jerseys and Bostonian loafers. Michael immediately turned to a life of pornography and crime, beginning as the prey of Times Square chickenhawks, and ending up as the leader of a Mafia-type cult that did cow mutilations for hire for rich hippie voodoo freaks. Heather would either become a gutter rat who loved gang-bangs, or a Massachusetts cod-catching Moonie fisherperson slated to die in a shooting war with Gloucester rednecks.

To change the subject, he asked, "What do you guys hear about the statue?"

The statue, a large and costly marble Hanuman idol commissioned by the Simian Foundation, had recently made its way across the seven seas from India to New York City. Right now (if Chamisaville gossip this past week was to be believed), the Hanuman was on its way west, and slated to arrive in town in time for a planned unveiling on Thursday, a gala event the funds for which were being raised right here, tonight, in the loudly rocking Cinema Bar.

Nancy said, "Apparently, they picked it up in a U-Haul at the docks today and they're on the way."

"Who's 'they'?"

"Baba Ram Bang, of course. And Iréné Papadraxis. And—"

Wait a minute. Who is Baba Ram Bang? Who is Iréné Papadraxis?"

"Baba Ram Bang is our guru. You should know that. The leader of the International Simians. He's this beautiful tubby little old man to whom we all look for spiritual guidance."

"And this—what's her name?—Papadipoulis?"

"Papadraxis. Surely you've heard of her. She's a Hungarian refugee and a former fashion model who's become a very famous magazine writer. She's doing a book on this whole thing. It's going to be serialized in *New Age* and *Ms*. Nikita has already contracted with a publisher to do a book on the saga of the Hanuman. We've actually paid for it with the advance."

"So she's riding across country in a U-Haul with a hundred year-old guru and a marble statue?"

"Plus the photographers, Rama and Shanti Unfug. And their little girl, Om. Surely you know them? They live in that big house next door to Eloy Irribarren's land."

"You mean Gail Furphy and Billy Unfug?"

"Recently they changed names. They flew over to India with Nikita last year and photographed the entire progress of the idol. They even came back on the boat with it."

"Sounds like quite a conglomeration of people in that U-Haul."

Nancy smiled. On her shoulder, Sasha bared his yellow teeth, in either a grin or a spontaneous death threat, then puckered his lips as if to obscenely kiss Joe, and gave a desultory flog to his little log. He was a ratty, half-bald, jaundiced beast with big eyes, small ears, a long tail, and tiny, wrinkled, very precise hands.

Although his children had visited there often, Joe had never actually been to the Ryan digs. Yet judging from Heather and Michael's stories, Sasha ruled that roost with imaginative terror. One day, Michael reported, when he lifted the toilet lid to pee, the dripping-wet monkey—who must have been hiding for hours awaiting a sucker—had leaped out at him, cackling, and damn near frightened him to death. Another time (according to Heather) the furry little fiend had eaten an entire box of Bradley's Crayolas. "And he didn't even puke!"

"But he shit a rainbow," Michael felt compelled to add.

"Fluff Dimaggio and Wilkerson Busbee are also with them." Nancy spoke lazily, oozing soporific sexy vibes.

Joe rolled his eyes dramatically: "Oy vay." Fluff, a former Seattle junkie refugee from the Boeing factory and currently a born-again Hanuman freak, played bass in Joe's ragtag rock band whenever they could get a gig. Wilkerson Busbee, another guiding light of the Simian Foundation's Chamisaville branch, was a successful local hippie entrepreneur, who controlled, among other things, a Winnebago dealership, a log-home-and-plywood-tipi franchise, an herbal tea company, a head shop (Tibet, Ltd.), and the Blue Star Taxi Service.

"They're planning to drive day and night," Nancy said. "They should be here by Tuesday."

"Well, I certainly wish 'em good luck." Joe waved stupidly back at her as he veered past the monkey paraphernalia into the bar. Sasha grimaced mordantly, then winked and sneered. Nancy cocked her head provocatively and called after him:

"Enjoy yourself!"

◆§

In the crowded and noisy bar, a band wearing EAT ME T-shirts was playing a song called "Why Don't We Do It in the Road?" The lead singer, Jeff Orbison, another Hanuman-nik, did landscaping for the Ragtime Flowershop in town, an operation launched recently by a young Bostonian, Gil Forrester, who had dropped out of law school to seek his fortune in less hyper environs. Last year, in a mountaintop Zen ceremony, Jeff had married Heidi Miniver's good friend, Suki Terrell, a petite girl with soft walnut-colored hair who had done some time at a Zen retreat near San Francisco called Tassajara. Only a month ago, in need of more space (both inner and outer), Suki had divorced Jeff, and he was floundering, planting boxwoods and marigolds by day, singing and boozing himself into a trenchant stupor every night. After a brief lesbian fling with Gil Forrester's estranged old lady, Adele, Suki could now be seen around town on the back of Randall Tucker's motorcycle.

The incestuous interrelationships among his friends and acquaintances never failed to amaze Joe. It seemed as if everybody (except him and Heidi) had at one time or another screwed everybody else. Often Joe hungered longingly for a part in the apparently easy sexual theater they were all engaged in. At other times, finding their nonchalant copulations horrendously tawdry, he was proud of himself and Heidi and their coherent and loving little family with its firm moral and ethical foundation. Not for them the bizarre shenanigans of Chamisaville's screwing-pool denizens!

Casting a nervous glance around the crowded bar, Joe ascertained that he knew at least half the people there. Starting with Skipper Nuzum, the decadent young securities whiz from Los Angeles—he owned this bar and the movie theater. Skipper was married to an eye-catching lady named Natalie Gandolf; she claimed to have been Cherokee in her previous life and kept a pet llama on their estate. Skipper himself, a large, flabby, sensitive, and educated gangster-poet with pitch-black hair, hangdog eyes, and a raggedy 1890s moustache that appeared always to be caked with molasses and dead flies, had flair. He wore leather vests (his wife, a Sumi vegetarian as well as a monkey disciple, wouldn't don anything made from animals), magenta silk shirts with mother-of-pearl buttons, and pre-faded flarecuffed jeans above polished J. C. Penney's work boots.

Tonight, Skipper was seated over at a table with one of his primary henchmen, Cobey Dallas, the Iowa farm boy to whom he leased both the theater and the cantina operations. Next to Cobey sat a lesser flunky—a ticket taker, an all-around troubleshooter and sometime accountant: Roger Petrie. A tiny, effeminate, Harvard-educated economist, Roger drove a repainted hearse, and his various uniforms invariably included black, long-sleeved turtleneck jerseys, a slim silver cross on a fragile silver chain, and scads of turquoise bracelets.

Cobey, an alcoholic Tiparillo-smoking entrepreneur, would have denied he had an anthropology master's from Kansas if anyone asked him. He saw himself as a cross between a Runyonesque Nathan Detroit and P. T. Barnum. A high-strung, inordinately intelligent huckster with aesthetic sensibilities, he perused T. S. Eliot and Richard Eberhart in his spare time and dreamed of somehow becoming a millionaire before he reached thirty. He wore a beret indoors and out, subscribed to *The Wall Street Journal*, and jogged seven miles a day. Annie, his wife, had a radio talk show—"The Chamisaville Forum"—on which she interviewed local culture heroes three times weekly.

Joe also happened to know that Cobey Dallas was trying hard to raise cash to buy Eloy Irribarren's land. In between Jeff Orbison, Adele Forrester, and Randall Tucker, Suki Terrell had had a brief secret fling with Cobey, and she had told Heidi that Cobey was embezzling from Skipper Nuzum, in hopes of amassing the bread to buy Eloy's virginal diminutive spread.

Actually, according to Joe's pal Tribby Gordon—the lawyer in charge of Cobey's (though not Skipper's) affairs (of a financial nature)—Cobey's accountant, Roger Petrie, was doing the embezzling. "In return," Tribby told Joe one day out on the Rio Puerco while they cast for trout, "Cobey has promised to deed to Roger the water rights once he gets the land." And the water rights, according to Tribby, would probably go, if sold to a new motel, hotel, or other business trying to hook up to town water, for at least ten thousand bucks an acre-foot.

Cobey himself made no bones about how he planned to develop that land. On the back acre he would build a Born-Again Laundromat, where Jesus freaks and other spiritual groupies could wash their clothes with vegetarian or herbal soaps, one-hundred-percent pure well water (guaranteed from the fourth aquifer), and completely biodegradable bleaches and other laundering agents.

In the front part of the property he hoped to construct an alligator wrestling pen and pool. The snouts of the small gators would be bound with leather belts so nobody could be bitten. And the prize to any tourist capable of pinning one of the beasts would be a miniature Bible, or a plastic cross that glowed in the dark, or a fluorescent portrait of Jesus. The theme, in keeping with the spiritual nature of his complex, would be "Wrestle a Gator for Christ."

One thing Cobey did not know: Roger Petrie was a double agent. He reported the embezzlements in detail to Skipper Nuzum as they occurred, and for a substantial remuneration into the bargain. In this way Skipper kept tabs on his financial empire. At least, so said Tribby Gordon.

According to Tribby, "Skipper figures he'll give Cobey enough rope to hang himself. He may even let it reach the point where Cobey buys Eloy's land. Then he'll lower the boom, file charges, send Cobey to jail, and grab the land as legal restitution for some of his losses."

"What does Skipper want with more land?" Joe had asked. "A million acres already isn't enough?"

"He couldn't care less. But Natalie wants it for the Simian Foundation: she's working hand in hand with Nikita Smatterling and Nancy Ryan to obtain it for the temple site."

Meantime, if what Heidi had gathered from Roger Petrie's ex-girl friend, Bliss Chamberlain, could be trusted, Roger himself had his eye on Eloy's property. He knew Skipper was going to lower the boom on Cobey once Cobey had the land, but he figured he could manipulate some money out of the embezzlements into his own bank account. More importantly, having separated the water rights from the land before Skipper's agents could ram the case into (let alone through) a court, he would sell them quickly to a buyer who'd already made a large downpayment (held in escrow) to assure them for himself once the deal went down. With all that instant cash, Roger would be in a position to buy out Eloy, if the old geezer was still involved, or to wield a heavy hand in any auction that occurred.

The buyer who had already made a substantial downpayment on the water rights was Eloy's flamboyant lawyer, Scott Harrison. Scott expected that he himself would wind up in control of the property, on which he planned to build a tax-exempt Universal Life Church, a tennis court, and a swimming pool. His major goal in life, according to his sometime mistress, Annie Dallas (who'd confided this to her good friend, the Cinema Bar waitress Diana Clayman), was to salvage Eloy's beautiful property (in Eloy's name) from the school of sharks intent upon either its ownership or dismemberment, and then grab it himself as payment for his services. He foresaw complications, however, sensing that Skipper Nuzum's convoluted procedures represented significant dangers to his own plotting. Hence he thought to tilt the scales in his favor by sewing up those gallivanting water rights if at all possible, even if, in the end, it turned out they could not be legally separated from the terrain in the manner he'd chosen.

Through all this, Joe's major ace in the hole was the fact that Eloy liked him and would try everything under the sun to see that he wound up with the property.

Joe had started toward the Nuzum-Dallas-Petrie table when Diana Clayman slipped an arm around his waist, giving him a squeeze. "What are you up to, Joe? You look terrible."

His heart deep-dived, his crotch prickled. Diana was twenty-five, a classics scholar from McGill, born and bred and bored stiff in Grosse Pointe, Michigan. She loved the ancient Greeks, gave poetry readings with one of the groups in town, roomed with two idiotic teen-age female junkies when not visiting her occasional boyfriend (a harbinger of malice known simply as Angel Guts), and always had car trouble. Her raven hair and snow-white skin aroused him. Her heroes were Robert Graves, Antonin Artaud, and Baudelaire. Joe had met her several times in bars accompanied by her menacing "Apache" with his horribly pitted skin. This sidekick posed as a silversmith: he refused to talk with white men except when drug deals were going down. Diana had enormous dark eyes and an altogether melancholy world-weary mien until she smiled. Then her face bloomed, her mouth radiated radiance.

"I feel okay," Joe said. "I mean, my kids are healthy, I just put some earnest money on a beautiful piece of land, and if everything goes without a hitch, we're gonna build a house this summer. It's all falling together. I'm gonna be a secure and happy man."

"Oh, you poor thing." Stretching, she brushed her lips against his cheek, touching almost hidden, yet impossibly full breasts against his arm. "You're gonna fit into a slot, Joe, it's so sad. You used to be beautiful."

For a second their eyes met—hers were so dark. Intimations of beautiful tragedy . . . smoldering sexuality. Her fingers fluttered off his shoulder . . . and then she was by him, carting two Coors, six Dos Equis, and a bourbon old-fashioned to a corner table.

Joe tried to suck in a deep breath without actually sucking in a deep breath: the air was so full of smoke that an honest-to-goodness inhalation probably would have triggered his asthma. Nervously, he cast about for Tribby and Ralph. Everywhere bodies cavorted, undulated, danced, and jabbered. Half the crowd was in costume. People wore outsized rubber ears, gorilla masks, Hanuman T-shirts. Several couples sported head-to-toe brown fur costumes made from dyed coyote pelts. Pink helium balloons, monkey faces painted on their silky rubber skins, bobbed and popped loudly. A dwarf, Ephraim Bonatelli, the wayward son of Chamisaville's Godfather, Joseph Bonatelli, was drunk and obnoxious as usual. At the top of his voice, as he toddled about snapping his teeth against the numerous plump rumps at his eye-level, Ephraim sang, "'Abadabadabadabadabadabadaba' said the monkey to the chimp!"

Joe spotted Eloy Irribarren. Across the room, seated at the bar, he wore an old straw cowboy hat, a faded dungaree jacket, overalls, and heel-less cowboy boots. One hand self-consciously clasped a beer; in his lap he guarded a small pile of benefit goodies—a rubber monkey mask, a Hanuman T-shirt, and a Speak No Evil, See No Evil, Hear No Evil statuette. The old man looked bewildered.

Joe took a step in Eloy's direction. But his progress was immediately arrested by the great man himself, Nikita Smatterling, a middle-aged (but svelte) Jungian analyst who dabbled, on the side, in everything from biofeedback and LSD therapy to aura adjusting and group gropes. He was the brains behind the local Hanuman craze, the founder of the Simian Foundation, and definitely a spiritual hombre for all seasons. The door to his eclectic vision and healing powers was always open: night and day disciples gathered at his feet. With some he drew mandalas; with others he rapped on Edgar Cayce and performed feats of psychic yoga. On Sunday mornings his students gathered for Sufi dancing. His Moslem name was Jamal Marrakesh. He had a tanned and powerfully wrinkled face with an iron jaw and startlingly vivid pale blue eyes. His smile could reduce granite to oily puddles; his white hair was the valley's most perfectly "leonine mane." *Handsome* was hardly the word to describe his fantastic stage presence. Had he chosen an acting career instead of this spiritual charlatanism, the man undoubtedly would have been typecast as God.

Rarely had he spoken with Joe. Tonight, however, he threw his arm around the budding convict's shoulders. "Joseph, m'boy, I want you to meet my good friend, Paula Husky."

A hefty, nubile girl with short-cropped blond hair and a peppy cornfed-healthy face glacéed with sleazy makeup, Paula couldn't have been more than sixteen. A transparent peach-colored rayon blouse and an even skimpier aqua miniskirt left her body definitely out there, in the spotlight, On a Platter. Drunk as a coot, she giggled, having a wonderful time.

"I just jumped the carnival," she explained. "I told Charley to shove it, and split. All I've got are these clothes on my back, but look at my luck—I've just met this adorable man. Christ I dig monkeys!"

This Adorable Man, Joe knew, had an official girl friend— Belle London (rumored to be the great-granddaughter of the writer Jack London)—and three children: Sanji, Tofu, and little Siddhartha. They all lived in a homemade mansion on a hillside north of town. After two years shrinking Navajos in Arizona, and twelve months counseling archcriminals in Soledad, Nikita had shown up in Chamisaville nine years ago to work construction jobs at the Pueblo's abuilding racetrack and Ya-Ta-Hey resort compound: immediately, he had commenced plying his maverick spirituality. Beige turtleneck jerseys under tweed sportcoats were his uniform. That, or fluffy-sleeved Pakistani blouses unbuttoned to the navel, exposing the mezuzah on a silver chain against his macho hairy chest. His public personality oozed sympathetic, friendly vibes. Yet Joe had never been much attracted either to the myth or to the man. He thought of Nikita, rather, as a spiritual bigwig on a cosmic power-trip who liked to get laid a lot.

To boot, he drove a pink Lamborghini.

"Joe's one of our little town's most highly respected sanitation engineers," Nikita boomed.

"Oh gosh," Paula chirped. "You mean you're the guy who's gonna try to pull off that big dope deal that starts tonight?"

Joe assumed he had heard incorrectly, excused himself, and, fending off the frenetic bodies, plowed through the crowd until he reached Eloy. "Mr. Irribarren," he gasped breathlessly, "what are you doing here?"

Eloy shrugged. "I don't know. They invited me."

A short, simple man in his mid-eighties, Eloy had a weather-beaten wrinkled face and arctic green eyes. His full head of neatly trimmed white hair was slightly mussed when he removed his hat; little wings fluffed out all over. A thin moustache gave his cheerful face a macho tilt. Wide shoulders and almost simian arms, a barrel chest, and small powerful hands completed the picture. A rope instead of a belt held up his loose-fitting dungarees.

Joe grimaced. "It's too loud. All these people are crazy."

Eloy sipped from his beer. "Every ten minutes somebody comes up to me and wants to buy my land. I'm a very popular man. The zopilotes are circling."

Joe asked, "What are those things in your lap?"

"Compliments of the house. That lady at the door gave them to me."

"What are you gonna do with them?"

Eloy smiled impishly. "I think I'm going to don this T-shirt and gorilla mask and rob the First State People's Jug of enough money to pay off all my debts."

"Ha ha."

"Don't 'ha ha' me, muchacho. If I want to, I can do it."

Alarmed, Joe said, "Wait a minute. What about me?"

"If I haven't robbed the bank by Monday a week from now, and you come up with the cash, it's all yours. If you don't come up with the cash, and I haven't otherwise solved my problems by then, I think I will rob the bank. It's worth a shot, anyway. We could even rob it together."

"But sir, you can't be serious." Here it comes, Joe thought frantically. I risk my life to raise sixty thousand dollars, but the day of the closing, Eloy waltzes into the damn bank wearing a rubber gorilla mask and a Hanuman T-shirt and gets himself blown away by Tom Yard (the EAT ME drummer moonlighting as a bank dick during daylight hours), and I'm left holding a bag full of money while the banks, the creditors, the Scott Harrisons, the Skipper Nuzums, the Cobey Dallases, and the Nikita Smatterlings carve it into little pieces.

"I'll tell you something," Eloy said. "In all my life I never would have thought to rob a bank. I obeyed all the laws. I trusted people and treated them like human beings. In return they annihilated my neighbors with every legal and illegal trick in the book. They cheated me in every money deal I ever made.

They robbed me of my insurance money, my Medicare, my social security when Teresa was dying. They have tried to dispossess me at every turn. So sometimes I wake up gloomy and feel like robbing their bank. I been too gentle my first eighty-three years."

Joe said, "Look, don't worry, I'll have the money."

"How will you get it? You found a genie in an old well who grants wishes?"

"My grandmother," Joe mumbled, lying through his teeth. "Her estate—"

"You're lying through your teeth."

"Hey, I'll get it, don't worry." A monkey mask hovered near Joe's shoulder—all ears? What in God's name had driven him over to Eloy Irribarren in the first place?

But the monkey mask saved him. It said, "Ho ming no kum chowki."

"Oh, it's you, Egon."

Egon Braithwhite being a randy fellow and former flutist with the Cincinnati Symphony. He had arrived in Chamisaville with novel-writing on his mind. His bucks he scammed by giving music lessons, tuning pianos, and making runs to western Kansas, where he bought old uprights for a song, refurbished them, and unloaded them on those of Chamisaville's new upwardly mobile denizens into music. He also held down a part-time job at the bus station four days a week. Part of his spiritual penance as a newly initiated Hanuman disciple was his vow to speak only in an invented Eastern language for six months.

Irritated, Joe replied, "Murasaki shikibu."

Egon said, "Toyatoami! Hideyoshi!"

"Fukada tanaka kawasaki!"

Eloy said, "Qué es lo que les están pasando, huevones?"

Joe explained, "He always talks like this. He took a vow."

"What kind of vow?"

Egon explained, "Shur op chop chitty mai mai!"

Eloy said, "We should send *him* to rob the bank."

Wearing a be-belled jester's cap and World War II aviator goggles, Ralph Kapansky materialized at Joe's other elbow. At Ralph's side was his enormous, dingleberry-decorated and constantly farting shaggy dog named Rimpoche. "Hey," Ralph said, "what's up? We been waiting for you."

Basically, Ralph was the most exasperating and obnoxious

SOB that Joe had ever liked. Around women he was a green chauvinist slime. A self-taught orphan who had had a remarkable rise producing records in the cutthroat rock world, at thirty-one too many acid groups had jarred loose the thread, and five years later Ralph lived alone in a tipi beside Tribby Gordon's Castle of Golden Fools (in which Joe and Heidi also resided). Frantically, Ralph dieted on molasses and lemon juice hoping to shave off a few of his 260 blubbery pounds. And gulped one Elavil and one Pertofrane antidepressant pill every 10:00 P.M. just to make it through the night. By day, when he wasn't being an expert, part-time maintenance man on the Forest Service's two helicopters, Ralph tried, from a two-hundred-dollar-a-month crib over Peter Caspian's Hairstyling for Men on the plaza, to write pornography, male adventure stories, and gothic novels, while awaiting inspiration for his first serious novel. Since inspiration of any kind rarely arrived, Ralph spent most of his daylight and nighttime hours wandering hepatically around Chamisaville hustling the ladies, and begging his life to begin again. Dying terrified the beautiful slob. If he made no killing on Joe's dope deal, Ralph had plans to move, with Rimpoche, to an ashram somewhere in India, near Raipur. Or was it Darjeeling?

"Where," Joe wanted to know, "is Tribby?"

"Over there. At our table near the exit."

"That guy in the gorilla mask?"

"Yup."

"And who's the female clown with the green rock in her nose?" The woman seated beside Tribby also wore a purple turban, green mascara, chalky powder on her sallow cheeks, glistening passion-pink lipstick, a bulky tie-dyed muumuu, and an acre of powder-blue poppette beads. A Tiparillo in a white plastic holder provided the proper finishing touch.

"She's a roadie I promoted in the Prince of Whales Café this afternoon. Name is Gypsy Girl. She's on her way from Bloomington to Mount Shasta to 'get a hit of those powerful vibes out there.' She's cool. Her head's a little tipsy, of course— I think she's got a retention span of three seconds. Too much glue before her adolescent years."

"We're just about to get involved in a major felony operation that is gonna require secrecy and nerves of steel," Joe rasped, "and you have to pick up some kind of Fellini grotesque with a rock in her nose?"

"Oh don't worry about her," Ralph said. "She's cool."

And he forged ahead, pushing across the bar. "By the way," he added nonchalantly, "apparently news of this coke your friend's bringing in on the two thirty-five bus has leaked around town. And certain parties aren't too happy."

Joe's heart went off the three-meter board in his chest and belly-flopped somewhere down around his ankles. His pores immediately ejected a gallon of nervous stench. Oh shit, he thought—the cops? Or worse, an incipient drug war? It had never occurred to him that they might be violating somebody else's territory, and that that somebody might take umbrage. But then, it had never occurred to him that anyone else, besides their little group, could ever find out.

In Chamisaville.

They reached the table. Tribby said, "Ah-hah, all the dastardly conspirators are in place, so we can begin." His voice came out muffled through the rubber mask. Underneath that mask, Custer-length prematurely white hair circled his half-bald dome. Tribby—or Theodore Reginald "Butch" Gordon, that is TRB (phoneticized to Tribby)—was an adventuresome maniac from Kitchener, Ontario. He had received a highly privileged private education in America from the ninth grade through college thanks to his hockey prowess. Next, he had triumphed at Harvard Law School and married a Cliffie named Rachel Parquielli, the cultured daughter of a Detroit Mafia family. Currently, she, like Joe's wife Heidi, taught preschoolers at the Shanti Institute. Tribby himself, somewhat haphazardly, plied a legal trade that had earned him the sobriquet "The Mortician of Marriages." Physically, Tribby checked in as five foot seven inches and 160 pounds of plump, coordinated murder on the ice, and a daredevil Hotspur off it. With impunity, he switched from hang-gliders to helicopter skiing in Canadian avalanche country. Easily bored stiff, he was one of the few people Joe knew who enjoyed instigating free-for-alls in bars. In Vietnam, in the same outfit as Ralph Kapansky, he had flown Cobra gunships, and piloted little Cessnas that called in air strikes, laying waste the jungle with napalm.

"Aren't we all being just a trifle too blasé about this matter?" Joe said nervously.

"What matter?" Tribby asked.

"He means the dope deal you guys are gonna put together with that stuff on the bus tonight," Gypsy Girl said giddily.

"Oh *no!*" Joe buried his head in his hands. "Who spilled the beans . . . Ralph?"

"Me?" Ralph swiveled his head to the right and to the left, looking for somebody besides his innocent self. "My lips have been sealed, old chum."

"Then who told her? Some stupid little bird in a banana tree?" He wanted to dive across the table and uppercut Ralph in his cynical rosy jowls. Sensing this, Rimpoche timidly growled.

"But I just guessed." Gypsy Girl's face registered alarm, then cunning. "Nobody told me, honest. I mean, you know, I heard some dudes rapping in the laundromat, that's all."

"Laundromat, shmaundromat!"

Tribby said, "Relax, it's all over town. Apparently Ray Verboten knows we're going to try and swing a deal in his territory and he doesn't like it."

Ray Verboten—Coke Kingpin of Chamisaville. What he didn't push, didn't get moved, or so the saying went. Some claimed that Ray reported directly to Joseph Bonatelli: others insisted that Bonatelli would have no truck with the snow— he scorned it for being an aristocratic, snobbish high.

Joe groaned, "But how could he find out? This was supposed to be a secret operation." Already he could see his house of cards was determined to crumble. He'd be lucky if only the entire army, navy, and air force was down at the bus station tonight. Right now, probably, the FBI, the state police, and local enforcement agents were setting up bugs outside the depot. They were arranging spotlights atop the Miracle Auto Supply building next door. And jamming their cameras full of infrared film in order to record every inch of the bust. Last but not least, no doubt they were snapping well-oiled clips bristling with dumdum cartridges into their Colt .45s and M-16 rifles, in case either Joe or his pal Peter made one false move.

LOCAL GARBAGE MAN AND PHILLY WAITER NAILED AT BUS
DEPOT WITH FIVE POUNDS OF UNCUT SNOW! STATE'S BIGGEST
NARCOTICS HAUL EVER!

Mimi McAllister, a dippy redheaded lesbian reflexologist who also worked for a woman's construction collective, bent over—in passing—and offered her snotty two bits: "Not to be a harbinger of bad news, boys, but you better steer clear of Ray Verboten."

Joe said, "I think I'm gonna ralph. Why didn't we just draw up our plans in the town hall, over the radio, during a city council meeting?"

Scott Harrison, six foot three inches of shyster hustler in his early thirties, impeccably attired in his Universal Life Church custom-made velour jumpsuit, landed on top of them for a second. "Hey, hey, *hey*," he chortled derisively. "Look what we have here—the French Connection brothers themselves!"

Joe shriveled, leered sickly, and attempted bravado: "What are you talking about?"

"What am I *talking* about?" Theatrically—who did he think he was, Kirby J. Hensley disguised as F. Lee Bailey?—Scott placed one hand against his chest, the better to accent his cheap raillery: "Word has it you've become the Meyer Lansky of the Chamisaville drug scene, José. 'That Joe Miniver,' they're all saying. 'He's gonna run Joe Bonatelli right out of town!'"

"Very funny, Scott. Go back to your graveyard."

"No, seriously, my friend. You think that by stepping on and marketing the sugar that's arriving on the two thirty-five A.M. bus tonight you can raise enough cold cash to buy out Eloy Irribarren? I'm getting a stitch in my gut from laughing! He owes me that land—every bush, every flower, every mouse turd on the place."

Joe mumbled, "We'll see. . . ."

"Well, you better take a Gatling gun down to the depot," Scott called back over one shoulder. "I heard Ray Verboten and his hippie asesinos are gonna ring your chimes the second that bundle lands in your hot little paws–"

Clapping hands over his ears, Joe prayed, as did little kids, that if he couldn't hear Scott's poison tongue, nobody else could either.

Tribby said, "It appears the entire forces of NATO will be on maneuvers at the depot tonight."

"Let's change the subject." Joe knew Tribby was correct, of course. But how could he quash his own tragedy? The die was cast: obviously, he was fated to spend the rest of his life in jail (if he somehow escaped the 2:35 rendezvous alive!). And all because he had wanted a piece of land on which to build a humble little middle-class home for his wife and darling kiddies. In China, he thought, this never could have happened. I would have had an apartment, a job, free medical care, and, most importantly, a role in my nation's history. Instead, he was doomed to perish in incarcerated exile, fending off sado-masochistic fags and lurid rats as big as tomcats.

"For argument's sake, let's pretend a miracle happens and you wind up with the cash to purchase Eloy's land." Ralph smiled benevolently. "What kind of house are you planning to build?"

"A big one," Joe whimpered. "All my life I wanted to live in a big house. I'm gonna make an octagonal tower with glass on all sides and a polar-bear rug on the floor. I'm gonna build a game room with a Ping-Pong table you won't have to fold up after every contest. There'll be solar collectors, a green-house. . . ."

Joe stopped. And for a moment he reveled in a typical fantasy. He had built the new house already and everything was Under Control. Joe's one great dream in life was to have Everything Under Control. An enormous woodpile—enough piñon to last all winter—cast its shadow against the house. Fragrant smoke issued from the chimney, dissolving against a glittery, iron-blue September sky. Yellow leaves zigzagged off cottonwoods by the irrigation ditch. The quarter-acre garden was so rich in vegetables you could hear the vitamins crackling. Tomatoes, tied carefully to proper sticks, glowed provoca-tively: squashes, neatly mulched, grew plumper by the minute; pumpkins, turned regularly, had ripened evenly. Humming-birds still nourished themselves at plastic feeders with bee-guards and ant-guards that actually functioned. All Joe's yard tools were stacked neatly in the garage—miracle of miracles, the kids hadn't lost an implement! In the game room, Heather and Michael played expert Ping-Pong: overcoming the tension that always made it impossible for him to instruct the children, Joe had taught them the game that summer. Nearby, seated contentedly before her loom, Heidi created beautiful wall hang-ings. Upstairs—in his tower—Joe was finally reading *Capital* by Karl Marx. In another room, best friend Peter Roth perused a Hemingway novel. As soon as Joe finished his current chap-ter, they would drop a Gouda cheese and a bottle of Wild Turkey 101 into a knapsack, and hit the Rio Grande for a three-hour trout bout before dinner. They would probably take the new Chevy pickup, unless Joe was in a Mazda mood and decided to select that fire-engine-red vehicle, equipped as it was (same as the pickup) with a CB, a stereo tape deck, and a Fuzz Buster. Yessirree, bob, Joe Miniver was *In Control*!

Ralph and Gypsy Girl exchanged wet, lascivious kisses and fumbled erotically under the table; Tribby sucked up a daiquiri through a straw stuck into a hole in his gorilla-mask mouth; Rimpoche whined and pawed Ralph's thigh, trying to sabotage the kissy-face—with one hand Ralph scratched the dog to shut up.

Forlornly, Joe said, "Apparently, everybody in town knows Peter Roth is arriving with the cocaine tonight."

Ralph begged to differ. "Everybody in town *thinks* they know. But it's all rumor. Nobody's taking it seriously. Chamisaville is like that. At heart I don't think anybody believes that Joe Miniver, Boy Scout extraordinaire and non-doper par excellence, would have either the guts or the inclination to get mixed up in such a dangerous and nefarious business."

"I don't believe it myself," Joe mumbled.

"So not to worry." Ralph nibbled obscenely on Gypsy Girl's painted cheek and scrabbled the fingers of his left hand behind Rimpoche's tattered right ear. "There won't be a single blood-crazed, trigger-happy hit thug at the depot—I promise."

Joe beseeched Tribby's glittering eyes peeping out through two little holes in the grotesque rubber mask. "What do *you* think?"

"I'm with Ralph. But what the hell, if anything happens, we'll just improvise."

"Maybe I need a partner at the bus station."

Ralph nixed that. "Crowds call attention."

"But what if Ray Verboten and a half-dozen armed nean-derthals catch me there alone?"

"Give him the coke, dummy."

"Just *give* it to him?" Joe was shocked. "It cost me my life savings—twelve thousand clams—for that cocaine."

"Is it worth dying for?"

"He's right," Tribby said. "If Ray Verboten says 'Gimme' you better let him have it."

"And then what—that's it? The end of our plan? Nobody gets hurt, and I'm out twelve Gs?"

Tribby touched Joe solicitously. "Easy, man, calm down. We'll simply switch over to plan B."

"What's plan B?"

Ralph had it scoped. "We go into training in Guatemala. Finally, when all is in readiness, eight of us sail a small catamaran up the Rio Grande to Chamisaville, disembark on the shores of Ray Verboten's estate, and, with our Uzis and Ak-47s spitting out a withering sheet of lethal pellets, we snatch back the sacred brick of uncut crystals, chop it up, and proceed to unload it as per plan A."

"Very funny. You guys are hilarious."

"Hey, listen, don't worry," Tribby said. "Nothing is going to happen. Who in their right mind would want to wait up for the two thirty-five bus anyway?"

Joe knew for certain now that he was doomed. They didn't care—after all, their lives and their boodle weren't on the line. No, only himself, Joe Miniver, had been selected for the Gangland Slayee Hall of Fame. Ahhh, he was only a mere speck, anyway, a tiny insignificant antlike blip on the asshole of humanity. Ten thousand human beings starved to death in India every day—anonymously. Twenty years from now what would any of this matter? Who would give a damn? Who would even remember?

Joe Miniver? Didn't he play second base for the New York Mets during the recession of 1989?

Naw, you're thinking of the guy that was a tailgunner on the B-52 that dropped the hydrogen bomb on Teheran.

Actually, fellas, Joe Miniver used to be a stand-up comedian from Keokuk, Iowa.

Meek and miserable, Joe said, "Well, just in case anything actually works out tonight, let's go over the plans for tomorrow."

"What's to go over?" Ralph tongued an earlobe. "You hit the airport at twelve noon with the stuff, the rest of us appear likewise. We fly off, cut the shit, stash it in three packages, land, and split. Five days later we reunite rich as ducks copulating in mud pie. What could be easier?"

"Sure." Tribby flicked ashes onto the floor. "What's tomorrow—Sunday? We should all be back in town by Wednesday rolling in bucks. You buy your land, I make a call to my broker, E. F. Hutton—"

Ephraim Bonatelli veered in front of their table, caught and steadied himself, then climbed on a chair and raised his Hanuman T-shirt, exposing an enormous little potbelly, on which he had painted flabby, passion-pink female lips. "Blabbleabbleglabbledabble," he sang in a rapidly disintegrating voice, "said the ape to the gorilla."

"Who's that?" Gypsy Girl wanted to know.

"A local dwarf," Ralph explained wearily.

"Beat it, Ephraim." Tribby glowered. "We're not in the mood."

"Blabbleabbleglabbledabble, said the apey to the gorilla!" Ephraim lost his balance but was kept from crashing to the floor by a dozen hands that reached out to catch him.

Gypsy Girl said, "I like him. He's *cute*."

Joe asked Tribby, "Are you scared?"

"You mean in general? Or specifically about our little adventure here?"

"The latter."

"No." His masked head shook slowly. "I don't think so."

"Why not?"

"Quién sabe? It's an adventure."

Ephraim Bonatelli said, "You're all creeps." He thumped his hairy little fists against his potbelly. "I eat scumbags like you for breakfast!"

"Will somebody order the dwarf to evaporate?" Ralph started pouting. "I find him very irritating."

"Oh no," Gypsy Girl cried. "Don't let him go. He's adorable."

"Scram, Ephraim." Tribby stuck another cigarette through the hole in his gorilla mask and lit it. "Make like a breeze and blow."

"Hey wait a minute." Joe was embarrassed by their crudeness. "That's no way to address a fellow human being, no matter how obnoxious. He has feelings, too."

"Yeah, I got feelings too," Ephraim croaked hoarsely. "So go fuck y'selves, scumbags."

"He's getting on my nerves." Ralph turned to Rimpoche. "Go sic 'im, boy. Tear 'im apart." Rimpoche's ears perked tentatively, even as he cowered at the sound of his master's voice. He gave Ralph a confused equivocal look of fawning temerity, with cautiously ferocious overtones.

"I like you," Gypsy Girl assured the malevolent gnome. "Sing that song again."

"Go fuck yaself, ya hippie whore."

"Hey, Ephraim." Tribby coughed as smoke caught underneath his mask. "Why don't you go bug Skipper Nuzum?"

Egon Braithwhite careened into their table; a beer glass tipped over. "Oops. Hirimangi basurai!"

"Wait a minute, wait just a minute!" Joe protested. "I can't hear a thing. Shut up, Ephraim! Hey Tribby, ask him to be quiet, will you? He's driving me crazy."

"I'm warning you, Bonatelli . . ." Tribby waggled a lean and menacing finger at the dwarf, who held his Hanuman T-shirt wrinkled up under his armpits.

"Touch me, shyster, and my dad will drop you into the Rio Grande in a cement overcoat."

"His 'dad.'" Ralph rolled woeful basset eyes. "How many times have I heard that one? Go ahead, Rimpoche—leap at his throat. Kill, big fella!"

"You better not mock me, fatso. I got a rod out in the car."

"Cement overcoats! A rod in the car!" Ralph snorted scornfully and slapped his thigh. "Ephraim, you watch too much television."

"Aw lay off him, sweetie. I tell you, he's really *cute*."

"C'mon, blubber face, hit me if you dare." Ephraim jutted his lower jaw, cocked his head, and patted his chin, offering it up as a target. "Go ahead, right here, you first. Whatsamatter, you chicken? Your dog wears fruit boots. Come on, lard ass, I dare you. *I'll murder you!*"

Caustic and laconic, Ralph replied, "Ephraim, if you don't take a powder mighty soon I may actually be forced to plant my reluctant fist in that bloated little belly of yours."

"Kiss my ass, blimp nose!"

"All right, that does it, so long creep." In a single fluid motion, Tribby raised himself half out of his chair, grabbed Ephraim by the throat, cocked his right arm, and nailed the arrogant little punk in the kisser. The crowd gasped excitedly. But Joe had had enough. He grabbed Ralph's arm and yanked himself erect, crying as he did so, "It'll be a miracle, it really will!"

"What will be a miracle?"

"If any of us come out of this alive."

"If you don't dream the impossible dream," Ralph clichéd after him, "you'll never know if you could have."

One eye murderously on Joe, the other eye apprehensively asking Ralph for approval, Rimpoche barked: "Woof! Woof?"

And Joe clattered downstairs.

❧

He reached the depot at 2:10, saddling himself with a twenty-five-minute wait. Parking in the Miracle Auto Supply lot next door to the tiny bus station, Joe killed the motor and tried to glance around without conspicuously turning his head.

Apparently, not a creature was stirring. Only a single light gleamed dully inside the station. At a desk behind the counter near some baggage racks, a relief driver (a G-man in mufti?) smoked a cigarette and sipped stale coffee. The station had closed officially at eight, and wouldn't reopen until 7:00 A.M. Joe wondered if six SWAT gorillas were crowded into the tiny men's room, or crouched behind the baggage counter, fingering the hair triggers of their shotguns, .357 magnums, and beanbag stunguns. Had they set up remote-control cameras to film Joe's meeting with Peter before they opened up? The question was: when the stakeout leader snarled "FREEZE!" could he raise his hands fast enough to avoid being ventilated by the notoriously trigger-happy crimestoppers?

A Blue Star taxi idled in front of the station. Listening to rock music on his radio, the hippie behind the wheel lethargically smoked a joint. Hippie? The joint seemed a little too obvious. The FBI always adopted blatant disguises, Joe remembered from his antiwar days: inevitably, they stuck out like sore thumbs. In fact, couldn't he distinguish the outline of a crew cut underneath that shaggy hairdo? The son of a bitch probably cradled a burp gun in his lap!

Until a few years ago, the only taxi service in Chamisaville had belonged to Juan Casados. One cab had worked the airport, another had met all incoming buses, a third scheduled regular trips to the Pueblo. Approximately two years ago, however, Wilkerson Busbee hit town. He had scammed a fortune in the Chicago commodities pits by the age of twenty-eight. But a sawbones had suggested his Type-A personality would land him on a slab in the morgue within a decade if he kept it up. Wilkerson promptly traveled out west for his health, and went into Winnebagos, tipis, herbal teas, head shops, and taxis. A brief price war followed in the last, but Wilkerson won handily because he had a fortune to squander and Juan ran a marginal operation at best. It had taken the local man fifteen years to accumulate three vehicles: Busbee started with a brightly painted

52

fleet of six cabs, daily radio spots, and weekly half-page newspaper ads. Ten minutes later Juan Casados became an assistant
sanding man at Eddie's Paint and Body Shop in the capital,
eighty miles to the south, and Busbee had the field to himself.

Joe's eyes wandered farther afield. Another car, a quasi-
familiar VW idled behind the taxi. In it a woman smoked a
cigarette. That was something new: female drug agents trained
in tactical massacre procedures? Or was she only the driver, a
decoy, a lookout poised to advise the burly agents crouched
on her floor when to pop up and open fire?

The woman said, "Hello, Joe, what are you doing here at
this godforsaken hour?"

Nancy Ryan, for the luvva Pete!

Such relief!

Eagerly, Joe barged out of the car, composed himself, and
sauntered over to Nancy's Bug. After all, they wouldn't dare
riddle him with slugs if an innocent bystander, and especially
a woman—a mother—stood to be injured by the fusillade.
Police departments had codes against that sort of outrage.

Innocent bystander? Suppose Nancy was in cahoots with
them. After all, the Simian Foundation wanted Eloy Irribarren's
land. Very possibly they had informed on Joe, fingering him
for this setup. Far from being a disinterested observer, Nancy
Ryan might be the spider at the heart of the web—his own
"Red Lady." She would duck below the window ledge of her
bulletproof car a split second before sharpshooters hidden in
the Miracle Auto Supply attic opened up, hosing him down
for good.

Aloud, Joe said, "Hi, Nancy. What brings you out at this
ghastly hour. Benefit's all over?"

"My son arrives on the two-thirty bus." Her serenity seemed
genuine. Her eyes betrayed not a glimmer of disquiet. In the
seat beside her, Sasha clutched a banana. He curled his upper
lip, snapped his menacing teeth, and made a guttural chirping
sound.

Joe squatted, bringing his face to her level. "How come
your kid—what's his name—Stanley?"

"Bradley."

"Yeah. How come he's arriving at this hour?"

"Carter flew in from Kansas City to the capital with him
this afternoon. But Carter doesn't want to see me, so I wasn't

allowed to drive down there and pick him up. In a nutshell," she grinned humorously, "that's my sad story."

Carter, her ex-hubby, did promotions for a professional football team. Several times, in the Prince of Whales Café, Joe had had long talks with Nancy: they had provided a barebones outline of her story. New Hampshire-born and -bred, and Radcliffe-educated, at twenty-one Nancy married (and divorced that same year) a nuclear physicist sixteen years her senior. There followed stints as a Kelly Girl, a publisher's receptionist, a reader at Random House, an editor, a tokenseller on the Manhattan subway lines, a research assistant for a Columbia professor, a copy girl at *Reader's Digest*, and an editor at Time-Life. She could call some shots by then, and soon started her own industrial consulting firm. The first man she hired was Carter Ryan. After the nuptials, she retired to have a child. Shortly thereafter, they started fighting about how to run the business: divorce followed. Momentarily depressed, Nancy attempted a half-hearted suicide that wholeheartedly failed. The prerequisite therapy raped her wallet for a while. But then, having determined that God helps those who help themselves, she hit the road in search of a new life. Parking the kid with an Akron-based brother, she arrived in Chamisaville, and spent six months at a Sufi Moslem retreat called Davishi in the Midnight Mountains an hour north of town. Then a friend turned her on to Nikita Smatterling, and in the middle of her first winter she stumbled out of the hills, bought a town house, and sent for her son. Stock income, Carter's child support, and the residue from their marriage settlement kept her comfortable enough so that she could tinker at a variety of odd jobs. During the short time Joe had superficially known her she had been a substitute teacher, a legal secretary, a salesperson at Ragtime Flowershop, a baby-sitter for the aged and the infirm, a therapist with the county mental health program, and an emergency paramedic with the county ambulance service, to name a few. She also rose quickly within the ranks of the Simian Foundation to become their all-powerful secretary-treasurer, a job, Joe surmised, in which she handled no small amounts of ready cash.

Nancy said, "By the way, I should have congratulated you earlier tonight. That Irribarren land in Upper Ranchitos is beautiful. How wonderful you can afford it."

"Well, yes, thanks," Joe said guardedly. Had she activated

a tape recorder in the glove compartment? Were two earphoned creeps in the auto parts basement crouched over a high-frequency receiver, listening to their conversational drivel, producing tapes that would send him up the river for life?

"If it's not prying," she said ingenuously, "however did you get that much cash all at once?"

"It would be prying." But then of a sudden something cracked inside, and he thought, What the hell? They had him, why protest? Better to give up, drop his guard, relax for a minute before his universe collapsed. "Actually, I stole the money. Me and three other guys, we robbed a bank in North Platte, Nebraska, ten days ago." Put *that* in your earphones, suckers!

A thousand percent nonplussed, Nancy smiled and said, "By the way, how's Heidi? Are you guys still together?"

"Why wouldn't we be together?"

"Well, I remember once, in the Prince of Whales, we had a long talk—that's all. At the time I gathered things were shaky."

"Things are always shaky. Who do you know that's basking in smooth sailing?" Sasha had bitten off the stem end of the banana. Slowly and deliberately, surgeon-careful, he peeled it.

"Me. I'm not shaky." Her smile was positively saintly. Her eyes had the intense luster of a morning star. Mata Hari disguised as a thirty-five-year-old Teen Angel?

Joe said, "You're twice divorced, you and Randall just canned it, you've held eighteen jobs in the past ten months, you once tried to commit suicide, and you're chain-smoking cigarettes hoping to drop dead of cancer before you reach forty. That's not shaky?"

She had an appealing way of thoughtfully nudging her lower lip with an upper tooth. The slightest little gap in the very center of her mouth remained even when her lips were sealed. And of course her eyes continued to emote an amiable luminescence. Beside her, Sasha finished peeling his banana, kissed it tenderly, and rocked the naked fruit in his arms as if it were a slumbering baby, cooing contentedly.

"The cigarettes are a bummer, I'll admit." She exhaled provocatively. "I've tried to stop. I actually once quit for almost a year, and wish to hell I had never started up anew. But I'm working toward it, I'll quit again, and this time for good. Then," she chuckled, "I'll be perfect."

Joe enjoyed teasing her. "You got no right to be so cocky. Every time we talk, your life is a mess."

"It's not a mess. It's just that things happen. But they always happen for a reason. Nothing ever takes me by surprise." Her serenity would have been galling had it not been tempered by an intricately powerful vitality.

Joe said, "Well, I don't know about you, but I can say one thing. I know that I certainly wouldn't mind a little break from feeling shaky every once in a while."

"That's not hard."

"What's not hard?"

"It's not hard if you're willing to work at it. Unfortunately, most people in our society are programmed into such terrible habits that they lose all sense of how to help themselves, of how to exploit their inner potential."

"Like, for instance, how do you help yourself?"

"No, I don't want to talk about it because you're not sincerely interested."

"Hey, honest, please—I *am* interested." He licked his finger, drawing a circle on her side-view mirror.

"Nice try, but I can tell you're not." A hint of sadness highlighted her smile, a flicker of sorrowful saintliness rippled across her forehead. "I think that if I were really to tell you where I am at, or how I believe that I could help you, you'd just make fun of me."

Reaching out with the same hand that held her cigarette, she flicked a piece of ash, or an eyelash, from the tip of his nose.

"See," she added. "Look at your expression. I can tell you're mocking me."

"You're wrong." Actually, he had a strong urge to embrace her. A kiss before dying—? She glowed like the color of bright autumn leaves heightened by a mist. Sasha quit lullabying his banana. Holding it in his right fist, he grasped the top of the pale-yellow fruit with his left hand and slowly squeezed. Plump, squashy lumps of banana meat bulged obscenely between his skinny prurient fingers.

"I wouldn't mock you," Joe said. "Scout's honor. I'm really interested. Sometimes I say to myself, I say, 'Joe, for Chrissakes, when are you ever gonna grow up? When are you ever gonna take the time to help your own self just a little?' Believe me, I'm often amazed at my own stupidity, my emotional immaturity, my ignorance. Take the fact that I got this lousy asthma—and the whole world knows it's psychosomatic, right? But I got it, and I can't seem to save myself."

"You could cure it, Joe. I could show you how to do it."

"Yeah, sure . . . but I don't have the patience."

"The main problem is that you must want to change before you can affect anything."

"Maybe, basically, I love the way I am," he said flippantly. "Maybe, basically, I love waking up at four o'clock in the morning gasping for breath. Maybe, basically, I love getting so frantic over my inability to keep everything under control that I almost faint from self-induced tachycardia attacks. Maybe, basically, I'm so in love with my own bourgeois angst that it'd be silly to ever dream about changing all that."

Her lips closed until only that sweet little gap remained in the center of her mouth: the tip of a single tooth rested on the cushion of her sexy lower lip. Her perfume tapped nostalgic roots, reminding Joe of high-school days, cashmere sweaters, and circle pins. *Christ, he was getting old!*

"It's possible," she said. "Most people are like that. But laziness isn't genetic."

Still jousting, Joe suggested, "Maybe we should set up a schedule. I could come to your pad three times a week for serenity lessons."

Her face grew intense and serious. "You may think you're joking, Joe. But I knew this was going to happen."

Her abrupt change startled him. Incredibly, his neck prickled. Likewise, his groin. It seemed he could almost feel something—a manifestation of sheer hippie bullshit—pass between them: *vibes*, god damn their eyes!

His stomach flip-flopped. His brain said, Whoa, boy, what are you gonna do, reach for a police informer that's into monkey gods? Sasha inspected his gooey hand curiously, tasted the pulp, made a face, stood, and, leaning forward, pressed his gushy palm against the windshield, leaving a nauseatingly gloppy handprint on the glass. Nancy seemed not to notice.

"You knew *what* was going to happen?" Joe's grin felt lopsided, out of kilter, foolish. "Don't you suddenly go mystic on me."

Calculating his concern, she lightened up, allowing a hint of smile to reappear. "Didn't you ever . . . before, when we occasionally met, and we had those long talks—didn't you ever sense that we had something important to share with each other?"

"I don't know. Share what?"

"I always felt an attraction between us. I don't necessarily mean sexual. It's nothing specifically in that realm."

Galloping back toward his own turf, Joe feigned astonishment. "You don't like sex?"

"I adore it. I just wasn't speaking of sex right now."

For no appropriate reason, Joe found himself spilling some private beans. "When I was younger, I used to believe that I could screw my way into salvation. I knew that was the only logical way to attain it."

"Really? Hmm. I suppose I've always considered sex something to get out of the way as soon as possible in order to truly open wide the door onto something special and profound."

"That's a funny way to put it."

"Joe, tell me truthfully: what are you feeling right now?"

How did we arrive at *that* tone of voice? he wondered in dismay, flabbergasted, as usual, by the Machiavellian complexity of women as opposed to the almost moronic simplicity of men. Or was it all an act for his benefit, allowing the drug agents more time to get into position? Joe quickly turned his head, expecting a human shadow to flit around a corner, or a glint to flash off a clandestine rifle barrel. But nothing stirred: the surroundings were abnormally subdued, quiet, suspended. Sasha had crushed the rest of the banana between his tiny palms and created a banana-mâché bas relief against the glove-compartment door. Every few seconds, as he forged his deliberate theatrical carnage, he cast beady eyes at Nancy and rattled his yellow teeth at her: she paid no attention.

"I dunno," Joe said. "I feel mostly hung over, I guess. I'm tired. But I feel good. Though it's been a long day."

"No, I mean right now. What are you *really* feeling? About yourself. And toward me."

"To tell the truth, I'm a little confused. Just a minute ago . . ." He faded, disliking the implications.

"'Just a minute ago . . .'" she prompted.

"Well, you know, I felt, I mean . . . my stomach did a flip. I guess you could say I felt attracted to you. That is, sexually."

She presented her profile. Even as smoke wafted from her nostrils, she clicked open a change-purse-style cigarette case, selected a fresh weed and balanced it between her lips, then

pushed in the cigarette lighter on her dash. Waiting for it to
heat up, she closed her eyes, apparently resting, the cigarette
stuck attractively between her lips, not dangling. Joe studied
her face. All its life had dissipated, displaced by the features
of an exhausted, tough career woman, a no-nonsense lady, a
remote professional person, and maybe not a stoolie after all.
But if her kid didn't get off that bus, he was in trouble. Maybe,
just as the Trailways arrived, he would grab her for a hostage. . . .

The lighter clicked out. Nancy pressed it against the tip of
her cigarette. Sasha scampered out the passenger window, swung
onto the front hood, and, just like a little boy, grinning idiotically, aiming his monkey dick with banana-pulped fingers,
he pissed against the windshield. Nancy exhaled languorously,
and pushed the washer button, squirting soapsuds against the
urine-stained glass. Switching on the ignition key, she activated
the windshield wipers, then asked, "Have you ever heard of
Alice Bailey?"

"Nope."

She replaced the lighter.

Joe said, "I think the problem between you and me is we
approach life from two totally different angles."

"'Problem'?" Facing him again, she reinfused her cheeks
with an almost mystical luster.

"Well, let's say difference, then." The monkey hopped onto
the top of the car and rat-a-tatted his fists against the skimpy
metal overhead.

"I think we should get together sometime, Joe. And talk.
Seriously. I mean, can't you *feel* it between us? Haven't you
always wanted to explore me one day?"

Joe shrugged, confused and embarrassed. A moment ago
his guts had lurched, the sexual pop had almost made him
shriek. Now she both angered and bored him; time to extricate
himself from the conversation. And be alert. Was that her role
in all of this—to divert his attention?

He used a timeworn escape route. "Well, you know, I mean,
maybe . . . that is . . ."

"I honestly believe there's really no need for anybody anywhere to ever suffer," she said.

"Hey!" His head spun around gratefully. "Here comes the
bus!"

Battered by torrents of relief, Joe jumped up: saved by The Bell! Then immediately his heart commenced pounding: Peter was going to descend from that vehicle. Carrying a suitcase full of cocaine? Or an airplane flight bag? Or would it be hidden in a tape recorder?

Veering off the North-South Highway, air brakes whooshing, the Trailways screeched past, traveled down an alleyway and turned around behind the station, then coasted forward to the loading door, facing the highway.

Joe spun around once, frantically expecting a dozen squad cars, cherrytops blipping and sirens wailing, to come screeching from all directions to nose-diving halts, pinning him, and Peter as he got off, in the circle of their glaring headlights.

When the doors hissed open, Joe staggered numbly forward and placed himself ten feet away, directly in front of them, his eyes squinched almost shut, awaiting the fatal bullet. Arms folded, unperturbed, a lit cigarette between her fingers, Nancy waited nearby, looking real good in a green-and-white-striped jersey, a knee-length denim skirt, and sandals. Sasha kneeled on the Bug's front hood, fiddling with the windshield wipers. To Joe, the world was deathly silent; the tension was unbearable; he knew the universe was about to shatter. . . .

A smallish boy appeared, sleepily rubbing his eyes with one hand, gripping a blue flight bag in the other. To say the least, the kid looked surly. Lacerating Joe with an evil eye, he limped over to Nancy and burrowed his head into her tummy. She hugged him gently but not gushingly as she asked, "How was the plane ride?"

"Shitty."

To Joe, Nancy said, "Plus ça change, plus c'est la même chose." She punctuated the saying with an appealing shrug, and, abruptly, he liked her again. With that, Sasha uncorked a jibbering shriek. "Oh dear," Nancy giggled. "His tail is caught under a wiper."

Nobody else got off. Had Peter foreseen the setup and jumped ship early? Perplexed, Joe waited. Then he paced nervously around the outside of the bus, neck craned, trying to see inside. Still, no floodlights sprang aglare: no loudspeakers ordered him to "FREEZE!" And so, taking another portentous deep breath,

he entered the vehicle and walked the length of the aisle. But
Peter was not on board. Not even in the lavatory, flushing
down the cocaine. Outside again, Joe backed away from the
bus, staring at it incredulously. He took a few hesitant steps
forward again, stopped, shook his head bewilderedly, and finally, facing the deserted highway, he blurted plaintively:

"You son of a bitch!"

Nancy had made no move to drive away. She stated the
obvious: "Your friend didn't arrive."

"But how could he . . . but he said . . . but I *talked* to him! I
talked to him just before he left Philadelphia. He gave me the
arrival times and everything. It was all planned."

"Maybe he got sick. Have you been at a place where he
could reach you by phone?"

"No. Would you believe this? I wish just once in my life
that some plan would function without a hitch! I'm so tired of
snarls! You hear me, God? *I'm tired of stinking snarls!*" And
if Nancy had not been a witness, he might have commenced
bawling.

All that waiting, all his terror, all his premonitions, all his
paranoia, all his arrhythmic heartbeats had gone for naught.
No cops had appeared, no dope had arrived, not even the evil
Ray Verboten and his sanguinary Verbotenettes had made an
entrance. What the hell was going on here, a Big Fat Joke?

The sullen driver was removing battered suitcases from the
cargo holds. "I had a friend arriving on this bus," Joe said.
"He's a muscular little guy, with curly hair and pop eyes and
a big nose. He was probably wearing a black T-shirt. . . ."

"Nah." The driver shook his head vehemently.

"Why don't you come over to my house?" Nancy suggested.
"I'll give you a cup of hot chocolate."

"I'd rather have a double shot of bourbon."

"Then you'll have to go elsewhere. I don't stock liquor."

"What are you, some kind of health nut?"

"I'm a vegetarian. And I don't drink."

"You just smoke two packs of cigarettes a day." Joe loved
it. The valley was crawling with freaks who shopped at the co-
ops, ate only organic edibles, practiced yoga three times a day,
and then blew out their anodes, cathodes, diodes, and guts with
pot, mescaline, acid, Quaaludes, you name it. They all dropped
dead at forty from hepatitis complicated by flashback traumas.

Nancy's face was a study in amused chagrin. "Like the saying goes, 'Nobody's perfect.'"

Given the hour and the situation, Joe knew he should go home. The evening's tension had left him exhausted, and anyway, now he had auxiliary plans to fashion. Where was Peter? And the dope? They probably couldn't meet in Tribby's plane tomorrow. Suppose Peter had been arrested in Philadelphia? Or elsewhere en route? He had better telephone Peter's wife, Julane. Though not tonight—no point in raising the alarm before his friend had had a chance to communicate, explaining things. I've suffered enough for one evening, Joe thought. What I need now is sleep. Heidi might worry if she awoke, finding him still absent. The day was over . . . good riddance . . . tomorrow would be better.

Yet Joe was caught in the grip of a childish truculence. He wanted to vent his relief, his anger, his frustrations. Or at least allow his disappointment to dissipate before heading home. Once more, for the ten billionth time, he had somehow been played for a sucker, been stood up again, been left holding the bag. He had psyched himself to be ready for anything—a shootout, death, life imprisonment, even success. Now he would have to prepare all over again: talk about fatigue!

Though technically he despised self-pity, Joe had decided to feel sorry for himself. And there was that hideously placid woman just sitting tight, smirking like a lobotomized ninny, totally in control of everything. Though the monkey had squashed a banana, pissed on the windshield, banged on the roof, and caught his tail in a wiper, she hadn't once flinched! Joe hated her. Yet he could use a transfusion of such equanimity. Her calm near the heart of his storm seemed very seductive. So why not have a little adventure, indulge his curiosity? After tonight's traumatic anticlimax he owed himself a favor. No point in trotting home obediently this empty-handed, especially when an explanation of utter disaster might await him there. "Joe, Joe, Peter got off the bus in Higginsville, Missouri, went to the corner café for a paper, and never returned!"

PHILADELPHIA WAITER, A MAFIA DRUG COURIER,
DISAPPEARS IN MID-AMERICA!
ROTH AND HOFFA BONES LOCATED IN SAME GRAVE!

"Oh all right," Joe grumbled artlessly. "I guess I'd like to come over for a quick hot chocolate."

Hardly had the words left his mouth than his entire innards lurched again, his groin prickled and contracted, he experienced a chilly sweat. Tonight hadn't provided enough sensations already: now he was going for broke!

"Follow me, then." Those words entered his ears sounding unlike any others she had spoken. It was as if they had been uttered in a foreign language. Loaded with positively thundering innuendo, they threatened to explode inside his head, splashing his brains all over the microbus.

"Ow!" Bradley shrieked. *"Ow, ow, ow!"*

"What's the matter?" Nancy asked.

"Sasha bit me!"

"Oh that silly Sasha."

"I'm gonna kill him, Mom! I'm gonna kick his guts out!"

"Now now, he didn't mean to hurt you dear. It was probably only a love bite, because he's glad to see you."

By the time, three minutes later, that he pulled up behind her VW in a Perry Kahn Subdivision #4 tract-house driveway, flight, pure and simple, occupied Joe's mind. "Go home, make sure the kids are covered," he urged himself. "Go to bed. Snuggle up against Heidi's warmth. Forget about Peter, forget about Nancy, forget about the coke, to hell with the land and Eloy Irribarren! There's still time."

Instead, he offered to carry Bradley inside. Thanking him, Nancy led Joe to the tiny concrete front stoop. Using no key, she opened the front door of her flimsy box-shaped dwelling. Sasha scampered in ahead of them twittering like a nervous bird.

"Don't you ever lock your door?" Joe asked.

"Nobody will rob me." She spoke with the type of assurance the pope might have used saying "I am a servant of God."

Joe had never entered a similar house in Chamisaville. A tiny three-bedroom ultra-tract building, it had one bathroom, a living room, and a linoleumed kitchen with a washer-dryer, a dishwasher, and a built-in stove. Clean as a whistle, completely deodorized, it seemed manufactured out of cardboard. Midnight-blue wall-to-wall carpet sheathed the living-room floor. Cheap gold drapes shielded the sliding aluminum windows. The few furniture pieces were modern Scandinavian, except for a large puffy couch. A single stained walnut bookcase housed a stereo set, an enormous color TV console, and many books on various aspects of psychic and spiritual experience, ranging from Alice Bailey and Elizabeth Kubler-Ross to Edgar Cayce and the Lao-tzu. All the walls were dominated by enormous Nikita Smatterling paintings. Garish, and clichéd, though somehow quite friendly, they featured wispy, cosmic monkeys dressed in flowing robes, and wrapped in brilliantly colored auras. Joe's immediate reaction was simply that they were pretty but lousy paintings. Not the subject matter, but the fact that so many of them abounded, bothered him a little.

While she puttered elsewhere, Joe put Bradley down, saucepanned some milk for hot chocolate, and checked out the refrigerator. Absolutely devoid of life's staffs—baloney, mayonnaise, Swiss cheese, marshmallow fluff—it teemed instead with vegetables, papaya juice, and jars of lecithin and tiger's milk. Groaning, Joe retreated to the living-room couch, from where—like a befuddled tourist who had just tumbled down a rabbit hole—he glowered uncomfortably at the fluorescent monkeys peacefully mocking him. Sasha entered the living room, grinned at Joe, then turned, proferring his neat little butt. He stuck a marble into his anus and pooted it out propelled by a fart, so that it sailed a few feet before bouncing to earth.

Five minutes later, while they sipped on the warm milk to a musical background of Emmylou Harris and "Delta Dawn," Joe asked, "How come so many monkey paintings?"

Nancy sat cross-legged on the blue rug in front of him. "I don't think you would understand if I explained, so I'd rather not explain right now."

They chatted about other things. Joe blithered through, nearly incapacitated by fatigue and disinterest. Life was a bitch. Half an hour ago he had been drooling for Nancy: but now he thought her silly, just another suburban housewife concerned about her kid, her vitamins, her interplanetary travels. Why is it, he brooded, that every twenty-eight-to-thirty-five-year-old single woman he had ever known came with a ready-made seven-year-old kid?

She disinterred the topic of their potential affinity for each other. A young Doberman pinscher padded threateningly into the room and sniffed him, then ambled to a corner, curled up, and started snoring with one eye open, glassily fixed on Joe.

A parakeet cage dangled in a corner: gradually, Joe realized that a small bird was perched atop, rather than inside, the cage. A thick candle, in a tall glass holder on the fireplace mantel, flickered. An incense stick burned beside the picture of a cheerful roly-poly gnome in a gold frame. A similar photograph leaned against a potted aloe vera plant on the kitchen counter. Another likeness of the same jolly elfin fellow helped clutter the bathroom window ledge, Joe discovered, when he ventured yonder to take a leak.

Sasha opened the desk drawer, removing a box of rubber bands. Squatting in front of the Doberman, he fixed a rubber band on his index finger, pointed like a gun, and shot the dog in the head. The Doberman growled, but Sasha blithely continued his game. Each time a projectile bounced off the dog's thick skull, it snarled irritably, but did nothing. Nancy ignored the whole scene.

About halfway through his hot chocolate, Joe's mood altered again. Pleasantly woozy, he gave himself up to drifting, answering her probes and inquiries good-naturedly and half-assedly without paying much attention. Things chugged, clicked, and hummed in her efficient little tract home, and to his surprise, once the initial shock wore off, Joe liked it. The place felt cozy. Not for ages had he sat in a house that wasn't crammed with spider webs and hundred-year-old vigas spilling dust down from dirt roofs onto ragtag conglomerations of colorful, secondhand (asthma-inducing) furniture.

After a while, her talk honed in on left-brain and right-brain people. A few complex German names that she threw out meant nothing. His cultural deficiencies started glaring. But eventually she got down to it.

"You know, Joe, I think it would be really interesting to have a relationship with you."

His stomach sent messages up to the brain: *Start functioning, kid. Wake up! Be alert!* "What kind of relationship?" he asked.

"That would depend. I really believe there's been a certain chemistry working between us for a long time. You may not have been aware of it, but I was every time we had a conversation. I definitely know that something between us was meant to be. Haven't you ever been able to focus in on the energy?"

Warily, Joe shook his head. "Not really. I don't think so." *Don't hurt her feelings*, an inner voice coached. *Get the hell out of here, turkey!* another voice warned. A third voice cau-

tioned, *Stick around, pal, something interesting might develop.*
A fourth counseled greedily: *If you want to, you can ball her.*
Then a fifth voice chimed in: *Ball her, idiot, and if you think
you were up the creek without a paddle before tonight, well
let me tell you something, Miniver, you ain't seen nothing yet!*

Was all of this innocent friendly palaver? Or, suddenly, was
he looking down the barrel of a very complex, very clever,
very devious human being with designs on his ass?

"I mean," he added, unwittingly sculpting his grave, "I've
always been attracted to you. You're, you know, you're a very
lovely woman. But..." In desperation, he grasped at a straw:
"Uh, how old is that Doberman, by the way?"

Nancy had become intense. Joe didn't understand it exactly.
Her speech sounded almost lazy, good-natured humor beamed
from her pretty eyes. On the surface she was just another genial,
casual chick, disarmingly regular and pleasant. Why then did
he flinch every time she opened her mouth?

"Tell me truthfully, Joe: would you like to start something
with me?"

"Start what? I mean, what do you mean when you start
talking about starting a relationship?"

"Well, naturally we'd have to define it. It wouldn't necessarily have to be sexual."

"But I'm getting all these sexual vibes."

"Of course, it *could* be sexual. But it doesn't *have* to be
anything, don't you understand? There wouldn't have to be
any pressure attached. It's the pressure that always confuses
people and scrambles their energy."

"But we're already friends. So in a sense, we've already
started something. Naturally, I'd be glad to continue being
friendly. I enjoy talking to you."

"It could be a lot deeper, however, than just the superficial
relationship we've had in the past."

"Yeah, okay. But I don't think I understand exactly what
you're driving at. I'm getting all kinds of confused signals."

"Suppose we made love. Tell me frankly, do you think you
would want to go to bed with me?"

Ah-hah! "If I wanted to hopelessly complicate my life and
lose my wife, yeah, I guess I could enjoy going to bed with
you."

"You don't really sound as if you'd like it, then."

"I wasn't aware that's what we were dickering over."

"Dickering?"

"Well, I mean, I didn't think . . ."

"It's not important, the sexual thing so much, as what we could give to each other if we just let ourselves get that close." Smoke issued languidly from her nostrils. "I think we could share some very relevant things."

Joe had a brilliant idea. It sent electricity all the way down into his toes, and beyond. "Why don't we shack up, right now, just once? Just for fun. Just for a lark."

"I wouldn't want it to be that way. That doesn't make any sense."

"But I got a wife, I got kids. I'm trying to hold a family together."

"I understand. Our relationship wouldn't interfere with any of that."

"But if we balled, how could that not interfere with my family? I mean, Heidi would shit a blimp."

"Well, of course, I don't know all that much about Heidi. But there would be no reason whatsoever for her to feel any kind of jealousy toward me."

"Wait a sec." Joe leaned forward. "Lemme get this straight. When you were married to old what'shisname, to old Carter. Suppose you decided to shack up with somebody else. You mean to tell me that that wouldn't have made him flip his biscuits?"

"Actually, we had what we claimed was an open marriage." She eyed him curiously—taking his measure?

"Did it work?"

She laughed, and her laughter mollified his pounding ticker. "No, of course not."

"Well, there you go."

"But we wanted it to work. We both knew that for either of us to be happy, it had to work. We just hadn't grown up enough, while we were together, to make it work."

"Although you are looking at a man who has registered thirty-eight years on the surface of this planet," Joe said, "it so happens that I have an emotional age, especially when it comes to sex and jealousy and other assorted accoutrements to the emotional rat's nest that surrounds the introduction of the penis into the vagina, of a three-year-old."

"It doesn't have to be that way all your life. You have so much potential, you just need to recognize it, that's all. That's why I'm really interested in you. I keep feeling that I could lead you into a realm that would really blow your mind."

"Blow my 'mind'?" he leered coyly.

She shifted, ever so slightly, but in a way that translated to him as icily provocative. The merest budging of a haunch called his attention to that haunch as an almost deliriously attractive portion of her anatomy. When she dropped her shoulders back a fraction, minutely altering the thrust of her bosom, Joe wanted to grind his teeth. How did people learn such tricks?

Sasha leaped onto a drape at the north end of the couch, by Joe's feet. He scrambled up to the rod, which popped free of the copper hook-holder, spilling Sasha, enveloped in the drape, back onto the couch atop Joe's ankles. Twittering frantically, the little beast punched and clawed at the muffling material, trying to free himself.

Nancy said, "If nothing else, perhaps we could try each other out, experimentally, just to see what might happen. Personally, I don't like one-night stands. I've never gone to bed with anyone simply to get my rocks off."

"Suppose you really feel horny, though, but you haven't got a steady old man?"

"I dislike it, but sometimes I masturbate. It makes me nervous, yet it's better than getting involved with somebody in an uncaring way."

"But if we made love—let's say if we went to bed right now—well, that'd be pretty cold and deliberate." Sasha's little fists continued to flail at the heavy material engulfing him. He chattered hysterically. But if Nancy could ignore him, then what the hell?—so could Joe.

"No it wouldn't, Joe. You're not hearing me. I don't feel that way about you. I think if we made love that something incredibly beautiful would happen. It might be a terribly intense and special interaction. We could create a whole new reality."

Okay—he had a hard-on. His shoulders pulsed with sexual anticipation. The bundle of drapery rolled onto the floor, unraveling in the process: Sasha popped free looking positively apoplectic, and sprang into Nancy's arms for soothing comfort.

"The problem is, Nancy, if we went ahead and balled tonight, that's all it would be, just a one-night stand."

"You say. But you can't possibly know before the fact."

"But I love my wife and the kids. I couldn't jeopardize that."

"You wouldn't be jeopardizing those things. I already explained that. Those things are precious beyond belief. Ours
would be a separate reality."

"Yet you're willing to mess with my family, and you have
no guilt?"

"I'm not 'messing' with them. You wouldn't go to bed with
me unless you wanted to. And if you wanted to, it means that
I have something to offer you that you're not getting, and you
know it. People reach out for things they-need. There are no
accidents in life."

Joe said, "I don't think I could trust you not to get involved
with me in a way that I couldn't handle."

"If you wanted to handle it, you could handle it. Easily.
It's merely a question of accepting your own needs and desires.
Without guilt."

"Listen: first off, I already got a relationship. With Heidi.
It's complex, aggravating, tenuous. Scary sometimes, also;
often bitter; and usually pretty loving." Sasha left Nancy's
embrace, plucked a newspaper from the wastebasket, and began
methodically tearing it to shreds. "And it's not just between
her and me, it's between her and me and the children—we're
all intertwined. From time to time, it makes me very happy.
It also has me climbing the walls. Often I think I can't take it
anymore, I need a divorce. Otherwise I'll be dead before I'm
fifty. Too much angst, it ain't worth it. Naturally, when I
consider divorce, I start thinking about other women, having
affairs, all the crap that goes on when you're out in the arena.
In fact, sometimes it feels like I've spent half my life tormenting
myself with sexual fantasies."

"Normal enough. We all do."

Sasha walked over to the Doberman and dumped an armload
of shredded newspaper onto its head. Gloomily, the dog snarled.

"Yeah, sure, but you should understand something. Even
while I'm tormenting myself I'm thinking I probably wouldn't
ever be able to act on one of those fantasies. Who needs to
jump right into another profound relationship? Not me. And
yet everybody always wants to get you into a relationship."

"Maybe you just never had the type of relationship that
would make you see how beautiful one could be."

"And you would offer that?"

"Let's put it this way. I've gone through plenty since I
divorced Carter and came to Chamisaville. I may not have all

the answers, but one thing I do know is that I'm not afraid anymore."

"Afraid of what?" Sasha quit tormenting the dog and turned on the TV.

"I'm not afraid to ask for what I want. I'm not afraid of what other people think—I used to be terrified of that. I couldn't shit, piss, or spit for fear of what other people would say. That's no longer a problem. I do what I want."

"Well, I guess you're lucky. . . ." Guns, bombs, and bullets cavorted soundlessly on the wide-screen Zenith. "I guess one of my major problems has been that I've spent an awful lot of time doing what I thought other people wanted me to do, or what I thought I ought to do, rather than what I myself really needed to do."

"That can be a fairly negative trip to lay on yourself."

"But the thing is . . ." He was straining awkwardly, convinced he shouldn't be revealing such private thoughts to this laid-back enchantress. "The thing is, much of what I feel I *ought* to do *is* important. My instincts, my conscience are good, ethical, valuable. For example, loyalty to Heidi. And keeping the family whole. Working to build roots, make the kids happy, create a solidarity in their lives with strong, familial love. . . ."

Sasha grabbed the sound knob and turned it on full blast.

"I agree with you a hundred percent," Nancy said. "Sasha, turn that down a little." She reached back and did it herself. "Honestly, that monkey." And then: "No other hopes and dreams could be more valid."

"And the other drivel that can torment me—sexual fantasies, wanting affairs, wanting to be in the hay with you right now—that's bullshit. It's very shallow."

"Not 'shallow,' Joe. It's just some other perfectly valid feelings and expectations and desires, that's all."

Sasha disappeared around the corner into the kitchen.

Exasperated, also almost woozy from anticipation, Joe said, "Look, let's say we decided to ball. Right now. In five minutes. Before I even took one sock off, I would have to make certain that you would abide by my rules."

"What are your rules?"

"First of all, I don't want a deep relationship. It would have to be a casual thing. I'm too messed up right now to deal with more complexity, thanks anyway. There couldn't be any love in it, you know? I would refuse absolutely to get emotionally involved. No commitments."

"What about *my* rules?"

Something crashed in the kitchen.

"What about them?"

"I couldn't start anything unless I knew it was open-ended. There would have to be room for all possibilities to happen. I could never be involved in anything so cold-blooded as you suggest. I know that it's very possible to love more than one person at a time, and I know that the real thrill in life comes from being open to emotional growth. Otherwise, relationships just turn into bummers, and I've done my share of bummers. But I've learned my lessons, I've graduated beyond that now."

"Then there's no problem." Joe leaned back, his wistful disappointment partially defanged by enormous sensations of relief. "I wouldn't start anything with you on your terms, you wouldn't start anything on my terms. Exeunt omnes, chased by bear. Thanks for the hot chocolate. Now I gotta run."

"I could brew you some more."

"What time is it?" He checked his watch. "Jesus, look at this, it's almost four o'clock in the morning."

Covered from head to toe by organic honey powdered with Ovaltine, Sasha staggered balefully out of the kitchen. Nancy said, "Oh dear, look at that stupid monkey. I wish you wouldn't go, Joe."

"What do you mean?"

"I wish you would stay here." She grabbed Sasha by one arm and lugged him, dangling unceremoniously from her hand, down the hallway into the bathroom, where she turned on the sink faucet, dumped him in, and began lathering his fur with shampoo.

Joe said, "But I thought we had just decided . . ."

"I know, I know," she called. "But I like talking to you. You give me this incredible—how should I say it?—you give me a truly *peaceful* feeling inside. Despite our differences, I really feel at ease with you."

"Well, sure, but, you know, it really is late . . . in two hours Heather will be awake."

Nancy appeared in the doorway, wiping sudsy hands on her jersey. Slowly, as she smiled, that luster emanated from her, infusing first her entire being, then spreading throughout the room. It was uncanny.

Joe said, "Well, uh, so . . ." Creaking erect, he went for the door and opened it. "I really gotta split. Like I said—look!—it's practically dawn."

Nancy approached Joe with fluid understatement like a swan waking, abundantly graceful. Close to him, she leaned against the door. In her bare feet she was shorter than he had suspected: he assessed her at no taller than five-three. That intrigued him. Most of his women, before and including Heidi, had been robust characters. And tall. His erotic fantasies often featured diminutive sexual partners. Her presence was making him weak; her perfume, tunneling like a masterful French burglar into the impregnable vault of his senses, had him reeling. In the bathroom, Sasha started sneezing; water splashed onto the floor.

"Joe, I know you have to go. But before you do, could I ask you for one small favor?"

"Sure. Anything you want."

"Would you hold me just for a minute?"

"Why not?" Cheerfully, he curled his arms around her.

"Umm. That feels good."

Joe nodded, gulped, swallowed. She wasn't kidding it felt good. Nancy Ryan was maybe the softest, most pliable, most criminally sensuous woman he had ever embraced.

"It's so sad," she murmured.

"What is?"

"I don't know. I guess that there's just no room in your life for me. It's funny."

"Yeah, it's funny all right." Melting like whipped margarine, Joe trembled. The world's hardest erection lay right across her sweet tummy like a molybdenum-reinforced crowbar. She pretended to ignore it. He couldn't get over how muffled and affectionate she felt. *Physically*. Joe pressed his hand against her back, the palm between her shoulder blades. The hand seemed to cover her entire back. Her mellow breasts created a fleecy whispery gel, an almost inessential pressure against him. Like meringue, like goose down. Did she flex her stomach against his conspicuous and embarrassing ramrod?—he couldn't be sure. Without exercising any constraints, her arms nevertheless trapped a heady delirium inside his body. No fingers had touched his shoulders like this since the days of puppy love. Her head was tucked under his chin; he could feel her damp lips against his collarbone.

"Gosh." She had such a relaxed, sleepy voice. "This sure

feels good. You're bigger than I imagined. You look sort of slight, you know? But you *feel* so solid."

"Huh. That's curious. You're not the first person who ever said that. I mean, people often tell me that their first impression is I'm slight. That's actually the word they use—'slight.' And then they're surprised when they see me in a swimsuit, or with my shirt off or something. Because I'm more muscular than they thought."

Conversation in this vein sounded as if he were in training for the Simpleton Olympics! But he went on:

"I used to be an honest-to-God athlete. I played three varsity sports in college. I actually got more varsity letters than anybody else in my class."

"How many was that?"

"Seven."

"In what sports?"

"Well, I played football for one year, but never lettered. I didn't return my sophomore year because that was one sport, on the college level, that I couldn't stand. It was brutal, overemphasized, no fun. In its place I ran cross-country, lettering in my junior and senior years. I also lettered in track. And for three years in hockey."

Maybe if he kept up this dramatic, intellectual patter, he'd wither on her imagination's vine and get off scot-free. They continued embracing each other as she sighed: "Brother, I could just stay like this forever."

"It's nice." All his muscles reverberated with the sort of wonderful swooning ache that could be caused by a sauna and a massage. His heart threatened to crack his sternum. Weak-kneed, addle-headed, he had forgotten the incapacitating excitement of holding another woman for the first time. For too long, thrills like this one had been absent from his prosaic wanderings. Heady stuff, indeed. Joe rubbed his chin against her hair, just a bit. She responded by very gently caressing the back of his neck. Joy, mitigated by an anguished desire to cry out like Adam over the loss of his innocence (not to mention integrity), welled up inside. His resolve was crumbling. Already fluid leaked out of his penis. Yet, wanting to groan "Let's make love," he held his tongue. It would have to be her move.

Something crashed in the bathroom.

Nancy said, "Would you just come and lie down with me for a minute?"

Barely able to croak it out, he said, "There's no point..."

"Nothing will happen. I feel terribly close to you right now, that's all. It would mean so much to snuggle for just five minutes."

Never one to go down without a fight, Joe mumbled, "But we already agreed..."

"I know. Don't worry. Nothing could happen anyway, I've got my period."

"All right then, if you want. Just for a minute, though. Then I really have to go. It's late."

Joe shut the front door and held her hand as she led him down the short carpeted hallway. He caught a glimpse into the first room on the left, which belonged to Sasha. On a single low coffee table sat a bonsai tree and an incense stick stabbed into a clump of clay. A lighthearted pretty Persian spread covered a sumptuous mattress on the floor. Atop the mattress lay a grotesque, six-foot-tall, passion-pink, blond-haired and buxom inflatable Japanese sex doll, her legs spread wide open, silently awaiting whatever transgressions a little monkey's pea brain could conjure.

Joe stopped. "Wait a minute—what's that?"

"It's Sasha's. He loves her. It was easier than buying a mate. And he never bites her—she's perfect for all his sexual aggression."

Across the hall, Sasha himself stood in the bathroom doorway, wrapped in a little pink towel, his teeth chattering loudly.

A wide double bed covered with a colorful puffy quilt dominated her room. A photograph of the guru, a candle, and an incense stick stood on her dresser. More metaphysical monkeys decorated the walls. Nancy settled luxuriously into the comforter; painfully, Joe descended beside her. Lying side by side, holding hands, they watched mysterious pluvial candle-cast shadows on the ceiling. Joe shook his head, destroying the image of a two-foot-tall monkey grappling with that latex amazon. Then Nancy rolled over and hugged him, burrowing her head against his shoulder again. A dead-quiet minute ensued. Nancy raised her head a little and kissed him. Their lips hung fire, barely touching. Her tongue tip sallied forth, laxly wetting his lips. Her eyes stayed closed, Joe kept his open. Nothing he could do would stop it now. He was fascinated by his inability to halt the process. Moments like this could make him believe that sooner or later the planet would be annihilated by a nuclear holocaust. Yet, despite the marital disaster in the offing, finally he was going to gratify some erotic curiosity. So what if, at the heart of the indulgence, dwelled his own self-destruction? Profound sadness and downright overwhelming melancholy guided one hand to her breasts. The other hand clamped her more tightly against him.

"Oh gosh," she said breathlessly. "This is sweet."

At first it happened gently, as if they had been old friends. As soon as he pushed her backward and had swung between her legs, Joe calmed down. The fear and trembling of anticipation was replaced by the act itself. She was flooded with goo: he slipped in easily. Nancy said, "Oh." They froze, savoring it, then began to make love. Her erotic passivity floored him. Instantly, he knew that he could do with her whatever he wished. A near-jibbering idiot moments ago, he was astonished by his sudden composure.

It had been over a decade since he had balled a woman other than Heidi, and yet he felt right at home. Holy mackerel—this was *easy*! Joe withdrew and toyed with her, gently teasing. He caressed her thighs slowly, touched fingertips to the sweet places on either side of her groin, inserted three fingers and massaged her clitoris lackadaisically with his thumb. She squirmed, murmured. After a minute, he backed up a little, lowered his head between her legs and nibbled gently, sending tremors up her body with his tongue. He sucked in all her wonderful tendrils and chewed them softly. Her fingers scrabbled lovingly in his hair; she arched, trying to press herself perfectly against his lips, teaching him how best to do her.

"Oh sweet baby..." The words scorched from a slow fire in her throat. Her thighs shivered against his ears. Her fingers slipped under his lips to play with herself as he sucked. He twanged her little target with the tip of his tongue, and Nancy squealed almost inaudibly: "It's so good...don't stop...please, finish me off...."

But he raised his mouth, whispering, "Not yet." She gave a disappointed, urgent murmur. Turning her over, Joe lifted her fanny into position, dropped his head again, and mooshed gobs of spittle between the crease of her buttocks, then deliberately probed her anus with his tongue. She gasped, saying "Sweet Jesus..." and "I never dreamed..." Joe reached for a pillow, slipping it under her belly, then pushed her prone. Straddling the backs of her thighs, he spread her legs out with his feet, arranged her arms at her sides, and gripped them tightly. Her ass bloomed at him, mushroom smooth and white, round and pornographic. From her open mouth saliva drooled onto the sheet. The wonderfully constricting muscles of her vagina sucked him in voraciously: plump gluteals settled against either side of his groin in a perfect fit.

Joe reached one hand under her belly to massage and manipulate again. "I'm gonna come," she hissed. "I can't hold back. . . ." At that, a real fondness for her, even a surge of love, rattled him for a second. He almost lost his composure. Her skin beneath him swelled with magical opulence, too good to be true, like puberty fantasies about movie stars. He could see her orgasm as it rippled throughout her happy frame. Joe warned himself desperately about the love as his own orgasm gathered—and then passed. His erotic tension was replaced by a bizarre, cold-blooded sensation as she squirmed spastically amid exclamations of "Oh dear . . . oh joy . . . oh my gosh . . ."

Dreamily, Joe licked his thumb and pried it into her anus. She gave a cry and her fingernails dug painfully into his flesh just above the knees. A feeling of panic arose. To be inside a woman and feel so *cold*. Joe wanted to holler "Stop!" and "I'm sorry!" and "I don't love you at all!" But he kept quiet. Yet he had never really screwed a woman just for the fun of it, just for the physical off—he had always felt (or thought he felt) *in love*—and his reaction was weird. He wanted to make it all right by saying, "I love you, Nancy, I really do." But that was crazy. Then the feeling subsided. Joe shivered from a chill and from a sense that this was wrong. Then suddenly, angrily, he banged into her a half-dozen strokes, thrust a final time, hard, causing her to blurt "Ouch!," and slumped, bending over to rest his breast against her shoulder blades. He buried his face in the nest of her neck, sighing in the kind of pain he would not dare express.

They relaxed.

An ugly phrase came into Joe's head, and repeated itself: *Find 'em, feel 'em, fuck 'em, forget 'em.*

Eventually, she said, "Wow." As he wilted inside her, Joe dazedly munched on her neck. What did they call this—"recreational sex"? Lazily, she readjusted. And queried: "Did you come?"

"It was incredible," he whispered, trying to sound sincere. "I loved it."

"I wasn't sure." She slurred the words sexily. "Don't move for a minute, whatever you do."

Exhausted, Joe lay there as if in a sleeper berth on a midnight train, listening to the wheels clack out a rhythm and a rhyme: *Find 'em, feel 'em, fuck 'em, forget 'em. . . .*

The telephone rang.

Nancy murmured, "Would you get it, please? I'm so comfortable."

Bumping into walls, bureaus, and paintings, Joe groggily maneuvered into the gloomy living room and snatched up the receiver. "Hello," said a high-pitched voice almost drowned in long-distance static. "Is this the Ryan pad? Are you Randall?"

"This is her place, yeah. But she's indisposed at the moment. And I'm not Randall, I'm Joe Miniver. Can I take a message?"

"Okay, but listen carefully, man, they're only giving us one phone call. This is Rama Unfug, I think you know me. I'm a photographer traveling with a group that's bringing the Hanuman statue to Chamisaville. But we ran into a little problem. The van got a flat in the Holland Tunnel last night during rush hour. We didn't have a spare. So Wilkerson Busbee hadda try and hike out with the tire to a garage, but he was overcome by the monoxide. This lady with us, Iréné Papadraxis, started mouthing off at the cops when they arrived, so they searched the van, found Fluff Dimaggio's lid of pot and a revolver he doesn't have a New York license for, and decided we must of ripped off the monkey god. They also discovered Baba Ram Bang doesn't have a valid visa to be in the USA. But that's not the worst of it. Baba Ram Bang's a diabetic, you dig? And somebody on the wrecking crew that towed us out must of stolen his insulin. So he's right on the edge of shock. You need to tell Nancy that the Simian Foundation had better wire some bread for bail and get a doctor to order these jerks to give us some insulin. And maybe somebody in Chamisaville knows a good New York lawyer who could figure out how to steer us clear of being detained under the Sullivan Law. . . ."

Back in bed, as best he could, Joe related the garbled message. Nancy said, "Oh golly, I'll be right back, don't go away." Joe lay there, semidumbfounded by her composure while she chatted pleasantly on the living-room phone for five minutes.

When she returned, he said, "How can you even begin to unravel that mess?"

Laughing, she snuggled in beneath him. "It's easy. You just don't panic. These things happen all the time. They'll be on their way again before noon."

Dawn glimmered faintly outside the window. Roosters crowed, a car started up. Heather would awaken shortly, rolling out of bed to perform her morning rituals. After taking a leak, she'd head for the kitchen, open the fridge, score a few swallows of OJ, then pad sleepily into the master bedroom and climb into the big double bed, snuggling down between her mom and dad for an extra hour of delicious shut-eye.

Only, where was Daddy this A.M.? Up so early, collecting garbage?

Touching his cheek, Joe was startled to encounter tears.

Nancy spoke cozily, her words a smidgen slurred. "Is anything the matter?"

"No, I'm okay. That lovemaking was wonderful."

The Doberman wafted silently into the room. Joe only realized it was there when the dog's velvety jowls brushed against his feet. He said, "Hey, what's with the mutt?"

"That's okay. He's friendly."

"He's licking my feet."

"He does that sometimes."

Joe rested on top of her while the Doberman slobbered over his feet. After it had run down that particular fawning course, the animal circled to the bedside, sat down, and stared at Joe: he returned the compliment. A plaintive note was struck by the dog's eyes: restless, sad, a trifle lost. Was that a slight squeak from its throat? Leaning forward, the dog laid its head on the bed, black nose only inches away from Nancy's face.

"What is this dog's name, anyway?"

"Bozo."

Joe raised his eyes from Bozo to her night table. Beside the clock-radio, a Kleenex box, cigarettes and an ashtray, a prescription bottle of Valiums, and a John Cheever novel, *Bullit Park*, stood another photograph of the jolly plump guru.

"Who's the guy in all these photographs?"

"Baba Ram Bang."

"The guy in the U-Haul with Wilkerson Busbee, Fluff Dimaggio, Iréné Papawhatsits, the Unfugs, and their daughter Om?"

"One and the same." Sleepily, she drawled, "I want a cigarette. Would you light one for me, please?"

Joe reached over the dog's head for cigarettes and a pack
of matches. Sticking a weed in his mouth, he lit it, and, without
inhaling, blew out a great cloud of smoke. "Okay, it's lit. . . ."

"Just touch it to my mouth and let me have a drag. But
don't move. I love having you against me."

Nancy tilted her head up a little. Joe placed the cigarette at
her lips. She sucked on it hungrily, making the tip glow brightly.
"Thanks, pal. . . ." Dropping her head onto the comforter again,
she released the smoke. "Oh, that's so heavenly." The dog
whimpered, coughed, complained throatily, and departed.

Joe held the cigarette, anticipating her demand for another
drag. Wide awake and growing antsy, he asked, "Am I crushing
you?"

"Not at all. I love it."

The parakeet flew in, circled the room twice, and alighted
on the clock radio. Chirping once, it fluttered onto Joe's shoulder. The tiny fibrillating heart sent tremors of miniature vitality
down through the bird's teeny-weeny feet. A minuscule doot
of hot shit splashed onto Joe's cool shoulder, and the parakeet
was gone again.

"What's the bird's name?" he cooed into her ear.

"Cheepy. . . ."

Cheepy and Bozo and Sasha: holy fuckin' mackerel!

Joe sweated, held there against his will, molded around her
feverish and delectable body. The real world beckoned. He
had to leave, jump up and run away like a thief, and face the
music at home. And learn what had happened to Peter. And
cook Sunday breakfast for the kids. And give Heidi an explanation—the truth? No! He would lie through his teeth!

The clock said 6:11 A.M. Joe's left leg had gone to sleep.
He shifted. Nancy gurgled, responding happily. She flexed first
the left, then the right buttock. Oh no, not again! Hard as rock,
with a barely perceptible thrust, he plunged once more into her
smoldering goo. She yodeled, "God I love it!" and squirmed.

Suddenly, a change in the electric nature of the air they
breathed made Joe look up. Bradley stood in the doorway,
wearing only a pair of Jockey briefs, holding Sasha's hand.
The parakeet was perched on his head. Bozo sat forlornly beside
the kid. All four of these beasties stared perplexedly at Joe

Miniver as he hauled, in no uncertain terms, Nancy Ryan's ashes.

Bradley piped, "What are you doing, Mr. Miniver?"

All Joe could think to respond was, "Please go away. Can't you see I'm touching your mother?"

TIPPED OFF BY A CHILD, VICE SQUAD BUSTS DEVIATE ADULTERER! ABANDONED WIFE ALERTS DRUG AGENTS TO BOLLIXED DOPE DEAL! MINIVER EXECUTED AT DAWN!

2
Sunday

Nine in the third place means:
The spokes burst out of the wagon wheels.
Man and wife roll their eyes.

An hour later, freshly scrubbed and tingling, his body humming from fatigue, apprehension, and a half-dozen other sensations that he thought had atrophied for lack of being tapped over the past decade, Joe steered his red-and-gold VW bus with the cracked windshield, taped-over side window, 190,000-mile track record in life, and advertising logo—MINIVER TRUCKING: WE HAUL EVERYTHING FROM SOUP TO HAY—onto the Chamisaville plaza.

Several years back the plaza had been a pastoral park. Shaded by enormous cottonwood and chinese elm trees, with a few flagstone walks, lilac bushes and flower gardens and old-fashioned benches, it had also been home to a Chamber of Commerce tourist information booth and a concrete pillbox housing the Chamisaville Police Department, whose roof constituted the fiesta bandstand. Then some CETA, SCUM, DARVAC, and other government-program funds had wound up hovering above the town coffers, offering to drop if the city fathers voted to renovate their park system. So naturally the town council decided to modernize the plaza.

Presto!—a gaggle of bulldozers, backhoes, water pumps, concrete mixers, bricklayers, carpenters, tree cutters, plumbers, and other assorted construction riffraff promptly descended upon the plaza. First, they knocked down almost anything that had leaves or looked quaint or was functional. Then they set to gouging, plowing, slicing, shoring, destroying, and battering the area with a truly joyous vengeance. When they finished, four trees remained standing in a solid brick-and-concrete mass of cantilevered ramps, cattywampused nooks, and reticulated crannies so cute and arty that the plaza now looked like the result of a brawl between the pioneering architect, Frank Lloyd Wright, and the tacky film mogul, Walt Disney. Dandified, black wrought-iron benches littered the brickyard, their backrests consisting of a Technicolor enamel depicting Howard Johnsonian revolutionary war soldiers and Victorian milkmaids. The town police pillbox still housed the cops, but it was topped by a circular gazebo and mollusc roof reminiscent of a thatched Polynesian hut. The Chamber of Commerce information booth had been reconstructed to approximate what the Taj Mahal might have resembled had it been built originally as an outhouse. Several ten-foot-high concrete pyramids with steep steps leading to their summits were closer to being anti-tank obstructions than children's play environments. A goldfish pond and fountain in the heart of the paved-over park had recently been filled in and planted (almost weekly) with petunias, because the original eighteen goldfish had survived less than twenty-four hours before they were eagerly devoured by starving Indians and gaga hippies blissfully zonked on twenty hits of Piccadilly acid.

This is not to say that the plaza was finished—not by a long shot. During Joe's three years in Chamisaville, the construction snafus from one end of town to the other had defied at least his imagination. Without exception, from January to December, all of the boomtown's main arteries and public gathering places were clogged by road crews, asphalt cutters, jackhammer drillers, backhoe operators, sewage technicians, bewildered hardhats manning bilge pumps, and befuddled macadam engineers slopping down hot mixes. You couldn't travel one hundred feet in Chamisaville without hitting a detour sign. Roads freshly paved in June were dug up in July, resurfaced in August, and chopped to smithereens in September. Getting from place A to place B in the rustic burg invariably entailed zigzagging through a veritable minefield of construction boondoggles so impenetrable and uncircumnavigable as to try the sanity of even the hardiest maze runner. What puzzled Joe was that Chamisaville had a very limited number of roads to maintain. Yet the variations on the excavation, sewage and water-line, pothole-patrol, widening, deepening, curbing, grading, regrading, and degrading themes that could be played by a relatively finite bunch of dedicated state and local highway sadists was infinite.

Hence, when Joe steered onto the plaza, he had to run a slalom course between festering wheelbarrows, blinker barricades, smudge pots, sump pumps, and signs announcing that his tax dollars were at work for a better America, before coasting to a stop at a meter in front of the Evergreen Drugstore next door to the Prince of Whales Café. Caught without a nickel, Joe warily canvassed the area to see if the cops' meter reader, Vaughn Tallyrand, was lurking nearby, hiding—as he often did—behind one of the portal garbage cans, which had been decorated, by local artists, with Picasso-esque and Braquian grotesqueries (during a beautification program sponsored by the Friends of Chamisa Valley) twenty-seven months ago.

Vaughn Tallyrand was the only meter reader in America who would distribute one-dollar fines at seven o'clock on a Sunday morning. Last Christmas—talk about injustice!—at 11:00 A.M., Joe had scored a parking violation when he left his car for thirty seconds to fetch the holiday papers.

But Vaughn, thank God, was nowhere in sight. Only a few folks stirred on the plaza. An ancient and venerated artist, Judson Babbitt III, was feeding bread crumbs to the pigeons. Dressed in a Persian-pink warm-up suit and beige Adidas, Suki Terrell, ex-wife of Jeff Orbison (of EAT ME and Ragtime Flowers fame), was jogging across the brickyard alongside Cobey Dallas; he looked resplendent in a midnight-blue running outfit and lime-green Adidas.

Joe locked up (he had been ripped off in Chamisaville—to the tune of several spare tires, all his tools twice, his scissors jack once, his checkbook thrice, and his groceries a half-dozen times—much more often than he had ever been burglarized in New York). He locked up, and entered the drugstore, where he purchased a *Rocky Mountain News*, an *Albuquerque Journal*, and a *Capital City Reporter* from the store's new owner, Lon Kennedy, a former Caribbean tour organizer for an Atlanta, Georgia, travel agency. Helpless in the morning before his "hit" of news, Joe was not, in this respect, a typical Chamisaville resident. Most folks he knew actually bragged that they never read the paper anymore.

Joe said "hi" to Scott Harrison; the lawyer looked devastating in a purple-and-green warm-up suit and lavender Adidas. He replied: "Hey there, lover boy!" Hurriedly, Joe slunk next door to the Prince of Whales Café for some caffeinated stroking before heading off to face the disasters certain to plague his day.

Immersed in the Sunday morning blues, Ralph Kapansky slouched at a front table, his back up against the jukebox, a cup of cold coffee hooked in his left index finger, his nose buried in the Sunday comics. His graying hair was ruffled, his eyes were pouched and puffy, his lips were set in a mournful snarl. He wore a gardenia-and-mauve warm-up suit and burgundy Adidas. At his feet, bloated, shaggy Rimpoche busily scratched at fleas.

Joe whacked his friend on the back, adopting a W. C. Fields drawl as he asked, "Ralph, m'boy, what's happening around the globe?" Then he dropped a quarter in the jukebox and punched out a Dolly Parton, a Merle Haggard, and a Theodore Bikel tune.

Glumly, Ralph said, "They flattened Beirut, they drowned Bangladesh, they kidnapped an Italian, they gave the Nobel Prize to a Nazi, and the Yankees already clinched the pennant three and a half months before the end of the season."

"But how come you look so horrible?"

"They called me to repair a goddam helicopter at one P.M. Then I was up all night doing a ménage à trois."

The jukebox rattled and wheezed in response to Joe's quarter.

"What are you doing, Joseph?" Ralph seemed genuinely alarmed. "Playing honky-tonk music on Sunday morning?"

"You looked sad. I wanna cheer you up."

Ralph assessed him perplexedly. "Sunday is a classical-music day, idiot. Where are your New York roots? And what are you doing up at this hour anyway on a holiday? We're not supposed to meet until twelve. Did the stuff come in with your friend on the bus last night?"

"What do you think?"

"Who's paying me to think?"

"Nothing came in on the bus," Joe said. "Not my pal, not the dope, nothing."

"What happened?"

"If I knew would I be sitting here griping to you?"

"I dunno, would you?"

"Oh Jesus." Briefly, Joe took stock of his surroundings. Only two other people were dining in the café at this hour. One was Diana Clayman's Apache friend with the pitted face, Angel Guts. Actually, Joe happened to know the man had no Indian blood. You could forget the black hair and slightly Oriental features, the eagle-feathered hat and porcupine-quill neck choker. Angel Guts was a Polish kid named Orville Jablonski from the Lower East Side of New York City. He had, at one point—way back in the mid-sixties—been investigated by the FBI for allegedly conspiring to assassinate Richard Nixon. This happened during his stint as a member of the RAT newspaper collective before it went entirely feminist. Nothing had come of the investigation, though. And by the time he drifted into Chamisaville last year, Angel Guts had his Apache genealogy down pat, just another East Coast pusher posing as a Native American, who, Joe had heard, often worked as a runner for Ray Verboten. He was leaning back in his chair, arms folded, staring straight into space, an untouched coffee at his side. The kid would sit that way—inscrutable, mysterious, hostile—forever.

The other dreg was a shadowy nameless little fart commonly referred to as Nick Danger. Bearded, belligerent, and preposterously antisocial, Nick was perpetually incognito'd behind and underneath a green Tyrolean hat, a brown Naugahyde trenchcoat, and one-way Acapulco sunglasses. The man carried a battered beige suitcase wherever he crept, and never spoke to a soul. He inhabited room 7 in the decrepit Dynamite Shrine motel and seemed to spend all his waking hours wandering aimlessly about town looking sinister.

Ralph said, "So did you call him up or anything?"

"Not yet."

"Why not?"

"Hey man, lighten up on the third degree, already. I haven't even had my coffee yet."

"You brought it up."

"No I didn't. You asked if the stuff came in last night."

Darlene Johnson, the World's Greatest Waitress, landed beside Joe, asking, "What are you so cheerful about this morning?"

"There's a law says I gotta walk around with a shit-eating grin on my face twenty-four hours a day? Come on, Darlene, gimme a break. I had a rough night last night."

Darlene said, "Did you hear about the Hanuman?"

"What about it?"

"Apparently their U-Haul was involved in a six-car crash in a New York tunnel. The statue was shattered and Baba Ram Bang is in a coma in the intensive-care ward of a big metropolitan hospital. Little Om, the Unfugs' daughter, went through the windshield, and a team of neurosurgeons at Mount Sinai Hospital are trying to sew her hand back on to her arm. It's horrible."

Joe said, "Not only that, but I heard Wilkerson Busbee had to undergo ninety days of rabies shots because he was bit by a rat that fell down through a tunnel vent under the Hudson River."

"Aw, c'mon, Joe—you're kidding?"

But he liked Darlene. Formerly, she had been a paleontologist connected to the Field Museum of Natural History. In Chamisaville she was always turning up as the chairperson of committees to save things, to Save the Whales, to Save the Farmer's Market, to save the Historical Old Roybal Home (though never the old Roybals). A tall lady in her late twenties whose physical appearance was often called "rawboned," Darlene had long arms, big expressive hands, and a startlingly powerful face, like Abraham Lincoln.

Joe ordered a fried egg, over easy, two link sausages, one piece of toast, a cup of Sanka, and a small orange juice. Actually, what he said was: "Darlene, gimme a cyclops, OE, side order of squeal—that's link piggies not patties—a small Florida sunshine, one toasted wheat, and a cuppa ersatz Joe."

She tapped him playfully atop his head with her pencil. "I bet you think you're funny."

"Who's funnier?" Joe called after her.

"Melvin Morgue! Frankenstein! Dracula!"

Ralph said, "Is she telling the truth about the Hanuman brigade?"

"Rumors. You know this town. An eight-year-old kid falls off his bicycle in front of the Tastee-Freez and scrapes his knee: five hours later Darlene serves Cobey Dallas his coffee and asks did he hear about the kid whose head was crushed under the metal treads of a backhoe in front of its own mother who at the time was gagging on a chicken bone at the Colonel's bucket of toasted pullets."

"Well, tell me this," Ralph said. "Is it true you balled Nancy Ryan last night?"

Joe tried not to blanch. "Where did you hear that?"

"Iréné Papadraxis called Natalie Gandolf last night to explain that they might be held up on account of a flat tire in the Holland Tunnel. Skipper and Natalie are throwing that preunveiling bash at their mansion Wednesday night, remember? So Iréné wanted to warn them it might have to be postponed. Natalie had a conniption and couldn't find any Valium. So she called Marilyn Tibby up at five A.M. to see if she had any, and spilled the whole story. Gypsy Girl and I just happened to be over at Marilyn's."

"I still don't see where Nancy and me come in."

"Iréné told Natalie, who told Marilyn, that apparently when Rama Unfug called Nancy to get bail money, a mouthpiece, and a piece of medical script for Baba Ram Bang's insulin, you answered the telephone at her place."

"I don't believe it! I'm a goner."

"There's more if you can take it."

"I can't, but you better tell me anyway."

"Okay. Soon as Natalie heard, and while she was flailing around trying to turn up a Valium, she decided she had better call Scott Harrison and ask his opinion on what sort of advice, re legal moves, she ought to call back to Iréné, or Rama, or Wilkerson, or whoever's personning the fort back there."

"Whoever's *what*ening the fort?"

"Please. Scott got pissed because it's five A.M., and he was shacked up with Suki Terrell: apparently she had a tiff with Randall at the Hanuman Follies last night and decided to ask Scott to teach her how to be a ULC nun. He told Natalie to call Nancy and ask the Simian Foundation to find somebody else to do their dirty work. So Natalie blurted to Scott that she didn't really want to call Nancy back because apparently she was having a blast shacked up with you."

"You're joking. You're a sadist telling me lies just for the hell of it."

"Wish I was, old boy. But Marilyn got a call ten minutes later from Suki Terrell, asking was it true that you and Nancy Ryan were doing a number."

"And Marilyn replied?"

"She says she told Suki to call Nancy and ask her."

"Suki didn't call Nancy," Joe groaned. "Not while I was there."

"No. But apparently Natalie called Tribby, to see if he would give any advice. So Tribby called a number in New York that I guess Iréné had given and he spoke with Rama Unfug. During the conversation, Rama happened to ask if you and Heidi had gotten a divorce. He was curious, you know, having heard on the grapevine that you guys might be his new neighbors. Naturally, when Tribby said 'No, why?' Rama told him that when he had called Nancy at five A.M., you had answered the telephone. So right away Tribby called me at Marilyn's and asked was the dope deal off or what? Then he explained to me that you were playing footsie with Nancy Ryan when you should have been entertaining your friend Peter Roth and five pounds of cocaine."

Morosely, Joe said, "I don't believe this is happening to me."

"Well, at least you nailed her. That's always fun."

"I didn't 'nail' her, Ralph. It was a nice experience," he lied, swamped with guilt and no doubt blushing crimson. "I actually enjoyed it."

"Okay. Congratulations."

"Screw your hosannas. I feel lousy. I never cheated on Heidi before. I wanted to plenty of times, but I never did."

"It's no big deal. The world doesn't explode."

"A lot you know."

"Look around you, dummy. Has the plaza been reduced to rubble? Are all the plate-glass windows shattered? Is Darlene nursing a couple of shiners and bleeding from the nostrils?"

"Thanks for the sympathy."

"Hey, it's not a big thing. Happens all the time."

"I don't care. I feel creepy."

Ralph tapped his shoulder good-naturedly. "Easy, amigo. You're not the first person who ever copped a little nookie out of season."

"I didn't 'cop a little nookie,' man. I happened to ball a very nice person, and—"

"What are you trying to say—you're in love with another broad?"

Joe said, "Why don't you refine the language a little? You make it sound so tawdry. Nancy isn't a 'broad.' She happens to be a very decent and complex human being, who is also sensational in bed."

"Bueno. So what?"

"This sort of transgression isn't my style. I don't *want* to cheat on Heidi. It feels so improper and . . . weird."

"Joe, in 1955, if you committed adultery, you might have had a problem. In this day and age, if you don't bag a few cunts on the sly, people will start thinking you're a faggot."

"I really wish you wouldn't use words like 'cunt' and 'faggot.'"

As Darlene placed Joe's breakfast on the table, Ralph addressed her: "Darlene, I'd like you to meet my friend here, Joseph Miniver, three-time winner of the Mr. Puritan Universe contest."

Joe threw up his hands. Darlene said, "Don't pay any attention to him, Joe, he's a wise guy. And a cynic. He writes pornography."

"What am I supposed to do," Ralph complained, "canonize him for falling from his state of original grace and yet remaining sensitive, compassionate, and concerned about the people involved who are going to be the victims of a terrible tragedy because he had the chance to slip somebody a stiff one and took it?"

Joe sliced open his egg, cut out a piece of it, forked off a chunk of sausage, arranged the egg and the sausage on a corner of his toast, and bit off the corner. Knocking it down with a slug of orange juice and a sip of Sanka, he moaned, "I'm dead. I blew it. What a shlemozzl."

"Relax. Just lie to her. Tell her you spent the night with me. I'll corroborate your story. We got to drinking and talking about literature up in my office after the bar closed. You got stewed and passed out."

"Didn't you just finish telling me that everybody from Natalie Gandolf and Scott Harrison to Suki Terrell and the Mormon Tabernacle Choir were informed by telephone, last night, of my whereabouts?"

Ralph said, "Listen to this: 'A melon farmer in Wyatt Earp, Missouri—'"

"Wyatt Earp, Missouri?"

"That's what it says here . . . 'paid his taxes to the IRS by tattooing his check on one of his own watermelons.' The IRS sent the melon to this guy's bank, and the bank cashed it. Know how they then canceled it?"

"I'm talking to you about possibly the biggest crisis of my life, and you have the audacity to start reading me stories about some kook—"

"They ate it."

"You're a big help. Thanks a lot, man."

"Here's another one. Dateline Maple City, New Hampshire. 'Local fish-and-game authorities recently arrested a woman named Ethel Sturgeon for killing a deer out of season. Mrs. Sturgeon said it wasn't her fault. She said she was sitting in her breakfast nook feeding the baby when an eight-point buck walked through the open front door. She was frightened for the child's safety. . . .' Says here the kid's name was Myron, age two. So she killed the buck. You know how?"

"You're an ugly human being. You really are."

"She beat the animal to death with a toilet plunger."

"You're lying."

"Read it for yourself. Says right here."

"I'll see you, *pal*."

"Twelve o'clock at the airport, right?"

Joe fished a sawbuck out of his front pocket, and dropped it on the table for Darlene as he addressed his hardhearted buddy: "Hope you enjoy the paper, knowing that Heidi is probably beating *me* to death with a toilet plunger, a scene you could have avoided by lending a slightly more sympathetic ear."

"'Neither a borrower nor a lender be,'" Ralph advised, dismissing his good friend by burrowing ever deeper into the Sunday newspaper. Rimpoche was still snuffling in his shaggy fur, nipping wee bugs.

As he plummeted out the jangling door, Darlene called, "Congratulations on your new relationship, Joe!"

Spinning to give her the finger, Joe didn't see the approach of Jeff Orbison—they collided. "Hey," Jeff said. "Where's the fire, man?" Sweat glistened on his dissipated plump face. He was wearing a yellow warm-up suit and mandarin-orange Adidas. A beaded headband kept his hair in place. His breath could have blown open a vault.

"No fire, Jeff. Life is a bowl of cherries."

"Say," the singer said. "What's this I hear about a gang of thieves that hijacked the Hanuman statue in New York, took Baba Ram Bang hostage, and shot Shanti Unfug in the chest during their escape?"

"What do I look like, the Simian Foundation's press secretary?"

"You were shacked up with Nancy Ryan when the call came through last night, weren't you?"

"Aw, do me a favor. . . ." Joe staggered down the sidewalk and swung into his bus.

Jeff said, "Wait a sec. I gotta talk to you."

Joe put the key in the ignition, and sat there, staring dully forward, wondering if he should commit suicide. Or, when he turned the key, would Ray Verboten's auto-bomb expert have done it for him?

"Speaking of Ray Verboten," Jeff said. "The word's out he's looking for you."

"I can't imagine why."

"They say you've got a shipment of smack coming in, and that you're planning to infringe on his market."

"It isn't smack, it's cocaine, Jeffrey. And it has nothing to do with Ray Verboten. Believe me, he's welcome to the territory."

"I'll be your bodyguard," Jeff said. "For two hundred a week. I've got a .357 magnum, and that ain't a Ping-Pong paddle. For an extra hundred a week I'll bring in Tom Yard: he's got a police .38. He actually used to be a cop up in Ouray, Colorado, before they caught him stealing the department's stash of confiscated Mary Jane."

"Thanks, but I think I can handle it." Joe felt dizzy.

"You okay? You look a little green."

"I feel a little green."

"Listen, I got just the thing for the mean old greenies in my car. You ever done cutworm moths?"

"Cutworm moths?"

"Sure, it's the latest. They pioneered it up at the Milky Way. They put all these cutworm moths in a box with a mixture of STP, PCP, and vitamin C in powder form. Those moths'll eat anything and apparently they really lap that stuff up. You gotta watch 'em close, though, because they don't live too long after they scarf the goodies, and you have to nosh them within ten minutes after they croak. In that time their chemistry does something special to the shit, and the rush that hits you is like taking off from Cape Kennedy for Lunar City."

"Thanks, but no thanks."

"Suit yourself. It's your funeral."

One deep breath later, Joe twisted the key. He elicited a glare from the dashboard's red and green lights, but only a *click*! from the starter. Cursing softly, he climbed into the back seat for his tools, then crawled underneath the bus and touched pliers handles to wire-connection points on the solenoid attached to the starter. Something gave a fluttering *clack*! in there, and dirt fell in his eye. He snarled and spent five minutes trying to knuckle away the pain.

Ralph's feet and Rimpoche's paws appeared at the edge of his car: "Everything all right under there?" Ralph queried imperiously.

"No thanks to you."

"Well, I'm going home. I need a float. You got me all tense in there."

"Bon voyage, bunghole."

But he had forgotten his change. Making a Dracula face as he cackled "the Master of the False Exit strikes again!," Joe slumped ashamedly back into the Prince of Whales and took—without a word—the seven dollars Darlene offered.

"What happened to your eye, Joe—you got punched?"

Ignoring her, he headed for the door.

"One other thing," she called after him.

Joe stopped in his tracks, but didn't turn around. Instead, he hunched up his shoulders and grimaced, like a man expecting an arrow to tunk between his shoulder blades.

"Tribby Gordon just called, looking for you. He says it's urgent you get back right away."

"Did he say what about?"

"He said he heard that your friend was on the Trailways bus last night when it was hijacked and dumped into the Rio Grande with all passengers aboard. He wanted to know if your friend was really in the intensive-care ward at the Our Lady of the Sorrows Hospital undergoing surgery to replace a severed hand."

"Ha ha, Darlene. You're a million laughs."

"He was *serious*!"

The door banged behind him. For some strange reason—his psychic powers were functioning—Joe thought to check under the vehicle's right rear wheel, and sure enough, his abandoned pliers lay there. With a stifled growl, he snatched them up.

Shifting gingerly, depressing and releasing the clutch with a delicate finesse (his throw-out bearing was almost gone), Joe muttered, "The light forces of Innocence and Righteousness triumph over the dark forces of Devious Technology yet once again," and steered his car out of the plaza, heading west.

"Oh damn!"

He had left his papers in the café. But on second thought, the oversight was probably a blessing in disguise. For no doubt the headlines he'd been too preoccupied to check out declared:

CHAMISAVILLE DRUG FIEND RAPES HANUMAN GROUPIE!
STATEWIDE MANHUNT PROCLAIMED!

Though a Chamisaville resident for only three years, the changes Joe had observed along Route 240 during his brief sojourn were stunning. A new house went up every day. Back when electricity entered the Pueblo and construction began on Joseph Bonatelli's dog-racing track and Ya-Ta-Hey Hotel complex, land in Chamisaville had been going for two thousand an acre. Now it had skyrocketed to nine, ten, sometimes fifteen grand an acre, with no end in sight. New houses, built exclusively by valley newcomers, inevitably combined the ridiculous and the sublime.

Old-style adobes, favored by Spanish-speaking valley denizens, had been solid, flat-roofed, one-story dwellings, so simple they seemed logical extensions of the earth. Unobtrusive, beautiful, and architecturally similar, for centuries their unpretentious sameness had added to the valley's feeling of community. In contrast, the new houses were explosions of individual expression gone awry. Every house was unique, an extension (call it a flaunting) of its owner's implacable ego. The design idiosyncrasies of each dwelling slobbered all over themselves. If fabricated of adobe, that mud was sculpted in Gaudiesque driblets. Ramparts, scaffolds, and turrets abounded. At every turn were corbels and arches and cantilevered patios, pyramids and towers ad infinitum. Enormous picture windows framed cinemascopic and panavistic views of Hija Negrita, the sacred mountain. Greenhouses proliferated like rabbits fed a diet of oysters and ginseng; banks of solar collectors reached toward the blistering sky. Bubble skylights let light stream into bathrooms where tubs were sunk into terrariums of banana trees, goo-goo vines, and pot plants. Two- and three-story frame houses shot toward the heavens like skyscraperitos, their flanks paneled with redwood, their roofs sheathed in Mediterranean-orange terra-cotta. Sky-lit and glass-sided studios seemed to stand on stems no sturdier than those supporting crystal champagne glasses. Behind beautiful stained-glass windows, you could see endless arrays of gourd-shaped flowerpots clutched in the folds of elaborate macramé Oriole nests. No staircase ever proceeded from point A to point B in a straight line: each one spiraled upward from the living room to the sleeping loft, or zigzagged from behind the organic banco in the sunken kitchen up to the second floor, from which a ladder rose to the staggered third floor, all the rooms modularly disposed to create separate but attached living quarters (guard that privacy, folks!), much like the nesting habits of paraplegic baboons.

In some of the old valley houses, residents had decorated their ceilings with splintered cedar or aspen branches, known as latias, lodged in a herringbone pattern. More often they had simply laid boards across their viga rafters and heaped on the dirt and tar paper. But in the new houses, craftspeople went berserk with latias, graduating from herringbone patterns to complex hexoglyphic designs of positively gaga spiritual significance. The old houses had been heated by wood, or by cheap butane heaters. In the new houses, solar technology ran rampant. Fireplaces were sculpted with Daliesque wit and intricacy, so crammed with nichos, and so inlaid with colorful stones and tiles (and hung with corn or chile ristras), that they resembled space-capsule cones in which mere burning logs would have seemed trite, if not downright nonsensical. Others installed superexpensive electric heating to go with their 26-inch color-perfect cableized TV consoles. A few people bought up old radiators in Colorado resort-hotel auctions, installing them in their modern houses. Daily, trucks, piloted by enterprising ex-advertising consultants, left Chamisaville to scour the Southwest, buying up collapsing old barns for a song, tearing them apart, and trucking them back home, where, as highly prized paneling—oh, that weathered look!—they could bring as much as sixty cents a board-foot, nearly three times the going price of finished lumber.

Steam rising from countless hot tubs seemed like emissions from myriad chubby little factories. There were swimming pools, too, and saunas, and Jacuzzis. And several dozen private tennis and paddle-ball courts.

Joe himself had dreams of doing his own house in some elaborate, farfetched style that was a "uniquely viable habitat" to go with the "aesthetic living" demands of himself, Heidi, Michael, and Heather. Yet occasionally, right in the middle of a reverie about pyramids, hexagons, A-frames, domettes, U-curves, rounded or mansard windows, sunken tubs and saunas, his balloon would suddenly pop, making him feel like a fool. Then he'd sit down and draw a one-story L-shaped house, such as they had been building for centuries in the valley before the newcomers arrived and instituted their architectural carnival.

Of course, wherever no elaborate dwelling punctuated the drawn-and-quartered fields on the way home, a simple white tipi extended its lovely inverted cone of slender aspen pole-tips toward the smiling bourgeois sky. It had been hundreds of years since local Native Americans bedded down in these smoky domiciles. Hence, the kooks inhabiting the dozens of tipis along 240 between the plaza and Joe's current lodgings were: a one-time Oklahoma DA turned jewelry czar, a potter with an NYU master's in child psychology, a former stock analyst with Bache and Company, a reflexologist who used to be a teller in the San Diego branch of the Bank of America, an ex-presidential financial adviser (under Gerald Ford), a onetime speech writer for Billy Graham, two ex-Moonies, and a female industrial nutritionist turned born-again plumber, who also did sexual massages for a privileged few (and much hard cash).

Squat beehive-shaped adobe sweat lodges next to the tipis were kept going day and night.

Occasionally, Joe felt bewildered and disheartened by the relentless development. Pizzafication, urbanization, *cutification*! What was the point to domes made of bottles or beer cans, or to family rooms fabricated from five hundred old tires? It was all too pat, too self-indulgent. Everybody was fleeing urban jungles and mind-fucking occupations to create a new life and a simpler life. Instead, they were trampling down the vineyards where the grapes of tranquillity had been stored, boldly and idiotically polluting the landscape with aesthetically relevant bullshit, and in the process re-creating only a semi-camouflaged image of the pernicious complexity they had hoped to escape.

Then again, Joe saw Chamisaville as his first real chance in life to create around himself and his little family a humane and compassionate ambience, something low-key, unexploit-ative, articulate, and (coincidentally) comfortable. A life with access to reason. Then Chamisaville could be a rainbow, a magic valley.

Joe beeped at Dr. Phil Horney and his wife, Gretchen, the head of Sköl Realty: she had arranged the deal with Eloy Ir-ribarren. Phil had recently taken Joe off Tedral and put him on Aminodur; the Tedral had given him hot flashes, cold sweats, and fainting spots before his eyes. They (the Horneys) wore matching forest-green headbands, sunflower-yellow jogging suits, and white Adidas with slanted maroon stripes. Joe waved, they returned the salutation. Aloud, though not so they could have heard him, Joe said, "Someday, you turkeys, I'll swerve and flatten an unsuspecting jogger, and I'm gonna run back and forth over the carcass until it's just a mangled splash of plum purple or cobalt blue against the asphalt of this bumpy road."

He was exhausted, and frightened. What had happened to Peter? How should he act with Heidi, what could he say? Confronted by this dilemma, did a man lie his head off, or tell the truth, hoping for mercy? Already, the whole town knew of his infidelity—how could he keep it from Heidi? And what about Nancy Ryan? Would she leave him alone? Perhaps all she had wanted was a one-night stand. Did he dare hope? Joe hated her, he hoped never to see her again. She had lured him into it against his will. Christ, such diabolically clever creatures! He was terrified of them all. Was Nancy capable of blackmail? Joe wished he were back in the bar last night with a chance to play it differently. Why hadn't Peter gotten off that goddam bus? It was all *his* fault.

Out of nowhere a thing swelled up under his diaphragm, making him almost dizzy—a wave of pure, unadulterated lust for Nancy Ryan.

"Oh shit," he moaned. "I'm just another cock, now, that went after just another cunt, now, in the screwing pool."

Shame! Remorse! How come his sexual moves could be just as banal as everybody else's erotic gropings? He was an insult to his own intelligence and sensibility. One greedy misstep, and he'd brought himself down to the level of a *True Romance* magazine, or, to coat it in a bit of intellectual sugar, a John Updike novel.

Yet suppose this Nancy Ryan affair opened the floodgates, releasing him from his puritanical hang-ups? Off he'd gallop through the valley's Ready, Willing, and Able—forget the cynicism involved—pulchritude. Joe Miniver, Traveling Stud. "Yes ma'am, I certainly *do* make house calls." He would cart his prick around in a fancy, velveteen-lined, fiberglass carrying case, as if it were a pearl-inlaid custom-made, two-piece pool cue. Why not? His truck, like a plumber's jalopy, would be full of his sexual accoutrements. Whips, chains, dildos, leather outfits, rubber scuba suits, tubs of Vaseline, sacks of scented condoms, jars of aphrodisiacs. A minifridge would keep the fresh seafood from spoiling: "Eat Oysters, Love

Longer." Every evening around five thirty he would open his eyes and spend twenty minutes stretching, yawning, and slithering erotically around on his satin sheets, waking up slooooowwwwwwly, sensuuuuuoussssssly. Then he'd check in with his answering service to see who was lined up for that night. "Hello, Joe—this is Diana Clayman. Would you be free around two A.M.? I got a feeling I'm gonna need that great big motor-driven Roto-Rooter of yours. . . ."

Joe started writing another in a long line of farewell letters to Heidi. He was always in the car alone when the urge hit to speak them out loud. Eyes glazed, barely paying attention to the road, his heart aching—how come he so often felt crippled with emotion? Why did his assessment of his needs, ambitions, and goals in life change so often? One minute he was truly in love, in control, happy, on top of the situation. But sure as hell the moment he settled into a smug frame of mind, whoever minded such things yanked the rug out from under, and he got hit by a nearly suicidal rush of despair.

"Dear Heidi, I love you, you know that. You will always be the most special person in my life. After all you're the mother of my children—" Uh, can that, Miss Pierson, she'd clobber me. It has a male chauvinist ring. Okay, from the top again—you ready? "Dear Heidi"—take two. "Fuck you, fuck women's lib, fuck being a house-husband, fuck the whole goddam shmeer—I want to be a male chauvinist pig! I *am* a male chauvinist pig, in case you hadn't noticed. I'm tired of the clothes you wear. When we first met you wore lipstick and mascara, miniskirts, garter belts and stockings and high-heeled slingbacks and transparent panties. Now all you ever wear are dungarees and sneakers and sloppy sweatshirts and you never wear rouge, you never wear perfume, you never wear lipstick. I'd give a million dollars, sometimes, just to hang out with a miniskirted, butt-wiggling little Kewpie doll again!"

Brilliant! Senility already at thirty-eight? "Erase all that, Miss Pierson, let's start from scratch."

Who exactly was Miss Pierson? And that really was Miss, not Ms., all you libbers out there, all you members of the Crypto-Lesbo-Commie-Whore-Fascist-Retaliation Society! Joe had never pictured her too closely. Call her just another mythical secretary who, coincidentally, wore tight fire-engine-red sweaters and had enormous jugs à la June "The Bosom" Wilkenson.

"Dear Heidi. I don't know how to tell you this, but I did something awful. Actually, I don't even know if it was awful or not. Probably it isn't, in fact. Probably it's just a routine thing that shouldn't even raise a half of anybody's hackles, except we are all caught up in a totally confusing system which doesn't know its moral ass from an ethical hole in the ground."

Too cute. Let's try it again, Miss Pierson.

"Dear Heidi. I don't know about you, but I know for a fact that I'm tired, I really am. I'm tired of all the chaos. I wonder where we are going together, and I can't come up with any answers. We seem to have lost the thread. I'm so sick of raging kids, of a house that always looks like the atomic bomb hit it, of shot nerves and sleepless nights, of tension, silent hostility, moodiness, anger, bitching—"

Joe paused, thinking it over, wondering if he ought to dictate in a few tears on the face of this self-pitying cliché clown.

One more time, Miss Pierson: from the top.

"Dear Heidi. Actually, if you must know, I just drilled this cunt on the other side of town. And if you give me even one iota of lip about it, I'm gonna emigrate to Alaska, become a powderman on the pipeline, marry an Eskimo, move to one of those desolate little islands up there crawling with foxes, and just hang out until I get my Berings Strait. Ha ha."

Ha ha indeed.

Veering too speedily around a corner at the deserted and crumbling Ranchitos Cantina, Joe swerved to avoid striking two nasty little black-and-white dogs—Mimsy and Tuckums—that charged his bus as if they meant to dismember it piranha-fashion. A right turn at this juncture would have taken Joe to Eloy's land; it lay three hundred yards along the hideously potholed road. Instead, he bore left, heading for his current digs (two miles farther south), trailing yaps, snarls, and growls like a string of wedding-day tin cans.

"Where will I live?" he wondered aloud; "if she throws me out?"

Even more gloomy to contemplate: Given a divorce, if the dope deal went down successfully, who would get the land, already retained in both their names? Would they draw straws? Would he have to sell it a week after risking his life to buy it in order to pay her off?

Enough! A hex on such vicissitudes! A simple human being (male) pokes the business end of his thing into another simple human being not his wife (but female), and the stock market shudders, thousands of dollars change hands, marriage counselors trade in their old automobiles for this year's models, real-estate agents add another wing to their houses, group therapists nail their shutters closed and fly to Saint Croix, divorce lawyers plan Hawaiian vacations as soon as the lucrative proceedings are over, and the thousands of greenbacks to be earned by two upper-crust sophisticated honkies disappear in a puff of emotional and legal hysteria. And what about the future lives of two adorable, normal, middle-class brats originally destined for fame, fortune, and security? Suddenly, Michael's cards are holding reform school, alcoholism, perhaps patricide with an ax, eleven years on death row, and finally—despite a last-minute conversion to born-again Christianity—the electric chair. Heather, lacking a father figure (or a mother figure, depending on who won in the divorce proceedings), is a pill popper and promiscuous by the age of eighteen, drops out of Sarah Lawrence, marries a Mafia bagman, loses him and becomes a high-priced call girl until her looks nose-dive, and eventually winds up as a lady bum wearing a grease-stained trenchcoat and stockings rolled down around her ankles, rifling trash baskets on Third Avenue, New York City, for other people's rejected goodies, which she stores in plastic-coated Macy's shopping bags.

Or maybe she would get off easy, at age seventeen, with a case of anorexia nervosa that would reduce her from 130 pounds to 63 pounds in six weeks.

"Help, help—*sharks!*"

       Joe's house—not his, actually, but rather Tribby Gordon's Castle of Golden Fools—loomed on the horizon. In return for room and board, Joe and Heidi had, over the last two years, helped with various aspects of construction. The house itself defied coherence: it was a ponderous figment of Tribby's whimsy, incorporating a dozen major materials, architectural styles, and protuberances that struck the eye, at first, as sheer anarchy. Tribby had designed and built the house largely by "playing it by ear." Constructed a room at a time with whatever materials happened to be on hand, the house was like a three-dimensional crazy quilt. It seemed part Bavarian castle, part sharecropper shack, part Navajo hogan, part solar dome, part log cabin, and part frontier fort. It had started as a one-room barn. Now it had eighteen rooms, six chimneys, two greenhouses, one trombe wall, and a large green pyramid housing the master bedroom.

Everything, of course, was in a disarrayed state of "almost completion." Windows had been studded into frames, but never puttied. Flaps of ninety-pound granular paper dangled over roof edges like the feathers of a queer molting bird, waiting to be trimmed. Walls made of adobe, and hung with chicken wire attached to nails, had waited two years so far for plaster. The forms had yet to be removed from one poured-mud flying buttress. Uneven viga butt-ends poking out from mud walls waited in vain to be trimmed to uniform and eye-pleasing extensions. Discarded lumber, wire, and rebar lay scattered among the weeds, rusty wheelbarrows, and inoperative cement mixers. A vast array of useless green hosing was frozen in silent writhes across the yard. Piles of beer cans, collected by Shanti Institute students, glittered destitutely, waiting to be bound into the six-pack blocks Tribby had used to construct several wings of his monstrosity. Dozens of birds nested under the overhangs, in little niches created by the turrets, gables, cupolas, eaves, and shoddy workmanship.

The Minivers occupied a second-story apartment consisting of a large living room, two bedrooms, and a kitchenette. Leading to their front door was an outdoor ladder which could, of course, be drawn up in case of attack. Atop their roof, underneath a green plastic corrugated awning Joe had erected, sat Michael's drum set, (hopefully) rotting due to exposure.

Heather, at least, had shown interest in the guitar.

When neighbors accused Tribby of creating a monstrous eyesore, he explained that the house was "creative," "functional," "a work of art," "a white elephant with sentimental value," "the best he could do under the circumstances," or "Chamisaville's own San Simeon." Ralph Kapansky, residing in a tipi upon the grounds, had a flair for pegging the monstrosity more accurately. He once described it as "an intergalactic shitheap." Another time he called it "a masterpiece by Frank Lloyd Wrong." In his lighter moments he suggested it was what happened when "California architecture fucked Victorian sensibility in disco heaven."

Once, when Joe asked Tribby why he had built the enormous, garish thing in the first place, Tribby replied, "Because it wasn't there."

Fearful and trembling, Joe entered the driveway, coasting to a halt among a passel of vehicles that resembled the stage setting for a play about Hiroshima. Rimpoche danced around the truck, barking his hydrocephalic head off. Well, this is it, Joe thought: the jig is up. Inside the convoluted excuse for a dwelling, Heidi awaited him with a rolling pin and a thicket of divorce papers. Beside her, FBI agents, Treasury, Firearm, and Tobacco flunkies, state narcotics bruisers, and local law-enforcement personnel eagerly tuned up their lie detectors, subpoenas, and rubber truncheons. In their midst stood Peter Roth, manacled and in leg-irons, his eyes puffed shut, most of his teeth missing, blood crusted at his nostrils. "Who's this bum?" Joe would growl. "Get him out of here. I never saw him before in my life."

Despite his bluff, the FBI's chief torturer grabbed him: another man clipped electrodes onto his testicles. "Heidi, *do* something!" Joe screamed. "*Die*, you male chauvinist swine!" she replied.

Unable to move, Joe sat tight. Everything he had worked for all his life was about to unravel; he couldn't understand why he had allowed it to happen. What insane alter ego had goaded him into risking his personal existence as well as a life term in jail for selling dope? Even if, somehow, miracle of all hallowed miracles, they stumbled to a successful conclusion on the cocaine front, what good would the money do him? For two hours in the arms of another woman he had thrown away his children, his unbuilt house, his wife, his promising future.

Opening the door, he got out. Joe ignored Rimpoche: the dog barked, growled, groveled, whimpered, and bared his teeth, not knowing whether to kill Joe or slobber fawningly over his feet. Standing beside the bus for a moment, Joe thought he could hear the planet draw in a slow sad breath and hold it. The script called for a last look around before the warden yanked that lever.

Sunday morning, Lower Ranchitos, Chamisaville, USA. Oh, Dem Golden Rockies!

Cool spring sunshine glittered in cottonwood trees whose leaves were young, more silvery than green. Early butterflies puttered above young alfalfa plants and budding timothy. Faintly, in the distance, sounded churchbells. Far to the left, across dozens of small pastures, every one of which harbored a new house abuilding, the Midnight Mountains presided over the valley like a melancholy judge frowning upon the frenetic (and criminal) development below.

Slim little airplanes dotted the sky. Some were gliders, circling thoughtfully, plying the thermals. On Sundays, the Coyote Glider Club did their thing. Heidi took lessons from Gil Forrester, dreaming of the moment when she could drift between sentinels of unruffled cumulus froth all alone. Though an acrophobe himself, for three years Joe had wished to go aloft for an hour, just to have that macroscopic perspective, not to mention a permanent memory of silken buoyancy. But he hadn't yet summoned enough nerve to risk everything on such an infantile whim.

Joe's 1947 Chevy pickup, known as the Green Gorilla, caught his eye. He scuffled over and leaned contemplatively against the hood. Rimpoche gave up and crawled into shadows beneath Ralph's 1953 Chevy two-door sedan. The warm metal of the Green Gorilla gave Joe succor. Every week, for the past two years, in the *Chamisaville News* classifieds, Joe's ad—featuring that hideously decrepit (but heartwarming) vehicle—had appeared:

> Need trash carted away, furniture moved, goodies transferred? Call for Joe Miniver and his Green Gorilla. We haul everything from soup to hay. 758–3989.

Joe loved that truck, and would miss it when he was just another number on the state's dole, manufacturing license plates fourteen hours a day. It was no great shakes physically, but Joe had kept it running. He constantly stuffed oatmeal into the transmission, plugging up holes; he broke eggs into the radiator, stopping leaks; and he went through a bar of Ivory soap every week, sealing the flak wounds in his gas tank. The truck had a quart-of-oil-every-twenty-miles habit: when Joe accelerated on the highway, it laid down an impenetrable smoke screen. Other marvelous details included: a reverse-gear trigger on the stick shift that constantly malfunctioned, vacuum-operated windshield wipers run off the manifold which stopped dead whenever he accelerated or climbed a hill; five-dollar voltage regulators that self-destructed so often Joe kept a box of a half-dozen in reserve under the front seat; a gas gauge, oil-pressure gauge, battery-charge meter, odometer, and speedometer that didn't work; a driverside window rusted open; and other byzantine quirks too numerous to mention.

Still, the Green Gorilla had conveyed him relentlessly from here to there. It had successfully hauled everything from dead cattle to granite boulders to the weighty loads of green piñon Joe cut every autumn with his two-hundred-pound solid-steel 1927 Pioneer chain saw (which dislocated his shoulders every time he used it). Loaded well above its stock railings, the truck had never failed to reach Chamisaville, where Joe sectioned the wood using a hydraulic splitter of his own fabrication. Then he retailed the logs for seventy dollars a cord. Good Lord, he mused, how many times had he rattled along dirt roads toting a full load of piñon during late October storms, his shoulders aching, his hands cramped (and frozen), snowflakes that fluttered through the open window plastering his chest and his crotch white, while he sobbed and croaked out rock-and-roll songs to keep his blood flowing on the interminable way home?

Heather's self-righteous little voice cut through his reveries.

"Boy, Daddy, are you ever gonna get it. Mommy's having a real conniption. Why didn't you come home last night? Your name is shit on a platter."

"Go wash your mouth out with soap," Joe said dispiritedly. "You got a filthy gab, Heather."

"I'm rubber and you're glue. Everything you say bounces off of me and sticks to you."

Glumly, Joe asked, "Why is she so pissed? What did I do that's so wrong?"

"You didn't come home last night. What were you up to, out messing around with all the chickie-poos?"

Joe stared at her, his face all squinched up in a puzzled, disapproving expression. Heather wore her pink, Easter-rabbit pajamas; they had feet and a ball of white cotton for a tail on her butt. Her perky blond hair was in double ponytails attached with rubber bands. A pair of Heidi's solid-gold hoop earrings dangled from the earlobes Heather had made her mother pierce nearly three years ago. And lipstick, of course. Sunday mornings being when she was allowed into Heidi's makeup paraphernalia (which Heidi never used anymore), she usually painted herself up like a Pigalle streetwalker. A fresh plum-purple maquillage on her fingernails completed the garish damage.

Joe said, "How did such an apparently nice little girl like you turn out to be such a despicable yenta?"

Heather twitched haughtily, flaunted her backside, and, as she strutted snootily away, called to him: "Boy, I wouldn't wanna be in your shoes. She's fit to be tied!"

Heather loved dramatic sayings. She picked them up at the drop of a hat, then overused them incessantly. She adored dramatic situations, also. Every time Joe and Heidi had a spat, she would approach Joe, asking, "Are you guys gonna get a divorce now?" When Joe snarled, "What are you, Heather, a lousy ambulance chaser?" she replied coolly, "I hope you get divorced, because then I would be able to have two mommies and two fathers."

"Why do you always refer to her as a 'mommy' but to me as a 'father'?" Joe asked irritatedly. "If she's your mommy, the least you could do is make me your daddy."

"You're too much of a grouch to be a daddy," she always replied.

And Joe always halfheartedly ordered her to "Go directly to your room."

Whereupon she usually held up her right hand, the knuckles turned toward him, all the fingers spread wide, sneered "Camouflage!," and flounced away, rubbing his nose in her insouciantly swinging tushy.

"One time in ten years," Joe shouted after her, "that I stay out all night, and she makes a federal case of it, my whole happy little family throws the book at me!"

"It's your own fault," Heather replied, without breaking stride. "I can't help it if you're a dodo."

"Up yours, Chicken Little."

"Hey, pipe down out there," came Ralph Kapansky's gravelly voice from the tipi. "It's Sunday morning. I'm trying to meditate!"

"They're gonna draw me and quarter me," Joe said miserably. "They're gonna emasculate me, stuff my private goodies in my mouth, publish in the newspaper that I'm an archcriminal and an adulterer, tattoo a scarlet A on my bosom, kick me out of my own house, take all of my money, maybe cut off my right hand Arabian-style, and send me packing."

Morosely, he walked over toward Ralph's tipi, halting beside the plump mechanic-pornographer's powder-blue sensory isolation tank. It was a large vinyl-lined casket half full of salt water, into which Ralph shut himself for hours whenever his internal stressometer demanded a hit of nirvana, altered consciousness, or becalmed brain-wave activity. That is, he entered the tank whenever in need of relaxation, and lay floating in briny uteral darkness until his alpha, beta, and theta brain waves and hypertension were back under control.

Joe knew at least a dozen people in the valley who had Float-to-Relax tanks in their backyards, garages, or game rooms. He had always mocked them, but right now he could have settled gratefully into Ralph's lukewarm womb, closed the hatch, and floated for an eternity in the soundless, gently sloshing neutrality.

"What are you meditating about?" Joe asked disinterestedly.

"If you'd only shut up, I could leave this blubbery old temple of the soul, and zip off to Anami Lok, wherein the sacred SUGMAD dwells."

"What's a SUGMAD?"

"You're kidding. You really don't know what the SUGMAD is?"

"No, actually I'm just asking the question to see if you know."

"Egads!" Ralph gestured to a third, invisible party. "He doesn't know what the SUGMAD is!"

"Forget it." Frowning, Joe slouched away. "I never brought it up. . . ."

All these minutes stewing on death row could drive an inmate bonkers: better to face the music. So Joe squared his shoulders and started climbing up the ladder to his second-floor domicile.

"Eckankar!" Ralph jeered good-naturedly. "The ancient science of soul travel! I'm off to see the SUGMAD, the mighty SUGMAD of Oz!"

Joe flipped him a finger.

Michael occupied a deck chair on the roof. He cuddled the cat, Barby Lou, in his lap, and was eating a bowl of Kellogg's Raisin Bran while reading the Gordons' Sunday funnies. In response to the boy's negative look, Joe asked, "What's the matter with you?"

"Nothing."

That was his stock answer: "Nothing." Michael, what happened in school today? "Oh, nothing." Michael, what happened in the movie last night? "Oh, nothing." His other habitual reply was "Okay." Michael, how was the football game on Friday? "Okay." Just okay? "Yeah." Anything special or memorable happen? "No, nothing." Ask him how he felt—it was always "okay." Ask him if he liked school—it was "okay." Did he enjoy his teachers? Sure, they were "okay." How about the lunches? "They're okay." What did he want to do that weekend? "Oh, nothing . . ." Of course, Joe realized that underneath Michael's imperturbable façade lurked a human being of diabolically complex dimensions who suffered excruciating torments and joyous revelations almost hourly. But right now, all Michael was prepared to divulge to grown-ups was his name, his rank, and his cereal brand.

"What happened to Dick Tracy this week?"

"Oh . . . nothing."

"Hey," Joe barked angrily. "How about a little more information, huh? How about some faint sign of intelligent life? I'm sick of your deaf-and-dumb moron act."

Smiling, Michael gave him the finger. "Fuck you, Daddy."

Too tired for threatening to throw his gawky, giggling boy off the roof, Joe returned the birdie and marched on. Occasionally, these displays of prepubescent insolence bugged him, but not often. Brought up in an atmosphere of terrifying formality in his own home, where sassing his father and various stepmothers was a capital offense, Joe had determined that his own kids would have it different. Let them heckle if they wanted, did it hurt anybody?

In front of the door he almost raised one hand to knock. Then, uncertain if a beautiful lady or a ravenous tiger awaited him on the other side, he turned the handle and entered his happy home.

A physical queerness gripped Joe, as if all his molecules were struggling to break their atomic bonds and in the very next second his body would disintegrate, fizzing off in a billion colorful directions like electrified New Year's confetti. Joe's awareness of himself, and of all the airborne energy in his home, was heightened to an absurd level, as it might have been during that split instant between the time a bullet left the barrel of a gun twenty feet away and drilled him right between the eyes.

The house, as usual, was a god-awful shitheap. Yesterday's sleeping bags and blankets, *Mad* magazines and sandwich crusts and Richie Rich comic books, and empty yogurt containers accumulated by the kids during their morning cartoon orgy still littered the floor around the TV set. Yellow Hot Wheels track sections were scattered everywhere as if blown to smithereens by miniature Nazis. Plastic imitation-marble chess pieces lay inertly here and there, as if slaughtered while frantically fleeing. Somehow, a towel or two, a pair of Heidi's panties, and a football helmet had joined the fray. Hundreds of tiny white pieces of chewed-up paper from Michael and Heather's last spit-wad war added to the mess. And newspaper pages in eighteen different two-page sections were perched atop various noisome heaps like large carnivorous butterflies. What is it about semimoneyed, middle-class, bourgeois families like ours, Joe wondered, that dictates we must live like this amid our own offal?

Off in a corner, Heather was putting a dozen dolls to bed in a mound of pretty pillows. She glanced up with one of those profound, all-knowing smirks Joe associated with children possessed by the devil or by sadistic psychic powers as exhibited in horror movies. Seated in a nondescript armchair, her lovely brown limbs swaddled in tennis whites and a maroon-and-yellow rugby shirt, Heidi was reading the newspaper. Classical music issued from the stereo. On weekdays it would have been James Taylor, or Laurindo Almeida and Salli Terri, or Gary Burton, or the MJQ. But on Sundays it was always Chopin, or Debussy, or the Brandenburg Concertos. Only when everybody had left the house could Joe play his funky old blues records: Reverend Gary Davis, Pink Anderson, Lightnin' Hopkins, and Big Bill Broonzy.

Joe fell head over heels into his buffoon pose. "Hey everybody, the prodigal returns! How come nobody was out to blow a fanfare when I came in the drive?"

Heidi said, "Hello, Joey, how are you?" Confirming his worst fears that he was a goner, her voice sounded like frosty fricatives squeezed through the wringer apparatus of an old-fashioned washing machine.

"Well..." Joe slumped into a wooden chair at the table they used for eating. "I guess everybody knows by now that our good friend Peter Roth blew it last night."

"He called," Heidi said. "I tried to get you at the bar, but they said you had already left. Then he called again this morning."

"Well, what's his frigging excuse?"

"They had a fight, he and Julane. I guess this time it was a really bad one."

"They always have fights. How could that stop him from coming? He spent twelve thousand of my dollars for that cocaine. There's a mini-industry awaiting his arrival."

"This time it was worse than usual."

"What's 'worse than usual'? They threaten to divorce each other every Tuesday."

"I'm only repeating what he said, Joey. If you don't believe me, why don't you call him up and find out for yourself?"

Her voice sounded so tight that if it were wound one more time it might snap out of her head in a great snarl of springlike vocal cords, a laryngeal Slinky gone amok.

Joe said, "You sound terrible, what's the matter?"

"Nothing."

"No, wait a minute, don't be stupid. It's not 'nothing.' You sound weird."

"If you don't know—oh, Christ, I don't want to talk about it, I really don't. It's too dumb." Lurching up from her chair, she whipped her lovely blond hair around like a colt, and, tears in her eyes, fled into the bedroom. Heather scorched her father with a smug, accusatory look of doom.

"Wait a minute—!" But the phone rang.

Peter Roth said, "Where the hell you been? What's going on out there?"

"I was waiting at the goddam bus station for you to arrive."

"All *night*?"

"Hey, Peter, do me a favor—"

"I called at one o'clock to save you a trip in to town, but you'd already split. Heidi said no sweat, she could find you and warn you off. I call again at eight o'clock this morning and it's like talking to the morgue out there. She says you never came home. What's the matter with you, shmuck, you lost all your sense of class? If you gotta take chip shots at another pussy, don't you have enough decency to be a little less blatant?"

Joe flushed angrily. "Uh, Peter. I was supposed to pick you, and a certain-little-commodity-which-shall-remain-nameless-on-the-telephone, up at the bus last night."

"What can I tell you? I hit her, she called the cops, I spent three hours in jail."

"You hit Julane?"

"Yeah, I still don't believe I did it. I spent two hours, though, baking a meatloaf. So what happens? The bitch comes home with her mouth full of garbage and starts laying it on me. I couldn't take it, I got mad. She grabbed the meatloaf and chucked it at me. I spent *two hours* working on that meatloaf! It had chopped onions, bread crumbs, the works. It was a piece of art, and Anna Magnani here, with a rose tattoo for brains, picks it up in her bare hands, burns the shit out of her fingers, and throws it at me!"

"Did she hit you?"

"Whaddayou mean, did she hit me? I boxed Golden Gloves; I played basketball at Temple. I got moves like Earl the Pearl. Did she *hit* me?" he reiterated scornfully. "Jesus Christ, Miniver, whaddayou take me for, bush league?"

"So what happened to the meatloaf?" What he really meant to ask was: "What happened to the cocaine?"

"Whaddayou think? Her dog ate it. I comb him every night. I tweeze out all his ticks. I take him for a walk on his leash every morning and every evening, and the ingrate sees a meatloaf skidding across the linoleum, he grabs it and gobbles it down!"

"But that's no reason not to—"

"I blew up. I went berserk. I started to beat the dog, so she opened her fat mouth and really lathered me in scum. I was shocked. I turned around and said, 'Call me that again, sewer lips, and I'll kill you.' So she called me that again, and what could I do? I *hadda* slug her!"

Joe said, "But that's absurd."

"Tell me about absurd. I almost broke all the knuckles in my right hand on her jaw. I also broke her jaw. And I loosened, it must of been, I dunno, maybe five, call it an even half-dozen, teeth."

"I don't believe it."

"I didn't either. I'm sittin' there on the floor, holding my hand and vomiting, cause it hurt *me* so bad, and she's over in a corner hollering for the cops in this hysterical high-pitched scream—I never heard *anything* that eerie. Like a banshee. And the dog's over in a living room corner cowering with meatloaf crumbs in its jaws. Not to mention that on its way over there it knocked the stereo off the coffee table. It was a Ufer, the best rig on the market. I had Banashak speakers. The system cost me over a grand."

"And you spent three hours in jail?"

"The neighbors called the cops. They actually showed up thirty seconds later. Last year our place got hit by a band of junkies, I arrived home just as one of the little glueheads was going out the fire-escape window with the TV. So I called for the gendarmes—they arrived *three hours* later! But my wife screams for a pig because I broke her jaw, and the place is crawling with uniforms before I can even properly crucify Lassie over there in the corner."

"So what are you gonna do?"

"Get a divorce, what else? She said I'm a brute. You know what she called me? A 'mentally retarded orangoutang' with an 'anemic dick.' I couldn't believe it. We used to hang around South Philly eatin' Pat's cheese steaks. I even held her hand in the Rodin Museum!"

Joe mustered his courage and said, "Peter, what about out here? What about the, uh, present you were bringing me? Plus you promised to help us build a house, remember? We were gonna catch a thousand trout."

"It doesn't sound to me like you'll be building many houses out there in the immediate future. Man, that woman was *hurting*. What's the matter with you that you could be so clumsy?"

"Listen, you don't know what's going on out here."

"I got ears," Peter roared. His wonderful belligerency buoyed Joe despite the writing on his own wall. "I'm a sensitive human being, maybe even an artist, I know when something stinks like week-old halibut. I talked to a funeral home this morning. Heidi sounded about an inch and a half east of suicide. How could you be such a prick?"

Joe said, "So you're not coming?"

"I broke the lady's *jaw*. She ain't only threatening a divorce, she wants to sue me. I wish the dog had choked on that meatloaf!"

"But . . . but what about the stuff you were supposed to bring?"

"What stuff?"

Talk about *obtuse*! "You know, the gift you planned to lay on us."

"Gift? You mean the cocaine?"

Ouch! "Hey, man, do you have to shout it out on the telephone?" Joe checked in all directions, expecting tommy-gun-toting G-men to burst out of the woodwork at the mere mention of the dope.

Peter laughed. "You think they got taps on our telephone? Man, are you paranoid. What have you ever done to warrant their professional scrutiny? Joe, you aren't even a medium-sized fish in their lexicon. In fact, you ain't even a perch or a stickleback!"

"Hey, I'm sorry but I'm very nervous. This is hairy stuff. I also happened to invest my life savings in the project, so naturally I'm eager to recoup the investment plus. I need the bread for a closing in nine days."

"So you'll have it. What's the problem?"

"I don't have the wherewithal for making that money. It was supposed to arrive last night."

"You talking about the cocaine?"

Joe cringed again. "I guess you could say . . . yeah . . . it's something like that. . . ." God, he had a terror of incriminating himself! He could just hear their ears flapping, their tape re-corders humming. How could Peter so blatantly ignore security precautions?

"Relax, José. Not to worry. I already put the goods on the bus before we had the fight."

"I'm not sure I follow."

"What do you think I'm gonna do, travel two thousand miles in the same vehicle with a suitcase full of coke? Some tipped-off Nazi halts the bus, ransacks the luggage, discovers the stash, and next thing you know I'm a suspect. Huh-uh, no sir, not me. I checked it through on the midday crate that left six hours earlier."

"You checked it through to Chamisaville?"

"I didn't send it to Anchorage, Alaska."

"What do I do, then—just go down to the station and claim a bag?" It seemed hideously simple.

"Sure, you can't miss it. A lightweight green airport bag labeled 'Cocaine—Handle with Care.'"

"You're *kidding*!"

"Don't jump out of your skin, dummy. It's in a cloth valise with a Scottish plaid pattern on the sides. Greenish and dark— I think the pattern is called black watch."

"Can you send me the claim check, special delivery?"

"Nope. I lost it."

"Suppose they know there's that . . . stuff inside?"

"You referring to the cocaine?"

"Yes, you bastard. They might have a stakeout at the bus station. Every day I read about some sucker who walks into a trap—picks up a suitcase, or claims a package at the post office."

"Lighten up, friend. You watch too much television. Yesterday I read an article said eighty percent of the crime in this country goes undetected, let alone unsolved. Now listen, I gotta hang up. This call is on a phony credit card and I don't wanna work up a suspiciously big bill."

"You're calling me *illegally*?"

"Don't shit a brick. I do it all the time."

"You mean some operator a month from now will ring me up asking who called on such-and-such a date, attempting to track it down?"

"Lie. You never got the call. Philadelphia?—where's that, a city in Nevada? Use your imagination. Oh, by the way. . . ."

"What?"

"In this morning's blat I read a little item. Apparently a U-Haul trailer carrying a sacred east Indian monkey statue bound for your home town had a flat tire in the Holland Tunnel yesterday and held up traffic for two hours. You shoulda read the names of the people in that U-Haul. Wait a sec—where is that paper? Listen to this mouthful. Baba Ram Bang. Rama and Shanti and Om Unfug. Iréné Papadraxis. Wilkerson Busbee. Fluff Dimaggio. They really got human beings monikered like that in Chamisaville?"

"Yup."

"Well about this monkey statue—whadda they call it here? A Hanuman. What's it all mean?"

"You're asking *me*?"

"There's somebody else on the phone?"

"I don't know, Peter. It's religious. You know—swamis, gurus, that whole scene. Now listen, I didn't get much sleep last night. I'm tired. . . ."

"I'll bet you are. Lots of luck. Ciao, sweetheart. . . ."

Dazedly, Joe said "ciao." If he had any doubts earlier, they were now dispelled: his ass was firmly caught in a royal sling. How could Peter come on so aggravatingly flippant?

Joe stared at the telephone for a moment after Peter had hung up. Hit by a sudden frost, all the green leaves on the tree of his upcoming summer had suddenly turned yellow. And, prompted by the chilly winds of his own stupidity and temerity, they were cascading in droves off all the branches of his deciduous hopes and dreams.

Heather warned, "God is gonna turn you into a potato."

"Not before he turns you into a Hobbit with leprosy."

"What's leprosy?"

"What I've got." Joe cradled the phone, closed his eyes, and walked into the moving airplane propeller of the master bedroom.

᪥

On the edge of their bed, hands in her lap, Heidi dismally confronted the floor. Joe experienced an abrupt surge of adrenaline: curiously, it created almost instant euphoria. With astonishing clairvoyance, he realized he was in so deep already, lying would actually be easy. As long as there existed an outside chance that the gossip hadn't reached Heidi, it was worth a shot. Why cultivate moral pretensions at this late date?

Flopping into another of their two-dollar easy chairs, Joe said, "Listen, I got drunk at the bar, I'll admit. I was nervous, so I really tied one on. Then, when Peter didn't show at the bus station, I crashed emotionally. Back at the plaza I found Ralph, and we rapped over a bottle of Black Jack in his office almost until dawn. Then we hit Marilyn Tibby's place for breakfast and a shower. That's it, kit and caboodle. I'm only sorry that I didn't phone.

The words had pirouetted off his tongue like tiny silver dancers!

"Nancy Ryan telephoned about an hour ago."

"Oh—?" Mr. Casual raised his eyebrows in supercilious unconcern (while a diamond-tipped dagger vivisected his heart like a Safeway butcher preparing chopped liver three minutes before quitting time on Friday). "What did she want?" He tried to make his voice sound as if he thought Nancy (*who?*) was on extended sabbatical in the Himalayas and not due back in town for years.

"I wouldn't even presume to guess."

"Well, I'll give her a call someday."

"She said it was urgent."

"What could be so urgent? I hardly know her."

"She said you left your watch over there last night."

"Oh shit." *Talk about perfidy!*

The safety cable to the Elevator of Life broke, and Joe felt himself plummeting swiftly toward his doom, a deafening whine reverberating in his ears as he plunged down the 102 floors of Sudden Catastrophe, aiming toward total disintegration against a concrete slab in the basement of Familial Tragedy at the bottom of the shaft.

"She said I left my *watch* over there?" That bitch! How could human beings be so devious? His first instinct was to strangle her—Nancy, that is. Then he felt sick. The whole town knew about his ram-bam with her, probably word would have reached Heidi by tomorrow, but he had to go and compound his predicament today by getting caught in a great and foolish lie that tarred and feathered him with gratuitous shame. What had President Kennedy said about life—that it wasn't fair? How true! Ridiculous as it might seem, their entire universe would now collapse because of a few banal hours trysting in a little tract home, surrounded by metaphysical monkey paintings employing the bright colors of cockatoo feathers.

Joe had a powerful need to explain it wasn't his fault, it was meaningless, her tears were stupid.

Heidi confirmed, "That's what she said."

"Oh."

They sat on their respective perches dully inspecting the rug. Sunshine pouring through the windows glazed her limbs the color of cinnamon butter. Such an apparition of middle-class health! A pretty phantom from Forest Hills! A debutante from south shore Long Island! Joe was going to miss his ever-lovin' woman rolling in his arms.

"It's so creepy," Heidi whispered. "I don't know what to say."

"I'm a little thunderstruck myself."

"What I don't understand is why did you do it with somebody like *her*?"

"Who would be better?" he snapped, surprised by the immediate anger her question aroused.

"I always thought maybe we could avoid this scene," Heidi remarked quietly. Silently, Joe pleaded with her to show an emotion other than this morose passivity. Why couldn't she stand up and grab a meatloaf?

"It's stupid," he admitted. "Obviously, I'm sorry."

"Well, I suppose I deserved it. I suppose we've been headed for something like this all along."

"I don't know, I really don't." Tongue-tied, embarrassed, he was out—way out—of his depth on this one.

"Now we're just like everybody else, Joey. You know what? I've been walking around these past couple of years feeling superior to all our friends because somehow we had avoided all the sexual bullshit going down out there. Somehow we were strong enough to be above it all."

"I know what you mean."

"Well, so much for my snot-nosed superiority. I sure had it coming."

"Look," he said lamely, "it didn't have anything to do with love or even honest attraction. It just happened out of the blue. Peter didn't arrive and I guess I freaked. It was a crazy accident. I feel so close to you and Heather and Michael. We're nice together, we have a wonderful family. I couldn't come with her—does that even count these days?"

"I don't understand what would make a person call up here like that. How could you fuck a woman who's that vicious? And spare me the sordid details, would you?"

Her bitter use of the word *fuck* to describe last night's experience angered him. "Let's not discuss it, okay? What's done is done. I'm sorry, I blew it. I take all the blame, it's all my fault."

"Oh, aren't you noble."

"I didn't mean it like that."

"All right, so what now? We just forget about it? Pretend it never happened?"

"I don't know. I have no experience playing this scene."

"You don't like me sexually?"

"That's a lie and you know it."

"What are we going to do, sweep it under the rug?"

"Yes . . . no . . . maybe. Unfortunately, right now I'm supposed to figure out how to retrieve a plaid suitcase full of cocaine from the bus station in time to meet Tribby and Ralph out at the airport at noon."

"God, you're gross."

"I can't just ignore it, can I?"

"Oh no, first things first, naturally. I'll just stay home and answer the telephone."

He hated her. Barely one hour a woman scorned, and already

she was playing the martyr role. Oh for the guts to break her jaw! Then he wondered, come nightfall, if he dared to grab some Zs under the same roof with her, would she stab him in the chest with a carving knife? Or would they never make love again?

Heidi blurted tearfully, "I think you're a first-class shitheel."

"You're right. I apologize. What else can I say?"

"Did you have to lie so blatantly? That makes me feel creepy."

"For what it's worth, I don't feel so hot myself."

"You're a lousy liar. You blush solid-crimson."

He shrugged pathetically.

"Why did you have to do it like that, then?"

"What would have been a better way? I walk through the door and announce to everybody within earshot that I just plugged this broad?"

"I'm amused—ha ha."

"Well, you don't have to rub it in—I know I'm a jerk. I blew it. I wish I hadn't, believe me. I don't know how it happened."

"How *did* it happen?"

"I really don't feel like rehashing the 'sordid details.'"

"How about it—was she a great lay?"

"I'm getting out of here." Joe stood up. "The longer that bag stays in the bus station, the more chance there is that somebody will discover what's in it. I'll take the kids. You're less suspicious if you have children."

"And I'll just sit around here stewing in my own juices, is that it?"

"I don't care what you do. I can't deal with it right now. Life is complicated enough."

"When will you want to talk about it?"

"Heidi, can't we take things one at a time?"

"Oh sure. And what does my master want me to tell her if she calls again?"

"Tell her to go screw herself!" Furiously, he strode from the room.

Heather looked up from her dolls. "I'm not going over to any bus station with a Fascist."

"Fine, great, beautiful." Joe stormed out of the house feeling breathless.

"Don't get a hernia!" was his witty and sarcastic daughter's parting salvo.

Of course, he had forgotten his glasses, his wallet, and his car keys. But he couldn't return to the lion's den. So the diabolical master of the false exit would have to pedal a bike!

On the way in to town, pumping his three-speed bicycle (with Michael trailing behind on a contraption with a raised banana seat, suicide handlebars, and a two-foot front-wheel extension that resembled a Hell's Angels' lascivious chopper), Joe crucified Nancy Ryan. Fortified by a bottle of Wild Turkey 101 and a handful of green pills, he kicked in her plywood door, strangled the monkey, axed to death the foaming Doberman, stuffed her kid into the washing machine and turned it on, chucked the parakeet into the dishwasher (added a box of Tide and spun the dial), collected all the metaphysical paintings and smashed them over her head (after first ripping off her clothes and committing a brutal rape), then slugged her insensate, dumped her into the bathtub hopelessly entangled in torn canvas and shattered stretchers, turned on the scalding hot water, and watched her drown.

"Jesus, people play dirty!" One thing for certain, anyway—he'd never see *that* diabolical weirdo again.

At the Ranchitos Cantina, Mimsy and Tuckums rushed them like kamikazes. Michael braked and cocked his BB gun. But Joe urged caution.

"Hold on, man, they won't bite. The thing we have to do is ignore them. If we do, they'll see we aren't a threat, and leave us alone."

"I hate dogs when I'm on my bike," Michael grumbled. "I wish I had an M-16."

"Just pedal along. Don't even look at them. I guarantee they won't touch us."

The dogs raised a fierce ruckus, snarling, foaming at the lips and snapping at their heels for about twenty yards. But they stopped abruptly upon reaching the perimeter of an invisible territory.

Joe said, "See? Listen to your old man, kid, and you'll grow up to be tolerant, wise, and magnanimous."

Michael asked, "What's gonna happen between you and Mom?"

"I dunno. Nothing. Why?"

"Before you came home she was really mad. She said she hoped you got drunk and slipped on a banana peel and broke your neck. What did you *do*, Pop?"

"Nothing. It's none of your business."

"How come every time I ask you a question about something important, you always answer 'nothing,' or that it's 'none of my business'?"

Joe said, "What happened to Dick Tracy today?"

"I forget. Pop—?"

"Don't talk to me right now, I'm in a foul mood."

"But that's not fair."

"Who ever said life would be fair?"

"She started crying and said maybe you and her weren't gonna live together anymore."

"Oh God, what's the matter with her? Did she announce it to the entire valley on a bullhorn? I swear, sometimes your mother has about as much brains as a newt."

"What's a newt?"

"It's a slimy little red lizard that lives under wet logs."

"Like a salamander?"

"Yeah, I guess so. I haven't seen a newt since I was ten."

Ed Diebold, hospital surgeon, Jaycee vice-president, and gung-ho Lion, drove by in his little red Toyota—Joe waved. A little farther along, Tad Hooten's gray Mazda zipped by. From the passenger seat Meridel Smatterling waved. Meridel's two kids from her former marriage to Nikita—Sanji and Tofu—had hair down to their gazots and spent twenty-three hours a day on skateboards, circling the plaza, doing tricks in the grammar-school macadam parking lot, or zooming dangerously down the hill leading from the 7-Eleven to the Safeway parking lot. Both Sanji and Tofu had been busted three or four times for smoking pot, which Joe happened to know they got from their father, who every year planted a lavish herb garden, including almost an eighth of an acre of German sweet basil, otherwise known as the best cannabis in town.

The next person to approach was Darlene Johnson's live-in lover, Spumoni Tatarsky, a jive little hypester so full of bull, so offensive, and so unalterably shallow that he positively gleamed with insincerity. Joe would walk a mile out of his way to avoid the man. Spumoni roller-skated around town wearing crushed-velour flame-purple jackets, pink shirts with ruffled paisley jabots, garish concho belts, turquoise rings on every

finger, and leather bell-bottoms. His five-foot-five-inch frame
was dwarfed by Darlene's six-foot body, but his ego was twelve
feet tall and growing. Spumoni lied like a hound, hustled like
a Times Square hooker, barked like a carnival barker, and just
could not be put down, embarrassed, or in any way turned
aside from his appointed rounds in life, which included pushing
every kind of bourgeois drug or narcotic on the market, from
coke through mescaline to LSD. Using laser beams, he manufactured hokey holograms and dichromates, which he peddled
from a dozen Chamisaville curio shops. Other scams dangling
on his repertoire included the mass fabrication of pornographic
scrimshaws etched on plastic ivory, and the relentless pursuit
of tail. Far be it from Joe to understand how Darlene could
even remotely put up with it. Spumoni's rampant mistresses
usually moved in with him and Darlene and their one-year-old
child, Moonglow Winterwind, whom Darlene lugged around
town in a deerskin cradleboard. Joe had heard rumors of as
many as three mistresses living with Spumoni and Darlene at
one time. Usually they were nubile teenyboppers, covered with
Tatoozies, who wore filthy granny dresses and work boots,
and, totally scragged from the pills, thrills, and spills they had
taken so early on in life, had become professional runaways
in search of a benevolent Charlie Manson.

So along came Spumoni on roller skates; Moonglow Winterwind was shoved into an old army knapsack on his back.
Spumoni wore a knitted (and earflapped) Norwegian Lapp cap,
a moth-eaten silk ascot, a T-shirt on which a tuxedo had been
painted, a red velour jacket with buttons made out of old silver
dollars, an enormous and voluptuous (and obscene) concho
belt, and leopard-skin flare cuffs. Moonglow's blue baseball
cap said "NAPA" on the front; the tyke's beautiful goat-fur
vest had to have come from Tibet or Afghanistan, no doubt by
way of Wilkerson Busbee's shop.

The last time Joe had conversed with Spumoni, the hustling
creep had so enraged him that they almost came to blows. Over
a crucial issue, too: had Tibet been a repressive society under
the Dalai Lamas? Joe knew the Communist revolution had
saved Tibet. All other Chamisa Valley newcomers believed
Tibet was one of the seven karmic centers of the universe. They
held that the Chinese Communists had destroyed one of the
most beautiful spiritual movements in the history of the planet.
And insisted that anything religious with Tibetan origins was

splendiferously sacred. Their fawning attitudes outraged Joe.
In private, he called them spiritual Nazis.

Give him credit, Spumoni could skate. Lifting one hand
sanctimoniously, he cooed "Peace, brother" while gliding by.
Joe veiled his eyes noncommitally, nodded, and managed to
hold his tongue as they passed like two shits in the night. Joe
retched, Michael frowned; they steered off the main drag into
the bus-station parking lot, and stopped.

꿍

Such luck! A bus being imminent, the station was
open. A thin frizzy freak slouched in a swivel chair at the
dispatcher's desk, his back to the door, browsing through *The
Autobiography of a Yogi* while keeping one eye on a funda-
mentalist Arkie Bible-thumper proselytizing on the tube.

Even as Joe banged one knuckle on the counter, saying
"Knock, knock, anybody home?" he spotted it, front and fore-
most in the baggage rack—Peter's suitcase! Moderately-sized,
and plaid as described. His thundering heart soared—was this
actually going to be easy? Might he sashay out of here in fifteen
seconds without a hitch, the proud possessor of his future land?
Joe's eyes quickly bobbed to either side, surreptitiously checking for feds, bloodhounds disguised as insurance-policy vending machines, or seeing-eye cameras high in the corners—but
the coast seemed clear.

He had to bite his lip to keep from giggling triumphantly.

The freak turned around at his knock: Egon Braithwhite.
Joe cried *Oh no!* as Egon grinned, revealing a toothless
gap. "Hi chop, Joe—durakabi?"

"That suitcase. The plaid one. I dropped by to pick it up.
Belongs to a friend."

"Mee kai chak—ruri ruri. Sakamajo."

"Hey, Egon." Still, Joe held his temper—after all, he was
almost home free. Smiling pleasantly, he said, "Couldn't we
forgo the lingo for a minute? All I need is that bag. Then I'll
be off and I won't bother you further."

Egon grinned back cheerfully, but expressed reservations
concerning Joe's request: "Joy kama wachi, no moy gallum,
sakamajo."

Joe replied, "Fee fi fo fum. Now listen, Egon. Please, I beg
of you—I don't understand what you're saying. But don't make

life any more difficult than it already is. I'm in a hurry, we got a million guests. Just hand me the bag—"

Egon shook his head, patiently explaining: "Wan up cholly fee goo rana rana. Pi san garalingo, mauchy, sakamajo."

"Oh for Chrissakes." Joe stepped over the low baggage platform. "Look, you don't mind, then? I'll just fetch this little baby myself."

Frowning, Egon leaped in front of him. "Chay no mi tai hi hirakistone, Joe. Si o minti, solly. Sakamajo."

All of a sudden, a nightmare. What did the brain-damaged piano tuner want? What was the problem? Or had he (Joe) forgotten that today was the start of National Insanity Week?

Calm yourself, all his inner mechanisms warned. But his sense of relief had been replaced by a premonition of danger. Somebody had put a hold on the suitcase—federal authorities in Newark? Saint Louis? Denver? Had Egon already pushed a secret button, or tripped a hidden wire, causing a light to blink and a buzzer to buzz in the county sheriff's office, where six enormous thugs outfitted in riot gear, gas masks, Mace guns, hand grenades, submachine weaponry, and scope-fitted sniper rifles awaited their marching orders?

A fly buzzed; the TV preacher blathered on; Egon held his ground. Joe backed up one step, forcing himself to be calm and friendly. "Uh, listen, Egon. Maybe we can work something out. Understand, I have all the respect in the world for your religious principles, believe me. I have a hundred-percent admiration for your ability to maintain the vow. But you'll have to admit, it poses some problems. Major one of which is I don't understand a word you're saying. So maybe you could cough up just one teeny-weeny little sentence in English to explain about the bag, then I'll be on my way."

Egon walked over to the bag, motioned Joe to approach, and, while fiddling with, and pointing to, the numbered claim tag on the handle, he said, "Toy ming no chow chow. Wokki wokki hey marinaki chicago. Sakamajo. Mooli fee tambouri."

"Something to do with the claim check?"

"Hi, raku pan." Egon nodded solicitously.

"You want the other half? The passenger's claim check?"

"Y rik no yama kai sanjury." Egon beamed, nodding vociferously, pleased as punch that Joe had understood.

"Egon, I forgot to bring it, man. But this is a small town— you know me. I'm not a thief, I'm not a robber, or a gangster.

I would never steal some total stranger's bag. Please, you hurt me with your insinuations."

But Egon wouldn't budge: orders, apparently, were orders. Amicably, with official coolness, he explained, "Mori stanislavki no tikki tikki pai monroe, kuba shrai sakamajo."

Joe's instinct was to nail the giddy boob with a right cross, grab the bag, and skedaddle. Fortunately, the voice of reason triumphed. If he called attention to himself like that, he might as well drive down to the state penitentiary and apply voluntarily for internment. No, better to keep a level head and a low profile in this matter.

In through the door came Chamisaville's answer to grotto groupies. Glowering menacingly, Nick Danger oozed across the linoleum and, with a surreal harrumph, slapped a ticket onto the baggage counter. Egon gestured apologetically to Joe, scooped up the claim check, and fetched a medium-sized cardboard box decorated with Japanese characters and colorful rising-sun stamps. Belligerently, Nick snatched it and took a powder.

Joe said, "Listen, Egon, lemme use the phone, okay? I'll call my friend, you can grill him in person. He'll describe the bag, give you permission to release it, and we'll both save ourselves a lot of time and trouble."

Egon made a motion with his fingers as if handling a small cardboard card: "Pider ab shat golly, runicifeeka potóto. Sakamajo."

Flabbergasted, Joe said, "I don't believe you're doing this to me." His entire body strained to leap forward, brain the moron, grab the valise, and flee.

Egon gave a bemused and rueful *You-can't-fight-city-hall* shrug: "Para ho mee no cum tsetse moro."

Joe said, "I dunno for sure, but suppose my friend lost the claim check—what then?"

"Hob knob er ob tsi guru muk luk."

Joe's temper strained like a good racehorse in the gate.

Michael said, "Pop, what is he saying?"

"You're asking *me*?"

Egon made a conciliatory gesture. His tone of voice suggested the solution was very simple. All Joe had to do was "Meri be baba cum shoji turificati pong sakamajo."

"Egon, seriously, pal. You lost Blues. All I want is the *bag*.

So how about just a paragraph in English? Then I'll know exactly what to do."

Back to the suitcase Egon went. Bent over, he pantomimed tearing a stub off the claim ticket at the perforation, and held up the invisible stub while explaining.

"Chari go mariboo sakamajo. See ri sakamajo. Pu quai sakamajo. Sakamajo."

"Sakamajo, eh?"

"Sakamajo."

Oh you son of a bitch! But aloud, Joe said, "All right, Michael. Apparently the man is gonna insist we deliver a claim check before he'll release the bag. No need to make a scene. Peter will just have to do without his clothes today."

"Uncle Peter? But I thought he didn't come in on the bus last night."

Joe glowered. "Button it, would you, moron? Just clam for a while."

"Fa shur ghonni boggle up lurifong?"

"Yeah, yeah, right on." Joe pushed Michael out the door ahead of him. "Far out, outtasight, and all that tommyrot. Oh Christ," he groaned once they were out of earshot: *"I'll emasculate the bastard!"*

"Dad?"

"Yeah . . ."

"What does 'sakamajo' mean?"

"Who knows? I forgot my Sanskrit dictionary. Probably 'claim check.'"

"In what language?"

"No language. He invents that crap."

"How come?"

"He took a vow."

"What's a vow?"

"Michael, I'm tired, I really am."

As they pedaled along further, Michael said, "Well, where now, brown cow?"

"Good question. I'm supposed to have a meeting at the airport in an hour. I can't believe that dumb ninny won't hand over the suitcase!"

"Why didn't you talk back to him in a made-up language?"

Joe pondered that as they cruised past the 7-Eleven. Nick Danger was lurking in the public phone booth, clutching his mysterious beige suitcase and the Japanese package to his chest.

Only a single vehicle, a hippie van with a CHICKEN RIVER FUNKY
PIE logo on the side, was parked in the Yellow Front lot next
door. Behind the wheel sat a hairy apparition, eating a banana.
Finally, Michael said, "I guess that wouldn't make any sense,
either."

Joe failed to respond. Already his mind was racing ahead,
deviously scheming. Before anything could happen, they needed
that suitcase—badly. The longer it stayed in the bus station,
glowing invisibly like a plutonium brick, emanating unsavory,
guilt-ridden vibes, the sooner its contents would be exposed.
Even if the authorities had somehow blunderingly stayed in the
dark despite all the clues scattered about Chamisaville like the
shattered refuse after a tornado, sooner or later they'd stumble
upon the answer, given Joe's miraculous facility to play himself
for a fool. Probably Egon would invite in some stray starving
dog for a watercress handout, and the dog, having been trained,
in a former life, to sniff out drugs at O'Hare airport, would
start barking at the black-watch valise, refusing to quit until
Sheriff Eddie Semmelweis arrived, put two and two together,
and opened the bag.

STRAY MUTT AND INCOHERENT GEEK BAG DRUG HOOLIGANS!
CRIMESTOPPER'S HOTLINE AWARDS 'EM $1,000 CLAMS!

Michael said, "Why do you need that suitcase?"

"Who wants to know?"

"Well, what's such a big deal about a crummy old suitcase?"

"Michael, it's not a 'big deal.' Uncle Peter checked his bag,
but couldn't get on the bus at the last moment, that's all. If
we leave the suitcase rotting in the bus station, somebody will
probably heave it back into a cargo hold by mistake, and carry
it off to Timbuktu."

My God, he thought, veering at the last second to avoid
catching a tire in a storm drain: that's *exactly* what'll happen.

Oh woe!

Think, he ordered his brain. They didn't have much time.
Obviously, they had to steal the bag. Okay, but how? He'd
recruit Ralph and Tribby. They'd wear ski masks. And black
gloves—no point in leaving fingerprints all over the place.
Driving up when the lot was deserted, they'd jump out, race
inside, and—while two of them held Egon—the third would
grab the bag and make a dash for it.

Brilliant! Egon only knew that the bag belonged to a friend of Joe Miniver. It might take the authorities all of eighteen seconds to arrive at Tribby's Castle of Golden Fools, warrants in hand, cherrytops flickering, walkie-talkies crackling!

Of course, if they found no evidence. . . . They could hide the bag in Ralph's float tank. Or better yet, fly it into the mountains in Tribby's plane, attach a parachute, shove it out over some high country clearing, and return later, when the heat had subsided . . .

. . . and the whole brick of coke had been devoured by junkie chipmunks!

"Brick" of coke? Joe was so hip to the dope scene he had no idea if uncut coke came in "bricks" or "leaves" or "powder" form.

He should have kept his mouth shut with Egon. Now, if he couldn't raise a claim check from Peter. . . .

Then Joe had a brainstorm. Hot dog! Here's what they'd do. Break in, leave traces, smash a window, bust the door, so what?—no problem. Quickly, they'd click open the suitcase, *remove the cocaine*, close the suitcase, and take off, *leaving the bag behind*! Let Egon report the break-in—the cops would never figure out what had been stolen. And no fingers could legitimately point at Joe.

"Brilliant!" Joe giggled out loud. "I'm an Einstein in a garbage truck!"

Michael said, "Is it something inside Uncle Peter's suitcase that you want especially?"

"Never you mind. I got it all figured out. Mr. Genius is in control."

"Is Uncle Peter's cocaine inside? If it is, you know what you could do? You could break into the bus station at night, take the cocaine out of the suitcase but leave the bag there, and split. Then nobody would know what had been stolen."

Calmly, Joe said, "Michael, why don't you run that by me again like a good little boy, all right?"

Michael ran it by him again.

Joe said, "Where did you hear about Uncle Peter's cocaine?"

"It's all around school. I think maybe Tofu Smatterling mentioned it. . . ."

All right, Joe said to himself. Don't panic, stay calm. If the entire grade school knew about the dope deal, there existed a real good chance that somebody else in town knew about that plaid suitcase, and was planning its removal. Yet unless they had been idiots, like Joe, and also demanded the bag from Egon, if it were stolen outright, Joe was the only suspect at whom a finger could point.

His overactive imagination immediately conjured up the following scenario. Under cover of darkest night, he and Tribby and Ralph broke into the depot and stealthily snatched the coke. That same evening others broke into the station and grabbed the entire suitcase, thus automatically casting the blame on Joe and his gang.

Obviously, then, after lifting the coke, they must leave behind a gang member to keep watch on the station, making sure nobody else broke inside, eager to abscond with the priceless goodies.

The thought wearied Joe—was there no respectable way out?

Michael said, "If you didn't want to steal the suitcase, you could sneak in and take the number off the claim-check tag and counterfeit the other half of it."

"How would I know what to make the counterfeit look like?"

"I could walk in this afternoon and ask for a baggage-check ticket, and you could copy off it, only changing the numbers."

Joe said, "Quiet a minute, I gotta think."

But so many possibilities offered themselves that his mind went blank. The scam was too complicated, overly riddled with traps that a single bumbling step could spring. He didn't want to play anymore. He wasn't tough enough. And anyway, if Heidi and he divorced now, Eloy Irribarren's land was a moot point, whatever the drug deal's outcome. At worst, the divorce papers would arrive on the same day some Capital City hanging judge put him away for life.

Trapped in a holocaust of his own devising, the only way out seemed to be for Joe to kiss off his family and the land, become a born-again Hanuman freak, and skip gaily down the yellow brick road to a far Eastern nirvana hand in hand with Nancy Ryan and Bradley and Sasha and Cheepy....

And Bozo.

Joe steered into Eloy Irribarren's driveway and stopped. The land, maybe one day (soon) his land, *their* land, lay ahead. If he wasn't killed in the process of trying to acquire it. And with that in mind, Joe wanted to see the terrain again, just to be sure it was worth it.

Panning slowly from left to right, his eyes riffled lovingly over the scenery. Ears pricked, Eloy's old brown horse, Geronimo, snorted softly. Three magpies and two boat-tailed grackles canvassed the shortcropped grass and horse-dung piles for tidbits. Tall cottonwoods awash in dead and dying branches from oyster-shell scale disease lined the property's road frontage. The field itself was thirty yards wide and a hundred yards deep. The Pacheco irrigation ditch was situated on its eastern border. Alongside the ditch ran another row of trees: silvertip poplars, a few honey locusts, a pear tree, and big, shabby chinese elms. Birdhouses for wrens, starlings, bluebirds, and flickers were nailed up high in the trees. The driveway, running along the southern side of the small meadow, was egregiously potholed. A flock of geese waddled up the rocky path noisily announcing their arrival.

"Whose horse is that, Dad?"

"It belongs to Mr. Irribarren."

"Who's Mr., uh, watchamacallit?"

"The man we're trying to buy the land from."

"How come his horse is still in our field?"

"It's not our field yet. And even if it were, he'll leave it here until he can locate another pasture."

"How come he wants to sell this farm if he doesn't have another one to go to?"

A trifle curtly, Joe said, "I guess he needs the bread. C'mon."

Taking their time, they negotiated the driveway on foot. Joe had such a lust to own the land that he couldn't stop himself from already considering it as good as his. This freed him to idolize the natural world he now (almost) owned as if only a few minutes ago God had touched it with a magic creation-rod, and everything from the ancient cedar fence posts to clover plants in the ditch were exhaling their first sweet breaths of life. Complex and contradictory emotions quickened his heartbeat. Last night's terrors and thrills galore mingled with an

129

apprehension (and awe) born of the fact that, for mere money, a person could actually *own* land. All of it could belong to him—this lovely grass, these majestic trees: even the horse manure dotting the front field had a heightened significance. It was valuable, it glowed, endowed with benevolent qualities, a precious resource fertilizing his front field. Or it would make his vegetables grow. In a pinch it could be burned as fuel. Had he no use for it, he could sell it to somebody else. No, perish the thought! Better it stayed right there. In fact, as soon as Geronimo was gone, Joe would kick that shit all over the field, spreading it evenly. And the grass would grow even greener. Then he would cut the grass, sell the bales—how many bales would such a field produce? What would the bale price be come autumn? Once cut, he could rent the pasture to a neighbor for grazing. At harvest time, they would sell squash, corn, and beets at the Farmer's Market beside the courthouse. Eloy had a big chicken coop; Joe would keep it full of high-caliber hens. They'd sell eggs, kill, pluck, and freeze their own birds, make cheese from their goats' milk, and, in October, slaughter a couple of hogs. And what about keeping on Eloy's beehives for their honey . . . ?

MINIVER FARMS, OF CHAMISAVILLE, WINS J. I. RODALE
"GREEN THUMB" AWARD!

Pausing atop the Pacheco Ditch culvert pipe, Michael said, "There's some water skeeters."

Joe positively tingled from the thought of owning his own water skeeters!

Michael said, "Hey, what was that *animal*?"

"A muskrat." Not only would they possess land, trees, fruit, and water, but they had purchased, as well, a partial share in a southwestern equivalent to the Bronx Zoo!

A large orange-and-black butterfly blithely bobbed toward them. Joe was flabbergasted. "Holy mackerel! A swallowtail!"

"You mean monarch," Michael chided.

"That's what I said."

Excitedly, Joe pointed out a twisted, pastel-blue bush beside the culvert. "That's a sagebrush plant, Michael. We own a regular Garden of Eden!"

"Do we own it already? I thought—"

"Don't think," Joe snapped. "It's bad for your brain."

A slight rise led to a wide rounded parking area. Here the geese mingled noisily with a dozen chickens, some guinea hens, several belligerent, thumping, posturing (and enormous) tom turkeys, two curious peacocks, and a bunch of Chihuahuaesque dogs named Sweetie Pie, Cookie, Honey, Fuzzy, Squeaky, and Daffodil.

Ay, such a racket!

A dilapidated pickup snoozed in front of the crumbling three-room adobe house in which Eloy Irribarren had lived most of his life. The truck's outer skin looked as if some baseball maniac had set up a pitching machine and fired hardballs at ninety miles an hour against it for a decade. The windshield was cracked, splintered, impossibly spider-webbed; the passengerside window was made of cardboard and silver duct-tape. The sides, the tail pipe, the rear fender and license plate were attached by snaggles of rusty baling wire. A twisted coat hanger jammed into a corroded gap in the right rear of the hood served as an antenna for a radio that apparently functioned.

Eloy still held a valid license and insisted on driving himself everywhere. Known around the valley as a one-man demolition derby, when out plying the highways and byways as if they were his own personal Dodg'em-cars rink, Eloy was assiduously avoided by all other motorists. Approaching cars a hundred yards away braked as soon as they recognized Eloy's pulverized Chevy, pulling way over to let him pass. Occasionally, on-coming drivers parked, jumped out, circled their vehicles, and dived into the roadside ditch as if escaping an overhead strafing. Those who did not pull over usually wound up careening onto soft shoulders, or plummeting into ditches anyway, as Eloy slalomed along, oblivious to it all.

Smoke issued from Eloy's chimney. Beside the house stood a vast and ragged pile of wood—piñon, cedar, lumber slabs, sawmill butt-ends, and silvery gray aspen trunks gathered at old forest-fire burns. Wood chips, from years of log-splitting, surrounded the house and trickled into the parking area. Duke, a grotesquely flea-bitten German shepherd, lay in the front of the shack's only door, eyeing them lethargically. On the roof, on the front stoop, in planters that might once have held flowers when the mistress of the household still lived, a pride of ragged cats sprawled, snoring, meowing, coughing up fur balls and vomiting grass, scratching in the dust to cover up turds, or glowering at bullyboy magpies. Conservatively, Joe guessed Eloy had fifteen cats.

And curled up within Duke's paws was an enormous tattered and one-eyed gray-and-white rabbit called Tuerto.

Several feet in front of the house, a quaint wooden structure protected Eloy's hand-dug well. The water dipped up out of that well by a hand-cranked bucket was crystal-clear and cold. Joe knew, because the old man had offered him a cup when they first started talking deal.

Off to the right, a pleasant murmur of animal and fowl sounds issued from the hodgepodge conglomeration of wire-covered pens that stretched for about thirty yards between the house and the small back field. Constructed of forty-year-old fence posts, warped lumber slabs, and all manner of chicken, sheep, and goat wire and screening, the chaotic, ramshackle pens housed an almost surreal zoo. Posed arrogantly against the skyline atop the goat shed, a peacock spread its gorgeous tail-feathers. Goats bounded eagerly around in a wooden corral, trying to leap out. Dozens of rabbits wrinkled their noses, sniffing indifferently, in a crazy, patchwork warren. A sow and six piglets snorted and chuffed beside a pen in which pheasants strutted nervously, their bright feathers glittering iridescently. More tom turkeys, hen turkeys, and chicklet turkeys occupied another jail. Pigeons cooed and fluttered in a green plastic dishpan, bathing themselves. Ten quail strutted around in their barren dirt pen, hunting tidbits. And in a far cage, Wolfie, a twenty-three-year-old timber wolf, paced patiently, awaiting his Alpo and Sunday morning stroll.

A miniature orchard was situated directly north and east of Eloy's tiny dwelling. It harbored a crab-apple tree, one green-apple tree, one Delicious apple tree, a pear tree, and several greengage plum bushes. Around them bees hummed busily. Eloy's garden area lay just to the south. Some dry cornstalks remained standing among patches of leaves and straw he had used for mulch.

The back field, another six-tenths of an acre, was planted in brome. Earlier, the old man had burnt off the dead grass. Now, streaks of carbon darkness were rapidly being obliterated by new spring shoots. A line of dry grass stalks running across the middle of the field like a mohawk haircut indicated where a Lovatos Acequia feeder ditch passed through.

A killdeer screeched over the field, glided, and touched

down with a bounce. Joe said, "Look at that bird! We'll even have killdeers! Do you think they'll nest out there?"

And, wise to the cornball proclivities of human beings, a meadowlark on a fence post unleashed its melodic riff.

Joe kicked down his bike stand and entered the back field. His eyes skimmed over the ground, marking alfalfa clumps, a gopher hole, a budding anthill that might have to be eliminated, and a black dung-beetle creeping along, its head to the ground, rump pointed skyward. Screeching, the killdeer jumped and winged away. Four more chinese elms against a fence delineated the eastern boundary: starlings, gathered in their branches, twittered noisily.

In the center of the field, Joe rotated several times ecstatically. "Michael, me boyo, what do you think?"

"It's okay."

"Just 'okay'?" Joe pushed his kid over, tackled him, sat on his chest, and poised a protruding knuckle directly above the boy's sternum. "If you don't say this is the most beautiful little chunk of natural nirvana you ever saw I'll give you the Chinese knuckle torture!"

"Ouch." Michael grimaced stoically. "You're hurting my stomach."

"Who cares? Let's go, punk. I want something more expressive than a stupid 'okay' out of you. Or I swear to Christ I'll tear you asunder."

Michael asked, "When we own the land, are you just gonna kick him out of there?"

"No, dumbbell, he'll move out. I'll pay for the land, he'll go someplace else."

"What if he doesn't have anyplace else to go?"

"Michael, do you know how much bread I'll give that old man for this place?"

Eyes squinched against the sunlight, Michael shook his head.

"Sixty thousand dollars."

"Oh."

"So the man could rent a castle if he wanted."

"How much exactly is sixty thousand dollars? What could you buy for it? Like how many cars?"

"Depends what kind of car."

"VW buses."

"New?"

"Yes. . . ."

"Well, I think about six."

Michael said, "I heard you tell Mom once that Mr., uh, you know, was in debt almost as much as he would get paid for the land, so in the end he'll wind up with almost nothing."

Joe jumped up. "Hey, kid, who's paying you to be a kill-joy?"

"Well, maybe we shouldn't buy it."

"If we don't buy it, somebody else will. You see, he has to sell."

"Why?"

"He's in debt and he's trying to get a decent price before they take it away and auction it off for a lot less than it's worth."

"Why don't we wait until the auction, then?"

"Because somebody else would buy it before the auction."

"You mean, no matter what, the auction can't really happen?"

"It could. But too many people have a vested interest in nailing this place down before that happens."

"Oh."

At the well, Joe said, "Watch this." He cranked up the bucket, and poured clear water into a tin cup he'd retrieved from a rusty nail. Downing a healthy slug, he pantomimed ecstasy while emitting a satisfied "ahhh." Then he tendered the cup to Michael.

"No thanks."

"I'm offering you real live H_2O, no fluoride, no chemicals, no asbestos fibers, no chlorine, and you have the unmitigated gall to say 'No thanks'?"

"Isn't that water polluted?" Michael peered suspiciously into the dark liquid rippling fifteen feet below them.

"Polluted? This is water in its natural state. Taste it. Champagne pales beside this elixir."

"But melted mung from that outhouse could be seeping into it. In school they said you're supposed to drill down to the third aquifer." He fired a BB that entered the water with an echoing *chug*!

"What are you shooting at?"

"My own face."

"Well, don't be killing any frogs. . . ."

Apprehensively, Joe knocked on Eloy's door. It took a while.

When the old man finally answered, Joe said, "Buenos días, sir. Are we disturbing you?"

"Disturbing me? Qué va! I always welcome a visitor. What's the weather like out here?—sorry I took so long, I must have been asleep. Though I didn't return from the fiesta until midnight, I couldn't sleep. I drowsed for a while, then all of a sudden I woke up, startled. There was a strange light coming into the house. So I went to the window and peeped outside. And you know what I saw? I know this sounds crazy, but I thought I saw an enormous angel drinking water at my well. I pinched myself to make sure I was alive, and went right back to bed. But I was up at five as usual, chopped some wood, made my breakfast, sharpened an ax, and then damned if I didn't fall asleep again."

Squinting, Eloy assessed first the high white clouds casting shadows against the mountains, then the direction of the breeze lazily tinkering with cottonwood leaves. His handshake was gentle: no squeezing, no pumping—it was simply there, relaxed and friendly.

"Who's this handsome little diablo?" Eloy asked.

"Handsome?" Joe tousled Michael's hair. "He's my son, but I sure wouldn't call him handsome. Ugly as sin is the way I'd put it."

Horribly shy with strange grown-ups, Michael hung his head, abysmally uncomfortable.

The old man asked, "What kind of a gun is that?"

"It only shoots BBs. It's a Daisy."

Michael muttered, "I can speak for myself, Pop."

"Give it here a sec." Eloy examined the rifle. Joe watched, fascinated: in the old-timer's practiced hands the gun took on a different dimension, acquiring the dignity of a weapon. Eloy worked the hand lever, took aim, and fired at a magpie cackling in the crab-apple tree.

Joe said, "Hey!" as the offended bird took off, scrawking loudly.

Eloy shook his head, running one finger down the tin barrel. Then he handed it back to Michael. "It shoots real low, son. You should adjust the sight."

Embarrassed, Joe nevertheless felt called upon to lodge a protest. "I try and teach him not to shoot at living things."

Eloy smiled, "You couldn't hurt a magpie at this distance with a BB gun. What day is today, anyway?"

"Sunday."

"I thought so." All his facial wrinkles seemed to explode as he giggled, giving Joe's shoulder a tap of recognition.

"By God, I missed church again. What do you think about that? The good Lord is liable to blight my tomatoes again this year, qué no? You folks aren't church people, are you?"

"Not us. I was brought up Episcopalian. But I quit going to church by the time I reached college."

"This whole valley used to be religious," Eloy mused. "Hell, they flocked to the Catholic church like flies to hot horse manure. Sunday mornings the entire valley reverberated from the chiming bells. Now it's like a spiritual circus—with dancing bears, and white horses, and elephants and clowns. But in the old days—"

He raised a harkening finger, the tip of which was missing: they listened for the faint echo of yesteryear's Sunday tolling.

Joe said, "Look, we don't want to disturb you. . . ."

"I'm so busy? Inundated with family and friends to care for? I want a game of cards with my neighbor, Elivirio Baca, I go to the camposanto. If my addled brain needs to ask my wife, Teresita, what herb is best for rheumatism, I make another trip to the graveyard. If, on a whim, I wish to ask my youngest son Larkin how's tricks, I got to wait until the one day a month they allow visitors at the state penitentiary—he went crazy three years ago in the La Tortuga and smashed a female real-estate agent on the head with a beer bottle. If I decide to share a cup of chokecherry wine with my eldest boy, Cruz, it's back to the cemetery again with a bottle and my broken heart— thanks to that place across the ocean, Vietnam. In all the ter-tulias for us old-timers . . . we convene on boot hill. It's grown mightly lonely around here aboveground. These days only the skeletons speak Spanish."

Joe said, "Well, you know, I mean . . ."

Abruptly, Eloy softened. "Don't be sorry. I should apologize. I know my bitterness is childish. Sometimes I hate my own bile. I stick my finger down my throat and try to upchuck it. I'm very lucky I lived so long, and had such a good life. But the day an old man in my position claims he's being molested by two young fellers like you will be the day."

Michael had a question: "Is that well-water polluted?"

"Yup, you bet it is."

Joe said, "Hey, Michael—who asked you to open that fat yap of yours?"

"You need to tap the third aquifer if you don't want it to be full of horse piss and human feces," Eloy explained.

Joe said, "But it tastes wonderful. And you drink it."

"I'm used to it. I guzzled it all my life."

The cheerful animal chatter, the sunshine glittering in apple trees, made Joe increasingly nervous. The land would not be his, really, until Eloy departed, taking his horse, his dog, his decrepit wolf, his one-eyed rabbit, and the rest of his menagerie, leaving the Minivers as sole proprietors of the diminutive estate. Meaning the animals were doomed. For what could Eloy do with all these beasts? Sell them, obviously. Or give them away. Suppose he offered them—gratis—to Joe? Ah, perish the thought. Yet the request was inevitable. And if Joe refused? He was condemning the animals to death. After all, what market existed for glue-factory horses, half-blind rabbits, and toothless wolves?

Heart sinking, Joe realized that the cacophonous group of flea-bitten barnyard critters would come with the territory. For sixty thousand clams, he would find himself the guardian of a bunch of useless misfits right out of a Buñuel film! The specter was horrifying. He'd have to borrow a backhoe, dig an enormous trench, and hire Jeff Orbison and Tom Yard to drive the flocks, herds, coveys, and gaggles into it, then cut loose with their .357 magnums and police .38s. . . .

CHAMISAVILLE'S OWN BABI YAR! SPCA FILES SUIT IN ABSENTIA
AGAINST BARNYARD "SHOCK-DOC"! MINIVER FLEES,
RUMORED IN PARAGUAY!

For such problems he was going to risk his life? Let the suitcase rot in that bus station!

Of course, until the old man and his charges departed, everything here belonged to Eloy. After all, it was his home; his history gave personality to each grass-blade and fence post; his kindness and concern had forged the personalities of the stock. So long as Eloy and his animals remained, Joe and the children and Heidi (if she hadn't already reserved a plane ticket for New York!) would be strangers on their own turf. Yet how could he broach the subject?

Gretchen Horney, at Sköl Realty, had promised to deal with

Eloy, alerting the law if he refused to budge. "Sometimes the old ones won't move, even after they've taken your money," she had explained. "I don't know why that is. Maybe they have a spiritual anchor to the land they're not strong enough to pull up."

Joe had posed this hypothetical dilemma to Gretchen: "Suppose a guy like Mr. Irribarren has no relatives and no place to go?"

"With what you're paying him, he could rent a room at the Chamisaville Inn for the next ten years."

"Yes, I know. But I mean, suppose he has no place to *go* to?"

Employing a Bic pen, Gretchen poked her wide round glasses up to the top of her head and regarded him wistfully. Finally, with a sigh, she cautioned: "Joe, there's not much room for emotions in the real-estate game."

Bueno. Maybe he should just hire Tom Yard and Jess Orbison to come over here and perform a hit on the old man himself. Or figure out a way to have him OD on cutworm moths saturated with PCP.

Eloy said, "You're going to build a house. A big house?"

"Well, we have plans to build, of course. But it won't be that large...." Confronted by the three-room, wood-heated, outhouse-serviced shack Eloy had raised a large family in, Joe choked on the rest of his sentence. Life wasn't tough enough, now God had decided to punish him for last night by making him freak out on a guilt trip over an eighty-three-year-old fox almost sixty Gs richer thanks to the Miniver largesse.

"If you would let me stay on a little longer after you buy the land, I could help you build the adobes," Eloy said.

"Uh, I'm not sure, that is, I mean, I don't know yet, well, if we're actually, you know, going to build with adobe."

Eloy shrugged. "Nobody builds with adobe anymore. They build with tin cans, they build with bottles, they build with plastic, they build with old tires. They build with peacock feathers. They even build with flyshit and Elmer's Glue."

Joe said, "We haven't exactly decided *not* to build with adobe. None of our plans have firmed up yet. I mean, after Heidi comes over to really inspect the land, the first thing we'll do is decide where to put the house. Then we'll make up our minds on what kinds of materials to use. Naturally, we'd have to price the various construction methods and play around with all that information. . . ."

Sadly, yet without real bitterness this time, Eloy said, "I built so many houses in my time. In the old days, nobody had cash—we helped each other. It was a community thing. We traded labor and knowhow with our neighbors. You could put your cows in my pasture for free—in return, I picked apples from your orchard. My wife Teresita was an enjarradora—she mudded a thousand houses, built fireplaces, plastered the inside walls with tierra blanca. In return, they gave us a side of beef, two lambs, sacks of freshly ground flour. When I visited Filadelfio's house, I could feel my labor in his walls. When I got drunk and fell over backwards in Tranquilino's kitchen, I was proud to see my handiwork in his ceiling vigas and latias."

He shook his head ruefully. "A bunch of us rode into the hills to cut timbers for Rudolfo Gurule's roof . . . and we raised it together . . . in a single day. Every year, Pablo Tafoya and Pancho Cruz and Jacobal Esquibel helped me to cut and stack my fields: Cipriano Martínez had a team of horses we all used for plowing. I even built the adobes for my daughter Maria's house when she got married. Six months after we plastered the outside, she sold it for a five-figure killing and moved to Califas. Now, when I drive around the valley, the ghosts of our togetherness sing to me mournfully from the fields going fallow, the dying apple trees nobody has cared to prune in a decade, the simple adobes that have been elaborately renovated by stockbrokers and hot-tub salesmen. . . ."

Ashamed (and angry and resentful), Joe wound up awkwardly fleeing with Michael. Facing Eloy, he had realized how much he hated being cast as yet another little gear in the machine steam-rollering the valley. Guilt foamed from his nose, mouth, and ears. At this rate, instead of one day aiding the Third World's starving billions by jousting against exploitative economic systems, he'd wind up tiptoeing through the carnage in Posturepedic brothel-creepers, karate pants, and soybean love beads, ordering kwashiorkored Biafrans to manifest themselves by becoming At One with The One while also, incidentally, sending their last dollars to the est Hunger Enrollment Project, which would, in return, send a pamphlet telling them how to feel good about dying.

Racing ahead on his bicycle as Michael called "Hey, wait up!," Joe wished he had never set any of this in motion. They should have moved to Wilton, Connecticut, or Barton, Vermont, where they could have displaced their own kind.

Instead, he was slated to go down in the record books as the son of a bitch who heartlessly ousted the Last Chicano.

Like miniature Hounds of the Baskervilles, Mimsy and Tuckums leaped shrieking and snapping from their gorgon's lair near the deserted Ranchitos Cantina.

"Bite me," Joe begged as they hassled his feet. Their hot breaths burned against the blue rubber Adidas sticker on his heels. "Go ahead, you creeps, sink those pearly choppers into my ankle, make this day complete!"

But although their spit sprinkled against his pantcuffs, Joe's theory of ignoring them proved correct. Raising a god-awful spine-chilling racket, their teeth clicking like castanets, the dogs followed them to the invisible frontier without taking even one teeny-weeny nip.

Michael went home: Joe pedaled out to the airport. Tribby and Ralph and Rimpoche had already arrived. They awaited him beside Tribby's pink-and-green Corvath 190. An exotic-looking barefoot woman with heavily mascaraed eyes, wearing a plum-purple gold-brocaded vest and filthy lemon-yellow harem pants, clung to Ralph's arm—another of his instant, sexual weirdos? Tribby leaned against one of the plane's wing struts in a lackadaisical, strung-out fashion suggesting a complete lack of bones. He wore a motorcycle helmet and a bluejean jacket, and had a black eye from last night's Cinema Bar rumble with Ephraim Bonatelli.

My friends, Joe thought sarcastically as he approached them. Upon whom I can count in my time of need: a shabby mouthpiece, a corpulent letch, a whacked-out teenybopper, and a filthy, chickenshit, bullying sheepdog!

Ralph said, "Joe, I want you to meet my good friend Gloria Halbouty."

"Hello, Gloria. Hi, Tribby. Ralph . . . guess what?"

"Your friend didn't arrive, but the dope's sitting in a plaid suitcase in the bus station under the all too watchful protection of Egon Braithwhite, who won't release it without a claim check," Tribby said.

"How in hell did you know that?"

"Rachel went jogging with Suki Terrell after she left Scott Harrison's place at six this morning, and Suki explained that she'd heard through Natalie, who called Scott, that Rama Unfug let drop you were shacked up with Nancy Ryan last night."

"That still doesn't explain how you know about the suitcase."

"Ralph told me."

"How did he know?"

"Your window was open when you screamed at your friend Roth on the telephone an hour and a half ago."

"That's the sign of a Type-A personality," Gloria said. "Really, Joe, you should augment your diet with a lot of Vitamin E."

Tribby said, "So we can't launch Operation Bald Eagle until you retrieve that suitcase from the bus station."

Joe said, "Wait a minute, I was screaming on the telephone *before* I went to the bus station."

"Must be a time warp somewhere." Ralph gave a genial shrug. "This has been a weird spring."

"Let's hit the clouds anyway," Tribby suggested. "The plane's full of gas. And we'll have more privacy up there."

Joe closed his eyes, terrified of dying. They were all squunched in together, packed like plump sardines. The dog sat a third in Joe's, a third in Gloria's, and a third in Ralph's lap. The light plane wobbled and bounced; struts and stays groaned, the engine whirred, clucked, spat, and chugged, lifting them off. Their wheels brushed sagebrush at the end of the runway. Rimpoche began whining. Ralph said, "My my." Gloria cooed, "Oh, I love it. I get so high in airplanes. It's a combined religious and sexual thing with me. I always feel closer to God. . . ."

"Gloria's a member of Women Aglow," Ralph explained.

"What exactly is that?" Joe's teeth chattered, and he dared not open his eyes.

"A Women's International Christian Fellowship organization."

"Meaning—?"

"She's a Jesus freak."

Caught in a wind gust, the lightweight plane shuddered and veered: Joe squeaked, "Oh help!" Rimpoche also yelped.

"No problem," Tribby said laconically. "I'm in total control."

"Let's talk fast, then. And return to earth as soon as is humanly possible."

"What's to talk about?" Ralph wanted to know. "You haven't got the suitcase. We can't cut the coke or package it. The scam is stalemated."

"Okay, how do I obtain the suitcase, then?"

"Walk in and snatch it," Ralph said. "Don't be such a Casper Milquetoast."

"If I do that, Egon might call the cops."

"So let him call."

"There's cocaine in that suitcase, Ralph."

"Remove it before the gendarmes arrive."

"Suppose they've got a dog that sniffs it?"

"There are no narc hounds in Chamisaville."

"You're missing the point," Tribby said. "If Joe takes the suitcase and Egon calls the cops, Joe's under suspicion. We don't want any of us to fall under their surveillance."

Ralph said, "Call your friend, have him send the claim check."

"He said he lost it."

"Then what we must do, of course, is steal the contents of the suitcase, without removing it from the bus station."

Tribby lit a cigarette. "Let's cut a hole in the roof. You guys can lower me with a rope. I'll make the snatch dangling in midair. There won't even be a footprint."

"Just a hole as big as the moon in the roof!"

Tribby said, "We could file a writ of *a certiori*, or *habeas corpus*, present it to Egon, and walk out with the bag."

"What do either of those have to do with impounding property?" Joe asked.

"Nothing. We merely flash some legal papers to Egon, impound the valise, and split. He'll never know the difference."

"Sounds pretty lame to me."

"We could divert his attention," Ralph said.

"How?"

"Lemme see. I could crash my car into the back of that old pickup he always parks out front whenever he's on duty. For good measure, I'll stumble outside and start blasting at his rig with a deer rifle, chastising it for getting in my way." While speaking, Ralph had rolled a joint and now offered it around.

Joe said, "That's absurd."

"Life is absurd."

Tribby had another plan. "We all don ski masks, waltz into the joint, and rob it. We make it look like a straight heist, grab a whole conglomeration of goodies, including the suitcase in question, then dump all the stuff in an arroyo after we remove the dope."

"So if they catch us they've got us not only for the coke, but for armed robbery as well? Brilliant!"

"It's the TV mentality," Ralph said. "The tubular method of problem-solving."

"We sound like a bunch of kids playing at cops and robbers."

Gloria added her two bits. "Maybe if I simply went in and asked him real nice for the suitcase. Usually you can solve just about any problem by being nice to people. The trouble with you boys is the roots of your solutions are belligerent."

"'The roots of our solutions are belligerent.' Nice phrase," Ralph said. "I like it."

Shrilly, Joe said, "Egon's an idiot. He won't even talk English. He's the belligerent one in this affair."

Tribby said, "Maybe we should forget the suitcase for a minute, and try instead to zap the opposition."

"Meaning . . . ?"

"We squeal to the State Corporation Commission and the attorney general about Skipper Nuzum's plan to let Cobey Dallas embezzle himself into a corner through Roger Petrie's sleight of hand. The package includes Cobey's deal to pay Roger off in the water rights. Then we dig up Xeroxes of the documents and back records pertaining to Scott Harrison's escrow account with Roger for those water rights, and mail them to the state bar association."

Ralph said, "Not to be a killjoy, but when has the state bar ever stomped on one of their own?"

"Granted. But lemme complete the scenario, at least. Harrison panics, grabs his dough to protect his ass, queers the arrangement with Petrie, and, out of spite, tips off Cobey that Roger is a bum. When Cobey tumbles to Roger's double-agenthood, he fires the little son of a bitch, gets drunk, and ineptly tries to kill him—thereby winding up in the state pen on assault-and-battery charges. Roger's so pissed off Skipper Nuzum suddenly never heard of him that he turns state's evidence on Skipper when the feds start auditing the convoluted shebang. Naturally, since it's really his wife, Natalie, and the Simian Foundation that Skipper's courting the land for, Nikita

Smatterling is implicated, and before you can say 'Yogananda,' the Simians have lost their tax-exempt status. Whereupon, their whole pious Chamisaville act collapses."

"Very funny." Joe grimaced. "During the seventeen years it takes this mess to unravel on the dockets, Eloy Irribarren croaks, Ray Verboten heists my suitcase and makes a quarter-million dollars from the stash inside, and the Tarantula of Chamisaville and his flunkies at the First State People's Jug foreclose on the land and carve it up into the Joe Bonatelli Memorial Condos for Christian Athletes!"

Ralph exclaimed, "Eureka, I've got it!"

"So talk."

"We purchase a suitcase exactly like the one Peter Roth sent. Then one of us travels down to the capital, buys a ticket for Chamisaville, checks the bag, rides the bus here, gets off, switches the claim-check stubs, and walks out with the wrong bag, which is actually the right one."

"Brilliant, except for one thing."

"Which is?"

"How you gonna switch the claim-ticket stubs?"

"Egon will be helping the driver unload or something."

Tribby said, "Even if it doesn't work, at least there'll be two suitcases that look alike in the baggage area, so that if anybody else gets wind of the loot to be had in that bag, they won't know which one to steal."

Ralph said, "How about this—we start a fire."

"Where?"

"In the bus station. Fortunately, all of us will suddenly arrive on the scene and help fight it. In the confusion we can grab the bag and head for the hills."

"That makes some sense, I guess. . . ."

But Tribby favored the second valise trick. "I even think I know how we could switch the claim-check tickets. One of us dresses up in some kind of official-looking uniform, enters the depot, lays a rap on Egon that he's such and such a baggage inspector for Trailways International, and putters around in the baggage area, putting stickers and little chalk marks on some of the suitcases, making the switch in the process, and we're home free."

"He knows all of us. We wouldn't stand a chance."

"He doesn't know me," Gloria said.

"Brilliant!" Ralph hugged her.

"Brilliant?" Joe couldn't believe he was trapped in an airplane with this gathering of terminal cases.

"Is what I would be doing considered illegal?" Gloria asked.

"Illegal, shmeagal—so what? It's what has to be done," Ralph said.

"But I couldn't do anything illegal. What would Christ think?"

"Christ has been dead for almost two thousand years."

Gloria rolled her eyes. "That shows how much you know."

"Wait a minute." Joe was perplexed. "You just took three tokes off a joint. That's illegal."

"Jesus says marijuana is okay."

Hollering, *"Oh shit!,"* Tribby lurched them sideways, trying to avoid a collision with a buzzard which had suddenly appeared dead center in front of them. Too late, however. The enormous bird smashed into the plane, was cut in half by a steel bar dividing the windshield, and, in a gory explosion of glass, feathers, and intestinal gore, slammed back through the compartment just above head-height, clipping all the passengers with assorted bits of offal, yet miraculously killing, or even wounding seriously, no one.

Ralph cried, *"God dammit!"* Joe bellowed, "NO!" and Tribby yelped, "Oh dear!" as the plane wallowed in an airless trough, threatening to roll. Gloria said, "Oh the poor bird!" Rimpoche uncorked an eerie, petrified howl, pissed on everyone, and struggled to leap clear of the plane. They held him down like zoo keepers wrestling a mammoth python.

Wind whipped at their hair; ears popped painfully. Papers flapped around, cudgeling them like madly beating wings. Buttons popped as their shirts were torn open. The blasting currents made it impossible to open their eyes—all except Tribby: he clanged down the visor on his motorcycle helmet, and said, "Hang tight, everybody, here we go."

"Are we going to die?" Ralph asked politely.

"Not if I can help it."

"God won't let us die." Gloria smiled reassuringly.

"God my ass!"

"I don't believe this is happening," Joe whimpered. "What did I step in last night? This is insane! I've had more bad luck in the last twenty-four hours than in the past thirty-eight years put together."

BIRD TO BLAME AS DRUG KINGPIN PERISHES IN PLANE CRASH!
DOG IS ONLY SURVIVOR!

Will Rogers, Buddy Holly, Rocky Marciano, and Joe Miniver. . . .

Joe *who*?

"Are we gonna crash?"

Tribby said, "I'm not sure. Everybody hang tight. Where did that bird come from anyway?"

Gloria started pouting. "It's not the bird's fault. It didn't ask for airplanes to be in the sky."

"Shuttup, Gloria." Ralph clapped one hand over her mouth.

"What kind of bird was it?" she asked, her words muffled and indistinct.

"Who cares?" What a dingbat! "How can you ask a question like that at a time like this?" Joe added. The hair battering his forehead and cheeks stung like thousands of tiny sadistic rubber whips. Rimpoche ceased to struggle and merely wailed in anguish like a dying wolf.

Ralph thought "It looked eagleish."

"My guess is a buzzard," Tribby opined.

Joe babbled, "As it went by me it resembled a chocolate pudding with feathers!"

"Is everybody okay?" Tribby asked. They were positively zooming down toward the mesa. "Is anybody decapitated back there? Is the dog hurt?"

"Incredibly, I think we're all right. Rimpoche is scared stiff, that's all."

"Well, keep on hanging tight. We'll be landing in half a minute."

"A crash landing?"

"Not if I can help it."

"What does that mean?" Ralph asked.

"It means there's the airport . . . here's the runway . . . looks like duck soup . . . grit your teeth, comrades, here we go . . . nice and easy . . . theeeeeerrrreee. . . ."

Wheels touched, they bounced a little, veered slightly, settled, sped smoothly along the runway for a bit, slowed down, drifted to a stop.

Ralph said, "Whew."

Gloria giggled nervously. "God saved us. Hallelujah!"

"What did God send the bird for in the first place?" Joe glowered malevolently. He actually pinched himself, astounded to be alive. Blood, gore, and bits of feathers covered them all.

Ralph said, "It looks as if a hand grenade exploded inside a haggis."

Tribby taxied slowly across the tarmac to his parking place. "I never for a moment had any doubts," he chortled, "that yours truly could rise to the occasion."

The plane halted; he killed the engines. Instantly lathered in silence, they sat there stunned and grateful and trembling.

Joe said, "I'm never going up in the air again."

"Planes are a thousand times safer than automobiles."

"Oh yeah? You can take that myth and shove it."

Ralph said, "We still haven't solved our suitcase problem."

Joe balked. "I'm sorry, I can't think about that right now. Look at me. Look at you, for that matter. Look at *us*. We're covered with *guts*."

"Maybe it was a sign," Ralph said.

"The bird? Of what?"

"Well, it could have been a warning. Maybe we shouldn't proceed with the dope deal."

Joe said, "What about my twelve thousand dollars?"

"What about it?"

"That's my life savings. I've risked everything to bring this off."

"Is it worth the rest of your life in jail?" Ralph asked. "Is it worth rats nibbling on your toes? And no TV privileges? And scarred murderers and child-rapists dragging you into their cells for asshole pussy?"

Joe left them, shakily maneuvering over to his bicycle. "I'll see you guys around the campus," he said, using his most surly tone of voice. "Forget the suitcase, I'll figure something out. I'll call you when we're ready to proceed again."

"God be with you!" Gloria cried. "Jesus will help you if you believe!"

"Send him over to my place around midnight, then. With a little black burglary tool bag and a nine-millimeter pistol full of bullets on his hip!"

❧

Ten minutes later, Joe had just negotiated a left onto Route 240, when a VW Beetle beeped in passing and veered onto the shoulder: Cobey Dallas hopped out, purposeful smoke streaming from his freshly lit cigar. He held up one hand, motioning Joe to halt.

"Hello, Cobey. What's up?"

"Your number, friend, if you don't watch out." Cobey smiled to prove he was only joking. But warmth rarely emanated from that golden-boy face freckled with auto-accident scars and boozy dissipation. Joe often likened Cobey to the insincere all-American guys who starred in TV programs—bland and healthy, and forever acting. Always finagling, Cobey was friendly only according to the size of the favor he desired from his mark. And everybody, in Cobey's world, was a mark. But he had silky blond hair framing a tanned and lovely—if neutral—fizzog, and he kept his body beautiful at the health spa. His clothes were custom-cut and western—ruggedly chic and slick, like a Hollywood cowboy. The cigar, Joe supposed, he affected to create an aura of mogul.

"My number?" wide-eyed Joe replied, all innocence. "How's that?"

"For starters, I hear you've decided to enter the drug racket. Word has it you just imported enough cocaine to keep Chamisaville loaded for a millennium."

"Oh, hey, Cobey, *please*. Where the hell—"

"Stop. Relax. Hear me out." The entrepreneur puffed; blue smoke billowed across his intent, cool-blue eyes. "First of all, you should understand I'm on your side. You need a promoter badly, and I'm a promoter. Here's the deal. If you and that fat letch and the hippie lawyer try to go it alone, you're doomed. That's not how things work in the dope underworld. They'll pop all three of you the second you put one toe in their water. What has to happen to facilitate the matter is somebody like me needs to assemble a package that'll keep everyone happy. And I can do that because I'm the best middleman in Chamisaville."

Blushing, Joe nevertheless insisted, "I'm not in the coke business, Cobey."

Cobey curled one of Chamisaville's phoniest friendly arms

148

around Joe's shoulder. "Ha ha, Joe—that's a good one. Course, I don't blame you in the least. How do you know where I'm coming from? Well, take the cotton out of your ears. Here's the riff. Ray Verboten controls the trade in our bucolic little burg. Auspiced, of course, by the Tarantula—Joe B. himself. For what cut, I dunno, that's immaterial at our level. Now, let's say you're sitting on maybe a hundred Gs of the devil's dandruff, maybe more. That's not big-time, but it's too much to ignore. Okay, Ray isn't gonna let you dump that on his territory scot-free—but he's a reasonable person. I know he could be persuaded to give you a piece of the action—maybe thirty grand—who knows? Maybe more. Under normal circumstances, that's how it'd work. Your cut would amount to what's called a finder's fee—you understand?"

"'Under normal circumstances'?"

"Yeah. But this ain't normal. You got an extra added problem."

"This is all hypothetical, of course. But just for laughs, what's my added problem?"

"He's a monkey freak—Ray is. And in cahoots with Nikita Smatterling, Wilkerson Busbee, and Baba Whosamadig—the Indian prune they're importing to bless the statue on Thursday. And Ray knows that the only reason you're trying to muscle a score in his territory is because you're working on a deal to buy out Eloy whatshisname, whose land the Hanumans wanna grab for their permanent gorilla shrine. So hell will freeze over—believe me—before Ray and his sharks will let you promote even Kool-Aid to that end. They'll run over you and Tribby and Sancho Panza with a battleship if you attempt to market even one gram of dope without their okay."

Joe gulped uncomfortably, wanting to wiggle his shoulders out from under Cobey's friendly clutch. Instead, he muttered ineffectually, "This is all very interesting, but—"

"Where I can save *your* butt, Joe, is as a disinterested outside party they're not on to. You turn over the stash to me, see? The whole kit and caboodle—don't withhold even an ounce— you could get a death ride, at this stage, just for having too much powder on your fingers. What I do, then, is very simple. I approach Verboten with the entire load and we work a deal. On the legitimate up-and-up. I tell him you got scared, chickened out, and sold it to me for your initial investment. That takes you out of the land rush in Ray's eyes. In return, he cuts me into the action at face value—that's maybe a sixty-forty split in my favor. You should remember, too, that the stuff is worth twice as much if Ray's dealing than if you are. And I pass on the bucks to you, minus my cut for fronting the shit, of course."

"And what would your cut be?"

"Approximately half of what you would have paid Tribby and the fatso—which should leave you with enough bread to buy out Eloy. Whaddayou think of that?"

"What kind of figures are you talking about?"

"How much coke came in on that Trailways last night?"

"I told you, Cobey—nothing arrived last night. This whole thing you're cooking up is a hypothetical reverie, remember?"

"Aw shit." Cobey withdrew his arm . . . but recovered immediately. He grinned, and, taking another puff, considerately faced sideways so that no smoke would irritate Joe. "Hey, friend . . ." The arm returned around Joe's shoulders. "I know how to facilitate these things. And right now I'm your only buddy in town. I'm on your side. You gotta trust me. If you can't trust me, who in this savage little community *can* you trust?"

Joe said, "Suppose I told you that I know you and Roger Petrie are embezzling bread from Skipper Nuzum in the bar-and-theater racket, hoping to buy Eloy Irribarren's land and transform it into a Wrestle-A-Gator-For-Christ emporium?"

The golden-boy face went blank. *What? Who, me? Somebody is talking to yours truly?* Then Joe was astonished by a transformation in Cobey's eyes. From all-American blue they changed abruptly to a cool yellowish green while narrowing slightly.

"And suppose," Cobey retorted with barely a hitch as his arm dropped off Joe's shoulder and he backed away toward his car, "that I was to tell you Ray Verboten, Skipper Nuzum, and three of Joseph Bonatelli's most intimate torpedoes are cooking up plans to break into the bus station tonight, grab that stupid black-watch suitcase full of tea cartons, and put a contract on your head if the goodies aren't there? So long, sucker—have a nice life."

Joe raised a protective forearm to ward off the pebbles and dust from Cobey's spinning tires.

"Oh me oh my," he whimpered stupidly. "The thot plickens!"

∽

Heidi was gone when he reached home. No doubt she had kidnapped Heather and Michael and made a run for the border.

Puzzled, irritated, and exhausted, Joe regarded their living room. The house seemed portentously empty. Dramatic and doom-laden thunderclaps crouched in all the corners and closets awaiting their cue. The vacancy of the air aroused little chills. Halfheartedly, Joe rummaged about looking for a suicide note, bloodstains, a tender (bitter, maniacal) farewell, an explanatory document. Already, their plane had probably landed at La Guardia. Well, so what? His foreheard throbbed, his eyes burned, his mouth tasted like rotten cotton, his shoulders ached; he flexed his fingers to rid them of cramps caused by gripping bicycle handlebars. It was time for a bath. A guy could only go so long crusted with buzzard guts.

In the bathroom, disappointed at the lack of final words scrawled in lipstick across the medicine-cabinet mirror, Joe dropped his trousers and started lowering onto the can when he noticed drops of urine splattered across the toilet seat. Michael, no doubt—and one of the kid's cardinal sins. Joe reached for the toilet paper. Three yards of the monolayered stuff had been unraveled onto the floor—another of the children's deadly misdemeanors. And Heather needed ten feet of the tissue simply to blow her nose. Someday Michael would piss on the seat once too often, and Joe would yank it off its hinges, tie it around the boy's neck, and force him to spend a year toting that albatross until he had learned to be a civilized human being!

Moments later, settling into the hot tub, Joe said, "Ahhh . . ." For two-thirds of humanity, such a self-indulgent treat would be a colossal luxury, an experience of stunning mystery and erotic magic. Yet he, Joe Miniver, scion of the garbage racket, archcriminal, flagrant delictodor, took it for granted.

Sloshing way down, he floated weightlessly. His body sighed, emitting tiny, satisfied burbles of gratitude. Tendrils of plants suspended from the shower-curtain rod tickled him forlornly, imploring him to be less of a bastard husband. Kiddie accoutrements—Heather's confetti-filled floating fish, Michael's mud-encrusted sneakers under the sink—broke his heart. All the everyday objects of an ordinary and loving life. . . .

Joe snapped awake split seconds before going under. Like tetrapods of yore, he crawled from the tub, snagged a towel, and limped into their bedroom. Accepted by the bed with open arms, he collapsed down through layers of comfort like a man drowning in silken roses. Yawning, Joe discovered he couldn't move—not even a pinkie. Gratefully, he waited for sleep to plant a morphine bullet between his eyes.

The telephone rang. Her lawyer? Scott Harrison? Joe gnashed his teeth. That son of a bitch! He was the kind of lawyer who would invite you to a party and charge ten bucks for the call! Heidi, out there in abogado waters, would be like a goldfish trying to navigate through a convention of sharks. Naturally, Joe would hire his good friend Tribby Gordon—the Mortician of Marriages. But would Tribby stand a chance against Harrison, a smooth-talking, Universal Life pendejo who drove a Pontiac Electra and wore those absurd velour jumpsuits and occasionally smoked a good cigar? Joe groaned. Scott Harrison versus Tribby Gordon, a long-haired chain-smoking, disorganized jock-hippie, who steered a battered '56 Volvo (missing one front fender) around town, and who was apt to appear in courtroom tieless, wearing J. C. Penney's workshirts, beige corduroys split at the kneecaps, and muddy fruitboots or old Weejun loafers torn at the seams. Plus moth-eaten socks, the colors of which did not match.

To make matters worse, Harrison worked out of a nit-pickingly clean office. File cabinets gleamed in all the corners, R. C. Gorman and Fritz Scholder prints adorned the walls, an efficient secretary and law clerk, Laura Hobbes, greeted visitors and typed up all the correspondence and briefs without a single flaw. Tribby, on the other hand, seemed to work out of his car. A battered old suitcase, and reams of legal motions, quiet-title suits, abstracts, letters, envelopes, transcripts, and state statute books littered the front and back seats and floors, stamped not by official seals and notaries' insignias, but with patterns of mud in neat herringbone rows from the soles of Tribby's tennis shoes.

Horror-struck, Joe recalled accepting a ride from Tribby. When you opened the door, the wind snatched several important-looking papers that you either grabbed in midair or retrieved from nearby puddles. "Just put 'em in back," Tribby rasped, "I'll sort 'em out later." As for the piles of hopes, dreams, and agonies on the passenger seat? "Just shove that garbage on the floor," quoth Theodore Reginald "Butch" Gordon. Onto the floor, that is, among more brutalized briefs, manila envelopes, important letters, tennis rackets, baseball gloves, and crumpled beer cans.

And this manifestation of a good-natured, irresponsible (brilliant, yes, but oh so distracted!) lawbooks was going to battle for his rightful share of the vehicles, the inheritance, and the kids?

Joe roasted in the sweat suddenly caused by this dilemma. If push came to shove, he'd have to select his friend, otherwise Tribby would be hurt. Yet his friend was a slob. Scott Harrison—on appearance alone—would run a real redeeming red-hot radiantly rotating legal ramrod right up the shyster-athlete's rosy red rectum!

The telephone ceased ringing. Could it have been Nancy Ryan with a message for his left brain? Or Heidi from the bus station, saying good-bye?

ढ़

Uneasily, Joe drowsed. All he wanted was sleep. But his exhausted frame, so full of electricity, continued humming. Sleep cuddled at his ears, whispered tantalizingly, and made his right arm and rib cage flush with soporific orgasm. Then it retreated, ruffled lax fingers in his hair, and hovered like a reticent sleaze, until, aggravated by its cockteasing presence, Joe suffered adrenal spurts just strong enough to keep him from going under.

Nancy Ryan . . . the plaid suitcase full of cocaine . . . the crippled airplane . . . Sasha gnashing his rotten yellow teeth . . .

At last it muffled his brain like a San Francisco fog: sleep. Or anyway, that no-man's-land just under the vapor where vivid dreams are a dime a dozen, and you surface occasionally, like a beaver or a whale, for a breath of groggy consciousness. Joe saw his kids being born, watched Heidi ride a horse, and lost them all in a vast field as they melted slowly into a snowstorm.

He awoke with a stifled cry of pain and loss just as Heidi—the real lady—sat down beside him.

Joe said, "I thought you were gone forever."

"Not yet."

"But soon?"

"Who knows. I suppose I should just laugh it off—isn't that what everybody else does? But I feel so tarnished."

"I understand."

"Do you? I mean, I thought we were running our marriage on a set of principles that had real meaning. Then suddenly you fall into bed with this slut who's fucked practically every horny letch in—"

"Hey! First of all, she happens to be an interesting and normal human being. Second of all, every middle-class inhabitant of this town in a similar age and economic bracket to ours *except* you and me has screwed practically every horny letch in this town, including all the people in your woman's group, and Suki Terrell, and—"

"How," she interrupted vehemently, "can you even in jest equate Suki with that—"

"It's a meat market, this absurd valley! And just because up until now we've been vegetarians, doesn't give you license to call people sluts because they happen to like a nice roll in the hay every now and then!"

Icily, she said, "Excuse me. Obviously, I had the wrong impression about last night. Didn't realize you two were so tight. How long have you guys been duking each other behind my back?"

"Aw, come on, Heidi. Why bait me with obscenities?"

"I'm sorry." She tossed her head angrily. "Let me rephrase the question. How long have you two been 'dating'?"

"You're a laugh and a half. Really."

"Well I happen to be *hurt*. . . ."

Wishing that he didn't have to deal with any of this, Joe accepted her into his arms. "Join the club," he admitted. "I don't feel very funny myself."

"The way you lied, I think, is what really brings me down."

"It was a one-night shot, honest. When Peter didn't get off that bus, I panicked."

"Actually, things have been pretty lousy sometimes between us. Sooner or later it would have happened."

"Things haven't been all that bad. We've had some pretty good times also."

"Oh sure. But in the end it's all boiling down to this."

"What's *this*? Not the end of the world. We don't have to give up, commit suicide, or move to Cleveland."

She burrowed her head deeper against his neck and hugged him for comfort.

"I know all that, Joey. I just feel so unhappy."

He held his wife. Her quiet tears burned against his throat. For a moment he was big, gentle, and worldly, protecting her. She snuggled the way Heather did in the early morning when she cuddled between her sleeping parents like a defenseless kitten. If only they could make love now, this nightmare might end. Their sex together had always been good. Comfortable, funny, loving—they had grown easy together, rarely careless. They could laugh, play, tease, dawdle—or be riotous, bumptious, faintly kinky, at home with each other's bodies, and rarely bored. Sometimes Heidi ordered him to be passive and worked him over slowly with deft, teasing little nibbles that he loved. Familiarity had bred no contempt. They still liked to collide suddenly in bizarre places and fuck each other to smithereens. Only a few weeks ago, at a party, Heidi had lured Joe into a strange bathroom under the pretext of helping to scout out a lash in her eye: but once behind the locked door, she had gone to her knees and hungrily sucked him. She had wound up straddling his lap on the toilet seat whispering prurient nothings into his fevered ears while a drunk banged on the door, wailing about his bladder. Regularly, on Sunday mornings, they lingered for hours in sunny sexuality. Somehow, they had retained an inventiveness resulting in quirky variations on timeless erotic themes. Only a week ago Joe had been inspired to lay his penis against her mons, and poke both his testicles, like grapes, into her vagina, where she squeezed them until his rubbing cock brought her off. Always, they had managed to soften bad times with intimate shenanigans, seeking forgiveness or solace in the clarity of their physical compatibility, happily orchestrating simultaneous orgasms that usually left them lighthearted and invigorated. Years of learning, trusting, and adventuring had nurtured this physical rapport. So how could I have placed it in jeopardy? Joe berated himself, squeezing Heidi softly as erotic juices began to stir. Then he realized their current dilemma could be solved by a considerate, funky lay—and with a grateful sigh, begging forgiveness, Joe tugged Heidi's hair gently, softly wrenching back her head, and touched his lips to hers, thinking they would make up now, and it would be all over.

Instead, Heidi pulled back and opened one eye: "I really don't want to make love with you, Joe."

Surprised, all he could think to say was, "You're upset."

"No shit, Shakespeare."

Triggered by her sarcastic, hostile tone of voice, Joe flared: "All right. Wonderful. What the hell."

"You know something, Joey? For things to collapse this abruptly, they must have been disintegrating for a while."

"We both admit it hasn't been nonstop peaches and cream."

Heidi stood up and nervously began to pace the room. "You know something crazy? I don't even *like* you right now. In fact, it's worse than that. I don't have *any* feelings for you."

"Heidi, let's talk later, okay? I'm so tired I'm hallucinating. You won't believe what just happened in Tribby's airplane. A buzzard crashed through the windshield. We could have been killed."

"Michael says the suitcase is still at the bus station."

"He ain't lying."

"So now what?"

Joe shrugged. "Unless Peter comes up with a claim check, we'll have to steal it."

"You mean on top of adultery and dope dealing, you could have an additional charge of breaking and entering, maybe even armed robbery, tacked onto your record?"

"Maybe we should discuss this later. Honestly, I'm all played out."

But she needed to talk. "After you and Michael left, I went with Suki Terrell to see Nikita Smatterling."

"You *what*?"

"I told him what happened last night."

"I'm gonna vomit! How could you—?"

"I'm sorry, I'm not an iceman, Joey. When the world caves in it helps to talk with somebody who understands."

"He's a charlatan! He's a creep! He paints monkeys! He screws teenyboppers!"

"He said he felt sorry for you."

"I feel sorry for *him*!"

"He said only if you were haunted by insecurity and pangs of sexual inadequacy would you haul off and pull a lousy trick like that."

"She wasn't a lousy trick, she was one of the best tricks I ever had."

Without missing a beat, Heidi said, "Nikita thinks we should go to a counselor. He said you would only do something like that out of a deep-seated hostility toward me that's probably been fomenting for a long time. He said it probably wasn't even a sexual act, per se, it was more like pure belligerence. And that if cantaloupes had recognized sexual properties, you would have accomplished the same thing by duking a melon."

"He's a shmuck! I don't want my private life aired in front of that . . ." He really *was* going to throw up!

"You don't have to be so superior. You know what he's talking about."

"The man is phony. He's greedy. He's—"

"Jesus, Joey, sometimes you can be boring."

Heather knocked on the door. "Mommy?"

"What is it, lamb?"

"It's the telephone. For Daddy."

"'Daddy' is right here, Heather. You can address me directly."

No way; not today. "Tell him it's a girl. It's Mrs. Ryan."

"Tell him yourself!" Joe snapped, sitting up. "He's right here beside your mother."

"I don't have to if I don't want to."

"Tell her I'll call back later."

"Mommy, she says to tell him it's important."

"Daddy knows it's important, Heather. Mrs. Ryan is a very special person in his life."

Women. One was vicious enough to call about his watch, the other would emasculate him with sarcasm in front of his own daughter. And the daughter, in cahoots with her mother, would seek to poison the paramour while at the same time assisting in the castration by handing over the sterilized scalpels, scissors, and other assorted tools.

Heather asked, "Can I come in?"

Joe hollered "no" in the same instant that Heidi said, "Of course, sugar." Heather opened the door and stood there, frowning cutely (and knowingly like a fox) so as not to grin triumphantly. Her teeth were crooked, she would probably need braces—eight million dollars to give her the perfect mouth for future blowjobs!

Heather asked, "What are you guys doing?" Such a sly, wise, and absurdly cute child. Half the people—half the adults, that is—in town, had already told her she looked exactly like

Tatum O'Neal. Five hours a day, already, Heather could spend at a mirror, combing her hair and daubing on eye shadow and lipstick. Three years hence, aged eleven, she would probably marry a forty-year-old Monacan prince, and commence flying around the world with Bianca Jagger, Andy Warhol, and John-John Kennedy.

"We're having a discussion," Heidi said.

"Actually, we're having a fight," Joe contradicted.

"What are you fighting about?"

Joe said, "Well, it seems that last night Daddy indulged in a slight indiscretion. . . ."

"Joey, I don't think we have to explain!"

"You're the one who's going to monkey gurus and announcing over a loudspeaker what went on!"

Heidi said, "Look, can't we just drop the subject in front of the children?"

"I didn't invite the little brat in in the first place."

"She's not a brat, dammit. Heather, leave the room this instant."

"You are *so* a brat!" Joe hollered. "You're way too big for your tight little britches! Next time Mommy and Daddy are having a spat let us fight in peace!"

Shrilly, Heather shouted, "It's not my fault the telephone rang!" Tears of theatrical rage spurted from her clever little eyes. "You're a gigantic fucker, Daddy!"

"Well at least she finally called me 'Daddy.'"

"You're cruel, you really are." Heidi added, "How could you speak like that to your own child?"

"We *all* speak to each other like that all the time."

Heather said, "Is anybody gonna answer the telephone or not?"

"Well, if your father won't have the common decency to talk to Mrs. Ryan, I will."

"The hell you say!" Joe grabbed an arm, yanking her roughly back onto the bed. Stark-raving naked, in three Baryshnikovian leaps, he landed at the living-room telephone.

Gulping, Joe closed his eyes. "Hello?"

Always, in the heart of a holocaust, there's one stultifyingly placid imbecile. The voice zipping across town through skinny electronic wires sounded like a cross between Marlene Dietrich and Tokyo Rose. Her low, breathy "hi" sent electric shocks fanning across his pectoral muscles; the nipples stiffened. Another impulse heading south passed his belly button going ninety and almost triggered an erection.

"Listen, Nancy, I can't talk right now."

She acted as if, dressed in a silk house robe, he were reclining in a black Naugahyde Barcalounger, sipping a homemade piña colada while lazily digging "The Waltons" on TV.

"I just wanted to call and see how you were."

"I'm great, really great. But listen..."

"Last night was fabulous."

Four feet away, her arms accusatorily crossed, her wide-legged stance like that of a miniature Jolly Green Giant, Heather tried to face him down. In the bedroom, Heidi had been transformed, no doubt, into the largest human ear ever recorded in the western hemisphere. "Look," he said into the telephone. "I'm glad. But right now I'm, you know, I'm at home with Heidi and my kids and I don't want to talk."

"I have your watch, Joe. I wound it so that it wouldn't stop. It's bad for the springs if you let them run down. *When am I going to see you again?*"

Joe hung up. Weirdos! Nudniks! Nothing else populated the world!

Heather asked, "Is she gonna give you back your watch?"

Heidi appeared in the doorway. "I'm sure Mrs. Ryan is going to give Daddy back his watch, darling. No doubt in person. And possibly even dressed in a see-through shorty negligee from Frederick's of Hollywood."

Her eyes, though slightly red and swollen, seemed maliciously humorous. A breath of apprehension from another world struck him. "Hey, where's Michael?"

"Possibly out committing suicide because of the shame visited upon our once-happy family by his sadistic father."

Suddenly, after all the pissing and moaning, Heidi had decided to be In Form. Clobbered, stomped, and humiliated; cheated, maltreated, and lied to; manhandled, insulted, and

159

damn near raped—for a moment, flabbergasted, she had been incapacitated, almost whiny. But now, ending her free fall with the yank of an emotional rip cord, she was In Control again as the colorful parachute of her inner equilibrium fluffed open and blossomed. Just that abruptly, an altogether different person inhabited her body. The one he especially loved—a chunky, sexy, brash dingbat with a head of wild ringlets, expressive happy eyes, a big nose, and a comically mobile mouth and no chin, a kind of rich man's Sophia Loren, a comedienne, a brilliantly instinctive person, a sexual lush as devious as the night is long, and as manipulative as the day is wide, with a heart on her sleeve as large as the moon, a tongue as acidic as a beaker of hydrocholoric chemicals, a resilience as fabulous as that of a trampoline, and an arrogance (and abrasiveness) that might have driven him nuts had he not admired her chutzpah with all his heart.

Oh suddenly, how fiercely he adored her!

     Self-assured, playing the woman scorned with gusto, Heidi strutted by him to the refrigerator. From here on in he had better gird himself, because there would be no more amateur histrionics.

She removed a carton of milk, a celery bunch, mayonnaise, and a tomato from the refrigerator, dumping them onto the counter. Riled, Heidi became a nosher. Even when not eating she had difficulty staying chunky, as opposed to fat (which Joe abhorred, an admittedly chauvinist hang-up). Her caloric binges could cause a terror in him.

At moments like this, Heidi took up smoking again. A pack of Winstons always resided in a top cupboard behind the Drano, the Raid, and the ant traps. Yanking over a chair, she retrieved those cigarettes right now, lit one up with a wooden kitchen match, and haughtily—viciously!—blew the smoke in his direction.

Joe retreated, waving hands to disperse the smoke—it might trigger his asthma. "Go ahead, give yourself cancer, see if I care," he taunted. "Eat yourself to death, become a blimp, your tits aren't big enough to support a potbelly."

"What do you care?" Heidi busied herself slicing a tomato

and smearing mayonnaise on a celery stalk. "You've found yourself another hussy."

"What's a hussy?" Heather asked.

Joe said, "Heather, why don't you go take a bath?"

"I'm clean. I took a bath last night."

"Then go to your room and cut out paper dolls."

"I don't wanna. And I don't hafta, 'cause you can't make me."

"I'll count to three," the biblical patriarch warned, "and if you're not in your room by then I'll yank down your smarty-pants and give you six whacks on a bare fanny."

A basically idle threat. Not because he wouldn't punish her, but because she was impervious to those whacks. Heather often deliberately disobeyed to provoke him, so that she could lie across his lap, eyes squinched and teeth gritted, taking everything he had to give her. This wasn't much, because Joe had a horror of hurting children. In the end, Heather would jump up and, a big arrogant grin splitting her cocky face, she'd sashay away, taunting her father: "Ha ha, that didn't hurt even as much as a mosquito bite."

"Next time," he always retorted, "I'll hit you so hard they'll stop you in El Paso for speeding!"

This time, however, so much emotional confusion convoluted the situation that Heather opted against a pink butt. Slowly, she repaired to her digs. Or anyway, to the doorway, where she stopped, turned, and defiantly faced them.

"Inside," Joe ordered. "*Inside* the room."

"I am inside my room. There's the line, right there, and my toes aren't even touching it. I did exactly what you said to do. Technically, I'm inside my room."

"Shut the door, Heather, or I'll bite your head off!"

She slammed it so hard all the glass in all the cupboards rattled.

Heidi said, "Your foul mouth certainly has produced a charming daughter." Her mouth was so full of junk Joe could barely distinguish her words. And all that food in her mouth triggered absolute panic. For eight years he had been telling her, "You should eat more carefully, you're getting fat." For the same eight years she had constantly replied, "What are you talking about? In the last three weeks I've lost ten pounds." Joe had often teased her with a joking refrain: when she least expected it, he would snatch her ample belly with one hand, announcing, "Ladeez and gennulmun, it sure took a lotta pasta to make this a-wunnerful panza!"

"Your foul mouth pitched the bottom half of every inning," he counterpunched.

A sudden *snap!* sounded at the nearby window: a lampshade spun half around as tiny glass shards sprinkled across the linoleum at their feet.

Heidi exclaimed, "What was that?"

"Some kind of gunshot?" And then he saw a hole in the window, a tiny round scalloped dot. Joe remembered that exact same hole from his days as a BB-gun-toting juvenile delinquent on Long Island, wearing—even on hot summer days—a football helmet, overcoat, and gloves in order to stalk similarly attired neighbors with his Red Ryder Daisy Special. Leaping to an open window, he yelled: "Michael!"

The kid had split, but he couldn't have gotten far. "Michael, I know you're down there! Come out from wherever you're hiding!"

Sheepishly, Michael emerged from behind the Green Gorilla.

"Get up here! Right this instant!"

"I didn't mean . . ." But why protest when life was hopeless? Christmas had come early, and his goose was cooked. Of all the accidental sins to commit, he had pulled off one of the real lulus. The only felony worse would be to put out Heather's eye with a pencil, or get caught setting fire to a cat. His morose shuffling progress across the yard indicated he knew very well he probably wouldn't see another BB gun, or weapon of any sort, until his forty-sixth birthday—if then.

The blow, consigning him, if not to hellfire and damnation, at least to a summer of pariahhood, had already fallen so hard that when Michael reached the front door he actually knocked.

"What are you knocking for?"

"Oh, I forgot." He opened the door, walked inside, and stopped in front of the coffee table on which sat a goldfish bowl teeming with sea monkeys.

Joe said, "I don't believe you just did that."

Michael gulped, half nodded, half shrugged, glanced sideways as if wondering could he make it to the window, leap through the glass, and give one last shout—"Vive la liberté!"—as he sailed down to a grisly demise among the tattered vehicles belonging to residents of the Castle of Golden Fools.

"Do you know how close that shot came to hitting your mother?"

Head tilted to the absolute nadir of head-hanging, Michael shifted uncomfortably and sniffled, no doubt wondering why society always had to read you the self-righteous riot act before it guillotined, garroted, electrocuted, stamped, shot, or gassed you to death.

"Suppose that BB had hit one of us in the eye?" Even as he spoke, Joe realized his words constituted the exact same phrase two billion, eight hundred thousand parents had uttered dating back from the present to April 13, 1927.

At his side, Michael held the gun—too late!—with self-conscious caution, pointed straight down at the floor the way his dad had taught him.

For his next trick, Joe was expected to confiscate the BB gun and break it savagely into pieces with his bare hands, as he had often threatened to do if he ever caught Michael using it carelessly. "You'd better treat that BB gun just as if it were a real rifle!" two billion, nine hundred thirty-three thousand parents had threatened ever since March 1, 1926. To which a similar number of slit-eyed brats straining to race around the corner and slaughter all the myrtle warblers in the pear trees had silently replied, "How can I treat a rinkydink little gun, that can't even shoot a harmless BB farther than twenty yards, like a real weapon, Dad?"

As a kid, Joe himself had had fantasies of kicking down his parents' bedroom door gangbusters-style and charging their connubial mattress firing little copper pellets from the hip in machine-gun fashion at his childhood tormentors, riddling their bodies with a million BBs that would penetrate only a millimeter under their skins, proving once and for all that even if you *deliberately* wished to off somebody with a BB gun it was an impossible task.

Perhaps, instead of smashing the gun, he would simply lean it in a corner where Michael could see it every day, but not touch it (under pain of instantaneous death) until his twenty-first birthday.

But Joe also remembered that previous image of himself, all decked out in his winter armor on a ninety-eight-degree day, thrilling to the *ping*! sound as tiny spheroids bounced harmlessly off his absurdly protected body, or one of his own shots stung the next-door creep in his unprotected derrière.

"Whatever made you do a thing like that?" Joe asked. "It's

crazy. You couldn't even have hoped to get away with it. You're the only person in this house who owns a BB gun."

"I know."

"Well?"

Michael tried hard not to cry. He looked about as dolorous as dolorous can get this side of the grave, until abruptly he blurted: "Well, you two are shits! You're stupid! I hate your guts!"

With that, he broke down, bawling. Tears rained upon the carpet, they splashed his sneakers. But, as if frozen, he remained rigid, the gun still held self-consciously at his side.

Heidi collapsed, rushing to cradle, cuddle, and murmur, "Oh hey sweet baby, don't cry, please don't cry, it's all right."

Beating back his own tears, Joe said, "Did you hear what he just called us?"

"Oh for Christ's sake, leave him alone, Joey—haven't you made us miserable enough for one day? Why don't you take a hike? Go crosstown and screw your new poontang, make *her* kid unhappy, *our* children have had enough!"

How easily contrite sorrow and tender warmth could turn into blazing, maniacal rage. "All right," Joe snapped, "that's exactly what I'll do, thanks for the suggestion!"

And although he could see in her eyes that she didn't mean it, Heidi nevertheless added insult to injury by suggesting: "Why not take a suitcase? Pack some clothes so that you can stay awhile!"

Joe bolted into the bedroom, tore drawers out of his bureau and bashed them onto the floor, grabbed handfuls of underwear, socks, T-shirts, and patched dungarees, thrust them all into a laundry bag, and then, with a last agonized look at the place, he tore off his wedding ring and flung it at Heidi—it bounced off her nose and landed in the sea monkeys! Joe raged past them and out the door, did an abrupt about-face and bulled through their anguish into the bedroom, where he gathered in his glasses, his wallet, his keys, and then literally catapulted himself blindly back through the scorched doom generated by his theatrics, only to bring himself up short on the doorsill again—he no longer clutched a laundry bag in his hot little hand! Unleashing the cry of a Job, Joe plowed through the ramshackle living room yet again, embraced the bag with a bloodcurdling yell, and roared between them once more with feeling, this time for good!

He sailed down the ladder, lost his balance, and did a shoulder roll into the yard. Heidi cast open a window, crying, "I didn't mean it, come back!"

"Go to hell!"

Flinging the laundry bag into the bed of the Green Gorilla, Joe tore open the driverside door so roughly it slammed back, almost dislocating his shoulder—he howled. Blinded by rage, ready to kill, foaming at the mouth, almost insensate, he punched the key into its slot, stamped on the starter, and the engine caught. Windshield wipers slapping time, lights on, and the radio blasting, Joe hit the gas, popped the clutch, and, in a great cloud of blue pollution, surged forward about eight feet, at which point his progress was arrested by the front grille of Ralph Kapansky's Chevy clunker, which had just fishtailed into the yard.

Blood in his eyes! Murder in his soul! Blue smoke in his lungs! On foot again, Joe bellowed in Ralph and Gloria and Rimpoche's direction, "Are you all right?" As soon as he heard Ralph's whimpering reply—"I think so"—he jumped onto his bicycle and, with his chest about to burst, raining heartaches over the valley like July-fourth fireworks, he pedaled onto the open road.

"Joey, come back!" Heidi cried. No way, though. He gave her the finger, toppled into a ditch, righted himself, and thought: I'm going insane, this is crazy, I'm gonna kill myself! But somehow he gained his seat and continued along the road, utterly dumbfounded by his incredible antics and irresponsible actions. In his ears rang the imploring plaints of Heather and Michael joining their mother's wails—"Joey, Daddy, Pop—*come back!*" while Ralph relentlessly honked his horn at him in execration.

Halfway to town, at that point where Mimsy and Tuckums exploded from their lair like fang-toothed U.S. Marines high on coke and patriotism and bent on his total destruction, Joe realized he was suddenly a man without a country. An emphatic exit, such as the one he had just pulled, prohibited any crow-eating, tail-between-the-legs, humble-pie reconciliations—at least for the foreseeable future. Essentially, he had renounced his worldly goods, his worldly woman and children, and the worldly roof over his head. This meant he had blown his prerogative to books, a telephone, food, and fatherhood. In short, as Heidi might have observed, he had severed himself from the whole shmeer.

In double short, he had bullied, shouted, adulterized, and pigheaded himself out onto the proverbial limb without a paddle.

And for what?

Joe slammed on the brakes, catching both dogs by surprise: they bumped into his rear wheel, scalping their noses. As they yelped, Joe grabbed up rocks and commenced pelting the mutts, intending to murder them outright. His first three stones missed; the fourth bounced off one dog's head, ricocheting into the grille of a brand-new Ford pickup just as the owner of that truck, Bertram Laidlaw, the right-wing dueño of Piccolo Gas Company, exited his front door dressed to the nines for a funeral, and shouted, "What the hell are you doing?"

Suicidal, afraid of nobody—so what if he dug his own grave? . . . good riddance to bad rubbish!—Joe screamed:

"Your damn dogs terrorize me every time I try to ride past on my bicycle! I'm sick and tired of taking their shit! They oughtta be gassed!"

"They attacked you?" Bertram narrowed his eyes suspiciously.

"They attack me! They try to bite me! For God's sake, man, if you can't keep them chained up, hang them from a tree with a piece of clothesline and let them slowly strangle to death!"

"Hey, mister, don't get a hernia." In the same breath, directing his comments at Mimsy and Tuckums, he commanded, "C'mere, dogs!" Whereupon, those two unrelenting administrators of canine apocalypse groveled obsequiously over to their Imperial Wizard. Joe immediately wished that he'd kept his mouth shut and simply pedaled on. Instead, in reaction to his moronic tantrum, this inhuman Minuteman was going to exact revenge on his behalf.

Bertram minced a single step forward and, like a professional place-kicker attempting a forty-seven-yard field goal, he booted Tuckums at least thirty feet, past the pickup and halfway across the road, then turned sideways and punted Mimsy so hard that she most likely would have landed a mile north of town had not the foot-thick, cement-reinforced brick wall of the Laidlaw residence interrupted her forward progress as she was but two feet high and still, like a good line drive, rising.

"You lemme know if either of those two cunts ever bothers you again," the gas man said laconically. He reentered the house, no doubt to wipe the blood off his storm-trooper cordovans.

Whimpering, Tuckums limped off the macadam as Joe hesitantly pedaled forward again. He wanted to approach the dogs and beg their forgiveness, explaining that he hadn't known . . . he hadn't meant . . . he couldn't believe. . . . His anger had been replaced by shame and trembling. Nothing he could ever do for those poor curs would atone for the misery he had caused them. Joe could picture it all too vividly: from now on, whenever he appeared, they would scurry to a safe place. Only their eyes would follow him accusatorily. He had destroyed their verve, their love of life. He had reduced them to cowering, simpering impotency. Guilt would finally force him to locate an alternate, and no doubt twice as inconvenient, route. That way, he wouldn't have to face the pathetic psychological wrecks that a slipshod moment of imprudence on his part had created.

ॐ

Worn out and thoroughly disheartened, Joe veered off the potholed dirt track bisecting the twelve-house Perry Kahn Subdivision #4 and coasted to a weary halt beside Nancy Ryan's VW. Sasha was seated atop the living-room couch, squeezing toothpaste against the picture window. Despite his abject disgust for himself, Joe's heart at once commenced fibrillating excitedly, threatening a tachycardia attack. As if that weren't enough, his trachia, bronchi, alveoli, and God knows what else in his pulmonar regions immediately reacted like a live oyster hit with lemon juice. We're off to the suffocation derby! Joe hoarded prescription jars of both Aminodur and Terbutaline in the medicine cabinet at home, right beside his metaproterenol inhaler. He also had cached jars of asthma pills in the glove compartments of both the Green Gorilla and the bus. Unfortunately, he carried no medical relief in his wallet (except a frayed condom left over from the eighth grade forlornly awaiting an adventure) nor in the basket of his bicycle.

"Oh dear," he muttered lifelessly. "I'm a goner."

Nancy's brightly lit eyes changed their expression to one of concern. As the Doberman slithered outside, belligerently shoving its nose into Joe's crotch, she said, "Are you all right?"

"I'm fine. I just can't breathe."

Freshly laundered, her hair glistened euphorically. Her low-cut aqua-green floor-length house gown resembled an opera dress more than a bathrobe. Her milky skin had a flushed, superclean tint suggesting it would melt in his mouth if only he could catch his breath long enough to chew on it. Though obviously she could not have known of his arrival, Nancy had nevertheless dabbed a trace of perfume behind each ear, an evocative teen-age scent that broke Joe's heart, reminding him of dance cards and the popcorn aroma of old-fashioned drugstores. He might have melted right there onto the stoop, wheezing to death as he asked her to marry him, had Cheepy not zipped out the door.

Nancy said, "Oh my God, the parakeet!"

At exactly the same instant, Bradley flew out of nowhere, attacking his mom, flailing at her chest, stomach, and crotch—tears spattered all over the place. He wailed: "You let him out! You left the door open! You let him get away! You did it *deliberately*!"

She smacked him atop the head, saying sternly, "Don't hit me. Go get the butterfly net."

Bradley raced off, returning promptly with a green plastic contraption which he hurled angrily at his mother: it landed in Joe's bewildered arms instead. Nancy strode past him, efficiently giving orders: "Quick, follow me, he always lands in Minissa's flowerbeds."

"Who's Minissa?"

"Tallyrand. My next-door neighbor. Vaughn the meter reader's wife."

The last thing Joe saw before blindly following Nancy was an accusatory glower—call it of hatred—on the kid's face, an expression so pure it could have stopped a pell-mell locomotive dead in its tracks.

The flowerbed, all of whose plants were solid plastic, occupied a ten-by-ten plot on the other side of Nancy's driveway. A structure in the center of it looked suspiciously like a wooden cross. Nancy dropped to her knees at the edge of the bed, calling, "Here, Cheepy, Cheepy, Cheepy, that's a good bird now." And when he drew closer, Joe realized the structure was a cross. No ordinary flowerbed, this was some kind of memorial for a person who had died.

"Squat down," Nancy said, "or you'll frighten him away."

"How do you know it's a 'him'?"

"I don't. We just assumed he was a he."

Perched on the cross, the bird preened its feathers. The name on the cross said: *Adrian*.

Joe hunched down behind her. "This isn't a flower garden, it's some kind of cemetery."

"Nobody's buried here. It's just a little thing Minissa did in memory of Adrian."

"Who's Adrian?"

"She was their daughter."

"Whaddayou mean 'was'?"

"She died last year of leukemia, poor baby. She was only seven. And the cutest little kid on the block. If you inch forward now, real slowly, I think we can get him. Swing at him from in front, he can't take off very well backwards. As soon as he's in the net, slam it down on the ground so he doesn't escape."

"I can't do that. What if somebody sees us? There's enough tension in this valley without throwing a couple of clumsy jerks into the middle of somebody's shrine to their dearly departed daughter in hopes of catching a parakeet."

Glancing around, Joe wondered if there would be no end to the disgrace this day was bringing him. At least ten people mowed lawns, sat on their front stoops drinking beer, washed their cars, or puttered in miniature gardens. Everybody in the neighborhood was outside, nosily glancing around.

"If we don't catch Cheepy you won't believe the freakout that kid will pull," Nancy said quietly. "Attila the Hun will remind you of Shirley Temple compared to that child if his bird flies away."

Joe handed over the butterfly net. "You do it. I didn't sign up for this gig. So far today I committed adultery, I left my wife and family, I scarred my children for life, I got hit in the face with a buzzard pie, I almost totaled Ralph Kapansky's car, and I caused the crippling of two harmless dogs. But I'm not gonna do a nose-dive into some poor lady's memorial garden to capture anybody's wayward parakeet!"

She gave his hand a gentle squeeze. "I understand."

Then, lunging forward, Nancy landed spread-eagled among the no-fade flowers, shouting triumphantly, *"Got him!"*

Eyes closed in humiliation, Joe wondered: Would it do any good to go door-to-door down this block, begging their forgiveness? Probably not. Slamming doors in his face, they'd order him back to his slut with her monkey paintings and the sacrilegious parakeet. On his return trip from the far end of the dirt road, suffering their taunts and blows in tragic, dignified silence, he would walk slowly—like Gary Cooper in *High Noon*—back to where Nancy (in the milky-white nude) awaited him with open arms. A rotten tomato would splash off his forehead; a brown banana would squish against his chest. And though small stones bruised him, he would not flinch. Even though human feces smacked against his nose, he would not lose his poise. . . .

"Come on." She took his hand. "Let's go."

Inside the house, Sasha had finished toothpasting the living-room window and was now off in a corner, methodically shredding newspapers. Cheepy fluttered onto the earphoned head of his mollified monster-owner (who was grouchily ensconced before the color TV watching "The Beverly Hillbillies"), and started preening. Joe said, "All I want is a bath and sleep."

He slumped on the toilet while Nancy drew a tub. Then she kneeled beside the tub, elbows resting on the porcelain, looking beautiful and sexy despite his frame of mind. The low décolletage of her silky aqua gown coyly revealed the delicate swell of one breast. Dozens of lascivious impulses were soon caught in an emotional crossfire inside his fatigued body.

"I knew you would come back tonight, Joe. All day I could feel it. It's almost eerie. I'd swear I have a direct line to your energy. I've been so happy. I just know it was meant to be between us. Are you an Aquarius?"

Not long ago, Joe had decided that he would decapitate, with his lethal kung-fu fists, the next person who asked him his sign for the purpose of learning about his personality.

Nevertheless, he merely said, "No."

"Oh?" Though taken aback, she seemed not at all surprised. In fact, her equanimity under fire amazed him. Nothing fazed this dame. Was she a Valium freak? Or on Lithium? Or Thorazine? "What *is* your sign?" Nancy insisted.

"'Caution: trucks turning.'"

Her eyes sparkled as her smile spread, emitting an increas-

ingly forceful light that soon flooded the entire bathroom.
Reaching behind herself with one hand, Nancy locked the door.
On her knees before him, she craned her long neck upward
and kissed him with slurry lips. Joe discovered her bare breasts
in his hands. She said, "Um..." He answered with a lazy,
melancholic grunt. By the time she cooed, "So sweet..." he
had nearly slipped into a coma of sexual arousal. While she
opened his fly, Joe whimpered like an abandoned puppy just
brought in from a killing blizzard and set down on a warm
hearth beside a bowl of milk. Nancy gave him the softest head
he'd ever known, holding him weightlessly inside her mouth,
barely massaging the tip of his penis by faintly constricting her
throat. Joe slipped his fingers gently into her hair, and begged
for a silky come. Catching him off guard, an "I love you" rose
in his gorge; only at the last second did he manage to quash
it—and once more his orgasm died aborning.

Hello, Valhalla, Joe Miniver speaking, fresh from yet another day on the hustings. Gimme a valve job, new points and
plugs, an oil change—don't forget to clean the filter—and
check the radiator too, would you?

Years peeled off the cinematic calendar. Joe luxu-
riated in ethereal aches. All his dreams held winning tickets.
In the past, whenever something threatened him, Heidi had
always said, "I'll protect you, Joey, I'll wrap you in a pink
cocoon of friendly vapor, I'll snuggle you in a pink cloud and
nothing will hurt you." Wrapped in that pink cloud right now,
Joe felt infinitely protected, "at one" (his subconscious believed
was the expression) with all of life, swaddled in cotton candy
and Christmas fiberglass, aswoon in the giddy warmth.
He dreamed of his 1.7-acre farm. Bees swarmed around a
dozen hives and among several rows of raspberry bushes planted
specially to make their nectar more delicious. In a gingerbread
shack the kids were squeezing the combs, extracting pure honey.
A modest and yet comfortable solar-heated house stood next
to the orchard. Their other energy came from a windmill, and
a Tesla coil tapping the earth's magnetic goodies. The garden
had cabbages as big as basketballs, strawberries as fat as val-
entines. Forty chickens in the new coop provided countless
eggs each day. Fruit trees groaned under the weight of apples,

plums, and pears. Eight sheep, a few cows, and Heather's
pinto pony grazed in their small fields. Outside, in the nude,
Heidi worked on the final painting for her upcoming one-person
show at the Houston Fine Arts Museum. Heather, whom some
had pegged as the next prima ballerina in the western hemisphere, was doing some free-form cartwheels on the lawn. In
the driveway, Michael showed two Yankee scouts and a handful
of metropolitan-newspaper reporters how he had developed the
phenomenal pitching control that had garnered him a multi-
million-dollar contract at the age of eighteen: he was throwing
Spaldeen pimpleballs through a knothole in the garage door at
thirty paces, just like his daddy had taught him. And Joe?—
well, Joe was in the back field training the new Irish setter he
would take grouse-hunting that autumn. . . .

The gossamer rasping of feathers against night air made a
laid-back bid for his attention. Though still asleep, one eye
opened. The enlarged shadow of a parakeet, somehow buzzard-
shaped, floated chimerically against the ceiling, then disappeared as the bird alighted atop the radio. All the wispy painted
guru monkeys whispered susurrantly and unintelligibly to each
other, the metaphysical world's equivalent of a Manhattan air-
well on laundry mornings, when all the Italian women hung
out their wash. Far down in the green netherworld of Joe's
romantic reveries, a thought formed. And, like a child playing
red rover, the thought began racing around down there, looking
for an opening through which to make a madcap dash for the
freedom of his conscious brain. Aware of its consequences,
Joe urged the troopers patrolling his lethargy to redouble their
efforts to keep him ecstatically snoozing. But when the thought
finally summoned the guts to make a dash for it, his troopers
blew it. And, with one eye on Cheepy, Joe surfaced just enough
to recall that he had blown his marriage . . . and needed to steal
that suitcase full of cocaine, fast, before some other criminal
beat him to the punch.

Into the valley of anxiety Nancy floated, naked except for
a cigarette. By the time she settled onto the bed, Joe had
managed to trigger his asthma again. Instant wheeze, folks,
and even Houdini couldn't have escaped the chains constricting
his chest!

Nancy peered intently. "Are you awake?"

"Yeah. I'm afraid so."

"The air in here feels tight. What happened?"

"I was just lying here, minding my own business, when I started thinking."

"You have to make your mind blank."

"How do I accomplish that? Swallow a beaker of acid? Touch a shotgun to my temple and pull the trigger with my toes?"

"Just close your eyes, take a few deep breaths. Let them out very slowly. Then think of a place where you'd most want to be, and go there."

" 'Go there'?"

"Picture a stairway, if you have to, and simply walk down it until you arrive at your dream place. Imagine a door, if you want, and open it and walk on through to where you wish to be."

"I can't."

"Everybody can if they try. If you're sincere about wanting to be at peace with yourself, you can do it. It's easy. I do it all the time. If you practice enough to get good at it, you can even travel back and forth in time. You can zip all over the world without 'actually' leaving your living room. Nikita does that regularly. Last week he had a conversation with Aristotle. Once he traveled so far forward that he reached the edge of the world's time. The sun was dying. The earth was covered by ice except for a small patch of the Amazon where he met an Indian from the Minamamo tribe named Kezar, who was among the last survivors on earth."

"Wait a minute—I can't *breathe* here. I'm worried sick about my children. I just told a wife I truly love to go fuck herself. I've got a suitcase in the bus station that holds the key to my future, but nobody will give it to me. Plus I'm a goddam self-indulgent, pussy-chasing, educationally privileged, self-ish-as-all-get-out rich hippie playing at being a garbage man, and you're talking about conversations with Aristotle and an Amazon Indian named Kezar?"

Being fazed was not one of the lady's strong points.

"I can help you cure your asthma if you want me to, Joe. And if you want to cure it yourself."

"How can I be cured—with a double pulmonary extraction?"

Using the butt of her old cigarette, she lit up a new weed. "You have to concentrate on making it go away. There are exercises. And I'll put you on our healing list."

"Do me a favor, don't put me on any lists."

"You don't have to do a thing. We'll simply put you down, and when we have our healing meetings we'll pray for you."

"Nancy, excuse me. But I don't want a bunch of Maharaji freaks setting their metaphysical meathooks into this kid's dilapidated psyche."

"It wouldn't hurt to try."

"All I want is my pills."

She placed her hands on his chest. The cigarette dangled from her mouth as if from the lips of a Parisian hooker in a Brassai photograph. She squinted slightly against the smoke. Cheepy flew from the radio to a lampshade, twitched his tail, and Joe actually heard the miniature *splat*! of a diminutive birdy caca hitting the dresser. Out in the living room, Sasha was engaged in something muffled and illicit. The dog growled: a thing went *thup*!....*squish*!....drool!....

"Don't move, Joe. I'll help you relax. With a massage." Her seductive hands elicited goosebumps. Her eerie tranquillity spooked him. Quaaludes? Ritalin? Or just a level dose of Smatterling? Joe envied her apparent equanimity. At the same time he wanted no truck with it. Let the spiritual folks do their broomstick numbers outside his bailiwick—he was a meat-and-potatoes man.

"I really want my pills," Joe pleaded. "If I take a pill, or squirt a little Alupent into my bronchospasm, I'll feel a hell of a lot better."

Oblivious to his whimpers, she let her hands coo over his muscles. Out of the frying pan—Joe thought as sheer dismay rolled over him like Notre Dame's charging linemen—and into the fire. In this rapidly degenerating town there was no such thing as a quickie, no such animal as the free lunch. Erica Jong could take her theory of the Zipless Fuck and airmail it to Ripley's Believe It or Not! Joe Miniver, Boy Nincompoop, sole survivor of history's most recent Donner expedition, had turned right, instead of left, at his destiny, and landed once more among the cannibals!

"If I don't get my pills real soon, Nancy, I think I'll die."

"I can take your asthma from you if only you'll let me."

Her fingers handled him like feathers with soul. Blood zoomed into his penis like New York novelists applying for Guggenheims and NEA grants. Joe responded by growing as mellow as if he were being electrocuted by a harmless furry current that individually stroked every one of the seventy trillion molecules in his body. He gasped quietly and murmured, "Don't you ever get tired?"

Her voice floated down at him from portentous ethereal heights: "When you come, all the asthma will drool from your body."

But same as before, he couldn't ejaculate. A vision of Heidi's naked body kept intruding. He was practically strangled by guilt. The find 'em, feel 'em, fuck 'em, forget 'em boogeyman delighted in a neon chanting that beleaguered his brain. Lord knows, though, she tried.

"You know something, Nancy—"

"Hush." She breathed heavily. The parakeet landed on her shoulder. Where was the Doberman—out hunting deer? In the hallway, the central-heating blower clicked on noisily. Sasha leaped onto the living-room drapes and they clattered, with a muffled rush of heavy folds, onto the couch.

The pills, man: he *still* had asthma!

Her body shifted slightly into a pose that apparently had special meaning.

"What are you doing?"

"Giving you positive energy."

"Not to be a killjoy, but I really would like to pop one of my own antiasthma little beauties. . . ."

"Shhh."

"Can I borrow your car? It'll only take a minute. I'm a careful driver, I swear." His lungs were filling up with cotton. His chin itched. The Asthma Hangman, a big black-hooded brute naked to the waist, wearing a necklace of confiscated adrenaline-injection capsules, tightened his hemp around Joe's windpipe. It looked like curtains for sure if he couldn't reach his pusher in time!

"Joe, it's one A. M."

Imitating jovial, good-natured flippancy, he said, "Give me the keys or else I'll bash in your head with the clock-radio and burn Bradley's feet and nipples with cigarette butts until he confesses where they're hidden."

"They're in the car. But if you insist, I'll drive you there."

"In the *car*? Aren't you afraid somebody will steal it?"

"If I projected those negative thoughts, sure, somebody might steal it."

"I'll go alone. You shouldn't leave the kid."

"He'll be all right."

"What if a burglar—?"

She chuckled. "In my world there are no burglars."

Sasha wanted to come. Joe said, "Does he have to?" Eyes twinkling, Nancy replied, "He doesn't *have* to, but he sure enjoys driving around."

Joe said, "I don't understand why you let him get away with creating such havoc in the house."

"Because of him, my house is peaceful."

In the VW, wearing only her robe, Nancy lit a fresh cigarette and started the car. Nearly frenzied beside her, Joe said, "Shouldn't you bring a purse, or at least your license? I mean, given that you're almost naked, suppose a cop stopped us?"

She gazed at him humorously and sympathetically. "A cop won't stop me."

"How do you know?"

"I never *ask* them to stop me. They used to pull me over all the time—before I understood—because I drive fast. But now it's almost as if I'm invisible."

They turned left onto Valverde: Nancy braked slightly to avoid flattening Nick Danger. Striding purposefully through the night shadows, clutching his singular valise to his heart, the mysterious little shtarker never glanced up.

A moment later, while crossing the North-South Highway, Joe cried, "Wait a minute! Take me to the bus station!"

"But it's all locked up. No bus arrives for at least an hour."

"Please," Joe begged plaintively, "just do as I say this once."

From the back seat, Sasha reached up stealthily, and suddenly pinched Joe's earlobe. "Hey, *ouch!*" Joe swung around angrily. Sasha leaped over the backrest, and crouched out of sight in the well between the seatback and the rear window. "That stupid animal just pinched me!"

"Sasha, you be a good boy," Nancy reprimanded him mildly. "Don't be flirting with Mr. Miniver."

Joe said, "Park in front of it, with your headlights aiming inside. I'll pretend I'm reading the schedule in the window...."

Nancy did as told. After checking to be sure they weren't under surveillance, Joe stepped down and sauntered nonchalantly up to the glass door. Pretending absorption in the arrival-

and-departure schedule, he peered into the gloomy station, searching for Peter's bag.

Instead he found himself staring into the beam of a flashlight held by a startled figure dressed in black and wearing a rubber gorilla mask, frozen in a frightened crouch, the black-watch suitcase in one hand—CAUGHT! RIGHT IN THE ACT!

Joe said, "Somebody's *in* there!"

Whereupon the world exploded. It seemed at first as if a gas heater had accidentally burst inside the station, so cataclysmic was the report of a gun going off. Almost in front of Joe's nose, the glass shattered, yet miraculously the bullet flung in his direction sizzled harmlessly past the ear Sasha had just tweaked. Old athlete that he claimed to be, Joe reacted instantly, flopping sideways in sheer terror, realizing as he fell that somebody had taken a murderous pop at him, fully intending to end his life.

Asked in a moment of tranquillity how he might be expected to react to such an outrage, Joe no doubt would have declared, "I'd collapse and play dead, or scramble the hell out of there." Confronted with the actual thing, however, his terror and astonishment were instantly replaced by outrage. "You son of a bitch!" he screamed. The *gall* of that intruder! Joe's fumbling fingers snatched up a medium-sized rock. And, instead of playing possum or scuttling off like a terrified crab, he lurched back onto his knees, and cocked an arm, prepared to hurl the rock at a protagonist toting lethal hardware and lugging the suitcase that held within it the key to Joe's aspirations.

Two more shots blahooied horrendously from within the bus station: glass bits and plywood splinters bounced off Joe's chest and shoulders as he fired his stone, but no hot lead projectiles thumped messily into his chest or forehead. Inside the depot, the masked gunslinger hollered, "Out of my way, you thon of a bitch, I'm coming through!" To Joe's astonishment, the robber leaped straight for him, suitcase in hand, and, in either a panic or an exaggerated show of derring-do, missed the door entirely, crashing through the plate-glass window like O. J. Simpson on his way to catch a plane.

Joe flung up one arm, warding off the fatal blow. Grunting hysterically, the barbarian crash-landed on top of him. The suitcase crunched into Joe's head and popped open, spilling several dozen chunky, rectangular boxes of herbal teas across the ground. The desperado's flailing body smelled of sweat, gunpowder, fear, and shoe polish. "Ah thit!" he wailed. A fist thumped Joe's shoulder; again the gun went off, this time almost in his ear. Squealing, Joe hit back. One fist glanced off the gorilla mask. A boot accidentally kicked his groin, as the masked man struggled to disentangle himself from their accidental union. "Which one ith the boxth?" he groaned, scrambling to gather in the containers. A gun clattered onto the pavement, and, surprised by his own murderous audacity, Joe grabbed it, swung it onto the black marauder, and might even have triggered a shot at point-blank range, had not the guy screamed in a near-falsetto voice, *"Don't thoot me!"* as, his arms full of boxes, he careened away. When, like a disoriented bird, he clipped the side of the depot building, boxes cascaded every whichway; he landed spread-eagled against the pavement. But this time he regained his feet instantly.

"I'll kill you!" Joe roared. But instead of pulling a trigger, he hurled the gun with all his might: it clattered harmlessly against those fleeing heels.

At which point, all hell broke loose.

A large gray 1957 Dodge van with a cow skull welded onto the front grille and a plastic skylight bubble on the roof veered out of the shadows and screeched to a nose-dipping halt. A psychedelic sign on the van's side said CHICKEN RIVER FUNKY PIE. Three doors opened simultaneously, and more men in black, wearing rubber gorilla masks, and including a diminutive figure that had to be a dwarf, sailed to earth brandishing machine guns, semiautomatic pistols, and a pump shotgun. With no further ado, World War III broke out in earnest. Guns, bombs, bullets, hand grenades, smoke, muzzle flashes, ricochets—you name it, it happened! Deafened by the holocaust, Joe hunched into a fetal position among the boxes, and prayed for rain.

Apparently, they wished to assassinate the original intruder. Incredibly, their hot lead, spewed about so liberally and unscientifically, failed to fell the zigzagging klutz, whose arms still hugged a dozen boxes. Instead, the sprinter stepped on a rake: the handle twanged up, as in an old-fashioned film comedy, brutally whacking him (vertically) across the face. He catapulted backward, spraying more boxes, yet again exhibited astonishing resiliency, almost reamassing his cargo before thudding to earth. In no time he was upright again, and bounding away like a frightened deer.

A Volkswagen microbus careened into the parking lot. Brakes locked, it fishtailed with a grinding wail of protesting rubber and a blazing horn into the Chicken River Funky Pie van. Metal crunched and crumpled, glass popped, motors yelped shrilly and hissed: steam arose. More black-outfitted goons disguised as apes emerged from the VW, pistols, rifles, and other assorted noisy accoutrements blazing.

Such turmoil!

The original fugitive collided against a garbage can and sprawled to the turf, landing in a heap of chattering oilcans and mushy coffee grounds. The Chicken River death squad continued their fusillade in his direction, even as they busied themselves near Joe, snagging tea boxes, which they dumped into a burlap sack. The dwarf hooligan screamed orders: "Get the boxes! Kill the son of a bitch! We need 'em all! Shoot that asshole! Gimme some more bullets! Die, scumbag, *die!*"

When the VW crowd had entered the fray, it seemed as if everybody must fall within the tornado of crisscrossing slugs creating a withering whirlwind of almost certain annihilation. Yet, though weapons were repeatedly discharged at point-blank range, everybody's marksmanship left something to be desired. Assailants cursed, ducked, lurched, jumped out of the way, crouched behind Nancy's Bug, the bus, the van, the corner of the depot, and did not fall. They slugged each other, toppled to earth only inches away from Joe, but bounced to their feet like Silly-Putty, unawed and unafraid. In the heart of such deadly choreography, Joe waited for a stray bullet to end his life. Chips of cement pelted his thighs, butt, and shoulders; bullets whined between his legs, searing his Levi's without causing an actual rent in the fabric.

Automobile windows disintegrated from errant shotgun blasts. The depot provided a seemingly endless supply of loudly erupting crystal. The original intruder survived his garbage-can collision, but five steps later he pitched into a ditch. Closer to the situation's core, the dwarf manhandled an empty tommy gun, wielding it like a baseball bat. Oofs, grunts, expletives, epithets, gurgles, and soft-nosed bullets mangled the airwaves as all parties involved continued gathering herbal tea boxes. One man secured an armful, only to lose it when tackled by another pug. Gunsmoke and dust, as thick as if laid down by a Hollywood smog machine, circulated among the scufflers. Joe had difficulty following the action.

Then, out of the corner of one eye, Joe caught a flash of beige fur leaping from Nancy's Bug. Sasha landed upright, apparently unnoticed by any of the free-for-allers. The monkey danced through a dozen flailing arms and kung-fu legs, snatched up a single box of herbal tea, gave Joe the finger, and obnoxiously scampered back to his mistress with his prize.

All the boxes were gone. Somebody kicked the empty suitcase. An order was given: "Let's scram!" The clumsy oaf who'd launched this bizarre episode heaved out of the ditch, but immediately tangled his legs in rusty barbwire coils and went down again. Screeching backward, the Chicken River Funky Pie van banged the VW bus, knocking it sideways: spinning tires kicked up spurts of stinking smoke. A horn was stuck. Hollering men piled into both vehicles. A final shotgun blast took out the microbus windshield. Other pellets, aimed at stars, chopped the pavement around Joe like hailstones: one BB actually pinged harmlessly off his head.

Minus a headlight apiece, the van and the microbus tore free of each other. The van's rear end smacked into the Miracle Auto Supply display window, setting off a burglar alarm. The microbus had a flat rear tire, but lurched onto the highway going sixty, sparks whizzing off the rim. The van swerved away in the opposite direction, its denizens imparting a few lead epilogues toward the VW crew.

Silence, but for the burglar alarm, dropped like a curtain upon a bad show; and only Joe remained to tell the tale. Seated dumbfoundedly in a glittering puddle of shattered glass and spent cartridge shells, he was unnicked despite the fire fight that had raged around him for those rabid moments. Obviously, he had lost the contents of Peter's suitcase, hence also his life savings, Eloy's land, and the hope of a serene and productive future.

Matter-of-factly, Nancy said, "Are you all right?"

"I think so," Joe gasped. "But I still can't breathe. Are you okay?"

"Of course. Now come on. We'd better leave."

"I don't know if I can walk."

"Try."

Joe raised himself gingerly, expecting to discover blood spurting from a hole in his thigh, to feel his steaming guts bulge from a gaping gut-wound. But nothing leaked or protruded from his trembling body. Apparently, all his organs were performing their crucial functions inside his body's fragile sheath. A miracle? Or just dumb luck. Incredulously, Joe said, "I'm not even scratched...."

Joe faced Nancy's Beetle, his jaw dropped open. "Oh my God—!" Her car had not suffered even a minute blemish. And inside it sat Nancy in her sexy bathrobe, lipstick glistening, absolutely unruffled, like one of those magic-show ladies in a large basket through which dozens of harmless sabers had been thrust.

"Look at your car..." Joe stammered. "How in the name of Christ did it avoid being hit...?"

"Hop in, please. You look awful."

Dizzily, Joe wrenched open the door. Crouched on the passenger seat, Sasha clutched the tea box to his chest.

"Sasha, sweetie, Mr. Miniver wants to sit down."

The monkey leered and plucked a booger from his nose. Grasping his tail in one tiny, scaly pink hand, he poked the tip of the tail up a nostril, swabbing around.

"Sasha, darling..."

Bounding fluidly, Sasha leapt into the back seat, still clutching the tea box.

Joe collapsed. Nancy turned the ignition key, and the engine started up without a whimper.

She said, "I wonder what that was all about?"

Dully, Joe moaned, "It's gone."

"What is?"

"Everything. My past, my present, even my future."

"Explain."

"They got it all."

"All what?"

"The dope in that suitcase. I just blew twelve thousand dollars."

"Joe, what are you talking about?"

"You honestly don't know?"

She nodded.

"Then you're the only person in town who doesn't."

"Doesn't know what?"

"One of those tea boxes held pure cocaine. That's how I hoped to buy Eloy's place." Joe buried his face in his hands. "I don't *believe* these past twenty-four hours!"

"Sasha picked up a box."

"Big deal. One out of thirty. Some odds."

"You never know. With just a little faith—"

"Do me a favor with your 'faith,' would you?"

"At least we could check."

"You check. I'm sick."

"Miracles can happen. All they take is a smidgen of belief."

"Sorry, pal, I'm plumb out of smidgens."

"Sasha," Nancy coaxed, "give me that box."

The monkey chattered busily, ignoring her command. He plucked at the box, forcing open an end tab. Turning completely, Nancy reached in back, and, soothing him—"There, there, that's a good little boy"—she wrested the carton from his arms.

Joe grumbled, "I'm gonna commit suicide. Actually, I might not have to. I'm being smothered by an invisible pillow. I want my asthma medicine!"

"First we'll check out this carton. It feels almost too heavy for tea."

"Oh sure. In the middle of a crazy gun battle the world's nastiest monkey grabs a box at random, and voilà!—a hundred Gs worth of cocaine."

"I wouldn't be at all surprised." Nancy pried open the end flaps.

"I would." Joe wallowed in melancholic self-pity. "The way my luck's been running, not only will it not be full of cocaine, but there'll be something horrible inside: a Gila monster, or a black-widow spider. It'll bite me, I'll drop into a month-long coma, and accumulate twenty-eight thousand in medical bills. . . ."

"I doubt God would have let Sasha risk his life just for a box of tea." Nancy pried up another flap.

"If that's the one with the coke," Joe joked leadenly, "I'll be a monkey's uncle."

"Well, here we go." Nancy opened the box and peered inside.

Sarcastically, Joe said, "And it's full of uncut cocaine, right?"

"I don't know. Does cocaine look like talcum powder?"

"Oh my God!" Joe sobbed giddily. *"It couldn't have happened, but it did!"*

Moments later, within sight of the Castle of Golden Fools, Joe realized abruptly that going after his Aminodur and the Alupent could be like trying to crack the Los Angeles Bank of America's Mosler vault without setting off enough alarms to bring the entire LAPD down on his head. If they parked on the road, and he tried to tiptoe into the yard and pinch his pills from the Green Gorilla, it was a million to one against pulling off the feat without triggering at least one dog, such as Rimpoche, who'd alert Tribby's three dogs, who'd alert all the people.

Quick decisions were needed, however. Another five minutes of reduced oxygen and his brain would sink into a permanent vegetal state anyway. So—what the hell? Since a racket was inevitable, he might as well be bold, Cast Temerity to the Wind, Seize the Day... Let a Thousand Flowers Bloom.

I. e.: Rush the joint, set off all the alarms, grab the prime minister, machine-gun his bodyguards, and split with the goodies before anybody could make a positive identification.

Joe said, "Drive in as fast as you can, stop by that green truck, see? I'll jump out and grab the stuff, leap back into the car, and you take off. It'll sound like the Titicut Follies— Rimpoche will go berserk—but pay no attention. The thing to do is do it so fast that we're long gone by the time anybody human can get their act together to stumble to a window and see what's up. Okay?"

The princess of Everything's-Gonna-Be-All-Right smiled serenly. "Okeydokey."

"Bueno. Turn off the lights. Now: on your mark... get set... *go!*"

Nancy peeled in, crossed the parking area, stomped on the brakes. Joe yanked a handle and slammed his shoulder against the door to pop it open. But he had locked it. The handle came off in his hand. And the door did not budge, not even by a hair. Excruciatingly pained, he shrieked, "Get out, I gotta exit on your side!" He shoved her onto the ground and, for good measure, trompled over her, scrambling to clear the Beetle. Enraged by his own stupidity, he gallop-limped for the truck, opened the door, dived into the glove compartment... and couldn't find the pills. Completely freaked, he threw papers, envelopes, maps, wrenches, screwdrivers, washers, inkless ballpoints, and fuses onto the floor, frantically searching for his pills—but no dice. Crying "Oh no!" he slammed the door and sprinted to the VW bus. Both the passengerside lock and the U-piece apparatus on the rear sliding door were broken, meaning the only sure way to enter was through the driverside access. But it was locked. "Jesus H. Fucking Christ!" Joe poked in the sliding door's vent window, reached down and flicked up the lock knob, grasped the outside handle, jamming it forward, and the contraption opened. Lurching backward, however, it also caved outward, knocking Joe down: he'd forgotten the iron U-piece attaching it to the outside runner was broken.

"You all right?" Ralph called. He was lying supine in his float-tank casket with the hatch open, reading a *Playboy* by a little night-light he had rigged up in there, while listening to a Neil Diamond record on a waterproof stereo speaker extension from the modular componented sound-shaped rig in his tipi.

Joe ignored him. Huffing now, half fainting from the asthmatic trauma induced by his bizarre exertions, he clambered into the car, leaned over the passenger seat, and rifled through the glove compartment, locating—hallelujah!—a plastic jar of Aminodur and Breathine. Three seconds later he was back at the Bug, lunging over Nancy to reach the passenger seat as he choked out fevered orders: "Let's go! *Hit that road!*"

Accelerating at a casual rate, she steered left, onto the paved road, and braked.

Joe babbled, "What are you doing?"

Her window was rolled down. "Listen."

"Huh?" Terrified by her strange behavior, he actually listened.

No quieter yard had ever existed. Lights remained extinguished in the Castle. Rimpoche was asleep somewhere, oblivious to the commotion. Benevolently, the moon—a wise old Santa Claus—smiled on the valley: *Accept this gift of my light, all you wee mortals; sleep like puppies for a change*. Countless stars, friendly nocturnal dimples, twinkled.

"See? You got all bent out of shape for nothing."

"I don't understand."

"It's all in how you feel. And in the kind of energy you project."

For his next trick, he would perform a pas de deux with the

childproof cover of his pill bottle. It crackled and twisted, but held fast. Nancy flicked on the headlights and they cruised off at a reasonable speed. Joe pressed his palm down hard, but the bottle remained impregnable. He banged the cover against the dashboard. No luck. Lodging the bottle between his thighs for leverage worked even worse.

"Have you got a hammer, a pair of pliers, a wrench, *any*-thing in this car?"

Negative: "The last time I had a flat tire was in 1972, and so—"

"Don't say it, please."

"Don't say what?"

"Don't say 'If you don't project a breakdown, you won't have one.' I've had enough of that drivel." *Stertorous* was an adjective accurately describing his gasping. He couldn't breathe. His chin and sternum itched, his inner chest felt as if it had been sandpapered by shredded gunmetal. Not for many a moon had he uncorked a lalapalooza like this baby!

"Stop the car, Nancy."

Joe tumbled to the pavement. He circled in front of the Bug, located a rock in the headlight glare, set his pill bottle on the macadam, and smashed it with a single heavy blow. Gathering up the pills, he popped one, funneled the rest into a shirt pocket, and, tearfully sobbing "This can't be happening to me!," he struggled to regain both the Beetle and his sanity. Once safely inside, both weeping and giggling, he cackled, "Carry on, Jeeves. . . ."

And they headed back for the barn, thus ending the first day in the Bachelor Bacchanalia and Liberated Life of Joe Miniver, Boy Klutz, All-Around Shlemiel of this Floundering Decade.

But he had that cocaine!

3
Monday

*To know how to take women
Brings good fortune.*

Sleep had not exactly tackled the entire unraveled sleeve of his spiritual woe, but it had applied darning needles to the more obvious gaps in that fabled garment.

Opening his eyes, Joe felt better. No matter that his head ached, his thighs twitched from cramps, one testicle had piercing shooting pains, and his heart was broken—if he could breathe, he was happy. Short of expiring in a violent plane crash, death by suffocation ruled the top notch in Joe's list of the Most Excruciating Offs populating the Grim Reaper's ugly repertoire. He'd sooner commit suicide by hammering a screwdriver into his ear.

All his life Joe had awakened with a hard-on so stiff it seemed reinforced by molybdenum, and this morning was no exception. He opened one eye upon a room fused with amaranthine premature morning sunlight that reflected heroically on his petrified peter. A right-hand probe discovered another warm body beside his thigh. Joe's theory had always been that an erection wasted was an erection to be mourned, and so, marveling at the lust inspired by this passive floozy engineering his vertiginous downfall, he swung lazily atop the lady and kissed open her eyes. Nancy murmured, "Um, nice lips." Seconds later, she gave a soft gasp. Her cheeks tantalizingly rosy from sleep, she said, "You know, for a nonspiritual person, you're a pretty good lover."

"'Pretty' good?"

Taking his head in both hands, she lowered him to her lips, planting a coo-shaped buss against the tip of his nose. On cue, Bradley banged the door Joe had providentially insisted they lock last night.

"Mom, I'm hungry!"

"There's some Cocoa Puffs in the cabinet beside the refrigerator."

Joe made a horrible face: "You feed him that kind of shit?"

"He adores them."

"According to the last government survey you get minus

189

four hundred seventeen vitamins in every box." He rotated
calmly inside her. "They cause breast cancer in laboratory rats,
and kwashiorkor in chimpanzees."

"What's kwashiorkor?"

"The Biafran starvation disease. Apparently the only thing
worse than Cocoa Puffs is agent orange, that chemical we
used to defoliate Vietnam." Such fun it was to twiddle her
nipples between thumbs and forefingers; Joe ogled the snowy
cascade of smooth curves that characterized her breasts.

"I don't want Cocoa Puffs for breakfast, Mom. I want Jimmy
Dean sausage and a fried egg and some hot chocolate in my
Ronald McDonald mug."

"You know we don't have Jimmy Dean sausage, we happen
to be vegetarians." She gave Joe a good-humored wink. "Every
morning he asks for Jimmy Dean sausage."

Reaching blindly onto the bedside table, she located a
matchbook and her cigarettes and lit one.

"Well, what am I supposed to eat?" Bradley pounded his
little fist emphatically against the door, as Joe raised her legs,
placing them over his shoulders.

"Make yourself a Morningstar Farm sausage. They're delicious."

"I hate that rubber meat. It tastes like sawdust!" The little
creep emphasized his anger with another palm against the doorway of their fuckatorium. Nancy blew smoke up into Joe's
face. Gripping both her biceps and grinning one of his more
dervish grins, he laid into her for a bit like a Manhattan air
drill, wondering: Could he shake her composure?

"What time is it, Joe?"

He checked the clock-radio: "Almost seven-twenty."

"Oh God! Bradley, are you dressed?"

"I don't have any clothes to wear. All my stuff is in the
laundry."

"Go to the bathroom hamper, find something semiclean,
and put it on. It's seven-twenty and you've only got fifteen
minutes until the bus comes."

Joe held her legs in a high and wide V, digging the dark
pubic tangle where his penis was lodged. Her thighs were a
little flaccid; he liked her voluptuous belly. Uninserting himself, he dropped his head between her thighs, inhaling as much
fur and oily tendrils as he could, nibbling, munching, sucking,
gumming, and drilling all over with his tongue. Arching, she

placed her non-cigarette-occupied hand against his head, and uttered appropriate, if whispered, sounds.

"I don't want to wear something from the hamper, Mom. Every morning I have to wear something from the hamper. I never get to wear any *clean* clothes. All the kids tease me."

"*Oh Joe, oh my God, oh you bastard*...Bradley, go find the clothes, go make a breakfast, and go to school!"

"I wanna come in. Why did you lock the door? What are you doing?"

"I have a right to privacy, darling. Now come on—you've only got, uh...twelve minutes."

"Is Mr. Miniver still in there with you?"

"Yes. Now listen—please. Mommy's tired. And you're big enough to get ready for school without my help."

"Is Mr. Miniver asleep? What's he doing?"

Mr. Miniver was flipping his mom onto her stomach and entering her from behind, thinking that if God hadn't invented female buttocks and the doggy position, Mr. Miniver himself would have spent the better part of his life in pursuit of realizing that invention. Or he would have died trying.

"He's just lying here, fast asleep. Now come on, Bradley, get cracking. If you miss the school bus I won't drive you there, you'll have to walk."

"If I miss the school bus I won't go!" Once more, he whacked the door for emphasis. Still working on the cigarette, Nancy exhaled smoke languidly while backing her butt up against Joe and almost triggering an orgasm.

"Don't move!" Joe said urgently. Cautiously, he stretched back his legs, lowered on top of her, and scooped his hands around to cup her breasts.

"If you don't do as I say, right now," Nancy threatened amiably, "you won't get any allowance on Saturday." Millimeter by slippery millimeter, Joe sank himself to the hilt. *"That's it,"* Nancy whispered lasciviously. *"Shove it all the way to China!"*

Twice, the little Nazi out there kicked against the door. "If you don't give me my allowance, Mom, I'll call Daddy and tell him to call the judge and the judge will put you in jail."

"What's he talking about?" Joe's right hand prowled around in her groin, then he raised the hand to her mouth, painting her lips with her own juices.

"In the divorce agreement he made me stipulate that a certain amount of his child support, which we list as alimony, has to go directly to Bradley in the form of an allowance."

"How much is it?"

"Two dollars every Saturday."

"Wow. When I was a kid I only got a quarter!"

Hungrily, she sucked on his fingers. Joe said, "What do you mean you stipulate child support as alimony?" Might as well bone up for his own immediate future.

"He gets a tax break if it's listed as alimony." Reaching for the bedside ashtray, she snuffed her cigarette, then played with herself as he slowly pumped.

Bradley called, "Mom, are you still in there?"

"Of course I'm still in here."

"It got awful quiet. What are you guys doing?"

"We're trying to relax. Now let's go, buster. Get dressed, get fed, and get going. And feed Bozo and Sasha too, before you leave."

"I fed them yesterday."

"They eat every day, just like you and me. *Oh golly, Joe, keep on moving just like that, oh Jesus you're good to me. Oh darling* . . . hey! Don't stop!."

"I have to or else I'll come."

"God forbid—not yet. This is too good. I want it to last forever."

"Mom, we're all out of dogfood."

"No we're not. I got a fifty-pound bag of Purina chow two days ago."

"Well, it's not under the sink beside the garbage can."

"Of course not, stupid. I put it in that space between the washing machine and the dryer."

"Jeez. Why didn't you tell me in the first place?"

"Don't go away!" she protested as Joe removed himself. *"What are you doing?"* Joe backed off the bed, dragging her half off with him. Her torso on the bed, her feet on the floor, he kneeled and tongued her again. Nancy gave a stifled, happy little gasp: the living-room telephone clattered. Bradley said "Just a minute," and returned to their door.

"Mom! Telephone!"

"Who is it?"

"I don't know. It's for Mr. Miniver. It's a girl."

Joe stood up and leaned over, grabbing both her forearms. "Tell her to call back later," Nancy said.

"I can't. She said it's very important."

"Who the hell *is* it?" Joe blurted, almost crippled by déjà vu.

"Mom, what's the matter with him?" the sadistic cherub asked with malevolent apprehension. "His voice sounds funny."

"Bradley, please darling, just go hang up the telephone. Then feed the animals and eat yourself."

"How can I eat myself?"

"You know what I meant. Are you dressed yet? You've only got eight more minutes."

"I'm almost dressed."

"What are you wearing?"

"My jodhpurs and my John Travolta sneakers and those socks that Daddy sent."

Nancy whispered, *"Oh God!"* as Joe made a new move. Out loud, she said, "How many times have I told you you can't wear those jodhpurs to school? They're old and moth-eaten. They look ridiculous."

"But I don't have anything else that's clean."

In the process of swinging Nancy off the bed to drape her over a footstool, Joe bumped against the bedside table, knocking a lamp onto the floor.

Bradley cried, "Mom, what was *that*?"

"I just tipped over the lamp reaching for my cigarettes, darling. Now come on, right away, put on another pair of pants and get out of here."

Oh she looked beautiful, spread-eagled above the thick, cobalt-blue rug. Joe straddled her in the leapfrog position, shoving it all the way past China into a Pakistani cornfield. *"Oh wow are you ever doing me,"* she tremoloed.

Crash! went something in the kitchen—something loud, heavy, splintery. An awful silence ensued. Joe quit moving: they both held their breath.

"Bradley?"

"What?" His voice came from right on the other side of the door. The little bugger had crept up on them.

"What was that god-awful noise?"

"Sasha made one of your plants fall."

"Are you all right?"

"I'm hungry! I'm gonna starve to death."

Prodded by Joe, Nancy slithered off the stool, landing face-up on the rug. Joe sat on her stomach, paddling her breasts, stroking her throat and lips. Then he let some drool fall between her breasts, smearing it around with his finger, reached for a pillow to boost her head, and whispered, "Press your tits together." She did. Fitting his penis into the slick groove between her exaggerated globes, he fucked that sexy crease.

"I don't care if you starve to death," Nancy said. Her eyes, as if facing a firing squad, were wide, her lips pursed as if to whistle.

Bradley whacked the door a dozen times, shouted "I hate you!," and stomped indignantly off.

In the background, Bozo commenced barking and snarling. Burglars? Porcupines? Joe touched the head of his cock against her lips, loomed above her for a beat, then lowered into her mouth until she gagged. He raised back, dangling above her lips. The orgasm began its swell from a thousand miles away, taking as long to reach its staging area as David Lean's galloping desert horseman had taken to reach the camera in *Lawrence of Arabia*.

In agony, Joe thought, Maybe I can talk it out. Aloud, as he touched his prick to the fat part of her lower lip, he said, "I'm almost there . . . you're such a sexy lay . . . Oh Jesus I . . . I—" But Nancy had heard the school bus rattle onto the subdivision drive: "Bradley?"

Came a surly growl from the living room: "What?"

"Here's the school bus!"

The front door opened, and Bradley shot back a final, defiant "I hate you!" as Joe tried to will at least the advance troops of sperm onto her lips. He could picture it, but failed to make it happen. In his mind the residue bubbled out and he guided his penis in a slow circle, laying jism—as if it were toothpaste—on her beautiful lips.

But only in his head.

Her alarm buzzed an hour late—there must have been an early morning blackout. It was time to rise and shine.

"I don't care," Nancy murmured sleepily. "I think you're sensational. What a stud."

When was the last time someone had called him *that*?

An hour later, when—as if ripped from too many lotus blossoms—he staggered in to the bathroom, Joe half expected to see Paul Newman or Marlon Brando reflected back at him from the medicine-cabinet mirror. Instead, what was this?—the same old Joe Miniver, and still up to his eyeballs in trouble. Marital trouble, financial trouble, scam trouble. It looked like curtains with Heidi and the kids; and now that he actually had the cocaine (though not his patron saint druggie, Peter Roth) in his hot little hands, how was he supposed to cut and distribute the white gold?

Apparently, judging from the evidence so far accumulated, he was determined to excavate the biggest grave yet seen in these here parts. Depression clobbered him. Weak-kneed, he plopped onto the toilet. Like, how, overnight, could he have abdicated every moral imperative giving his sloppy, yes, but also loyal and eminently ethical, life meaning?

Once it started, where would it end—in a John Berryman Icarus act? In Fitzgeraldian delirium tremens? In Hemingway-esque shotgun blasts? Or in some scathingly devious Sylvia Plathology?

When, clad only in pink bikini briefs, she ambled past the bathroom doorway, the woman who had turned him on only a heartbeat ago, appeared slump-shouldered, potbellied, flabby-assed, and pigeon-toed, the epitome of suburban housewife-hood, and about as alluring as a potato.

Joe washed, scrubbed his ivories using her toothbrush, shared a cup of coffee, helped resuscitate the smashed plant, snarled at Sasha (who gestured obscenely in return), and made three false exits, returning for his glasses, his wallet, and the carton carrying $100,000 worth of cocaine. But then, finally he *ran*.

Six years had gone by in the last forty-eight hours!

Head down, instinctively slaloming through joggers as he verbalized yet another letter to Heidi—"Did you think you were being clever when you called this morning, is that what you thought?"—Joe almost knocked down Ralph Kapansky. Veering, he braked and would have crashed had Ralph

195

not grabbed the handlebars. Rimpoche danced clumsily around the bike, yapping befuddledly.

"Is it true?" Ralph asked.

"Is what true?"

"Have you left Heidi? Are you getting a divorce? Are you going to marry Nancy Ryan?"

"That's what I like about this town, Ralph. Scott Harrison drops a banana in Safeway, and Diana Clayman picks it up and hands it back to him. One hour later, in the Prince of Whales Café, Tribby Gordon tells Darlene Johnson that he heard Diana flogged Scott's log in front of the Kitty Litter, they were both busted, arraigned, and jailed, and, while in the local hoosegow, Diana hung herself with her own panty hose."

"Hey, man, aren't you overdoing it a little?"

"I'm sick of the rumor mill, Ralph! I'm sick of the lack of privacy! I'm sick of living in a nouveau-hippie town where hordes of filthy-rich, college-educated welfare cases playing poverty fooseball blunder scurrilously around the valley spreading doom and gloom like a bunch of banana-republic, machine-gun toting, Fort Benning-trained sadists!"

"Speaking of gun-toting, old sport—what the hell happened at the bus depot last night? I'm surprised to see you alive. Somebody told me you were practically vivisected with hot lead around midnight."

"That's a semiaccurate description."

"Apparently they got the suitcase."

"How'd you know about the suitcase?"

"Rachel Parquielli was talking to Suki Terrell, who mentioned it."

"Where did she hear about it?"

"I'm not sure. But I think Diana Clayman spilled the beans."

"And she found out how?"

"From Angel Guts, who else?"

"*I* didn't tell Angel Guts."

"I know, I know. But he found out somehow."

"Well, for what it's worth, our scam is still alive," Joe said nervously. "Last night Sasha leaped into the fray and nabbed the one box that held the cocaine."

"Who's Sasha?"

"Nancy's monkey."

"Where's the dope?"

"Right there." Joe nodded at the tea carton in his basket.

Aghast Ralph said, "You're just carting it around, out in the wide open, like *that*?"

"Do I have a choice?"

"Well, shit, man, suppose somebody knew? You're a sitting duck."

"How could they know? Everybody who's interested must think everybody else but me has it."

"So what are we supposed to do now?"

"First I go to the café and catch my breath."

"We'll have to meet again."

"Not in Tribby's plane!"

"But we have to cut the stuff and unload it fast," Ralph said. "Can I take a peek?"

"No, dummy—sheesh!"

"Okay. But what's the plan?"

"I haven't the faintest. Peter was the key, and he blew it. So right now the logistics are up for grabs. But I'll figure out something and be in touch."

"You should be wearing a bulletproof vest!" Ralph called out cheerfully as Joe pedaled on, slumped morosely over his handlebars like a country mortician suffering from a spinal fusion on his way to claim a rural corpse.

Two joggers wearing large earmuff-shaped transistor radios listened to rock music from KKCV or KWIK as they cantered along. The earmuffs enraged Joe. He wanted to stop, knock down the joggers, and tear the offensive gadgets off their lame brains while beating them soundly:

"I used to run cross-country in college! I looked at the trees! I smelled all the smells of nature! I listened to the birds singing! *What the hell is the matter with you zombies?*"

Face frozen in a clandestine snarl, Nick Danger scuttled across the road, clutching his mysterious suitcase and muttering angrily to himself.

The Prince of Whales creaked at the seams from a ragtag gathering of colorful expatriates. Tea box safely tucked under one arm, Joe chose a table occupied by Tribby Gordon, Diana Clayman, Mimi McAllister, and Jeff Orbison. While he was at the cash register buying a newspaper, Ralph and Rimpoche jogged in and flopped down at the same table. Joe returned, unfolded his blat, and, mimicking buffoonish surprise, said, "My oh my, they're still fighting in Beirut."

Tribby said, "What's this I hear about you and Heidi?"

"I give up—what did you hear about me and Heidi?"

Ralph stroked his beard. "In front of all these wonderful people, Tribby, we wouldn't want to be indiscreet."

Tribby said, "What's the secret? Channel eight had a roving reporter over in the PK Subdivision Number Four last night, and on the eleven P.M. newsbreak the whole valley got a four-minute shot of Joe and a-certain-somebody-not-his-wife-who-shall-remain-nameless engaged in some very funky anatomical hijinks."

From then on it was all downhill. Joe ordered one egg, toast, a glass of orange juice, and Sanka. Taken aback by his sulky manner, Darlene said, "Don't you mean you'd like one cyclops, OE, slice of toasted wheat, side order of squeal—that's double links not patties—and a glass of Florida sunshine?"

But Joe was in no mood for it. "Hey, just bring the food, Darlene, and cut the palaver, I got a headache."

"Male chauvinist pigs," Mimi huffed scornfully. "Every time you turn over a rock in this valley some liberated house-husband's skeleton jumps up and bites your nose."

While Joe tried to read, they talked. At first, Mimi carried the ball. A health nut, and a reflexologist who carted wooden barrels to clients' houses and manipulated their tootsies for a double sawbuck, she lived in a La Ciénega tipi and was blind as a bat. She refused to wear glasses, however, figuring them to be debilitating eye-crutches. "Without glasses, I can force my eyes to get better." Because Mimi was on the fifth day of a water fast, they discussed the pros and cons of that.

Water fasts, Hanumans, reflexology—Joe rarely participated in such erudite discussions, being basically a meat-and-potatoes man.

Ralph soon began extolling the virtues of colonic enemas. Jeff Orbison claimed the healthiest way to crap was squatting—and that's the way he defecated, even on a toilet. Next, vegetarian diets used up ten or fifteen minutes. Mimi said many vegetarians blew their scene completely by overloading on carbohydrates. Diana Clayman postulated that everybody was freaking out because their air had become overloaded with negative ions. Tribby informed them that on his morning KWIK astrology program, Pancho Nordica had predicted money for Leos, love for Aquarians, and heartbreak for Pisces. He had also urged his listeners to eat more bran and Top Ramen, and "cut out the Jujyfruits."

Tiring of gastrointestinal themes, they ran down the Morning Disaster Report, a regular feature of the Prince of Whales, and tuned into religiously by the 4,837 people in this town (sarcasmed Joe Miniver while pretending to fanatically devour his newspaper) who were writing novels. Norman Mailer never said it, but he might have had he visited the place: "Just give me ten minutes in the Prince of Whales Café, and I could write a two-thousand-page novel about Chamisaville."

What else was new? Drunk for the eleventh time in as many days, Cobey Dallas had gone on a rampage last night. It ended when he tried to smash his Volkswagen Beetle into the La Tortuga, where, apparently, Suki Terrell (with whom Cobey had had an affair) was sharing a number two combination plate with the EAT ME drummer, Tom Yard.

Terry and Perry Kahn were in trouble also. Terry resembled a great many newly arrived Chamisaville women Joe knew. Three times weekly she had dance classes at the Chamisaville Art Association auditorium. She acted in two plays every year and taught part-time at the Shanti Institute, where all three Kahn kids were educationally interred. In winter she took her offspring skiing, and raced in the Nastar events herself. She was blond and blue-eyed, tense, and very competitive. They were charter members of Tennis Heaven and spent six hundred dollars a summer on memberships and lessons alone. All the children took piano lessons. But Perry was straying way off course. Three years ago he had been a handsome young developer, fresh out of Miami real estate and construction. Then he started smoking dope and playing the guitar. After cleaning up on his first half-dozen subdivisions, he seemed to lose interest. His hair grew long, he adopted a colorful headband. When he and Joe occasionally met, Perry babbled about psychic energy and psychedelics. Rumor had it he was into some heavy shit—LSD, mescaline, maybe mushrooms. Perry this past year had grown filthy, gentle, absentminded, and abstract, as Terry panicked. "You know what?" Perry had told Joe one day. "I'm really losing interest in making money." Last week he had run off to a Colorado ashram where he hoped to learn the art of psychic healing. And Terry was at the end of her rope. Yesterday she had complained to Mimi McAllister: "If that man becomes a hippie-do-gooder, I'll commit suicide!"

Pearly Stan, a man with a silver eyepatch who had leased the La Lomita Dance Hall from Wilkerson Busbee, had jumped town last night, taking all the money and leaving his employees in the lurch, some to the tune of a thousand dollars. According to what Cobey Dallas had told Tribby (when Tribby bailed out Cobey early that morning), just before he split, Stan had offered to sell County Sheriff Eddie Semmelweis information on all the local dope dealers and buyers, but Eddie had refused, the county sheriff's LEAA stocked coffers being semi-low after some untoward embezzlement. Eddie also told Cobey that Nikita Smatterling had tearfully staggered into the station last night to report that his elder kids, Sanji and Tofu, were getting ripped on Moroccan kif every day, and making daredevil junkets out underneath the girders of the Gorge Bridge, where passing motorists could hear them singing the best of The Who while dangling a thousand feet above oblivion. As an afterthought, Nikita admitted to Eddie that he had just poked a pistol into Ephraim Bonatelli's stomach and pulled the trigger. Ephraim, apparently, had entered the Cinema Bar around closing time last night, wearing a gorilla mask and waving a pistol and had threatened to kidnap (and sink his sexual meat-hooks into) Nikita's youngest child, beautiful, seven-year-old Siddhartha, the blessed progeny of a brief union between Nikita and a hippie woman, originally from Scarsdale, named Rachel (Wisebaum) Whitefeather. She had spent time up at Davish right after that eclectic Sufi commune was founded by Nikita and some of his friends during their off-hours from Pueblo construction jobs.

Eddie S. had held Nikita for almost thirty minutes (outrageous!) until Belle London appeared at the jail accompanied by Tribby, to post a ten-thousand-dollar property bond for his release. Over at the Our Lady of the Sorrows Hospital, the diminutive Bonatelli's heart had stopped thrice during the night while doctors Phil Horney and Ed Diebold labored to save the warped little scumbag. "Stable" was his most recent listing. Rumors had it the senior Bonatelli had not yet decided whether to put the contract on Nikita for traumatizing his kid or for failing to eradicate the useless little bum.

In no mood to promote this balderdash, having found himself—these past few days—traveling uncomfortably close to the core of commensurately puerile shenanigans, Joe slowly chewed on his breakfast and pretended to read the newspaper. Yet his big-lobed ears were flapping. Oh for the guts to scribble down all these stories during the act of their telling! Of course, when he glanced up, surreptitiously letting his eyes probe each animated face in their group, Joe realized that he was ensconced in a den of similarly intentioned vipers. For although all heads were cocked in attitudes of conversational alertness, their heavy-lidded eyes had that half-glazed, introspective look of fireside cats, as they attempted to memorize choice goodies while frantically wishing for the chutzpah to withdraw their little notebooks and scribble frantically, indelibly capturing the rich mishmash of sardonic and histrionic information going down that could be money in all their Nobel banks one day.

Eager to get up, get out, and be gone, Joe couldn't move. He was held spellbound by the gossip. And anyway, where could he retreat to now that he had no home? While they talked of recent flying-saucer sightings on the gorge rim, Joe wondered: how could he ever face Heidi and the children again? While Ralph Kapansky described his recent aura-adjustment down in Alamogordo, New Mexico, Joe wondered how, even if he managed to raise the cash, he could evict Eloy Irribarren from his adobe shack, thus giving himself, however humble, a home.

They were discussing the Kabala—the Tree of Life. Somebody was thinking of joining that born-again women's Christian group called Women Aglow, where "they actually speak in tongues." Somebody else had a friend who had recently joined the Hermetic Order of the Golden Dawn. They discussed bi-orhythms and decided how to pull a "cosmic trigger." Ralph mentioned that he had met a lady, a millionaire tourist from Cincinnati, last night. She had offered to fly him to her Ohio digs where they would do a kundalini copulation in front of her videotape machine. Mimi said in her former life she had been—no kidding!—a grizzly bear in Yellowstone Park. "That's how come I'm a lesbian today." Joe failed to see the connection, but nobody else had a problem with it. Where had she picked up this fascinating tidbit about her past?—from Nikita Smatterling, of course. Not only could the man paint ethereal monkeys, but he augmented his income by being a Past-Life Reader as well.

That is, when he wasn't wearing a loincloth and a pink

turban giving naturopathic massages down in the "body cubicle" of Wilkerson Busbee's Spa and Sauna.

Mimi McAllister ran down the latest on the Hanuman scene. Somehow, the Eastern contingent had been sprung from New York City despite the lack of Baba Ram Bang's visa, and Fluff Dimaggio's Sullivan Law violation. Yesterday afternoon, Nikita Smatterling had received a telegram from Wilkerson Busbee saying that Baba Ram Bang (that ninety-three-year-old Darjeeling mystic who, in a previous incarnation, had missed selection as the Tibetan Panchen Lama by a mere millimeter) had expressed a desire to see Sahdra (formerly Penelope) Pinkerton and her belly dancers perform at the Cosmic Banana Café. . . .

I should have a tape of this conversation, Joe thought. Nobody would believe it. A ninety-three-year-old diabetic east Indian ether-brain sitting at an outdoor café table in Chamisaville, USA, eating an alfalfa-sprout sandwich and guzzling Red Zinger tea, surrounded by graying hippies in turbans, rice-paper shirts, and aoki sandals, watching a bunch of middle-class honky women (outfitted in diaphanous turquoise and salmon-pink crepe) calling themselves Sahdra, Meshak, and Jamila (who used to be Penny, Peggy, and Paula)—undulate like Egyptian ecdysiasts.

And it's only the first Monday morning in June!

Then, apparently, somewhere in Ohio, the Hanuman bearers had run into trouble again. It all started when Iréné Papadraxis, who liked to tipple on a flask of cream sherry as they zoomed along, got drunk and, reacting to the hot afternoon sunshine, stripped to the waist. Almost immediately, the driver of an oncoming eighteen-wheeler jackknifed his rig, and Wilkerson had to swing off the road to avoid certain death from the catapulting trailer spewing chickens. Nobody was hurt, but they ended up jammed into a culvert. When police arrived on the scene, Fluff Dimaggio handcuffed himself to the precious Hanuman statue and swallowed the keys—a security precaution in case the cops locked them in jail. Baba Ram Bang retired to a nearby patch of rest-area lawn exclusively reserved for dogs and went into a deep meditative trance, refusing to move when law officers gave him orders. So they arrested the mystic. Rama Unfug tried to film the arrest for evidence in a later brutality case, and was promptly kayoed with a billy club. For good measure, they smashed Rama's camera, at which point Shant

Unfug kicked an officer in the groin, and Om Unfug whacked his kneecap with her Creative Playthings wooden mallet. Arrested en masse, they were all now cooling their heels in the Clarion, Ohio, hoosegow, even Fluff Dimaggio. The cops had transferred him, and the heavy statue to which he was chained, eleven miles in a lumberyard forklift.

"They'll never make it by Thursday!" everyone wailed.

Closer to home, various catastrophes and happy adventures were happening to people Joe knew only peripherally. The ex-husband of a woman named Sarah had driven in from Rochester last night and kidnapped her two children because he didn't like her living with Sam Halaby, a metaphysical teacher claiming to be on his last incarnation (and damn glad of it because he wanted never again to return to this scorched and degrading earth).

Several folks just in from the Wolf Creek Pass Film Festival claimed to have met George Raft . . . and they had never done so much coke in their lives.

Joe said, "During the three years I have lived in this town I've heard that everybody and their brothers and their little sisters and even their dogs and their cats and their canaries toot coke like banshees, yet I've never been in a room where people were sniffing, or quiffing, or whatever the hell it is they do."

Diana said, "You're kidding. The only place they don't do coke in this town is in Foodway!"

Rumor also had it that a very rich guy had arrived in town seeking to finance an expedition of unscrupulous well-armed hippies to travel down to Lake Titicaca for the purpose of snatching the Golden Sun Disc of Mu, a precious stone belonging to the head of the Brotherhood of the Seven Rays, Aramu Muru.

They talked about housing and land, about buying and renting and building and house-sitting and financing and searching.

"How you gonna find an acre of land anymore?" Jeff Orbison asked testily. "When Suki and I first hit this valley you could find land for a few thousand bucks an acre. A week ago, my next-door neighbor sold his half-acre for thirteen fat ones."

"To who?"

"I think it was Ray Verboten."

Mimi said, "I happen to know that Ray's first day there he sold the irrigation rights to the new Sonic Burger so they could

get hooked up to city water. You know for how much? Eighteen
thousand dollars."

Everybody whistled. A great helium bubble of despair rose
to the top of Joe's skull, doubling the intensity of his headache.
No grace, no compassion, no class existed in the real-estate
game. The Chamisa Valley was like a slave market, or a whore-
house. An entirely new breed had taken over the town and its
once outlying, now incorporated, communities. Despite its
pseudo-hip ecology-conservation rhetoric, when this new breed
assessed landscape, all it saw was dollar signs. They rational-
ized, pretended, lied through their teeth, paid lip service to the
Sierra Club, and brought in the backhoes. And Joe was one of
them, too, wasn't he? Just another ego with money in his
pocket, looking for a Chicano or a snail darter to stomp.

Mimi was trying to buy land from a freak named Baldini
Miller: he was moving to Bolinas because he felt the Shanti
Institute was too eclectic for his children. Too, the violence
vibes emanating from the Pueblo's sacred mountain were too
much of a downer. Her dealing for his half-acre and a hogan
had been going great until Baldini put an ax through his foot
eight days ago. With that, in an attempt to get straight with
his karma, the freak had taken a vow of silence.

"Every time I go over there to clinch the deal, he just stares
at me tearfully and shrugs," Mimi said angrily. "His old lady,
Ipu, keeps hitting him with a broom and ordering him to speak,
make the deal, and grab the bread so they can split. But he
merely continues to shrug, cry, and point at this big blood-
soaked towel wrapped around his foot."

"How much does he want?"

"Eighty-one thousand."

"Wow! Where are you gonna score that kind of bread?"

"I have it all figured out. Part FHA, part family loans. Where
do any of us get our money?"

Crazy Albert, a bearded and barefoot florist, entered the
café lugging a newspaper carrier's sack full of pink and green
carnations. Beatifically smiling, he glided from table to table
dumping handfuls of flowers in front of the patrons. Joe had
heard that Crazy Albert had his own greenhouse in which he
grew nothing but these carnations. Apparently he lived on a
trust fund, compliments of a bigwig relative at ITT.

Joe simmered, feeling crazy. The air jumped and bubbled
with weird molecules of clarity that exaggerated his hearing,

tricked his vision. A rush of animosity labored hard to clear his body. He had an urge to bash down his fist, tip over the table, and go ape blaspheming his cohorts: "Parasites! Fascists! Egomaniacs! Sexfiends! Me-crazy jingoists! Amoral fuckfaces! Neophyte Nazis!"

What rough beast, its hour come at last, had slouched into Chamisaville to be born again?

Diana Clayman's hand thoughtfully scrabbled at the back of his neck. "Joe, are you okay?" Her voice issued from a distant place. And even though Joe wanted to pay attention, he couldn't stop listening to the others. "I don't know," he murmured, barely able to hear himself. Instead, he heard Ralph doing a rap on some fine mescaline that he'd dropped recently up at one of the Little Baldy Bear lakes north of Chamisaville. Totally ripped, Ralph had caught rainbow trout on tiny flies during a savage hailstorm: he called it one of his most classic, all-time highs. At the next table, three people Joe knew only as Tammy, Vern, and Newlin were having a simple conversation—yet to Joe their words seemed lunatic.

"Why didn't you give me some more room? I felt like you were crashing in on me, cutting off my space. And I needed that space."

"Maybe your energy just had to go somewhere else for a while. . . ."

"I started to realize I don't even know what your trip is about. . . ."

"Apparently, we just don't share the same kind of reality."

"But I hear you, really. I understand where you're coming from. I know we could continue to have an ongoing relationship if we would just manage to be more open, especially sexually. . . ."

"We got rid of some of that anxiety momentum for a while, but then we started laying negative trips on each other. . . ."

"There was too much deception and the vibes were getting all fucked up by unnecessary distractions. . . ."

"You needed another space to sit in. You're not very centered at all. I was really worried. I thought you were on the brink. . . ."

"I love you all, I really care about you, I really care about people, but I'm not reading you very clearly."

"Yeah, I know. My etheric is all out of whack."

"When we discovered that you really needed that time and space, we were able to give it to you, because we understood your creative anxiety...."

"I think of lot of my problems stem from the fact that in my last reincarnation I was a mandarin sorcerer...."

"Well, all you really need is love...."

"Yes, love is the only important thing...."

The crime scene made its appointed rounds. Somebody had set a fire in the theater last night, trying to burn it down. An artist friend of Mimi's had parked her car on the gorge rim and walked off a ways to sketch; on her return, all four of her tires were gone. Somebody had lost a toolbox from the back of his truck while parked at the A&W the other evening. Three days ago, after shopping at Foodway, Tribby had placed the groceries in his unlocked Volvo, then entered Wacker's to buy birthday candles. While he was thus engaged, a thief ripped off the groceries.

"So what kind of freedom do we really have in this country?" Joe said dully.

"Don't start," Ralph warned. "I'm not in the mood for your wishy-washy communism."

"You people aren't ever in the mood for anything," Joe said bitterly, staggering to his feet horrendously startled because he was almost crying. For a second his hands paddled the air helplessly, like a disoriented seal begging for its life. Turning, then, he stumbled against his chair, knocking it over, and, chased by Rimpoche's neurotic barking, he fled from their puzzled, accusatory gazes.

He was surprised, out on the sidewalk, in air he could breathe again, to find himself supported by Diana Clayman. Secreting saliva, he fumbled in his shirt pocket for an Aminodur, popped the pill, and exclaimed, "What's the matter with me?"

"It'll be okay," she soothed. "You're just strung out. You've been going through some heavy shit, haven't you? When was the last time you logged a decent night's sleep?"

Joe faced her, honestly perplexed as he tried to catch his breath. "What are you doing here?"

"You look like you need a friend."

"You don't appear so hot yourself. Who gave you the shiner, the Polack Apache with bad breath?"

Grinning toughly, Diana said, "Who else?"

Joe gave her more than a cursory glance. She had lovely dark and smooth hair. The skin around her large, dark eyes was wrinkled and slightly red. She had a curved nose—call it a sort of Greek beak—a thick upper lip, and a full, slightly jutting lower lip. His eye was attracted to a small deformity, a grouping under her chin of three or four large black hairs that had obviously been plucked or cut. She wore an overlarge army jacket (with the name Wiggens across the pocket), faded dungarees, and sandals. Her head only came up to his chin.

Joe said, "Excuse the hysterics. I'm not my usual cheerful, shit-eating-grin-personified self. Momentarily, I've lost the thread."

"What happened?"

"Who knows. I'm sick of it already. It's so banal it's pathetic. I feel like some kind of Woody Allen cliché. I can't stand the fact I've become a neurotic bourgeois bum just like everybody else...."

"Hey, kick back a little. You don't need to thrash yourself like this."

"Right out of nowhere I blew it with my family. I started balling a woman I don't even know. I just spent twelve thousand bucks to buy some pure coke to sell to buy land and a little house I probably couldn't even move into anyway because I'm afraid to evict the old geezer living there. Last night somebody tried to kill me for that dope. But I don't even know if I'll have a family to live on that land with if I do make the score. I can't *believe* these last two days!"

She put her arm around his waist. "Join the crowd. Angel threw me out last night. He came in around two A. M. dressed in black and choking inside one of those Hanuman gorilla masks. We had a fight. I drove out onto the mesa and slept there. It was beautiful. And the first decent night's sleep I've had in six months."

"So here we are: Two Lost Souls on the Highway of Life."

She tossed her head. "I don't care, I'm used to it."

"Used to what?"

Her eyes narrowed, indifferently hostile. "It used to be I went around looking for some kind of punch line in my life. I was like Candide, you know?—in search of Pangloss. I thought eventually you could reach some sanctified place where important events would happen, and it would all coalesce into something meaningful. But now I know the secret to existence is understanding that life is just something you do until you die. It's how you kill the time until there isn't any more time to kill. So I don't get upset or discouraged about it anymore."

"For Christ's sake, how old are you?"

"Twenty-five."

"You look younger."

"I feel older."

After a brief pause, Joe said, "Would you do me a big favor, Diana? Go back inside and ask Ralph for the key to his office, tell him I gotta use the phone."

"Go back in there yourself."

"I can't. One more false exit, and I swear I'll commit suicide. I'm not ordering you around—honest, I'm begging you for a favor."

"All right, I'll go."

As she departed, Spumoni Tatarsky roller-skated across the plaza, heading straight for the Prince of Whales Café. He carried a briefcase full of (either) Acapulco gold or a bunch of those cheap hologrammistic pendants known as dichromates. Resplendent in a black velvet top hat, formal tails decorated by crocheted pink-and-crimson roses, and a railroad engineer's striped coveralls, he resembled a funky Uncle Sam. Playing the movie-star-avoiding-paparazzi-during-preliminary-hearings-for-his-trial-on-charges-of-murdering-his-internationally-famous-playgirl-wife-by-clubbing-her-to-death-with-a-toilet-plunger, Joe hid his face. And, after his regular salutation—"Peace, brother"—Spumoni skated right on by into the Prince of Whales, trailing an odor of marijuana, incense, and dank armpits.

Nick Danger appeared, scurried across an open area with his scabby suitcase tucked securely under one arm, and then disappeared.

A cute little blond teenybopper, wearing a white turban and flowing robe, approached Joe and handed him a rectangular, blue, bookmark-sized card with "The Great Invocation" inscribed on it. The fourth and fifth verses said:

> From the center which we
> call the race of men

Let the Plan of Love and Light
    work out.
And may it seal the door where
    evil dwells.

Let Light and Love and Power
    restore the Plan on
Earth.

Joe asked her: "What is The Plan?"

"I beg your pardon?"

He called her attention to the card: "What does it mean here
when it talks about The Plan? What is The Plan? Communism?
Capitalism? A screen pass to Franco Harris on two?"

She smiled sympathetically and drifted prettily away.

Had the moon been up, Joe would have howled at it.

Ralph Kapansky's miniature office never failed to
amaze Joe. The man had once earned millions, yet here he
was, camped in a stark cubicle with not a picture on the wall,
seated day after day at a Salvation Army grade-school desk
hacked half apart by the crudely gouged names of a thousand
Guillermos, Josés, and Marias, surrounded by three cardboard
boxes filled to overflowing with crumpled wads of rejected
pages and a zillion cigarette butts. A bookcase held a couple
of dozen male, girly, and fuck magazines, a few cheap pornographic novels, a handful of Al Goldstein's *Screw* newspapers, and copies of *A Farewell to Arms*, *Mrs. Bridge*, *Ulysses*,
a repair manual for Pratt and Whitney bubblecopters, and *The
Bhagavad Gita*. Hanging from a pink ribbon around her neck,
a semideflated life-sized sex doll graced the wall like some
lascivious polyester poontang from a demented avant-gardian's
screwball imagination. On the desk sat a battered old Reming-
ton, an ashtray, a ream of cheap sixteen-pound duplicator paper, a telephone, and an electric alarm clock. A single sheet
in the typewriter held the following:

and Bill's prick was in her ass, Joe's cock was in her cunt,
and Larry's fat succulent shlong, was in her mouth. In a
cage on the nearby table the myna bird

"How can your imagination flower in such a depressingly banal atmosphere?" Joe had once asked.

"Who's asking the imagination to flower? I just want to get my foot in the door and earn a few bucks—later I'll worry about art."

Diana said, "You don't mind if I crash, do you?"

"Be my guest."

"Thanks." Her back against the wall, she slid straight down to the floor. Giving him a weary, playful wink, she tipped slowly sideways, laying her head on her hands, tucked up her legs until the knees almost touched her chin, and instantly fell asleep.

Joe regarded her for a minute, affected by her vulnerable posture. The large sleeves of her jacket almost covered her hands. Her toenails were painted dark burgundy. Joe shook his head, dropped the cocaine onto the desk, picked up the phone, and dialed Heidi: Heather answered.

"Hi, sweetie, how are you?"

Her voice sounded like that of a fifty-year-old former Parisian call girl who had recently gone straight (after a thirteen-year stretch in the Bastille) by starting a small aerospace information industry: "What do you want?"

"What do you mean 'What do I want'? Heather, this is your father speaking."

"I know who it is, for Christ's sake."

"Don't swear at me, kid. You're only eight years old."

"I'll be nine in September."

"Big deal. Listen, lemme speak to your mother."

"If you come back here and try to live with us, Michael and me are gonna run away," she said tightly.

"Look, Heather, I'm sorry, I know this is a big mess. But skip the recriminations, huh? Save all the venom for your autobiography, and right now lemme speak to Heidi."

"She's in the bedroom."

"Well, how far is the bedroom from the telephone—four steps? What happened—you caught muscular dystrophy suddenly?"

"She doesn't feel so good. Last night she killed a whole bottle of Black Jack and we watched 'Star Trek' together. Captain Kirk got trapped in this weird interphase and they almost couldn't beam him back on board. Spock had to take over the *Enterprise* while these creepy things called the Aoleans were weaving a time-warp fabric around the spaceship. It put weird vibes in the air and into all of them. McCoy and Mr. Sulu tried to kill each other. They wound up in straitjackets down in the sick bay. Except for Spock, of course, because Vulcans don't have the kind of feelings that could be affected."

We should all be so lucky. "Heather, that's nice, I'm glad you had fun, now—"

"We didn't have *fun*, stupid. Nobody could go to sleep, and Mommy was getting drunk. Guess what Michael did today?"

Joe heard Michael in the background shouting, "I did not! You shut up you little stoolie or I'll bash your teeth in!"

"He shot a chickadee with his BB gun." She sounded so prissy and self-righteous Joe wanted to slug her.

"It couldn't of been a chickadee, Heather. They all went into the mountains. Now listen—"

"We fed it to Barby Lou. She loved it."

"Heather, if you're trying to get my goat, it won't work. I'm too tired. Now do me a favor, go fetch your mother. . . ."

"I think maybe she's asleep. She was awful sick last night. She said if you drove her to an early grave she would come back as a ghost and haunt you until she drove you crazy and foaming at the mouth."

"That's great. Now cut the crap and go tell her I'm on the phone and we need to talk—it's important. Hey, how come you guys aren't in school this morning?"

"We're staying home to make sure that if she upchucks anymore she won't gag to death on her own puke."

"Heather—!"

"I'm going. Don't get a hernia. . . ."

The phone clattered, banged, clunked. A high, static-filled crackle entered the airwaves. Joe felt sick and apprehensive— then he heard breathing on the other end. "Hello?"

Michael replied shyly, "Hi, Daddy."

"Oh, hey, Michael. How you doing?"

"I'm okay."

"What's happening over there?"

"Oh . . . nothing."

"Wait a minute, what do you mean 'Oh nothing'? Heather just told me Mommy drank a bottle of Jack Daniel's last night and got sick as hell. That isn't 'nothing,' is it?"

"I guess not. Are you coming home?"

A plaintive note in his son's voice suggested Michael was close to crying. Immediately, Joe felt weepy himself. He said,

"I dunno yet. Sure. Probably. That's why I gotta talk to your mother. What's Heather doing in there, reading her her constitutional rights?"

"Mommy's awake, but she just ran into the bathroom."

Oh Lord! The universe, a relatively stable conglomeration of potentially volatile atoms for eleventy (as Heather would say) billion years, had chosen the last three days in which to finally collapse.

Michael asked, "Where are you, Daddy? Are you over at her house?"

"'Her'? I'm in Ralph's office on the plaza, where do you think I am?"

An embarrassed, choking silence bristled on the other end.

Joe said, "What's this about shooting a chickadee?"

"It wasn't a chickadee. Heather don't know shit."

"She 'doesn't' know shit."

"I know. It was actually—"

"'Doesn't,'" Joe interrupted. "Don't say 'don't' know shit, the proper word is 'doesn't' know shit."

"Oh, all right."

"Well, say it."

"Say what?" He was totally confused.

"Say 'doesn't.'"

"Doesn't."

For some insane reason over which he had no control, Michael's thickness made Joe furious; he could barely contain his temper. "The goddam sentence, Michael, should have been, 'She doesn't know shit!'"

Sounding like something from a gloom-riddled nether region beyond the Styx, Heidi's voice came over the line. "*Who* doesn't know shit? Me? What did you call up for, Joey, to rub salt in our wounds?"

"I was talking to Michael. He acts like good grammar is illegal. How come they aren't in school? You figured it was more educational to stay home and kill chickadees and watch Mommy vomit?"

"It wasn't a chickadee, it was a stupid English sparrow."

"Well, who gave him a license to terrorize nature with his BB gun? As soon as I leave the premises for ten minutes, suddenly there's a total breakdown in discipline, and it's open season on every little animal in the valley?"

"He's upset, Joey. When he shot the bird I asked him how

come, and he said he just felt like killing things. Frankly, I don't blame him. I feel like killing things myself, right now."

"I don't feel so hot either."

"Oh, the poor widdle icky-tums. Did you stop a bullet or something in that bus-station shootout last night?"

"No, but I could have."

"Don't you mean 'should' have?"

"You don't have to be totally nasty. Aren't things tough enough without the Cleopatra act?"

"What's that supposed to mean?"

"What's what supposed to mean?"

"'The Cleopatra act'? It's just another of your meaningless references to some kind of historical or glamorous thing or person or metaphor that's supposed to gloss over the fact you have nothing relevant to say. Not only that, but how in God's name can you pimp around accusing Michael of immorality, when you're creeping through gunfights trying to steal a hundred thousand dollars worth of illegal cocaine. Some gall!"

Joe waited a beat before asking, "You through?"

"I don't know. Give me a minute. . . ."

"It doesn't interest you, I don't suppose, that last night I actually wound up with the stuff Peter sent, does it?"

"Isn't that a double negative? 'It doesn't,' and 'I don't suppose,' and 'does it,' all in the same sentence?"

"Ha ha."

"Well, I can't believe your cruelty, Joey! Why don't you dance on over here and pour boiling oil on the heads of your two little babies? Because when you left yesterday you hadn't quite finished the job!"

"Heidi, if we tear each other apart like this we won't get anywhere."

"Where are we going?"

"I don't know. That's why I called. I mean, it's stupid to stay apart like this. The whole thing started as a simple accident. . . ."

"Oh no you don't! As long as you're sleeping with that mongoose, I sure as hell don't want you near my house, my bed, or hanging out around my children."

"In case you forgot, they're my children also."

"Oh, excuse me. Of course. Why don't you come over and pick them up, then, and lead them over to Miss Spiritual America's place, and let them watch the two of you doing your celestial carnal act?"

"Heidi, what is the matter with you?"

"I'm pissed. Didn't you ever hear that expression, 'Hell's got no fury like a woman scorned?'"

Incredibly, he heard himself saying, "'Hell *hath* no fury like a woman scorned.'"

"What did you say?"

"Hell 'hath.' Listen—"

"No, wait a minute. What were you doing, *correcting* me?"

"It's not important. Really. Now listen—"

"No, stop. I want to get this straight. You were correcting me, weren't you? 'Hell *hath* no fury like a woman scorned'— is that it? I hope so, Joey. I really don't want to have any imperfections that might cause you to look askance at me or—"

"Stop!" he hollered. "Didn't you hear me? I got the coke! What am I supposed to do next?"

"Shove it up your ass, Frankenstein!"

In a rage, gasping for air yet once again, Joe slammed down the instrument, waking Diana.

"Hey," she muttered groggily. "Take it easy." Closing her eyes, then, she smiled and resumed snoring.

The phone jangled: Joe jumped a mile. "Hello?"

The Marlene Dietrich of the Perry Kahn Subdivision #4 unleashed her tantalizingly breathy salutation: "Hi..."

"Who's this?"

"What do you mean, 'Who's this'? It's me."

"Who's—oh. You. What are you...how did you..."

"I called the Prince of Whales. Darlene gave me this number. How are you?"

"Fine, wonderful. Hey Nancy—"

"I miss you. I'm still glowing all over...."

"Look, I'm sorry, I'm waiting for an important call, I'll talk to you later."

"Anything wrong?"

"No, everything's fine. Hunky-dory squared. It's just things are also a little, you know, complicated. I mean, in my life right now there's a certain amount of sturm and drang going down. Like for starters, yesterday Michael shot a chickadee."

"Do you have pills? Are you breathing okay?"

Joe realized that inside of perhaps a week her equanimity would drive him either insane or to murder.

"I'm sorry, Nancy, I got to hang up. Good-bye. . . ."

Diana opened one eye, croaking, "Who was that?"

"Jimmy Carter."

"Oh." Adjusting her diving weights, she floated under again. Her face was pink from sleep. Flushed, warm, and innocent, she seemed an angelic little bum. Enormous and tragic feelings of love moved Joe for a second. They could hijack a plane to Cuba together. Or else scurry away from Chamisaville under cover of darkest night, buy a cozy farm up around Bozeman, Montana, and spend the rest of their days trout fishing on the Bitterroot River.

Joe found his dilemma hard to believe. Played by Ray Milland, he could see himself slumped over a shiny mahogany bar in his own *Lost Weekend*, a burnt-out case before forty. Incredible to reflect that only forty-eight hours ago he had been halfway certain that they could convert the drug deal, buy the land, and gloat (as a family) over a future thus assured.

Instead, with the unsparing brutality of a shtetl pogrom, everything seemed to be collapsing. It only remained for him to bumble into a life sentence while trying to unload the coke, and the tragic farce would be complete!

Joe sighed loudly. The paragraph on the typing paper in the machine before him focused. After contemplating it for a moment, he decided to complete the sentence which began "In a cage on the nearby table the myna bird . . ." Three minutes later he wrote: ". . . was caught in a paroxysm of heinous and deleterious anticommunism that threatened to cauterize the only friendship it had ever had."

"Are you okay?" Solicitously, Diana sat up, circling arms around her knees. She rested her chin on her arms. "You don't look so hot."

"Oh, I feel like a million dollars."

"Bullshit."

It was impossible to face Diana. Joe harbored a mixture of hostility and sexual attraction for her. And fear, also. What did she want? Kicked out of her own digs, had she attached herself to him like a waifling puppy?

Joe said, "Now that you have no place to stay, what will you do?"

"I'm not worried. I never expected anything better. I have friends. I'll get along just fine."

"How come you came to Chamisaville in the first place?"

"I just drifted here with a guy. He made jewelry and wore a turquoise turban. Then he split and I stayed. I lived with a couple of girls for a while—Josie and Patty. But they were crazy. Patty was only sixteen and pregnant: she'd been up at Alexander's Ragtime Crash Pad. Josie was eighteen—she came here from Santa Cruz with a People's Templer who ditched. She was into booze, and any kind of dope, and boys. The house was like the men's restroom at a football game, only instead of lining up for the urinals, they were lining up for Josie. She hated it, but said it was punishment because in a former life she had been an Egyptian gypsy who had stolen an emerald goblet from King Tut's tomb. One night she cut her wrists and ran up to the plaza covered with blood and singing 'money can't buy you love'—the Beatles' song. About that time I got it on with Angel. It was a little better than the house with Josie and Patty, but not much. Angel gets off on being mean. In his previous incarnation, by the way, he claims to have been a mild-mannered Negro clerk in Bloomington, Indiana, who'd been unjustly imprisoned for embezzlement by a jealous Caucasian lover who happened to be the local DA, and he was stabbed to death in jail by a Communist faggot. So this time around he's determined not to let anybody make any moves on him, not ever. And I must say he's certainly a surly son of a bitch."

"But I mean, why did you come *here*? What did you *want*?"

"'Want'?" She shrugged. "An alternate life-style? Pie in the sky? I don't know. Adventure?" She smiled wistfully. "I had some friends back in Indiana who said Chamisaville was far-out."

"But what do you want to be when you grow up?"

She uncorked her captivating lustrous smile. "It doesn't matter. Whatever happens, I'll adjust. You only make yourself miserable messing around with a lot of phony goals."

"What about marriage? Kids?"

"Someday I might have a kid. But I'll never get married. For sure, I won't worry myself sick wondering how my life is gonna turn out."

"You're depressing me."

Standing, she walked behind him, put her arms around his neck, and touched her lips to his earlobe, imparting a delicate kiss. "I'm okay, Joe—honest. I'm a pretty tough cookie and

I like my life. Don't shed any tears for this lady. Save them for yourself."

Reaching up, Joe took her hand. "Why do you say that?"

"Well, you seem like a semifragile soul. You're old-fashioned, also hip, and you don't believe in either one."

"Screw you. Let's get out of here."

"Where are we going?"

"I don't know about you, but I'm heading out to Tribby's castle. I have to talk with Heidi and see my kids. Then—I dunno. I need a place to stay. I have to move this coke. . . ."

"I own a tent."

"So what?"

"Maybe you would let me pitch it on your land for a while?"

"It isn't my land yet."

"But you put up the earnest money."

"Granted. But it might look funny. . . ."

"To who?"

"Oh, who cares anymore? You're welcome to try. Just ask the old man—Eloy Irribarren—for permission, okay?"

"Hey, thanks." She gave him another hug, another sweet kiss. "You're a gentleman and a scholar, Joe Miniver."

"In my previous incarnation they called me Mr. Big."

"Don't beshry. . . ."

She was gone, leaving him alone again and terrified of this Brave New World into which he had floundered, a swingler's madhouse with liberty, if not justice, for all. Though Joe started by thinking about Heidi and the kids, he wound up, split seconds later, fantasizing about Diana in bed. Her white thighs considerably muffled his hearing; her fingers plucked at his lips; she smelled like snow when it was still falling. Her cheeks were like unutterably soft ice. Her heavy breasts fell into his hands, and he molded them with trembling fingers into near-bursting happy globes. The phone rang, and without thinking he answered.

Nancy Ryan said, "Will you be home for dinner tonight?"

"Will I be *where* for *what*?"

⊷ട

When he pedaled as surreptitiously as possible past their lair, Mimsy and Tuckums remained beneath the Laidlaw pickup, nursing their broken ribs, punctured lungs, and dreams of revenge. Joe heard a disheartened snarl and caught an ambiguous glower from the darkness under there. Assailed by guilt, he also gave them the finger, wondering why he had never summoned the guts in his simpering lifetime to punt an animal—a child, a wife, an enemy—as had Bertram Laidlaw yesterday. No matter how they misbehaved, Joe's kids would never know the humiliation of being battered children. No matter how she taunted and tormented him, Heidi would never be able even remotely to conceive of what it was like to be an abused and battered spouse. Often Joe wished he could liberate the King Kong inside his fumbling, semicompassionate, quasi-gentle body. CIRCUS ELEPHANT GOES AMOK, TRAMPLES WORLD-FAMOUS CUB SCOUT! The release offered by murder, maiming, and other *m*-words (marauding, maliciousness, and malevolence to name a few) had to be wonderful. He admired the ability, nay, the passion, of a Nikita Smatterling, who could, in defense of his principles (and his child), stick the snout of a loaded .38 into the plump belly of such a goon as Ephraim Bonatelli and pull the trigger. My God, what a purge! Dig those lurid headlines! Flee those police dragnets! "Using a machine gun borrowed from a black disc jockey, Joe Miniver, age thirty-eight, a Caucasian drug kingpin, went on a rampage last night. After blasting his wife and kiddies while they were watching a 'Kojak' television program, Mr. Miniver assassinated his paramour, one Nancy Ryan, her child Bradley, and the Ryans' pet monkey, Sasha. Then, leaving a swath of death and destruction across Chamisa County, Mr. Miniver escaped on foot into the thickly forested Midnight Mountains. . . ."

"*Mr*. Miniver!" Jesus H. Effing Et Cetera! As Don Adams, playing secret agent Maxwell Smart on the old "Get Smart" TV show, might have said: "Aha, it's the old *New York Times* 'Mr' So-and-So trick!"

What was behind such formal reverence for propriety? "Then, having razed, burned, pillaged, and raped Poland, Latvia, Estonia, Slovakia, Rumania, Hungary, and other assorted countries, *Mr*. Hitler gassed six million Jews." "From his perch in the Texas tower, *Mr*. Whitman then proceeded to kill everybody he could get in his telescopic sights."

Joe swerved to avoid squashing a tarantula, and this action just may have saved his life. For as he prepared to hang a right off 240 in the direction of Eloy Irribarren's place, there was a roar and a screech of underinflated rubber heralding the approach of a kamikaze-like assassin. A van hurtled by Joe, skidding sideways, even before he realized he was under attack. Hot exhaust scorched his pantleg, and a hollow *whump!*—as if he had actually been creamed broadside—shocked the air. Through a boil of dust and pebbles, as he tipped over, Joe recognized the Chicken River Funky Pie vehicle. Spinning tires whined, pelting Joe with more dirt and gravel; then the panicked van clattered off, bucking down the road doing eighty. Joe had caught no glimpse of a driver.

Standing, he brushed himself off, amazed, once the dust had dissipated, at how silent the moment became. Benevolent sunshine warmed his earlobes; no noise tarried; tree leaves shivered mutely in a teasing breeze. He could have been killed, but the day remained uneventful, soporific, sensual.

It had happened so quickly, Joe's heart wasn't even drumming loudly. In fact, maybe the van's driver had meant no harm: perhaps he or she had simply applied the brakes suddenly—having forgotten to bring their shopping list—and turned around. . . .

A kingfisher, perched on a telephone wire, eyed the Pueblo River water. Then a butterfly landed on a cornflower.

Joe stopped and dismounted in order to savor the walk along Eloy's front field. Although he knew it was emotionally dangerous to do so (given that he was far from owning the little farm), Joe nevertheless felt—each time he ambled slowly up the potholed access road—as if he were further claiming this small, beautiful territory for himself, his family, his heirs. The longer he allowed trees, leaves, last autumn's dry weeds, and driveway rocks to burn into his memory, the more they became his, acquiring a slightly Miniveresque personality because of the sensibilities he washed them in, recreating their uniqueness in himself.

Today, however, three men in the front field marred the serenity of this vision. Nikita Smatterling, Skipper Nuzum, and . . . Scott Harrison? Joe did a double take. Nikita waved; his stentorian voice boomed: "Hello, Joe!"

"What are you guys doing?" Joe flushed like a spiteful owner, wanting to kick them off his property. The poison of their presence made his stomach clench.

"Just getting the lay of the land for Thursday," Nikita responded. He said something to Skipper Nuzum, who swept his hand obscenely through the air, indicating a portion of the pasture in a way that seemed to claim it forever in the name of the Forces of Evil. Joe's heart sailed into his mouth, clammy perspiration burst from every pore. He knew Eloy had rented the site to the Simian Foundation for the Hanuman unveiling. But seeing those three clustered together was like coming across maggots on the corpse of a virgin.

Joe shuddered and gazed elsewhere.

All his ribs mewling plaintively, gaunt Geronimo limped slowly toward the driveway. He looked like a goofy police artist's composite sketch: mule ears, basset-hound eyes, ostrich legs, the gait of a sorely dismayed pole-vaulter. If ever a horse resembled a bad joke, this one had to be the quintessential punch line. Still, a flicker of alertness made intelligent the droopy eyes. The flabby velvet nostrils dilated curiously, picking up the Miniver scent. Or perhaps its odor detector was threading delicately through currents of horse dung, alfalfa pollen, green leaves, and apple trees, searching for the aroma of sugar cubes. At the fence, reeking of pathos—or was it bathos?—the horse snorted feebly. Don't throw us out, the animal seemed to be saying, referring not only to itself, but to its master, Eloy Irribarren, and all the other animals. We have no place to go. We are old, and should have been venerated in our old age. Instead, we're alone, cast out, at the mercy of the financial tides.

Moved to attempt communication, Joe touched Geronimo. He cupped the furry nose, and felt hot breath against his palm. Geronimo twitched one ear, but stood perfectly still, eyes closed. A piece of Joe's inner being donned a plumed helmet, adjusted its tin gauntlets, and galloped down his arm to joust with the sensitivities of the thirty-six-year-old beast: the world equinely perceived. Breezes slowed, the wind melted instead of blowing, nature adopted its lackadaisical bluff. Leaves detached from the mighty cottonwoods voyaged simplistically on the poignant ether, taking forever to settle atop life's unending banquet (for a horse).

Immense sadness, triggered by the three background men, flooded Joe's body. There was too much to lose in life, including life itself—it seemed unbearable. How could he live without his children, assimilating that emptiness, accepting the irrevocable mistake, becoming used to the absence of his gangly, wiseass daughter's body in his borning bed? Threats to the very survival of the planet were psychic tremors traveling up through earthworms, pebbles, and timothy roots into the unshod hooves of a derelict caballo; they coursed through Geronimo's meat, muscle, and blood to his lungs, then hitched a ride on the hot breath that arrived eventually in Joe's palm, transmitting to him an immense forlorn apprehension that everything he considered precious might be lost tomorrow, no matter how he abetted, or abjured, the process. The Amazon Basin, bigger than Australia, containing one-third the earth's forests, a fifth of its water, and generating half the photosynthesized oxygen, was no longer a vacant wilderness. In fact, if current development by the Brazilian government continued, it would be a desert by the year 2002. Elephants and lions would be extinct before Michael and Heather were old enough to vote. In Waterloo, Iowa, people were finding ortho nitroaniline—a bladder-cancer-causer—in their drinking water. All across the nation, Americans were inadvertently guzzling arsenic, trichloroethane, and 2,4-5 T, to name not even a few. In Italy, terrified of kidnappers, the kinds of people who fostered such pernicious chemicals were investing so heavily in bulletproof vests that stores couldn't keep them in stock. All across the Yankee homeland, every day in every way, murder was the name of the game. In Sausalito, a fifteen-year-old flower child is found wandering nude (having been raped), both her arms hacked off below the elbows by a man with an ax. In Ypsilanti, a man kills two people in the parking lot of a saloon, offs somebody else in a tool-and-die shop, goes home, shoots his mother, then executes his father and stuffs the body in a freezer. In New York, a quiet man, exasperated because his wife had a job and he didn't, beats his spouse to death, then methodically and fatally bludgeons one crippled offspring, another deaf, blind, and mute son, and finally an adopted daughter, after which he sticks his head in an oven, trying to commit suicide. "Bob always seemed like a sweet guy, a marshmallow," said a neighbor. "But there was a lot going on inside his head." Babies in Third World countries suffered severe malnutrition from drinking watered-down American instant formulas their mothers couldn't afford in the first place. And the price of cocaine was 120 bucks a gram. *Progress*, the slogan had been saying for years, *is our most important product*.

Geronimo whinnied softly, shifted slightly. Clouds overhead sat in the sky like deaf-and-dumb children on their haunches laconically observing ants. Swollen with grief, Joe wondered if he could make it through the next ten minutes. Bitter tears welled—my God, after so many years without sobbing, his waters had finally burst! He had a great humble urge to race home and embrace Heidi and the kids, squeezing them tightly against his bosom, protecting them as he swore undying love. His emotions couldn't sit still for a minute. It seemed as if every tree within eyesight would evaporate when darkness slipped over the mountains and glided across the plain, creating a snakelike fantasy of night. Oh, that whirlwind of death was about, clobbering anything that twitched or peeped!

Frightened, excited, and stymied, Joe said, "Geronimo, you're a pathetic excuse for a hayburner." Taking his hand away, he pushed his bicycle up the driveway. Geese honked as he approached; Sweetie Pie, Daffodil, and their irritating ilk bounced and cavorted, yippety-yapping. Tom turkeys puffed out their chests and thumped menacingly. A peacock screeched and cats meowed.

Yet something was wrong. Too strong an air of inactivity permeated the little adobe ruin. He's dead, Joe thought instantly, neck hairs prickling. Things weren't convoluted enough, now he had an eighty-three-year-old corpse on his hands!

Petulant dismay oozed into his body as he neared the house. If Eloy was dead, even if Joe could raise the cash by next Monday it would do him no good—he'd be out of the game. The Scott Harrisons, Nikita Smatterlings, and First State People's Jugs would fight over this raggedy-ass piece of earth until nothing remained except Holistic Laundromats, Universal Life bungalow monasteries, and retirement condominiums.

Duke, the immortal wonderdog, opened one eye halfway, focusing the bleached pupil on Joe.

Trying to erase his fear with false joviality, Joe said, "Hiya, Dukie—how's the old pup? Fit as a fiddle and bopping with all the bitches?"

Releasing a long, slow exhalation, Duke let his eyelid droop closed again. Joe figured he breathed only once every seventeen minutes. In fact, Duke had probably died two years ago, but some bizarre canine instinct, inherited from a race of animals used to surviving under adverse conditions, had kept him going, even if—albeit—with the metabolism of a hibernating frog.

Joe knocked on the door. Awaiting a reply, he gazed around,

surveying the property, the world, the sunshiny and impassive weather, the lazybones clouds and the lumbering magpies. Quite consciously, he sucked in a final moment of tranquillity, prior to entering the shack and finding the old man twisted grotesquely halfway out of the bed, drenched in his own blood and vomit, his last excruciatingly painful doomsday paroxysm evident in his horribly glassy eyeballs.

Joe knocked again. Silence seeped back at him through the keyhole like a malevolent genie. "Just when everything was going so good," Joe ridiculed out loud, "*this* had to happen."

For good measure, allowing the body in there ample time to resurrect itself and bid him enter, Joe knocked a third time, banging his knuckles hard enough (he grimly and fervently hoped) to waken the dead.

What's the absolute of zero—zilch squared? Joe strained his ears, trying to will a chirrup from the deadly vacuum behind the door.

Had the head been gnawed off by rats? Would Eloy's bowels have loosened, unleashing heaps of noisome defecation? Joe turned the handle: the door wasn't locked; it opened an inch. Then stealthily, feeling sick to his stomach, careful not to make a sound, he pulled it back closed.

Ghastly premonitions had his hair standing on end. Duke's slow sighing—his second breath in the past five minutes—came so unexpectedly that Joe jumped.

One of these days, he could hear Heidi vituperating at him, *you're gonna wake up dead*. By making an offer the sick old geezer couldn't afford to refuse, Joe had partially captured this delectable chunk of virgin earth, causing Eloy Irribarren, a far more noble human entity than ninety-nine percent of the Comic Cookies (including—let's not be stingy in assessing guilt—Joe Miniver himself) pizzafying this valley, to die of a broken heart.

Well, maybe not quite yet. When Eloy opened the door, saying "Oh, hello there," Joe nearly did a backflip. "Hope you haven't been waiting for long," the old man said. "I'm a little deaf. And I move kinda slow, anyway."

In his hands, Eloy held an old, octagon barrel, lever-action .30-.30. An ancient, yet freshly oiled, leather bandolier for holding rifle cartridges was draped over one shoulder. Around his waist was a simple gunbelt and holster. A wood-handled, double-action, old-fashioned revolver, probably a .38, rode snugly in the holster.

Joe said, "What's with the hardware—you going hunting?"

"Hunting for money." A twinkle lighted up his cool green eyes.

"I'm not sure I follow."

"You'll excuse me if I speak frankly, then?"

"Of course."

"I'm not sure how to put this—maybe I better just say it out straight."

"That's the only way." A chill spread up from Joe's groin, ruffling his body, causing a cold sweat.

"Bueno. My understanding, then, is that you won't have the money for my land by next Monday's closing. As I interpret it you had hoped to raise the cash by selling a certain item which arrived on yesterday's bus. However, apparently last night that item was removed from the depot by force, and is now in the hands of others. That can only mean that I am now at the mercy of my creditors, a situation I had hoped to avoid."

Joe said, "No, you don't understand—a miracle happened. I wound up with the coke."

"Oh."

"The only problem is that the guy who was supposed to help us market it never showed." Joe waved his hands helplessly. "So I'm not quite sure how to begin. . . ."

"Then maybe I should go ahead with my own plans."

"I don't follow."

"I'm gonna rob the bank."

"But that's crazy!"

"Why?"

"Well, I, um . . ." Joe fumfered. "I mean, you're what, eighty-three years old? They have guards. And seeing-eye cameras. That bank dick, Tom Yard, he's nuts—he'll shoot to kill. And because you're the only Chicano left in the valley they'll know immediately . . ."

"I'll wear a monkey mask and a Hanuman T-shirt. Like all those people involved in the depot fracas last night."

"But those guys were insane!"

"Who in this town, these days, isn't?" Eloy smiled sheepishly.

Joe hung his head. "Look, I'll admit I'm ashamed of what I'm doing. By nature I am not a drug pusher. But I just ran out of options."

"These are hard times; we're all desperate. Who worries

about morality anymore? My morality is my geese, and that cottonwood tree, and my piglets. I think I would kill human beings to ensure their existence. Only animals and flowers are moral these days."

Joe said, "Somebody actually fired a gun at me last night."

"But they missed, thank God."

"They could have killed me, though. And so could somebody plug you if you try to rob the bank."

A trifle shyly, ashamed of his own bravado, Eloy said, "When you need money you make a withdrawal."

"At least wait until I try to pass the coke."

"Isn't that dangerous? Aren't they always mangling hippies who deal drugs?"

"'Mangling'?" Joe gulped. Then he thought a moment, and said, "On second thought, maybe we could rob the bank together. You're an old man. I might come in handy."

"It would be dangerous," Eloy said quietly. "You're too young to risk such dangers."

"I have to risk them one way or another," Joe said melodramatically. "I've got nothing to lose. Plus I figure if I wasn't killed last night, I'll probably live to be ninety."

"Then tomorrow we rob the bank?"

"Tomorrow?" Joe blanched. "That's too soon. First you have to case the joint. Then you make a plan. Suppose it's a timed vault? You have to coordinate everything. How were you planning to do it?"

"Walk in, point my gun at a teller, and demand the dinero. I'm not a complicated man."

"That's no good. You have to smoke out possible stumbling blocks and make contingency plans. Study the bank, assess the tellers. What are the guards' habits? How do we neutralize bank patrons once we announce it's a holdup? Finally, we have to make sure we can get all the money we need in a single heist so we don't have to return for more."

"In the old days around here, people just walked into the bank, made a threat, and filled a burlap sack with greenbacks."

"That was the old days. Today is a whole new ball game. We might want to steal certain securities instead of cash. Or maybe stock options or certificates of deposit. Should we rob the place in broad daylight, or blast our way into the night-deposit vault early Sunday morning after all the bars have dumped in their weekend receipts?"

Eloy said, "I'm tired of all these modern complexities."

Joe admitted, "Me too."

"What will you do with your drugs if we rob a bank?"

"I'll try to unload that first. I think the bank should be our backup scam."

"When should we plan the robbery?"

"I don't know. I'll have to think...."

"Think fast," Eloy said somberly. "It's already Monday."

"Don't worry, I got the fastest brain in the West."

But already he could see the headlines:

OLD MAN AND SPASTIC SIDEKICK BUNGLE BANK JOB! GETAWAY
CAR HAS FLAT TIRE! INEPT PAIR NABBED WITH $17.00 TAKE!

Eloy said, "It's hot out here. Why don't you come inside for a minute? I can offer you a beer."

The old-fashioned cluttered darkness smelled musty and cool—and of apples and autumn. It enveloped Joe in a reverence he associated with classic daguerreotypes. Standing quietly in the main room, he glanced around while Eloy went in back to fetch their drinks. Everything in the neat hodgepodge glowed with a wonderful warmth. Colorful weathered statues of various saints occupied several nichos carved into the thick mud walls: Joe recognized only San Ysidro, the farmer's patron, with his plow cart and a silver fish on a thin thread in one hand. The walls were largely obscured behind photographs, some in black dime-store frames, others contained by crude hand-tooled tin frames that had a primitive beauty. Joe pinpointed a young Eloy in a cowboy hat and chaps beside a skitterish horse. A fiftieth-wedding-anniversary picture had been taken most recently. In others, family members and friends posed self-consciously with wives, husbands, offspring, 4-H animals, school classes. One little girl, at least thirty years ago, seemed unbearably precious in a Communion outfit. Another rascally barefoot kid, missing teeth, wearing bib overalls, grinned obnoxiously beside a huge, beribboned county-fair pumpkin.

An intricate colcha embroidery lay over a puffy, rainbow-colored patchwork quilt on the bulky double bed. Two candles in brass holders were silhouetted behind gauzy white curtains on a window ledge. A kerosene lamp with a smoky chimney stood on the simple hand-hewn table where a lowcut cardboard tray held a dozen three-inch-high tomato plants. On one wall a crinkled rattlesnake belt, a thickly oiled leather bridle, and red chile and chico ristras hung beside shelves that contained old canning jars filled with dried fruits—apples, apricots, pears. A pistol in a handcrafted leather gunbelt dangled from a wooden peg. In two ceramic crocks on the floor under the table, wine—probably plum in one, chokecherry in the other—was fermenting. The odor palpitated within the autumn atmosphere of the tranquil, vestigial room.

Eloy returned, loosening the cap on the beer; the other was tucked beneath his arm.

"It's not icy," he apologized. "Three years ago I had them cut off the electricity. It surprised me how much better I felt at once in the kerosene glow and candlelight."

"I like your house a lot."

"So do I. It fits like a shell. But sometimes I worry, because the past is over—qué no? When the bitterness takes over my body, I want to throw the saints in the garbage can, tear the pictures off my walls, and reinstall electricity. Sometimes the sorrow squeezes my heart, causing a pain not even a hundred Alka-Seltzers could cure. Then I want to order myself to grow up. 'Get modern, Eloy. Shed your outdated skin. Learn to survive in a new age. Accept a different magic.' I should buy a suit and take a jet ride to New York City—I've never been in a plane. That way, I think I might live longer. But when push comes to shove, I can't change. So this valley, now, is killing me. Every day, since Teresita ran away and died, Chamisaville is a knife in my stomach, causing a terrible pain with each nasty little jerk."

What could he say? Joe toed the edge of a rag rug, eyes avoiding Eloy. The floor was spotless: despite busy surroundings and the plethora of old mementos, everything was clean.

"Look here." Eloy sat on the edge of his bed. "This is a tape recorder." He lifted it off the night table: a wire stretching from the instrument disappeared under his pillow: he removed a mike-shaped speaker.

"The state library loans these out to old people in their education programs. You can learn while you sleep. I have tapes on mathematics, American history, psychology, sociology. I can't listen while I'm awake—they befuddle me. But over the years they have reached me a little while I'm dreaming."

With a chagrined chuckle, he replaced the recorder on the night stand. Joe noticed that whatever Eloy touched—even his beer bottle—he handled with respect.

"Well, I'm just an old fuddy-duddy, I guess." Eloy took a short tug. "And I guess you can't teach an old perro new tricks."

Silence. To get them on a less uncomfortable track, Joe called Eloy's attention to a faded color photograph of a small adobe house whose outside walls were decorated with pretty murals within which cows grazed, magpies floated, and the Virgin of Guadalupe sparkled sweetly.

"That house is beautiful. Who does it belong to?"

"Years ago—way back at the start of the Great Depression when the hot springs were first discovered and the tourist industry began to transform this valley, many local people were intoxicated with the promise and adventure offered by progress, American-style. And when they first received real cash from working in the recreation and development industry, it was a fad among some folks to have muralists decorate their houses. At one time we had dozens of such dwellings, and many were very lovely. But about fifteen years ago they began to disappear. The original owners sold out, and the new patrons were embarrassed by the childlike and religious pictures defacing their homes. So they painted or plastered them over, and pretty soon most of the murals were gone. My son Emilio was an amateur photographer: he took that photo of Filiberto Tafoya's residence, the last surviving painted house in the valley. Which they knocked down last year to make way for a Sonic Burger."

Eloy sighed and giggled apologetically. "Excuse me, I'm beginning to sound like an incarnation of La Sebastiana."

"What's that?"

"Death."

Joe said, "This must once have been a very attractive valley."

"It still is, in a way. But before, it was our home. For better or worse, it belonged to the people who lived here. I'm not saying we were great saints or especially compassionate people. We got drunk, and poisoned the air with malicious mitotes and perpetuated our share of ugly movidas and thoughtless chingazos. But what we had that was very valuable was a sense of identity and community. We were a part of this home that had a continuity of almost four hundred years—much longer for the Indians at the Pueblo, of course. We were caretakers of the land, like our abuelos and our bisabuelos before them. The land and the people belonged to each other. The mountains and vegas lived in our hearts instead of our pocketbooks. Then they discovered the hot springs and the development began. At first we were excited to have hard cash in the valley. It promised so many good times and fabulous adventures ahead. We all embarked on a magic journey together into the American dream. Radios, automobiles, an airport, motels and art galleries and swimming pools. . . ."

Pausing, Eloy wiped a dash of foam off his upper lip.

"Nobody realized at first they would take it away from us. Nobody understood concepts like 'free enterprise,' and 'competition,' and 'looking out for number one.' Our survival on the land had always depended on mutual aid. My well-being and your well-being were interwoven. We couldn't get along without each other. But then . . ."

Eloy shook his head. And Joe sat at the table, waiting.

"You see, all of a sudden the survival rules changed. Overnight. Everything, including the souls of the *plebe*, were up for sale. Most of us couldn't adapt fast enough, and were rubbed out in the hurricane. The new rules made no sense. Traditional loyalties meant nothing. A people accustomed to counting on each other were suddenly pitted against each other. Most of us never had a chance. And now, finally, I guess it's over. The character of my home is different. Nobody has—what's the word?—*intimate*, I think. Nobody has an intimate stake in the land. People come and go, buying and selling. For three hundred years, an adobe house probably stayed within the same family—but in the last decade it may have had five or six different owners. Life here has become a . . . commodity? Yes. People, alfalfa fields, even the mountains, it seems, change hands overnight. The newcomers have few true loyalties to Chamisa Valley traditions. A selfish and self-indulgent God rules the present; and the future is entirely out of focus."

Eloy stopped, swirled the last drops of beer in his bottle, then swigged them noisily.

"Excuse me for giving a lecture. I'm only a retired farmer—qué no? I am different from many of my extinct compadres because I understood the process. I studied it for years and fought it as the means to survival. And now I have the distinction of being the last old geezer to fall. Me and my horse, Geronimo."

Laughing in a deprecating manner, Eloy stood up and gestured with the empty bottle. "We used to save glass bottles—
they were precious. We refilled them time and again for years.
Now they throw them in fields to maim horses, or smash them
on roads to puncture tires. . . ."

Joe said, "Listen, I better get going. I promised Heidi and
the kids . . ."

"You're right to run, Joe Miniver. I even bore myself when
I fall into this mood. But thanks for the loan of your ears. . . ."

~§

          Departing the nineteenth century, Joe slalomed ap-
proximately three hundred yards through the joggers before
being hit broadside by the future. At a beep to his rear, he
swerved onto the shoulder. A diesel Mercedes parked beside
his bicycle, and, leaning over to open the passengerside window, Skipper Nuzum, in all his leather and turquoise splendor,
hailed him in a patronizing, authoritative accent that gave an
order while asking a question:

"Hey there, Joe—got a minute?"

A chill blast of air-conditioned luxury, coupled with jarring
rock from the tape deck, pelted Joe's face: his stomach churned.
Here it came, round sixteen in the Eternity Junction sweepstakes!

"Sure," he replied jovially. "I'm just a wayfaring troubador,
out on a relaxing cruise—shoot."

"I hope nobody has to go that far." Skipper shouted to be
heard over the jarring music he could have quelled with a mere
flick. His grin was reminiscent of those old Cobey Dallas eyes.
Wide and healthy and lacking any connection to the real thing.

But who was Joe to quibble over labial semantics?

"I've been meaning to speak to you in private, partner.
You're a hard man to pin down."

"I figure it's better to be a moving, rather than a stationary,
target," Joe joked, wondering who had invented this particular
repartee.

"That's not funny, man. You don't seem to realize the nature
of the position in which you are."

In which I are? Joe tried, and failed, to meet Skipper's
large, sad eyes. He must have garnered millions, back in L.A.,
disarming the opposition with those morose intimations of

internal weakness and poetry. His shaggy moustache completed the look of an ascetic, sincere, fuddled, almost cuddly, almost bear of a man. But then the smile hit—bright, flashy, somehow totally intransitive, and his face matured, exuding a bold and almost frightening confidence. He must have parlayed it into the incredibly ample perks of a true California gunslinger, intimidating by always keeping others off-balance. All the moves, in Skipper's lexicon, were his to make first, and control absolutely.

"I've been hearing all sorts of strange tales on the grapevine," he barked, one of those space-age geeks, apparently, who felt more comfortable, and domineering, yelling at his foes through the blare of a radio, the babble of a loud tube. A syndrome not unlike that of folks who must sleep with the lights on? Joe wondered.

"Such as . . . ?" he said aloud.

"I understand that you and a friend from Palermo broke into the bus station last night and ran off with a little item worth a bundle that belongs to Ray Verboten."

Calmly, though his heart thundered, Joe said, "Number one—I have no friends from Palermo, Skipper. Number two— we didn't 'break into' the bus station last night. Number three— it doesn't belong to Ray Verboten, it belongs to me."

"I see." Skipper barely blinked. "Now here's my proposition, Joe—and listen carefully, I'm a busy man, I don't want to repeat it. I happen to know there's no way you can legally wrest that land from Eloy Irribabble. Scott Harrison has a more legitimate claim, the First State People's Jug could foreclose tomorrow, I could snap my fingers if I wanted, buy up all the promissories by five o'clock this evening, and own it fair and square. But I'm a reasonable man, and I take it you are also. No need for anybody's feathers to be unduly ruffled. I mean, hey, I talked to Nikita Smatterling earlier, and he was fit to be tied. All his life he worked hard to find the right place for a permanent Hanuman shrine, and now look how bollixed the supposedly straightforward negotiations have become. To make matters worse, I understand Joseph Bonatelli might even launch a power play, either through his bank or on his own—God forbid—out of spite because you imported that little item on the bus without his okay."

Hail Mary! Joe thought: at least somebody was cautious enough to employ a euphemism for the cocaine!

"So it makes no sense, Joe. Why do you want the wrath of potentates hanging over your head? It's a one-way path to perdition when you embark upon the black-market packaging and distribution of things such as that item you possess. Suddenly, nobody likes you, everybody grows especially defensive, and very greedy. It'll be one of the great races of the year to see who nails you first—the long arm of Eddie Semmelweis, the blunt club of Ray's enforcers, or the icy inimicable cruelty of the Tarantula's wrath. I'm scared for you, Joe—honest. All of us who like you are terrified. The puddle into which you've jumped is bottomless."

Into which I've jumped? Icy inimicable cruelty? Wouldn't Heidi love to sink her choppers into *this* turkey!

Astonished by his own wiseapple aplomb under fire, Joe said, "You just offered a proposition?"

"Right. So listen carefully, Joe. I don't wish to repeat myself—"

"Could you turn down that fucking music?"

"Huh?—oh, sure." Skipper twiddled a knob; wailing Fenders and dyspeptic Moogs gurgled into a slightly lower register. "Now as I understand it, you and your wife Heidi are heading for divorce. That means even if you somehow effectuate a miracle and swing a deal for Eloy whatshisname's property—"

"Irribarren," Joe interrupted coolly, amazed to hear himself on the attack. "Eloy Irribarren."

"Sure. Whatever. So let's take the most inadvertent hypothetical miracle that could occur. You somehow live long enough to parlay your radical ineptness into possession of that property—then what happens? In the divorce settlement, Heidi gets at least half . . . or maybe the whole thing. These judges in Chamisa County, Joe, they go to the highest bidder. And if you think I'm a big roller, you should realize that Mr. Bonatelli and his associates could sprinkle me with salt and eat me for breakfast. Are you paying attention, Joe?"

"Yes sir."

"Then you have to admit the odds are stacked heavily against your favor. Of course, I should further mention that already every narc in town has you under his microscope, and the second you make a move to score bread for even one gram of that item they'll foreclose on your freedom like a pack of jackals annihilating a wounded antelope."

"Sounds bad," Joe said, beginning to feel woozy.

"'Bad' is hardly the word I'd employ. You happen to be a very little person about to swim into a very big fishnet."

"I still don't understand the proposition."

"Okay. Let's see if I can elucidate. You're a nice man, a fairly honest and straightforward person who just happened to stumble into a monumental mismatch. But I for one like you. And especially I hate to see anyone get hurt. No need for that, correct? We're all neighbors in this valley. And with a little effort we should be able to coexist peacefully. So my proposition is as follows. What did that item put you out? I'll meet that sum in cash and throw in your overhead costs as a favor because I hate to see anybody lose on the deal. In return, you deliver to me the item, and I'll place it where it belongs."

"That's it?"

"You don't look convinced."

"Frankly, I'm not."

"Consider the alternatives."

Joe said, "Suppose I go to the state's attorney general, informing him of your plan to eliminate Cobey Dallas from contention for Eloy's land by collaborating with Roger Petrie in his embezzlement from your own business ventures? Then suppose I could dig up evidence that Roger was also double-crossing you by selling the water rights to land he doesn't own (which have nevertheless been deeded to him by Cobey in return for his collusion in bilking you) to Scott Harrison, who's busily trying to cover his own bets just in case he can't grab the land for legal fees involved in defending it from folks like you and the Tarantula's First State Jug and the Our Lady of the Sorrows Hospital Mafia?"

Skipper blanched, but recovered neatly. "The AG would laugh at you. He's my brother-in-law."

"Ah-*hah*." Joe nodded circumspectly.

Abruptly solicitous, Skipper said, "Maybe we could work out a different deal. I hear you and Nancy Ryan have become pretty close. Let's say you two actually tie a knot once you're divested of Heidi and the kids. All right, now here's a distinct possibility. We all know the Simian Foundation desires the land for the monkey shrine—that, quite frankly, is my concern with this whole botched caper. Should you choose to join the foundation, I'm sure that I could convince the board of directors to make you a voting member of the stockholders' association.

You turn over your item so that it can be disposed of properly, and in return you win a partial ownership of that property, which can then be promptly dedicated to the spiritual well-being of thousands of conscientious disciples throughout the valley and across the nation. I can't in all conscience believe, Joe, that you'd allow narrow, self-seeking interests to conflict with the greater good."

"If I don't buy that land, Eloy certainly won't sell to any of you."

"'Sell'? Joe, he's not selling that land. He doesn't even own it. He's just squatting on it until the necessary paperwork can be done to hand the terrain over to whom it properly belongs."

"But if that happens it'll be divvied up into little pieces. A dozen creditors will chop it up like hungry barracudas, and it won't be good for anything."

"Hopefully we could avoid all that. Such a finale would be a real shame."

"But the way I figure it is that I'm the only person, right now, who has an honest shot at obtaining the land whole."

"What about this, then? You need money to buy from Eloy? Good. I'll hand you the money—all of it—sixty thousand dollars, before the bank closes this afternoon. Naturally, we'll sign an agreement that the land goes over to me. As a finder's fee in the land deal, you get double the offer I just made to you for the purchase of that item. Naturally, I receive the item, in conjunction with the land, once Eloy Whosit signs over all the pertinent deeds and quitclaims to you."

"Meaning you finagle land worth sixty grand for that price plus twenty-four Gs and some odd shekels over that ceiling, and then recoup that investment by unloading a hundred Gs of cocaine? And I wind up with no place to build a home for my future, and only twelve thousand dollars beyond my initial investment for all the risks I've endured?"

"Tell you what," Skipper rebounded calmly. "You front for me on the land, and I'll give you back your initial investment plus six thousand dollars. And you're allowed to keep half of that certain item to do with as you please."

"But you said every narc in the county is waiting to pounce. You just told me if they don't get me, Joe Bonatelli or Ray Verboten, or God knows who else will. Right now, that cocaine is absolutely worthless to me."

"Precisely. So why am I even talking deal with you, Joe? If you turn over that stuff to me, free of any charges whatsoever, and front the purchase of that land for me for the usual ten percent commission, perhaps—and this is even a long shot—I could at least save your ass. To go beyond that, frankly, I'm not at all prepared."

"Then it's all gibberish. You're not proposing a thing."

Skipper sighed, straightened back behind the wheel, and frowned morosely. "Ah, what the hell, Joe. You're a pigheaded fool, and already I'm late for my flight to Ohio. My number is in the phone book. Call me whenever you change your mind."

At the punch of a button, the passenger window hummed shut. Meekly, Joe waved, trying to figure out what, if anything, had just transpired. In the final analysis, only one thing seemed certain: he couldn't win for losing in this game.

"'Flight to Ohio . . . ?'"

The Castle of Golden Fools seemed deserted. Although on the surface apparently nothing had changed, everything Joe looked at bore an elliptical tinge, a foreign essence. Only a few hours down the road of separation, yet already the house, trees, battered vehicles, and yard were relating to him as if to a stranger. Even the air seemed indifferent. Joe coasted to a stop beside the Green Gorilla. For a spell longer he dared not dismount and approach the now-neutralized house. He was like a man approaching a disaster; no life existed here. Right around the corner, for sure, he would stumble upon bodies galore, blood-soaked shower curtains, and dripping red butcher knives on the kitchen floor.

Furtively, Joe reconnoitered the second-story windows. But no curtain fell back into place; no telltale sunlight glinted on a rifle barrel; no sign said TEXAS SCHOOL BOOK DEPOSITORY. And anyway, the bus was gone. So Heidi was out there somewhere seeing a divorce lawyer, getting stroked by Nikita Smatterling, crying on Suki Terrell's shoulder . . . or buying a gun.

When he opened the door to their apartment, Joe was flabbergasted. No dirty socks, Tinkertoys, old newspapers, or vacuum-cleaner hoses were spread across the rug. No jelly knives, apple cores, or half-filled coffee cups littered the tables and ledges. No sleeping-bag "nests," holdovers from Saturday's

cartoon time, cluttered the floor before the TV. And somebody
had actually vacuumed and scrubbed the rug: it didn't smell of
cat pee, it wasn't filmed with squashed Play Doh, BBs, corn-
flakes, pea-shooter pea seeds, broken crayons, dust furries, and
children's dirty underwear. And in the kitchenette—miracle
of all miracles—somebody had torn down half the grotesque
kiddy pictures taped to the Frigidaire, the smudged black area
around cupboard and drawer handles had been Baboed clean,
and three potholders, lost for two years, were hanging on hooks
beside the newly scrubbed stove.

No question about it, the place was picked up, neat, positively spotless.

At first, Joe was stunned. Then, remembering all the times
he had bitched about the bourgeois shitheap they inhabited, he
felt touched, almost tearful. Too late, finally, they had heeded
his words. In hopes of bringing him back? Or out of guilt,
finally, for driving him away? Or had they only been able to
get it together at this late date because previously his shabby
personality among them, his presence, had been a catalyst that
forged the mess despite his fervent desire for physical law and
order in the limited space they occupied?

Cleaned up, the apartment also seemed cold and foreign.
As if everything related to his former life had been eradicated
overnight: the Khrushchevian deStalinization of Joe Miniver,
by his wife and ungrateful kiddies. Had it been done deliberately to offend him? Probably. Joe could picture Heidi in Nazi
cap, black boots, and a whip ordering the kids about. Michael
worked the vacuum cleaner, Heather wielded dustrag and furniture polish. Frantically, they scrubbed as she screamed: "I
don't want any traces of him left, not even a herringbone
footprint from his sneakers in the dust. And especially *no trace
of his smell*! Nothing! Fini! Kaput! Michael, over here, *quick*!
Suck up this feather from that damn jacket of his!"

Joe collapsed into their lone armchair. He cradled the tea
box of either his salvation or his total perdition. Suddenly, he
felt nauseatingly mortal, as if a major heart attack was already
abuilding inside, his veins and vessels twitching, molecules in
the blood around his heart metastasizing, coagulating, photo-
synthesizing—whatever all the coronary thrombo-technicians
did just before the shit hit the fan: ten minutes from now he
would be dead. And a half-hour from now, when Heidi and
the kids came through the door, how would they react? Michael

would be genuinely sorry; but his son was the only ally he could count on. Heather would take it in wiseass stride: "Oh dear, Daddy's dead. I'm glad he didn't die in bed." Heidi would hold up one hand, advising caution before they launched the celebration. "Wait a minute, kids, maybe he's only playing possum. Ever since I've know him he's wanted to be accidentally declared dead, so that he can hear and read all the hosannas in his eulogies and obituaries, like Hemingway in Africa."

So they would spend several minutes shooting his toes with the BB gun, applying lit matches to his fingertips, and sticking hatpins into his buttocks, making sure he was deceased. Then Heidi would filch all the money from his pocket, split it three ways, greedily read aloud the benefits in his life insurance policy, and they'd dance around his carcass, shouting "Son of a bitch, we're rich! We'll bury Daddy in a ditch! We're *rich*, you son of a bitch!"

Yet suddenly he was struck a poignant blow. After all, if life was tragic, wasn't it also truly rich? And chock full of beauty and vitality also? Abruptly, Joe wanted to live forever! Come hell or high water he absolutely *must* acquire Eloy Irribarren's 1.7 acres of land! On it he would create a magnificent garden like the one Monet tended for the latter half of his life. Wisteria trellises and grape arbors! Japanese bridges over the irrigation ditch! Blooming orchards! Delphiniums! Eight-foot-tall sunflowers! Rose bushes! Poplar trees! From the mountains he would retrieve little aspens and make a grove. On transplanted spruce trees, come wintertime, he'd hang suet balls for the chickadees. A little nirvana on earth! He would build a bunch of birdhouses to specification and nail them up in the chinese elms: wren, starling, and bluebird houses, also flicker boxes. And beehives for honey. A backhoe would excavate a small pond; he'd plant cattails and lily pads, and stock a few trout, a handful of snail darters. Redwing blackbirds would warble in the rushes, a virginia rail would appear. Come autumn, ruddy ducks, mallards, and goldeneye would spend a few days on their way south. Muskrats would build a domed lodge. Wood ducks would nest in a box on a pole in the middle of the water. When it froze in December, they'd have skating parties. Long ago, he and Heidi had frequented Central Park's Wollman Rink: courting days. Joe flashed briefly on being young, madly in love, and loaded with dough . . . stroking around that rink, flaunting his hips at each stride.

For a beat, he felt soft and muted and lazy—tranquil and private. At the core of existence, despite all the heartaches and woe, lay such a private dream.

All his life Joe had wanted a pond. All his life he had hoped to see a bald eagle in the wild. All his life he had looked for bears in the forests. All his life he had fantasized about making love to a Hollywood sex symbol (female gender). All his life he had been a jerk.

Glumly, Joe reached over and picked up the telephone, staring at it. Then, of a giddy impulse, he placed the mouthpiece against his crotch, and, making his voice low and mollifying like a professional newscaster's, he said:

"Hello out there, sex fans, this is John Cameron Miniver bringing you exclusive interviews with erotic celebrities. Today, it's our good fortune to have with us here in the studios Mr. Paul Withington Penis, noted authority on cloacal spelunking and author of the well-known bestseller *Vaginal Troglodytes I Have Known*. Say hello to the folks out there, Mr. Penis. I'll have you know, by the way, that this broadcast is being beamed by satellite to over twenty-one different countries overseas including portions of Afghanistan and the Soviet Union, and is being carried live on all armed-services networks for our fighting boys *en outre*. So we are facing an audience even larger than the one that tuned in for the Thrilla in Manila, that last incredible Ali-Frazier fight."

Adopting a high, prissy voice, Joe said, "Hello, folks. It's a pleasure to be here with you tonight, John . . . Doc . . . Ed . . . a real pleasure."

"Okay, thank you, Paul. Now, as I was saying at the top of this show, we've got one of the largest audiences out there ever to tune into a program like this. And I'm sure a lot of those people have personal problems that fall within the sexual realm. So for my first question this evening, I'm gonna put it to you straight and hard and I sure hope you won't give me any limp answers."

In a falsetto voice, Joe replied: "Tee-hee, tee-hee. Oh that's funny, John, that's a real gas. 'Limp answers.' You'd really 'prick' my balloon if you could, wouldn't you? Tee-hee."

Assuming his newcaster's voice, Joe said, "Actually, Paul, I'm not out to 'prick' any balloons. But when you came into the studio tonight and we were talking just before we went on camera, you seemed so 'cocky'. . . ."

From the open doorway, Heather said, "Daddy, what in hell are you doing?"

"Doing?" *Oh help, trapped again!*

One of Joe's strongest childhood illusions had been that grown-ups were actually Grown-up People. In Control. He had believed, for example, that they had order in their lives, and that their personal worlds hummed along smoothly. He had firmly believed that come adulthood not only would he *not* be afraid of the dentist, but that when he did go, *it wouldn't ever hurt.* He had also suspected that grown-ups never cried. Most of all he had admired grown-ups and been awed by them because they weren't flawed and weak and confused like kids.

His children, anyway, wouldn't have that illusion to kick around when they matured!

"Heather, how long have you been standing in the doorway?"

"What are you doing to the phone?" she insisted. "Why are you talking to yourself?"

For a split second he actually fantasized that he could explain, in some rational manner, the fact that he was conducting an interview with his cock in front of a hundred million viewers worldwide. Then he opted for a more logical explanation:

"Actually, I was just sitting here being stupid."

"That's a relief," the precocious little brat said. "At least you weren't doing anything different than you usually do."

"Come over here." Joe hung up the phone. "I wanna knock your block off."

"No thanks."

"Come over here then because I wanna hug you and give you a kiss."

"You'll just hug me and say sweet things to get in my pants, then you'll run away with somebody else," she said crassly. "No dice."

"Hey! Where did you learn to talk like that?"

"Wouldn't you like to know?" Oh, that sassy punkette! Flouncing her butt as she approached, Heather started to walk on by, heading for her room. But Joe reached out, fast as a rattlesnake, and grabbed one arm:

"Hey, Miss World Snootiverse—hold on a sec. This is your daddy begging for a smack!"

He swung her into a bear hug and went for a kiss. But she squirmed powerfully, twisting her head away. Joe persisted, until suddenly he realized that she meant it. In fact, Heather was crying. Horrified, he relaxed his hold. "Wait a minute," he mumbled. "What's the matter, sweetie? I love you."

"No you don't, you motherfucker! Otherwise you never would have run away!"

"I didn't run away." Joe shook his head, vividly convinced that he was creating one of those indelible psychological scars on his daughter that would brand her an emotional cripple for life—she'd become a lesbian, an alcoholic, a photographer like Diana Arbus. "But watch the language, would you?"

"You say 'motherfucker' all the time!"

"I don't call *you* a motherfucker."

"Yes you do, you called me a motherfucker plenty of times!"

"When I'm playing around, maybe I call you a mother-fucker—sometimes. But I would never call you that when I'm serious."

"Well, you're a son of a bitch then," she sobbed.

"No I'm not, you don't understand—"

"Yes you are!"

"No I'm not, dammit!"

"Yes you are! I hate you! You stink!"

"Shuttup Heather, or I'll spank you!"

"Go ahead and spank me! I don't care!"

"But I don't *want* to spank you, sweetie. What's the matter with you, anyway?"

"You're chickenshit, then! Mommy says you're chicken-shit!"

"Well, the next time you see Mommy, tell her to go fuck herself and keep her goddam opinions to herself."

"Why don't you tell her yourself?" Heidi said calmly from the doorway. "Or are you too afraid?"

Joe let go of Heather: she roared away in a defiant, miserable bound.

"Hello, everybody," Joe said morosely. "It was awfully nice of you to invite me into your happy home like this. But I'm afraid I can only stay a minute."

"Oh Joey, Jesus, would you lay off the cute theatrics for once?" Heidi crossed the room and dumped groceries on the kitchenette table. "As maybe you noticed, some of us are a trifle edgy today."

"Where's Michael?"

"How should I know? I think he ran away."

"What do you mean, you *think* he ran away?"

"We had a fight. He called me a whore, took his BB gun, jumped on his bicycle, and pedaled off to who-knows where?"

"You got to be kidding."

Heidi sighed, snapped open a beer, and sank into a chair at the kitchenette table. "It's the truth, Joey. I was so furious I just let him go. I figured he'd return as soon as he shot a sparrow, or put a BB through somebody's chicken-coop window, or shattered a half-dozen pop bottles alongside the road. Then, when he didn't show up, I went out searching. I checked Eloy Irribarren's, thinking he went there looking for you—but no dice. Then for about half an hour Heather and I drove all around. We covered La Ciénega, La Lomita, Borregas Negras, and Lower Ranchitos, stopped for some groceries, and came home: still no Michael."

"Did you check out Ralph's float tank? If that little son of a bitch snuck in there again and peed in the salt water—"

"It's the first place we looked. When I lifted the hatch, Ralph was inside, floating on top of a plump woman with an emerald in her nose."

Joe groaned, "I don't believe it. What happens now?"

"I'm open for any suggestions. I'm tired and I'm really demoralized."

"Did you call the police?"

"Not yet. I mean, suppose he's at a friend's house?"

"Did you call anybody?"

"Tribby and Rachel, Suki, the Baileys, and Jane Zuckerman. Nobody's seen him, nobody's heard a word."

"I bet Michael went across town to kill *her* with his BB gun," Heather said.

"Her who, Jane?"

"No, *your* her."

"Heather," Joe groaned, "do Mommy and Daddy a favor and don't talk until you're spoken to, all right?"

"I can talk if I want. It's a free country."

"Free country?" Joe snarled. "Who feeds you that shit!" Something in his head went *ping*! "Is it a free country for all the millions of gay people that Anita Bryant's trying to burn at the stake? Is it a free country for all the blacks and Chicanos and Indians who can't get into law school or medical school or into a decent housing project unless they burn down a ghetto to prove they're sick and tired of being exploited and culturally genocided into oblivion? Is it a free country for our twenty-five million alcoholics, our ten million junkies, and the other one hundred eighty million of our people who are manic-depressive pill poppers that spend ninety percent of their salaries on psychiatrists? Is it a—"

"Joey, for God's sake, stoppit."

"—free country for the millions and millions of people that we have incarcerated in one of the most extensive prison systems on earth? Is it a free country for the ten million New Yorkers who are afraid to go out after five for fear of being mugged? Is it a free—"

"Joey! Jesus *Christ*."

"—country for all the people who get murdered in America, and for all the people who get robbed, and who get killed in car accidents? Is it a free country for all the kids that graduate from our lousy high schools as semifunctional illiterates? Huh? Tell me about this *free* country! Heidi, who feeds them this junk . . . ?"

They were all crying: Joe, Heidi, and Heather. Shocked, Heather stood in the middle of the room, staring at her father, tears flowing down her cheeks. Head buried in her arms, Heidi's voice was muffled as she sobbed, "Joey, just shut the Christ up, *please*."

"Look at you and me!" Joed wept hysterically. "Look at us! The beneficiaries of the best education money can buy, upwardly mobile middle class, every advantage on earth! Look at all this *freedom*! Look at Skipper Nuzum and Jeff and Suki and, and look at all *that* freedom! Everybody's so happy in this country with all their freedom! Freedom," he spat, turning to aim his final invective at their only daughter. "Don't you believe it for a minute."

"Joey, geeze, *can* it."

"'Cause it's bullshit!" he sobbed. "It's propaganda! Freedom to choose between thirty-seven different colors of car or flavors of ice cream *does not a democracy make*, little girl. And don't you ever forget it!"

With that, he ran out of steam. Nobody moved. Joe wondered: had he flipped out? Right before their eyes had he gone nuts? Apparently. Heather said, "You're crazy, Daddy." Snatching an orange from the coffee-table bowl, she heaved it at her dad, galloped past him to her room, and slammed the door.

"She's right," Joe whimpered. "I'm crazy. I'm sorry."

"What about Michael?"

"I'll go look for him."

"Where?"

"I don't know. I'll drive around. Do we still have that elk call? I'll go stand in the middle of a field somewhere and blow it until he comes arunning."

"Joey, what's happening? This doesn't make any sense."

"I don't know. Go read Gail Sheehy, I sure don't have a pipeline to any answers."

"I'll come with you."

"No, you better stay with Heather."

"What if you don't find him?"

"Then we call the cops. No, actually, we can't call them."

"Why not?"

Joe displayed the tea box. "Because it makes no sense to call attention to yourself when you're sitting on a potential hundred Gs of cocaine, does it?"

"I'll call the cops," Heidi said darkly, "If I have to."

Ignorant of human follies, the yard was enchanted by the glowing dusk. Even the Green Gorilla, bathed in luminescent butter-yellow light, seemed to have a magnified importance, like a museum object—precious, beautiful, unique. Love for landscape, colors, and smells momentarily stopped Joe. Greedily, he sucked it all in, needing the transfusion. A kingfisher rat-a-tatted by. Peepers and crickets had commenced their evening racket. Sweet puppy clouds, and the darkening mauve sky behind them, were reflected in the Green Gorilla's spider-webbed windshield. Tiny mosquitoes floated through the last brilliant light; tree leaves were paralyzed by an airless crescendo of mood. The earth was captured for a moment, its heart revealed. Absolute silence governed the planet, as if somewhere, somehow, the first oxygen-breathing fish was emerging from the sea to crawl about clumsily on terra firma; it gulped in an initial breath of air and filled out fledgling lungs.

What precocious magic could deliver a reverie like that? Michael had fled—or had he been kidnapped by Ray Verboten, to be held for ransom? Heather hated his guts, and already, at age eight, she was scarred for life. Heidi was counting ways to ream him in a divorce. A woman he had screwed only twice had asked what time he would be home for supper. He was sitting on a hundred Gs of coke with absolutely no idea of how to market it without being killed. Eloy Irribarren wanted to rob a bank, and Joe had foolishly promised to help in hopes of somehow forestalling *that* idiotic move. And Diana Clayman was pitching a tent on land that he lusted for, desperately, but would probably never own, unless a miracle occurred.

And yet the world, caught in a hollow of evocative color—nature, the endless pietà!—moved him to feel a sensation that could only be described as tragically sublime.

He should have flung out his arms: Here I am, Charlton Heston, ready to inherit your throne! But a last vestige of good taste came to the rescue. Instead, pretending not to notice a large stain of transmission oil on the ground near the rear of the vehicle, he entered the Green Gorilla, spent ten minutes firing it up, daintily wrestled the trigger-outfitted gearing lever into reverse, backed up, swung around, and, the gear shift grinding and clunking horrendously as he manipulated it, Joe headed off in a gusty cloud of blue poison to search for Michael.

The truck rattled, bumped, hiccoughed, skipped a few beats, lurched, swayed, and carried on. Exhaust seeped up through the fire wall, so Joe rolled down the passenger window. Under his butt seat-springs howled in execration: only three layers of duct tape in a crisscross pattern lay between him and a royal goosing. Ay, Mama, he loved this old truck! It was all he had left that he cherished. Bury me in this truck, boys! Air-freight it to Varanasi and burn me alive in it on the banks of the putrid Ganges! Actually, properly embalmed, his feet lashed to the brake and clutch pedals, his hands strapped to the steering wheel, the bed chock full of piñon wood, he wanted to be pushed off the mesa into the Rio Grande Gorge. Let the boulders and the foaming waters consecrate his body to the Great Unknown!

Heidi believed in an afterlife: in reincarnation. Joe couldn't see it. Living in a town surrounded by people absorbed in their former lives and reincarnations and in their future lives and immortalities (and in interplanetary-spirit jamborees and en- counters of the third kind, and in astral hitchhiking and nether beings, and in deathbed guides and 1,112 easy ways to attain nirvana)—living in a town like that, Joe had nevertheless been unable to come up with a necromance any more complex than:

when you're dead you're dead. When it was over, you stopped—period. No feeling, just blankness, all sensations ceased. The human spirit—The Soul—was nice to have when alive. But it ceased to be when you died. No reason to feel bitter or cheated, however—he had no complaints, he wasn't scared. Life on earth was what counted. For some reason, Joe had always mistrusted every manifestation he ran into of spiritual pie in the sky, from cryonics to Catholicism, from devil worshipers to Hare Krishnas. He could understand the artificial continuation of a particular spirit, say a writer's in his books. But beyond that—?

"Hey, wake up, turkey!"

He had driven a mile without searching for Michael. Joe slammed on the brakes, forgetting he had to pump for ten minutes before they'd even begin to catch. The truck continued at thirty miles an hour for a ways, then began slowing down because, after all, he had taken his foot off the accelerator.

A female hippie hitchhiker stood forlornly beside the road. Joe's immediate instinct was to hit the gas pedal, peeling away in a cloud of dust so thick she couldn't identify the truck (meaning that next week, when by coincidence he met her at the Cinema Bar, she wouldn't be able to say, "I know you, you're that son of a bitch in the Green '47 Chevy with license plate number AKJ-one eighty-four, who refused to pick me up last week when I was trying to flag down a car for help because my daughter was back in the house, choking to death on a chicken bone!")

However, because of some atavistic guilt in his genes, Joe could almost never pass up a hitchhiker, even though he hated giving lifts, especially to hippies. For starters, they were usually stoned, or in one weird place or another that made Joe uncomfortable. Often they pulled out six and a half pounds of Moroccan hash and offered to turn him on. And from that moment until he left them at their destination, Joe was terrified of getting stopped by the fuzz for a traffic offense, or on the mere suspicion of being suspicious. And, unable to prove his innocence, he'd pull a life term for trafficking in controlled substances. Too, nobody in this part of the country, especially hippies, ever had a logical destination, such as the center of town, or a well-traveled crossroads. Invariably, they lived sixteen miles off the highway up a grade-X dirt road liable to flash-flooding any hour of the day or night. And, because it was snowing, or too hot, or the hitchhiker was sick or drunk or stoned (or nine months pregnant), Joe always felt obligated to make the detour. This often resulted in an hour's delay in his life (usually for an important meeting that could cost him a three-thousand-dollar hauling contract if he was late), or a flat tire, or perhaps a broken axle. Other hitchhikers might prove surly, and spend their time trashing their old ladies, or gringos. Driving back from the Pueblo last year, he had picked up a drunk obnoxious Indian kid who asked if Joe was local. When Joe said yes, the kid replied, "Guess I can't describe the local points of interest for a buck, then." When Joe asked about his destination, the kid cracked, "I'm not getting off, this is a hijacking. Take me to Cuba." Still attempting to be friendly, Joe talked about Cuba. The kid replied, "What was the name of that guy down there— Geeborba?" "Guevara." "Yeah, him. I'd like to grab his balls and squeeze them seventeen times." When they reached the overcrowded town and were simmering in a traffic jam, the kid kept remarking, "Geez, there's hardly anybody in Chamisaville these days." Finally, he ordered Joe to drive him to a liquor store and buy him a bottle: "I can't get it myself, I'm underage." Joe refused, the kid called him a cocksucker, and they almost came to blows.

Other hitchhikers said nothing, but made him so nervous by their sinister silence that Joe became convinced they intended to rob him, put a bullet in his head, and dump him in a sandy arroyo where he wouldn't be discovered until the only way to identify him was through his dental records. Better them, though, than some of the talkative ones who drove him nuts. Each year a few gay thumbers made passes which Joe mishandled abysmally, trying to reject the advances without offending the advancer. He had a terror of hurting feelings, especially of strangers, and, even more especially, of homosexuals.

Occasionally, Joe pretended he couldn't stop for a certain hitchhiker by making exaggerated pointing signals to the right or to the left, smiling with sympathetic "what can I do?" sadness to indicate he was turning off the beaten track just up the road a few yards. But this led to elaborate and time-consuming deceits. Horribly aware of the hitchhiker's eyes following him just to make sure "that cat in the green Chevy wasn't just another honky middle-class bullshitter," Joe often clicked on his blinker and turned onto the very first path that appeared,

praying it wouldn't deadend at the digs of some trigger-happy
redneck holding a grudge against hippie vehicles.

The Green Gorilla ceased its forward progress and stalled.
As the girl ran toward the truck, Joe removed the ignition key
and circled around to unlock the passengerside door. Panting
heavily, the girl arrived. Heavy-set, pregnant, dressed in what
looked like colorful rags, she also wore athletic socks and
hiking boots. Her dirty face was tear-streaked. As Joe fiddled
the key in his broken lock, she blurted desperately: "Oh wow,
man, am I glad to see you. Jesus, is this ever a heavy day. I
mean, like, what a fuckin' bummer, you know? Do you know
my old man, Othello?"

"Othello?" Rolling down the window, Joe pinched the tidbit
of broken passengerside lock-knob poking above the win-
dowsill hole, and tried to prod it upward. Instead, a rude *clack*!
inside the door indicated some crucial mechanism had gone
awry.

"Othello. You know, man. He's a big, heavyset dude with
a walrus moustache, drives a 1957 Dodge van with a cow skull
welded on the front grille. He used to be a bouncer at the La
Lomita until that one-eyed dude, Pearly Stan, ran away with
all the bread."

Vaguely, Joe remembered he had seen the cow-skull van
around. He recalled a plastic bubble skylight, psychedelic head-
paintings on both sides, and a sign saying CHICKEN RIVER FUNKY
PIE. But he was distracted and couldn't recall exactly where
he'd seen it last.

So he nodded: "I guess so, maybe, sure." And wondered:
what kind of a human being is it who, when his son runs away
(desperate, unhappy, and bearing a firearm into the bargain),
and there's only an hour before dark in which to locate him,
winds up parked beside the road jawboning with what looks
like a cross between a yak and a professional crackpot about
her Chicken River Funky Pie van driver?

Joe tugged on the key: it wouldn't budge. He yanked hard,
but it was stuck.

"Damn."

"He's gone, man. And I don't even know where he split
to. We used to live up at the Family, but I couldn't take all
the PTSes. And anyway, Bill Dillinger, man, he's heading into
this real weird place, like, he's really putting out some weird
ego trip and I didn't wanna hang around him anymore, you

know? Their whole inner-reality program is on the skids. So me and Othello found this really groovy little place, it's right back there, across that field, see? It doesn't have any running water or heat right now, but the price is right—only a hundred and fifty a month. And the vibes are wonderful. He's almost a Clear. I'm a Pre-Clear and also a pretty heavy SP. But for a while, there, we were really moving up The Bridge together fantastically. Then this morning—wow. The stars must be all messed up. I'm running this goddam negative karma you wouldn't believe. Othello went out last night and didn't return until two A.M. He was really uptight and doing a whole bunch of Overts. We had a big fight and couldn't do any Word Clearing at all. And then he just split—barefoot! Can you dig it? I threw an I Ching and it told me I shouldn't even of got outta bed this morning. But I gotta find him, man. I really love him. This is such a beautiful place to live—why are we all so unhappy?"

Joe said, "Lookit this. My key's stuck in the lock. Not only can I not open the door, now I can't even start the truck, 'cause the lousy key's stuck in the lock."

"It's me, man. I wanna be an Upstat, but every place I go I screw up all the ions in the air. I don't know why I keep pushing all the wrong Buttons. I need a hit of something, man, I really do. You got any shit in the truck? Some reds...a popper, maybe? Or even a little grass? I really could use a hit of *something*."

Joe stared at her, wondering who was writing this script. He said, "How'm I gonna get this key unstuck?"

"Don't ask me, man, I'm not very mechanical."

"Well, why don't you quit messing with the ions for a minute, so I can get my key out?"

"I don't know how to," she sobbed. "Ever since I left Chicago, I don't know what's the matter with me. But I keep having all these ARC breaks. One week after I landed in the Family, I got gonorrhea. Then some tithead I never even met before got me pregnant. I dunno what's wrong with me. My Flow One, Flow Two, and Flow Zero are so fucked up I can't see straight. I don't know if I can live without Othello, man. He was my Auditor in Chicago. He was the biggest Win I ever had. You gotta help me find him."

"I can't get my ignition key out of this door."

"Where could he go without his shoes on?" she hiccoughed

bewilderedly. "You know what he called me?—a 'stinkin' gorilla.' Then he smashed our E-meter and ran away. If I don't find him I'm gonna kill myself. I'm so blue . . . and I'm broke. I couldn't buy a nickel bag if you paid me to. God knows what's wrong. I *hate* falling off The Bridge. Mars or Jupiter must be all screwed up. Wow. What a bummer! I bet I'll be a Pre-Clear forever!"

Locating his toolbox under the front seat, Joe assaulted the door paneling with screwdrivers, pliers, a socket wrench, a hammer. As he worked, in a frenzy of trying to stay calm so he wouldn't freak out entirely, Joe puzzled over his own bad luck. Where had he learned this heartrending ability to step in shit?

Talk about karma!

"Do you think he'll come back?" she persisted. "If he left without his shoes, he'll return, won't he?"

"Frankly, all I care about right now is getting my key out of this door so I can start this truck."

About then, it dawned on Joe that he was approaching the problem incorrectly. He had to remove the paneling to get at the lock apparatus. But he couldn't pop the paneling unless he opened the door. And the door was locked. So he had to separate it from its hinges. But the hinges weren't exposed. Therefore, he must crawl underneath the fender to find them. Or take out the fire wall, hoping that he could somehow wedge himself around. . . .

Grabbing the hammer, Joe backed out the driverside door, circled the truck, and, like a maniac, began swinging the hammer—*blam*!—attacking the keyhole area—*whack*!—smashing it as hard as possible with every blow—*k-blonk*!—and cursing it for good measure while the girl looked on horrified: *wham*!

"Hey, you shouldn't treat machinery like that, man. Cars have feelings too, you know."

"This isn't a car, this is a truck"—*k-tunk*!—"and trucks don't have any feelings"—*bang*! "Not this old, they don't. General Motors didn't start"—*smash*!—"putting feelings into trucks until 1954." Emitting a grunt, he launched a final blow—*k-thud*!—then grabbed at the key . . . it slid right out.

"Ah-*hah*! The human brain, with its infinite grasp of superior technology, triumphs again!"

"Wow, man, are you okay? You're reeking with Overts and Withholds!"

"If you want a ride, get in the driverside door."

The girl backed away uneasily; she had even stopped crying. "I don't want a ride, man. Not with you. You're on a really scary ARC break. I bet your Theta never went Exterior, did it? What are you on, anyway?"

"On?" Joe swung into his truck. "What am I *on*? Let me tell you. I'm high on smack, whacked on meth, I just dropped six tabs of some very heavy acid, smoked a doobie, snorted half a gram of coke, and ate a PCP cutworm moth pizza, and boy do I feel ripped!"

Fuck this drug culture, he thought as the Green Gorilla surged away from her. Miss Pierson, take a letter. "Dear Fidel Castro. My name is Joe Miniver, I'm thirty-eight years old, I used to be in New York advertising. But then I came out west and became a garbage man. However, I am not so sure, at this point in my life, that the United States is the right place for me. I have always had sort of Socialist leanings, and was wondering if you ever let Americans emigrate to Cuba. Do they need garbage collectors in Havana? Other skills I have is I could probably develop into a good canecutter, I used to be a pretty fine athlete. Two things, though: is Scientology legal in your country, and do you have any figures about the Cuban climate's effect on asthmatics?"

It was dark. No point in continuing. Better to return home, admit defeat, maybe even call the cops, though he was terrified of hailing fuzz. Suppose Michael was just hanging out at a friend's house; or had decided to hit a movie. Joe didn't think he could face the sneering reproach in their hostile police eyes if that happened. Not to mention that they must have heard rumors about his dope score. And no doubt had been apprised of the bus-depot conflagration last night.

A chill entered the cab. Joe's window wouldn't rise, but the passenger one wound up, thus he could eliminate the cross-current. Reaching over, he turned the handle, but nothing arose from the slot. Instead, he heard a tinkle inside the doorframe of shattered glass bits rattling around.

Another accepted entry for Ripley's Believe It or Not! Another five dollars in his pocket! His remarkable penchant for being an incalculably retarded moron might one day make them all rich!

❦

Home again, home again, jiggity-jog.

Heidi and Heather were seated at the kitchen table, slurping up hot chocolates.

Joe said, "You'll never guess what happened."

Heidi replied, "It's all right, we found him."

"You did? Where?"

"Over at your friend's house. Nancy just called a few minutes ago. She's bringing him home."

"Well, gee . . . that's good. What's the matter? You guys look funny."

"Michael shot Sasha with his BB gun!" Heather blurted. "He hit him in the eye!"

For a second, that didn't register: "Sasha?"

"The mean old monkey that bites," Heather explained. "Mrs. Ryan said he shot him three or four times, but the one that really hurt was smack dab in the middle of his eye."

"Wait a minute. He ran away from here, rode all the way over there, and shot the stupid monkey?"

"She's very upset." Heidi smirked. "Bradley started screaming, and then held his breath and managed to prolapse his intestine, which apparently he hasn't done for over three years. And this time it isn't pinworms. She's driving Michael home right now."

Joe sat down. "He *shot* the monkey? Who is he, all of a sudden, Clint Eastwood? Teddy Roosevelt?"

"The monkey's in pretty bad shape. They were about to rush it down to a Capital City vet. Nancy said if that monkey dies it'll be awful. She was in tears. I gather the beast is sacred?"

Joe said, "Aw, really. Who *is* writing this script?"

"I told her we'd pay all the vet bills, of course."

"Naturally. Tell her I'll buy another monkey if she wants."

"I'm sure she would love to have you buy her another monkey. I didn't realize she was a Hanuman worshiper. What do you two do together, pluck lice from each other's fur?"

"One more wisecrack, Heidi . . ."

"Oh, pardon me, I forgot. And of course, I should have remembered—there's that unveiling on Thursday. Do you know,

251

Miss Whosit sounded just a trifle pleased? Perhaps Michael, where nobody else could, finally ruffled her composure?"

"You're starting a war, I'm warning you. . . ."

"Oh me oh my. Shut mah big ol' mouth."

Footsteps clumped up the outside ladder. White as a sheet, Michael appeared in the doorway. Behind him, Nancy said, "Here he is," and fled.

Joe cried, "Hey, wait a sec!" and sprang to the door. "Nancy!"

"We can talk about it later, Joe. Right now I have to get back to Sasha."

"I'm sorry!" Joe called into the darkness, his words lost in the chattering of a VW ignition. "He didn't mean—!"

Back inside, Michael was proceeding like a rusty robot toward his room when Joe said, "Stop in your tracks. Where do you think you're going?"

He froze, but didn't answer.

"Boy, Michael, you're really gonna get it," Heather gloated.

Joe said, "Shut up, Heather, or I'll beat you to a pulp."

"I didn't do anything," she snapped, insulted. "I didn't shoot the monkey."

"You're shooting off your mouth, and I don't like it. Besides, it was a grubby monkey and probably deserved to be shot. So if you haven't got anything helpful to say, keep it buttoned."

Heidi flared. "Just because you happen to be committing adultery with a Hanuman freak doesn't give you the right to treat your daughter like dirt."

"'Dirt'? But she has no right—"

To Michael, Heather said, "Where's your BB gun?"

"They took it," Michael admitted hoarsely.

"Who's 'they'?"

"Nikita Smatterling. And his friend—they smashed it."

Joe exclaimed, "They *what*?"

"First Nikita Smatterling broke it over his knees, then his friend took a sledgehammer and bashed it to smithereens and threw it in a garbage can."

"What about your bicycle?"

"They let me bring that back."

Joe wanted to give the kid a medal. But for appearances' sake he had to be stern: "Why in hell did you shoot that monkey?"

"I don't know."

"But people don't just go out and shoot other people's pets

for no reason, do they? I mean, even Hitler knew what he was doing and why."

Heidi said, "I don't think we need to compare our son with Hitler."

Michael mumbled, "I guess I was pissed off."

"We'll have to take the vet bills out of your allowance, you know."

Michael nodded dismally—he knew. Between the broken window and the maimed monkey and the dead English sparrow and a dozen other peccadilloes he'd performed both long ago and of late, he had not really received an allowance during the past year. And probably would not score another Saturday handout until he reached sixty-nine.

"What if Sasha dies?" Heather chirruped.

"Will you shut up?" Joe snapped.

Heidi pleaded, "Don't talk to her like that," at the same time that Heather said, "Well, what happens if he *does* die? That's murder."

"It's not murder if you kill a monkey," Joe said. "Murder's just for killing people."

"Well, what is it called for a monkey, then?"

"I don't know. Monkeycide. Don't ask so many stupid questions."

Heidi said, "Joey, let's stop for a minute. Let's all take a breather: allee allee in-come-free. Michael, darling, you look hungry. How about some split-pea-with-ham soup and a PB and J?"

Joe asked, "Am I allowed to eat something here, too?"

"If you want."

On tenterhooks, they prepared to share a meal. Heidi opened soup cans, lit a fire under a large saucepan, and added water. Joe made peanut-butter-and-jelly sandwiches. Heather set the table. And Michael—without being asked!—fed the cat, and even forked some turds from the catbox into the garbage can. They circled each other on tiptoes, acting very formal, as if the meal somehow fell in the category of such events as the Job Interview, and they were all afraid of blowing it.

Things remained calm until they sat down and Heather bit into her sandwich. With a great *phwoop*! sound, she spat out the mouthful as if it were cyanide, exclaiming, "You put *butter* on my sandwich!"

Joe held his temper. "So what? Butter can kill? I always spread a little butter on my sandwiches."

"I *never* put butter on my sandwich. I hate it. *Yuk!*"

Momentarily defensive, Joe thought: Good Christ, have I already forgotten my family's likes and dislikes? But before he could labor for too long in such a bitter vineyard, he thought: What gives that snotnosed little Gidget the right to spit out her sandwich? Whereupon, his despotic character asserted itself: "I don't care if you don't dig it. In this family, you take what you get and like it."

Where—given his record for the day—Michael mined his audacity, beat Joe. But the next person to speak was his son, and the gist of his comments was:

"I never have any jelly on my sandwiches, Dad. I just like butter and peanut butter. When you add jelly, it tastes kinda pukey."

Incredulously, Joe exclaimed, "What is going on here? What is this—the court of Louis Quatorze, and Mr. and Mrs. Stuck-up Rockefeller just paid a visit? What's *your* complaint?" he belligerated Heidi. "You like it with butter and jelly, but no peanut butter? And you can't eat the sandwich unless it's cut in half, but not so that each half is rectangular—each half has to be triangular?"

"Joey, ever since they were born, practically, you and I have been making sandwiches to the specifications they just asked for."

Joe was growing faint from anxiety, anger, guilt, bewilderment. "I don't care." Even though he knew the only loving, noble, and sensible thing to do would be to shut up, he couldn't stop himself. "I'm sick and tired of harboring a couple of spoiled and thankless little brats! When I was growing up if I had ever spit out part of a sandwich, I would have been banished to my room for a week, and then executed at dawn the following Monday! Your kids, my kids, every middle-class kid in America has been spoiled rotten! I can't stand it anymore, I really can't. I'd like to see these two little bourgeois morons kicked out of this house, I really would. In another five years they'll both probably be walking around in pinstripe button-down shirts, with navy-blue turtleneck jerseys underneath, and brown corduroys, and Bostonian loafers, looking like Caroline and John-John Kennedy!"

Heather said, "It takes one to know one." Michael cast down his eyes and squirmed.

Joe said, "You kids are gonna eat those sandwiches if I have to shove them down your throats!"

Heidi said, "They don't have to do anything of the kind. I see no reason under the sun to force people to eat what they don't want to eat."

Joe said, "But you don't understand. Their attitude about the sandwiches is the same kind of idiotic reasoning that leads to racism."

"Joey, isn't that a pretty big jump—from peanut-butter-and-jelly sandwiches to racism?"

"You don't know what I'm saying, do you? You really don't."

"I don't see the point?—yes, that is correct. You're not making any sense."

"Any kid who would spit out her peanut butter sandwich for the reasons Heather just cited is gonna grow up to be a stock manipulator and a racist," Joe stormed. "And probably a Fascist. I absolutely guarantee it."

"I'm not fast enough yet to be a racist," Heather said calmly.

Joe missed it completely. Off-balance, he asked Heidi: "What did she just say?"

"Ask her. I think it's both insulting and patronizing to talk about a child in the third person in that child's presence. Especially when that child is a girl, and has enough chauvinistic strikes against her without her father adding to the damage."

That did it. Joe slapped at his soup bowl; it skidded across the table, landing in Heidi's lap. Thrusting dramatically to his feet, he savagely ripped apart his sandwich, throwing one portion at Heidi, and beaning each of his offspring with the other pieces. Then he made a mad dash for the door, where he turned, à la Zorro, to launch a final speech. Oh, it was dumb, and wrong, and ridiculous! But having gone this far, he might as well finish the job. No way was he going to eat crow, now, not in this cul-de-sac he had prepared for himself:

"You just let them get away with it, Heidi! You don't care! You're just gonna let them turn into a bunch of stuck-up, capitalist *preppies*!"

Jaws dropped. All three of them gaped at him as if he were a flying saucer, its retro rockets firing, settling to a touchdown on earth.

Heather yelled, "Daddy, you're having a nervous break-down!"

Heidi shouted, "Joe, just *go!*"

Joe hollered, "Where am I supposed to go to?"

"Her house! Tahiti! Who cares?"

"Go to *hell!*" Heather suggested. "Go *crazy!*"

"I'm sick of that kid's foul mouth," Joe warned Heidi. "If she's gonna talk like a guttersnipe let her go live in a gutter."

"If you hadn't fucked Nancy Ryan," Heidi wailed, "Michael never would have shot that damn monkey!"

"They are gonna be storm troopers when they grow up!" Joe couldn't resist saying.

Heather accused: "You already *are* a storm trooper, Daddy!"

"Joey, get out of here! Go away!"

"When are we gonna talk?" he raged. "What—we'll just stay mum and hope something works out?"

"Talk about *what*, for God's sake?"

"Would you believe, *us*? You and me! This so-called marriage! Our happy little family! Our living arrangements! The beautiful house we were gonna build together this summer!"

"I hardly think this is the time—"

"There are no right times in life, Heidi! If we always waited around for it to be the Right Time, nothing would ever get done!"

"Well right now I want you to be gone!"

"Great, thanks a lot, I'm going!"

"So don't just stand there," she sobbed. *"Get out of here!"*

"I don't wanna go out there!" Joe shrieked at the top of his voice. *"It's a cold, cruel world out there, teeming with idiots!"* Shakespeare . . . ? He added: *"It's a tale, full of sound and fury—!"*

"Go," Heidi pleaded. "Just go! go! *go!*"

Suddenly, what had seemed life-and-death crucial to Joe a moment ago became patently absurd. He moaned, "I can't go." The sight of their big, wide-open, tormented eyes whammied by pathetic despair, set against soaking-wet features twisted in clownlike misery, broke his heart and raised a chortle at the same time.

Puzzled, wary, and infuriated, Heidi said, "If you don't go, I'm calling the police."

"What's my crime? Who did I kill? What did I steal?"

Astonished, Heidi said, "You're actually *smirking!*"

"This whole thing is preposterous."

For reasons even the most astute theologians, psychologists, and sports commentators would never understand, Joe's spirits had started to soar. He was enjoying the whole ludicrous Felliniesque imbroglio.

"Please go," Heidi sobbed.

Joe let his voice drop to normal. "So long everybody, it's been good to know you." And, tipping an imaginary Maurice Chevalier hat, twiddling an imaginary cane, he did a brief jig step, then slyly soft-shoed out of there.

Down by the Green Gorilla, inspiration—a three-hundred-watter!—flattened our cavalier boy. Joe ransacked the glove compartment for a soiled piece of typing paper and a pen. By starlight, leaning against the front hood, he wrote, *I love all three of you.* A cursory inspection of the surrounding terrain soon turned up the correct-shaped stone. Joe wrapped the note around it, went into a baseball windup (doing a double-pump-and-knuckle-dusters like big Don Newcombe), then reared back and tossed a strike through the southern window of their living room. And, as he pictured them unwrapping the rock, Joe fired up the Green Gorilla, cackling in ecstasy!

Downright euphoric, firmly convinced he was one of the planet's most original and far-out human beings, Joe was about to sail onto the open road, bound for glory, when, from up high in the starlit darkness, Tribby Gordon called: "Hey Miniver! What's going on down there?"

At first Joe was startled: the voice, like that of God, seemed to be firing at him directly from heaven. Then he remembered Tribby's crow's nest atop his bedroom pyramid, and hollered back:

"It's nothing! Just a little domestic squabble!"

"You're breaking my windows, man! That's a tenant no-no!"

"I'll buy you another, shmuck!"

"Come up here a minute! Let's talk!"

"I can't! I'm afraid of heights!"

"Oh bull! Come on! I'm waiting! I'm smoking some dynamite shit up here!"

Joe quelled the truck, thinking: I hadda throw the rock. Me and my big fat inspiration!

Not that he wished to avoid Tribby, It's just that, for some reason, the tattered lawyer had made his crow's nest almost impregnable. You reached it not by navigating a sensible indoor or outdoor stairwell, or even by ascending a seminegotiable gizmo such as a ladder. Instead, you latched onto a large rope dangling from a lightning rod atop the pyramid and more or less belayed yourself up the side of the house and the treacherously steep pyramid cone. One slip, of course, at the higher elevations meant, if not instant death, at least a passel of broken bones. Razzed unmercifully by Tribby, Joe had clawed his hair-raising way to the top of the pyramid perhaps a half-dozen times, in mind-boggling terror every second. In fact, fear had made him so woozy that he had always lunged the final yards on the brink of fainting and doing an Icarus into the yard below.

Tribby, naturally, scrambled up and down the rope with the blasé dexterity of a monkey.

Joe whined, "Do I have to?"

"Absolutely."

"Aw, shit . . ."

Nevertheless, he descended from the Green Gorilla, approached the side of the house, grasped the rope, and winced as terror sheathed his body in clammy goosebumps. Then, seeking to avoid the absolute hysteria that might strike if he overly circumspected the task ahead, Joe jerked himself aloft.

As he tugged himself painfully along, the soles of his feet went numb; shortly thereafter his calves became deadened. Joe gritted his teeth and would have closed his eyes had he dared. Everest was more human. A whimper, a gasp, a grunt—Joe tried to will himself on high. His fingers grew numb; his head buzzed. After the usual eternity, he found himself at the edge of the crow's nest, a square box shaped somewhat like an inverted sled, railinged on either side. Two people, in a squeeze, could camp in that rickety coffin.

"Come on in, Joe. The weather's great."

"Now that I'm up here, how the hell am I gonna get down?"

"You always ask that question."

"I still can't comprehend why you insist on making the route so dangerous."

"It isn't dangerous. It's a routine climb. You just think it's dangerous. But the real peril comes from you *projecting* fear. I never feel insecure."

"Just wait. One night you'll topple out of this box. We'll find you in the morning with a broken neck."

"If I toppled out right now I'd sail away into the stars. Now look up for a minute, ferme la bouche, and be awed for a change."

Joe obeyed. As always, despite his anguish over the precarious rope scene, he was floored by the aerial display. Nothing stood between them and eternity. Though only forty feet aboveground, the pyramid peak seemed light-years closer to the universe. Barely scathed by a polluting atmosphere, the stars sizzled in bold precision. The busy symmetrical beauty of twice as many constellations proclaimed immortality. Meteors, which would have been invisible from a second-story window, zipped through the bewitching clarity. Joe took no stock in the magic of pyramids, but all the same he had to admit . . .

Smoke from Tribby's joint was rich and pungent. One whiff and Joe's brain slithered sideways—he giggled nervously. "Want a drag?" Tribby asked. Joe declined: one toke would render him insensate and he'd pop free of their hazardous perch, experience a split second of euphoric zero-gravity, then punch against the earth so hard that his brain would squirt out of a split-open skull, zooming across the yard like a sloppy fluorescent softball until it collided against a tree: *shplat!*

Tribby said, "What happened at the bus station last night?"

"All hell broke loose."

"I know that, dumbbell. What I mean is, how did you rate the goodies?"

"You're not gonna believe this, but Nancy's monkey picked up one carton of tea. . . ."

"And it was in that carton?"

"How did you know?"

"Actually, Wilkerson Busbee told me this afternoon. I just wanted to double-check."

"How come you talked to him?"

"I've been retained to spring them from the Clarion, Ohio, slammer. Wilkerson had already been briefed by Skipper Nuzum, who learned the details from Natalie. She apparently called Nancy—concerning the logistics of spiriting that imbecilic Hanuman crew from there to here—and I guess she let slip that Sasha had been the hero of that rather convoluted moment."

"Sasha—egads. Don't remind me."

"Michael picked some moment to perform his perfidy."

"You heard about *that* already?"

"Rachel was having coffee in the Prince of Whales when Nancy phoned for help and Nikita Smatterling gallivanted off to the rescue."

"Jeesh."

"I wouldn't worry about it. Our main problem now is what to do with the dope."

"Oy vay!" Joe exclaimed.

"What now?"

"I left it in the apartment."

"Go back and fetch it."

"I can't. I made an exit."

"What sort of exit is worth a hundred thousand dollars?"

"An emphatic one."

"No comprendo."

"Don't try. I'm just sick of being a scatterbrained gangster. I'll climb back on The Bridge tomorrow."

"Heidi won't do something irrational?"

"It's her future as well as my own."

"Well . . . okay. Want me to bring you up to date on some of the more peripheral developments around that land?"

"No, but go ahead."

"Skipper Nuzum dropped by the office today plumb gorged with bile. That shootout last night pushed his panic button. He wants the DA to move on Cobey's embezzling toot-sweet, as the saying goes. Rumor has it Cobey was one of those deranged depot marauders. So Skipper says it's time to nail Cobey, double-cross Roger Petrie when he proffers a hand for the payoff, and make Eloy an offer he can't refuse. Naturally, he assumes you'll be out of the running."

"He doesn't know you're helping me unload the coke? Cobey does."

"If he did, would I be the first to know?"

"No, but he wouldn't keep you on a retainer either, spilling all his plans."

"He might. To throw me off the scent, keep me occupied. This way I'm a foil against certain parties while he makes secret moves elsewhere."

"You want to hear one of those moves? Earlier today, Skipper stopped me on the road and tried to buy me off. He also assumes Heidi and I will split up, so that even if I land Eloy's acres I'll wind up unloading them to pay her off. Then, in about five minutes of fast talking he threatened my life, offered to buy the dope—first, at my original investment, then double that, then he asked me to be front man for him in purchasing the land for an eighteen-grand finder's fee, plus half my own shit. After that, he said if Nancy Ryan and I tied the knot, they'd make me a stockholder in the Simian Foundation. And he wound up ordering me to hand over the coke gratis and front the land for a ten-percent finder's fee. All that, of course, is on top of Cobey's earlier roadside offer to make a deal with Ray Verboten, on my part, for the coke and turn over to me half of whatever he could wrest from Ray. I blew it again trying to neutralize him by coughing up what I know about his plot to grab enough bucks for Eloy's property by embezzling from Skipper. He left in a huff."

"Hmmm. Well, that might not hurt us too badly. At least they know we have a few aces up our own sleeves. Cobey I figure we can ignore—though Skipper can't. In fact, I bet he still won't muzzle me on the Cobey D. case, even though our cards are on the table."

"But that's crazy—isn't it?"

"Like a fox. While I'm preoccupied zapping Cobey and suffering Roger's sure-to-be-outraged invective, he's out there plotting with Nikita Smatterling and F. Lee Bailey, for all I'll know, on how to directly bugger Eloy, with or without your help."

"But Eloy won't jump at his cash if I'm still in the picture."

"Without the dope, he figures you're not in the picture."

"But I have the coke."

"I know that, you know that, even Skipper knows that. But he's also aware that you don't know squat about how to package, much less unload, it. And through Ray Verboten, and other lesser functionaries, the word is already out in the dope hotspots of the Southwest not to touch our scam with a ten-foot reefer. That way, any Chamisaville sale we try will have to be on the black market, and we'll have to wade through hell to stir even the faintest play. Because anybody who buys from us is telling every other pusher around to go fuck themselves.

And Skipper figures that's as good as if we had no coke at all."

"I haven't pushed a gram, and already I'm blacklisted."

"On other fronts, Scott Harrison may or may not have been implicated in the fracas last night. Regardless, this morning he filed suit in district court against Eloy, figuring he had better move fast to offset the Dallas-Petrie-Nuzum troika. At best, he'll snarl the property in filibustering litigation so that even if you score the cash, Eloy won't be able to sell. If that fails, Scott may blow the cocaine whistle on us."

"I'll tell the judge about Scott's water-rights pact with Roger. That amounts to outright collusion between Roger and Cobey and Scott in the Nuzum embezzlement caper."

"Don't forget, though, that Skipper's been cooperating with Roger in order to nail Cobey's ass. They're all on the take from each other. So if it came down to an actual court fight, they'd all suddenly back off, join hands, and present a united front against you."

"I'm not sure I understand the logic, but I suppose that makes sense."

"I've been mulling over this situation all afternoon, and I've finally arrived at a fairly astute analysis of the situation."

"Namely?"

"It's a can of worms." Tribby giggled and exhaled iridescent marijuana fumes.

"I'm not laughing."

"But you got to admit it is funny," Tribby said gently. "It's like one of those whacky sexual Victorian farces where you can't tell the players without a program."

"To round out the picture, then, maybe you should know this. When I chatted with Eloy this afternoon, he had assumed somebody else won the dope last night, and was planning to rob a bank."

"I know."

"How could you know that?"

"In the bar on Saturday night he mentioned it to Diana and she and Rachel got to reminiscing about one thing and another. . . ."

Joe said, "This whole crazy shtik is absurd."

"I think it's a rather amusing scenario."

"But who stands a chance?" Joe said miserably. "When I

start seriously kibitzing the game, I don't seem to be holding many cards."

"One thing I don't understand is Nancy Ryan's role," Tribby mused. "Theoretically, she's Smatterling's stooge. When you two got it on, I figured she meant to addle your brain so you couldn't act. Or to split you and Heidi, thereby rendering the land-purchase pointless. Both of these goals she seems to have achieved without even raising a sweat. But why, then, sic her monkey on the tea box? Without it, you're not even a twenty-to-one long shot for that property."

"You mean you think that bitch seduced me in cold blood just to blow my shot at Eloy's farm?"

"Why else would she be doing you up in such style?"

"Maybe she thinks I'm cute."

"Well, I can only look at the developing patterns."

"The sex is very heavy."

"Bravo."

"You're not impressed?"

"Not as impressed as I am by the fact that she threw a curve last night by putting the coke back in your hands, when all she had to do was ride out the gunfight on the sidelines and turn the keys to Eloy's palatial estate over to the Simian Foundation."

"You actually figured all along that was the reason she and I started balling?"

Tribby shrugged. "I got a puzzle. I'm trying to collect pieces and fit them together." He pointed skyward. "It's fun, a titillating game. Like drawing lines between all the bright twinkles overhead to make a dipper, a crab, a scorpion...."

"Wow." Joe was momentarily overcome. "It sure is beautiful up there."

So they sat, bewildered, placid, thoughtful. Joe said, "I'm beginning to think this whole antic is doomed. I'll never score that land. It's crazy. All my life I assumed I had a natural-born right to all the middle-class amenities. I mean, how much is one-point-seven acres and a house of my own just big enough for a four-person family? That's what capitalism is all about. Every time I click on the TV, or look at magazine ads, there's a million good-looking Mommies and Daddies and Kiddies and pet Doggies and Kitties leaving a spotless suburban garage in their road-tested, thirty-one mpg, rotary-engine chariots, looking so happy and secure it's obscene."

"But we all know they're miserable. The promoters just want us to think they're happy."

"If we know they're unhappy, why do we buy it?"

"Because we *want* to be happy, idiot."

"But we know beforehand that crap *won't* make us happy. So why am I risking my neck—"

His words slurred, slightly mocking, Tribby said, "Listen, why worry about it? Something will come up. Meanwhile, the adventure makes it all worthwhile. Tomorrow we'll all meet and devise an infallible plan."

"Infallible," Joe murmured caustically. "Why don't you smoke another couple dozen joints?"

"Hey, America is perfect, Joe. We'll figure out a way."

"I dunno. How come I feel so blue?"

"You got them old Nirvana Blues," Tribby giggled irreverently. "Things are so good they make you sorrowful."

"Tell me about it," Joe sarcasmed gloomily. And added: "Screw you and your Colombia two-toke."

"Did you hear that, Universe?" Tribby guffawed. "Mr. Idealistic here is growing cynical!"

&

Cynical? Not really.

Ten minutes later, halfway to Eloy's land, his single headlight flickered and failed. Joe pumped the brakes, and, several hundred yards farther along, coasted to a stop. As soon as his eyes grew accustomed to the darkness, he shifted into first, and continued on steering by starlight. The ghostly landscape of enormous hovering cottonwoods and warm yellow houselights extended a hand of reconciliation. The small snowcap on Hija Negrita burned like a lyrical fire of ice. His brief spell atop the pyramid hadn't been so bad. In fact, though he hadn't smoked, Joe felt mildly giddy. He even chortled about his dramatic weighted note. Oh for a photograph of their startled faces! Anthony Quinn had no more Zorbaesque stranglehold on life than did Joe Miniver right now! His blood fluttered like wind-caught daffodils! *I wandered lonely as a cloud...!* His ego inhabited the coordinated panache of a Romanian gymnast! A magic moment, one of those that occasionally usurped his paranoia no matter how hard he struggled to be wizened and tight-assed, had captured his soul. Joe Miniver cruising down the starlit boulevard in his headlightless Green Gorilla right after a catacylsmic horror show with his rapidly-becoming-ex-family, was a pure rhapsody. Where these natural highs hailed from, he did not know; but God forbid he ever try to look them in the mouth, either!

Soaring was the only answer.

A skunk waddled across the road. Silver light glinted off the wings of a veering bat. The nocturnal frog-babble created a summery Christmas sound. Joe wished he could float along, without headlights, on a night like this, forever.

Slowly, he jounced up the potholed driveway to Eloy's spread. Geronimo waited patiently in the front field, an ancient argentine apparition. Joe stopped in the middle of the driveway and switched off the ignition. The horse whinnied softly. Both his hands draped over the steering wheel, Joe shut his eyes and sang:

> *Tell my why*
> *The stars do shine.*
> *Tell me why*
> *The ivy twines.*
> *Tell me why*
> *The sky's so blue . . .*
> *And I will tell you*
> *Why I love you.*

Then he abandoned the truck. Breaking off a weed, Joe fitted it between his teeth. *God that tasted good*! He tiptoed up the driveway, praying that he wouldn't trigger the howls of Eloy's menagerie. No lights burned in the small adobe. Joe had caught the chihuahuas, turkeys, and geese off guard—nobody made a peep. Her car—Diana's—was parked in the shadow of the old man's sagging pickup. She had pitched her tent, right on the edge of Eloy's six-tree orchard. It was larger than Joe had suspected: a real live-in nylon house that might have slept eight.

No lights shimmered inside. But when he said, "Diana? Are you in there?," her whispered reply came back: "Sure. Come on in."

Joe unzipped the mesh flaps, and, on his knees, entered the silken womb. Seated cross-legged on her sleeping bag, wearing only panties and a radiant white T-shirt, Diana was brushing her long hair. Starlight, strained through thin membranes, blurred the highlights in her features, and softened shadows.

"How did it go?" she asked.

"All right, I guess. You didn't have any trouble?"

"Not a bit. That sweet old man helped me pitch the tent."

"That's nice."

"He certainly loves this place."

"Yeah, I know." Guilt over his lust to obtain it punched Joe in the solar plexus.

"He planted all these fruit trees, and most of the cottonwoods," Diana said. "And the honey locusts. And the four little aspens years ago. It's fascinating to hear his stories. When he and his wife built that little house on this land they had barely reached twenty. There wasn't another house within a mile. He dug that well by hand and lined it with rocks. He's a funny old guy, really loves to talk. He told me a great story."

"Which was?"

"Well, unlike a lot of old-timers around here, he liked coyotes. In this area they used to run rampant. Sometimes he and his old lady would sneak out before dawn and sit in the apple trees training binoculars on the coyotes when they trotted through the pastureland."

"Huh." Her enthusiastic riff on the old geezer he must soon evict if he came up with the cash to buy the land made Joe queasy. How could he deal honorably with Eloy? The answer, of course, was he couldn't. Joe wondered petulantly: why was it that God never gave anything even semi-nice, without making you pay for it through the nose?

Diana's brush generated electrical sparks as she tugged it slowly down through her full mane. Joe said, "Hey, look at that."

"At what?"

"All the sparks in your hair."

"I have beautiful hair. Do you think I'm pretty?"

Pretty? Joe hesitated, put on guard by her voice. It wasn't quite innocent; it contained traps.

"I think you're attractive. Especially when you smile. And you have a beautiful body." Her large breasts, revealed by the T-shirt, surprised him. They were sizable enough to be described as pendulous; they were beautiful—and, for her slim body, oversized—globes. A letch for her abruptly keelhauled Joe. The moody nocturnal light, combined with the friction sparking in her hair and the T-shirt outlandishly hailing her breasts, had his heart mildly fibrillating.

"My tits are too big. I've always been ashamed of them."

"I like 'em big."

"Well, whatever. It's neither here nor there."

"Where is it?" he joked.

"With sex?"

"Well, sure—if you want."

"I don't know. People always beat up on me a lot. I put out a bunch of energy, I attract men. It's really easy. But then it seems that violence always happens. Never have I even found a man who remotely understood me."

Joe studied her body, her facial expression, the lax way (the provocative way) she stroked her hair. It added up to a come-on. But not her voice. It came from a curiously remote, perhaps even dangerous, place.

"I guess all in all," she said confidently, "you could say I'm a pretty cute chick. Still, men have to be careful with me. I'm really vulnerable. I'm more naïve than you would believe."

Joe had been prepared for idle chatter, a brief noncommital rap, and then perhaps she would let him shack up beside her. But he had known, the second he entered, that a heavier adventure lay in store. Already he had a hard-on. Which in no way guaranteed he'd have the courage to propose they ball.

"How did it go with your wife?" Diana asked. "Okay?"

"That's hard to say. We had a fight. I threw a rock through the window. But you never know."

"Are you guys in love?"

"We were. Sure, I guess we still are."

"But you might get divorced?"

"Right now everything is up in the air. It's a crazy limbo—"

"I don't ever fall in love. I can't stand nostalgia. Or any kind of romantic crap. Sometimes people make me so sick. . . ."

Joe studied her eyes: was she being hard just for effect, trying to calculate, from his reactions and his answers, whether he was safe or a potential rapist?

"There's no point in being cynical," Joe said. "As for love— well, you just never know." Talk about insipid!

"I can't stand jealousy trips," Diana said quietly. "Everybody always gets jealous and then the whole thing falls apart. I don't give a damn what anybody I'm with does in their spare time. And I don't expect anybody to care about what I do. But as soon as you get together with somebody, they always want to put you in an emotional cage. Then it winds up violent when I want to get out."

"'Violent'?"

"Well, I've been raped almost a dozen times."

"How did that happen?"

"Sometimes it was guys I knew, sometimes just people. I used to hitchhike a lot." Her voice sounded so hostile. Yet the brief smiles she released were vintage coquette: they gave her a sultry, partially tragic bloom. Beyond that, her breasts seemed to be pleading: *Touch me, feel me, knead me, fondle me, heft me, slide your dick between me, suck me, crush me, you big ol' hunk you!*

"You should at least be sensible about when you hitchhike," Joe said. The usual preliminary weakness induced by his high-falutin lust was usurping his motor activities. Not for a million years had he dreamed she could be this attractive. Yet if asked to explain, he could not have defined the origins of her sexual affluence. Her manner and tone actually seemed a-carnal: yet her eyes sparkled with cockteasing energy. In the back of his mind, a faint warning bell jangled: cuidado, muchacho, this one might be a real lulu!

"I've always picked up people that interested me," she said. "I never worried about sexual proclivities. In that way I guess I'm terribly innocent. On the other hand, I've had men stick with me for months, even though I wouldn't make love with them. Something profound in me keeps them interested."

At a loss for coherent replies, Joe remained silent.

She said, "You'd like to touch my breasts, wouldn't you?"

"Well, I can't deny..."

"Go ahead. You can feel them."

Reaching for her, Joe wondered, What's wrong with this girl? His fingertips touched that swollen flesh; thrills banged into him like bullets. Her brush halted. She cocked her head, listening to a faraway jester, but her dark eyes had locked into his. Against his fingers her fat nipples burgeoned like inflating steel nubs. Laying down the brush, she tossed her silky tresses. Her lips were framed in an all-knowing superior smile. Why so uneasy? Joe asked himself. Was she in too calculated a control? One hand hefted her breast, assessing weight, texture, consistency. When he twirled, between his thumb and index finger, a nipple, she arched slightly, but her hands made no move to touch him. Not aroused . . . ?

"Your tits are wonderful. They're like Baggies full of vanilla pudding."

"You're so romantic."

"You said you despised romantic crap."

"What you just said is romantic crap disguised as good-natured jocular teasing."

Winchlike, her breasts tugged him closer. He pushed her back gently, scrooched up even with her face, and was about to settle his lips over hers, when those dark eyes stopped him.

"You're so calm, Diana." His own heart was pounding.

"I feel calm."

"Are we going to make love?"

"That's for me to know and for you to find out."

They kissed lightly. With his tongue-tip, Joe traced a line around her mouth. Her arms refused to embrace him: they were flopped loosely atop her sleeping bag and amid the rubble of her personal effects scattered around the tent. How to interpret such passivity? When he pressed against her large, soft lips she responded a little. Her tongue was rough, but beneath him her body seemed astonishingly pliable.

Joe squirmed against her, but she didn't reciprocate. When he licked at a nostril, she murmured, "Stop it, I don't like that."

From her face, he traveled south to those breasts, burrowing happily into the plump Eden, snuffling and sucking through the T-shirt fabric, working over the fantastic nipples until he could almost hear their tiny squeaks of erotic bliss. Her right hand alighted tentatively in his hair, guiding him without pressure. Joe rocked and rolled with her a little, feeling his oats, yearning to screw. She flopped around with him, but initiated no active moves. Her eyes remained wide open, her all-knowing smile never for a moment flickered. She had a tiny waist, slim hips, a tight little butt, lovely legs. Yet something was wrong. When finally he dared slip a hand into her groin, she stayed his hand. "No, Joe. I don't want you to."

They kissed some more, rolled around, thrashed a bit. Joe hugged hard, wanting to squash her body into his own. She bore it quietly until his bear hugs got out of hand, then whimpered, "Ouch, you're hurting me."

Cued by her words, Joe realized he wanted to hurt her. Because of her passivity, her incredible body, and that unnerving smile, he wanted to kill. "I won't hurt you," he re-assured. "I just want to make love."

Abruptly, her hand began stroking his head. "You poor boy. You're so hungry."

True, so true. The fever of his passion was painful: his groin throbbed, his heart ached. Various pleas sprang to his lips: *Please God, just let me fuck her, and I'll never ask you for anything again. I even promise to join the church!* And: *I love you, Diana, I don't know why, but I really do! I'd sell my soul to the devil for just a half-hour inside your jeans!*

Leakage from his penis had gooeyed her thighs. Joe strained, convinced that if they didn't make love, he'd go crazy. In his arms, her weight and shape and peculiar darkness of soul conspired to make her more sexually desirable than anybody on whom he had ever taken a bead. Crushing against her, he pumped . . . then turned her over and achingly ground himself against her tiny buttocks, nuzzling in her hair, against the nape of her neck.

"I'm gonna enter you," he whispered into one ear.

"No you're not."

"Hey . . ." he whispered, "what's the matter?"

"Nothing's the matter."

"Then why can't we make love?"

"Because I don't think I want to."

Peeved, Joe said, "Then why are you letting this happen?"

"Because I feel sorry for you, I guess."

"'Sorry' for me?" He drooped atop her, panting, so erect he thought his penis might shatter. "Why 'sorry' for me? I'm fine."

"You seem so hungry."

Joe thought: I'm learning something about life. I'm learning that when everything seems perfect, when it looks as if I'm on the brink of an Erotic Adventure Personified, that only means it's going to be ten times more blatantly aggravating than all the other situations I've been in that began with two strikes obviously against them.

Reaching underneath, he cupped her breasts, and refused to let the dream die. "Why don't you want to make love, Diana?"

"I didn't say that. I only said I don't want to with you right now."

"Well, if not now, when?"

"Look, if you want me to, I'll go down on you."

"Come again?"

"'Go down on you' is an expression meaning I'll suck your cock."

"I know *that*—geez! I just don't believe what you said."

"Well, that's the way it is."

Joe pushed off, backing up a little so that he was sitting on her legs. Beautiful hair was tangled across her shoulders, around her head. Her arms, outstretched in a lax way, gave her the appearance of a child about to make a facedown snow angel.

"I don't understand you at all."

"Take it or leave it."

"I'll leave it." Joe slipped his hand up under her T-shirt, pressing his palm lightly against the small of her back. "You're not turned on by me. Are you a lesbian?"

"God, you're such a typical male. I wonder if there's any man anywhere in the United States who's sophisticated enough, or liberated enough, not to ask that question of a girl like me."

"I can see why you get raped." His anger, oddly enough, was tempered by curiosity: she interested him a lot. And he added: "Well, let's just forget about sex."

"I said I would go down on you if you want."

"'If I want.' What about you? I wouldn't want a blowjob if there's no reciprocal passion attached to it."

"See what I mean? You're a slave to old-fashioned romantic notions."

What could he reply? "Actually, you just manufacture a false feeling to justify the sex," Diana continued. "You think you feel passion, or love, or whatever, but it's phony. Ten minutes after ninety percent of the men alive screw ninety percent of the women alive, nobody feels a thing. The passion ends as soon as they get what they want, which is usually just a hot body to aid masturbation."

Meekly, Joe said, "But I enjoy sex. I think it's fun. For both people. You don't have to be committed for life just to share some erotic warmth."

"Bullshit." Her tone was whimsical, calm—not at all unfriendly.

A woman's voice outside the tent said, "Joe . . . ?"

"Who's that?"

"It's me, Nancy. Can I come in?"

"No, wait a minute! How come I didn't hear you drive up?"

"There's an old pickup blocking the driveway. I only want to see you for a minute."

"But . . . I mean, I'm not alone, I'm in here with a friend."

"I don't mind."

"Well, *I* do. Nancy, what are you doing over here?"

"I just thought you would want to know all about Sasha."

Oh God! He had forgotten the monkey. "Of course I want to hear all about him. But—"

"You can come in," Diana said. "It's okay with me."

Stooping, Nancy pushed aside the flaps and entered. Diana didn't bother turning over to say hello. Embarrassed, Joe squatted as far away as possible from the woman he had been astraddle only seconds earlier, thinking: If I somehow manage to fast-talk my way back into Heidi's good graces, I'll never leave the family again. It's too cold, cruel, and absurd out here in the Real World of swinging singles.

Nancy's red swollen eyes and tearstained face lit up a little. She didn't seem at all to register Diana's lascivious, almost naked body languidly stretched out at her feet. She said, "Hi. Gosh, it's good to see you. After that asthma attack last night, I was so worried. And of course I was terribly upset about Sasha. And then I thought I'd better see you because you might be going crazy with guilt feelings. And I didn't want you to punish Michael."

"I'm okay. Of course I was worried. . . ." Joe had never felt this trapped, ashamed, uncomfortable. Plainly, he was a hopeless neophyte in the ruthless mating game. He was also a shallow, hideously self-centered bastard. He clamped his teeth to keep them from chattering. "It's been a confusing day."

Nancy asked, "Are you spending the night here? Or do you want to come over to my house and wait for news about Sasha?"

"Well, I . . . uh . . . um . . . actually, I'm really tired. Everything at home is so bollixed up. I think I need to be alone for a while. I'm right in the middle of a very heavy ARC break."

She gave him a funny look. "I'm so worried about Sasha. The next forty-eight hours are crucial."

"I bet. I'm really sorry. I don't know what to do." If he acted like a brainless spastic maybe some crazy deus ex machina would take pity and save him!

"You know, you did promise that you'd be over tonight, Joe. Remember? If you hadn't promised, I wouldn't even have bothered to come over."

"I promised? When was that . . . ?"

"Hey." Gently, she touched his knee. "It's all right, I understand. You don't have to panic."

Diana exclaimed, "Whew, it's getting hot in here." Sitting up, she grabbed the T-shirt hem and stripped off the garment. Her breasts jounced provocatively and settled. "There, that's better." She smiled piquantly.

Nancy said, "Well, I left Bradley alone, so I better be running along. He's almost in shock about Sasha. I am too, of course. I don't know what I'll do if that poor monkey. . . ."

"Michael didn't know what he was doing," Joe said. "It was a terrible accident. . . ."

"I know, dear. . . . Now I have to go. . . ." Yet at the doorway, her unflappable composure (as Joe had known it would have to sooner or later) suddenly cracked. Twisting until it became a parody of ugliness, her face released those great time-honored equalizers, tears, in droves. "It's just that you *promised*!" Nancy added: "I was fixing such a nice meal for you when Michael arrived and started blasting. . . ." Then she fled.

"Wow," Diana commented acerbically. "That lady is a professional."

"She really loves the monkey," Joe said protectively. "And what's the big idea of shedding the T-shirt? Man, you're *crude*."

"You're calling *me* crude?"

"You didn't have to do that."

"Your hypocritical apologies about that dumb monkey almost made me puke."

"You took off that shirt because you wanted to hurt her and make me uncomfortable."

"I figure if you got 'em, you might as well flaunt 'em."

"I don't like your games," Joe said.

"Don't give me that self-righteous drivel. It's all a game. All you had on your mind ten seconds before she appeared was nailing me. Then suddenly you reek of insipid apologies. Only, you can't go console her because you think you still might have a shot at me tonight. Now, usually I'm neither this crass nor this crude. But that woman is a heavy gameplayer, don't worry about her—she can take it. I'd worry about myself, if I were you. Remember, you get A's for being a shitheel, but you're also a babe in the woods. She'll eat you for breakfast and spit out your bones."

"What about you?"

"I'm a different kind of person. Other games amuse me."

He had been morally and emotionally drawn and quartered. He had been shamed and made to feel small. He was a wishy-washy, ethically pathetic, not even macho, ratfink. The need for solace sent pleading supplications—like uplifted hands in a Bangladesh breadline—out from his heart. Joe pushed Diana over again, embracing her with all his might. His lips, pressed against a hollow in her throat, burned against a pulsing artery. Uncomfortably diminished in his own eyes, he held to her tightly, wanting to cry. Whatever had happened to the myth of the macho assman? This was no fun at all. Becoming a target for ridicule and scorn was all his pussy-chasing would ever net him. That, and a total loss of human dignity. A thousand Sashas would dance on his grave!

"If you want," Diana murmured timidly into his ear, "you can fuck me now."

Joe almost killed it by hollering "What?!?" Self-preservation tempered by greed made him look before he leapt. When he was quite in control, he said softly, "I don't understand."

"Oh for Christ's sake, you don't have to 'understand' everything in life. I'm ready now. That's all. It's okay. Just be careful. . . ."

The lovemaking was like drinking champagne out of family-heirloom glasses under the watchful scrutiny of his grandmother, his mother, and his great-grandmother, at a Thanksgiving dinner in 1947, knowing that if somehow he broke or damaged the impossibly valuable (and fragile) vessel, his name would not only go down in Miniver Infamy, but three generations of ghosts would hound him into eternity. She was tight, surprisingly small, shockingly frail: once inside, Joe almost feared to move. "Don't come in me," she litanized, her body tensed, terrified of his orgasm. "I don't want a baby, I really don't want a baby, I don't *ever* want a baby." After a while, Joe realized it would be a sexless screw. Withdrawing tenderly, he embraced her, saying "I'm sorry." He felt terrible. She said, "No no, it's my fault, it's always my fault. I'm just scared of men, that's all, I don't know why. But I'm terrified. And it's never been any different, not with anybody. Just *please* don't make me pregnant, I'm begging you."

"I won't. It's all right, Diana. It's over."

A tear seeped from the corner of that tough little cookie's tightly shut eye.

"I'm really sorry." The sensation for Joe was of having violated something truly precious. "If I had known...but I couldn't tell from the way you act. You seem so tough."

A wry grin broke through her tears. "That's me: the toughest scared-shitless kid on the block."

"Have you made love much?"

"Are you kidding? I hate it. Now I'm going to live in terror until I get my period." Sitting up, she reached into a wrinkled paper bag and removed a bottle of Maalox.

"I didn't come. Honest."

"It doesn't matter. It's like, if I got pregnant, I know I wouldn't have the guts for an abortion. But I couldn't stand to have a kid, either. I don't ever want children. I don't like any things you can get attached to. As soon as you start loving something, it gets taken away, or it dies."

"That's not always true."

"It's true enough." She unscrewed the Maalox and guzzled down a generous amount.

Joe said, "If you don't want kids, I mean, this is the modern age—there's a million styles of contraception. Rubbers for me, diaphragms, the pill, foam, an IUD."

"Everything you mentioned for me, except the diaphragm, is dangerous or detrimental. And with a diaphragm, you never know."

"Haven't you ever enjoyed making love? Or just being in a relationship?"

"I don't know. Once or twice maybe. But it always falls apart. I don't know how to handle love or make it work out. I'm not tough enough. They always wind up exasperated, beat the stuffings out of me, and take off. Now I don't really want anything with any kind of so-called love in it. Because love is a bum rap. All love means is sooner or later I'm gonna get it. I thought you were going to beat me up and rape me tonight."

"Never."

"They always say 'never.' If I hadn't given you a green light, you would have wanted to kill me."

Not him, he was different. Joe had a brief fantasy: He would tame this hardened child, teach her to make love voluptuously, look forward to it, adore her own body...they'd make a child. Blossoming into a rare beauty, she would come to cherish and revere him with a loyalty and trust he had never known.

(For the purposes of the fantasy, he would forget that to

cultivate her into such a superlative being he would have to abandon a loving wife and two beautiful children who'd cling frantically to his clothing like kittens about to be drowned as he left them!)

Rousing himself, Joe wandered barefoot into the back field, and took forever urinating, his head thrown back, admiring the stars. How could so few, who had so much, be so miserable? The sky was so clear he could almost hear the constellations sizzling. Diana Clayman was beautiful, healthy, sexy, intelligent, and a basket case. Bright moonlight on the mountainsides defined each individual pine tree; the silvery sheen on their branches made it appear as if a warm summer snow had frosted the somnolent hills.

Back in the tent, when he stretched out beside Diana, something hard and uncomfortable lodged against his back. Reaching underneath the blankets, a bathrobe, and some clothing, Joe latched on to a revolver, a six-shot, double-action, .22 pistol. It was loaded.

"This is your gun?"

"I always carry a weapon. I don't think I would be afraid to use it."

Joe inspected the piece, frightened by it.

"I'm the only guy in this town I know who doesn't own a gun," he said thoughtfully. "Maybe I'm the only person in America without a piece. But please don't tell anybody."

"Why not?"

"I guess because then, if the word gets around, a whole bunch of robbers, muggers, and other assorted riffraff will lay siege to my house, knowing I couldn't kill them."

"Why don't you have a gun?"

"I'm scared. I doubt I could shoot somebody, even if my life depended on it. I figure, too, that if they know I have a gun they'll come after me with guns. Beyond that, one of my kids could find the pistol and accidentally blow his or her brains out. Heidi and I might have a terrible fight and in a single insane moment of emotional uproar one of us might grab the betsy and do a job on the other. Finally, every now and then I sink into almost suicidal depressions, and that's no time to have a weapon handy."

She hugged him. "If you're going to be in the cocaine racket, you better learn to carry a gun."

"I keep three large stones under the table beside the bed," Joe said sleepily. "I can throw very accurately."

Diana murmured and began drifting. Unable to dehorn himself while pressed against her, Joe rolled away, tucked up his knees, and awaited sleep. Instead, he barely sagged under the surface and was accosted by unnerving dreams: lyrical, sexual, unintelligible. Little sparrows flitted through his hands, but he couldn't grab them. Sometimes his fingertips touched their feathers. Diana was a business secretary in a typical office. Joe traipsed in and out, seeing her about indeterminate things. Eventually, he summoned enough nerve to touch her: she didn't mind. Then he lured her outside, onto a stairwell landing, and awkwardly hugged her, intensely conscious of great feelings of love.

When he surfaced his heart was pounding uncontrollably. He was covered with goosebumps and unable to breathe. Carefully, on all fours he crawled outside. Chilly night air reinforced the goosebumps. Stepping awkwardly over pebbles and twigs, terrified he would awaken Eloy's flocks, Joe reached the truck, located a bottle of auxiliary pills in the glove compartment, popped two, and returned to the tent. Until his breathing returned to normal, he sat upright, willing himself to calm down.

The bottom line in all of this was that he had no idea how to cope with sexual freedom. After twenty years of avidly (and surreptitiously) thumbing through *Playboy*, Joe was no closer to understanding from where those jocks, studs, and slimebags derived their smug self-assurance. Hadn't he longingly daydreamed a million times about strolling through life with a pipe in his mouth, a superior sneer, and a bevy of Lainie Kazans and Jayne Mansfields clinging to his muscular arms? "Buenos días, Heff, how's it going? I was just down in the sauna balling Miss October. Now I'm headed for the solarium where Miss July and Miss December are waiting. Why hello there, Miss February . . . what's that? Sure, be delighted . . . I can probably fit you in right after five . . . eh? Oh, of course, by all means, bring your whips. Say, Heff, loan me a little of your Borkum Riff, would you?—I'm all out. Thanks. And by the way, could you give me a lift to the Cannes Film Festival in the Big Bunny—you can? Swell. Bye-bye . . ."

Puerile fantasy! And one that had competed with another heavy daydream also featuring himself, although this time as a balding and toothless, yet dignified old bloke posing respectfully beside a seventy-eight-year-old Heidi for their golden-wedding-anniversary photograph. Despite his years, Joe positively glowed with health and pride, having just returned from Oslo after accepting the Nobel Peace Prize. He had earned it for his distinguished career as a world-renowned radical leader who, after seventeen years of heroic sacrifice with a small band of faithful radicals high in the Rocky Mountains, had descended onto the Great Plains, leading America through the fantastic upheaval that had established an egalitarian Marxist-Leninist State which had finally created liberty and justice for all. History had appointed Miniver, at long last, to select a governing junta made up of women, blacks, Chicanos, Catholics, and Puerto Ricans! His name was more revered than that of Castro, Allende, Camilo Torres, Luis Turcios-Lima, Eugene Debs, Che Guevara, Frantz Fanon, and Ernest Hemingway. And all because of an exemplary life in which he had been a model husband and father, a tireless revolutionary, a compassionate humanitarian, a nonsexist, nonchauvinistic, totally unselfish (not to mention visionary) human being.

Diana twitched, emitting little squeaks and groans. Joe thought about his family. No doubt Heather had already moved in to sleep with Heidi—she always did whenever Joe spent a night away from home. Heather needed a bed the size of a football field to sleep on, she thrashed about that much. She never bothered Heidi, though: his wife loved to cuddle, she enjoyed Heather's octopus appendages flung around her. The few times Joe had let Heather sleep with him when Heidi was elsewhere had been dramatic failures. In her sleep, she would literally kick him out of bed. Relentlessly, he kept shoving her away. But two minutes later she would return, grinding her teeth, elbowing him in the ribs, kicking him in the balls. In exasperation, at 3:00 A.M., Joe would end the experiment by carting her back to her own bed, shaking her awake, and ordering her never to sleep with him again.

Seated upright, Joe reflected on things almost until dawn. He felt so sad, tragic, beautiful. He tried to think about selfishness, narcissism, lust, the general preoccupation with narcotics, and the absurd difficulty of buying land and a house. Then he nestled beside Diana, quietly circled his arms protectively about her, and fell asleep vying for the title of Loneliest Man On Earth.

4
Tuesday

Six at the beginning means:
He gets his tail in the water.
Humiliating.

❧

"Hey, dad," Michael shouted. "Are you in there?"

Diana tapped his shoulder, blew softly in his ear. "Your kid's calling, Joe. Hey, meshuggeneh, wake up...."

"Mrmph?" Joe opened one eye, disoriented. Then, as the gist of her message sank in, he awoke, alarmed. "Who? Which one?"

"I think his name is Michael."

Hoarsely, Joe called, "Hello?"

Michael said, "Hi, Daddy."

"What time is it?" Joe groped in the refuse for his Timex. "Where's my reloj?" he grumbled. And in a louder voice: "Michael, how come you ain't in school?"

"We're going. But my bike got a flat tire. Those two dogs charged us, and we had a crack-up in the ditch. I don't know how it happened, but the tire is flat."

Would he ever, in his life, know the luxury of sleeping late? It seemed there hadn't been a single day, in the last thirty-eight years, when he had not been summarily aroused by alarm clocks, parents, or kids long before the sun had even halfway accosted the eastern horizon. If they got divorced instead of buying Eloy's land, Joe thought, then while his share of the coke boodle allowed for inactivity he'd make it a point to sleep until noon!

"What's the matter with the bus?" Locating the watch, he fumbled to attach it.

"We missed it," Michael admitted, without bothering to lay on much contrition. Heather added, "Mommy had an eight o'clock appointment with Nikita Smatterling."

"Is that Heather out there with you?" Joe gravely pulled on socks, then buttoned up his shirt.

"Who didja think he meant when he said 'we'?" Heather's snotty voice asked.

Joe grimaced at Diana and gestured comically: *See what I have to put up with every day? Ain't you lucky—you're single!*

"Who are you in there with?" Heather added.

281

"None of your business. A friend."

"Which friend?"

"Hey, Heather—" Joe tugged on a sneaker and fumbled with the laces. "Do me a favor, don't worry about it. You got time enough to be a yenta when you grow up."

"Are you in there with 'her'?"

"I mean it," Joe threatened. "Curiosity killed the cat."

Michael asked nervously, "Are you gonna give us a ride?"

"Yeah, I guess so." Joe leaned over, kissing Diana goodbye. "Only this is the last time I ever give you two slobs a lift when you miss the bus, y'unnerstand? I'm sick and tired of your inability to dress, eat, and get out the door in the morning. It's very inconsiderate to me and your mom. . . ."

His standard rap, one he'd recited, almost without variation, ever since Michael metamorphosed into a professional lollygagger five years ago. Did they even *hear* it now?

Heather complained, "It wasn't *my* fault we missed the bus."

Michael begged to differ. "Yes it was. If you would've just eaten your Cocoa Puffs faster we would of gotten out there in plenty of time."

"Cocoa Puffs?" Joe howled.

Heather's self-righteous goody-goody smarmy-bitch voice answered: "Mommy bought us a box yesterday."

Holy Toledo! Absent two days, and the entire moral structure of the family collapsed! "How could she do something like that?" Joe turned away from Diana, facing the tent flap like a Christian about to confront the arena. "She knows I don't allow that poison in the house. Each box contains a grand total of five thousand calories and one vitamin. You eat that stuff you'll die of malnutrition in a week!"

"They're neat," Heather teased. "I'm glad you don't live with us anymore. Mommy said if we're good she's gonna get us some Nestlé chocolate tomorrow."

"If she does, I'll murder her!" Touching Diana's thigh goodbye, Joe plunged into the sunshine. "She knows damn well we're supporting the Nestlé boycott, and why!"

Both kids were a mess. Michael's shirt was filthy; his knobby knees poked through shredded bluejean fabric; he wore one blue and one red sock; and mud-caked sneakers. Heather's pink jumpsuit seemed to have been laundered in vomit; 2,001 knots decorated her frayed laces. Obviously, during these past traumatic days, they had blown the laundry run. With heartrending vividness, Joe pictured the kids scrabbling madly through the hamper, searching for something—anything—to wear. Why was it the children of rich folks always looked like ragamuffins, whereas poor kids always seemed spick-and-span?

Neatly wetted down, except for the cowlick, Michael's hair, at least, toed the line. Tied by fluorescent green yarn, Heather's locks hung in dual ponytails. They both chewed gum.

Gum? "Where'd you get that gum?"

Heather shot right back: "It's Trident, Daddy. It's sugarless, and you allow us to have that."

"It better be Trident. Because if it isn't—" Then he noticed Heather's grotesque fingernails and gagged. She had Magic Markered them every color in the rainbow. Joe bawled, "What in Christ's name did you do to your fingernails?"

Heather pouted, inspecting her hands. "Get off my case, Pop."

"What are you trying to do, grow up to be the dreamboat of every male chauvinist pig in America? When are you gonna learn to play soccer? Next thing, it'll be Barbie and Ken dolls!"

"All my friends say my fingernails look pretty."

"All your friends got their taste in their assholes. Now come on. Leave the bike here, Michael, we're already late."

Eloy Irribarren was seated in a sunshine-flooded chair beside his door, smoking a cigarette. He waved. "Buenos días."

"Can't stop, Eloy. Gotta rush the kids to school—they're late."

"I'm gonna turn over my garden today," the old man called. "This is perfect weather."

My garden? Joe's heart sank. Maybe on his way back from school he should stop at the county sheriff's office and beg one of those irresponsible thugs to drive over on Monday morning two minutes after the closing to evict the old man (and his dying dog, and his dying horse, and the rest of his ancient barnyard charges) before Eloy got the impression Joe was a soft touch who'd let him and his herds, flocks, and gaggles stick around ad infinitum.

Even contemplating a move that vulgar gave Joe the willies. Every winter newspaper across the nation published gruesome stories about how a ninety-year-old woman named Mildred Polinski, living alone and on welfare, froze to death during a cold snap because the landlord kicked her out, or the gas company turned off her supply. This summer, AP and UPI would run stories featuring Joe Miniver, the Beast of Chamisaville, who kicked a sick, eighty-three-year-old man off his property. And that man (a member of an oft-exploited minority group) was found two days later in a ditch, dead of (a broken heart and) exposure. Militant Chicanos (allied with AIM, the SCLC, and the NAACP) would publish Joe's mug shot in all their newspapers: "Here's the honky who done it, bros!" When the Socialist revolution triumphed, his photograph (or wax replica) would be installed in the Bigots Hall of Fame, along with George Wallace, Sheriff Rainey, and George Lincoln Rockwell.

"Hey," Heather exclaimed, "there's a note on your windshield."

"I'm not blind, I've got eyes." There were two notes, actually: Joe stuffed them into his pocket without taking a peek.

In a hurry?—trust the Green Gorilla not to start. It had not been cold last night, but that made no nevermind with the cantankerous vehicle. If even a slightly chill mist had settled on the hood, Joe was in trouble.

He cranked over the engine for a minute—the battery immediately threatened to conk out, so he swung into phase two. Locating a can of Quik Start in the glove compartment, Joe banged open the hood, removed the air cleaner, gave the carburetor a double squirt of the pressurized ether, jumped into the truck, and she coughed right up. He depressed the accelerator for a moment, warming it up, then tumbled out, replaced the air filter, slammed down the hood, returned to the truck, and only then remembered that he had no reverse.

Heather cared little if she never got to school. But Michael nervously twitched his fingers and licked his lips. Little sores festered around his mouth; everybody always cautioned him not to lick his lips. Of course, the more you asked him not to, the more self-conscious he grew, and the sores multiplied.

Delicately triple-clutching his way into first, Joe said, "Michael, put some Chapstick on those sores."

"I forgot my Chapstick. But they don't hurt, honest." Michael's main task in life was to try and put everybody at ease by assuring them his mini-leprosy really didn't hurt at all.

"Check out the glove compartment. Maybe there's a tube of bacitracin."

They lurched forward and rocked over the irrigation ditch. By swinging wide and skimming past the woodpile, an old clothesline, and the back of Eloy's truck, Joe managed to forge a circle and head out in the right direction. Unaccountably, Old Duke, the inventor of canine lethargy, suddenly scrambled erect, barking and snarling, and furiously chased them—slaloming between geese, ducks, wayward turkeys, and flea-bitten tomcats—down the driveway, ordering them never to return.

Heather asked, "Does that dog bite?"

"He's a killer." Absentmindedly, Joe reached in his pocket for the notes. "Two days ago he ripped my pants to shreds before I finally beat him away with a log." Unfolding the larger paper against the steering wheel, he turned it around so the message was rightside up. "They say last year he attacked three little eight-year-old girls skipping through the back field, killing two, and putting the third in the hospital for a month and a half with one leg chewed off at the knee, and her left arm severely mangled."

"You're full of it, Daddy."

The note said:

Dearest Joe,
After the way it has been with us, I don't see how you can wind up making love with that woman. I know you are a free person, and also a grownup adult, but you must be very careful with her—she has so many negative vibes. And she is the sort that takes energy from you but doesn't give any back in return. You are such a lovely person and I would hate to see you hurt by her. You're not a self-destructive person, but she is. I'm sorry if I bothered you by coming over last night—I didn't mean to intrude. When you love somebody it's important to let them have their own space. And if you love someone, you should support them in anything they choose to do. So I'm sorry I cried last night, that's not like me at all. I just hope you are careful, and that I am able to see you soon, for you make me so happy when I am with you.

I miss you terribly,
Nancy

PS Sasha is "critical" still, but listed also as "stable."

He unfolded the other, slightly more cryptic, epistle:

> Miniver, you keep it up,
> and you're dead.

At nine on a school-day morning, Heather now actually had the brass balls to ask: "Daddy, can we go to school by the Seven-Eleven way and stop for an ice cream?"

Joe snorted, facing her almost admiringly. Where had she gotten the panache? "You're nuts, Heather. After a healthy breakfast of Cocoa Puffs and what—Kool-Aid?—you're asking me to feed you an Eskimo Pie, a Fudgsicle, a Super Tango, or a . . . what are those enormous things called, the really hideous, fat, cone-shaped, grisly, blue-colored blobs?"

"Malt Crunch Bombs!"

"Never. You kids are sick. By the time you reach your teens you won't have any teeth, all your hair will fall out, you'll have rickets, sickle-cell anemia, and beriberi."

"Well, at least we need lunch money," Michael noted.

"If I give you lunch money, you'll probably ditch school at noon, trot up to the plaza five and dime, and blow it all on Jujyfruits, Pop Rocks, and Gatorade."

"No we won't."

"Bullshit. That's what I always did as a kid."

"Uh-oh, Spaghetti-O!" Heather rolled her eyeballs.

A second later, Michael drew Heather into a whispered conference. Emerging from the huddle, Heather said, "Daddy, if you're not gonna live at home anymore, will you at least come over tonight and wrestle?"

One lesson years of parenting had taught Joe was never, *ever* tell kids outright, unequivocally, "Yes." Because they'd hold you to it come hell or high water. They would make you feel so damned guilty about promising something you couldn't deliver that you'd wind up delivering something you had never meant to promise. The cardinal rule, in answering kiddy requests, was: Always Equivocate.

Joe said, "We'll see."

Heather never gave up. "Well, if you can't come for a wrestle, could you at least drop by and play us some songs when we go to bed?"

"I dunno. Maybe. Can't say for sure."

They lapsed into a brief silence that Heather killed. "Daddy, do you believe in the Monkey God?"

"What? Who says?"

"Don't get a hernia. I was just asking."

"Nobody in this town just 'asks' a question like that."

Michael said, "Everybody's talking about the unveiling on Thursday."

"Who's everybody? What do you mean?"

"Oh . . . just people in school," he said evasively.

"We had monkey cookies at lunch yesterday," Heather reported self-righteously.

"Monkey cookies? At school?"

"In art all this week we had to draw gorillas and chimpanzees and spider monkeys," Michael informed him.

Joe was shocked: "They're not supposed to teach you religion in the schools."

"Are Hanumans religious?" Heather asked.

"Hanumans . . . ?"

"What *is* a Hanuman exactly?" Michael wanted to know.

"It's God disguised as a big monkey," Heather replied. "And if you don't believe in him, he punishes you with a stomachache, or takes you to the devil."

"God doesn't look like a monkey," Michael said. "She's crazy, isn't she, Dad?"

"God knows karate, smarty-pants." Heather displayed a feisty fist. "He could knock your teeth out with one little chop."

"No he couldn't, could he, Dad? There's no such thing as God, is there?"

They had been over this a dozen times: Joe never knew exactly what to say. "Well, *we* don't happen to believe in God.

I mean, not like there's an actual person up there, you know, an old woman with white hair and a long flowing beard—"

"God's not a woman!" Heather said. "He's a man!"

"Nobody knows for sure. God could just as well be a woman as a man. I mean, if there was actually a God at all . . ."

"Then he could be a monkey if he wanted to, couldn't he?"

"Don't interrupt, Heather, Or I'll karate-chop *your* teeth down your throat."

"But you just said—"

"Heather, shuttup. I haven't finished what I was saying."

Arms folded stubbornly, she couldn't resist further needling. "Well, what you were saying was dumb."

Joe said, "Jesus, I hope they pass the Equal Rights Amendment and draft you to go fight in Nicaragua."

"What's the Equal Rights Menendent?"

"It's a law that says women have just as much right to do anything that men are doing. It'll probably even force us to rewrite the Bible so that God is a hermaphrodite."

"What a maphrodite?"

"A half-man, half-woman thing."

"With a penis and a vagina?"

How did he get into these things? "I don't know, I suppose so."

Michael said, "Then God could fuck himself."

"Or herself."

Heather said, "Somebody painted a monkey with a halo over its head in the girl's lavatory yesterday."

"Forget the monkey. God isn't a person, or an animal, or a real being at all. God to me is just a word to mean the essence of everything human. It's a metaphor for the . . . for the personality of humanity, I guess."

Blankly—he'd lost 'em, but fast—they muttered, "Huh."

"But you don't want to go around telling people there is no God," Joe said. "They might not understand. Also, many folks believe in different interpretations of God, and they get upset if you claim there is no divine critter up there, punching buttons, concocting plagues, guiding wars like a maniacal three-year-old. The whole concept is such a philosophical mare's nest that the best thing to do is lay low. Don't worry about religion until you're old enough to start drinking."

Heather said, "Well, what about the Hanuman?"

"Forget it. It's a false idol."

Michael said, "Tofu Smatterling came up to me yesterday and said if I didn't say I believed baboons were holy, he would punch me out."

"What did you reply?" Joe asked angrily.

"What could I say? He's bigger than me."

"All this monkey talk is pernicious garbage. Forget it."

A beat and a half later, Heather opened her fat yap again. "Everybody says you're fucking a monkey-lover."

He should have exploded. Instead, he sagged, at a loss for words. *You dug this grave*, his brain said. *Now lie in it*.

Embarrassed, Michael said, "You're really dumb, Heather. Jesus Christ."

Joe moaned, "Leave her alone, Michael: I asked for it. Now do me a favor and shut up for a minute, okay?"

Heather said, "Before we shut up, can I ask one more question?"

"All right. But just *one*."

"Okay. What about angels?"

"I give up. What about them?"

"Is there such a thing?"

"You're asking me?"

"Well, Sanji Smatterling said he saw this great big ol' angel hanging out in the Seven-Eleven telephone booth yesterday."

"Oh Heather, you're crazy!" Joe guffawed.

"I am not crazy. Am I, Michael?"

Her brother hemmed uncomfortably. "What about when we heard Mr. Irribarren tell us about the angel, Dad?"

"That's it!" Joe snapped. "Enough! You had your question. Now stifle."

A quarter-mile later, Joe pulled into a parking lot opposite the ramshackle grammar school, and said, "We're here. Scram. You're late."

"What about lunch money?"

Joe forked over the dough and stepped down. As they piled out the driverside door and raced pell-mell for the building across the potholed street, he yelled, "Wait a minute—how about a kiss good-bye?"

"You didn't shave," Heather cackled. "I don't wanna get my face all scratched." And then she suddenly flung up her hands, jutted one hip, did a quick jive two-step, launched a mockingly obscene cheer—

"Had a little monkey
Took him to the country
Fed him on gingerbread;
Razzle, dazzle
Kick him in the asshole,
And now my little monkey's dead!"

—and fled.

Joe settled behind the wheel, closed the door, and faced in the direction they had gone. All at once life seemed overwhelming and hopeless. Sensations of loss and of longing half smothered him. Just possibly, he might never again cohabit day in and day out with his children. After a divorce, Heidi might split. Or he'd move to Altoona for some obscure but inevitable reason. Then he would see his children only occasionally, on a weekend visit, during their summer vacations. How could they survive without Joe around to offer protection, answer their silly questions, provide wishy-washy explanations about Hanumans and God, and condemn them for noshing Cocoa Puffs? His heart threatened to break. He felt like throwing a maudlin drunk. Would he simply, from never being around, fade out of their memories? In later years, would they recall the wrestling matches, the bedtime songs, the weekend nights in sleeping-bag nests when they had watched "Star Trek" together right after the ten o'clock news? How could Michael become a Little League all-star without a father to play catch with? More to the point (feeling sick to his stomach), could he pull through without them?

As always, clutching that enigmatic suitcase, Nick Danger scuttled across the road . . . but Joe barely noticed.

His vision had blurred: he struggled not to let tears fall. An awareness of his own vulnerability made him shudder. Time for something to eat. Then he'd locate Heidi, sink to his knees, and beg forgiveness. Screw the cocaine—it wasn't even remotely worth the risks involved. What they shared as a family was precious: how could he have placed it in such jeopardy these past few days?

Joe ripped the monkey-cartoon death-threat note to shreds and dumped the confetti out his window. Trailing a remote aura of menace, Nick Danger disappeared around the corner of a building. Then a bullet-shaped hummingbird zipped through the driverside window, colliding against the passenger door. It flopped backward onto the seat, cold-cocked and not even quivering: its tiny feet, toes splayed, poked up stiffly out of its teeny-weeny tummy.

Never had Joe viewed a hummingbird up close. Timidly, he cupped it in his palm, astonished by the achingly precise workmanship in the minuscule feathers and in the powerful wings. The shiny ruby and olive colors seemed more like the luster of jewels than of a living thing.

Joe waited for a sign. Gradually, the weightless thing quivered, blinked its eyes. A sharp, speedy tongue flicked out one side of the needle-thin bill. Quicker than the eye could catch, the hummer turned over. Beady eyes, no bigger than the gems inside expensive, precision Swiss wristwatches, glared at him, assessing survival chances.

"It's okay," Joe soothed. "Go ahead, kid. Fly away. I ain't gonna hurt you."

Joe blinked his eyes, and justlikethat the broadtail zipped off, so fast he had no clear impression of its departure. There had been no little push as it jumped up, no flutter of wings—nothing, just a lightning-quick "now you see me, now you don't."

In the center of his right palm lay the smallest feather he had ever seen, a positively exquisite piece of fluff.

Then a mischievous breeze tooled into the cab, and, although Joe emitted a heartrending "Wait a sec!," it plucked up the almost microscopic shaft and carried it off to Never-Never Land.

The joggers were out in full force, huffing and puffing in their rainbow warm-up suits and color-coordinated earmuff AM and FM radios. Probably a fortune could be accumulated insuring automobiles against jogger-related accidents, Joe thought, as he chugged warily toward the Perry Kahn Subdivision #4. Or vice versa. Every year at least a dozen gasping Chamisaville runners were poleaxed by wayward autos. Especially those with earmuff radios—they never heard any vehicles coming. Too, among joggers, the newest fad form of suicide was veering into the path of an onrushing Pontiac. Also, more and more murders involved first-degree vehicular homicides, as angry husbands and miffed wives nailed their aggravating spouses with the family station wagon while those partners were out Staying Fit in Order to Live Right. A great problem for the insurance companies, in such cases, was that many such acts of mayhem did not result in instant death. Old-style ten-ton wood-paneled Chevy and Ford station wagons would have made perfect murder weapons. But today's light-weight Toyotas and Datsuns lacked real killing power: and murder attempts often resulted in agonizing manglings, vege-tablizations, and other similarly gruesome injuries that stopped short of death and entailed years of lingering hospitalizations (and litigations) that could break even the wealthiest insurance conglomerate.

On Santistevan Lane, a crew of eight hardhats, manning a bilge pump, two jackhammers, a portable generator, and a backhoe, had gathered around a large cavity out of which steam and irregular burps of sewage water flowed. Joe braked, steer-ing into the Guadalupe church parking lot where he managed to forge a circle, arriving back on the artery headed in another direction. Placitas Road seemed like his best bet for an alter-native route across town. But it was soon blocked off by an enormous machine laying down a hot mix. The machine was followed by two gravel trucks and a large four-wheeled iron roller flattening the hot mix, trailed by a bulldozer gouging up the just-laid macadam. Joe braked again, executing a hairy U-turn that almost landed him in a ditch. He idled momentarily, aimed west yet staring east at the simultaneous road-building-and-destroying operation, trying to understand the paradox. Then he guessed that LeDoux Street might land him across the North-South Highway. Thirty yards short of his goal, however, even that innocuous and seldom-used path was blocked off by a crew of fifteen men, a bulldozer, a large watering truck, a backhoe, and a crane attempting to set a concrete four-way sewerline-junction-fitting into the flooded earth.

Chamisaville had a semifunctional new sewage plant in Ran-chitos Abajo, completed two autumns ago. Already, it was badly oversubscribed. But recently the city fathers had wangled a half-million dollars for sewage-system expansion. The project entailed placing sixty miles of trunk lines underground: the construction involved had staggered the picturesque little vil-lage around the clock for the past year. Of course, once the trunk lines were buried, both private citizens and municipal organizations would be forbidden by federal law to hook into it, given the inadequate capacity of the new sewage plant. The plant itself could not be expanded, however, because the valley's rapidly depleting water table could not be tapped any further to form additional fecal slurry necessary for moving more shit.

Joe was only a mile from the plaza. But to get there, now, he aimed south along Suicide Lane, driving two miles down through the Perry Kahn Subdivision #6. At the Our Lady of the Sorrows Hospital on Valverde he turned left and hung another louie a scant half-mile later, onto the North-South Highway. There, due to a jam created by a cement mixer and six men fashioning a totally useless, surfboard-shaped island in the middle of the road, Joe had to turn right onto a Santistevan Street detour. On Santistevan, the bumper-to-bumper traffic was completely veiled in a thick, dusty smog. Last week, in the *Chamisaville News*, Joe had read that this picturesque little town, in clear Rocky Mountain air at seven thousand feet, was one of the state's four most polluted areas. Its airborne particulate poisons rated favorably with the air over two uranium mines, an open-pit copper operation, and a power-plant complex whose pollution had been the only man-made crap visible to the first astronauts circling the globe.

A perfect environment for asthma!

Regulars dominated the Prince of Whales when Joe stopped for breakfast. Silhouetted in the doorway, he wondered whether to enter, sit down, and make believe nothing had happened, or turn heel and flee. For when, responding to the doorbell's jangle, everybody (in unison) glanced up with varying degrees of recognition, Joe suddenly thought: I've become one of the lead clowns in this circus.

Ralph Kapansky held forth at his regular corner table by the jukebox, on his eighth coffee already, procrastinating, as usual, from writing filth. At his feet, Rimpoche dreamed—twitching—and stank to high heaven. On his left, Tribby Gordon had disheveled hair and uneven facial stubble. His jacket dribbled fluff out of flak holes, his sneakers had no shoelaces; several legal briefs were scattered on the table before him. Had he spent all night atop the pyramid blowing potent numbers while gooning at the stars? Or, more to the point of how he looked, had he gotten careless and tumbled off his perch at 3:00 A.M.?

Also enveloped in smoke wreaths at their table was Jeff Orbison, Suki Terrell's ex, EAT ME's lead mouth, and a gun freak into the bargain.

Off in a corner sat Nick Danger, his eyes lost in dark shadows cast by the Tyrolean brim: he was sucking something up through a straw, and clutched his battered suitcase to his lap.

The only other solitary person around was Diana's old pal Angel Guts. He glowered at the world from underneath the floppy brim of an old-fashioned cowboy hat.

Two shoved-together tables accommodated Nikita Smatterling and his entourage, including a saffron-robed bald-headed holy man with a spot on his forehead; the radio astrologer Pancho Nordica; Nancy Ryan's ex-Hanuman-nik lover, Randall Tucker; Sam Halaby, the metaphysician on his last reincarnation and hubby of Sarah (whose children by a former husband had just been kidnapped); Baldini Miller, the silent one, with his bandaged foot and his wife, Ipu; Ray Verboten, the valley's biggest coke dealer and rising Miniver nemesis; and Roger Petrie, embezzler supreme, double agent, and dark horse in the Eloy Irribarren Land-Grab Derby.

At another table sat Bernard Laver, the Tennis Heaven pro Skipper Nuzum and his wife, Natalie Gandolf, and the tattoo artist, Noelle Paxton, accompanied him. The craggy-faced but intriguing woman with them Joe had never seen before. She wore one-way dark glasses, gold hoop earrings, a black turtleneck jersey, a Guatemalan sash, black pants, and knee-high high-heeled beige suede boots. In the old playground days, the boys would have said:

> Hubba hubba
> Ding ding
> She's got
> Everything.

At a third table, Egon Braithwhite was bending Wilkerson Busbee's ear, no doubt with ersatz Indonesian slang phrases. Abruptly, Joe flashed: Wilkerson Busbee? Wasn't he supposed to be locked up in an Ohio jail? Wilkerson's two-way taxi walkie-talkie crackled even as he violated the Nestlé's boycott by washing down his lox and bagels with Pero.

Then Joe realized the rest of them were present also: Fluff Dimaggio and the entire Unfug family—Rama, Shanti, and Om. Bleary-eyed and doomed-looking, Fluff had a broken arm; Shanti and her angelic butterball daughter looked fresh, pert, and lively. Rama crouched off in corner shadows, an eight-millimeter camera stuck in front of his face like a pig snout, filming the scene.

The bald geezer in yellow must be him, Joe realized—Baba Ram Bang. And the hubba-hubba lady?—who else but Iréné Popapopcorn, the big-city journalist!

Somehow, they—and their statue?—had arrived.

Instinct suggested flight, if only on the grounds that Ray Verboten and one of his alleged henchpeople, Angel Guts, were on hand. Yet habit spurred Joe to enter the abuzz joint. Why he felt so equivocal, beyond his fear of Ray Verboten, was a puzzlement. Perhaps in his former life as loyal husband and trustworthy father, Joe had always been a spectator in the Prince of Whales, enjoying its messed-up denizens' colorful woes from a secure haven Above It All. But now a change had occurred. And his revulsion for this crowd must stem from the fact that he had fallen among the heathen. Their hideous scars, banal emotional tribulations, and fatiguing little holocausts now had something in common with his own traumatic dilemmas. Rudely gone, though not forgotten, was that superiority complex he had wielded for so long. Screw the abyss: it was absolutely no fun bumping elbows with all the other gargoyles and fallen angels!

Egon Braithwhite called out: "Ho ming no cum chow ki!"

Annoyed, Joe nevertheless replied: "Hideyashima. He ho gum shur crap."

"Moyo mookie! Pi shediyeshi!"

"What does all that mean?" Natalie Gandolf asked him as he passed her table.

"Beats me. He took a vow, remember?"

The foxy stranger laughed. "Oh my God!" Joe couldn't quite pinpoint her accent: it sounded too guttural to be British. "That's simply marvelous! Natalie, who is this ludicrous and wonderful man?—you must introduce us."

Natalie said, "Joe Miniver, Iréné Papadraxis. Joe is the best garbage man in Chamisaville."

"Superb!" She tipped her glasses down, glancing up over

the rims so that Joe could see her green, heavily mascaraed eyes. "I don't believe I've ever met a real garbage man."

"Iréné's a house guest," Natalie explained. "I suppose you've already heard the wonderful story of her escape from the Clarion, Ohio, jail last night?"

"Nope, and I'm the only one in here who hasn't, aren't I?"

Iréné giggled. "I still can't believe we're here. It was a miracle! Skipper was absolutely unbelievable."

Joe opened his mouth to ask what had happened, but Egon Braithwhite stood up and interrupted again. "He hishi pata-*po*po!"

"Moishay! Dayan! *Tak*ayama!" To Natalie, Joe said, "I was talking to Tribby last night on his pyramid, and as far as he knew these guys were still in prison."

"Tribby's a horse's ass. Skipper and Scott Harrison and Ray Verboten flew to Cincinnati yesterday and rented a helicopter. Ray has connections in Cincinnati."

"Such ruffians!" Iréné shivered delightedly. "What ugly people!"

"Didn't they get the job done?" Nikita Smatterling called triumphantly from the other table.

"Those hooligans broke my arm," Fluff Dimaggio grumbled.

Shanti Unfug's self-righteous Baltimore hillbilly voice said, "Well, if you hadn't chained yourself to the Hanuman, they wouldn't of had to."

"If I hadn't chained myself to it, Mr. Bull Connors there that Clarion flatfoot, woulda lugged that marble monkey to the dump!"

"It's not a 'marble monkey,'" Nikita corrected. "It's a sacred statue."

Joe said: "So they rented a helicopter and a couple of thugs?"

"And a Lincoln Continental." Iréné beamed excitedly.

"I liked the part with the smoke bombs," Wilkerson Busbee said effusively.

Shanti Unfug added her two bits: "I thought we were goners when that machine gun started chattering. My little ol' heart just about did a backflip."

Joe said, "They broke you out of jail?"

Skipper smirked and twirled his moustache. "We put hooks on the four corners of the thing and carried it off."

"I don't follow."

"It was a portable classroom they had rigged up as a jail. Ray and his boys donned black suits, crept in, and attached the cable. Then the copter swooped in, grabbed the whole shooting match, and carted it off to a soybean field where we had a plane and a smaller copter waiting."

Joe said, "Sounds like a busy night."

Skipper smirked nonchalantly. "Oh no, it was just another ordinary day in the life."

Natalie addressed Joe, "So the unveiling takes place as planned—on Thursday. You'll attend Wednesday's bash, of course? And bring Heidi. Or Nancy. Or that little waitress—or bring all three, whatever gets you off. Joseph, you're beginning to flaunt quite a reputation."

At another table, Ray Verboten had overheard Natalie's comment. Winking at Joe, he spoke to Natalie in a chillingly jocular voice: "A guy could strangle himself on such a reputation."

The first time Joe had laid eyes on Ray, he had instinctively disliked, and feared, the pusher. Ray affected a semiwalrus, old-timer's moustache. He had high cheekbones and pale blue eyes, always wore elaborately tooled cowboy boots, ribbon shirts, a fringed buckskin jacket, and a Resistol ten-gallon hat. His skin was sallow and debauched, his eyes absolutely frigid, his voice cruelly mellifluous—the quintessential Aquarian hoodlum.

Egon Braithwhite must have been drunk, or on cutworm moths. "Noguchi! Kurosawa! *Pijama! Pijama!*"

Embarrassed and humiliated at being singled out by the jerk, Joe nevertheless felt compelled not to insult Egon by ignoring him: "Toyota murasaki shikibu!" Extending his hand to Iréné Papadraxis, he added, "I'm pleased to meet you. Thank God you all escaped from there alive."

"The pleasure's all mine, believe me. Maybe we'll meet again at the party." The hand that he gripped was covered with a bunch of smooth precious rocks resembling amber marbles set in baroque silver claws. Joe pinched her fingertips gracefully, and executed a charming bow.

"He's weird, but sweet," Iréné told Natalie as Joe again voyaged toward Tribby and Ralph.

Nikita Smatterling raised one hand. "Joe. C'mere a sec, would you?"

Joe veered, smelling trouble. When your kid shoots a monkey in a valley overpopulated by Hanuman freaks, the writing is on the wall.

"You know everybody here, don't you?"

"Just about." Joe nodded as he spoke their names: "Pancho, Randall, Sam, Baldini, Ipu, Ray, Roger." He had skipped the troll in the blond wrapping paper.

"And this is his holiness, Baba Ram Bang," Nikita said.

Joe could think of no reply except, "Pleased to meet you, I'm sure." The guru remained mute, staring sleepily at a fly on his nose.

Nikita came right to the point. "I hear your boy Michael shot Nancy Ryan's monkey Sasha yesterday." Though stentorian, his voice was also extra-suave, proving that anything he said promoted the interests of peace and love, brother. Not to mention groovy. Joe, on the other hand, immediately wanted to punch the professional do-gooder in the jaw.

HIPPIE GARBAGE MAN GOES AMOK, ATTACKS FAMOUS GURU, THEN IS KILLED BY LIGHTNING BOLT FROM HEAVEN!

Kiddingly, Joe said, "I understand you were here in the café when the call came through."

"Precisely. And we were just talking about that. We're a bit perplexed. Not one of us can imagine why he would do such a thing. What do you think makes a child attack an innocent monkey?"

"I dunno. What is it that makes a disciple of peace and charity stick the snout of a loaded revolver into the stomach of a Mafia dwarf and pull the trigger?"

"Ah, touché, Joe." But Nikita was one of those aggravating people whose aplomb could never be shaken. "You make your point."

"What point?" Ipu Miller, a big, belligerent hippie, was not so easily neutralized. "The dwarf threatened a child. The monkey never did anything to anybody."

"You say!" Joe flared, even as he wondered: How could I find myself engaged in this ridiculous and puerile repartee? "That monkey is a royal pain in the ass who torments everybody!"

Randall said, "Christ, Joe, you're pathetic."

Hoping to avoid fisticuffs, Nikita held up his hand. "Please, everybody, calm down. We're not here to accuse each other.

t's plain to see, however, that Joe doesn't know much about monkeys."

"Monkeys, shmonkeys—I know a furry shitheel when I see one."

"What a monkey is, and what he isn't is all in the eye of he beholder," Nikita pontificated. "You know, of course, that Nancy is heartbroken. But she's bearing up beautifully. Little Sashy is right now lying on a slab with three intravenous tubes n his body and an oxygen mask over his face."

"Tu tu *toots*ie! Moshi!"

Back to his tormentor, Joe gave Egon the finger.

Ray Verboten said, "You know, man, you seem to be trespassing in a lot of areas where you aren't exactly welcome."

I deserve it, Joe thought. Of my own free will I walked into his Star Wars bar. Nevertheless, his dander was up. "My life s my own business," he replied coolly. "So you just keep your cotton-picking fingers out of my slice of the pie."

"My, *my*." Ray smiled icily. "Is that a threat?"

Pancho Nordica had some good advice. "Friends, we shouldn't hassle each other. Joe, please don't be offended. I've alked with Nancy, and believe me, she has faith in you. She's a beautiful and compassionate human being. Given that the unveiling of the Hanuman is imminent, we just don't understand the omen, that's all."

"What omen? Michael ain't religious. It happened for ordinary reasons. Heidi and I are on the outs. I'm seeing another lady. Michael got upset. All he could think to do was seek revenge on the pet of that other lady. I mean, he can't shoot us, right?"

Roger Petrie said, "It's not quite as simple as that. God has a strange way of choosing his messengers."

"How do you know God is a him?"

"What?"

He had to open his big mouth! "Well, you said 'him,' referring to God. What makes you so sure God isn't a woman?"

Baba Ram Bang squirmed, raised two fingers, and in thickly accented English murmured, "Coca-Cola."

Ray Verboten adjusted his leather lapels. "You're violating the rules, man. Don't talk down God. You reek of lousy karma."

"Does he do coke, too? Does God smoke marijuana?"

"Hey." Ray petitioned others at the table, silently ordering up their instant support. "Somebody loan me a baseball glove,

so I can play left field where all this flak is coming from."
And to Joe: "You got a very fat mouth, bro. Cuidado."

Nikita gestured for reason. "Please. We only diminish each
other with these niggling contretemps."

"You're a crackpot." Ipu Miller sniffed angrily. "I bet you
sicced that kid on Sasha to sabotage the unveiling this week."

"Hoyo! Babaru! Samurai!"

Out the side of his mouth, Joe snapped: "Ti ti mo*bush*i! Hi
pee jo!" To Ipu, he said, "My kid didn't attack your statue.
He shot a filthy little monkey with a masturbation complex!"

Everybody at the table booed. Ipu turned crimson: "He tried
to murder the spirit of the Hanuman."

"Wait a minute, friends." Probing into his knitted purse,
Nikita located two pears. Using a restaurant knife, he quickly
sectioned them into many pieces. "We will all eat of this fruit
and establish harmony again."

Joe wasn't that hungry. "No thanks. I hate pears." Spinning
to leave, he almost bowled over Rama Unfug: the cinematog-
rapher was peering through the lens of his Bolex, grinding it
out. "What is *he* doing?" Joe whined angrily at Nikita. "Filming
this whole charade?"

Nikita pushed the fruit at him: "It's prasad."

"Prasad, de Sade—I don't like pears. Thanks anyway."

Ray Verboten held up one hand. "Hey man, you're incredibly ignorant. Prasad is blessed food. You don't just refuse it."

Pancho elucidated: "It's been left all night under the Hanuman's U-Haul. In that way it's been sanctified."

"Eat," Rama urged. "I want a picture of this for the record."

To Ray, Joe said, "What are you all of a sudden, *religious*?"
Ipu screeched, "You're crazy, Joe!"

"*I'm* crazy? You people are sitting here, seriously suggesting
that because my kid plugs this odious monkey an Indian statue
blows its vibes? And the biggest drug pusher in the county
starts laying a God trip on me?"

Baldini banged his fist on the table, bouncing plates, knives,
forks, and glasses, and broke his silence vow. "Get him out
of here! He's corrupting the prasad!"

At the same time Ray Verboten yelled, "*Your* pot is calling
my kettle black?"

Rama said, "Back up a little, Joe. I can't get everybody
in."

Joe pleaded for reason. "Look, I'm hungry, I need to order breakfast."

"First you should eat of the prasad. . . ."

Egon added his two bits: "Yukio! Papa*do*shi! M*iki*maus!"

Baba Ram Bang sneezed as Randall called after Joe, "Maybe we'll sue!"

"So sue, already, you bunch of banana-gobbling hypocrites!"

Iréné Papadraxis howled gleefully: "I'm going to put him in my book! He's priceless!"

Oh me oh my, Joe whimpered silently. Whatever could have induced me to dig such a deep and gloomy grave this early in the day?

BODY OF CHAMISAVILLE HERETIC DISCOVERED AT DUMP!
APE SIGN CARVED INTO BELLY! MANGLED CORPSE
OF HERETIC'S SON LOCATED IN ABANDONED WELL!
RELIGIOUS PERVERTS SUSPECTED!

Ralph was in his usual form. "Will you welcome, please, Joe M. Casanova, assman, monkey-baiter, and all-around hell-raiser supreme." Desultorily, Rimpoche growled at Joe, then cast a baleful glance at his master for approval.

"That's not funny, Ralph." Joe sank into a chair. "Your sense of humor is out to lunch."

"I only call 'em as I see 'em."

"Well, get a new pair of glasses, shmuck."

Tribby hated arguments not initiated by himself. "Please, no hostility. My analyst expressly forbids it."

"Analysts," Joe scoffed mournfully. "Fuck psychiatry."

"He's superior." Ralph gestured to Tribby. "He just told Ray Verboten to shove it, and it's all the rest of us who are crazy."

"I couldn't help it. Who do those arrogant cosmic cookies think they are?"

"You blew our cover," Tribby accused.

"What cover?"

"Well, for starters it might interest you to know that up until a minute ago I actually had a buyer for that coke."

"What coke?"

"Yours, dummy!"

"Kee *fash*ima! Hara *kir*i."

Tribby asked, "What is it with you and Egon, Joe? What language is that?"

Joe said, "Hi, Darlene. Lissen, babe, gimme a usual, would you?"

"A usual?"

"Yeah, you know. A fried egg, over easy, single piece of wheat toast, couple of link sausage, a small orange juice, cup of Sanka, black, no cream."

"Lemme see if I can translate that into English. You want a cyclops, OE, side order of squeal—that's link piggies not patties, slice of wheat singed and soaked in oleo, a midget of Florida sunshine, and a cup of ersatz ink, hold the moo juice."

"Gracias, Darlene. You get an A."

Their repartee made her bold. "Say, what's this I hear about you and Diana?"

"Oh shit!" Joe threw up his hands.

"*Sanjuro! Boca ku! My tai!*"

Joe addressed his friend, the pornographer: "Do me a favor, Ralph, and make my nemesis over there shut up, would you? Tell him I got a headache."

"Am I my brother's keeper?"

Darlene bent to whisper in Joe's ear. "I heard that her ex-old man caught you both stark-naked in a trailer home that belonged to Marlon Brando and took a shot at you with a twelve-gauge shotgun."

Joe grimaced. "Geez, Darlene, news sure travels fast."

"Well, frankly, I didn't believe it."

"Thank you for that, anyway."

"Sure. I mean, after all, what would Marlon Brando be doing with a trailer in Chamisaville?"

"*Bashi, bashi!* No tickee no washee!"

"Did any of the pellets hit you?" Darlene asked. "I don't see any visible wounds."

"He's sitting right over there. Why don't you ask him yourself?"

"Who?"

"Angel Guts."

"Who's that?"

"Diana's ex, for pete's sake!"

"Ah-*hah*. The plot thickens."

To Tribby, Joe said, "What did you say about the coke?"

"Never mind. It wasn't important."

"Who wants to buy it and for how much, dammit!"

"Well, I rapped with Natalie early this morning. She heard hat I might be in a position to broker it."

"And . . . ?"

"Sheesh ka bob! *Po*go!"

"And so she needs a load for the party Wednesday. Aparently something in Ray's apparatus is temporarily jammed. A plane crashed near El Paso yesterday when he was in Cinninati. So that puts you in the catbird seat."

"For about how long?"

"I figure until they kill you."

"Oh wonderful."

"Once you sell it, though, the heat's off."

"For how much?"

"You're not going to like this."

"I didn't ask if I was gonna like it."

"Twelve thousand dollars."

"That's what I paid Peter! It's pure stuff! It's worth a hundred rand! I already told you her stupid husband offered me *double* hat yesterday, plus a stockholder's position in the Simian Founation!"

"You also said you told him to go screw himself, and he vound up threatening your life, for free. Natalie's acting inlependently of Skipper: it's her own scam. 'I'll be doing Joe a favor to take it off his hands,' she says. 'And Skipper need never know.' With it, apparently, you're considered a dead nan. Without it, at least you could breathe again."

Stubbornly, Joe said, "I didn't come this far to accept that ind of a ripoff."

"Suit yourself. I'm merely the humble intermediary."

"As per our plan we'll dilute the goods ourselves, package t, pass it, and get rich."

"I've been thinking about that 'we.'" Tribby's eyes became hifty and evaded Joe. "And I've come to a conclusion that he odds are against us."

"Like for instance?"

"Shagatsu! Feen *jon*! Bu *beri* chop!"

"Like for instance I got a phone call at three A.M. this morning. A rasping voice threatened to castrate me with a rusty nife if I even touched the contents of your herbal tea box."

"So you're chickening out?"

"I wouldn't say that."

"What would you call it, then?"

"I'd say I'm merely keeping you abreast of the alternatives."

"What about you, Ralph?"

"Well . . . ahem. It occurs to me that just possibly the fun has gone out of this wild and woolly little caper."

Joe said, "I don't believe it. Everything's falling apart. Nobody has any guts anymore."

Tribby said, "Heidi told me you told her to flush the coke down the toilet, anyway."

"My God! I never . . . When did she say that?"

"At three thirty A.M. when she banged on my door after *her* three A.M. phone call that threatened to kidnap Heather and drop her in the gorge."

"Oh."

"Gentlemen." Spumoni Tatarsky plunked his slick briefcase onto the table. Leaning over Joe, he crowed, "Feast your eyes, dudes, I got the perfect Christmas gift for the little lady."

"Holograms! Dichromates!" Tribby covered his eyes. "Fie and begone, Tatarsky. I already heard your spiel."

"*Christmas*?" Ralph made a mocking, disgusted face.

"Wait a minute. Do not judge me so quickly." Spumoni's thin fingers snapped open the locks and flipped up the lid, revealing a velvet-lined display case harboring monocle-sized glass discs on which three-dimensional images had been imprinted by means of a laser beam, in the process called holography. Attached to the rim into which each monocle had been set was a slender silver chain. 3-D images contained within the monocles were of Marilyn Monroe, Charlie Chaplin, a clown, a puppy, a rose, and an old-fashioned Colt dragoon pistol. Spumoni handled them with obscene familiarity, as if he intended to perform lewd tricks. He arranged them dangling from the open lid; they twirled, catching the sunlight, reflecting prismatic beams.

"This stuff is beautiful." Lying flat on the nearby tabletop lashed snugly in his deerskin cradleboard, Moonglow Winter wind started crying. When Darlene delivered Joe's breakfast her sharp elbow nudged Spumoni in the ribs. "The kid's crying Spumoni."

"I'm selling—screw the kid. Listen, look at that imag Joe—have you ever seen anything more beautiful?"

"It's intriguing. How do you obtain that 3-D effect?"

"Are you actually interested? Or are you just bullshitting me?"

"Would I ask if I wasn't interested?"

Spumoni craned his neck down to within inches of Joe's face. "Everybody asks, even if they're not interested. They ask by rote. But they really don't give a damn. They think they're being polite, but they never listen to my replies. They're all enveloped in their personal ego trips. Nobody cares anymore about anyone else's art. It's this fucking capitalist system."

"Hey!" Darlene shoveled three platters onto the Nikita Smatterling table. "The kid is crying."

"The kid, the kid!" Spumoni looked momentarily infuriated. "I'm an artist, I've got genius in me, and all she can do is badger about the kid. What do I have to do, *die* to be appreciated?" He raised his wounded voice for the entire café to appreciate. "A little crying won't hurt the brat. I'm *selling* these gentlemen here—my friends. They're interested in my *art*! Now—hello again Joe, Ralph, Tribby. Listen, you guys are about to be rich. So if you don't buy one for the little woman for Christmas, how about for her birthday? Or what about this beautiful Marilyn Monroe for the Fourth of July? Be the first kid on your block—"

"Ba *ro*jo! *To*jo! *Ho*Jo!"

"What is with that guy?" Spumoni asked. "A cleft palate?"

Tribby said, "These dichromates are nice, but, you know. I mean, how much are they?"

"It costs me twenty, twenty-five bucks to do one. Normally, I sell it for thirty and break even. I don't make a nickel after I pay the guy who shoots them with the laser. But I'll sell one to you for a quarter-yard because I want you to become acquainted with my art. If you do, I'm sure you'll tell all your friends about me. I mean it—this is the creative wave of the future. The reason I'm poor is I'm way ahead of my time."

A voice from another table said, "Take off those fuckin' roller skates."

Spumoni cast a furtive glance at Angel Guts. "He's jealous, Joe. He wishes he had thought of this. I already have the patent registered. And I got an investor in Denver who's gonna put up five hundred thousand dollars to construct a mass-production lab. Buy now while you're still alive."

"Suji! Borokata *wa*ki!"

"Man, that guy gets on my nerves," Spumoni admitted. "I

mean, I don't mind it if a dude does his own thing—what the hell. But that lingo, man, that's too weird."

Ralph said, "Hey, Spumoni, we're eating breakfast."

Tribby turned to Joe. "I haven't been fishing in a month. I'd like to quit work early this afternoon. We could go out to the La Lomita highway and fish the Rio Puerco. It's supposed to be good on dry flies again. What say?"

"Fishing? Tribby, you just told me Heidi got a three A.M. phone call. How can you think about fish?"

"Take the twelve Gs," Tribby hissed, "and run. I'm sorry. But I think it's the only way. I got a feeling Natalie's fronting for Verboten, to save his face. But either way, somebody's trying to avoid bloodshed."

"For you guys, I could cut ten whole dollars off the price," Spumoni insisted. "I could let you rob me for twenty dollars. If your conscience could take it, my pocketbook could take it."

"The *kid*, Spumoni, come on!" Darlene's eyes flashed as she pocketed a tip. "If you can't keep him quiet, don't bring him in here while I'm working. If I get fired, we're dead."

"The roller skates, you hippie bum—take 'em off!"

"My roller skates happen to be a part of my personal art, Angel. They are an extension of my body. They don't just come off, like that."

"He sleeps with them on." Darlene slid poached eggs and an eggsalad sandwich in front of Baba Ram Bang.

"*Churi, chu*ri! Moo goo *gai* pai!"

"Is that you I'm looking at, Miniver?" Angel Guts tipped forward, squinting through his menacingly opaque sunglasses.

Joe nodded and gulped. "Hi, how you doin'?"

"Why you shit-can mother-sucking skull-fuck!" Angel Guts rose unsteadily. Next, as if bouncer-propelled by the seat of his pants, he flew through the air, hitting Joe's table going sixty. "*My dichromates!*" Spumoni cried. The table collapsed and flipped; glasses, plates, and silverware cascaded through the air. "I'll beat your brains in, cocksucker!" His wild hay-maker connected, instead, with Spumoni's jaw. "Hey!" Nikita Smatterling wailed. "Boys!" Natalie Gandolf shouted. Rimpoche barked, then squealed in terror. Joe pivoted, and, like Tony Dorsett breaking yet another long one, he swiveled out of the enraged killer's grasp, bumped into (and knocked over) Nikita Smatterling, and lunged for the exit. Yet for a split second, as in a nightmare where molasses instead of blood filled the veins and (fleeing from mortal danger) he could barely move his limbs, Joe was caught up in traffic. Almost everybody in the Prince of Whales had risen, either to go to the aid of, break up, or flee, and Joe found himself paddling frantically through bodies as if they were a school of obstinate and curious fish blocking his escape from a man-eating mako shark. Desperately, he pawed between Pancho Nordica and Bernard Laver. For an interminable instant his freedom was threatened by Ipu and Baldini Miller. But he managed to thrust them aside, and, with a final agonizing leap, he reached the door and kicked it open, tripping over the prostrate body of Mimi McAllister, who had been entering the café when Joe's dramatic exit bowled her over. Joe squirted toward the fresh air of his salvation just as his attacker providentially skidded on a piece of the Hanuman prasad and did a pratfall: his bone-handled Bowie knife slashed through the air, its razor-sharp blade sliced a neat line down the back of Joe's shirt and parted the cloth between his buttocks—yet it didn't touch his skin! The deadly blade then missed Joe's flying heels by millimeters, thudding into the wooden floor with a sickening crunch, embedded so deeply Angel Guts couldn't wrench it free. Instead, the Polish Apache lay in furious frustration, his knife twanging back and forth, and Joe made good his escape.

"Pora shagatsi Mina*mata!"*

Somehow, Joe maneuvered the Green Gorilla back onto Ranchitos Road. Like a clever Indianapolis 500 racing driver weaving through an eighteen-car pileup on the first lap, he circumvented three construction sites and dexterously avoided the usual herd of joggers. Down the road a ways, Mimsy and Tuckums were back in form, charging his car as if they intended to piranhasize it in sixty seconds flat. But he arrived safely at the new land. Duke opened an eye a sixteenth of an inch, saying hello; the one-eyed rabbit, snuggled between the old cur's paws, merely twitched its nose. Joe sat behind the wheel for a moment, calming down. A half-dozen turkeys surrounded the vehicle, huffing and thumping. Geese honked, a peacock screeched. Diana's car was gone. Eloy Irribarren labored in the garden area, shoveling over the earth. The placid sky, harboring but a single indifferent cloud, belied Joe's surreal morning.

Floating dreamily, cottonwood fluff took forever to touch the earth. A thin, patchwork layer of fuzzy whiteness covered the already-worked section of garden. Bits of whiteness, like poetic lint, clung to Eloy's sweatstained hat. He wore a spanking-clean blue workshirt, faded dungarees, cowboy boots. And although he didn't dig fast, he sure worked steady. Instantly, Joe envied the old-timer his apparent tranquillity, his absorption with weather, trees, the garden, animals, tools. Eloy overturned a thick clod, and rested for a beat, staring at the hills; then he jabbed his spade into the ground again. The shovel blade was rounded from a million hours of use over the years. Handling it once, in the shed, Joe had never been so personally moved by a piece of cold equipment. The wood had been spliced, glued, and secured with tightly wrapped baling wire: the blade was thin, sharp, half worn away. The smooth handle smelled salty. Eloy's hands were so tough he worked without gloves.

Joe waved: Eloy doffed his hat. The falling cottonwood fluff made the man resemble a sentimental figurine in an old-fashioned paperweight. Smitten by an intense yearning for the peace of mind guiding Eloy through his constructive days, Joe gulped. The ancient codger didn't have much, but he had dignity. Already I've blown it, Joe thought. "My chance for an honorable life," he explained out loud.

Before approaching Eloy, Joe checked in at the tent. Diana had left a note—or, rather, a poem that (needless to say) caused yet another lurch in his arrhythmical style:

> Even after you left
> This morning
> I could feel your presence
>   curled up like a cat around me.
> I opened the flaps, and
> Although it was 70 degrees out,
> It was snowing:
> White cotton...
>   ...so soft...
>   ...with Mercy.
>
> You carve an ache in my heart.
> I am afraid.

Please don't be cruel
And I won't hide from you.

Diana

"What about *me*?" Joe groaned petulantly. "Did it ever occur to you that *I* might want to hide from *you*?"

Then he wondered: Is everybody so lonely and paranoid that even a shmuck like me—because he stops short of outright murder—looks good? In his hand he held the verse as if it were a lost and hungry kitten, a literary waiflet, a ragamuffin Keane poem: a teardrop stained its painted prose. The moral being driven home, in spades, was that Nobody Is As They First Seem. Also that: Sooner, Rather Than Later, People Turn Out To Be Mordantly Human. All the unattainable cinematic glamour, that for years had catalyzed his yearnings, was nothing if not a royal Saturday Night Ripoff. Even so, as he folded the poem and slipped it into his wallet, Joe flashed briefly on Iréne Papadraxis in the Prince of Whales Café. Now *there* was a professional human being among all the amateurs crowding this town. A New York literary gun moll with a Greek moniker by way of Hungary, and maybe even a thirty-eight-inch chest? Jeepers, creepers! Nobody like that—not in those kinky boots, shiny black pants, and silky tight jersey—could be just another sniveler on the brink. In the middle of the party tomorrow night, she would catch his eye with a faint nod, and he would follow her upstairs and along a thickly carpeted hallway, to a luxurious guest bedroom. "One moment, Joseph. . . ." She slipped into the bathroom, and a short spell later reappeared wearing an ermine-chromed see-through silk lounging robe, and silver high-heeled slippers. "A trip around the world," she murmured, "is not—contrary to popular belief—a vacation." Joe swooned toward her crash course in aphrodisiacal shenanigans.

There you go again, Heidi complained. *"Aphrodisiacal shenanigans." What the hell does that mean?*

"It means never having to say you're sorry," Joe replied, and headed for Eloy Irribarren.

Leaning on his shovel, the old man looked very picturesque. He grinned toothlessly and shook Joe's hand. His wrinkled and sunburned face reeked of a sly good humor. "Did you get cold in the tent last night with your wife?"

"No, the weather was nice. But she isn't my wife, just a friend."

"Everybody these days has 'friends.'" He wagged his right hand, floppy at the wrist, back and forth. "I got married at eighteen, widowed at eighty-three, and that was it. What's the matter, your wife doesn't like this land?"

"Oh, no, she likes it fine."

"But you had a fight?"

"I guess that's accurate."

"These days, everybody fights." Lazily, they stared across the back field. A pair of killdeer fussed noisily near the shallow ditch traversing the field. In a minute, Joe figured, one of us will squat, select a twig, and start scratching pictures in the dirt. Or perhaps they'd pick up a clod of earth and crush it while gazing soulfully eastward.

Instead, Eloy continued his analysis of modern society. "It used to be that everybody knew whose children belonged to who. Nowadays, if you know whose kid belongs to who they give you a medal and send you to the university."

"Oh, it isn't that bad. I know my kids belong to me."

Eloy shrugged and thrust in his shovel blade. "In the old days, people had respect for each other." The dirt was chockfull of bright pink worms. Eloy slashed the clod apart, vivisecting a dozen squirmers. Such careless brutality toward members of the slug kingdom made Joe flinch. How typical of the gap between generations, that Eloy could excoriate today's loose morals while nonchalantly butchering worms, even as Joe, a flagrant example of modern immorality, grew queasy over the heartless dismemberment of fishbait.

On the other hand, where did this decrepit (and theoretically almost homeless) octogenarian get off even *insinuating* castigation of the middle-class moron who held his well-being in the palm of his (also) calloused hand?

I'll kick out him and his feeble dog and his one-eyed rabbit and his antique horse! Joe snarled. For sixty thousand dollars, I don't need some masculine reincarnation of Carrie Nation and Billy Graham speechifying pompously every time I commit some dinky sexual transgression! The second I own this place I'll strangle his turkeys, drown his chickens, and execute his goddam senile wolf!

Finally, what the hell was he talking about—the Old Days? In the Old Days the Spanish waltzed in and castrated the Indians: rebelling Indians then butchered the Spanish. Everybody raped, pillaged, and plundered to their heart's content. They kidnapped each other, selling the human booty into slavery. They boycotted witches, believed in the Evil Eye, condoned patróns, and died at thirty of malaria, syphilis, tuberculosis, and the common cold. To hell with the Old Days!

Thoughtfully, Joe drawled, "This is pretty durn good-looking earth."

"That's because it *is* good earth. Not too much caliche. I take care of it, too. I feed it goat manure, horse dung, leaves. For years I have pampered this ground. My gardens are beautiful. You'll see."

Joe closed his eyes, seeking to block out an image of himself as Hitler, ordering a final solution. Trying to make it sound offhand and innocuous, he queried: "Have you had any luck yet finding another place?"

Eloy grinned. "Qué va? Where would I look?"

Joe said, "Well, you'll have all that money. You could probably get into those low-income Operation Breakthrough houses they built last year."

"And do what?"

Die. Lounge around. Water a geranium. Attend senior-citizen luncheons at the county HELP center. Sit in a chair in the driveway watching twenty-eight other decrepits slumped in rockers watching each other. So Joe backed off a trifle:

"Well, yeah, I suppose you're right. But those houses do have indoor toilets. And gas heat. And you must admit that's not bad come winter."

"All my life I used an outhouse—why change now? And as for heat—if I couldn't chop wood I'd drop dead. My muscles would say, 'Eloy, Eloy, why hast thou forsaken us?'"

Miserably, Joe said, "Yeah, I guess I see your point." Guilt worked him over like a professional rubber-hose man. How could he, in all conscience, buy out this crusty old fart? Eloy was the only semi-noble human being left in the valley.

Eloy said, "Have you had any luck, yet, raising the money?"

"I'm working on it."

"Yesterday afternoon I bought bullets for robbing the bank."

"You'll just get killed," Joe wanted to say, but held his tongue. The bottom was falling out of his hopes; even his anger had been defused. Although he knew that an individual should believe he could actively take charge of his personal destiny as well as the direction of history, right now he felt powerless, flustered, cynical, inept, incongruous, and hopeless.

So Joe gave up. "You got another shovel? I need the exercise."

"In the shed." Eloy stabbed in his own spade and grunted, turning over more earth.

They worked together, sweating under the high sun, chatting amiably even though Joe felt lousy. His biographers wouldn't believe this one. An all-American upper-class, college-educated, and lily-white boy tries to pull off a coke number in order to buy land from an itinerant gardener and sheep farmer with a second-grade education, and winds up dead, or in jail for life. Or he successfully dumps the coke, buys the land, and then can't move the sly old bird out. No house can go up because the analphabet's shack can't come down. In the end, our hallowed scion of the power structure winds up living in a tent and working as tenant labor for the doddering sheep herder, who survives to a hundred and nine. *Unless* he is killed in a bank robbery five minutes before Joe is to hand him the purchase price, in which case the banks, lawyers, probate courts, and creditors gobble up the estate before you can say "José Miniver!"

But the first sane physical moves he had made in three days soon worked their magic. Joe calmed down. Taking off his shirt, he reveled in the bright heat, and in the smell of damp earth, crushed leaves, old horse dung. Almost sexually, sunshine bruised his tingling shoulders. A peculiarly energetic laziness laid siege to his ulcer-oriented body, and triumphed. All his troubles seemed so far away. Reason returned, and he knew that Tribby was correct. If he could come out of it with his twelve Gs intact, he was way ahead of the game. Perish the greed that desired this land. Joe relaxed. And at the end of an hour, he was grateful to the old man for sharing this mundane endeavor.

They paused, contemplating their work. The symmetry and richness of that exposed terrain, freckled with white fluff, pleased them both. Joe asked, "What do you usually plant here?"

"Over there, where you see the old stalks, that's obviously corn. Those humps are where the squash—scallop, summer, zucchini—and the pumpkins go. Then I plant two rows of avas—horse peas, in your American lingo. And snow peas and regular peas. And ten rows of beans. Couple rows of carrots, beets, potatoes. Mustard greens, spinach—and over there, that green row already sprouting, that's my garlic. It comes up automatically every year. I have tomato plants in the house. And the chile grows back over there, in the corn."

"It must be a lovely garden."

"I dry many things in the autumn. Squash, apples, pears. I harvest enough beans for the winter, and chile, and corn. I make chicos and use them in posole. I pack some apples and pears in straw and eat them for months. Same with the beets and carrots, although, depending on what the cavañuelas say about the winter, sometimes I just mulch them in their rows and pull them when I need them. You can feed your family year-round from a little garden like this."

Joe pictured the garden. A minute ago his greed had ebbed: now lust for ownership flooded back into his veins. Yet benign thoughts launched a glowing altruism. Eloy could stay on as caretaker of this land he had loved and nurtured much of his life. His deft hands would keep it healthy and productive, pruning the fruit trees, mulching rose bushes, mowing their new lawn, tying up suet balls for the chickadees at Christmastime. The old man would always be on call to cheer Joe up with a bit of Old Days doggerel, or a slew of pithy observations. . . .

For the next hour or two, they discussed land. Eloy demonstrated which dead apple-branches needed cutting and told why fruit saplings shouldn't be left to grow around the parent tree's roots. He explained what it meant to say that alfalfa was a "preataphyte," and went down on his knees to caress a clover plant rising in the back-field brome. "Two autumns ago," he recalled, "I saw these burnt brown clover seeds beside the La Ciénega road, stopped and picked a bagful, and sprinkled them in my field. Of their own accord, now, they are spreading."

Some weeds were undesirable; Eloy cursed vehemently and tugged them out by hand. Each time they passed a clump of horseshit, he kicked it, saying: "You got to spread the wealth around. If I had a tractor I would drag this field. But I don't, and nobody else does either, these days. so I won't."

In a corner of the back field had sprouted a small group of thistle-burr plants. "For the last ten years I have dug out these leaves at least three times every summer," Eloy grumbled, "but I never manage to kill every plant. I hate this weed. Its burrs destroy Geronimo's mane and his tail."

For eleven summers sparrow hawks had nested in that particular dying cottonwood tree. Occasionally, Eloy opened his pocketknife and cut, and ate raw, a wild asparagus spear. He also pointed out a nondescript weed called calíte. "You Americans would probably call it wild spinach. Prepared with onions, a little chile, and garlic, and fried in oil, it's delicious."

At Wolfie's cage Eloy paused. He opened the door and attached a plaid leash to the alert, flea-bitten animal. Joe marveled at how the infirm beast seemed to glide over the ground on tiptoes, his paws an inch above the dirt, as if he were swimming through the air using an elegant, effortless stroke, never tugging at the leash. With them, now, he quartered the terrain silently, sniffing carefully, peeing wherever piss was called for, listening intently to Eloy's monologue, and from time to time, with an easy twitch of his head, snapping flies and grasshoppers out of midair, gulping them down in a single swallow.

So Eloy's random observations metamorphosed into a grand tour of the property. Joe got a first-hand look at the oystershell-scale disease attacking four fragile aspens along the garden's southern border. Each hand-cut fence post delineating the property boundaries had come from a special place in the Midnight Mountains. Two sagebrush plants along the eastern fence Eloy had brought in off the mesa about a decade ago: he loved the smell of chamiso after a rain. Each wooden headgate along the Lovatos Ditch had a story. Tiny lateral ditches leading to the garden, to the orchard, to the sweet-pea vines had a pertinent history. Soundly castigating a gopher hole, Eloy wondered aloud why one son of a bitch always survived his extermination efforts.

In the northeast corner of the back field, where Geronimo had overgrazed, the area had been usurped by wild lilies. Stooping, Eloy scrutinized an old meadowlark's nest. "They build here, and half the time their young are drowned when I irrigate. But they always try again. I like their music, though I always wondered why God gave such a beautiful song to such a common bird."

As they wandered, Eloy used his shovel to assassinate a thistle plant, knock down a careless weed, and clear an offensive clod from the as yet dry ditch. He scratched a kitchen match on his zipper and flicked it into dead ditch grasses; they caught fire immediately. While the grass burned, Eloy talked about the acequias. Wolfie's eyes grew heavy-lidded as he dreamily focused into the smoke.

"It's all over, I'm afraid—irrigation farming. I'm the only person who cares that water still runs in this ditch. There isn't even a commission anymore. And for eighteen years I have been the mayordomo. Though only a lateral off the main ditch, it's almost a mile long. Every year, all by myself, I clean it. This year, this week, in fact, maybe you can help me. Three years ago I went to court against the state engineer, who tried to declare it non compos mentis. I won my case."

He grinned good-naturedly. "On three other occasions, in the past five years, I've gone to court to stop a newcomer from building a house or a garage or a tennis court on top of my acequia. All the newcomers along this ditch hate me, they can't wait until I die."

A little later, as he pried open a brittle milkweed pod and thumbed out the silken seeds, Eloy said, "When the ditches die, the land dies. And when the land dies, what interests me in people also dies. Do you know how much they are paying now—the Town of Chamisaville, for example—for water rights to a little plot like this?"

"I'd guess a lot."

"Up to twenty thousand dollars."

Eloy spoke not bitterly, but with an extreme sadness Joe found quite touching.

He continued introducing Joe to the property. Every year, up in that birdhouse, starlings nested. The pretty red bug nibbling on his hat was an elm beetle. Skunks often wrecked his corn; the best way to combat them was to leave a radio playing among the stalks at night. Often, during irrigations, a trout, or a couple of chubs, wound up splashing in the field. Muskrats honeycombed the ditch bank: Eloy shot at least a dozen every summer. Three years ago a weasel he could never trap had killed almost twenty of his chickens—then it had moved on. Those trees, which hadn't leafed out yet, were honey locusts—they always matured a month after everything else. The front-field grass was largely native, with a little timothy thrown in. You couldn't excavate in the field because it was solid rocks, part of an old stream bed. The water level was only a few feet below its surface.

Eloy's shadow darkened an anthill. "To get rid of these hormigas, I pour gasoline on them." Later, his hand settled proudly atop a rickety fence post. "Normally, I only use cedar posts. But this is an old pine log I brought out of the mountains eleven years ago. If you can't afford creosote, just save the old stuff when you change your car oil, and soak the underground part of the post in it—the wood will hold up for years."

Several times he stooped, picking up baling-wire strands, which he wound into hoops and draped over the nearest fence post. "Wherever you are," he intoned religiously, "always save a piece of wire. With it, you can repair the world, even your soul."

Eloy knew every inch of the land by heart, every weed, every animalito. "My wife planted this little snowball bush in 1962: in July it will be covered with white balls of flowers." A rosebush had been around since 1958. And: "We got the sweet-pea seeds from Francisco Naranjo in 1949."

He opened the rickety door to a chicken pen, and gathered a handful of eggs. In a shady area carpeted by dandelions, Eloy rested momentarily on a disintegrating blue bench. Wolfie snagged a large blue dragonfly and settled on his haunches, chewing reflectively, savoring the taste.

"I built this bench for my daughter, Teresa, in 1928," Eloy said. "I made her little dolls out of cornhusks, and she would sit on this bench, under a different crab-apple tree that finally died, making up games for her dolls to play."

Bemusedly, he fingered a rusty nail almost covered by the bark of a silvertip poplar. "My youngest boy, Larkin, built a treehouse here during the war."

Halting at a certain spot in the back field, he said, "Right here is where I found one of my sheep dead in the summer of 1956. She slipped out of the corral, and before I noticed her escape, she had eaten too much alfalfa. In minutes she bloated up and died."

Fascinated, Joe watched the old man stake out the land, sharing its history with the potential new owner. Right about here, in 1947, a favorite horse had stepped in a gopher hole and broken its leg. Right over there a daughter, Adelita, and her new husband had discovered a killdeer nest a week after their 1951 wedding day. Some charcoal shards in the grass pertained to a shed that had burned in 1943—struck by lightning, by God! Some now-wild yellow iris had been cultivated near the sweet-pea vines by another daughter, Marta, in 1936.

All the hollyhocks surrounding the little house had arrived on the wind and proliferated of their own accord.

By the end of the tour, Eloy had Joe close to tears. By what right could he—an easterner, a college-bred, self-indulgent, morally reprehensible idiot—come in and take over, calling this miniature farm his own, in one fell swoop annihilating the historical vibes with his alien presence? Joe was surprised that flowers didn't wither when touched by his shadow as he lumbered along clumsily behind Eloy, bald-facedly exhibiting his ignorance of nature every time he opened his mouth. For a mere sixty Gs, it seems, he could purchase (and become caretaker of) a man's soul. And how (after a tour like this, and the historical intimacies shared) should he be so lucky as to raise the cash, could he order the old boy to scram? Eloy Irribarren belonged to this cherished piece of terrain: Joe would always be a brazen interloper. Better he should retreat, tail between his legs, letting them as had legitimate claim to the place—through years of toil, love, and everyday living—run out their string.

Bewildered by conflicting emotions, Joe slumped against Eloy's adobe hovel and basked with melancholy peacefulness in the soothing sunshine. Eloy drew up a bucket of icy well-water, poured some into a platter for Wolfie, and drank from the tin cup himself. The old wolf licked his chops after drinking and, with a careless, lightning jab, plucked a little black beetle out of the air. He tasted it for a second, found it undesirable, and, pursing his lips, spat the bug out like a watermelon seed.

Yes—Joe ached to own the land. He also did not want the onus of ownership. He was wavering about risking his neck to unload the coke to obtain the bread to swing the real-estate deal. On the one hand, he fervently hoped Heidi would flush the dope down the toilet, sparing him the agony of actually purchasing this sacred land. On the other hand, if she actually did that, he would strangle her!

Suddenly, his heart thundered, his brain pulsed, his guts throbbed. Caught in a cerebral dust devil, thoughts intrabuffeted giddily. He had such powerful lusts; he also wished to do the decent thing. He was terrified of Ray Verboten . . . he would kill to possess trees and flowers . . . the risks weren't worth it . . . he needed Heidi and the kids . . . he wouldn't mind another shot at Nancy Ryan, either . . . he would help Eloy rob the bank . . . he was going crazy.

In the warm sunshine, Joe's teeth chattered.

Eloy splashed half a cup of clear water into the dust at his feet. A hummingbird buzzed between them. The day had become ultra-lazy. Chickens scratched in the driveway, clucking soporifically. Turkeys lay on their sides, ruffling feathers in the dust.

How could they kill this way of life?

Eloy said, "I'm hungry. It's time to eat. . . ."

✒

But as they relaxed beside that well, passing the tin cup of icy water between them, a late-model celestial-blue pickup towing an orange-and-white U-Haul pulled into the driveway and stopped. Behind it a jungle-green 1967 VW microbus screeched to a halt. Crouched on its roof, face obliterated behind the snout of his eight-millimeter Bolex, Rama Unfug assiduously immortalized the scene. Doors in both the pickup and the bus opened: Shanti Unfug and Iréné Papadraxis emerged from the VW, Nikita Smatterling and Ray Verboten descended from the azure cab. Using a pair of pliers, Nikita promptly began to snip at the barbed-wire fence, making a gate.

Eloy murmured, "Ay, qué sinvergüenzas!"

Joe said, "What the hell are they doing?"

"Bringing the brass monkey. You know I rented the pasture for their unveiling."

"But they'll destroy everything. They'll trample the grass and defecate in the ditch. . . ."

"I needed the money."

Without thinking, Joe said, "That badly? What for?"

"Food. Lard, flour, coffee . . ."

"Oh shoot . . . I'm sorry."

"Don't apologize."

As the pickup entered the field, Geronimo whinnied nervously, and Iréné Papadraxis walked up the potholed driveway toward them, a slick sexy vision in her Acapulco shades, black body-shirt, midnight-purple stretch pants, and those knee-high spike-heeled leather boots. Her outlandishly sexy gait made Joe's groin prickle. But his heart thundered, because—embarrassed for his aged companion—he also hated her. Viewed through Eloy's campesino prism, what a Martian! In the background, Nikita and Ray, Shanti and Rama shouted orders to each other, taking over the field, determining crucial place-ments for the U-Haul. Dressed in daffodil yellow, Om Unfug danced through the short grass, chasing imaginary butterflies of love.

Serene and peaceful clouds reflected obscenely in Iréné's one-way shades. Nearing them, she smiled. "Hello, Joe—so we meet again." Imprinted in black, every hair and minuscule nub around her nipples jumped at Joe like carnival shouts. Though angry, he also had a rising hard-on.

"Hello yourself," chirped Mr. Casual. "How have you been?"

"And this, I take it, is Mr. Iddibabben?" When she pushed those obnoxious glasses into her hair, green eyes leaped out with beautiful icy hauteur. Her smile—admittedly a turn-on—seemed pained. She extended her hand.

"Irribarren," Joe corrected.

Amusedly, Eloy accepted the handshake. "That's my name. Don't wear it out."

"I hear you're one of the most fascinating men in the Cham-isa Valley, Mr. Irribarren. I'm writing a book about the Han-uman and its unveiling on Thursday. I'd love for you to tell me a little background about your place here...."

Joe squirmed, averting their eyes, and retreated to the Green Gorilla as Eloy, accepting her request at face value, launched into a gentle, peaceful dissertation on his beloved terrain. Embarrassed at the way she provoked him sexually, Joe had to cop at least three surreptitious peeks at her lascivious body before he could start the truck and flee. But halfway down the driveway he pumped himself to a stop.

Nikita Smatterling and Shanti Unfug waved; Ray Verboten gave Joe a neutral, hired-killer stare.

"You guys shouldn't have cut the fence like that, without asking his permission," Joe called out.

Ray Verboten quit conferring with Nikita and started toward the driveway. He came on slowly, like a slick old-fashioned gunslinger. A funny sensation squeezed the day. Like a camera lens focusing down, Joe lost contact with images on his pe-riphery. Until abruptly Ray Verboten seemed to be coming at him through a tunnel, or in a spotlight—no other earth, people, or noises were involved. Magpie calls receded, Om's laughter evaporated, Geronimo's nervous whinnies died away. All Joe could hear was the menacing *swish-swish* of Ray's boots in the grass. It took him forever to arrive. He circled the truck to the driverside window, placed a foot on the running-board, and poked his impassive cruel features up to the open window.

"Joe," he said, in a mockingly bored voice, "I'd like to personally invite you to the unveiling of this Hanuman on Thursday . . ."

"Gee, thanks," Joe muttered, angrily fighting off his queasiness, begging his heart to be tough.

". . . *if* you're still alive."

Joe said, "Fuck you," popped the clutch, and clattered off in a dignified, gallumphing huff.

JERK WHO SPAT ON HITMAN FOUND DEAD WITH CROWBAR
STABBED THROUGH CRANIUM!

    A few minutes later, Joe found himself grinding to a theatrical halt in the parking lot of the First State People's Jug. He quelled the engine and kept still for a moment, knuckling his aching eyes. A direct route to Tribby's office had been his official flight plan; yet at a crucial juncture he had unwittingly executed a left instead of a right, ending up at the portals of Chamisa County's premier financial institution.

Tom Yard—all six feet five inches, Stetson hat, and Sam Browne belt toting a .357 mag of him—leaned against the main portal, smoking a hand-rolled cigarette. He waved. Returning the salutation, Joe experienced a guilty lurch somewhere east of his pancreas. If they really wound up robbing this sucker, Tom would be their major obstacle. Two years ago an Oklahoma drifter named Darvil Cummings, disguised in a blond wig, a shirtwaist dress, and spike heels, and his diminutive sidekick, Judy Moravek, a waitress he'd picked up only the night before at the Chamisaville Inn, had tried to do a heist in Tom Yard's domain. Blowing his cool when the teller fainted, Darvil yanked a toy German Luger from his purse and ordered everybody in the room to freeze. Only Tom Yard refused to go gelid: instead, he grabbed his own pizzolover and decked the Okie with a single shot right between the eyes, depositing half his brain against the wall clock thirty feet away, over the personal-loans department. When Judy Moravek tried to flee, Tom fired four more times: each slug spun her around on her feet so that she resembled a frenzied ballerina during that brief, horrific instant before she shattered the glass partition to auto loans, riddled beyond repair.

Since then, nobody had fucked with the First State People's Jug.

Half paralyzed by fear, Joe remained seated, casually casing the joint through discreetly hooded eyes. Probably, they would have to ice Tom Yard even before the robbery commenced. Park right about here, dismount feigning abject indifference, stroll into the money bin with checkbooks drawn, saunter up behind the cold-blooded oaf, pull out an army .45, and empty the clip into that Frankenstein, praying at least one projectile would scramble a vital organ seriously enough to deck the fanatic behemoth.

And don't forget to cock the goddam gun beforehand, either!

"Brilliant, Miniver! Positively brilliant!" All he needed right now, to make his life complete, was a murder rap on top of everything else!

Little boys playing cowboys and Indians had more grown-up approaches to the cultivation of robbery and mayhem. Joe Miniver, in his fourth decade, was a downright vestal moron.

It couldn't work. The notion was absurd. Eloy can't have been serious.

Joe opened the door and slouched past Tom into the bank. Cool air enveloped him like sophisticated female arms. Approaching the high-ceilinged hushed room from the perspective of a criminal made him slightly dizzy. An invisible force squeezed his testicles; a large drop of lemon juice landed on the raw oysters of his internal abdominal organs. And his buttocks tingled.

Assuming a nonchalant pose at a central check-writing table, Joe allowed his eyes to wander around lazily. Five tellers currently handled a half-dozen customers. On a deposit slip Joe wrote: *five tellers*.

A bank officer reached over a low walnut barricade at the west end of the marble-tiled floor, fingered a buzzer releasing the catch on a thigh-high partition door, bumped the door open with her hip, and trotted briskly past two tellers into the open vault. Joe checked the time—were those little flecks of dried brain material around the clock, or only a minor rain seepage from the roof?—and wrote on his deposit slip: *3:17, vault open*.

For a moment he counted functionaries. Added to those five

tellers against the south wall, were seven higher officers seated at ponderous walnut desks among partitions and glass cubicles along the north side of the room. Eloy would have to cover them, while Joe terrorized a teller.

He wrote: *7 officers, north side—Eloy.*

Oops, here came that chic lady out of the vault: he'd forgotten about her. During the real thing, an extra, unaccounted-for person popping up like that could blow the entire show.

He followed her back to her desk, and noted: *One more officer . . . check vault.*

Barely had he finished writing, however, than a short, pudgy woman in a navy-blue skirt and white blouse appeared in a doorway on the western edge of the room, having just climbed upstairs from what must be basement offices.

Cover stairwell . . . downstairs offices.

Next, a mechanized voice greeting a drive-in banker made Joe realize that through the archway just behind the row of south-side tellers, at least one, and possibly two, drive-up personnel were hard at work.

In fact, here came one now—a slim aristocratic woman in her early twenties: she clickety-clacked westward behind the tellers and spent a few seconds leafing through the current depositor's records to make sure a check would clear.

Don't forget drive-up windows!

A seeing-eye camera mounted high on the wall over the bank manager's desk east of the tellers' windows seemed to peer directly at Joe. He stared at it lackadaisically for a few seconds, before realizing the exact nature of seeing-eye cameras; and, in a sickening adrenal spurt of panic, he wondered, Had that goddam remote-control TV just filmed his eyeballing and note-jotting venture?

Did those things transmit pictures all the time, forging videotape cassettes that could be played back in a courtroom against him? "Now Mr. Miniver, let me call your attention to approximately three-seventeen on the afternoon in question. If it please Your Honor, we would at this time like to draw the shades and activate our videotape machine. . . ."

Joe knew absolutely nothing whatsoever about the habits of fiduciary seeing-eye apparati. Suppose a man downstairs, whose sole purpose in life was to monitor transmissions from aboveground, was right now phoning County Sheriff Eddie Semmelweis to report a suspicious-looking character upstairs reconnoitering the spread in a most provocative way while scribbling surreptitious notes on a deposit slip?

"Wake up, Joe. Get out of here, nebbish!"

By the time his crumpled deposit slip landed in the bottom of a tall, empty wastecan, Joe was almost at the door. A foolish grin and an innocent shrug took care of Tom Yard; then he practically sprinted for the Green Gorilla. But as the door slammed and Joe hit the starter button, a terrible thought illuminated the crimson light bulb in the puffy cartoon balloon above his head. *They had the act on videotape, including the way he'd crumpled that deposit slip and left it behind as evidence!*

"Better get it back, shmuck, fast!"

But if he returned so quickly, obviously flushed, and nervous as a trapped jackal, they'd nail him on the spot. It would be over before he had even decided if they should rob it or not.

Could they put you in jail simply for casing a joint? Or for mulling over a criminal idea?

Tom Yard was back inside, no doubt eyeing everybody and fingering the release strap on his holster, just waiting for a nerd like Joe Miniver to burst through the doors and start scrabbling around in wastebaskets. Joe could see it vividly: Just as his fingers touched the crumpled deposit slip, Tom cut loose a barrage; the first slug severed his spinal cord. Bent double, Joe's body sagged, crunching into the bottom of the can. And with a terrible clatter, he tipped over—immersed in tin from the waist up—and rolled noisily across the floor, leaving a sanguine trail, ignominious death personified!

Joe giggled nervously: what an absurd vision! After all, having done nothing, he was still as innocent as the daisies. But it would be crazy to rob that bank: they didn't stand a chance.

🙞

    Joe fired up his jalopy. But just as the Green Gorilla was about to hightail it out of that parking area in order to attack, with joyless abandon, the clogged arteries of Chamisaville's open road, the snout of a large army Colt .45 automatic slid through the driverside-window area and settled against the tip of Joe's blackhead-studded nose.

A voice, muffled behind one of those grubby gorilla creations, said, "Hello, Joe, what're you up to? Cathing the moneybin for a pothible heitht? Thath a no-no, my friend."

"Me? Who? What?" Oh my God, here it came for sure: *Eternity*! Joe's first instinct was to stick fingers in his ears, thereby at least avoiding the noise. But his second, more to the point reaction, was to budge not even a millimeter.

"You and me are gonna take a little ride," the gorilla mask said, "Ith that okay by you?"

"Do I have a choice?"

"Thure. You could make a break for it and I could crothet the entire texht of Revelationth acroth your back in hot lead."

"Some choice."

"Bueno. Jutht hold it thteady, then, while I thircle around to the other thide, you got that?"

"I won't make a move. I wanna live. . . ."

The guy was six feet tall, and scrawny. An acquaintance, perhaps, the lisp a ridiculous disguise? But what did he mean, "take a little ride?" Like Jimmy Hoffa? Were cohorts out there in the bushes and the brambles waiting to measure Joe for a cement overcoat and toss him unceremoniously into the Rio Grande after poking the muzzle of a .45 against the back of his head and giving him a one-way ticket to Hades? What else did gun-toters do when they took you for "a little ride"? I better make a run for it, Joe thought. Open the door, tumble out, gallop screaming (and zigzagging) for the bank . . . *too late*! The gorilla mask climbed through the passengerside window, and settled in beside Joe, poking the .45 uncomfortably into his ribs.

"Juth do what I thay and you won't get hurt, Joe. Now, let'th pull out of here—thlowly, inconthpicuouthly—no horn-blowing."

"The horn doesn't even work," Joe whimpered scornfully.

"Tho much the better. Turn left here."

Joe hung a louie onto Placitas Street and braked for a hardhat brandishing a Stop flag before a busily excavating backhoe.

"Ignore him, Joe. We're in a hurry."

"But I'll hit the backhoe."

"Thcrew the backhoe; you can thircumnavigate it."

"But . . . I . . . all right . . . okay! *Ouch*. You don't have to prod me with that thing."

Yet as he began to swing around, the flag man leaped in

front of the Green Gorilla, screaming, "Hey, buddy, who do ya think ya are? I said stop! Are you blind? Look at my flag!"

Inclined out the passenger window, the gorilla mask aimed at the loudmouth. "We happen to be prethed for time," he said calmly. "That'th what thith .45 automatic ith all about."

The flag man blanched. "Okay, excuse me, sir. I didn't understand. *Hey Bill, get that fucking machine out of the way, we got some folks in a hurry here!*"

A hundred yards farther along, the gorilla mask ordered Joe right onto Santistevan Lane. Cutting up to the North-South Highway, they turned left again, heading north toward the Dynamite Shrine complex. A mile below the shrine, they swung into a macadam driveway running beside a high adobe wall of the old McQueen estate, which now belonged to the mysterious and ubiquitous Tarantula of Chamisaville, Mr. Joseph Bonatelli.

Nervously, Joe said, "Why are we coming here?"

"Ever been inthide theeth inthcrutable wallth, Joe?"

He indicated no, almost paralyzed by fear.

"Then thith'll be a real treat for you."

Joe gulped. His kneecaps tingled. He had an urge to gun the truck, fling open his door, spin the wheel, and tumble out, praying not to break his neck, at least making a stab at escape. But as soon as he thought of it, the plan seemed stupid. His captor would pull triggers the second a door flew open. By the time Joe landed he'd be sawed in half by high-powered slugs. No, he stood a better chance if he just kept his mouth shut, acted stupid, and prayed for miracles.

A meadowlark atop the wall yodeled melodiously; black-and-white Clark's nutcrackers played noisy games in the tops of fir trees visible above the high adobe barriers. Joe slowed down: in the middle of the driveway a large raven was gnawing on a dead rabbit.

"That'th you and Mithter Bonatelli," the gorilla mask joked.

"Which one is me?" Joe yukked, trying to kill his panic with a moronic pleasantry.

"Ha ha. You're a barrel of laughth, Joe."

A large metal gate barred access to the inner sanctum. But as Joe commenced braking, his kidnapper produced a remote-control apparatus, aimed at the gate, and pushed a button: the elaborately scrolled iron doors swung open: the truck puttered smoothly inside.

Their tires crunched against polished Florentine gravel. Crocuses, hyacinths, and daffodils lined the route. Croquet wickets gleamed by a goldfish pond at the foot of a budding weeping willow tree. Although bright daylight, gas lamps burned atop antique wrought-iron poles. Robins tugged fat worms out of the carefully manicured lawns. A large Saint Bernard, oblivious to their incursion, playfully rolled in the grass, toying with a cow skull beside a luminescent blue spruce tree. Stone lions guarded the front walkway; the Green Gorilla coughed to a shuddering halt in front of them.

"Journey'th end, Jothé. Out you go."

"Why are you bringing me here?" Joe descended from the stinking truck. "What's going on?"

"That'th for me to know, and for you to find out."

"But I'm innocent. I haven't done anything. I'm just a two-bit everyday shmuck."

"Joe, pleathe. Thkip the heartth and flowerth. I only do what I'm told to do. Don't make it hard on me." With a menacing jerk of his big gun, he ordered Joe around the truck and between the lions.

"I'm not trying to make it hard on you. I just don't understand. I don't even *know* Mr. Bonatelli."

"But he knowth all about you."

Flagstones, flanked by hydrangea bushes, hollyhocks, tall jaune irises, and other assorted rainbowalia, carried them to the leaded glass door of the mansion. Joe cast a last frantic glimpse around as his captor punched the doorbell. A zillion trees, bushes, leafpiles, little grottoes, bubbling streams, and goldfish ponds studded the lush grounds. They could bury me somewhere, Joe thought, and I'd never be found. The job would probably be done with a gun muted by one of those tennis-ball-can-looking silencers. Or perhaps one goon would strangle him with piano wire, while another repeatedly ice-picked him in the chest.

His head cried, "Make a break . . . run away . . . karate-chop this turkey . . . grab his gun . . . head for the hills. . . ." But his arms were paralyzed, his feet stayed glued to the flagstones—even his fingers had gone numb.

A Pueblo maid opened the door. Grasping Joe's elbow, the gorilla mask said, "Let'th go," and propelled him inside. Joe barely had time to register a regal interior of Persian rugs, sixteenth-century French étagères, original Flemish art, and

Tibetan draperies, before they passed through lovely french
doors onto a patio beside a heated swimming pool, where a
very fat man wearing a blue beret, a gaudy Hawaiian shirt, a
black European bikini, and beach clogs sat in a white metal
patio chair with his pinkie-ringed hand resting atop a circular
glass and latticework white metal table.

One-way sunglasses hid his eyes: below them, cruel teeth
and fat lips clenched a Havana cigar. A pet ferret on a pink
leash attached to the leg of his chair dozed on the warm tile.
A single yellow rose protruded from a silver bud vase on the
glass-top table. Beside it lay a Magic Marker pen and a grapefruit.

"Well, I got him, Mithter B. Here he ith. Thigned, thealed,
and delivered." He poked the .45 snout against his own ear,
nudging an itch.

Forehead wrinkled in a prepossessing scowl, Bonatelli assessed Joe, lips pressed together, accenting his bulldog jowls.

Joe said, "Hello, Mr. Bonatelli."

"Hello, Joe. Welcome to my humble abode. Won't you sit
down, please?"

A plump, menacing hand indicated the other metal deck
chair. Gingerly, Joe settled into it: the springy legs squeaked;
he jounced uncomfortably.

"You want me to get you anything, Mithter B.?" The gorilla
mask asked.

"No, that's all right, Algernon." Bonatelli raised his pinkie-
ringed finger, probing thoughtfully in a large, flabby nostril.
"We won't keep you here but a minute, Joe. I just thought we
had better meet, get to know each other, so to speak." In a
rather obscene way he deserted the nostril and adjusted a testicle.

"Well, you know . . . it's a real nice place you got here . . ."
Joe fumfered inanely.

"I earned it by tolerating no interference in my business
interests, Joe." Bonatelli spoke almost gently, yet his words
so reeked of menace that Joe's heart almost ceased. He nodded
stupidly.

"Yessir, well, you know, I can certainly understand that."

"Really?" Bonatelli exhaled cigar smoke almost dreamily
and parted his lips as if to threaten further, but remained mute.
Thirty seconds, during which time Joe sweated cats and dogs,
ticked by.

"I'm not sure what you mean," Joe said at length, hoping to break the scary silence.

"Now Joe, please. Don't act dumb." Bonatelli's smile complemented his mellifluous voice. He opened a sharklike mouth, revealing gold-capped, irregular, rotten teeth. The mouth stank of power and corruption. It was permanently adjusted into a scornful sneer. "I dislike wasting time."

"I don't want to waste your time, sir. I mean, I didn't even ask to be brought here."

"*I* brought you here, Joe, because I want us to reach an understanding." He released words slowly, giving an impression of selecting them very carefully before opening his mouth.

"About what?"

"Please." Bonatelli turned his face slightly and raised both hands as if to ward off an unpleasant odor. "These things are understood. We don't have to spell them out. That would be in bad taste."

Joe nodded dumbly, wondering, What next?

Bonatelli removed the cigar and pursed his ugly lips. Though facing Joe, the one-way shades made it impossible to tell if his eyes were open, closed, or fixed on the swimming pool. Inside, Joe shriveled. His mouth was dry and chalky, his tongue had swelled. His palms were sticky with fear. Quite clearly, he had never been this close to annihilation. His gorilla-masked kidnapper had grown unearthly still, as if the inner human being had evaporated in the withering presence of the Tarantula of Chamisaville.

"Joe, I'd like you to do something for me." Bonatelli leaned forward, and, with a passel of noisy creaks, he grasped the grapefruit, handing it to Joe. "I want you to take this grapefruit, and with this pen—" his other hand picked up the Magic Marker "—I'd like you to write your name across the skin of this thing."

Hesitantly, Joe accepted the grapefruit from the gangster—and the pen. Were they booby-trapped? Would they explode in his face? What kind of a joke was this anyway?

"I don't understand," he said.

"You will."

Joe uncapped the Magic Marker. He checked Bonatelli, who observed him with deadly disdain. "You mean . . . just like . . . I mean . . . write my name on this grapefruit?"

Nothing about Bonatelli moved: but, from the vibes implied by the sneer and the scowl, Joe figured Yup, that's what the man had said. So he tore his eyes away from those shades, and, feeling sublimely ridiculous, as well as mortally threatened (while garish headlines flickered across his faltering brain), he started printing his name around the equatorial circumference of the large yellow fruit.

BABE "MORON" MINIVER ICED GANGLAND-STYLE BY SELF-
AUTOGRAPHED GRAPEFRUIT! KLUTZ SUFFOCATES WHEN NOSE
IS JAMMED INTO LETHAL SNUFFER! BONATELLI RELEASED ON
OWN RECOGNIZANCE IN BIZARRE MINIVER EXECUTION!

Finished, he recapped the pen and placed it on the table.

"That's good," said the Capo di Tutti Capo in Chamisaville. "Now, give me the grapefruit."

Joe obeyed. Lips pursed, the fat man revolved the fruit in his hands, inspecting Joe's name, then he gave it a choppy sideways toss—the grapefruit landed in the swimming pool.

"The gun, Algernon." Responding to Bonatelli's just-barely-snapped fingers, the gorilla mask almost tripped over his big, sneakered feet, lunging to deposit that .45 in the fat man's powerful, pudgy fist.

Eyebrows arched, Bonatelli dramatically fingered the weapon, giving Joe his money's worth. No more cold-blooded pistol had ever settled into a crueler mitt. Joe hoped they wouldn't hang him upside down in the plaza and spit upon his broken corpse. Bonatelli seemed more likely to butt-whip him insensate than to pull a trigger.

Instead, that sourpuss blob swung his attention to the grapefruit bobbing in the swimming pool. Raising the heater, he took deliberate aim, making certain the menace soaked in. Just before the heartless little giant squeezed off a shot, Joe realized, somewhat joyfully, that he was only being symbolically eradicated here: water geysered into the air about three feet off-target.

Impassively, Bonatelli fixed his sights on the yellow globe and let fly; the report of a bullet that again missed by a mile deafened Joe.

Inwardly enraged, to judge by the teeth clamped down on his cigar, Bonatelli leaned forward slightly and emptied the clip at the bobbing grapefruit. He came close: the yellow ball bounced and jiggled in the froth created by impacting slugs . . . but it also remained unscathed, pristine—whole.

Incredulously, Bonatelli confronted the swimming pool through his hostile lenses. Joe bit his lower lip, suppressing a screechy giggle. The Tarantula of Chamisaville, hoping to paralyze his hapless prey with fear, had instead almost capsized him with slapstick.

"Another clip, please." Bonatelli spoke without taking his eyes off the object of his animosity and derision.

Algernon scrambled in his pocket to produce more firepower. The fat man fumbled with the .45, looking for a button to punch, releasing the clip. Evidently, however, he had not been on the business end of a betsy for many a moon. His big blunt fingers slithered helplessly around the gunmetal while Algernon dangled in suspended animation above him, offering the loaded clip. Finally, Bonatelli disgustedly handed the gun to Joe's kidnapper, and said softly, "You put it in."

Algernon complied and returned the pistol to his boss.

Bonatelli aimed . . . and fired. The lead slammed into chlorinated agua, and, had the grapefruit possessed a tongue, hands, and ears, it would have waggled the tongue tauntingly while sticking thumbs in said ears and wiggling its fingers nyah-nyah-nyahingly.

Another careful bead . . . and one more bullet splatted harmlessly into the drink an armlength away from a bull's-eye. Quietly, Bonatelli removed the cigar from his mouth and placed it on the table. Then, veins protruding from his forehead, he concentrated mightily—and cut loose, splashing water from here to Timbuktu, but leaving the object of his wrath unscathed.

With that, the crime boss shuffled erect and held still for a moment, teetering as his rolls of flab joggled, resettling according to the new location of gravitational pull. His black bikini disappeared underneath doughy drifts of pink flesh. Seated, he had seemed enormous to Joe: but erect, although he must have weighed close to three hundred pounds, Bonatelli couldn't have topped five feet, three inches. Dully enraged, obviously in spiritual pain, Bonatelli waddled over to the edge of the pool, extended his right arm at a downward slant, and aimed very carefully at the grapefruit six feet away merrily bobbing in the limpid water. Even at that distance, Joe heard the gangster suck in a long, rasping breath . . .

Blam! Pause. *Blam*! Pause. *Blam! Blam! Blam!*

Fruitlessville.

Joe couldn't help it—he snickered. Fortunately, nobody

heard as his irreverent scorn was lost in a final explosion.
Airborne, the grapefruit remained as perfect as a full moon. It
splashed down unblemished, "Joe Miniver" blaring out for all
the world to snarl at.

Apoplectic, but in control, the old gangster flung his weapon
into the pool. Tightly, he said, "Go in there and get it."

"Yeth thir!" Algernon gamboled clumsily to the edge of the
pool, pinched his gorilla nose, and jumped in feetfirst, soaking
the Tarantula of Chamisaville from his belly to his tiny pups.
Too late, as he grappled for the grapefruit, Algernon realized
the water was over his head.

"Help!" He glubbed and gurgled, went under, kicked into
the air again, screamed *"I can't thwim!,"* and sank like a marble
tombstone.

To Joe, Bonatelli said, "Save him."

"Me?"

Obviously tired of being beleaguered by assholes, Bonatelli
tilted his head slightly, firing dumdum bullets of icy boredom
through the one-way shades. All kinds of piano wire, ice picks,
and shallow quicklimed graves commuted themselves in that
glance. Overcoming his astonishment, Joe leaped up, gallivanted to poolside, heroically plunged into the drink, and grabbed
the gorilla mask, lugging him a few yards to where his feet
touched the ground.

Bonatelli made an acerbic gesture with his cigar. "Now
retrieve me that fruit."

Obediently, Joe clumped through the water in his soggy
clothes, plucked up his namesake, and propelled himself over
to the pool's edge, depositing the invincible fruit at Bonatelli's
elegantly coiffed toes.

The fat man raised his left foot and brought it down hard:
SQUASH! Pink pulp and bitter juice sprayed out, catching Joe
in the kisser. He blinked, splashed water, went under, and
surfaced in pain and gasping.

"Now take a powder, termite," Bonatelli snarled, waddling
back to reclaim his cigar and settle slowly, like a large python
laboriously coiling itself after noshing a tapir, into his deck
chair.

Joe fumbled into the shallow end, hauled himself onto the
warm tiles, and for a moment wavered, bewilderedly staring
at Joseph Bonatelli. That's it? All over? Chamisaville's leading
businessperson had troubled himself to snatch Chamisaville's

leading fool and most inept drug-dealing neophyte, in order to annihilate a symbolically tattooed grapefruit right before his terrified eyes . . . and nothing more? Where were the 280-pound sadistic enforcers waiting to work him over with rubber hoses? How come nobody had broken his fingers in the men's room, or shoved needle-sharp bamboo shoots underneath his fingernails? They hadn't even cattle-prodded his testicles! Or given him until sundown to make like a breeze and blow this constipated burg!

"H-how do I get out?" Joe managed to stammer at last, almost disappointed by his unexpected freedom.

"Same way you got in," said the dignified, deadly blob.

"Through the house?"

But having dismissed him, the fat man had turned deaf. So Joe backed away, convinced it had to be a trick, waiting for the sky to fall. As in a James Bond movie, the grisly son of a bitch would trip a button with his foot, and the tiles would open up, dropping Joe into a pit full of gorgeous peroxide blond amazons with steel-fanged vampire dentures, razor-sharp metal fingernails, and needlelike, four-inch-long dart pasties over their lovely nipples.

Yet the gangster chief sat in his chair, immobile and undeadly, imperviously smoking a cigar; while in shock, the gorilla-masked man named Algernon tarried meekly, submerged up to his chest . . . and the juice from the smashed grapefruit dribbled slowly across the shiny tiles, seeping into grassy cracks like albino blood.

A small army-green bubble helicopter appeared overhead and began descending toward the Bonatelli lawn. A white sign on its side said U.S. FOREST SERVICE. But that was no Floresta flunky at the controls, Joe thought, as the copter drew closer. In fact, had he not known better, he would have sworn that the diminutive figure inside was none other than the Tarantula's mortally wounded, hospital-ridden offspring, Ephraim by name.

Bonatelli's gravelly voice interrupted his reverie: "Goodbye, Joe."

Nobody, not even the maid, was around as Joe squished obsequiously across priceless Persian carpets and out the already open front door. Neither man nor beast leaped at him from the bushes as he scurried for the Green Gorilla. And no snipers took potshots at him from high up in the spruce and elm trees as he collapsed behind the wheel and reached for the ignition key.

Wait a minute! whoa boy! Alto! *Stop*!

So *that* was their gimmick. At the switch of a key, the dynamite bomb lodged against his fire wall would detonate, pulverizing the Green Gorilla, and airmailing Joe Miniver, in multidimensional flesh confetti, to the four corners of Chamisa County.

"Jump out and check under the hood!" a voice cried.

Whereupon one of the world's most chickenshit and off-the-wall reasoning processes interceded. "If I do that," Joe replied, "they might see me and be offended that I don't trust them. Or maybe he'll think I'm hanging around, trying to spy on his helicopter."

So with squeezed-shut eyes and gritted teeth, he flipped the keys and pounded the accelerator. A *baroom*! sounded, but only of the engine catching. Barely daring to open his eyes much more than slits, and miserably hunched over, hoping to absorb the shock of an explosion should one come, Joe peeled out, shotgunning the Bonatelli mansion with bits of Florentine gravel.

No invisible, molybdenum-reinforced, unbreakable wire stretched across the driveway sliced off his truck's cab, gruesomely decapitating Joe in the process. And his tires triggered no Claymore mines or Bouncing Betties that might have hamburgered his vehicle with him in it. The gates, of course, loomed as an obstacle. When he dismounted to open them, would some cackling becloaked monster in an ivy-shrouded tower observing him via a remote-control TV screen, throw a switch to slam 100,000 volts through the ornate gate-handle as Joe's fingers closed over it?

Instead, the wrought-iron portals opened as if by magic when he approached them. And, if not exactly whistling Dixie, Joe egressed much as he had ingressed—whole, hale, and bewildered.

He was free, back into the actual world, with nothing to remind him of the surreal adventure except a soggy costume!

Tribby Gordon's office was located on the second floor of a shabby prefab hovel situated a quarter-mile north of the post office. The building also housed a pawnshop, Noelle Paxton's tattoo parlor, and three hippie jewelers. Joe counted "One, two, three..." waiting for Tribby to terminate a coughing fit, then opened the door. Peering through opaque layers of cigarette smoke resembling a Dickensian London fog, he spotted his frazzled pal seated behind a beaver-mound pile of legal papers surrounded by a half-dozen butt-laden cut-glass ashtrays, reading a copy of *Trout*, by Ray Bergman.

"Hard at work, I see." Joe left open the door, hoping a miraculous breath of fresh air might clear out the place before he collapsed from smoke inhalation or suffered a fatal asthma attack. "It's nice to know that when you pay a man fifty bucks an hour, he's sparing no effort in diligently prosecuting your business."

"Don't come to me with your problems, Joseph. Let Scott Harrison handle your divorce. I'm tired of flakking marriages for my friends: they never pay, and hate me in the end anyway. Did you bring extra flies?"

"I got a whole box. But how come, every time we go fishing, I always have to supply all the flies?"

"I'm a busy man," Tribby grumbled. "Do you know what the divorce rate is in this county? Three out of every two marriages end up in divorce. The average live-in relationship, nonwedded, after which the concubine—male or female—sues for half the property, lasts three months. Every day at least twenty new dwellings involving these basket cases start construction. Every afternoon I have to spend at least two hours driving around the valley, handing my card out to lovey-dovey couples who'll be tearing each other apart like Siamese fighting-fish as their dream houses near completion. Did you bring the coke?"

"I haven't been home yet."

"Heidi still has it?"

"I told you—I left it there last night."

"What about Natalie's offer?"

"You mean as opposed to her husband's bagful of propositions?"

"Need I repeat that you said he wound up by threatening meatgrinders?"

"Granted. But . . ."

"Well?"

"Oh sure. I suppose it makes sense to accept her offer. But today I spent hours over at Eloy's land and it's so beautiful it breaks my heart."

"Why don't you think about it, then? No hurry. We got lots of time . . . an hour, two hours. Maybe even two hours and forty-five minutes. Don't want to rush into anything. But the fish are awaiting, let's split. Later we'll talk."

"First, I think I should tell you something."

"So tell."

"I got snatched by Joseph Bonatelli a few minutes ago."

"'Snatched'?"

"Kidnapped. Some lisping thug in a gorilla mask took me at gunpoint out to the don's digs for a meeting with the Tarantula himself."

"Hmm. How come you're all wet? What happened?"

"I'm not exactly sure. I think he tried to threaten me by shooting a grapefruit with my name on it. But he missed. And I wound up jumping into his pool to save his errand boy—my kidnapper—who couldn't swim. As I was leaving, a little Forest Service helicopter started to put down on the lawn, and, if I didn't know better, I'd say that the dwarf was behind the wheel."

"Which dwarf?"

"Joe's kid—Ephraim."

"He's in the hospital with a bullet wound."

"I said 'if I didn't know better.'"

Tribby frowned, then squinched up his entire face perplexedly: "One thing that makes sense—that little jerk can fly."

"How do you know?"

"I kept bumping into him in Vietnam. His dad must have paid the army to drop the height requirements. He used to pilot a Huey gunship wearing a chartreuse jumpsuit with a naked woman in silver cowboy boots on the back."

"What would Bonatelli be doing with a Forest Service helicopter in his yard?"

Tribby shook his head. "Look. Let's talk in the car. The trout must be up."

"Before we leave, I gotta borrow the phone."

Joe dialed the house, hoping that Heidi would decide these issues for him. She had flushed the cocaine down the toilet. Or, thinking it cake mix, Heather had ruined it with water and burned it up in her Easy-Bake Oven. Joe was about to hang up after eight rings when Heidi answered breathlessly. Joe said, "Listen, this morning the kids asked if I could come over and wrestle tonight, after supper."

"Joey," she said plaintively, "just for the record, what are you up to? What are you doing? What's happening with us? Don't you think we ought to have a discussion or something to figure out where we're at and why, and where we're going? So that we could either separate formally or stay together or get divorced, or just do *some*thing? We need to articulate an arrangement; I can't stand this ridiculous limbo."

"Well, sure, I don't see why not."

"I mean, I have no idea what you think, or why you left, or why you started screwing that Reichian Pollyanna, or why—"

"Maybe we could leave other people's names out of our conversations," Joe said tightly.

"How am I supposed to refer to her then, as 'her'? As 'it'? As 'she'?"

"How about if you don't refer to her at all?"

"But why has all this happened in the first place if it wasn't because you wanted to ball old whatshername? Do you want a divorce? Are you two planning a July wedding?"

"Nobody's getting married—Jesus!" Stop, he cried silently. I'm calling you up because I *love* you! I want a reconciliation!

"Well, Joey, you're so goddam wishy-washy. It's like all of a sudden you decided to float around out there acting stupid—it doesn't make any sense. Your official midlife crisis isn't due for another six years! If you're in love with her, I could understand. I might not like it, but at least I'd understand."

"Hold on a sec. Get off your high horse. For starters, three days ago you told me you didn't want me in the house."

"Would you want me in *your* digs if I was out there screwing some cockteasing religious fanatic who kept calling the house while *you* were here and asking me to come over for a roll in the old sackeroo?"

"Do you have to be so gross?"

"Yeah, I think maybe I do. What's the matter, Mr. Morality

here doesn't want his eardrums tainted with crude talk? Pardon me. I'll have to reread my Emily Post."

"I don't see any point in coming over tonight if all you're interested in is seeing how many bitch-points you can score needling me. I mean, we're supposed to be at least semirational human beings."

"I'm not trying to score bitch-points. If that's the way I sound, apologies to the pope. I'm just not accustomed to this role, that's all. In case you're interested, I happen to feel a bit humiliated."

"Well, uh, I guess I can't blame you for that."

"Thanks for all your compassion. But why don't you save yourself a lot of grief and take the compassion and shove it you know where."

"Heidi! All I wanted to know was could I wrestle with the kids after supper?"

"They're your kids, too. You don't need permission. I'll leave, if you want. I'll call up Scott Harrison, see who's available in the screwing pool, and go have myself a wonderful time doing S and M with some SOB or R and R from Doyle, Dane, Bernbrenner, Katusco, and Loblolly."

"Will you calm down, please? You're getting hysterical."

"Actually, I'm not really hysterical." Heidi calmed down immediately. "I've been doing some thinking—I know, that surprises you. But do me a favor, don't make your usual crack, that you thought you smelled wood burning, all right? It wouldn't sit well right now."

"I had no intention—"

"Fine. Just double-checking, you know?"

"And so?"

"And so I've been thinking this whole mess is probably a very good thing. I've been tired of this town for a long time, I've wanted to return to the city. Now I have a made-in-the-shade opportunity to pull up stakes and try New York again."

"You *what*?"

"You heard me."

"Yeah, but, I mean, well . . . shit."

"My sentiments exactly."

"But you can't just . . . I mean, those are my kids, too. Hey, Heidi, what's the matter with you anyway?"

"*You* left home, Joey. You walked out, deserted us, and started fucking Miss Ethereal over there. Not a court in this country would give you custody. Not only that, but naturally we'll have to sell the land and split the take—"

"*Sell* it? We haven't even *bought* it!"

"That's right. 'We' is the proper word. But now that it looks like 'we're' not going to be a 'we' any longer, I want my half of that land, in cash. It's not cheap to move back to the city with two young children."

"Wait a minute, shut up, would you? What are you talking about, moving to the city, selling the land? Five days ago you were in love with the land. We're gonna build a house, put down roots—"

"Things change. Five days ago you weren't racing around town sticking your penis into every vagina that gave it a coy little wink."

"Heidi, you got a garbage-mouth."

"Hell *hath* no fury like a woman scorned."

"Oy vay, stop—all right? Listen, I'll come over tonight, I'll play with the kids. And after they're in bed, we'll talk, okay? This is absurd."

"Maybe I have a date tonight. I was in a bar this afternoon and I met this really super-fab-groovy Texan from Dallas who looked like a real stud. He invited me over to his pad in the Holiday Inn—"

"Do you have to be this ugly?"

"I don't know . . . but everything I am I learned from you the last few days."

Joe said, "One thing I ought to make clear is if we buy the land, we can't sell it. Not while Eloy is there. He has nowhere to go. He's sick. If we kicked him off he'd die in forty-eight hours from a broken heart."

"Joey, you'll hand that 'poor little old man' sixty thousand dollars in hard cash that you risked all of our lives to secure. I'm sorry, but I can't—"

"He's spent his whole *life* on that property! He knows every weed. Every leaf and grass-blade is an extension of his soul."

"Four days ago you told me that as soon as we gave that old goat the heave we could start building."

"But that was before—"

"No buts, mister. I want my cash. I even figured it out, in case you're interested. Half of sixty Gs is thirty grand. But if we hang on to the place for just six months, we should be able to sell for eighty."

"Heidi, you're sick. Where's the stuff in that tea box?"

"You mean the cocaine?"

He shuddered. "Does everybody have to advertise it explicitly over the telephone?"

"It's in a safe place. Don't worry."

"Don't worry? You got a three A.M. phone call last night from a killer who threatened to kidnap Heather and drop her into the gorge, and I'm not supposed to worry?"

"How did you know that?"

"Tribby. He got the same call."

"Tribby's untrustworthy. I love him as a friend, but I think we should cut him out. He has cold feet."

"My *own* feet are freezing! I was kidnapped by none other than Joseph Bonatelli this afternoon. He made me write my name on a grapefruit, and then he smashed it right before my eyes."

"What's that supposed to mean?"

"The adventure is loco. The usual channels are closed off to us. They'll stomp us royally if we try to unload that stuff on the open market. Ray Verboten, Skipper Nuzum, Cobey Dallas, and Joseph Bonatelli himself have already threatened my life. We've been blacklisted. But Tribby at least knows how to get me my money back, and that option's the only one makes any sense."

"You want to sell it for twelve thousand dollars?" Heidi shrieked.

"Believe me, at that price right now it's a bargain. Heidi, they *mean* it when they talk about dropping Heather into the gorge!"

"Over my dead body."

"Precisely. Now listen—where is that box?"

"I know where it is, and it's none of your business. If you're so chicken, I'll handle it."

"You'll *what*?" Who had she metamorphosed into overnight, Alice Capone? "Heidi, it's not worth it, honest. I would rather you flushed the coke down the toilet, really. The longer that junk is in our possession, the sooner something horrible could happen. Suppose they broke Michael's back? Or threw a hand grenade!"

"You and your imagination! It got us into this, and now all you can do is whimper and order me to flush twelve thousand dollars down the toilet. Well, let me tell you something, Joey. If this is a trick, I'm not buying it. You can't fool me anymore. If we're going to be divorced, I want my thirty Gs. No male chauvinist pig is screwing me out of that. I want mine. Then we'll be even steven and you can proceed with your amorous lunacies without any more interference from these quarters."

"I hate to say this, Heidi, but you're giving me the creeps."

"You *are* a creep, Joey."

"I'm gonna hang up now, I feel sick."

"Welcome to the club."

"But, it's just that you sound like...I mean...God. Like Zsa Zsa Gabor."

"What's that supposed to mean? Another of your coy, cloying, meaningless allusions that are supposed to make people believe you're actually much cleverer than they might at first glance suspect?"

"Zsa Zsa Gabor, lame-brain! She's always getting divorced and cleaning up in the settlements—get it?"

"No need to shout."

"What are you trying to do, rape me? Destroy everything? Kill our kids? Right before my eyes you're turning into every ugly, vicious, capitalist greedy cliché in the book!"

"*I'm* turning into?"

"Just because I was confused and screwed a person I don't give a damn for doesn't mean you have to turn into some kind of bloodsucking John D. Rockefeller in a skirt."

"You needn't denigrate her," Heidi said with diabolical tranquillity. "She's a human being too, you know. And also a woman. Who, no doubt, like all the rest of us, has been trashed since time immemorial by zhlubs like you who just like to find 'em, feel 'em, fuck 'em, and then forget 'em."

"Whoa!—did you just *defend* her?"

"Well how do you think *she* feels?" Heidi bleated. "Lord knows why but she may have honest loving feelings toward you, and you mock her behind her back. You treat her like dirt. She has a vulnerable impressionable child who would probably like a daddy. But instead you enter their lives—this cold-blooded Fascist who deserts one family in order to viciously exploit another. Then for the frosting on your Nazi cake, you send Michael over to assassinate their monkey. Naturally, I feel sorry for them. And, incidentally, your callousness makes me upchuck."

"'Callous'? When have I ever—"

"Let's drop the subject, okay? Finito. Kaput. I'm not interested."

"You can't just accuse me of all those horrors and then tell me to drop the subject."

"Can't I?" Her increasingly arctic tone made him shiver. Out of his league in this thing, he was obviously going to have his head, not to mention his balls, handed to him on a platter before he could cry "uncle!" And not just by Heidi, but by Nancy and by Diana also—all three of them at once, in fact. Not to mention what Ray Verboten and Joseph Bonatelli and their ilk had in store. Joe pictured himself a week hence, parked on the mesa in the Green Gorilla, a pistol in his lap, adding the final touches to a will before planting a bullet in his befuddled noggin. Heidi would have departed by then, having scored the coke on her own for a hundred thousand clams, absconding with his kids and all of his cash equity. Citing his spiritual bankruptcy as an excuse, Nancy would have deserted him for good. Diana would have left because he refused to beat her up. Completing the rout, having successfully robbed the First State People's Jug, Eloy Irribarren wouldn't even allow Joe onto his sanctified terrain to say adios to Wolfie.

Tribby pointed anxiously to his watch. "It's almost five o'clock. The trout should be hitting."

Joe covered the mouthpiece. "Trout? I'm talking to a lunatic, and you're concerned about trout?"

Tribby displayed all his snaggleteeth in a lopsided grin. "The trout will only be hitting for two hours. The lunatics go on forever."

Heidi asked, "Who are you talking to?"

"Nobody."

"Why did you muffle the mouthpiece? I could hear your palm squudged against it. You're calling from her house, aren't you? I don't believe it. You're incredible. You know what you remind me of? One of those Nazi doctors who got great glee out of experimenting on people and watching them suffer. Really, Joey, I'm dumbstruck."

Joe said, "For your personal information and edification, I'd like you to know that I happen to be in Tribby's law office, in case you're interested."

"Bullshit. You lie like a flounder."

He was on a grammar-school playground again, playing the dozens!

"I believe the proper expression is 'lie like a hound.'"

"God, you're funny. If you're in Tribby's office, which I doubt, put him on."

Joe handed the phone to Tribby: he contemplated it as if it were made of molded dog-turds. "What am I supposed to do with this?"

"Talk to her. Say hello. Give her your name, your rank, your serial number."

"I'm a shyster, man, not a marriage counselor."

"Just for God's sake say hello, will you please?"

"It's all right," screamed a teeny voice issuing from the mouthpiece. "I can hear him! I believe you! Joey? *Joey!*"

"That'll teach you to accuse me of lying," he crowed.

"Well, I can't trust you anymore. You've turned into some kind of a frigging Bluebeard."

"Believe it or not, I'm not having so damn much fun out here, ravishing all these beautiful maidens."

"Oh gee, tough beans. I'm crying crocodile tears."

"I bet you are. I bet you just sit there, managing the lousy switchboard, gloating over all the field reports coming in to your flapping little ears concerning my clumsy adventures and imminent demise."

"Ha ha. Joey? I'm sitting here in *rubble*. I'm sitting here in a rain of *ashes* trying to figure out if I'm supposed to go fishing or cut bait. I asked Adele Flannigan what to do, and she said, 'Lock him out, throw away the key, hire a good lawyer, get all his money.' I asked Suki what to do, and she said 'What can you do? The grass isn't any greener elsewhere, only different. Try and work it out.' I asked Sally what to do and she asked me back what did I *want* to do? I said I didn't know, I couldn't think of any options that made sense. So she said 'Fight fire with fire. Go out and have an affair and he'll come crawling home, slavering jealousy and contriteness from his lips like rabid dog foam.' But there's something I really don't understand."

"And it is . . . ?"

"Everybody makes it sound as if having an affair is like going to the store for a loaf of bread. But I think they're nuts. I look at men right now, they make me sick. Sometimes, out of the blue, I even feel like slugging Michael for no other reason than that he's a man."

"He's a little boy, Heidi. And if you even lay a finger on him, so help me God—"

"Stop it, Joey! Good Lord, I'm not going to hit him!"

"Well, what are you doing even going around *thinking* that kind of thought?"

"He's a male. He's got a dork. He even has some of your mannerisms. Someday he'll grow up and be a man and start leaving footprints on the women he's trompled. And I don't think there's anything wrong with hating him for that."

Joe said, "We're not getting anywhere. I'm gonna hang up. But I can assume, can't I, that it's okay to come over tonight?"

"Trout," Tribby whispered urgently, pointing at his watch. "This can wait, the trout can't. I haven't been fishing in a month. All day I looked forward to right now."

"What's Tribby saying?"

"Nothing important. Look, do everybody a favor, Tribby, and shut up, huh? I'll be off in a minute."

"*One* minute."

"I'll be off, all right? Don't get a hernia."

"He said 'trout,' didn't he?" Heidi's voice slid back into a dangerous register. "I did hear correctly. That's exactly what he said."

"I've got no idea what he said. I wasn't listening."

"The two of you are going trout fishing, aren't you? Really, Joey, you're fantastic. Right before my very eyes you're turning into a goddam *Martian*. I don't even know you anymore. It's like your chest opened up, your . . . your breasts swung open like a couple of saloon doors, and your heart fell out, dressed in black, wearing double six-guns and a Jack Palance mask."

"Are you on a drug? Are you drinking?"

"I mean, I'm sitting here at home, trying to be cheerful for the kids, whose lives are in danger, feeling so rotten I can barely move, and you're out there blithely fornicating and trout fishing, Pee—yew!"

"Damn it, Heidi, I am *not* going trout fishing!"

Astonished, Tribby hollered "What?" at the same time Heidi declared emphatically, "Yes you are. I'm getting those vibes. I can tell from the tone of your voice you're blushing."

Frantically, Tribby hissed, "Whaddayou mean we ain't going fishing? I canceled two appointments."

Joe muffled the receiver. "I *know* we're going fishing, dummy, but if Heidi finds out . . . I mean, you should listen to the crap I'm tasting on the other end of this wire."

"We don't have all day," Tribby urged. "Hang up and let's hit the road."

"Hey, Heidi, come on, please—I'm gonna hang up now. Tribby's waiting for a call."

"That's another lie. Keep it up, brother, and all you'll have to do in September, to have enough wood for the winter, is cut off your nose."

"Ha ha."

"I talked to Nikita again this afternoon."

"Oh, and what did Mr. Magic have to say?" Joe made imploring gestures toward Tribby: the lawyer grimaced like a trussed man on a plank heading for a buzz saw.

"He said he thought we could work it out if only you weren't so stubborn."

"That hypocritical egomaniac is a phony!"

"That's your opinion."

"What have you decided to do—march into the ocean with the rest of the lemmings?"

"He listens to me, Joey. Your opinion to the contrary, I think he's a wise man."

"He's evil! He's like a green, carnivorous slime! I can't believe you suddenly started to take him seriously!"

"Oh, Jesus!" Joe could practically hear teeth gnashing. "Sometimes I hate you so much I think I would get great satisfaction from pouring Drano on your balls, I really do."

Joe whined. "But you used to ridicule the man! Not two weeks ago you called him an ego-eater."

"That was two weeks ago. But thanks to Suki I've learned that he happens to be a very astute and serious and beautiful human being, the opinion of some Philistines to the contrary."

"Two days ago you asked me if Nancy and I picked lice out of each other's fur!"

"That was two days ago."

Before Joe could clap his hand over the receiver, Tribby howled, *"Trout is what it's all about!"*

"I heard *that*," Heidi snapped vindictively.

"Tribby, what's the matter with you, man? You're supposed to be on *my* side."

"It's five-thirty, dammit. We've already lost half an hour."

"But Heidi and I are trying to hold together a very fragile situation. I can't be bothered right now with piscatorial considerations."

"Yes you can," Heidi said. "I'm hanging up."

"Before you do, let's get one thing straight—Nikita Smatterling is a power-tripping guru who'll embrace any faith if there's a convert and a painting sale in it."

"You've become totally intolerant, Joey. You're practically a Fascist."

"*Fascist?*"

"You leave home on the spur of any whim, get drunk, spend all our grocery money, screw the neighborhood divorcees, and cavalierly trot off trout fishing while the wife and kiddies are at home, in shock, sitting on a pile of cocaine, their lives threatened by midnight callers, trying to piece back together their shattered lives—and if that isn't a Fascist, what is? Should I add anything else like Conspiring in Secret with Lawyer Friends in Order to Nail Wifey Before She Even Knows the Legal Battle Has Been Joined?"

Joe sighed wearily. "I thought you were hanging up."

"I changed my mind."

"Well, I think *I'm* gonna hang up."

"Just like that, without deciding anything? Without letting me know if you're coming over tonight, or what?"

"Way back at the start of our conversation, all I wanted to know was could I come over or couldn't I, that's all. But you hadda make a federal case out of it!"

"Oh, I like that. Very cute. *I'm* to blame. *I* made a federal case out of it. *I* decided to invest twelve grand in uncut cocaine and then chickened out of marketing it. I suppose I'm also to blame for screwing Miss Archangel over there, too?"

"Wow. You really got me that time. The connection there I totally fail to comprehend."

"I drove you to it, right? My frigidity in bed? The fact that my chest isn't big enough? The fact that two weeks ago I denied you a screw because my cunt hurt, and that drove your poor sensitive poetic little body out into the cold cruel world to seek gratification with the first tushy that batted an eyelash, right? It's *my* fault, because I don't understand you. It's *my* fault because I always burn the toast in the morning. It's *my* fault because, after I cook dinner and vacuum the house and sew the kids' clothes, I'm so tired out that I can't muster it to look glamorous enough for Joe Miniver, boy superman, who, when he comes home smelling like a garbage truck, wants to get hit by Anita Ekberg and Lauren Hutton all rolled into one."

Tribby rolled his eyes and said, "Later, turkey." Trailing bitter cigarette smoke, he slouched unhappily out of his office. "Don't bother locking the door when you split," he growled. "I never lock it. I hope someday they steal me blind."

"Wait—*Tribby*! . . . Heidi?"

"Go ahead. Go with him. I'll tell the kids Daddy can't come over to wrestle because he went fishing."

"Aw, you're crazy." Joe sagged. Hopeless, hopeless, hopeless. They both sounded crazy. Though they each had a fairly decent command of the English language, they'd forgotten how to talk. Some main emotional bearing was worn out, and the meaning of language could no longer turn on it.

Joe shouted, "Murasaki Shikibu!"

Snidely, she droned, "Fuck you, Joey," and hung up.

Unable to breathe, fumbling in his shirt pocket for a pill, Joe leaped to catch Tribby.

⊷§

In the Green Gorilla, slowly chugging southward, they soon reached the first impasse. A backhoe, a dump truck, and a Sno Cone Wagon had skidded into a large pit the backhoe had been digging. Present was the usual generator, coughing out rotten steam, providing electricity to run the usual bilge pump, which spewed every whichway a noisome underground liquid with the viscosity of oil and molasses. Joe veered onto a detour road without hitting anybody. A few seconds later their route was blocked by a Custer Electric Co-op cherry picker parked diagonally across the road while some geek in a fuchsia hardhat, suspended thirty feet above the world, futzed with a high-tension wire. Irritated backed-up cars honked deliriously, causing the geek to pause often in order to give them the finger.

Tribby moaned, "It's a quarter of six, man. I just gotta catch me a trout."

"What can I say?—we're trapped."

"Cut across that field."

"How can I? It's fenced."

"Forget the fence. If I don't catch a trout tonight, I swear to Christ I'll go off my rocker. I haven't relaxed in a month."

"If I break the barbwire, they'll sue."

"I'll defend you, gratis."

Joe gunned the engine, spun the wheel, popped the clutch, and they jounced off the detour road, smashed through the fragile rusted strands, skidded along a soggy stretch of the lowland meadow, barged through one more wire barrier, and jounced onto Martyr's Lane. It led them back onto the North-South Highway, where immediately they slowed to a crawl behind a huge yellow truck spewing gravel and an enormous road-building machine laying down a hot mix. A small army of hardhatted ants puttered in the hot mix with rakes and hoes and other more industrial-looking implements. Blade lowered, a bulldozer trailed this snail-paced team gouging up the still-sizzling tar and gravel and tossing it in hot crunchy heaps onto the shoulder, causing much consternation among joggers.

Tribby said, "Pass 'em, god dammit."

"It's not our turn. The girl is holding out her Stop flag, in case you didn't notice. There's also cars approaching from the other direction."

"Forget the flag, forget the cars. Joe, if you got no guts in life, you'll never gather any blue chips."

"They'll throw me in jail. And what's this crap anyway? You're the one trying to bail out the coke scam for peanuts."

"I'll defend you. On the house. The coke deal is different. Right now we're talking about *trout*. Come on, goose it!"

Joe goosed it, swinging into the oncoming lane. The flag girl shrieked, an oncoming car veered onto the shoulder, and, as Tribby desultorily sucked on a cigarette, they rattled past the machinery, almost hit the southernmost flag girl, and swerved back into their lane.

"You see?" Tribby said. "It's easy."

"I'm gonna have a heart attack!"

"Before you do, where's the extra flies?"

A hundred yards further along, at the single stoplight decorating the mouth of the plaza, another bottleneck had developed: the traffic light was broken. City police had not been notified early enough to avoid the seven-car collision that had promptly resulted. Now six cops, four wreckers, and the assorted drivers were trying to disentangle the mess.

Tribby wailed, "This town used to be a humane place! You could go from A to C by way of B!"

"We'll get there." But Joe did not at all believe his own words.

While they waited, stewing in various juices, joggers trotted by, positively zooming. Heading north against the flow, Scott Harrison waved gaily, his eyes full of menacing double entendres. Head thrown back like a champion racehorse, he pranced into the distance with the superior gait of all joggers whizzing past automobiles locked in a traffic jam.

Jeff Orbison stumbled spastically into view. His face was crimson, his arms flailed, he winced at each step like a man with painful shin splints.

Next, tossing a V sign, Spumoni Tatarsky skated by. "Peace, brothers!" He pretended not to notice when Tribby snapped him a bird.

Its blue-and-red light blinking feverishly, a wrecker in reverse crunched sickeningly into a healthy vehicle. Two cops started yelling at each other, a third cursed at the wrecker's driver, horns went bananas.

Tribby remarked, "It's six-fifteen. I don't believe this is happening to me."

"Picturesque Chamisaville," Joe crooned sarcastically, "situated high in the beautiful southern Rockies in the easygoing land of mañana, where three cultures exist in perfect harmony, trout streams abound, and the genteel hospitality of her denizens will make your vacation stay one of unbridled joy and relaxation."

Ralph Kapansky sneaked up behind the driverside door: his "boo!" made Joe jump. "Is it true," he mocked sympathetically, "that Heidi just flew off to Reno with Nikita Smatterling and the kids?"

"Hey, Ralph . . ."

"I'm sorry, old boy, really. If there's ever anything I can do. . . ."

Trailed by an anxious, lumbering Rimpoche, off he cavorted on tiptoes, his maroon-and-white jogging outfit shining like a Christmas bauble.

Ahead of them, the pompous guru himself, Nikita Smatterling, threaded through the jam leading Baba Ram Bang. In midroute they detoured around Nick Danger—his hat brim hid his eyes, his spidery arms hugged that battered suitcase as firmly as ever.

"What the hell is he guarding in that bag?" Joe asked petulantly.

"You're asking me?"

"He's *never* without that creepy suitcase."

"Maybe there's a miniature dialysis machine inside."

"Very funny. Listen, do you know anything about that sinister little gangster?"

"Absolutely nothing."

"Have you ever even said hello to him?"

"Me? What kind of fool do you take me for!"

"One of these days," Joe threatened quietly, "I'm gonna knock that secretive little son of a bitch on his ass and tear open that suitcase."

"Maybe there's limbs inside," Tribby mused. "Like from a baby or an unlucky girl friend he murdered."

"Or a lifetime supply of Preparation H he won in a raffle. . . ."

Tribby said, "I hear Sasha's still in the emergency ward of Tim Eberhardt's Pampered Pets down in the capital."

"You heard correctly. What's on the grapevine today about the incident? Are thirty people in saffron robes, wearing monkey masks, gonna hit the castle tonight at midnight, mug me with gats made out of weighted bananas, kidnap Michael, cut off his lips, penis, and big toes, and offer them to the Great Monkey Spirit, so that no whimsical deity out there will hassle the unveiling on Thursday?"

"I don't know about that. But of course people are upset. They think it's an omen."

"*Omens!*" Joe said scornfully. "An innocent kid, disturbed by family troubles, takes it out on an ugly monkey who's bugged him unmercifully for the past three years, and they want to make a federal case out of it."

"I know. But you ought to hear Nikita Smatterling on the subject."

"Nikita stuck a gun into the belly of Ephraim Bonatelli and pulled the trigger. Don't talk to me about his rights to piety."

"Ephraim is only a human being."

"Can they sue?"

"I doubt it. Damages for assaulted monkeys aren't exactly big-time settlements these days. Fish and Game, on the other hand, might hit you with a couple hundred dollars, plus court costs, for letting your kid poach out of season, without a license."

Joe felt like whining. "What happened all of a sudden? Three days ago I was on cloud nine. Life had never been better."

"For what it's worth, you're beginning to get quite a reputation in this burg. This morning I heard you were out in a tent on Eloy's land shacked up with Nancy Ryan, Diana Clayman, and Heidi all at once. Must be nice work if you can get it."

Joe buried his head in his arms. "You 'heard.' This town. I love it. What else is going around?"

"You mean aside from that three A.M. phone call?"

"Yeah."

"Well, I suppose you should know the latest on the Cobey Dallas–Roger Petrie–Skipper Nuzum axis. Now that the Hanuman is in town, there's all kinds of jockeying going down. More people are in cahoots than meet even the most practiced eye. Yesterday, as you know, Skipper was just about to nail Cobey, double-cross Roger, and initiate you into the fraternity of the Golden Apes. Like I said, he even asked me to draw up some papers. Today, I learn I'm supposed to forget it. Maybe you poisoned the well by telling him to shove it. Then in almost the same breath, I hear on the grapevine that Scott Harrison withdrew his suit against Eloy. And Cobey and Roger appear involved in some kind of fancy footwork to cover their bets you so arrogantly flung into Cobey's face during your tête-à-tête. Something big is in the air. Curious alliances are going down. Everybody is scrambling. It smells, all of a sudden, as if there's a lot more money in the kitty than just the bucks riding on our dope scam. But I have no idea what it is: nor can I figure out how they're gonna get Eloy's land. Or even, suddenly, if anybody truly wants it anymore."

"So what else is happening?" Joe said dispiritedly, utterly confused by the opaque innuendos of everybody's pending shenanigans.

"Oh, you know, all the usual lewd and crude and juicy. Re you, it's Joe the Satyr, Joe the Sadist, Joe the Stud, Joe the Chauvinist Pig, Joe the Et Cetera."

"What happened, Tribby? One minute I was sitting pretty. The next minute . . ."

"That must mean you weren't sitting so pretty to begin with."

"I guess so. All my life, all my married life, anyway, I lusted for other women, other adventures, other things. But I kept it in control. I figured I could handle it. I assumed it would always be there, one of those minor ordeals you got to suffer all your days just for being born human. But I never felt really threatened by it."

Tribby lit up another cigarette, and glowered at a young woman, wearing a black Lone Ranger mask, rounding the corner. She looked ravishing in a hot-pink muscle shirt, silver shorts, and powder-blue sneakers. He gawked as she jogged past two real-estate offices, an art gallery, and J. C. Penney's approaching them. In her hand she carried a small bouquet of plastic violets.

"I dunno what to say, Joe. We all got our devils."

At the last moment, drawing up to them, the female jogger veered, tossed the violets through the passengerside window, and sprinted away like a streak of greased lightning.

The no-fade violets bypassed Tribby, landing in Joe's lap. "Don't touch them, it's a bomb!" Tribby shrieked, but Joe knew better. Immediately, his eye had caught a note affixed to the bouquet, and he had read its words:

> If this had been a bomb, you
> would be in heaven right now.
> Think about it.

Joe handed the note to Tribby—the lawyer read it and frowned. Then he crumpled it into a small wad, dropped it out the window, and said, "Forget it. You were saying?"

"I wanted to ask: What about you? I mean, you and Rachel, your lives together. Are you loyal? Do you cheat on each other? Is sex a big deal? What do you want from your life? What are your ambitions? What do you hope it all adds up to? What—"

"Stop."

Joe stopped, immediately embarrassed. He had rarely asked intimate questions of his male friends. Curious all his life about how other couples loved each other, Joe had rarely had the guts to quiz a pal on his love life. Mostly, he had joked about getting laid and had seldom delved into love. Often he envied the way women could bare their souls to each other. Men seemed hopelessly alone, and sadly vulnerable in ways that women, up to their eyeballs in the diabolical machinations of men, wouldn't care to understand.

Joe had always feared that if he started probing intimate levels with another man, a homosexual confrontation (accusation, proposition) might develop.

Talk about straight jackets!

"Just answer one of those questions, then," Joe said warily. "Any one."

"Well, about life, I dunno. I want to make some money, finish our house. We'll have kids, I suppose. We've both cheated on each other, but we survive. Sex is sort of a big deal but it's funny."

"'Funny'?"

"I can't figure it out exactly. We fuck a lot and it's usually semidramatic. But I often feel I'm, like, pretending. You know? Acting. Like if it were really left up to me, maybe I'd be happy screwing once a month in the missionary position for the rest of my life. Occasionally all the hoopla gets me down."

"Huh." Joe was growing increasingly articulate as the days went by.

"At the same time, naturally, I kind of envy you, breaking out of the marriage, nailing all this interesting pussy, that sort of thing."

"But it's a cliché. It's what everybody does."

"Well, sure. But if I do it, see, I'm aware all that wonderful pussy has feet of clay. Not to mention what my own insecurities would do to me in the rack with a relative stranger. But when I see you gadding about and hear the rumors, you come across as a regular Hugh Hefner, a legend in your own time."

"What about your goals in life?" Joe asked timidly, convinced that any second now Tribby would cut him short, leaving them both horribly uncomfortable.

"I dunno. I make it from day to day. I used to believe in a very definite structure. But over the last few years I've seen that structure dissolve. Right now I'm just watching other people and waiting."

"You smoke like you're trying to kill yourself before you hit forty."

"If I kill myself I kill myself."

"You're not afraid of death?"

"Yeah, I'm afraid of it."

"You don't sound frightened."

"Let's put it this way—I have a desultory fear of it, but I can't be really bothered, you know? I think in the last few years I've become rather lethargic about everything. Yet I weigh consequences—I'm not a total fool. If I figure out something like our coke scam isn't worth it, I'm smart enough to back down."

"What about passion?"

"Passion? Something seems to have stolen it from me. That's funny. Five years ago I would have bought a machine gun and gone after Ray Verboten. Nowadays, it so quickly becomes a pointless adventure. But I feel passionate about catching trout, I guess. . . ."

"Me too. I feel like I could kill to get to those fish right now."

"If I had that machine gun, I'd jump out of this frigging truck, mow everybody down, grab one of those bulldozers back there, clear away the autos, then race off to the Rio Puerco before dark, tie a size-twenty renegade at the end of a ten-foot tapered leader, and, with the most delicate finesse you ever saw, battle a two-pound brown for a half-hour before I finally brought it to shore. I'd clean and gut it on the spot, and eat it so fresh the flesh would still squeak every time I took a bite. Passion," he finished wryly, exhaling smoke out the window. "Oh me, oh my."

Joe said, "Sometimes I feel passionate. But I can't sustain it. My body's in constant turmoil. One minute I have highfalutin ideas about the Nobel Prize, a marathon fuck, the idealization of romance, building a house, creating a picture-book farm of Eloy's land—but then I lose it. I can't seem to sustain any emotion except confusion."

Tribby nodded. "In my youth I was such a fanatic. For hockey. For trading cards. For pet gerbils. Inevitably, I went overboard. I even had a passion for the law at one time. Tell me: do you think it's a necessary part of growing up, of growing mature, or of accepting your place in society, to lose all that passion, to cease being that kind of idealist?"

"All I know is that when I see an old person, let's say like Eloy Irribarren, who still has all this passion and idiotic enthusiasm for something . . . his old dog, his decaying horse, his treasured land . . . I experience enormous surges of envy. Sometimes I feel terribly run down at thirty-eight. How do you reach seventy still feeling fresh and peppy and passionate?"

"Tell me something," Tribby said after a pause. Out there, lines of automobiles extending north, east, south, and west from the traffic light had hopelessly clogged the area. There was no way to haul out the immobile autos once wreckers had them in tow. It appeared as if nobody would escape until helicopters had removed three hundred impacted vehicles.

"Yeah?"

"What you're doing now, messing with these women—are you enjoying it?"

"There's moments. One minute I'm excited, next minute I kill it with guilt. I can't seem to enjoy anything for very long. I'm terrified of consequences."

"That happened to me a couple times. Any pleasure I might of received I killed with guilt. Just sort of casually fucking somebody for fun—recreational sex is what they call it, right? It's pretty difficult."

"I wish I could learn how to enjoy myself," Joe said longingly. He wanted to confess that so far, during all his amorous adventures, he hadn't even been able to come. But such a revelation seemed impossibly intimate. "I wanna have gusto," he added. "I wanna live big, I wanna be happy. Instead, I bungle everything. And I'm exhausted. Right now my Theta couldn't punch its way out of a paper helicopter."

"What's a Theta?"

"A place where they show movies and act in plays."

All of a sholem, Tribby snapped his fingers and exclaimed, "Wait a minute . . . *I got it!*"

"Oh?"

"Listen to this—wow! Talk about passion! We'll rob their highfalutin Hanuman!"

"Come on, man. It must weigh a jillion pounds."

"No, that's easy. When you mentioned the helicopter I had a great idea! Holy Toledo, folks!" Tribby clapped his hands. "This is beautiful!"

Joe shivered, already appalled by the upcoming lunacy.

"It'll be a cinch," Tribby exclaimed gleefully. "The copter's a natural. Ralph has a set of keys to both the Floresta's birds. And I can fly 'em—no problem. Did you see the U-Haul it's in? Does it have a cable harness? Didn't they already ferry the thing out from Ohio like that? Oh boy!" Tribby quivered with joy. "We'll snatch the monkey and hold it for ransom!"

"Wait. I heard somewhere that it's insured for over a million bucks. With bread like that at stake, they'll have the FBI crawling over this town like fleas on a hot dog if somebody pinches it."

"So what? We'll fly the statue into the mountains and drop it into a lake!"

Joe said, "Aw, come on, Tribby. That's insane. Forget it . . ."

"But listen—"

"Shut up. *Please*."

It was getting dark. Both men fell silent. Tears paced behind Joe's eyes, nudging sentimental triggers with their bootheels: sad and vulnerable, lost and lonely. Dust reeled, ebbed, and eddied; cops shouted, horns blared; rosy-cheeked joggers threaded happily through the bottleneck, inhaling pure carbon monoxide. Over it all levitated the moon, pretty, powdery, svelte.

Joe projected himself onto the Rio Puerco at dusk. Where the water flooded grassy fields at a beaver dam, he waded slowly, barely sloshing, casting superbly. Velvet-brown animals swam past, undisturbed by his presence. Against the nearby hills, silvered in moonlight, horses stood quietly under the thick branches of junipers, watching him. Pale steam fluffed from their nostrils. His fly disappeared, he gave a tug, and was attached to a fish. It stayed under, never jumping, and fought with unorthodox passivity. Joe soon headed it. Something patient and gentle transcribed its fight, something unconnected to the death throes of trout. Finally, Joe urged it to shore and, carefully, with a smooth sweep of his arm, he swung it onto the damp grass at his feet. The thing on his hook was not a trout, but a pale, opulent naked woman about a foot long. Joe closed his fingers over that soft albino form. She squirmed tiredly in his hand. It was like holding the yearning for passion again.

"One of my problems is I don't feel very useful," Tribby said after a while. "To tell the truth, I doubt that being involved in pursuits of self-interest is really that gratifying over the long run."

"Well—" Joe started to say, but Tribby cut him off.

"No communism, Joseph. I ain't in the mood for it. If I can't talk about ripping off the Hanuman, then you certainly can't hand me any Socialist crap."

So Joe clammed up and returned to that sensual little woman he had just fished from the water. And they sat there, waiting for deliverance, while it grew dark.

Elsewhere, out of sight if not out of mind, sleek brown trout dimpled still waters, snagging the hatching caddis fly.

∽§

In a sad and provocative mood, Joe arrived at the Castle of Golden Fools. Discounting the Hanuman-snatch idea, that brief rap with Tribby was the first faintly intelligent and meaningful conversation he'd had in ages. When his lawyer friend had finally whimpered "Fuck the trout," bid him good-bye, and left the still-trapped vehicle, their parting had been muted and self-conscious. Joe had been touched by their discussion: all appearances to the contrary, words could actually sometimes be used to communicate!

Often, at the end of a long day, Joe would relax in his quiet vehicle at dusk, basking in that lazy pause between his job and the jabberwocky atmosphere of family doings. Those were among the only moments he ever captured entirely for himself. He cherished such lackadaisical sojourns in delectable limbo. Right now, as he gathered courage to head inside, Joe's mood was both plaintive and introspective, yet also semi-cheerful. Clouds representing the carnage of his past few days had parted, allowing him a glimpse beyond into the possibility of compassion. He had pretty much decided to forget Eloy's land, let Tribby (screw his wild ideas!) broker the cocaine for twelve Gs, and put all his energy into recapturing what he'd had before but never fully appreciated. Given ideal conditions, it wasn't too farfetched to believe that with a snap of his fingers he might erase his erratic behavior, wipe the slate clean, and enter his peppy little domicile as if nothing had soured. Joe closed his eyes: Heidi was cooking fried chicken and humming "Si mi chiamano Mimi" from *La Bohème*, happy to have completed a good painting today; Heather was fashioning a magic doll-house from blocks, paper flowers, pillows, and old jars; and Michael was lounging before the roaring fire, reading *Boy's Life*, his hands unstained by bird, window, and (attempted) monkey murders. . . .

It's over, Joe thought. Just like that. He was astounded. All the recent turmoil, all the lust, indecision, curiosity, and just plain cussedness that had caused it, was done for. In a minute he would climb up and enter his house as if he had never left it, gently greet his children, kiss Heidi fondly, and say, "I'm sorry." Tearfully, they would accept his apology. The family, as a single unit, would embrace. After a good wrestle, they might play songs, or even watch Johnny Carson on TV. After the kids crashed, he and Heidi would sit at the kitchen table over coffee, bemusedly hashing over Joe's recent escapades, commenting wryly on the convoluted silliness of humanity. Then: to bed, to bed, you sleepyheads. Between exquisitely clean sheets they'd effect tender easygoing sexual reconciliation. After that? A slumber so rare and beautiful he would awaken next day as refreshed as if he had abruptly turned twenty again.

Mesmerized by this vision, Joe descended from his mythic wheels. Breathing in deeply and gratifyingly, he decided, "I'll never have asthma again." And, firmly convinced his strange odyssey had forged in him a significantly matured human being, Joe tripped the light fantastic upstairs. Thank you, Peter Roth, for not coming! Almost euphoric from anticipating their reconciliation, he thrust open the door, exclaiming, "Hey, everybody, I'm back!"

Michael sat in the middle of the living-room floor doing a jigsaw puzzle. A large white bandage arrangement somewhat resembling a hockey goalie's mask obliterated two-thirds of his face. Yet both his black-and-blue eyes were visible as he looked up at Joe in terror. Over at the kitchenette table, outfitted in a floor-length pink nightie, Heather was painting her fingernails with a polish so poisonous it was a miracle the entire family didn't expire from the fumes every time Heather loosened the cap.

And Heidi was nowhere around.

Taken aback both by Michael's headgear and by Heather's absolute indifference to his jovial appearance (she couldn't even muster brief eye-contact as she said, "Hullo, Daddy"), Joe stalled momentarily, at a loss for words. Then unexpected anger flared, and he almost hollered "Look up and *greet* your father in a civilized manner when he enters the happy homestead, you little creeps!" But he had just enough presence of mind to avoid that riposte and the antagonisms it would trigger.

Refiring his positive engines, Joe piped, "Hey, what's up, gang? What'sa happen? Where'sa you mommy?"

"She went to bed."

Heather's professionally frosty voice instantly made Joe want to leap across the living room crying "banzai!" in order to brain the snotty little brat!

"So soon?" Joe fumbled, checking his watch. "It's only eight fifteen."

"She said she didn't feel good."

Joe couldn't believe how much fury Heather inspired in him simply by not looking up. Coolly cocking her head, she inspected the glistening poison on her fingernails, a scary female gesture guaranteed to break hearts and chill testicles.

"What was the matter?"

"I don't know." Heather further stoked his rage by articulating her speech too clearly. "She said you cared so little about us that instead of coming over to wrestle and play the guitar you went trout fishing with Tribby Gordon."

"She did not say that," Michael contradicted. "You're making half of it up."

"Well, it's almost exactly what she said." Heather altered the tilt of her head, inspecting the fingernails from a freshly provocative and murderous angle.

"She went to bed 'cause she had a headache," Michael said.

Joe asked, "Michael, what is the matter with your face?"

He mumbled unintelligibly.

"What? Speak up." How many billions of times had Joe begged Michael—a diabolical mutterer, mumbler, and word slurrer—to pronounce his words carefully, so that occasionally his listeners might catch at least the general drift of his pronouncements.

"They broke my nose." Michael averted Joe's penetrating stare.

"*Who* broke your nose?"

"I don't know. A bunch of guys jumped me."

"What guys, where?"

"They beat him up on the playground," Heather said. "It was Triple Threat Tucker, and Tofu Smatterling, and—"

"You shuttup, you little shithead!" Michael snapped angrily. "Nobody asked you!"

"I can talk if I want to. It's a free country."

"I'll *kill* you if you open that fat mouth of yours one more time!" Michael threatened.

"I'm not ascared of you." Heather inspected her nails calmly from yet another disinterested angle. "You're not even as big as flyshit."

Joe said, "Heather!"

"That's my name, don't wear it out."

"Jesus Christ!" Joe wailed. "What's the matter with you kids? I asked a simple question. Michael has a broken nose. As your father it seems to me I've got a right to know who smashed it, and how, and why."

"It was just some kids." Embarrassed by the attention, Michael had turned crimson. "That's all."

"What kids?" Joe neglected to add: I'll kill them, I'll sue their parents, I'll track them down and beat them into bloody pulps with my plumber's wrench!

"Just some guys," Michael squirmed. "I don't remember who."

"I told you," Heather said. "It was Triple Threat and Tofu Smatterling and Boo Tenace and Jonah Nordica—"

"You shuttup, Heather, or I'll stick your head in the toilet and flush it!"

Joe's bleatings were almost incoherent. "Why did they jump you? Why did they want to break your nose?"

"I dunno. . . ."

"It's 'cause he shot Sasha." Heather dabbed at her left pinkie nail. "It's 'cause he fucked up the unbailing of the Hanuman."

"Un*veil*ing, sweetie. U*veil*ing."

"That's what I said, unbailing."

"No, listen to me—you're getting sidetracked by the labial *b*. It's not a *buh* sound, it's a *vuh* sound . . . Heather, dammit, *look up when I'm talking to you!*"

Taking her own sweet time, she lifted veiled eyes that spewed at him innuendos of bald recalcitrance, boredom, and hostility.

The bedroom door opened and Heidi appeared, hair half covering her eyes and fluffed in sleepy disarray. She wore white cotton briefs and a tattered Snoopy sweatshirt.

"What did you do?" she croaked hoarsely. "You weren't tormenting us enough from a distance so you had to return and twist the needles in person?"

His jaw dropped. Unjustly accused, adjudged guilty for a heinous crime he'd had absolutely no intention of committing, outrageously misunderstood and cavalierly dumped back into the excrement at just that moment when he had felt himself shining, clean, wingèd, and ready to soar, Joe stammered non-sensically for a beat, then located his tongue:

"Wait a minute, what is this—a loony bin? When I opened the door, all I held in my heart was love. All I wanted was peace and forgiveness and just a minute to make my case. But you lame-brained piranha fish won't even allow me five words on my own behalf."

Heidi said, "Let me get this straight. You came back here with love in your heart in order to call us 'lame-brained piranha fish'?"

"I didn't *plan* to call you anything, dammit! I planned to enter this house with a little humility and see if maybe we couldn't patch things up. Instead, I'm greeted by a trio of wiseasses who can't shut up long enough to hear my apologies because they're too busy scoring points."

"I was asleep, Joey. Don't include me in your accusation. I was trying to rest because I'm a bit exhausted, in case you're interested. And then you swagger in here, bellowing at the top of your voice—"

"Oh no you don't. I wasn't 'swaggering.' I was calm and cool and collected. Then I happened to notice that my kid's face is swaddled in bandages, so I asked who did the damage, that's all. But do you think either one of these mongoloids here would give a straight answer?"

"I gave you a straight answer," Heather protested. "I know who did it. I saw it happen!"

"Squealer!" Michael spat with astonishing vehemence. "Stool pigeon!"

Joe said, "You mean you watched them break his nose and you didn't even try to help him?"

"They were all bigger than me!" Heather's arrogant eyes widened in outraged innocence.

"I wouldn't want any help from any girl anyway," Michael said.

Joe turned on him. "What's the matter with a girl? Why did you say that?"

Michael had received enough feminist brainwashing to realize he'd made a cavernous goof. In lieu of defending himself, he clammed up.

"Women happen to be just as good fighters as men." Joe wondered unhappily how in the name of God Almighty they had landed on *this* particular rap! "Not only do they make good doctors and excellent parachute jumpers, but they are also exceptional warriors. Who do you think did half the fighting in Vietnam, enabling that backward, poorly equipped country to defeat the most powerful military machine ever assembled? Who do you think makes up half the Chinese army? Who do you think some of the most skilled black-belt karate experts in the world are? Women! That's who they are!"

"Yeah." Heather chimed in. "Women hold up half the sky, y'know."

Joe ordered his daughter to stifle. "You don't have to goad him any more than you already have."

Dripping venomous sarcasm, Heidi said, "That's right, Heather, darling. Despite Daddy's liberal rhetoric, he doesn't want you ever to forget that little girls should be seen, not heard."

Joe protested. "Wait a minute. I don't see any reason why she has a right to taunt Michael while I'm reading him a riot act."

"So you told her to shut up. Of course, why not? Men have been telling women to shut up for ten thousand years."

"She's not a 'woman,' she's a little child. On top of that, sometimes—including right now—she's a real brat! And besides, I can't make her be quiet any other way. She never listens to me. Michael never listens to me. You never listen to me. In fact, *nobody* ever listens to me. I might as well scream at the stars."

"Why don't you try *not* screaming, for once. You might find communication would improve immensely. It seems that your method of making a point is to yell so loud everybody's intimidated whether they think you make any sense or not."

Joe said, "I give up, I really do. You win. I don't believe

it. I blew it again, you're right, it's incredible, I'm sorry, good-bye."

"Wait a minute. Don't leave."

"Why? What can I accomplish here?" Those old debbil tears commenced again. "All I have to do is cross the threshold, and everybody acts like I'm a fox that just entered the chicken coop looking for a fat pullet. *Frenzy! Feathers everywhere! Cackle, cackle, cackle!*"

"I hate to say this, but you bring most of it on yourself."

"I know. I got lousy karma, right? Last week, what was his name, that freak from Alexander's Ragtime Crash Pad? He was walking down the highway shoulder at ten P.M. when a car of teen-agers pulled over, jumped out, and beat him insensate with clubs, chains, and hammers. Now he's lying in the Our Lady of the Sorrows Hospital paralyzed from the neck down and doomed to be a vegetable forever. So I'm sitting in the Prince of Whales—when was it? I guess about last Thursday—talking about it with several people, among them Jeff Orbison and Spumoni Tatarsky, when you know what that fucking Spumoni said?"

They stared at him.

"You know what he actually *said* to me?"

Michael shook his head. Heather locked her eyes expectantly into her father's face. Heidi said, "What?"

For dramatic emphasis, Joe added, "I mean, you know, these are supposed to be semi-intelligent human beings we're dealing with here. Granted, Spumoni is a trifle weird, but the guy actually went to college; he's got a piece of paper says he earned a degree. And Jeff?—that man actually has a doctorate. He's a PhD!"

Joe halted: they waited.

"So you know what went down?" he repeated, enraged, the spittle flying.

"For God's sake, what?"

It happened. The entire lesson—the point of his story, the thing he wished to prove—abruptly dislodged from his brain and slid sideways. Joe drew a blank. In the heart of his rage, at the apex of his moral, he blew it. Mouth hanging open, he stared back at them, perplexed, slightly bemused, and then horrified. On the threshold of an important punch line, his mind had bailed out.

Dumbfounded, Joe remained frozen, his hands raised in a

pertinent gesture the reason for which he had completely forgotten. After a few puzzling seconds had ticked away, he had
to admit: "I forget."

"What do you mean, you forget?"

"I forget what I meant to say. I don't even remember what
I was talking about."

"Karma."

"Karma?" It rang no bell.

"Yeah, karma. And Jeff Orbison's PhD."

"But why? I mean, I was on the brink of saying something
important. . . ."

"You were talking about that guy from Alexander's Ragtime
Crash Pad who they almost killed last week," Heather offered.

"I know that, dummy. But what was the *point*?" Joe knuck-
led his eyes, then ran fingers back through his hair, guessing
that sometime over the past few days he must have been deftly
lobotomized by some duendi prankster employed by that particular devil in charge of ridiculing dignity and promoting overt
idiocy and shame.

Heidi said, "You baffle me, Joey. One minute you're talking
about chicken feathers everywhere, next minute you're ranting
about some wounded jerk from Alexander's Ragtime Crash
Pad."

"Yeah, but why? I mean, there was a point. The freak, and
the crash pad, and Spumoni Tatarsky. . . ."

Bewildered and defeated, Joe sat down. Or anyway, he
started to settle into their lumpy Salvation Army chair when
Heather shrieked, *"Daddy, don't!"*

Don't what—rape her? Plunk down atop a venomous cobra?
Set his butt into a fauteuil booby-trapped with punji sticks or
the kind of plastic device used by renegade French army officers
protesting Algerian independence?

Joe halted, shaped like a question mark, halfway there.

"You're gonna sit on Baby Erica!"

Grappling beneath himself, Joe located a small raggedy doll
wrapped in wax paper and pincushioned with needles. A paper
taped on her forehead said: "Erika, kidnee and hart."

"We were playing hospital," Heather explained. "Erika's
sick."

Distastefully, Joe assessed the doll. "What's with all the
needles?"

"She's getting a cute puncher for her kidney."

"A what?"

"A cute puncher for her kidney. That's what the Chinese people do. They put you on a table and stick needles inside you and it makes you better. They can even stick a needle in your neck and cut your brain open if they want."

"Acupuncture," Joe slumped wearily into the chair. "The word, Heather, is acupuncture."

"That's what I said, a cute puncher."

Superior Michael begged to differ. "It's not 'a cute puncher,' Heather, you moron. It's 'acupuncture,' just like Daddy said."

"I am not a moron. You're a moron—"

"Quiet!" Joe literally wrung his hands. "We really don't need to argue over who's a moron right now. It's not in the script."

From the refrigerator, Heidi selected a beer. She offered the can to Joe: "Want one?"

"Sure, why not? Beer makes it great."

She remained there, her knee propping open the door as she pensively scanned the Frigidaire's jumbled innards. Apparently, she had decided to drive him crazy, for nothing rattled Joe more than to see somebody wasting God knows how much electricity (one-sixteenth of one-tenth of one-half a milliwatt?), and spoiling God knows how much food (one-tenth of one cell in a celery stick?), by gratuitously leaving the refrigerator door ajar. It had long been a heavy bone of contention between them. Heidi could watch the inside of a refrigerator the same way most people gooned at television.

"Heidi, maybe if you leave the refrigerator door open long enough an owl will fly in and start nesting."

She replied, "I can't decide what I want—but I've got it narrowed down to one of two things, either the strychnine or the cyanide."

"Very funny."

"You started it with your snide owl comment."

"Well, in case you didn't notice, electricity costs money."

"Joey, if I hold the refrigerator door open for twenty seconds, what's that going to cost extra at the end of the month— eighteen demimils?"

He was too tired to answer. Ten minutes inside this house, and already his body, which had arrived in the pink of condition, was dismally fatigued.

Michael abandoned his puzzle and whispered in Heather's

ear. She listened raptly, then asked, "Daddy, are you gonna wrestle with us tonight?"

"Sure, why not? Maybe I can bash Michael's nose so bad he winds up breathing from his asshole."

"*Da*-ddy!"

"I'm all right," Michael pleaded urgently. "You won't bug my nose. It doesn't hurt at all."

"So let's leave it like that. Thank God for small favors."

"Aw, Daddy . . ."

"But I'm okay," Michael insisted. "I won't even let my head get near you. I'll just wrestle with my feet."

"Lemme paint for you the scenario," Joe said wearily. "Eighteen seconds after we begin, I heave Heather off my chest, and she lands on top of you, who've got me in a scissors grip. Quite by accident, of course, her elbow, driving backwards and downwards to break her fall, drills into your shnoz like a jackhammer, not only rebreaking your nose, but sending ninety-seven razor-sharp splinters of cartilage and bone up into your brain, either killing you instantly, or damaging that part of the cerebellum controlling your immunity system, meaning that for the rest of your life you'll have to live in a germ-free bubble, which will cost us all our savings in the first three weeks. . . ."

"I'm tired of your doomsday bullshit." Heidi took a noisy, challenging drag from her beer. "If he wants to wrestle, let him wrestle. If you don't want to, at least be honest and say so, don't blame it on Michael's nose."

"If I smash his nose again and we have to rush him to the emergency room, that's thirty dollars just to walk through the door," Joe said angrily. "I don't understand where any of you people are coming from, I really don't. How can you be so cavalier about a broken nose?"

"I could wear my football helmet," Michael suggested hopefully.

"Oh great. You wear your football helmet, then *I* get at least a broken nose, or just possibly, a concussion."

"It won't hurt his nose to wrestle," Heather pleaded. "Come on, Daddy, *please*?"

"No. It's crazy. Haven't we got enough free bad luck without going out and deliberately recruiting some more?"

"Well, that's too bad." Heidi released a pregnant sigh. "I know Michael and Heather were looking forward to it. They so rarely have a chance to interact with you these days."

"If you had a broken nose would you wrestle?" Joe asked incredulously.

"Yes, under the circumstances, I think I would."

"Under what circumstances?"

"Well, these. I mean, you promised, Joey. And I don't think this is the best time in the lives of our children to begin breaking promises."

"And you really think I won't hurt his nose?"

"Not if you're routinely careful, no."

"Can you guarantee something horrible won't happen?"

"Sure, I guarantee it. All you have to do is exercise a modicum of constraint. Of course, I realize that for you these days that presents quite a challenge—"

"All right, I'll wrestle. Just so long as we make one thing perfectly clear. If that nose gets clobbered, I ain't taking the rap."

Both kids shouted "Yaaayyy!" Heather assured him. "Don't worry, Daddy, we'll be extra special careful." They raced from the room.

Joe called, "Where are you going?"

"Uniforms!"

Heidi smiled. "There. See how easy it is to make children deliriously happy?"

"But if his nose gets clobbered again . . ."

"It won't. Believe me."

"How can you be so sure?"

"Because I *said* it won't. I promise. I guarantee it."

"Just so that everybody understands it's not my fault if—"

"No ifs, Joey. It's simply not going to happen."

Who had she been talking to, Nikita Smatterling again? Joe cleared furniture to the side. Then, with much grunting and cursing, he retrieved the double mattress from the master bedroom, and dumped it in the middle of the living room. Removing his shoes, he assumed a lotus position on the mattress, folded his arms, and adopted an evil, leering expression. The kids returned. Michael wore a baseball cap, a Luke Skywalker T-shirt, Jockey underwear, and purple knee socks. Heather sported a Japanese bandanna, a red body-suit, and white bobby-sox.

Joe raised his hands, the fingers bent like monster claws, gnashing his teeth. Gleefully, the kids pranced around the mattress, swerving close then leaping away as his deadly talons

swiped at them. Briefly, they huddled, planning an attack. Joe
gestured menacingly and snarled out his usual bag of derisions:
"Come on, you lily-livered lilliputians, I dare you to attack.
Come here, you chickenshit little scaredy-cats, I wanna crush
your heads like eggshells."

The preliminaries endured about five minutes. Michael and
Heather positioned themselves on either side of him, Michael
shouted "One, two, *three!*" and, simultaneously, they charged.
Joe embraced their jet-propelled bodies with an "oof!" and the
wrestle began.

Their momentum knocked him over sideways. Their goal
was to pin down his arms, and knuckle-drill his sternum. They
rarely succeeded, but had fun trying. At the penultimate moment, Joe always worked himself free in a frenzy of grunting,
gasping, and blasphemy. The kids continuously shouted orders
to each other: "Get his arm, Heather. *Get his arm!*" "I can't.
He's got me in a headlock." "Well, then, pinch his ass!" Ass
pinching was acceptable torture. Likewise, foot tickling. The
kids constantly shrieked and jerked spastically, kicking away
from Joe's fingers scrabbling in their armpits. Gently, he tossed
them all over the place. Constantly, he pinned down one kid,
and, like a moustachioed black-hatted villain tormenting a rail-
road-tracked victim, he threatened to do horrible damage. But
the free child always pounced to the rescue in the nick of time,
leaping on Joe's back, bowling him over, and hollering, "I
gots him, *get away!*"

Joe loved it. What cornball theater! He gasped, gurgled,
grunted, groaned, hissed, wheezed, whimpered, threatened,
and pleaded. It was rough play, yet they rarely got hurt. Everyone understood the physical limits of the game. In fact, as he
flopped and tussled, Joe felt almost relaxed. He loved the way
they became intertangled in a big ball of fulminating arms and
legs. Especially he loved the absolute thrill wrestling gave to
Michael and Heather. Their eyes sparkled with champagne
energy. They pranced, swatted, and danced like cavorting kittens. Joe believed this wrestling was the biggest immediate
pleasure he could give his kids.

In the heart of this particular frenzied loving tussle, Joe
started drifting. Tranquillity settled into his body as the kids
tugged on his arms and legs. The world became a sunny place,
and easy to comprehend: gentle, innocent, compassionate. He
fantasized that he should do this for a living: Joe Miniver,

Professional Wrestler of Children. They were contorted amo-
rously around each other in a delirious helium atmosphere,
lighter than air, wonderfully insouciant and happy. Joe threatened to commit unbelievably horrible mayhem upon their wiry
little bodies; he became inebriated on their giggles. Oh wow,
he thought. Everything's gonna be all right! Heather and Michael, Renaissance angels, fluttered their creamy golden wings,
and collided against his body like enormous holiday kisses.

Bam!

The usual, sickening collision. Even without seeing it, Joe
knew that the back of Heather's head had crunched into Michael's broken nose.

For a second, the usual stunned silence ensued—that hesitant, totally dead period before the squall. And then:

Not noise, so much, as blood. As if a gigantic pig-bladder
hanging over their heads and full of the stuff had been stabbed
open with a knife, they were—all three of them—instantly
drenched in crimson. Then they rolled away from each other,
Heather in tears, Michael on his knees, his head against the
mattress and his ass in the air, making queer, shocked, guttural
sounds. Finally, maybe ten seconds after the fact, Joe heard
Heidi's shout: *"Oh no!"*

In the next instant, it seemed as if ever since the kids' births,
his life had been a series of traumatic emergency situations
interspersed with a series of drills preparing for traumatic situations. Heather commenced bawling, not from hurt, but because she had caused such damage, and knew that the best way
to stave off blame was to feign pain and hysteria. Michael was
in too much agony to cry. Spouting blood, he allowed himself
to be grabbed, hoisted, and carted unceremoniously down to
the car by his father, while his mother trailed behind wailing,
"Oh God! I'm sorry! You were right! I'm sorry! Oh, God!"

How sweet it is! a tiny portion of Joe's brain managed to
gloat through all his emergency adrenaline. *Vengeance is mine!*

The bus starter clicked and went dead. Frantically, Joe
grabbed the pliers, clobbered his head diving under the right
rear tire, jumped the starter, scrambled back into the car, and—
brrrrooooom!—they were off.

Juan Fangio, starring in—dahdle-a-*dah*-de-*dah* . . . *charge!*—
A Race Against Death! They made it, as somehow they always
did, to the hospital. And burst through the emergency-entrance

door. As usual, nobody was on duty. No nurse, no doctor, no ambulance driver, no paramedic. Nobody but a janitor maneuvering a mop and a bucket was on hand to stem the bloody flow.

Heidi pressed a soaked T-shirt to Michael's face while Joe raced off to locate a doctor, a nurse, an anybody. Yet no one moved in the hallways; the head nurse's station was deserted. An eerie air of vacuity permeated the hospital. My kid will bleed to death, Joe thought in a panic, because today is some kind of special hospital holiday:

PRESIDENT PROCLAIMS NATIONAL DOCTORS' GOLFING TUESDAY!

Desperately, he pushed open the nearest door and plummeted inside. Nikita Smatterling (seated in a chair beside a vase of colorful carnations on the night table near Ephraim Bonatelli's slightly raised bed) looked up without demonstrable surprise. Ephraim himself, clothed from head to toe in a chartreuse jumpsuit and looking decidedly chipper, sat in the lotus position on his own pillow. On the other side of the bed, Ray Verboten reacted to Joe's precipitous entry by clapping his Resistol onto his head and leaping upright. Egon Braithwhite had been standing at the foot of the bed, nearest the door—he turned, startled, and exclaimed: "Pi shidonoi bessi mamaba!" Beside him stood the stoop-shouldered little shtarker himself, Nick Danger. His suitcase lay on the foot of the bed—its lid raised—facing away from Joe.

"Whoops, pardon me!" Joe spun a hundred and eighty degrees, yanking shut the door as he bolted away.

A nurse emerged from the ladies' can. Grabbing her arm, Joe stammered "My kid . . . !" Almost at a run, he led her to the emergency-room area, where she dialed the doctor on call: he was in the middle of dinner.

"I just remembered," Joe gasped.

"What?" Heidi hugged Michael tightly, stroking his hair, whispering, "It's okay, lovebird, it's okay."

"What I planned to say when I began that story about the freak who was mugged into vegetablehood."

"Joe, I think this is hardly the time—"

"Spumoni said it was his own fault for putting out a lousy karma."

"Whose own fault?"

"The freak's. He said it was *his own fault* for getting beaten to a pulp, because he must have been putting out really lousy karma."

"Who said—?"

"Spumoni Tatarsky. And Jeff Orbison agreed. Can you believe *that?*"

Now came the Incredible Coincidence. Hurrying through the emergency-room door, little Bradley screaming to high heaven in her arms with one of his eyes already swollen shut and yellowing like a puffing grapefruit, came Nancy Ryan. Her face radiated serene concern; a cigarette dangled from her lips. Her outfit consisted of a blue terrycloth bathrobe and embroidered Chinese slippers.

Settling beside Joe, she noticed Michael's crimson deluge and shouted (in order to be heard over Bradley's hysterics): "My God, what happened?"

"We were wrestling!"

"What about the doctor?"

"He's coming! What happened to Bradley?"

"I was in the bath! Somehow he caught the parakeet, threw it into the dryer, and turned on the machine! It was cooked to a crisp by the time I discovered it! So I spanked him for the first time in—three years, I guess! Enraged, he ran outside, picked up a big rock, and smashed himself in the face with it!"

In this way, Joe thought (seated between the two women and their mayhemmed offspring), America is busy building the leaders of tomorrow. For only upon the firm foundation of today's healthy youngsters can the civilized glory of our manifestly destined future be assured.

Dr. Phil Horney arrived; confusion ensued. Both Joe and Heidi wished to enter the ER with their wounded child, but Heather wasn't allowed. She threw a fit when ordered to remain in the corridor, inhaling Nancy's smoke and Bradley's eardrum-shattering howls. So Heidi accompanied Michael, and Joe stayed outside, seated in a vomit-orange plastic cafeteria chair, flanked by a grim and martyrish Heather, and Nancy and her hysterical offspring.

Right off the bat, Nancy's incredibly blasé style threw him for a loop. Unperturbed by the howling dervish beside her, she chain-smoked, smiled cheerfully, and seemed totally disinterested in her son's predicament. She neither ordered Bradley to clam up nor offered much solace. Joe quite admired her aplomb. Especially as she seemed much more intent, now that Heidi had departed the field of battle, on furthering their relationship however possible, given (of course) the limitations of these awkward circumstances.

"My God," she whispered conspiratorially, "have I ever missed you since yesterday morning! How did you feel after our sex together?"

"Very nervous," Joe admitted uncomfortably.

"I felt heavenly. That was one of the most incredible experiences of my life."

Speaking out the side of his mouth (to frustrate Heather's flapping ears), Joe said, "Well, it wasn't bad, I'll admit."

"Our baby is going to be the most beautiful child created between two people ever," she murmured blissfully. Bradley continued his alarmingly shrill protestations, and Joe's eardrums started to ache.

His heart also went *k-flomp*! at the mention of "our" baby.

"Hey, Nancy, what are you talking about? I didn't even—"

"A woman knows." She exhaled luxuriously, as if they were actually conversing in a relaxed and sensual manner after a particularly gratifying lay, while stretched languorously between pristine linen coverlets.

"I don't want any baby."

"How can you speak like that after our times together?"

"Nancy, I want to cut it off. Break up. End the relationship. I don't know what happened."

She smiled her lazy, know-it-all, heavy-lidded, come-on affectation. "I do."

Joe opened his English-foreign language phrase dictionary, selecting a time-honored standby: "None of this makes any sense. It's crazy."

She opened her Hipster's Cosmic Dictionary of Astrologically Inspired Catchwords: "That's where you're wrong. It makes perfect sense. All my life I've known something like this was going to happen with somebody like you. The minute we met in the bus station my body began feeling as if it needed to be pregnant. Even Sasha's tragedy is relevant, because Michael's act, terrible as it is, hasn't changed my feelings for you one iota."

Joe flipped rapidly through the pages of *his* dictionary, searching for that other old standby to be used with aggravating repetition in case of emergency: "I don't know what you're talking about."

"I'm talking about *us*." She pronounced "us" the way Sir Edmund Hillary might have pronounced "Mount Everest."

Joe fumfered. "Listen, Nancy, back off a little. I don't want what you want."

"You say that now, Joe. But when you're inside me you're not saying that at all."

"Then I don't ever want to be inside of you again."

She took his news with infuriatingly placid lack of concern. "It's all right. You've already trusted me with the most profound gift anyone can give anybody, ever."

"But I don't *want* to give you that gift! And besides—"

From the emergency room came a piercing howl. No doubt Phil Horney was perpetrating an unnecessarily brutal obscenity upon Michael's traumatized beak. Bradley showed few signs of slackening his outrage, although his howls now lacked a certain vitality. They had become dreary and monotonous, assembly-line exclamations, the pathetic bleats of a child advancing beyond exhaustion, his howls triggered by the memory of how to execrate. Heather's eyes remained stoically fixed on the opposite wall. No doubt her incompetent little mind was trying to deal with the psychological impact of having disfigured (perhaps brain-damaged) her older brother for life.

Said Nancy: "I hear what you're saying, but words are often the least reliable indicators of what a person really means. Right now, you think your left brain is in control of how you actually relate to me, but the actual message I'm getting from you is very different. I'd say that your right brain truly dominates your feelings toward me, and they're coming through loud and clear."

Whereupon Bradley fell asleep right in the middle of an elongated yelp, and Heather spoke for the first time: "Thank God he shut up—the creep."

Joe said, "I don't like it when you say I'm saying something I'm not saying."

"I would expect you to say that, but I'm reading your aura and, believe me, it's wonderful."

"My aura?"

"It's so warm, so outgoing, so loving. If only you could realize it."

"What do you mean, 'my aura'?"

"The glow around you. The emanation from your color chakras."

"You're saying you can actually *see* some kind of light around me?"

"Very clearly. Your vibrations are incredibly powerful. Of course, your etheric has a tendency to come and go with your moods. But why delve into it here? I doubt you're ready for any of that yet."

"What does it look like, my aura?"

Her loving, adulatory gaze also seemed almost mocking. Smoke fluffed from her gently grinning mouth as she said, "Well, I'll tell you one thing—the red is fantastic."

"What does that mean?"

"It means you're very sexy...."

Heather had been eyeing a distant vending machine. Thinking to catch her old man in a weakened condition, she said, "Daddy, I need a quarter to get something from that machine."

She had miscalculated. Eternally vigilant, ever alert, Joe lit into her wearing his full battle regalia:

"Can you have a *quarter*? For *that* shit? For packages of phenol benzoate lacquered in propyl glucose, garnished with rithium nitrite to preserve the freshness and flavor of a quarter of a teaspoon of peanut butter?—Hah! I'm upset, Heather, I'll admit, but not *that* gaga."

"All it costs is a lousy quarter," she nagged grumpily.

"The price ain't the problem, sweetie. That shit is so full of chemicals it causes cancer in twenty-four original ways six hours after you eat it."

"When you were a kid you ate all that junk. You even said so a million times."

"In those days nobody understood nitrosamines and sodium nitrite. But I absolutely refuse to let you fill your lovely little tummy full of that venal crap."

"What's 'venal'?"

"Bad, rotten, nasty."

"Oh." In the next breath she asked: "Is this her?"

"Is who what?"

"Is that lady 'her'?"

He should have caught on, but recent events had him a bit addled. "Who?"

"The one that calls up on the telephone all the time, that you're fucking?"

"Hey, man, cool it! What business is it of yours anyway?"

"It's account of her, isn't it, that I'm almost a orphan?"

"'An' orphan," Joe corrected. "Heather, let's drop the subject, okay?"

"Her name is Mrs. Ryan, isn't it?"

"Why don't you ask her yourself? I'm sure that the sound waves caused by your voice will reverberate in coherent patterns across her eardrums."

"Huh?"

"Just ask her *yourself*, dummy. Stop playing the fool."

Defiantly, Heather folded her arms. "I don't want to ask her myself. I won't ever talk to her again in my life."

"Hey! Cut the stupidity!"

"How can I? I don't have a knife."

"Humor," Joe explained to Nancy. "I'd like you to meet Jack Benny in drag."

"Well I think only a rotten creep would wear a bathrobe in public." Tears welled in Heather's eyes. "I don't think it's fair for her to be fucking you instead of letting you be our father."

"I'm still your father, Heather. And stop using 'fuck.'"

"Not anymore, you aren't. You're just running around shacking up with every Jane and Barbara that twitches their butt at you, trying to win the Fornication Sweepstakes."

Joe's eyes became suspicious slits. "That's not your own expression, Heather. You didn't make that up. Who said it?"

"I did so make that up. Just now."

"The hell you say. Is that the way Heidi talks to you kids about me? 'The Fornication Sweepstakes?' Wow—I don't believe it!"

Such betrayal! To nobody had Joe ever said an uncomplimentary word about his wife. He took great pride, even while intimately joined with Nancy and Diana, of never having trashed Heidi. But while he had been keeping their relationship clean and private, she had been bad-mouthing him to the kids, trying to capture their little hearts and minds (and loyalty) for the no doubt messy divorce proceedings in store.

"It's not Mommy," Heather insisted. "I told you, I made it up."

"Yeah, and the pope wears fruitboots. The way you said it was like a parrot imitating somebody else. 'The Fornication Sweepstakes'—shee-it! That bitch has gall!"

Marvelous, self-righteous rage took command of his sanity. When Heidi walked out of the emergency room, he would demand an explanation. He might even threaten to have her declared legally insane in order to snag the kids in a custody battle: FIRST TIME EVER, HUBBY WINS BRATS + ALIMONY! No need to ditch Nancy after all. And she focused—did Mrs. Ryan—her fanny raised at him invitingly . . . what a gluteal target! A lust spasm twitched in his nether regions. He wished to unleash cries of frustration, joy, and eternal ambiguity while asking the old Jobian interrogatives: Why so much suffering, God? Why me? Basta ya! Stop hacking off my arms and my legs! Lighten up, Lord, a little peace and comfort in my old age, if you will!

The emergency-room door opened, and Michael and Heidi emerged. Michael's face was scrubbed and cleaner, his eyes were blacker, he wore a fresh goalie's mask. Heidi looked ashen and chastened. The nurse said, "You sure have a brave boy there, Mr. Miniver." Phil Horney added: "Yeah, that oughtta hold him for a while. I wouldn't let him wrestle for a few weeks, however. Heidi says that's how he reinjured it—apparently you were wrestling with the kids only a few hours after he broke it?"

"It wasn't my idea. She forced me into it."

"*I* forced you into it?" Heidi's jaw fell on the floor and bounced. "I said you could, but don't start blaming me. You didn't have to follow my advice."

"Wait a sec. When it happened you fell all over yourself apologizing."

"I was distraught." Her frost fogged his cheeks. Taking Heather's hand, she led her two children toward the exit.

To the doctor, Joe said, "Did you hear that? *I* didn't want to wrestle with the kids. But she made me feel so guilty that I finally gave in. And look what happened. Exactly what I *said* would happen!"

Heidi whirled like an expert gunslinger, firing a broadside before Joe had even started to slap leather. "That's right, go ahead, tell everybody! Air all of our dirty linen in public! That's become your style, these days, hasn't it?"

"Well, you don't have to blame me for something that *you* set up!"

"I'll see you around the campus, Joey. Have a ball with your concubine there."

"Heidi—!"

Swish, bam, slam!—they were gone.

Joe said, "What's the matter with everybody? Have they gone crazy?"

Phil was embarrassed. "Well, uh, you know. With accidents like this people tend to become flustered."

"But that boy of yours sure is a regular little trooper," the nurse piped cheerfully. "Now what have we got here?" she asked Nancy, referring to Bradley, who was slumped in his plastic chair, noisily cutting Zs.

Joe banged out the swinging glass Exit door and sprinted for the bus. Heidi gave a muffled shout; a blurred scrambling took place inside the vehicle. When Joe reached the car, all the windows were rolled up, all the doors locked. Joe whacked the passengerside window: Heather stuck out her tongue. Michael lay on the rear seat.

"Let me in, dammit! You can't leave without me!"

Heather displayed her most pugnacious, malevolent grin, and nodded her head up and down, indicating that they sure as hell *could* leave without him—For Reals. Heidi switched on the ignition key, but all she got was a *clunk*!

"Hah, see? You don't even know how to start it. Now, open up. *Come on!*"

"I'm not going anywhere with you, Joey. Not tonight. Not ever again. I don't believe the way you're acting. It's despicable."

From the back seat came Michael's pathetic cry: "I wadda go hobe."

"We're going home, sweetie. Just as soon as Daddy backs off and allows us to split."

"Daddy's going with you." Joe pressed his nose against the sliding door's window. "I happen to be just as much your parent as Heidi is."

"It's nice of you to be so concerned," Heidi said. "Maybe

you'll even find an extra five minutes between your erotic appointments around town every week to drop by and say hello to your children."

"I think you're having a nervous breakdown, dear. You've flipped. Now come on, dammit. Open up!"

"You are *not* traveling home with us, Joey. I mean that absolutely and irrevocably. I refuse to negotiate."

"How you gonna start the car, then? Beg for a miracle?"

"I am going to hand you the pliers out the vent window in hopes that you still have enough common decency left in your body to go under the car and jump the solenoid so that I can take my sick and suffering child home."

"You'll run over me while I'm under there."

"Joey, *please*. Your imagination is too vivid."

On his way around to her side, Joe paused, licked his finger, and wrote ꓘƆUℲ across the spiderwebbed windshield.

"Very clever," Heidi sarcasmed. "Now please, we're in a hurry."

"What about me? I got no wheels. What am I supposed to do?"

"I'm sure that Miss Cosmic Bathrobe in there will take very good care of you."

"You're ugly. You know that? You're really developing into a very ugly human being."

"It takes one to know one." Heidi poked pliers out the open vent window.

"Why do we have to see who can most insult the other all of the time?" Joe was thoroughly demoralized by the whole situation. "It's stupid."

"I didn't start it, Joey. I didn't blow off our marriage at the bus station last Saturday night."

"Ah, screw you." He swung around the VW, made a grotesque face at Heather, dropped underneath the car, and applied the plier handles to the pertinent connecting points. Immediately, Heidi started the car, slammed it into gear, and drove away; the right rear tire jounced over his thighs.

Incredulously, Joe hollered, *"Ouch!"*

Heidi slammed on the brakes, crying out, "Oh no! What was I *thinking*!" And, while Joe writhed in pain, convinced that both legs were shattered, she tried to escape from the bus. But once the broken lock knobs had been pushed down, the only way to pop them was with the key, from outside. Frantically, Heidi rolled down the window and leaned out, trying to accomplish the maneuver upside down and backward. But she hadn't enough leverage to open the door.

Oblivious to the latest drama, Michael groaned, "I wadda go *hobe!*"

"*I'll sue you!*" Joe screamed. "*They'll declare you mentally incompetent! They'll throw you in jail!*"

"Joey, I didn't mean—"

Heather's window wouldn't open—the winding apparatus was broken. So Heidi climbed in back, flipped up the sliding-door lock knob, and, because the interior handle was broken, reached through the vent window and jerked up the outside door handle. The sliding door popped out, but, because the U-piece attaching it to the body runner was broken, it sliced downward, clanking against the pavement, then fell outward, flopping over, and yanking Heidi, whose arm was trapped in the vent window, with it.

Her turn to scream: "*My arm!*"

Heather wailed, "*Mommy!*"

Joe jumped to his feet. Surprise, surprise! Not only could he walk, but he felt only a fraction of the pain he had been prepared for. Apparently, his legs were completely unbroken, an altogether embarrassing development, given the circumstances.

The tilted door was still attached by its bottom arm to the car's lower runner. Heidi's twisted arm, bent through the vent window, was pinned underneath the door, crushed against the pavement. "It's broken . . ." she gasped. "Oh shit, I never felt a hurt like this!"

"Here." Joe fumbled. "Lemme lift this . . . okay . . . can you pull your arm out? Quick, I can't hold this up forever . . . come *on*—!"

"Joey, it *hurts!*" She was crying. Heather sobbed, Michael whimpered. As it often did, something went wrong in the accelerator system, and abruptly the engine started racing with a high-pitched piercing rattle.

"I know it hurts, Heidi. But you gotta free it from . . . *there!*"

She slid off the door, gripping her arm just below the elbow. The bent wrist looked sickening.

Joe helped her to her feet. Heidi whimpered, "What are you doing? Take your hands off me."

"We got to get back to the emergency room."

"I'm not going back in there!"

"Don't be stupid. Look at that wrist. Come on, Heidi, grow up for ten minutes."

"You grow up. If we go back in there, I'll never live it down."

"Oh wow." Joe forced his wife to move. "If you *don't* go, I'll break your jaw, I swear to it!"

She protested, then relented. Guiding her toward the hospital, Joe called back over one shoulder: "Heather, turn off the damn car."

"There's no key!"

"There *has* to be a key, sweetie. You can't remove it from the ignition while the car's still running."

"I did," Heidi said faintly.

"Come again?"

"I don't know why, but it popped out when I yanked. Joey, I hate that car! Just once in my life before I die I want a new one!"

"If we buy a new car we won't have money to start the house."

"Who cares? We're gonna be divorced, and we don't have any money anyway."

"Tribby says he can unload the coke and get my twelve Gs back. So we'll have that, anyway."

"Not unless Tribby goes after it in a rubber suit and a snorkel."

"Not unless what—?" Behind them, the bus made a sound like a gunshot, shuddered, and stalled.

"It went off by itself!" Heather called, as Joe opened the glass door and ushered Heidi inside.

"I didn't run over you on purpose," Heidi whimpered, as Joe knocked on the emergency-room door. "Honest. You've got to believe me."

"What did you say about Tribby and the dope?"

"I just wasn't thinking, Joey. Are your legs hurt?"

"A rubber suit and a *snorkel*?"

A nurse appeared, stating the obvious: "You're back again." A blast of Bradley's pained howls hit them like an anguished flock of fleeing birds.

Dazedly, Joe said, "It's my wife. She just broke her arm."

The nurse screwed up her features. "It wasn't broken a minute ago, was it?"

"No, listen, it's a long story. Maybe you could give her a shot, for the pain, until Phil's free."

Nancy circled the operating table upon which her child lay screaming his guts out while Phil Horney sutured. Placing an arm solicitously around Heidi's shoulders, she said, "Oh you poor dear."

"Tell her to keep her fucking paws off me," Heidi whispered weakly. Then she fainted.

Joe, Nancy, and the nurse kept her from hitting the ground. Grunting and cursing, they lugged her to a chair; the nurse rummaged through steel-cabinet drawers, hunting for smelling salts.

Joe murmured dreamily, "I'll be right back. I better check on the kids."

Seated beside Michael in the back, Heather stroked her brother's head. Joe checked the ignition, the front seat, and the outside lock on the driverside door, then asked, "Where's the keys?"

"We don't know."

"But what did she do with the *keys*?" Joe gnashed his teeth. "She had to have them to start the car."

"We didn't take them."

"I'm not accusing you of taking them, Heather. I'm simply asking: did you see what happened to them?" On his hands and knees, Joe scoured the floor up front—fruitlessly. A rubber suit and a snorkel? In back he tore through old *National Geographics* and scattered tools, shredded newspapers and greasy rags, tennis rackets, an old shoe, and a thousand other items, most of them dump candidates, but came up empty-handed. Next, he scrabbled without luck through the glove compartment, then pawed through all the garbage lining the windshield dashboard—Bic pens, supermarket game stubs, envelopes containing shopping and chore lists, and two dozen rotted, shriveled brown applecores: but he found no keys.

Outside, Joe wrestled up the sliding door, checking the pavement underneath it, which coughed up no keys.

Heaving the door up against the car, Joe fitted the broken U-piece into its proper slot on the upper runner. After some awkward prodding, he managed to shut the door again, and lock it.

A town cop had sidled up behind him during this operation. "Say, buddy, what's going on here?"

"Officer, you wouldn't believe me if I told you."

"Try me."

"We just brought my kid in for a broken nose. That's him on the back seat there. Then, while we were leaving, this door fell off with my wife's arm caught in it and broke her wrist. So she's in there now, having the wrist set."

"I see. Do you always park your car in the middle of the road, or is tonight a special occasion?"

"I don't understand."

"Well, mister, maybe I can clear it up for you. This here portion of macadam happens to be the entrance and egress portion of the driveway for the emergency room. If a ambulance was to come in here right now, carrying a life-or-death patient, your car would be blocking it."

Without thinking, Joe corrected the man's grammar: "'An' ambulance."

"That is correct. Now, that portion of the macadam back there, see? With the concrete parking dividers and the slanted yellow lines, that's for hospital parking. And that is precisely where this heap should be."

"I know sir. I apologize. But right now I can't find the keys."

"It's immaterial to me whether you can find the goddam keys, mister. Your car is in the wrong place, and it's breaking the law. So I'm gonna have to give you a citation."

What to do—flare? Attack the son of a bitch, grab his gun from its holster, and—

STATEWIDE SEARCH LAUNCHED FOR COP KILLER

"Reliable sources with the State Bureau of Investigation claimed, early this morning, that they were closing in on the hideout of Joe Miniver, maniac cop killer, who is apparently holed up in a cave in the foothills of the Midnight Mountains just north of Chamisaville. Authorities believe that he is heavily armed, and has enough ammunition to service a small army. At 4:00 A.M. this morning, two armored vehicles were flown from the capital to Chamisaville in a pair of transport helicopters. State police spokesperson, Gary Slocum, informs us that Miniver has vowed he will never be taken alive, and police fear he may choose to die in a fiery exchange of gunfire rather than give himself up. However, on the off-chance that such a

confrontation can be avoided, Miniver's two children, Heather
and Michael, were driven to the area where their father is holed
out, and at right this moment they are speaking to him over
police bullhorns, begging their daddy to give himself up. . . ."

In the background, Nick Danger slunk out of the emergency-
room exit and scuttled off, his mystifying suitcase thudding
softly against one thigh.

Joe said, "Look, sir, I'm really sorry. Maybe my wife has
the keys inside, I dunno. I'll go in and check."

"And leave this car camped here, illegally, a public nuisance
as well as a real danger to life and limb if an ambulance should
have to deliver somebody or cart a stiff away?"

"Well, then I'll try to push it back over there. Maybe you
could give me a hand?"

"You're very funny, buddy. I get paid to enforce the law,
not to push vehicles around."

Joe said, "Heather, into the driver's seat, quick! I need you
to steer this car."

"I don't know how."

"It's easy. Now come on, hurry up. Do what I say, or this
fucking cop is gonna throw us all in jail."

"One more cussword out of your mouth, buddy, and I'll
haul you in." He was standing back from the rear of the bus,
writing the ticket.

"Heather!"

"I'm scared, Daddy. I don't know how to steer it."

"Get in the goddam driver's seat right now! Or I'll drop
your pants and give you a thousand whacks on a bare fanny."

Hesitantly, his miniature Flo Nightingale deserted her dying
charge and settled in the driver's seat. Joe reached through the
window and grabbed the wheel. "See, all you have to do is,
when I'm pushing it, turn the wheel like this, in this direction,
you got that? Good. Let's go."

"Okay, Daddy."

His back pressed against the front of the bus, Joe bent down,
grabbed the bumper, lifted up, and heaved backward with all
his might. It was easy. The light car rolled effortlessly across
the flat macadam, achieved the parking area, and collided—
crunching softly—against the cop's cruiser.

Joe let go the bumper and leaped around to the driverside
door, through which he must pass to step on the brakes so the
vehicle wouldn't roll forward again. But of course the door

was locked, and he had no keys. And by the time he had scrambled through the window, shoving Heather roughly aside as he reached down desperately with one hand to hit the brakes, the bus had proceeded lazily forward again, halting exactly where it had been before Joe pushed it. And by the time he resituated himself in a right-side-up position, facing forward, the cop stood at the passengerside door demanding that he "roll down this window, mister."

"I can't, sir. The handle is broken."

The cop circled cautiously to Joe's side of the car and drew his gun.

"I want you to descend from that car real slowly. And I want to see your hands at all times. I don't want no more jokes, no more pranks, no more false moves. Try anything funny and I'll kill you, understand? Now: open that door, and get your ass out of that vehicle."

"I can't open this door, sir. It's jammed."

"I'm not buying it, buddy. Now, you don't have much time left, you really don't. Open that door right now!"

"I have to crawl out the window." Joe's throat was so dry his voice squeaked. "Honest, sir, I *can't* open this door."

"Very well, then." The cop raised his arm, pointing the gun at Joe's head. He held the weapon in a classical grip, steadying it by clasping his right wrist with the left hand. The sensation engendered in Joe by this current tête-à-tête was otherworldly. A ringing commenced in his ears, and his brain reacted accordingly—it cringed, and Joe felt worse than faint. It was as if a bullet was already headed for that gray matter, which, in the next split instant, would splatter against the roof and the driverside window. Joe moved his lips to make words—"I can only get out through the window." But thanks to his constricted throat and ringing ears, he couldn't hear himself speak.

He gave up, convinced it was all over. Closing his eyes, Joe expected his life to pass in review. Instead, after a few seconds (or an eternity), the jangling stopped, and distinctly (with a downright eerie clarity), he heard Nancy Ryan salute the cop.

"Hello, Vern. Why are you pointing that gun at my friend?"

"You better stand back, Nancy. This lug's crazy."

"No he's not. He's simply distraught. His son broke his nose, and then just a minute ago, in a freak accident, his wife

Heidi broke her wrist. She's in the emergency room under Phil's care right now."

"He's fucking with me," Vern said tensely. "He backed his goddam car into my cruiser."

"Oh come on. I'll vouch for him. But first put away that silly gun."

"Not until he hauls his ass out of that car and I can see all of him."

"Joe, you better get out of the car," Nancy coaxed. "Open your eyes."

Joe opened his eyes. "I can't get out the way he wants me to, Nancy, because the door's jammed shut. So I can only crawl out the window."

"Well, then, crawl out the window."

"But he said he would kill me if I crawl out the window."

"Oh come on. Vern? I'm surprised at you. You won't hurt him if he crawls out the window, will you?"

"Aw . . . I guess not."

"He guesses," Joe mumbled with meek scorn. "What kind of assurance is that?"

"See what I mean, Nancy? He's an arrogant prick. That kind is usually dangerous."

"Vern, he's the least dangerous person I know. Scout's honor. Now Joe, climb out the silly window. Hurry up."

"If he kills me it's your fault." What a clammy, all-encompassing terror had now taken over his body!

"He won't shoot, darling. I've enveloped you in a cocoon of pink clouds."

Just what he needed—a cocoon of pink clouds! Guaranteed to stop .357-Magnum bullets any day! An impenetrable shield of cotton candy! But he moved anyway, hesitantly poking his head out the window. Awkwardly, like a colt being born, he oozed out farther. Eventually, as one hand sought a grip on the roof, and the other grabbed for the outside rearview mirror, he lost his balance, was airborne briefly, and thumped against the pavement.

"Up against the car," Vern ordered. "Quick! Spread your legs—that's it. And your arms, too."

Joe did as he was told: Vern slapped him down for hidden weaponry, removed his wallet, and flipped it open.

Nancy said, "See? There was no need to worry. He's just a regular little old human being."

"Well, why is he acting so funny then? Turn around, Joe."

Robotlike, Joe obeyed. Vern had holstered the gun. He handed over Joe's wallet. Whereas a minute ago he had looked ready to kill, now the cop seemed almost scared. He had pulled a gun unnecessarily on a law-abiding (though perhaps momentarily deranged) citizen, who might be within his rights filing some sort of police brutality suit.

"Listen, uh, Joe. Maybe I was a little hasty, there, with the betsy. You know. Just last week a partner of mine was blown away by this hopped-up freak with a piece over a routine traffic violation. So I'm a little nervous, you dig?"

Joe tried to speak, but could only dredge forth a squeak.

"Vern, you're super." Nancy stood on tiptoes to buss his cheek. Approaching Joe, she asked, "Are you okay?"

"But he has to move this goddam car into a parking place," Vern warned. "It's a menace in the middle of the roadway here." As an after-thought he handed Joe a citation for illegal parking, bald tires, a cracked windshield, an expired safety sticker, a broken taillight, and for colliding with a police vehicle.

"You see?" Nancy cuddled up against Joe. "Everything turns out all right if you just have faith."

Like Amelia Earhart, Vern disappeared.

"Faith in what? And how do you know that thug, anyway?"

"We dated for a little bit last year. He's really not a bad guy."

"He almost killed me."

"He was probably scared. People always act funny when they're frightened."

Relieved and exhausted, Joe said, "Well, all I want to do right now is pick up Heidi and go home."

"I'll wait just to make sure everything is all right."

Bradley focused in the background. "I don't wanna wait, Mom. I wanna go home."

Staggering toward the emergency-room entrance, Joe thought: *Kids!*

When he emerged again, a shaken and drained Heidi leaning on his arm, they still had no keys. Joe said, "I searched all over the car, but I couldn't find them."

"Don't look at me, Joey. They're not in my pockets. I don't know what happened."

"Can't you think? Can't you remember? How can I start the bus without the damn keys?"

"I don't remember anything. I'm sorry."

"Oh boy. When it rains it pours."

"Go ahead, dump on me. Everything is my fault. I haven't tasted enough gas, yet, this evening."

The devil, disguised as a smiling female cheerfully smoking a cigarette, stepped out of the shadows. "Why don't you guys let me drive you home? Joe or somebody can return to find the keys later."

"I'd rather hitchhike." But Heidi's meek declaration totally lacked pizzazz.

Gratefully, Joe accepted her offer. "Thanks for hanging around, Nancy. Kids, climb out of the bus. . . ."

Packed like sardines on the drive to the Castle of Golden Fools, the adults tried to remain mute while the kids exchanged amenities.

"Get off my foot, Bradley. You're squashing my foot."

"No I'm not. I'm not even *near* your stinking foot."

"Bradley, dear, don't say 'stinking.' Be nice."

"Daddy, Bradley's standing on my foot and it *hurts*!"

"Shuttup, Heather, we're almost home."

"Well, he's killing me! Ow, ow, ow!"

"Bradley, darling, move your foot, would you, please? if it's on top of Heather's."

"It is not. And anyway, I can't even budge. I'm getting squashed. I can't breathe. Michael's elbow is stuck in my guts."

"Michael, move your elbow, okay?"

"Where cad I moob id to, Dad? I'b id a straid jagged. Bradley id crudhing my hib."

"Bradley, are you crushing his hip?"

"I can't help it, Mom. There's too many people back here."

Joe said, "Here, I'll move. Heather, change your position on my lap. Ooff, *Jesus*! Michael, see if you can squunch your leg over a little, huh?"

Heidi said, "Maybe I can move my seat forward and give you some more room back there."

"No, I'm sorry," Nancy apologized. "The gizmo that loosens the passenger seat is rusted, it doesn't work."

"Well, we're almost home anyway," Joe said. "Come on, everybody, let's see if we can hold out a few minutes longer."

"Pee-yew," Heather exclaimed. "Who just laid a grenade? Bradley, did you cut that fart? I bet you did."

"Shuttup, Heather."

Bradley screeched, "Mom, I didn't cut a fart! Make her take it back."

"You did so," Heather accused. "It had to be you." She started to make gagging sounds. "Help! I can't breathe!"

Joe said, "Heather, when we get home I'm gonna kill you."

"I'm not afraid." She stuck out her tongue. "Blaaah!"

Bradley cried, "Mom, tell her I didn't cut a fart!"

Nancy swung her head sideways. "She knows you didn't cut a fart, Bradley. Nobody's blaming you for anything."

"Yes they are! Make her take it back!"

"I can't make her take it back, dear. That's silly."

"Take it back, Heather," Joe snarled wearily.

"Why should I take it back if he really did?"

"You don't *know* if he really did or not. And I can't stand this bickering. So take it back, dammit, or I swear on a stack of Bibles I'll tan your hide so thoroughly when we get home that they'll be able to cut it up and make saddles with it."

Michael said, "*You* probably fahdded, Hedder. Id's alwaids duh wud dat fahds dat accudded edrebody else ob fahdding."

"I did not! Daddy, make Michael be quiet! He's a liar." Poking her face to within an inch of her brother's bandaged visage, she chanted, "Liar! Liar! Pants on fire! Hanging from a telephone wire!"

Heidi added her two cents: "Joey probably farted. But he's too chicken to tell anybody. That goes with his new role in life as a professional snake in the grass."

"Heidi, I hate to be picayune, but that was gratuitous venom."

"Still, it's probably true."

"I didn't fart, dammit." Her accusation was so absurd and unfair that he felt a heat rising. If he let it build unchecked for another thirty seconds, he would probably reach forward and strangle the bitch in her tracks, broken wrist or not.

"*I* farted," Nancy said pleasantly. "Please excuse me." She exhaled another rich billow of Lucky Strike exhaust and, abruptly, Joe couldn't breathe.

"Heidi, open the window a little, would you please?"

"I can't. I'm shivering. My teeth are chattering. I think I'm getting a fever."

"But I can't breathe. I left all my pills and the inhaler in the bus."

"Oh screw your asthma, Joey. I'm sick of your emotional crutches. When are you ever going to grow up?"

Joe said, "Stop this car, Nancy. I'm getting out."

"But we're almost there."

"I didn't ask you where we *were*, I asked you to stop this car."

She pulled over to the shoulder and braked. Using her left hand, Heidi opened the door and leaned forward. Joe pried himself out, lost his balance, and crashed into the ditch, enormously relieved to be free of those claustrophobic quarters. Fresh air embraced him with a delirious rush.

"Good riddance to bad rubbish," Heidi snorted, slamming the door.

"I'll see you around the universe, asshole!" Yet as the car chugged off, Joe suddenly remembered again, and hollered in panic: "What did you mean about a rubber suit and a snorkel?"

"What the hell do you *think*?"

Then they were gone, and Joe sat there, incredulous, astonished by their infantile interactions.

A dozen cows mooed appreciatively. Filtered through spring mists, the moon was balanced atop a Midnight foothill, trailing wisps of soft yellow fog like angel hair. And Joe Miniver, child of scorn, reeled to his feet like a punch-drunk fighter wondering in what direction salvation lay. Overhead, a billion stars twinkled imperviously. To them, the human condition didn't mean squat.

But then he thought: "She's lying. She'll market the stuff herself, after we're divorced, and live high on the hog forever after."

A skunk trotting across the road peered at Joe inquisitively. But then, deciding this human had probably had enough for one night, it merely flicked its tail in a neighborly fashion and waddled on, disappearing into the ebullient shadows.

◆§

With a pebble he was too pooped to excavate in his shoe, Joe limped halfway up the driveway, cursing softly. Geronimo answered his muffled exclamations with a soft whinny. The horse stood in the center of Eloy's front field, nosing around the Hanuman U-Haul. Incredibly, despite a million-dollar price tag on the monkey god, nobody was guarding it.

Joe glanced around once, uneasily, just to make sure nobody like Angel Guts or Ray Verboten or Cobey Dallas crouched in the branches of a nearby tree, fingering an infrared sniper gun. Then, slipping between barbed-wire strands, he approached the U-Haul. Geronimo whinnied again and backed off, suspiciously awaiting further developments.

Head cocked, Joe listened for a sound: for a clock ticking, an electrical humming, for anything from inside that prosaic trailer indicating life, security precautions. Maybe somebody slept inside, arms wrapped around a sawed-off twelve-gauge shotgun full of double-ought buck loads. Or perhaps a pair of Indian king cobras came wrapped around the idol to protect it from infidels. Then again, Nikita Smatterling and his underlings might simply have wrapped the whole kit and caboodle in a pink cloud for safekeeping. In fact, most probably, they figured the Hanuman's safety was ensured by its own positive vibes.

Circling the battered red-and-orange trailer, Joe inspected the padlocked doors. He reached out to touch the mammoth steel contraption doing the job . . . but stayed his hand, paranoid—abruptly—about fingerprints. Suppose Tribby and Ralph slunk over here tonight and absconded with the goods? It'd be typical of his luck that the one clue cops could extract from the empty, shattered vehicle at the bottom of a ravine would be a single Miniver fingerprint on the lock!

A steel cable, probably a relic from the Clarion, Ohio, caper, still packaged the trailer. A large metal ring, such as a gymnast might use, poked up from intersecting cable strands at the center of the U-Haul roof. No doubt they had used an immense grappling hook to make the connection when they whisked the statue away from the previously airlifted hoosegow in that soybean field. And Tribby wanted to swoop down like James Bond on this field in a Floresta bubblecopter. . . .

HELICOPTER HEAVIES HEIST HANUMAN! MINIVER MANGLED
BY MONSTER HOOK DURING MANEUVERS!

In the grass beneath the U-Haul, some fruit was cooking . . . or anyway, absorbing the kind of vibes it needed to become prasad—celestial radiation. Joe wondered: did Hanuman freaks with pacemakers have to steer clear of potent statues?

Stooping, he spitefully selected a heavy peach, bouncing it a few times in his palm, liking the heft of it. As his teeth sank in, would lightning bolts erupt from the sky directly overhead? Or would a bestial voice, with tantalizingly human undertones, issue forth in a growl from the U-Haul's interior? Tempting the fates, Joe took a healthy bite. Sweet juice dribbled over his chin . . . and a thousand owls hooted, frogs croaked, crickets uncorked a symphony of dazed screeks, the moon slid behind a cloud. Sudden thunderheads coagulated and clotted over the sacred mountain: nature prepared to go bananas.

In Joe's mind, that is. Outwardly, his chomp provoked nothing more delirious than another inquisitive and slightly demanding whinny from Geromino, who conquered his temerity and clomped forward, seriously interested in a piece of the action.

Well, why not?

Three delicious apples later, the horse burped appreciatively, whisked some misbegotten moon-struck fly off his haunch, and retreated, allowing digestive juices to have at it unmolested.

His palm placed against the scratched metal of the U-Haul, Joe waited in vain for a vibration. While he waited, he tried to assess where he was at. A few crickets chirped: he missed the katydids from his youth. And where oh where were all the whippoorwills of yesteryear? And the *fireflies*? If God was so god-awful good, how come She couldn't invent fireflies above six thousand feet? Would his children never know the ecstasy of gamboling through thick dewy grass in their kiddy feet chasing the blinking little buggers through sweet muffling currents of nocturnal air?

As if in answer to his prayers, a teeny-weeny star plummeted out of the sky, halted its descent right above Geronimo, and languidly floated toward Joe, blinking lazily. The horse tossed his head, emitting a puzzled, guttural harrumph. Joe was so surprised his jaw fell open, and he gaped, thoroughly astounded. In fact, for a few seconds it was as if his limbs had been frozen by some sort of extraterrestrial stun-gun: he couldn't move, his heart stopped, his body experienced a sensation that seemed akin to what he might have felt had somebody punched

an air needle into his belly button and commenced pumping
him full of helium. A hit of euphoria, mixed with terror, clobbered his brain . . . then, casual as you please, the minuscule
neon insect floated into his open mouth and lodged in his throat.

Joe doubled over, coughing, gagging, trying to expectorate.
Spooked, Geronimo galloped away. Joe shook his head, flailed
at his mouth with his tongue, dropped to one knee, and thrust
an index finger between his choppers, frantically digging for
the obstreperous bug. For a second or two, he thought he might
die. "Holy shit!" he croaked. *"I don't believe it!"*

Then he managed to cough the thing free. With thumb and
forefinger, he plucked it off his tongue. And knelt in the grass,
frowning at the slimy, black, mangled lump on his finger, trying
to make out its surviving features in the silvery moonlight.

"This just didn't happen," he whispered in dismay.

But it would certainly teach him to swagger around cavalierly devouring somebody else's prasad!

"Psst . . . *Miniver!*"

Joe jumped, spun around, and, had he been packing a rod,
would for sure have slapped leather and drilled the surrounding
obscurity like a wildcat oilman in the east Texas petroleum
fields, circa 1930.

Instead, however, he found himself face to face in the gloom
with the diminutive, braceleted accountant known as Roger
Petrie. Against his black turtlenecked chest, a silver cross glowed
phosphorescently.

"Jesus, Roger—you scared me!"

"Why are you feeding their fruit to a horse?"

"Why are you creeping around here like some kind of lugubrious Dracula? Planning to filch the monkey and hold it for
ransom to raise bread to hire a West Coast mouthpiece to keep
you out of leg-irons when the legal apparatus of this godforsaken state starts snuffling in the garbage of your embezzlement
and water-rights affairs?"

Oh, that silvery dancing tongue! When he was hot he was
hot!

Taken aback, Roger said, "Where did you hear that?"

"Oh, hey please." Now that his initial terror had passed,
Joe practically gloated. For this was one buzzard at his own

level he knew he could keelhaul. "You know this town. Scott Harrison floats a double sawbuck into escrow lining up that H_2O Cobey promised you for doctoring Skipper's books, and the great pinball machine in the sky over Hija Negrita Mountain flashes a giant TILT that even astronomers at Mount Palomar come in their pants over."

"Very funny. Who's writing your gags?"

"Would you believe Cobey Dallas? Skipper Nuzum? The Tarantula of Chamisaville?"

"Seriously, Joe. I didn't come here for you to mock me."

"I'm tired, Roger. All the convolutions surrounding these monkey maneuvers have got me down."

"Me too—I can honestly sympathize. It's getting out of hand. Nobody knows whose side anyone is on anymore. All the traditional loyalties have gone down the drain."

"So you're here to make me an offer I can't refuse?"

"Sarcasm, Joe, is the cheapest form of humor. You don't need to put me down just because I'm a small fry."

"Okay, what's the deal? Cobey sent you? Or Skipper? Joe B. threatened castration unless you figured out how to stop me before I cut off my nose to spite my face by blowing the lid off everybody's illegal finaglings to do Eloy out of this choice piece of real estate?"

"You insult me, man, but I'll ignore it for the moment. More important considerations are afoot."

"Don't tell me, lemme guess. Cobey knows you're a double agent, but he can't alienate you because once Skipper hauls him into court, his survival, vis-à-vis your testimony, depends on influencing you to perjure yourself—probably by threatening to squeal on your deal with Scott Harrison re the water rights. Plus what Skipper doesn't know, but Cobey probably does (thanks to a careful review of your handiwork), is that you've been skimming off the embezzlement into your own account, hoping to zoom unsuspectingly out of nowhere to grab this land for yourself before anybody understands how it happened. Only problem is, word recently leaked out that Scott got cold feet once he heard Skipper had plans to spear Cobey and you into the bargain in order to cover his own tracks. So you need a new alliance, and here I am: Mr. Patsy on the half shell."

"That's a farfetched synopsis. What kind of drugs are you taking?"

"Fair enough: make me a liar. You wandered by simply to wish me good luck in the upcoming holocaust."

"Are you quite finished, Joe? Because if you've gotten all this snide bile off your chest, I'd like to say something."

"Speak, memory."

"It's very simple. I think Skipper's prepared to let both Cobey and me take a rap. He even met with Scott Harrison today, probably because Scott realized Skipper's jig was up unless he forgot his own selfish interests and joined the big boys."

"Does Cobey realize you were reporting his embezzlements to Skipper and getting paid for it?"

"That's a lie and a gross fabrication."

"So proceed."

"There's not much more to tell. The Hanumans are stymied because Eloy's in love with you at this juncture, and the last hope for this land to survive intact is before it's out of his hands. Scott Harrison is blocked because Skipper's threatening to tell the bar about his deal with me. Cobey can't make a move, really, because the second he does, Skipper will initiate proceedings to have him thrown in jail. I'm in trouble because I worked with all three of them, performing illegal gambits. You can't get to first base because the dope scam is preposterous, and lethal into the bargain. And anyway, even if you could manage it, you'd have to unload the land to pay off your ex-wife. But I think I have a solution of sorts."

"Mainly . . . ?"

"We form a partnership."

"Roger, save your breath."

"No, wait. You give me the coke—I can step on it heavy and fence what looks like the entire package to Natalie Gandolf for twelve Gs, while retaining at least half the stuff to make a killing elsewhere—maybe in Boulder . . . I know some people there. With the twelve Gs, I can cover myself in Skipper's books, so that when he lowers the boom on me and Cobey, I'll be clean as a whistle. Meanwhile, we step on the other half of your cocaine and market it for the full price, split fifty-fifty between us. The proceeds should be enough to buy out Eloy Suchandsuch, and we split the land down the middle. How does that grab you?"

"No."

"Why?"

"You're crazier than all the rest of them. We could get killed."

"I don't think you understand, Joe. Plans like this work. You have to be bold. It's how the world goes round."

"Sure, but I have a better idea. Lemme run this up a flagpole, see if you salute it. There's a million dollars worth of insurance on this monkey god—we'll pinch the thing and hold it for ransom. I know a guy who pilots helicopters. What we'll do is swoop down, snatch it with a grappling hook, fly it off to the Midnight Mountains, and drop it into one of the Little Baldy Bear lakes."

Roger blurted, "Aw, shit man—now *you're* crazy."

❧

By flashlight, Diana was reading a copy of *I, Claudius*. Joe mumbled "Hello," and collapsed among her tattered blankets, old ski jackets, and dirty bluejeans.

"What happened to you?"

"What *didn't* happen to me is more like it. Man, am I bushed."

"I heard all hell broke loose in the Prince of Whales."

"The Prince of Whales?" Joe had trouble remembering. Events clattered around in his fatigued noggin with kaleidoscopic caprice. How had the day commenced? Where had he spent most of his time? A police officer had pointed a cannon at his head. He had teetered emotional millimeters from prematurely ending his blithering stay on the face of this tattered globe. Blood, bandages, incoherent squabbling, downright biblical confusion. Joe Bonatelli had squashed a grapefruit. Had Nancy or Heidi claimed to be pregnant? Who had a broken nose? And had he caught trout with Tribby, or only dreamed of escaping that traffic jam? What had they planned to do with the cocaine, if anything? Or had Heidi really meant what she said about the rubber suit and a snorkel?

"What happened in the Prince of Whales, Diana?"

"Depends on whose rendition you take for the gospel."

"I'm all ears." Joe stretched out, enormously relieved to be off his feet. He wriggled his shoulders into her raggle-taggle bedding; his aching muscles whimpered gratefully. He cleared his throat, ridding last vestiges of that arcane glow bug.

"Darlene Johnson says you threw a plate at my old friend,

Angel Guts, and he stabbed you three times before Nikita
Smatterling and his retinue of cosmic gangsters broke it up.
She claims they rushed you to the hospital on the brink of
death. But when I called there, my friend Gail Jackson said
nobody ever checked you in."

"I didn't arrive until later."

"Gail did say something interesting, however. This afternoon, when she went to give Ephraim Bonatelli his juice, he
wasn't around. One of those inflatable Japanese sex dolls occupied his bed instead."

Joe nodded stupidly and blotted out implications of that
bubblecopter landing in Joe Bonatelli's backyard.

Diana continued: "When I stopped by the Cinema Bar to
see if Roger Petrie had any houses for rent on his bulletin
board, he said that you and Egon Braithwhite had tipped over
three tables and beaten Angel Guts half to death with catsup
bottles. Then, when the police came, you and Egon and Spumoni Tatarsky threw a cop through the plate-glass window,
and wound up being arrested for violating ten thousand laws
and ordinances. But, of course, when I checked at the jail,
they hadn't heard of you either."

"You know, I came within an inch of having my brains
blown out this evening." And then he remembered: the bus
was still sitting there, blocking ambulances, gathering traffic
tickets, and, no doubt, infuriating Officer Whosamadig, the
Fastest Gun in the West. Joe's heart did a forward two-and-a-
half with a full twist, and entered the water down there splash-
lessly.

"Mimi McAllister had the best version of the day. She said
that after Angel Guts vivisected you with his Bowie knife, you
crawled outside and were run over by a garbage truck. She
insisted your body had already been flown back to Rhode Island
for burial."

"Why Rhode Island? I've never even visited there."

"She mentioned a burial at sea. But that's not all—dig this.
Rumor has it plans are afoot to steal the Hanuman, make it
disappear, and collect the insurance."

"Oh yeah? Who's doing the stealing?"

"Mimi wasn't sure. It's pretty convoluted. Somebody thought
maybe even Nikita Smatterling is in on the play. Apparently,
that writer—what's her name—Iréné somebody, actually wrote
a scenario for the ripoff. The idea being to create an adventure

for her book that'd make it sell like hot cakes, and bring in revenues to the Simian Foundation hand over fist."

"How do they plan to pull off the scam?"

"You won't believe this. But apparently they intend to hijack it, using a Forest Service helicopter piloted by Ephraim Bonatelli, and drop it into a high-country lake until the insurance is collected and the heat's off."

"Is it only this town that's crazy? Or is all of America gaga?"

"What *really* happened at the Prince of Whales, Joe?" Shyly, Diana touched his shoulder.

"I don't even know." Joe frowned, trying to recall. "Egon kept shouting at me in that phony lingo—why does he pick on me? Everybody was flogging me because Michael plugged Nancy's monkey. Then all of a sudden your ex-sugar daddy came flying through the air like a Polish Superman hoping to slit my throat. So I ran."

"You poor misunderstood little boy." She hunched over beside him. Their hips touched. On her elbows, gazing down at his face, she pursed her lips thoughtfully and quietly shook her head.

He touched her cheek. "Well, at least you're beautiful."

"You don't have to brown my nose. I know what I am. I have an interesting face, but that's all."

"Hey, you should lighten up on yourself sometime. Learn to just flow with it."

Gently, she poked a finger into his chest. "I do all right. I can take care of myself."

"You and your gun and your terror of men."

"I'm not afraid of you anymore. You're nice. You may be the most gentle man I ever met. I was so startled when you didn't slug me last night. Anybody else and I would have awakened this morning without any teeth."

"Well, now you know. Beneath this fierce exterior there beats a heart of molten marshmallows."

"You don't even have a fierce exterior." She drew aimless little patterns on his chest: his penis tingled. "You know what you look like to me?"

"I couldn't guess."

"You're like somebody who simply wants to be a good guy, but you know that good guys finish last. So you try to fool people by acting tough. But underneath you're nothing but a whimsical child. And you're all perplexed inside because you know you're supposed to act like a grown-up but you don't *feel* like a grown-up. Of course, constantly you pray that no-body finds out, because once they discover you're not a mature person they'll skin your ass and hang it from a belfry."

"Oh, I dunno." Joe allowed himself to grow lazy despite the nagging image of a misparked bus in the back of his mind.

"I do."

Diana leaned forward. Her lips dangled tantalizingly above his face for a moment, then settled upon his mouth. Such pliable meat! Joe closed his eyes; his hands sought her breasts. Her tongue probed across his teeth. She backed off an inch and murmured, "I want to make love with you tonight. I'm really sorry about yesterday. But it's been so long since I could trust anybody."

"I don't know. Maybe it's easier not to make love. I'm all confused. Sometimes I think I'd rather be friends with women. I don't know how to be a good lover. Also, I don't think I want to lose my family."

"I can tell you desire me a lot, though."

"I know, but—"

Her mouth silenced him. They rolled together, back and forth, lazily rubbing up against each other's bodies. They bur-rowed about in the tangled bedding, licked each other's noses, and undressed slowly. Momentarily hovering above her, Joe was captivated by her fragile, opulent torso. Her pale throat curved like a plume of snow; luminescent white breasts flooded her chest and the biceps of arms clamped against her sides. What bewitching and achingly textured material! Moonlight, starlight, distant streetlamps—their auras filtered through the tent's transparent roof, laminating her skin in a frighteningly evocative radiance. The effect was so powerful, Joe almost cried, "I love you!" But he rejected it as he would have rejected his own doom. The visual image of her was so strong it threat-ened to cripple him, so Joe closed his eyes and sank slowly onto the woman. Holding her tight, he stayed inserted, scarcely moving, aching to break down and destroy his life by promising her the moon. How wonderful it would be to give in, accepting another human being absolutely without strings attached. Melt-ing into her body, into her soul, dissolving...merging ...emotionally readjusting...until all the anger, suspicion, paranoia, game playing, jealousy, selfish hungers, greed, and stupidity evaporated, and nothing but clarity remained.

"Oh," she whispered faintly, "how I love you."

"Don't say that." His voice was tiny.

"I can't help it."

"*Please* don't say that, Diana."

"I can't help it."

"But we hardly know each other. I don't love anybody."

"Yes you do. Whether you admit it or not, you love me."

"No ..."

"Yes."

"Oh help ..."

"It's all right. I'm here ... I'll take care of you."

Obviously, the only solution to his sexual gluttony was suicide. Warm snow fell through his body. He wanted an orgasm to seep through all his pores, caressing Diana's flesh, making it sprout goosebumps that would prickle back against him like soda bubbles. "I love you" rose in his throat, but he choked it back, determined to survive. She constricted her muscles, lovingly squeezing his cock.

"I'm not afraid anymore, Joe."

"I am."

"I know, but don't be. Everything is all right."

"You don't know anything."

"Yes I do. I'm wiser than you think."

Enveloped in wings, powdered in carnal down, locked in a babysweet embrace, Joe was touched by an angel's wand. His body puffed up and cried out for the blowsy fluff of satiation. If he could only let go, they would drift through the apocryphal land of Dreams Come True. It was so close. Almost intoxicated by fear and longing, Joe dared not move even the chromosomes in a molecule. An orgasm wailed for release; his testicles ached; he wanted to give up and accept the rare and exquisite mood of such vibrant despair, such powerful and radiant and melancholy blues.

Perfection of sorrow, perfection of grace? Eyes open, Joe regarded a hand—his or hers? Actually, it belonged to both of them. Joe was still hard inside her. Tears bloomed at his eyes. An incredibly strong, undiluted sensation of orgasm tarried in his penis, pulsing like a quasar—but he could not, he would not, let it go.

A moment later, Joe brooded over this strange woman. She

reminded him of Thomas Hart Benton's *Persephone*. Moonlight glistened provocatively against the damp curves of her belly, breasts, and shoulders. Her throat was caught in aching beauty. Despondently, he viewed her as some pure and unnatural princess spirited into his prosaic life from a long-lost Xanaduvian region. Her skin had been pampered with tepid mosses for generations; her body *was* her soul.

Joe contemplated Diana as he might a work of art. For this suspended moment her perfection was overwhelming, intimidating. Giddy laziness invaded his muscles. He breathed oxygen strained through rarefied champagne filters. Sorrowfully, he relaxed. He felt beautiful, also extraordinarily melancholic. A heavenly minute ensued as his eyes, trained on her poetic form, gradually unfocused. Where had he been transported to all of a sudden—Anami Lok? All colors and objects ran together, until Joe visualized her as a fuzzy indeterminate pristine glow in the center of an infinitely mollifying universe. There was no need to make sense out of things, or to feel responsibilities or obligations. Something had cast a spell, and he was bewitched. He suffered from those old Nirvana Blues. If his life were to end right now, he probably would be crowned a saint. They'd fly him—in a presidential jet, no less—to go on view (for a fortnight) at the Vatican, before he was embalmed, placed in a glass sarcophagus, and retired to permanent public display in the basilica of Saint Peter's.

"The sweetest fuck..." she whimpered, falling asleep (and completing the phrase from her dreams), "that I ever had."

Where *were* those keys?

It resembled a long-distance telephone connection with Kabul: "Joe? Are you in there?" *Fzzt... crackle... ping...*

"Huh? Whuzzat? Who...?"

"Is that you?" *Burp... gurgle... glug...*

"Who?"

"Joe Miniver." *Chakata... chakata... chakata...*

"Uh, yeah, right away. Who's that?"

"It's me." *Drone... hum... clickety... clickety...*

"Oh." Which me? Floundering like a child caught in ocean breakers, Joe flailed upward into a poor semblance of groggy rationality. His brain was detached, lost, adrift. He lunged for the surface, stroking frantically toward the light, and banged his nose against the bottom. "I'm asleep." His words were made unintelligible by muffling cobwebs. "What time is it? Where—?"

"Can I come in?"

"No. Wait a minute!" He awoke.

Stretched out nude in a nest of rumpled blankets and old clothes, Diana looked tragically clean and natural—a perfect little girl.

"Who is it?"

"It's *me*. I came to take you back."

"Back where?" Who the hell was talking? Several gears in his head were stuck. The connection eluded him.

"Back to the hospital," she said.

"The hospital?" A sickness in the family? A loved one about to kick the bucket? Was somebody having a baby?

"Are you all right?" she asked solicitously. "You sound funny."

He felt funny. Sleep held onto him with savage tenacity. *Morpheus as Epoxy!*

"Yeah . . . I'm fine . . . sure. Hi."

"Hi. Are you positive I can't come in?"

"Well, I, uh, I mean, you know—right?"

"Joe, don't be silly."

"Wait a minute . . . I'll come out. Is it nighttime or daylight? What day is this?" Dizzily, he crabbed onto his knees, crawled forward, and poked his head through the flaps into a night as dark as Russian owl hoots. Staggering upright, he wavered incoherently, a veritable senile oaf.

"We can't go if you're naked, Joe."

At first, even as he peered through the dark, Joe could not connect her face to a personality and a name. Then finally his brain woke up. "Oh, it's you, Nancy. Jesus. . . ."

"Who did you think it was?"

"I dunno. I'm riddled with sleep. I feel like a geriatric nitwit. Maybe I inhaled a drug. . . ."

"It's only ten o'clock."

"So what are you doing here?"

"I came to drive you back so you can find the keys and fetch the bus."

"The bus?"

"It's over at the hospital. Joey, what's the matter with you?"

"Mom," a child called from back in the driveway, "I wanna go home!"

"In a minute, Bradley. You hush now, dear."

Joe said, "Lemme walk around a little." He shook his head and slapped himself. Then, stepping gingerly in his bare feet, he advanced onto the garden area spaded over that afternoon. Earth, cold and damp, crumbled between his toes. What had happened to the cocaine? He couldn't remember, but a sense of disaster rode his aching bones. Joe shivered, accepting the jolt, and became a semi-intelligent, partially functioning human being.

Joe dressed, and got in her Bug. Heading out the driveway, Nancy said, "We're planning a healing tomorrow at daybreak for Sasha."

"You're *what*?" Joe stared into Eloy's front field, where the Hanuman U-Haul, leafed in misty moonlight, glowed eerily. Geronimo's soft, unhappy whinny hurt his heart.

Nancy reached over, tousling his hair. "You're funny, Joe. You're the most comical guy I know."

"What exactly is meant by a 'healing'?"

"I'm a member of a healing group. We've decided to get together especially to heal Sasha. It's very simple."

From the back seat, Bradley broke his sourpuss pose. "I always hated Sasha, Mom. I hope he dies."

She chose to ignore him. "Joe, is there anything wrong with a healing?"

"It's stupid."

"Why?"

"For starters, Sasha is a really creepy monkey."

"A purely subjective opinion."

"He's right, Mom. Once Tofu Smatterling and me were building a castle in the sandbox, and Sasha hopped down and kicked apart the castle. Then he made a caca where it had been."

"You see?" Joe grinned smugly. "Anybody who knew that monkey hated its guts."

"That's because most people don't really understand what Sasha is about."

"You bought him in a pet store, Nancy. He isn't the Son of God."

"All of us—creatures, all things—are the sons of God."

"And daughters."

"Granted."

"Well, where does it say in the Bible that Jesus Christ shat on sand castles?"

Patiently, she handled his belligerence. "You realize, of course, that you are completely missing the point." Her smile was so aggravatingly sympathetic and tolerant that he wished to erase it with a bolo punch. "And missing it deliberately, I might add, just to provoke me."

"No, seriously. I don't understand. Michael plugs with his BB gun a dime-store ape that's into pornographic antics and child abuse, and suddenly my kid is a pariah being hunted down and mugged by gangs of the Cosmic Mafia's offspring. I don't get it at all."

"That was very unfortunate. It's because they were children."

"I still don't understand."

"Unfortunately, that's because you're not a spiritual person."

Bradley insistently tapped his mother's shoulder. "Remember what happened last year, Mom?"

"I don't think I care to hear it, dear."

"Remember when Mary Beth Eisley came over and Sasha threw a rock that hit her on the head."

"That kind of story right now has no positive effect on anything at all."

He continued whapping her shoulder. "But that's not all, Mom. Don't you remember? She cried a whole lot, and got real tired, so you put her to bed for a nap. But while she was asleep, Sasha sneaked through the window with a spoon he stoled from the kitchen, and he jammed the handle into one of the holes in her nose and made it bloody."

"Bradley!"

"But that's not all, either. Remember? He jammed it in so far you were afraid to take it out by yourself. So we hadda drive her to the hospital with a spoon stuck up her nose."

To rollicking Joe, Nancy said, "I fail to see what's so humorous."

"A spoon rammed up her nose by a monkey? You fail to see the *humor*?" Joe couldn't help it, he sputtered and ho-ho'd until the tears fell like rain.

Spurred on by his show of approval, Bradley reached into his sack for another yarn.

"Remember the time Sasha shoved a banana down our toilet? It got jammed in there somewhere, and the plumbers had to take the toilet out of the bathroom into the yard and push the banana out with a Roto-Rooter?"

"Bradley, I'm going to ask you not to talk about Sasha anymore, sweetie."

But the kid was on a hot streak. He tapped Joe's shoulder. "Did my mom ever tell you about the time Sasha carried my football onto the roof and dropped it down the chimney when we had a fire going in the fireplace? It exploded and blew flames all over the living room. A curtain caught on fire, and our house almost burnt down."

"That's what I like," Joe wheezed between derisively merry gasps. "A real spiritual monkey."

"Bradley, we really don't need this kind of talk right now. You're exaggerating anyway."

"No I'm not, Mom. Honest. You know that. Remember when Rufus was over at our house once, and we were having peanut-butter sandwiches and Kool-Aid for lunch, and Sasha hopped onto the table and pissed in the Kool-Aid?"

Joe slapped his thighs, banged the dashboard, and nearly swooned, rocked by gales of laughter. "Hey, wow, dig that crazy monkey! Oh Lord, oh Lord! I do hope he survives! That monkey should get a medal! Where do I sign up for the healing group?"

"You're welcome to participate, if you want."

"I *gotta* participate. A whole bunch of people are actually going to meet for the purpose of salvaging the soul of this little monster? Ooo-ee, baby, ooo-ee!"

"First of all, Sasha's not a monster. Second of all, if you're going to mock the proceedings, I'm afraid I can't invite you."

"I won't say a word." Joe sobered quickly. "I'll keep my mouth shut, I won't even smirk, nothing. I'll be so good you won't even know me."

"All right. I guess so then. Well, here we are. . . ."

"Wait a minute." Joe blinked. "How did we drive from Eloy's to the parking lot without detouring around twelve thousand construction sites?"

"If you don't want to be hassled by them, you aren't. That's all. It's simple."

The bus hadn't moved since Joe deserted it. A barrage of parking tickets and traffic citations had accumulated underneath

the left-hand wiper. Under the right-hand blade, an evilly
scrawled note on scented pink paper said:

> Your hours are numbered,
> Miniver!

"I already searched everywhere for those damn keys," Joe
said dispiritedly. "We'll never find them. Heidi probably
chucked them into the bushes. Or, in her confusion, flushed
them down the toilet."

"The trouble with you, Joe, is that you have a negative
mindset. If you really wished to find the keys, and thought
about them positively, you could make them materialize."

"I bet."

"It works. Don't knock it if you haven't tried it."

Joe climbed through the bus window, and pawed through
all the garbage again, wondering as he did so: Why haven't I
cleaned this car? Why is it always a mess? Why must I always
spend twenty minutes searching for a simple tool? What is the
matter with me that I can't maintain order, avoiding all this
aggravation? To a T, he resembled that "Peanuts" character,
Pigpen, the kid who automatically got dirty even while standing
completely still in a sanitized and hermetically sealed room
immediately after a bath.

Nancy stubbed her toe against something that jangled. "Oh,
here they are."

"You're kidding!"

They dangled from her fingertips, glittering like diamonds
and rubies. Above them sparkled her eyes: beautiful, serene.

She licked her lips. Mercury-vapor light gave them a luster evoking nubile high-school girls from a million years ago.

"You're weird," he whispered, accepting them through the window.

"I'm just an ordinary person. You think I'm weird because you don't understand some crucial truths, that's all."

"I'll follow you home, Missus Ryan."

"That would be neat."

Ay, dig that loving warmth pouring from her eyes and her pursed lips! He had a hard-on and wanted to grab her and fling her down roughly onto the macadam or across her Beetle's hood, letting her know just how grateful he was for the vixen in her that could arouse such vital lusts.

"Mom," Bradley whined abrasively. "I'm hungry."

Oh weren't they all!

ॐ

Ever the relentless sleuth, on his way out Joe stopped by the hospital's north wing. Only a bed of bedraggled tulips, through which he tiptoed, stood between him and the window of Ephraim Bonatelli's room. Though dropped, the Venetian blinds had not been entirely closed: slits of yellow light fell across his face like inverse jail-bar stripes. Straining for one more inch of height, Joe peeped inside. . . .

And gulped.

"Holy sh-*tit*sky!"

Joe's nose, pressed against the cool glass, tingled at such a sight. His blood ran icy in veins that had had their fill of nerve-shattering trauma for one day. Beads of chilly sweat sprouted across his forehead. Muscles in his buttocks contracted uncomfortably, as if a sadistic phantom were probing at his anus with a peacock feather. His testicles said, "Ouch!"

"Son of a bitch," Joe muttered huskily, and he backed off, instinctively hunched.

Time to change his name, grow a beard, scour the tips of his fingers with acid to destroy the prints, locate a skilled engraver to falsify his passport, and purchase a one-way ticket to Rio!

Instead, and more in keeping with his current resources, Joe practically duck-waddled back to his bus, slithered around to the driverside door making sure that his body provided no

targetable silhouette, and eased up behind the wheel. But when
he reached for the ignition key, a voice said, "You start this
thing, dingbat, and they'll hear you, they'll come barreling out
of that room like bloodthirsty gangbusters!"

So he wrenched it into neutral, descended and, grunting
inaudibly, heaved with all his might, pushing the bus another
thirty yards along the flat pavement before entering, turning it
over, and racing uptown to the La Tortuga Bar for something
to quiet his nerves and, hopefully, to blot out the latest atrocity
molesting his overloaded, ingenuous little brain before he sought
further solace in Nancy Ryan's everlovin' arms.

                              ⮧

        But fate promotes strange tricks on her chosen pro-
vocateurs.

Bound for Nancy Ryan and, he had thought, for yet one
more round of sexual hijinks before calling it quits and retreat-
ing to the safe haven of hearth and home, Joe detoured into
the plaza for that quick belt of alcoholic stimulant to calm his
fraying innards.

Clogged from his ass to his tonsils with qualms, Joe nevertheless tried to hide his blossoming panic by blithely tripping
the light fantastic into the La Tortuga. He settled gaily at the
deserted bar and ordered a triple daiquiri, straight up, with an
extra glass of neat tequila on the side.

And then, in line with the script guiding recent events (and
leading, no doubt, to ultimate censure, exile, deprivation, disease, and total humiliation), Joe felt a presence at his elbow,
a perfumed breath behind his ear. Expecting eternity, he heard
instead a thickly accented voice say, "Hello there. What is a
nice boy like you doing in a place like this?"

Iréné Papadraxis.

Talk about the fickle and convoluted motives behind destiny's incomprehensible rationale!

But to then coherently dissect the mysterious logic that could
lead a fellow from that apocalyptic near-orgasm with Diana,
through those powerful juicy cravings for Nancy, to finding
himself in the buff only tantalizing inches away from the rosy
nipples of a Hungarian Greek in Skipper Nuzum's heated swimming pool, was beyond Joe's powers of analytical mumbo
jumbo.

Iréné said, "Well, here we are."

Joe nodded, thunderstruck. The exquisitely tiled pool they had to themselves. Underwater lights accented the sensual emerald undulations. The impossibly fluffy grass of a thick green lawn had only recently been mowed; the scent of fresh cuttings was intoxicating. Weeping-willow branches languorously brushed against the manicured carpet. Thirty feet away, a dim row of grottoesque lights glowed through the sliding glass doors of the ballroom area of the otherwise darkened mansion. Sleepy jazz music tinkled through the air: vibes, a husky sax, bass notes that advanced like lion paws carefully traversing the greensward. Naturally, in the obscenely clear and bright heavens, a billion stars laughed silently. The orange moon was so big and pregnant it seemed to have been huffed into being by a mysterious oboe.

There you go again, Heidi said. *What in hell does that mean?*

Mean? Who cared. Here I am, thirty-eight-year-old Joseph Whosamidig Miniver, snatched from the craw of deadly dangers to suddenly and finally encounter myself at the culminating moment of every *Playboy*-reading pud pounder's macho dreams. Like magic, this wishy-washy Marxist garbage man and roué manqué—in One Fell Swoop—had landed himself at the apex of capitalist erotic expectations. For such an experience as this Sammy Glick had slit throats, Scrooge McDuck had pinched pennies, Citizen Kane had accumulated empire. For such an experience as this a Possum Trot shoe salesman bought a Georgia lottery ticket, a Polish immigrant mortgaged his future to buy a tenement, a big-nosed little boy from Beaver Falls, Pennsylvania, spent eighteen hours a day spiraling a football through a swinging tire. And yet he, Joe Miniver, after only four days on the prod, had simply taken a desperate turn into the plaza, and toppled down a rabbit hole into a fantasy where the sum total of all his sexual longings collided, delivering up that for which he had often plaintively murmured he would have sold his soul to Satan to obtain. And wonder of all wonderful wonders, apparently it wasn't going to cost him a nickel!

Hard-ons?

Don't make him laugh. What was that thing twanging straight out from his groin down there in the undulating emerald if not something comparable to the best baseball hickory that North Carolina could supply, and pointed with the unerring instinct of a blue-chip field retriever at the holy grail waiting there behind her tangled bush?

Oh no, not to worry. Now that he was miraculously *here*, this boy was not about to blow it, not on your life, not for all the tea in China, no sirree!

This one was as good as signed, sealed, delivered, cashed, receipted, stuffed, and hung on the wall. *Oh my God, Joe, you're incredible!*

You better believe it!

It was so corny, he laughed. Peals of his happy tune scattered like doves with whistling wings into the fragrant night.

"Why are you laughing?"

"I can't help it. This is a fairy tale. I feel ten years old."

Her hand, a hungry cruising trout, glided through the water.

"*This* doesn't feel like you're ten years old."

Joe wished to savor it as long as possible. He needed to absorb this most perfect body he had ever seen. He wanted the mere sight of her to caress him until he could stand it no longer. He wanted it to be like abstaining hungrily from attacking a marvelous dessert. A fine mist rose off the warm water. Joe remained immobile, but for the hands at his sides that lazily paddled the tepid water, just as a fish laconically moves its fins while balancing in one place.

When her fingers closed over his enormous war club, Joe didn't budge.

"Nice," she said.

"Mmmm."

"How come you're grinning so wildly? I've never seen anything like it."

"I can't help it, Iréne. This is incredible."

HUMBLE CAMEL DRIVER RECEIVES AUDIENCE AT THE WHITE
HOUSE! KING DESERTS HIS THRONE FOR COMMONER!
IMPOVERISHED SHEPHERD DISCOVERS BABY JESUS IN
BETHLEHEM MANGER!

For how long—call it forever?—did they stall, her fingers softly clutching his dork as the mollifying waters of his dream lapped against her ripest bosom?

She cocked her head. "Are you all right?"

"Am I all *right?*"

"You seem strange."

"I'm happy. I'm euphoric."

"I'm so glad." Her voice lacked a little something, though her eyes seemed friendly enough. Faintly, Joe suspected that the intensity he felt for the moment was not totally mutual. She'd been here before. She was accustomed to the setting, and to that mammoth thing in her hand. Quite possibly the experience was old hat.

Such thoughts dissipated with the mists. After a ten-minute eternity, Joe ceremoniously lifted one hand and cupped one breast as if it were a sacred chalice. Her nipple nibbled at his fingertip. And Joe feared that all the hunger and anticipation of pleasure accumulating inside his humble salt-of-the-earth body might cause him to burst.

Or else lightning, inadvertently released from his penis before they reached dry land, might electrocute them both!

"My God," he murmured.

Speaking inaudibly, Iréné dropped her eyelids and began to rhythmically squeeze his prick. They drifted together, embracing. Eyes wide open, Joe tilted his head, scanning the heavens. He expected comets, shooting stars, a rare silver night bird, the explosion of a leftover firework that had been hanging in weightless ether for a year anticipating this moment.

Urgently, she clasped him tightly and rubbed his erection between her straddling legs. He tried to crush her against him so that she couldn't move. "Wait, Iréné . . . just a few more seconds . . . we've got plenty of time."

"I need you." Her hips were grinding. "Come on, let's go inside."

Inside? People had been shot for lesser heresies!

"It's okay. Just a little bit longer. I want you out here."

She nipped and slurped at his neck, his collarbone. When her teeth sank into his shoulder he winced and almost cried "ouch!" When she spoke, her voice had changed. Huskily, a trifle humorously, she demanded: "I want you. I can't wait any longer."

"Oh please." Joe fought off something that was happening to him—the unthinkable: a tiny bit of disintegration around the fringes of his Perfect Moment. "Let's not rush it."

"I want that big cock inside of me." *Ay, spare me such crudity!* The words, her tone of voice, hurt his ears. And here came more of the same: "I want you to fuck me with that iron dick until I scream. Do you think you can do that?"

"Oh don't talk right now. Let's just be quiet. . . ."

Her teeth again—"Ouch!" And fingernails—"Hey!" Joe had always mistrusted women who let their nails grow that long. Obviously, they rarely used their hands to a useful purpose.

"I want to consume you," she gasped theatrically. "Come on, let's go inside."

"I want to screw you here." Joe had difficulty keeping his voice seductive, cool, macho, unblemished by the first gust of panic goosepimpling his inner flesh. "Let's fuck in the water."

"I've got some amyl nitrate back in my room. I want to cop it while you ream me. You're so strong. God, it's so big I'm afraid you'll butcher me. There'll be blood all over the sheets."

Yuuucch!

"No it's not. It's only normal. I measured it once. It's just six and a half inches exactly. The American average."

She raised her mouth and began slobbering all over his lips, cheeks, chin. Her tongue-tip twirled into one nostril. "You're wrong, Joe. It's much bigger than that, I can tell. It's almost eight inches. It's a real peter. When we get inside I'm going to do everything to you. I can deep-throat it. I'm going to shove three fingers at once up your asshole. . . ."

Ouch again!

Joe drew back his head, trying to avoid her anaconda tongue. Her thighs churned around his erection . . . although it wasn't as hard as before. Incredibly, it was dying. "Don't talk dirty," he whispered. "You don't need to to arouse me like that."

Too late. She had entered a whacked-out trance. "I want you to come in my mouth, Joe. I want that fantastic shlong in my mouth right now, I want to drown in your sticky come. . . ."

"I don't think I ejaculate all that much semen. . . ."

"Ooooohhhhh those balls," she crooned ecstatically, wrenching them painfully. "They are so swollen with jism. I want you to smear it all over my tits. I want you to shoot it up my ass. I want you to shit on my stomach and rub it all over me. . . ."

Joe said, "Let's go into shallower water." He led her from the four-foot to the three-foot area. While she kept up her obscene patter, he guided her to the pool edge and got between her legs. But the thing was half-limp now, pathetically rubbery. And all the joyful and sexually urgent sensations had evaporated. In fact, if she kept it up, he knew that for certain—

egads!—the thing would die completely, and he'd be staring down the terrifying barrel of impotency.

Impotency!

"Not here." Iréné shook her head. "In my room. I've got some poppers. . . ."

Joe fiddled with himself. He pressed it into her thick pubic hair, felt for a hole with his fingers, but couldn't pry it open because it was dry and chalky—underwater? Yup, believe it or not, even underwater. Yet all his life he had thought. . . .

This was getting clumsy.

"Turn around." She obeyed, letting his hands manipulate her, even as she repeated: "Not here, Joe. It isn't comfortable." She shivered. "And besides, I'm cold."

"It's okay. Just let me . . ." Oh how had the romance and sensuality fled so abruptly? Desperately, he wanted to make love in the heated pool, under the stars, soothed by the weeping willow, enveloped in the redolence of freshly barbered Kentucky blue. Instead, frantically, Joe shoved his pathetic nub between her perfectly shaped buttocks, and humped away, attempted to revive it. His shame expanded. As the clumsy seconds ticked away, he felt increasingly like a man sweating in a glass booth on television, struggling to answer a sixty-four-thousand-dollar question. Teeth gritted, he silently begged God to take a break from such cruel pranks, allowing his humble servant on earth, Joseph Miniver, to reclaim that potent hard-on so that he could stab this gorgeous garbage-mouth before she ordered him, with November ice in her voice and eyes, to get lost.

But no such luck.

Sinking against her, Joe gave up. Reaching around, he apologetically enveloped her breasts. Attempting to sound at least lamely humorous, he admitted, "I lost it."

"So I noticed. *Now* can we go inside?"

As she departed the pool ahead of him, a soft lump sailed out of the darkness, landing in the water beside Joe. Startled, he heard a scurrying off in the bushes, a grunt, and scraping sounds as a largish person scaled a wall. And he knew, even before he gave it his attention, what the thing that bumped gently against his tummy would be.

Another stuffed, popeyed little monkey, of course. And in a note, protected by Saran Wrap, pinned to its furry potbelly, was the usual redundant admonition:

> If this had been a bomb, Joe,
> you'd be eating an eternity sandwich
> right now!

He had entered the pool raunchy, cool, and cocky—a real bad dude. He exited like a bedraggled kitten somebody halfheartedly had tried to drown. Yet in honor of the Stiff-Upper-Lip Theory of Existence, he maintained an ear-to-ear shit-eating grin—the most painful smile of his life.

"The water's too hot, I guess," he apologized.

Wrapped in purple terrycloth robes, compliments of the Nuzums, they hurried into the mansion.

"I didn't want it in that damn pool anyway. I tried to tell you."

An hour earlier, the wall-to-wall white lamb's-wool rug in the kitchen had triggered in Joe paroxysms of decadent ecstasy: such a thrill (unbeknownst to all those who'd listened to his quasi-Marxist patter) to experience total irresponsibility! But on the trip back his toes curdled against the lavish decadence as he slunk queasily through that citadel of imperialist corruption.

Her room was a lime-green sanctuary muffled by drapes and another precious carpet on the floor. Kneeling, Iréné pulled an airline satchel out from under the kingdom-sized waterbed. She zipped it open and rummaged through the contents, removing vials of pills, jars of ampules, packets of powder.

She said, "I hear you're trying to enter the dope racket. But I suppose it's just my luck you don't toot coke or anything, do you?"

Helplessly, Joe shook his head. He actually stammered as he asked, "Wh-where did you hear th-that?"

"Natalie told me you're sitting on five pounds of pure shit she's hoping to score for the party tomorrow night. With a load like that you could blow this silly little town to Alaska and back."

Morosely, Joe said, "Maybe you better tell Nancy that I think my . . . uh . . . ex-wife flushed it down the toilet this afternoon."

"You're kidding." Her jaw dropped.

"I don't know for sure. Maybe she's lying just to get my goat."

"Ray Verboten will kill you both."

"You know the man?"

"I met him this afternoon. What is a greenhorn like you doing trying to play in the big leagues? I had a friend in the Apple, his name was Toby. He got mixed up on the dealing end of some smack. You know what they did when he made an independent move on another man's turf?"

Though he felt like a character in a bad TV movie, Joe said, "What?"

"They gouged out his eyes, punctured his eardrums with knitting needles, shot him point-blank in the forehead with a 357 Magnum, cut off his head and his left hand, and dumped the entire mess on the Gansevoort Pier Halloween night, two years ago."

"I'll be darned."

"Well, excuse me a sec, will you? I gotta freshen up."

Iréné zipped into the bathroom. Hesitantly, Joe positioned himself in front of the four-paneled dressing-table mirror and gestured obscenely at his traitorous body. Yet, it didn't look bad. He had good biceps, only minor waist flab, and strong thighs. Though a tiny bit short, his legs were muscular. Same with his hands. He put one behind his back, testing a mono-appended look. His ears could have been smaller. But all in all, for thirty-eight, he looked okay. Not a stud, but no bleep, either. All of a sudden, however, out of a sheer idyll he seemed to be fashioning a disaster. Suppose—God forbid!—that this woman left believing him to be a nerd: impotent, unimaginative, square . . . maybe even—gasp!—gay? What kind of abysmally cruel overlording factotum out there could play such a joke on this feeble earthling?

FROM JAWS OF VICTORY, MINIVER SNATCHES SHAME, BLAME, DISGRACE, AND HUMILIATION! "I OFFERED HIM THE MOON BUT HE BLEW IT," SAYS FRUSTRATED SEX SYMBOL.

Not to mention, in the late-breaking editions:

MINIVER BODY, SANS CABEZA, LOCATED IN CHAMISAVILLE ALLEY! HEAD DISCOVERED BY CHILD IN PLAZA DRINKING FOUNTAIN! COPS CITE "TERRITORIAL DISPUTE" AMONG NARCOTICS SUPPLIERS! "HE TOLD ME TO FLUSH IT DOWN THE TOILET," SAYS WIDOW! LAWYER PAL BARELY SURVIVES MAULING BY TRAINED WILD ATTACK DOGS!

Iréné reappeared, smiling distantly. Extending a hand, she said, "Let's go." Her eyes were funny, wide open yet lopsided. Just as they settled onto the wonderful bed, Joe realized he was way out of his league with this woman, in this house, on this bed.

Her arms and legs enveloped him. "Now," she whispered, crudely coy, "we're going to get it on, you and me. Relax, lighten up, enjoy."

But how to relax with a head full of regrets and self-recriminations? Suppose Heidi actually had flushed the coke? She snagged his cock and jerked it roughly until Joe murmured, "Ouch, please don't." Self-consciously he tried to generate an erotic drive in himself by kissing her brutally, biting her lips, crushing her tits. Maybe they could sell Natalie a box of talcum powder and use the cash to fly to Brazil? She urged him on breathelssly: "That's it, come on big boy, hurt me with your teeth, I like that, uh-huh, that's it, bite me *harder*. . . ."

But the more he tried, the less he succeeded. His teeny nub down there had no feeling whatsoever: in fact, his entire abdomen had gone numb. It wasn't fun; nor romantic. Suppose that junta in Ephraim Bonatelli's hospital room chose to throw him off the Gorge Bridge instead? Or forced him at gunpoint to swallow four pounds of Pop Rocks, and then sat there, cackling, as his body exploded?

Desperately, Joe sucked on her breasts, splashed saliva against her belly, and spent five minutes tongue-gouging her vagina. *Enjoying yourself?* Heidi leered. *Birdy num-num, Joey?* Iréné writhed and jammed his face into her pussy, which was every bit as dry as he was limp. "Please, dammit, Joe, I want you to ram it in hard!"

Hard, already! Heather pointed a mocking finger at him: *Oh Daddy, you're just too weird!*

"In a minute." Joe surfaced, raising his face even with hers. "Can't we slow down and be quieter and more considerate? I need to be gentle." Tears had gathered at his eyes, but she could not notice. As soon as they commenced, Iréné had shut her eyes.

Incredulous, she said, "Gentle?"

"Just for a minute. I'll never get a stiff like this. It feels forced . . . and self-conscious. I'm sorry."

"Whatever you say. You're the boss."

"It'll be okay soon." Why wouldn't she open her eyes and

look at him? "I just have to get used to you. You're so different." All they needed was a wad of chewing gum in her mouth, and an electric light bulb overhead.

THE KILLERS KICKED IN THE DOOR, POLICE SOURCES SAY, AND OPENED FIRE WITH TOMMY GUNS, KILLING THEM BOTH!

"Is something the matter with me, Joe?"

"No, no, no. I'm just not used to you. You're very beautiful. And also the sexiest woman I've ever been with. You have an incredible body. I feel off-balance, that's all."

"Don't sweat it." Her hollow voice came from an insipid, drugged place. Almost feverishly, she toyed with his cock again. "This gig is duck soup."

Joe placed his fingers on hers to stay the painful hand job. What Bridge was this he was falling off of—the Verrazano-Narrows?

"Let me do you," she urged tensely. "Why are you so uptight?"

"I don't know...."

Joe gave up, lying back; he stared at the ceiling. Iréné kneeled over him and began to chew, suck, and lick. His heart swelled with a mixture of shame, sadness, despair. He wished to embrace Iréné, holding her protectively, convincing her that it was all right. To avoid enduring another second of this clumsy tragic scene he wanted to ask for her hand in marriage, suggest they have a child together, buy a cottage in Wilton, Connecticut, groom the kid for Exeter. *Oh Heather, Oh Michael, I hope you never grow up!*

"Come on," she muttered angrily. "I can arouse this bastard, I know I can. Everybody says I give incredible head."

Everybody says!

But she did. Her teeth never touched. She woggled him in her mouth, doing suction routines he couldn't believe. She had great teeth—braces as a child? They never nicked him. Tantalizingly, she tickled his nuts. And then she drilled one of those long expert fingers right up his ass.

Joe arched, released a silent howl, but somehow kept from slugging her. Every pain relay station in his body clanged out four alarms as she reamed his intestine and fellatiated his penis with superstar techniques.

COPS REVEAL GRECO-HUNGARIAN NOVELIST MOONLIGHTED
AS NARCOTICS HIT-PERSON!

Finally, Joe coughed out: *"Stop!"*

"No! Give me two more minutes! I know I can do it! *Relax!*"

"You can't," he sobbed. "I'm sorry." Latching onto her head, he forced her mouth away. At last her eyes flew open. Gasping, she blurted, "You . . . you gibbering *dumbbell!*"

"I'm really sorry. It's all my fault." His tears meant nothing to her. She was "out of it."

"Well, Jesus! Wouldn't you know it? If they gave out Academy Awards for bad luck I'd have a bathtub full of Oscars."

His foot wasn't inserted quite deep enough into his mouth, however. So Joe gave it a final shove. "It's crazy. This has never happened before."

The look she humiliated him with he richly deserved. "Thanks a lot, pal. You know, you got real class."

"I didn't mean . . ."

"I know what you meant. I've been around men."

"But . . ."

"Screw your 'buts,' Joe. Get dressed and clear out."

"But I can't leave like this. It's horrible. It was so wonderful out by the pool. I felt great."

"Be brave, sweetie. It happens every day."

"But now you probably think I'm a real creep."

" 'Probably'?"

"I had that coming."

"Well, you've already expressed what you think about me: so we're even. There's your clothes. Chop-chop."

"If we could only wait a few minutes and calm down. And if you weren't so rough, or so demanding, I think—"

"Hey, friend: come on. Don't waste any more of our precious time."

Forever after Joe would remember this moment as the end of his sexual career. Anger hit with a rush and he almost fainted. For a split instant he considered attacking her: he wanted no witnesses. I'll knock her down, commit rape, and then—using the small marble lamp on the bedside table—I'll beat her brains to a pulp. The thought lasted for only a second, yet during that time he actually gestured in her direction. What followed, accompanied by an explosion of breathlessness that immediately rendered him a cripple who couldn't have raped for a million dollars, was a sensation of utter disgrace. Emotionally he would never be able to live down a self-induced beating like this.

Would she, Joe wondered, self-consciously yanking up his trousers, tattle to Natalie about their lurid nonadventure? If so, he was a goner. It would take eight minutes for Natalie to telephone her first thirty friends. He'd never be able to look another pal, or lover, in the eye again.

Dressed, buttoning his cuffs, Joe pleaded, "Look, I'm really sorry. I blew it. I'm ashamed. I wanted you too much. I was too excited. I don't know how else to explain it. I don't have much experience in these things. I only left home three days ago."

She faced him briefly, looking empty and bored. "Oh, it's okay. What the hell. Nothing ventured, nothing gained." Then she turned her back on him, sauntered over to a closet, opened the door, and retrieved a large object from inside.

Joe was flabbergasted. "What is *that*?"

"Don't you know?" She held up the life-size inflatable Japanese creation for his edification. "It's called a Darling Don. He's a companion piece to their female creation."

Barely able to see, Joe fled, looking for blaze marks to guide him back toward the life he had almost lost.

◄§

The bus was idling. Yet where to go? Not home, not after this evening's debacle. They probably had bureaus, chairs, maybe even the refrigerator stacked against the door in case he returned. From now until a divorce decree became final, he and Heidi would probably communicate solely through their lawyers.

And as for Nancy . . . ? Right now Joe was convinced that he would never make love again.

Diana's tent, then. But if she had awakened at any time between his abrupt departure and his return to find herself stone-cold alone just minutes after their liltingly potent assignation, chances were she'd be awaiting him with her gun cocked. . . .

A rational solution, perhaps, to all his problems.

The crotchety engine idled noisily. Like a heartless gangster, loneliness attacked his vulnerable chakra points. Half-frozen Bowery bums wrapped in urine-soaked weekend editions of the *New York Post* had nothing on Joe Miniver, a formerly compassionate garbage man, cheerful father of two, and semi-decent husband of one, who had unaccountably lost his way, a syndrome which was no more tenable for being (apparently) the good old American Way.

What self-destructive catalytic enzyme had been triggered last Saturday night? And why? If only he could prove the adventure was worth it. If only the value of his losses had been replaced by emotional, spiritual, and physical accumulations of similar worth. But the ledger was a mess. "I break our hearts, therefore I am." An American Descartes in Swingler City. "If only Peter had gotten off that bus!" But Peter, having hay-makered Julane's jaw, had enough troubles of his own.

What was happening to everybody? Hey God (you non-existent werewolf!), I don't see any sensible pattern emerging from this anarchical circus of Boschian dingle-prancers with red roses flopping out their assholes, bells on their dunce caps, and nasty crab-pincers attached to their colorful breechclouts! Trapped in eggshells of ego, and shivering under the shadowy spell of leering angels flapping pterodactyl wings, they eat strawberries with drugged malevolence, crying "Help!"

That does it, Heidi shrieked. *Joe Miniver, the world's greatest vapid-mouth!*

The farcical turmoil of his past few days twitched before his eyes like the cardboard pictures in a nickelodeon. Apprehensive and awkward nude women struggled to free themselves from enormous enveloping sheets. Out of their open mouths poured miniature kids covered with blood, and tiny smashed looms, trailing pretty fibers. Carnations snowed into traffic jams. Balancing dichromates on all his fingers, top-hatted Spumoni Tatarsky pirouetted in a circus arena: he was surrounded by guitarists, tennis players, joggers, fugitives from learning, and prissy PhDs. Siddhartha this and Nikita that cantered on-stage, flying guru kites on silver strings. Every seventh person wandering through the carnival was a mysterious, trenchcoated Nick Danger arriving from nowhere . . . bound for oblivion, clutching a tattered suitcase. Hands flailed, tearing off spiffy clothes. Silly pink bodies wiggled and squirmed, screwing each other. Helicopters zigzagged overhead, dangling large grappling hooks, trying to snag priceless granite idols. Lawyers meandered, tapping shoulders, collecting money. Ipus, Baldinis and Baba Ram Bangs and noisy dwarfs in chartreuse jumpsuits tumbled along chaotically, sniffing incense and toot-

ing coke. "Biff, bam—thank you ashram!" Grapefruits fell out
of the sky, smashing emphatically on poolside tiles. Key words?
How about *equity*, *love*, *sex*, *coke*, *space*, *death*, *cosmic*, *spiritual*, and *pornography*?

For starters.

Off to the side, leaning against his shovel and amusedly
looking on, stood Eloy Irribarren, a little white-haired old man
who could have been God.

Joe shifted (*grind! clunk! grate!*) into first and tarried no
longer at the Nuzums' Tara.

He puttered through the deserted streets of the little city.
Steam snaked eerily from dozens of construction pits, sewer-
line breaks, gratuitous holes in the ground. What kind of fool
would burn all his bridges before consolidating a trump card
for his new future? For perpetuating the myth of the Zipless
Fuck, Erica Jong ought to be lined up against the wall and
castigated severely by means of dumdum bullets, steel-jacketed
slugs, and other lethal projectiles.

Sex. Violence. Cocaine.

Joe drew a weary breath. His glazed eyes canvassed the
darkened town. Caught in a commercial riptide, even at 2:00
A.M. Chamisaville's stores sizzled in an orgy of sputtering neon.
Sourpuss cops glared at him from their dented cruisers. Everywhere he turned a law officer scowled: idling beside the Tastee-
Freez, circling the First State People's Jug, shining flashlights
into the glass-and-girder mess of Safeway's abuilding southern
branch. Cars were still parked in front of Heavenly Bodies,
the new topless disco joint. Lavishly chromed late-model vehicles mingled with a few old pickup trucks in front of Irving
Newkirk's X-rated lodging enterprise, the Sexational Porn-atel.
Inside, couples gallivanted on Magic Fingers beds while watching *Deep Throat* on closed-circuit TV. Intrigued by such sin,
Joe had never dared spend a night, even though he and Heidi
had joked about it occasionally. Now (and forevermore?) he
had no more desire. The lure, merely lurid, was dead for him,
dissolved.

Curiosity had killed this cat.

Joe mewed plaintively and swung into the 7-Eleven parking
lot: he braked near the outdoor public telephone. After first
casting about for muggers dressed in black and wearing rubber
monkey masks, he dialed home. Heidi's groggy voice inter-

rupted the eighth ring: "Jesus Christ, you son of a bitch, who's this?"

"Me—Joey. Heidi—"

She hung up on him.

He located two more dimes and redialed. This time she pleaded with him: "Joey, what time is it? I'm exhausted. I'll bail you out in the morning. G'night. . . ."

"Heidi, I'm not in jail!"

"Thank God for small favors. Now seriously, call again in the—"

"This is important: *don't hang up*! I got no more money."

"Joey, are you completely nuts?"

"What did you mean about the septic tank, the rubber suit, and the snorkel?"

"What did I what about what?"

"The septic tank, the rubber suit, and the snorkel, dammit!"

A puzzled silence greeted this exclamation. "Heidi, are you still there?"

"I'm here. But the question is, where are *you*?"

"The Seven-Eleven phone booth."

"I mean inside your head, Joey. What do you mean—septic tanks? Rubber suits? Snorkels?"

"In the hospital parking lot you said Tribby would need a rubber suit and a snorkel."

"You mean a scuba suit?"

"Is that what they're called?"

"Joey, it's two A.M."

"But what did you *mean*?" he sobbed.

"About what?"

"About the fucking rubber suit and the snorkel!"

"Apropos what, exactly?"

"Apropos the stuff that came in on the bus."

"The cocaine?"

"*Must you*, over the phone? Don't you have any regard for security precautions?"

"If this is a lecture, pal, I'm hanging up. . . ."

"Please," Joe pleaded. "Just tell me, and I promise, I'll never bother you again."

"I don't know what to tell you, Joey, because I haven't the faintest idea what the hell you're talking about."

"Did you flush the cocaine down the toilet or not!"

"That's for me to know and you to find out."

Click.

Benumbed, Joe stared at his feet. He was standing on a large, rather pretty feather. Stooping painfully, he plucked it off the dirty concrete and twirled it in his fingers, puzzled. From what sort of bird had it fallen? Nothing he had ever seen around here. It could have belonged to an eagle, perhaps, but what eagle had such creamy, pearl-colored plumage? The burnished feather was luminescent; it seemed to glow as if infused with some kind of otherworldly, quasi-electric energy.

Tribby Gordon's ancient Volvo eased into a parking place near the phone booth. "Hey, José. What time is it?"

"Time?" Joe blinked uncomprehendingly into the single headlight. Ralph Kapansky rode shotgun beside Tribby—he crickled the fingers of both hands at Joe by way of greeting. From the back seat, Rimpoche snarled uncertainly.

Tribby said, "Yeah. I came in for cigarettes, but the store is closed. My watch must have stopped."

Dazedly, Joe said, "I think she flushed it down the toilet."

"My watch?"

"The cocaine."

"Who?"

"Heidi."

"I'm out of cigarettes and you're wasting my time with cocaine stories?" Tribby yanked his stick shift into reverse, and swung around, calling as he did: "It doesn't matter, man. Ralph and I are on our way to check out the helicopters. But first we gotta catch the La Tortuga before they call it quits! Come on out to the Floresta helipad behind the district headquarters on Valverde in fifteen minutes! We're developing a foolproof plan!"

Joe paddled away the exhaust fumes with his rarefied feather. The empty parking lot jeered at him heartlessly.

Nick Danger turned a corner, glanced surreptitiously in Joe's direction, shifted his suitcase from under his right to under his left arm, and scurried into more protective shadows. Then the Chicken River Funky Pie van cruised down the street, veered into the 7-Eleven parking lot, and accelerated suddenly, heading straight for Joe. But even before he had time to react, the driver spun his wheel, and, as the van fishtailed, a package sailed out the passenger window, landing at Joe's feet. For a split second, as the two earthbound tires squealed, Joe thought the odd vehicle was going to flip. Instead, aiming in the op-

posite direction, the van settled onto all fours, and screeched
away.

As for the package?

Just another toy monkey with a miniature toy .45 automatic
in one hand, and yet another cheerful exhortation pinned to its
chest

We will bury you!

❧

       Before Joe could escape, a mauve Datsun coasted
through the stale penumbra to enrich his nightmare.

Resplendent as always in one of his ULC custom-made
velour jumpsuits, Scott Harrison appeared less than arrogant
as he contorted his tall, athletic frame out of the little vehicle
and brushed a speck of tarnish off his fuzzy lime-green outfit
before addressing Joe.

"Mr. Miniver, I presume? What has you out amongst all
the nocturnal creepy-crawlies, pal? Scouring around for a million dollars? Planning, perhaps to take a powder on the little
wifey before your court date lands on the docket?"

"Hello, Scott. Spare me the rod, huh? I'm pooped."

"And well you should be, according to all I hear. The grapevine's been positively ecstatic over your exploits."

Scott ran a hand through his short, barber-clipped blond
hair. His face reminded Joe of famous retired football quart-
erbacks gone soft as TV announcers who hailed from Oklahoma
Baptist neighborhoods. His jumpsuit was unzipped to expose

an ample expanse of sexy chest curls, his fingernails were
cleanly manicured, he wore an expensive Seiko digital watch
and Nacona cowboy boots. He exuded an impeccable smell of
male after-shave lotion. And seemed—curiously—somewhat
ill at ease.

"Scott," Joe mumbled, "I was just leaving."

"This will only take a minute. But it could salvage what's
left of your life."

"This town is positively reeking with altruists."

"You need an altruist, my friend." Scott's enormous quart-
erback hand adjusted a bulge in his tight crotch. "From all the
info I've accumulated, I'd say you have just about played out
your string. You know, for a very unimportant fingerling in
the Chamisa Valley's fishbowl, you sure have stirred up a passel
of enmity, Joe. Not since the Richard Nixon dartboard became
a best seller have I witnessed so much antagonism directed
toward a single personality."

"I'm through with the telephone, Scott, so it's all yours."
Joe started to swing around him, heading for the bus.

"Not so fast, man. We have things to discuss." Scott's ham
hand touching Joe's shoulder suggested the cramped power of
somebody who had perhaps worked up to a karate black belt
in Japanese health spas.

"Bueno. Have at it, I'm all ears."

"Good. For the moment we'll forget the little contretemps
between you and Heidi. That's all cut-and-dried, and one for
the courts. And I certainly wouldn't want to violate my client's
trust by hashing out the divorce logistics with you."

"I can certainly appreciate your integrity." Joe wondered
where was it, the assembly line that produced all these hype-
sters?

"On other fronts, I think I can speak frankly, however."

"Such as?"

Scott frowned, brushing another distasteful fleck off the
raised nap of his carefully brushed shoulder. "Such as, for
starters, the fact that your insistence on trying to buy Eloy
Irribarren's land is making a lot of people very uncomfortable."

It was too late—Joe hadn't the heart, or the stamina, to
prolong a snide and sardonic repartee. Dully, he allowed his
listless eyes to roam the cigarette-and-Coke-can garbage lit-
tering the parking-lot gutters. Let the big lummox wheedle to
his heart's content, it was no skin off Joe's exhausted butt.

"Maybe I should outline the impasse just a bit," Scott continued. "We all know you'll never peddle a single gram of coke in this town—that's an irrefutable given. In fact, you may never even get the shit back from Heidi—she'll hold it as collateral. But as long as you keep Eloy Irribarren on a string, thinking you might come through, the works remain mighty bollixed for the rest of us interested parties."

"Apologies to the pope. What else can I say?"

"Say nothing until I'm finished. Let me outline a few repercussions your stubbornness could cause, that's all." As he adjusted his crotch again, a highlight sparkled off his diamond-inlaid fraternity ring.

"You probably know, Joe, that various parties are interested in Eloy's primo spread for a number of diverse reasons. Cobey Dallas, Roger Petrie, yourself, the hospital, the bank—the list goes on and on. As Eloy's lawyer these past two years, naturally I myself have come to feel an intimate concern for the future of that beautiful property."

"Though not, of course, for the beautiful man who lives on it."

"Eloy's irrelevant, Joe. His day is over. He had a good life, but it's time to push on. You can't stop progress. That land is simply too valuable to remain in the hands of an unambitious agricultural octogenarian. It's being wasted."

Joe said, "Scott, I really would like to hit you, or knee you in the balls or something, but I'm afraid you'd beat me to a pulp."

The lawyer ignored him. "So we come to the heart of the problem. Theoretically, Eloy's property belongs to me. He owes thirty thousand in legal fees. I have the water rights tied up in a separate deal, just to be on the safe side. Your wife has retained me to defend her in divorce proceedings that she'll pay for in Eloy's property should you successfully land it despite yourself."

"But if you're disbarred for making a deal with embezzlers on those water rights, how the hell will you claim that property for legal fees?"

Scott chuckled self-assuredly. "I've covered myself. When I heard that Skipper was gonna nail Cobey and Roger, I went to Skipper and offered to turn state's evidence against them both to make it look like he'd never colluded with Roger to burn Cobey's ass. Naturally, he had to agree, because if not,

I could have taken him down with me. That's just simple business arithmetic, Joe—nothing to it."

"So now you're allied with Skipper and all the other monkey freaks and gangsters—big deal. They'll make you a stockholder in the Simian Foundation, but that won't buy you a Universal Life Church in Eloy's back pasture."

"Correct, it won't. Which is where you come in."

"Me again? Oh my." Though he had little strength left for laying it on thickly, Joe tried anyway. "Don't tell me, lemme guess. With my help, you could bypass all the convolutions, snagging the property fair and square and all for your little old lonesome. Here's how it works. I convince Heidi to turn over the cocaine to you, now, and you lay it on Ray Verboten, who gratefully hands you half its street value—let's say fifty Gs. To that you add ten grand of your own bread, and we strike a deal—you and me. I buy the land from Eloy before all the grace periods expire next Monday, and we own it, half and half. Only I won't own it for long, because you'll see that Heidi gets my half in the divorce proceedings, and she'll have just enough time to quarter it once before you claim it in legal fees. How am I modulating, good buddy?"

Scott swung around abruptly, contorted back into his peppy little gas-saver, and fired it up. "You'll be sorry," he grumbled petulantly. "I don't think you even remotely understand the power or the antagonism of the people lined up against you."

"If *you're* not afraid to try and double-cross them," Joe called after him, "why should I be?"

Or was that *Why be I should?* He needed lessons from Skipper Nuzum!

ᴥᔣ

It wasn't much bigger than the basketball playground on Sixth Avenue at the Fourth Street subway entrance, Joe thought, drifting, with his engine cut and the lights extinguished, into a U.S. government parking place, labeled Naylor, RB, near the chain link fence surrounding the Forest Service helipad. Two small utility bubblecopters were chained down on the white-lined macadam. In the northeast corner stood a prefabricated forest-green tin shack and a gas pump. Beyond the fence loomed a large, open-faced aluminum hangar.

Already engaged in nefarious skulduggery, Tribby and Ralph

pawed over a copter by flashlight, apparently impervious to the dangers of discovery. When Joe stepped from his bus, Rimpoche lurched up from his servile stand directly underneath the bird and barked. Joe hoot-whispered, "It's me, shut that damn dog up!"

He heard Tribby snarl, "Stow it, mutt!" Ralph replied, "He's no mutt, the dog has pedigree!" "Pedigree!" Tribby scoffed. "That bloated mongrel's genes couldn't paw their way out of a paper bag!" "I beg your pardon," Ralph joked noisily. "How can you cast an aspersion on such a felicitous incarnation of canine regality?"

During this exchange, Rimpoche continued barking.

"Hey," Joe cried bewilderedly. "He'll blow our cover!"

"Shuttup, Rimpoche!" Ralph yelled. "I'm sick of your atavistic stupidity!"

"It's all right now," Ralph called boldly. "He got the message."

Joe cringed. "You don't have to shout. Christ, you make more noise than the dog!"

"*I'm* making noise?" Ralph blustered, offended. "Look who's shouting at *me!*"

"Why don't you come a little bit closer?" Tribby suggested in a loud, echoing voice that no doubt could be heard the length and breadth of Chamisa County.

"Sure," Ralph chorused. "After all, you're our kind of man."

What's the penalty, Joe wondered as he climbed over the fence and dropped noiselessly onto the helipad, for trespassing on government property, for tinkering with government helicopters? Five concurrent life sentences? Immediate execution for being a Communist spy?

THREE MOUSEKETEERS SURPRISED BY GOVERNMENT AGENTS
AT FLORESTA HELIPAD! BULLET-RIDDLED BODIES SENT TO
WASHINGTON D.C. CRIME LAB FOR IDENTIFICATION! SURVIVING
MUTT DRAWS LIFE SENTENCE FOR BEING WATCHDOG!

"Oh shit!" The flashlight clanged to the floor of the copter, rolled out the open door, and dropped to the pavement, shattering.

Joe jumped a mile; Rimpoche shrieked.

"You clumsy oaf," Ralph giggled. "How can I show you all this stuff in the dark?"

"Hand me back that lamp," Tribby said. Joe obeyed, eying the deadly rotors above his head. He had heard stories of people who had been decapitated, walking into the still-whirring blades while boarding or disembarking. They gave him the shivers. Then he turned his attention to the shattered glass on the ground.

"What are you doing?" Tribby asked, banging the flashlight against his palm, hoping for a miracle.

"I'm collecting all the pieces so they won't have any evidence. Are you guys touching anything up there? Try not to leave fingerprints."

"I touch these choppers every day," Ralph said lightheartedly. "These are my babies. I oil their gizmos and grease their whatchamacallits. I center their little mechanical souls so nobody will fall out of the sky. Don't worry about fingerprints."

"Well, I hate to be obtrusive, wiseass," Joe said petulantly, "but what's the plan?"

"Easy." Tribby patted a dark, gleaming handle that resembled a gear-shift lever. "I can fly this baby, no problem. And there's a basket back there, with a rescue rig, according to Ralph. Chains, steel cables, grappling hooks, wounded litters—the works. All we got to do is fly over to Eloy's place, grab the monkey, buzz off into the hills, and drop it into one of the Little Baldy Bear lakes."

"When?"

"You're not gonna like this."

"Try me."

"About a half-hour before they unveil the Hanuman on Thursday."

Joe sat down with a thump. "You're right—I don't like it. Couldn't we figure out a better time?—like at the height of the Easter pilgrimages? Did you call up all the leading national newspapers and magazines, asking them to send reporters for the show?"

"That sarcasm is very puerile, Joe." Ralph waggled a chiding finger. "The time slot, as anyone with a little less of a knee-jerk reaction might have guessed, isn't exactly of our choosing."

Tribby explained: "The two copters are signed out across the board except for a couple of afternoon hours on Thursday."

"But that's insane. You can't snatch the statue in front of all those people!"

"We got no choice."

"It's an absurd plan. They'll shoot you out of the sky. They'll see who we are."

"We'll wear masks."

"It's too dangerous. How could it possibly work?"

"I figure it this way." Tribby slipped from the pilot's seat and settled in the doorway, legs dangling, kicking against a metal strut. "First off, we have the element of surprise on our side. Nobody could possibly imagine that a helicopter would swoop out of the sky in broad daylight and cop their precious idol."

"Oh no? Suppose somebody on their side is planning the same thing? I told you about that helicopter I saw over at Bonatelli's place. Well, listen to this. Diana told me tonight that Bonatelli and Smatterling and God knows who else are concocting a plan to steal the Hanuman for the insurance. And to create a caper that would give Iréné Papadraxis a best-selling book that'd keep the Simian Foundation in shekels forever. She also told me that rumors have it Ephraim Bonatelli is piloting one of these babies with a grappling hook to grab the U-Haul and drop it into a high-country lake until the heat's cooled off."

"You're kidding. You made that up."

"Don't I wish. But here's the icing. I was at the hospital earlier tonight, and I took the opportunity to peek through the shades into Ephraim Bonatelli's room. And guess what I saw?"

Ralph said, "We're all ears."

"Well, they were all in there——Ray Verboten, Ephraim, Egon Braithwhite, and Nikita Smatterling. I'd seen them earlier when I barged in looking for a nurse after I rebroke Michael's nose wrestling. But now two others had joined their Apalachin—guess who?"

Ralph said, "The Tarantula himself, and Skipper Nuzum."

"How'd you know that?"

"It figured."

Joe said, "They had a map on the wall, and Joseph Bonatelli himself was pointing to one of the Little Baldy Bear lakes. And guess what else?"

Ralph and Tribby shrugged.

"The dwarf was playing with a toy helicopter. It had a string attached, and at the end of the string dangled one of those furry little toy monkeys."

"Oh my."

"One thing else."

"There's more?"

"They had enough hardware scattered on the foot of Ephraim's bed to commence World War Three. And Ray Verooten was busily loading it up with fresh cartridges."

Tribby let out a long, thin whistle. "How do you like them apples? Gawd *damn*!"

"The audacity," Ralph moaned. "The utter, nihilistic audacity of it all."

"Capitalism," Joe moralized self-righteously. "In its climax stage."

"No communism, Joseph. I ain't in the mood."

"You're never in the mood."

"We still don't know for sure if that's exactly what they're planning," Ralph said. "And certainly we don't know their timetable."

"Why all this big charade of Ephraim going to the hospital in the first place?" Tribby asked.

"Who knows?" Joe dropped the glass bits into his front shirt pocket. "My guess is it was to throw people off the scent. It gives him an alibi—no? How could he be pirating Hanumans if he's in the hospital with a bullet wound?"

"It's fantastic." Tribby shook his head in admiration. "How could two groups in the same town come up with the identical farfetched idea at the same time?"

"It beats the odds." Ralph nodded sagely. "It sure as hell beats the odds."

Joe said, "What's to prevent us from cruising into Eloy's field, say, tonight, and just hooking that unguarded U-Haul to a trailer hitch and driving away?"

"Somebody would spot us: this town's too crowded. And we still couldn't ferry it high enough into the hills. It has to be whisked away, real fast, and disposed of immediately, as if it were swallowed up by an act of God. Any slower process, and we'd never escort it through the commotion to a safe haven."

Joe said, "What about the dope? Is that closed off completely?"

"Forget the dope. They've shut us down there. But this . . . this is just crazy enough to work. *If* we can arrive there first."

Dispiritedly, Joe said, "So what's the plan?"

"I'm not sure yet; it needs more thought. But here's what

I envision so far. Ralph rides with me. Naturally, between now
and Thursday he's made an extra set of keys, so that when we
jump the helipad in our monkey suits, we don't have to worry
about getting airborne. After that, it's fairly simple. We pop
over to Eloy's place and hover above the U-Haul. Ralph drops
a hook, captures the brass ring, and off we go."

"All those people will climb onto the U-Haul. They'll pull
you down out of the sky."

"That's where you come in."

"When you hear us coming, you start a ruckus to divert
everybody's attention," Ralph said.

"Oh come on!"

"I'm serious. You launch a free-for-all. Attack Nikita Smatterling. Tear off your clothes and kick over the cooking pots.
Grab the old geezer, what's his name?—Baba Ram Bang—
and threaten to slit his throat with a butcher knife. We'll leave
that to you—the diversionary tactics."

"If it seems too deliberate, they'll know I'm implicated."

"So don't make it too deliberate."

"How can I make a free-for-all look undeliberate in a convention of Peace-Love-Groovyniks?"

"You'll think of a way." Tribby dropped to the ground.
"Come on, Ralph, I've seen all I need. Let's split." Headlights
were swinging up Valverde Drive. "Here comes somebody."

Tribby had discarded the broken flashlight on the copter's
floor. Ralph's foot now dislodged it by mistake. Rimpoche
howled when it landed on his head, and, acting reflexively, he
sank his teeth into the nearest object, Joe's leg.

Joe screamed, Tribby clapped a hand over Joe's mouth,
Ralph kicked Rimpoche, hissing *"Ta guele!"* and the headlights
of the approaching vehicle went off. In fact, the car screeched
to a halt, backed up in a frantic whine of rubber, and peeled
away in the other direction, still blacked out.

Pungent dust drifted across the helipad. Ralph said, "Now
who do you suppose *that* was?"

The moon popped from behind a cloud, bathing all three
conspirators in a spooky, aluminum-cruel luster.

The sky, apparently, was going to be their limit.

Slowly, Joe negotiated the maze until he arrived at Nancy Ryan's ordinary little cardboard home. Bedeviled by moths, the porch light glimmered invitingly. Wearing that sexy blue terrycloth robe, Nancy stood in the open doorway.

Joe asked, "What are you doing up?"

"I had a presentiment you'd be along. Isn't that nice? In fact, I know you won't believe this, but I reeled you in."

Like a trout? They embraced, but Joe pulled away quickly. The corner of his mouth was sore—from her hook? Gingerly he touched it. "I can't mess with you, Nancy. I'm all confused. I need to forgo sex for a while."

"There's nothing to be afraid of."

"Ha ha." Joe flopped onto the living-room couch, shucked his sneakers, tucked his hands between his thighs, and closed his eyes.

"Oh Joe," she murmured, sniffing him, abruptly saddened. "If you keep this up, I'm afraid you'll paralyze your kundalini."

"Just let me sleep. I'm so tired."

Lightly, her fingers fantasied across his forehead: maybe her lips flicked past an earlobe. And her breath fogged one cheek. Just before he went under, Joe mumbled, "I know why you're doing all this. You wanted Heidi and me to break up, so that even if I sold the coke, we'd have no reason to buy the land, and the Simian Foundation could grab it for the Hanuman. How much are they paying you to ruin me?"

"Tais-toi, my sweet," she cooed into his left ear. "Everything is going to be all right."

Then he was gone, sinking down through layers of quilting azure moss until he settled languidly into thick webs that enveloped with a fatiguing softness. They could have pilfered his soul right then, and he wouldn't have known the difference. Surely molecules joined together, forming a Nick Danger: he opened his suitcase . . . something shapeless and macabre croaked duskily. And monkey cupids wearing black eye-patches and smoking reefers paddled through the somnolent ozone, lips puckered lasciviously, whispering about Pre-Clears, kundalini, E-meters, and the SUGMAD.

5
Wednesday

Nine at the top means:
He brings increase to no one.
Indeed, someone even strikes him.
He does not keep his heart constantly steady.
Misfortune.

Wednesday

~ॐ~

A light blue humming nudged him calmly but firmly toward consciousness. Joe clung to sleep as if to a childhood security blanket, but no dice. Though the sound was relaxed and empathetic, it insisted he awaken and gulp in dawn air. An almost supernatural light infused the room. Like the strange indeterminate luster that often floods mountains shortly before dawn, a luminescent pre-auroral glow bewitched the air. All nature was counting to ten, silently, at that precise moment when the last nocturnal flake shakes hands with the first presolar spark.

Joe sat up, mystified, also a trifle frightened. An angel seated in a nearby armchair observed him benevolently. By no means your run-of-the-mill angel, this one was rather large, chunky, and bearded, obviously male and mighty macho. It leaned back against an enormous pair of burnished nacreous wings. A bright halo hovered saucerlike above its head. The halo never remained in the same place for more than a second, yet maintained a fairly stable position up there, given that it was the real thing and not attached by any rods, coat hangers, or other wirelike gizmos from some school's fifth-grade Christmas pageant. The Bunyanesque creature had small but cheerful blue eyes, a nose borrowed from some over-the-hill, oft-tagged heavyweight pugilist, and plump, almost effeminate lips. Large rough hands were clasped in appropriate piety before the chest; and the beefy body was swaddled in yards of creamy linen, as per the great sixteenth-century Italian masters.

The angel said, "Hello."

"Who are you?"

"That's really not here nor there, Joe." The voice, incongruous in light of the monster body, was higher than Joe's, and contained a faint lisp.

"But why are you here?" Joe rubbed his eyes and plucked at the air in front of his face, seeking to rid himself of invisible webs tickling his nose.

"Well, quite frankly, Joe, you're blowing it."

435

"I need an angel to tell me that?"

"The authorities in charge thought an angel might make more of an impression."

"For what it's worth, I already got the message."

As its blue eyes noncommittally roamed the room, the angel pursed its lips in an irritating prissy manner. "The question is, Joe, what are you up to? Why are you grappling through such a rash of puerile indignities toward some calamitous termination of a life that once held so much promise?"

"Look, I need your analysis like I need a hole in the head."

Above it all, the angel smiled tolerantly. "Sometimes we all need a pal to lead us out of these predicaments, my friend."

Anger was rising. "Listen, Mister, you're wasting your time with me."

"Maybe we could talk just for a minute." Utilizing a large ham hand, the angel flicked an ash flake off the tip of its nose. The hand seemed weightless, detached from the arm. Yet it also reminded Joe of a well-dressed athlete's hand, manicured and powerful, used to throwing touchdown passes and slipping inside size 38C brassieres. All it lacked was a Super Bowl ring. Figuring maybe he ought to pay a little more attention, Joe straightened up.

"I really don't want to discuss it," he said. "I'm a fool, and I know it, so what more do you want?"

"More to the point, Joe, is what do *you* want?"

"Sleep wouldn't hurt. I'm very tired."

"Ha ha. I was referring, of course, to what you might desire over the long climb."

"Haul."

"I beg your pardon?"

"The expression is 'over the long *haul*.'"

"Ah, I see. Well, Joe, they told me you might be a trifle recalcitrant, but I'll admit I didn't expect to find you quite this cynical and acerbic."

Joe yawned, mumbled a halfhearted "excuse me."

"But what do you want to *do* with your life? Certainly you have no wish to rupture all the bonds of loving it took so many years to solidify?"

"Hey, wait a second, man. Where are you coming from? What do you know about the pressures I'm up against? You want to save me, go talk to the Nikita Smatterlings and the Spumoni Tatarskys, and the Pentagon warmongers, and the pederasts and the purveyors of porn who've corrupted me with their movies and their magazines and their sexy advertisements ever since I hit puberty—don't lay it all on me! Go flog William Westmoreland and Richard Nixon, and . . . and John D. Rockefeller and all his legatees. Go—"

Hands up, the angel patted the air soothingly. "Whoa, Joe, please. Calm yourself. No need to start spouting Tinkertoy Marxism. Nobody's on trial here."

Were all angels capitalists? Joe said, "What is this then, an interview for sainthood?"

The angel had weird skin. It kept changing hues, one minute almost flesh-colored, the next minute mother-of-pearl. But what most irritated Joe was the apparition's insistence on coming on a little too debonair. The toga, for example, was a trifle too custom, more St. Laurent or Givenchy rather than from the tailor shops of God.

"I'm merely here to give you a prod, Joe. I'd like to draw out the sensible, compassionate, and loving instincts you possess. I'm here to guard the aspects of your personality conducive to creativity."

That did it—talk about pompous! Joe lunged.

He had expected his fist to rocket straight through some kind of foggy material, knocking over the armchair as he landed spread-eagled against the floor, an object of ridicule, while the angel circulated above, going "tsk, tsk." Instead, his fist collided with something heartily tactile, and the fight was on.

It ended almost immediately, however. For such an apparently muscle-bound character, the angel turned out to be an astonishing jellyfish. It cried "Eek!," gurgled when Joe's fist crunched against the Adam's apple, and flipped out of the armchair with surprising ease when Joe grabbed handfuls of toga material and yanked. Joe landed atop the angel, his limbs momentarily trapped in great folds of linen and enormous rattling feathers. Then he got in a nice little right-left-right combination as the angel shrieked, "Oh dear, stop it, *please!*" Blinded by fury, Joe filled his fists with feathers and jerked, tore at the hulky scaredy-cat's beard, boxed its ears, and in return received only a mild-mannered pittypat knee in the groin. Then light, as if from a flashbulb, burst into the room. An elegant whoosh followed. Thunder rattled the windows, causing monkey paintings to dance off the walls. And with that, the angel split. Leaving Joe behind, in the center of the room, his hands full of plumes, while hundreds of other feathers zigzagged about in the air, pulling a riff the opposite of autumn leaves by slowly rising up against the ceiling. Over there, next to the wall heater, Nancy Ryan demanded to know, "What's going on here?"

Stupidly, Joe shook his head, unable to speak. Icy sweat shrunk his testicles: his life wasn't worth a dime. For what could be worse, in the great lexicon of all lexicons, than mugging an angel as if it were some common atheistic thug? Ray Verboten would look good compared to the vengeance that feathered lug had at its command. *Floods! Pillars of salt! Plagues of locusts!*

He had hit bottom, all right, and there had been no bounce.

The only consolation was that now he had nowhere to go but up.

"Up?"

Joe shuddered.

∾§

"Jaya Hanumana gyana guna sagara, jaya kapis tihun loka ujagara."

Come again?

Afraid of where he was, terrified of where he may have been transported during the night, Joe hesitantly opened one eye, blinked, and then remained very still, playing possum lest they realize he was alive and light into him, flails glistening.

But this was no congregation of gods—Norse over here in bone-and-copper helmets, Saxon over there in fur loincloths and silver gauntlets—but instead a grouping of perfectly normal human beings, most of whom Joe knew, gathered in some kind of rite not of immediate national (that is Amurrikan) origin. . . .

The healing of Sasha, by Jove!

Dawn: Joe stretched open his eyes. About two dozen of them had gathered while he slept. Nikita Smatterling and his kid, Siddhartha, Randall Tucker, Spumoni Tatarsky and Moonglow Winterwind, Pancho Nordica, Crazy Albert, Baba Ram Bang, Baldini and Ipu Miller, Ray Verboten, Natalie Gandolf, Suki Terrell, Jeff Orbison, Nancy Ryan (and Bradley), and several other folks, adorned in turbans and little gold slippers, whom Joe did not immediately recognize. Some sat in yoga positions on the floor, softly chanting. Others occupied ordinary chairs, their heads thrust backward, singing in a lilting monotone. Only Bradley and Siddartha had open eyes staring at the idol in the middle of the rug: A stuffed monkey smothered in Crazy Albert's fluffy dyed carnations.

Not a real stuffed monkey, but a toy, rather, a scrufty brown-and white doll with big furry ears and mocking popeyes. Like a whacky little gunslinger from the Amazon, it gripped dual plastic bananas. Gaily colored ribbons decorated its throat and tummy. One ribbon supported a button, a relic from bygone decades: "Make Love, Not War."

"Yuga sahasra jojana parabhanu, lilyo tahi madhura phala janu."

The instant Joe's scrutiny alighted on Nancy, she opened her eyes. Although in midrefrain, she smiled, and, without causing a disturbance, rose, circled outside the healers, and settled on the couch beside Joe.

"What are they saying?" he whispered.

"We just said, 'When you were young, you leapt high and swallowed the sun, thinking it to be a sweet fruit.'"

"Ah-hah."

Her cheeks glowed. She seemed imperially clean, infused with generous tranquillity. Their hands touched. Dawn light settled against her dark hair like a transparent silk prayer against polished ebony. Her throat was as smooth as the surface of a white stone molded for centuries by flowing water.

"Apana teja samharo apai, tinon loka hanka te kanpai."

"Meaning—?" Joe prodded.

"'You are self-radiant. The three worlds tremble at your thunderous roar.'"

Until the recitation ended, Joe kept his eyes on Nancy's face: it had grown uncannily pretty, flushed with the innocent power of a believer in a Way To Be. Her bright, sentimental conviction had him enthralled. He fantasized living together for the rest of their lives, Nancy captured always in this immediate mood, forever charged with this spiritual radiance that seemed almost unbearably simple and good. God, her beauty was dazzling! It stirred eerie mellifluous longings. In her resided possibilities of ecstasy. They would live surrounded by lighthearted weather and easygoing folks with modulated voices, bare feet, white clothes, and genteel manners. And no brash hang-ups stemming from ambition, alcohol, materialism.

" 'Oh Lord, make my heart your abode.' "

Silence. Everybody joined hands. Peace poured into the room like water filling a clean porcelain bathtub. Spellbound, Joe barely dared breathe. All windows were closed, allowing light in, but keeping the silence from leaking out. As it grew, the pressure of it increased. With every passing second the silence became more portentous, until Joe thought he could bear it no longer.

They held hands, concentrating on the funny flower-laden doll. Their silence became so overwhelming, that Joe suddenly thought he must risk eternal damnation by breaking it with some idiotic remark. They had sucked the noise out of an electric wall clock, they had engulfed the noisy colors of Nikita Smatterling's fluorescent monkeys, they had even digested the turbulence of dust dancing in dawn's first sunbeam, which landed—where else?—squarely upon the dime-store Hanuman lathered in flora.

But just as Joe believed he must utter a sound to salvage sanity, somebody said, "Hello, Sasha."

Another person added, "How's it going—better I hope?"

A third healer offered, "Keep a stiff upper lip, Sasha. We're with you, kid."

Then everybody opened their eyes at once. They smiled, nodded at each other, and commenced normal conversations. Nancy excused herself, heading off to fix some tea. Suspiciously, Joe assessed this conglomeration of cosmonauts, who came across very cool, very calm, very collected—infused with Inner Light and Infinite Understanding. Joe wondered if this sort of séance could actually hasten the recovery (or stall the demise) of a gangster monkey that shat on sand castles and shoved spoons up little girls' noses.

As if in answer to idle conjecture, the telephone rang. Nancy said "Yes?," listened for a second, then addressed the gathering: "Oh dear, he died."

They joined hands, exclaiming joyfully: "Our prayers are answered! He joins the others in the eternal happiness of heaven!"

Into the phone Nancy said, "What? Oh gosh, I'm sorry. . . ." Again, she spoke. "I made a mistake everybody. I didn't hear correctly. Sasha hasn't died, he has *revived*."

Again they all sought each others' hands. "Our prayers are answered! He joins the rest of us in the eternal happiness of life on earth!"

Joe did a double take, scratched his head, and realized his bladder was about to explode. Bolting upright, he dashed into the bathroom, where a single carnation floated in the toilet bowl, and somebody, using soap, had drawn a gawky monkey on the medicine-cabinet mirror: it had a halo above its head.

He was splashing water in his eyes when Natalie Gandolf appeared in the doorway. Her hard, pretty face had a momentary spiritual softness.

"Hello, Joe, how's it going?"

A warning bell rang in his head—*bong!* And a headache suddenly flared. Cautiously, he dabbled at his damp cheeks with the corner of a fluffy towel. "Can't complain," he replied warily. "I'm still alive."

"Though maybe not for long."

"Ho ho *ho*."

"Tribby called late last night. He said he's not sure, but he thinks Heidi flushed the cocaine down the toilet. Or anyway, that's what you told him. When I passed the news to Ray, he suggested the toilet rap was a ruse to make him call off his dogs so you two could then unload the stuff in secret."

"I only gave Tribby what Heidi told me on the telephone. Why don't you call Heidi?"

"Ray did."

"And?"

"She said it was none of his business."

"I don't have it," Joe whimpered. He stared at his pathetic features in the mirror. "I don't even have my original twelve thousand bucks. Apparently, I also don't have a wife anymore. And I've lost my children into the bargain. If Ray Verboten wants to kill me, tell him he's welcome to, I don't care anymore."

"You should know the rumors are flying fast and furious. Somebody said you were casing the First State People's Jug yesterday, with an eye toward robbing it. Others think you and whatshername, the waitress—Angel Guts' ex—and Eloy Irribarren are sitting on the dope, with an eye toward marketing it later when the heat's off."

"Natalie, I think the only way to resolve the impasse is for Ray to assassinate me, my kids, Heidi, Diana, and Eloy, and anybody else who has even a microscopic acquaintance with the affair."

"Of course, Tribby could be bullshitting me for the benefit of your interests."

"You better off Tribby, then, on general principles."

"My party is tonight," Natalie threatened softly. "I really could use that stash, Joe. Ray's in a bind ever since his plane crashed. I'll tell you what: providing you don't tell anyone, I'll up my offer five thousand dollars, cash, if you can deliver it before five P.M. Nobody else has to know . . . strictly between us two."

"I don't have it. I don't even know if it still exists. And if it does exist, I don't know where it's hiding, Boy Scout's honor. Heidi said yesterday the only way I could recover it was with a rubber suit and a snorkel."

"You mean a scuba suit?"

"If you insist."

Her fingertips fluttered off his shoulder. "Will I see you this afternoon, Joe, before my party?"

"I really can't promise anything. Apparently I have little say in the matter these days."

"I'll tell Ray not to do anything rash. Not just yet, anyway."

"Thanks," Joe mumbled to her back as she floated away.

HEIRESS BEFRIENDS LOWLY GARBAGE MAN:
"NATIONAL COMPASSION WEEK" PROCLAIMED!

Eyes bloodshot and swollen, wrapped in her ski jacket and huddled refugeelike in a corner of the tent, Diana yelped "Where have you been?" as she lunged for his embrace and held him tightly, head burrowed into his armpit, her body shuddering from heartfelt sobs.

Joe said, "Listen, I'm sorry. . . ."

Apologies. By the time all this ended, he would be so riddled with guilt that not even a life spent groveling on his belly, only the whites of his eyes showing, would constitute sufficient repentance. How could such a simpleton go so complexedly astray? How is it that a person he scarcely knew could cling so tightly? How bad (how sad) must be the national emotional state that endowed its citizens with such a hair-trigger on the

pistol-shaped frame of their dependencies? The moment a shred
of kindness or a blivet of semi-compassionate sex touched their
crucified sensibilities (and expectations), they collapsed, becoming maudlin effigies of human beings, incapable of rational
thought, let alone survival. What kind of society even allowed,
let alone catered to, a Jack the Ripper like himself?

"Stop me, lock me up, envelop me in chains, kill me quick,
before I murder again!"

Deaf angels inhabited heaven. He was on his own. Time to
be a man, make a clean breast of it, tell the truth. He was too
far gone to keep procrastinating. Salvation could only be earned
by coming clean and taking his lumps, by facing Diana—
without a blindfold or the crutch of a last cigarette—like a
man.

Joe opened his mouth, fully intending to break it off can-
didly, showering her with the bitter truth. Instead, he lied like
a trooper.

"I got nervous about the car," he explained haltingly. "I
couldn't sleep. So I got dressed and walked into town. But
then I couldn't find the keys. I must have spent two hours
tearing that damn vehicle apart. I felt like an FBI agent searching for subversive literature in the house of a suspected Weath-
erperson. I even crawled all around that parking lot on my
hands and knees. But around three A.M. I finally threw in the
towel. By then I was too tired to walk back here, so I limped
over to Ralph's office and crashed there for a few hours. This
morning I returned to the hospital at daylight, and guess what?"

"What . . . ?" Ay, such a bedraggled, forsaken, forlorn, and
much-too-tightly-clinging kitten!

"In two minutes I found the keys. You know where?"

"No."

"Lodged in a tire tread. The car must have rolled over them.
Ain't that a kicker?"

"You can't leave me like that, ever again. I mean, after last
night, after that incredible loving. I woke up, I don't know
exactly when—probably around midnight—and you weren't
here. God, that was devastating!"

"Wait a minute. Two days ago you were trying to brainwash
me into a state of cynical detachment and sardonic objectivity
re romance. You said you couldn't stand sentimental bullshit.
What happened?"

"Things change. I fell in love."

They clung to each other silently for a half-hour, until Joe sprung a bad cramp in one thigh and twisted away from her, shrieking. She smiled as he thrashed painfully and cursed, pummeling the delinquent muscles. Wonderful highlights glistened on her cheeks. Even in pain, Joe was reminded that all of us, no matter what our physiognomy, have our moments of soul-rattling beauty. And he seemed defenseless against these moments. His firmest resolve could be melted by a smile, a provocative pose, or thoughtfully pursed lips. He could be enslaved by a gesture, enraptured by a sentimental melody, hog-tied by the promise of tenderness.

At heart, all he really wanted out of life was to be a lovable buffoon, liked by everybody, with an impeccable social conscience.

Sooner or later, for the nation (for the world) to become a sane and humanistic place, a shattering and violent revolution would probably have to occur. Yet Joe doubted he had the courage to pick up a gun. In his revolutionary fantasies he saw himself as an invaluable arbiter, beloved and trusted by both sides, responsible for the crucial liaisons that ultimately forged a just and reasonable (and lasting) truce.

In other fantasies he saw himself brutally drawn and quartered at the first bugle call to holocaust, disdainfully cut down and spat upon for being a lily-livered and ineffectual sissy on the barricades who nobody, on either side, could stomach: a Fraidy-Cat without the courage of his convictions.

Yet he didn't want to cause actual physical *bodily* damage in the upcoming conflagration. Although it might be argued that, on his own this past week, and without my assistance from the John Birch Society, the National Association of Manufacturers, or the American Nazi party, his sordid escapades had caused enough hurt to give him Ku Klux Kredentials for life.

Joe blurted, "Diana, it's no good."

"What's no good?"

"This. Us. You and me."

A mother bids her child farewell in front of the exterminating oven. Their fingers touch. Then, with a gunbutt, the mother is prodded through a metal gateway toward her doom: the child stares after her, stunned, bereft in a way impossible to imagine for anyone who did not experience the Holocaust. The camera pans in to a close-up of the child; her expression is beyond torment; her face is familiar.

It is Diana.

She said, "What do you mean?" Instantly, her cheeks flooded with salty water.

"It's stupid. It won't work. I'm not tough enough or crass enough—oh hell, I dunno. How did I ever get myself into all this? I thought it would be easy. I thought everybody was out there, carelessly duking each other on a billion whims, having a ball. Instead, every time I knock on any door, the meek of the earth, crippled by dreams of warmth and kindness and security, open up."

"You can't leave me." She looked utterly terrified. "You're the first time in—Jesus, six years?—that I trusted somebody to be decent. Last night, for the first time ever, I mustered the courage to accept real loving. You can't just throw me away."

"But you said . . . but I didn't . . ."

"Look at what happened, Joe. Look at what *happened*."

"It didn't mean that to me."

"I don't care what it meant to you. You can't just walk around being totally irresponsible for your actions. You have to answer to a conscience, you know. Moral imperatives are involved when you love somebody like we did last night."

"Oh, Christ . . . nobody understands."

"The way last night was is the way people make love to have a baby."

He could see it now: "The Bureau of Ciphers and Statistics announced yesterday, in Washington D.C., that due to an enormous and unexplained rash of illegitimate babies in the American Southwest, that region has violated every government ZPG ordinance on the book and has been placed on natal probation for at least a year. A major factor in the sudden increase superseding all birth and fertility guidelines, Joseph P. Miniver, was arrested recently. A dozen thick rubber bands were wound tightly around his offending member, initiating a process somewhat akin to that used in dehorning cattle. After a week, due to restricted circulation, Mr. Miniver's penis will atrophy and eventually dry up, painlessly dropping off. Commenting upon his punishment, Mr. Miniver said, 'I deserve it, I really had it coming (no pun intended).' Asked how he planned to carry on a sex life once the operation was completed, Mr. Miniver

stated, 'I'm not quite sure, but I know one thing: I've got
nowhere to go but up.'"

"I never said I loved you, Diana. For sure I don't want
another baby."

"The way you speak is irrevelant; your actions contradict
everything you say."

"I'm sorry. But we just aren't on the same wavelengths."

Life wasn't melodramatic enough, however: now the gun
appeared in her hand. Joe groaned, "Oh shit!"

"You didn't just say what you just said, did you? You can't
mean what you say you're meaning, can you?"

He performed another in a long and undistinguished line of
hopeless gestures. "I can't say I didn't say what I said. I can't
pretend not to mean what I meant."

"I'll kill you, then."

Joe was astonished by his lack of panic as he spoke. "What
can I tell you? Please don't kill me."

Then he heard a hollow thunderclap that seemed silent, like
a noise from a dream: shock waves skidded through his body
as if he had been struck a dull blow by a very heavy, yet
somehow slow-moving, leaden fist. The tent instantly filled
with smoke, through which, with utmost fascination, he perceived Diana's astonished eyes suspended weightlessly in the
ether, unattached to any facial features. He had no clear idea
of what, exactly, had happened. What flashed into his head
was the idea that somehow the tent had absorbed a volatile gas
and popped like a balloon pricked by a needle. He heard his
voice say "Hey!" although the word took forever to swim up
through his body and escape the prison of his mouth. Diana's
eyes promptly swooped backward, and disappeared. In their
stead arrived the tent's ceiling, almost lost in pungent gunpowder smoke.

In short, without any clear idea of how he had gotten there,
Joe was lying on his back.

Diana's face hove into sight. Her lips moved, obviously
speaking words, but he heard nothing. The violent ringing in
his ears saw to that. Joe tried to read her lips. She repeated
the same statement several times, to no avail. His ability to
concentrate on her lips was hampered by a squall of mysterious
hail-sized pellets that stung his forehead, nose, and cheeks. He
recognized them as tears at almost the same moment he de-
ciphered her lips:

I didn't mean to shoot you.

Tongue-tied, he couldn't reply. Yet his brain functioned superbly. It's clarity belied the maudlin nature of this uncomfortable misadventure. He had been shot by a distraught woman, probably by accident. Obviously, although she had known the gun was loaded, Diana had not meant to pull the trigger. His supine posture could be explained by the fact that a tiny lead projectile no larger than a third of a pinkie had entered his body somewhere—where?—at a high rate of speed, damaging certain crucial muscles, tissues, nerves, organs, and bones seriously enough to impede the natural functioning of his motor locutor. Joe wasn't worried, though naturally, in passing, it occurred to him he might be dying. An unfortunate circumstance, given his youth. In fact, he hadn't accomplished much of note during his thirty-eight years on earth. Looking on the bright side, though, his death would solve a lot of personal problems he'd managed to forge over the last five days. At best, he wouldn't have to start a rumble among a lot of blotto monkey freaks while his maniac friends played Super Thief in a stolen helicopter.

The cup is always half full, qué no? Joe laughed, although he could not hear himself doing so. In fact, how to tell if he was, in effect, laughing? Perhaps he simply had a desire to laugh, but, because the bullet had nailed him in the throat, or the chest, or the chin, he no longer possessed the physical equipment to realize such a desire.

Out of curiosity, Joe tried to wiggle his toes. He succeeded, and exalted that feeling yet remained down there. If nothing else, he was not (apparently) slated to lose the use of his feet.

Diana fled. Joe stayed absolutely still, unwilling to risk further physical experimentation. Any movement could aggravate his wound, causing intense pain, even death. After all, if the bullet was lodged against his aorta, any slight shift might dislodge the slug, allowing his life to geyser out of a wretchedly gaping wound.

Or the lead might be embedded in his spine, one tenth of a millimeter away from paralyzing him for life.

Joe's brain commissioned a platoon of sensory soldiers to march outside the perimeters of their protected hamlet in the oblongata region, in search of the wound. They reconnoitered his arms uneventfully, and tip-toed through the yukky, swampy regions of his abdominal cavity without sighting any ruptures,

foreign objects, or viscous fluids that had leaked from their
proper tubes or holding tanks. Proceeding south with all due
caution, they hacked through a thick jungle of thigh meat on
the banks of the sciatic nerve, then probed kneecaps, calves,
femurs, and ankles. At last, in the Antarctica of all flesh, where
metabolism shone but a few hours every day, they sent a cable
back to the oblongata region, claiming to have discovered nothing. So Joe ordered their retreat. In fact, he vacuumed them
up swiftly, a precipitous move, granted, but one which may
have avoided the anguish that could have been triggered had
they double-checked his body on the return journey, accidentally discovering where he was wounded, and how badly.

In due course, his ears stopped ringing. Actual sounds returned. The early morning chatter of magpies; a distant truck;
the persnickety whine of a little machine somewhere doing a
little job. Idly, Joe wondered: What's going to happen? Where
had Diana run to—to fetch Eloy? To call a cop? To send Heidi
to the rescue?

Probably she had just run away, terrified, leaving him there
to die like a dirty dog, his sweet young blood staining the
freshly overturned earth of land he would never own now, no
matter what.

Such a price he had paid for this greed to own a little piece
of property!

How to attract attention, calling for help? Joe could neither
move nor speak. Of course, he had not absolutely proved his
immobility. He simply feared that by budging he might dislodge
something crucial, and be dead three steps out of the tent. Plus
the mere thought of discovering where, and how badly, he was
injured gave him the heebie-jeebies. And as for speech?—
suppose that instead of words, only grotesque and horrifying
gurgles emerged from the depths of his rent esophagus. . . .

Left to him, then, were limited alternatives. Perhaps, by an
extreme effort of will, he could float himself astrally over to
the hospital. Or, lacking the intensity of belief to suddenly
dominate a technique he'd actively pooh-poohed all his adult
life, maybe he should tackle the problem at a lower level. Could
he generate enough ESP to hail Nancy Ryan before he expired?

Joe nixed that. After all, if she saved his life he would be
indebted to her forever. And the point right now was to extricate
himself from damning liaisons.

Leaving—would you believe prayer?

"Oh Mighty God, please don't let me die. If you save me, I promise I'll be good. Also, I'll never ask you for anything else again. Just this once, have a heart, let me live. I promise, I'll be a changed person. I'll reunite with the family. I'll give all my extra pennies to the March of Dimes. I'll even go to an Up With America concert. . . ."

Joe stopped. Aside from registering a full ten on the Maudlin-Meter, it was stupid to beg for mercy from a figment of humanity's imagination in which he believed almost as intensely as he believed in Santa Claus.

Another face, a slightly smaller dirigible than Diana's, materialized overhead. Chubby cheeks covered with jelly, matted and dirty strawberry blond hair—her large blue eyes inspected him with childlike inquisitiveness.

"Hi, Mr. Miniver."

Saved by a three-year-old Peace-Love-Groovynik!

"Hello, Om." Hot dog, no horrific gurgles!—his voice sounded normal.

"What's the matter with you?"

"Somebody shot me. Now listen, Om. Listen very carefully. . . ."

"What did they shoot you with, Mr. Miniver?"

"With a gun. Now Om—" The face disappeared. "Om?" It reappeared, accompanied by the gun held in pudgy clumsy fingers. "Now listen, sweetie. . . ."

"Is this the gun?"

"Put that down, dammit! It's dangerous. It might go off again."

Once more, the face retired. Joe dared not turn his head to follow it for fear a wounded disk might slip, killing him on the spot.

"Where did you get shot?" Om asked, in sight again.

"I don't know. It isn't important. But right now—"

"Did they shoot you in the heart?"

"No, Om. Now listen to me—"

"Did they shoot you in the head?"

"No—hey! Do me a favor, hush up a minute. This is very—"

"My daddy says guns are dumb."

"Right, guns are dumb. God bless your daddy."

"He says if you mess with a gun it will turn around and shoot you because of all the bad vibes."

"Very true, very true. Now come on, Om, hear me out. Would—"

"Did you shoot yourself?"

"Jesus—hey, kid? Have a heart. Lemme finish a sentence. I might be dying."

"If you die, you go to a place that makes you very happy. You shun't be scared of dying, it's beautiful."

"Om, I need help. Go fetch your mommy and daddy. Tell them Mr. Miniver is hurt."

"My mommy's not there."

"So go tell your daddy."

"He's not there either."

"Well, who the hell's over there? Call your baby-sitter."

"I don't have a baby-sitter. Rama says I'm big enough to take care of myself 'cause I got good karma."

"Where did they go?—your mom and dad."

"The foodstamp office."

"But they can't simply leave me lying here."

Om asked, "Do you have lots of money?"

"I don't know. Hey, look, listen, do me a favor—"

"My daddy says you're a filthy-rich dope pusher. He says you're gonna build the biggest house in the neighborhood."

Fuck your father. "Om, go get help. Find Mr. Irribarren. Tell him that Joe is shot and lying in the tent."

"There's lots of butterflies out there. My favorite is the one with the orange wings."

"I know, I know. Michael has a big collection, too."

"I don't have a collection. You shun't kill butterflies. If you kill them, all the flowers will die. You'll get sick, too."

Butterflies! "Om, maybe *I'm* dying. I need help immediately."

The face floated away, but the voice remained. "Once I founded a butterfly in the bathtub. It stayed there and laid a egg—"

"'An' egg." *Shit!*

"—and so we couldn't take a bath for almost two weeks until the egg hatched into a teeny-weeny caterpillar. Then my daddy put the caterpillar on a matchstick and let it go outside, and we could take baths again."

"Om, no more small talk. Seriously, you have to find a grown-up."

"My dad's got a movie camera."

"I know, I know." He could tell she was growing bored and he didn't want to drive the flaky little poseur away before his message was embedded in her kiddy noggin. "Please, I'm *begging* you, Om. Honest to God, I'm hurt."

"If you're hurt, my daddy says you can fix yourself. You just pretend you're not hurt and it goes away. The hurt isn't really in your arms and legs and tummy; it's in your brain. So nobody has to be hurt, ever—really."

A preview of things to come? Would Shanti Unfug, kneeling over his prostrate body, explain that the only reason Diana fired was his bad karma? No doubt she'd cure him by enveloping the bullet (embedded deep in his vital regions) with a pink cloud attached to a psychic thread. One jerk of the thread (by her mind), and the slug would pop clear. Then she'd heal the wound with a mentally created dose of color-coordinated chakra bullshit, crowing as she did so (and as he expired!), "There, see? It's easy if your head's in the right place, Joe. Joe . . . ? Can you hear me, Joe? Oh jeepers—*Joe!*"

Not to worry, however. A couple of Nikita Smatterling's fluorescent-pink monkey duendis, trailing mysterious wisps of colorful mist, would accompany him safely to the Other Side, where, like a seventeen-year locust shedding its crackly exoskeleton, he'd discard his Joe Miniver disguise, and zip himself up into the identity of his next reincarnation. Which, given his luck of late, would probably be as a hunchbacked short-order cook with a cleft palate and secret yearnings for a sex-change operation so he could win tennis matches at Forest Hills!

"Om—?"

Om had split. No doubt she was back out there, skipping merrily through his field with dozens of butterflies perched on her chubby fingers, proselytizing their tiny souls, ascertaining that their insect karma was cool, that nothing but love radiated from their stupid little butterfly hearts.

These ruminations were getting him nowhere. Yet what to do? How to act? Joe felt somewhat flushed, and aggravatingly unable to localize the place and extent of his wound. Was he bleeding to death, or so superficially wounded his eventual rescuers would titter and sneer while pointing at Joe the Shlimazl, who for eight hours mistook a mere powder burn on his left pinkie for a fatal injury?

Double-checking, Joe wiggled his left pinkie: it appeared to be in perfect working order.

He heard a rustle, fur rubbed against mosquito netting, then something sniffed at his cowlick. A *National Enquirer* headline flashed into his unaccountably lucid brain:

WOUNDED GARBAGE MAN EATEN ALIVE BY SKUNKS!
CHAMISAVILLE RESIDENT BECOMES SEVENTH MUTILATION
KILLING OF THE YEAR!
GUNSHOT VICTIM'S THROAT SLIT BY PET FERRET!

But when two large gray ears appeared on the periphery of his vision, he realized that once again his imagination had played him for a fool.

Eloy's rabbit, Tuerto, hopped onto his stomach and sat there for a moment, its one good eye staring blandly at Joe. Heaping insults atop humiliation, the animal stiffened peculiarly, stretched its neck slightly forward, and (Joe could tell from the little blast of heat that tickled his belly) laid a bunch of pellets on his navel. Then it twitched one ear and hopped away.

Not only would the doctors titter and point, but now the emergency technicians who arrived to pick him up for the ridiculing MDs would bust into guffaws over the rabbit shit on his stomach, laughing so hard they might lose hold of a stretcher handle, causing a lurch that would completely destroy his almost severed spinal column. Given their macabre sense of humor, if he survived they would probably arrange him on the operating table with that collection of turds still intact. And *then* wouldn't those damn physicians have a laugh at his expense?

He wouldn't pay the sons of bitches! Let them try and collect! For saving his life he'd tell them all to fuck off. Better yet, as soon as he could walk again (after years of Moscow steroid treatments and physiotherapy in Baden-Baden swimming pools), he'd go underground, return to Chamisaville, and methodically off every quack who had mocked his misery, killing them in grotesque ways, slowly, one by one, by emasculation, by evisceration, by cramming stethoscopes into their mouths, by stabbing rectal thermometers through their hearts, by shoving sigmoidoscopic instruments into their ears!

For another hour he lay there, incensed by the ignominy that would be his fate if discovered with a bunch of rabbit turds on his stomach. By flexing his belly maybe he could bounce them off. But if his wound was there, any untoward strain could cause him to park it for good. Yet presentiments of humiliation gnawed at him like a hungry rat. *"Psst, Mary, did you hear that when they found Joe Miniver, he had rabbit turds on his stomach?"* Ever after, in this sick little village, he would be known as the Rabbit-Turd Kid. An invisible RTK would be emblazoned on his character. He would have to leave town, moving, say, to Quinter, Kansas. But even there his reputation would follow. In the local clinic after a near-fatal asthma attack, the attending physician would demand his records from Phil Horney in Chamisaville. And the truth—since Phil no doubt would have written: *Patient arrived at ER with superficial dilation of pupils, a lowered pulsebeat of 57, a small bullet wound on left-hand side of the body just below the pectoral muscle, and a little pile of rabbit shit on abdomen approximately 13 centimeters above the navel*—would out. Every time he walked down the street to buy a paper and eat breakfast in Cathy's Cornbelt Café, dozens of big, beefy, Czechoslovakian wheat farmers, wearing Oshkosh, B'Gosh bib overalls, and seated at the wheels of their John Deere tractors, would point their blunt, calloused fingers at him and snigger in Slavic accents: "Dots him, Olaf, duh vun dey found mit der robbit turds on der pupik. Hee hee hee."

She she she.

It it it.

Ay, Dios!

Weariness made his bones creak; his muscles sighed. A shadow—of an enormous bird?—rippled against the sunlit material overhead. And—was he dreaming?—an enormous thing landed outside. Joe waited—should he be apprehensive or terrorstricken?—for something to happen. Sure enough, the flaps parted, and, before he could say "Oh God!" the angel he had mugged earlier loomed overhead, grinning sadistically. It had a black eye, a raspberry on one cheek. The wings had been repreened, but several gaps, caused by missing feathers, existed.

"Well," said the bearded seraph. "We meet again. And in slightly different circumstances, I might add."

"What can I say? This time around I'll admit it, I'm helpless."

"You can't say you didn't have it coming."

"'You didn't have it coming.'"

"You know, if I were you, Joe, I'd curb a little of my

arrogance, at least for the time being. You aren't exactly in the catbird seat, right now."

"I'm not afraid of you."

"Who asked for fear? The point isn't to be afraid of angels, Joe. The point is simply to be humble enough to listen when they bend close to the earth, their wondrous tales to tell. Who knows, you might learn something."

"Like what?"

"Like—" But just as it appeared the apparition would drop a few pearls, it frowned, and leaned over, squinting to focus more closely on Joe's stomach. "Hold everything, what's this?"

Here it comes, Joe groaned. Slavic wheat farmers, tittering doctors, and snide emergency-ambulance technicians aren't punishment enough. Leading the whole retinue of jeering barbarians is a goddam moth-eaten angel that more closely resembles one of heaven's flea-market specials than a figure of mythological potency!

"Do me a favor," he begged, "don't say anything. I'm in no position to defend myself."

"You've got rabbit turds on your stomach."

"Bright deduction, Dick Tracy."

"Where did they come from, Joe?"

Joe figured, I won't answer: I'll refuse to play the game. Only with silence can I salvage a shred of dignity.

But he fumed and stewed, wanting to bag the clumsy beast riling him. Wiggling his right-hand fingers, he ascertained that they still functioned. Then, in a daring departure from the inertia he'd tolerated on the belief that absolute immobility might save his life, Joe let his hand stray a few inches until it reached the cool metal of Diana's pistol. Gradually, he worked the pistol into his grasp. And, moving his arm but slightly, he pointed the gun upward at the angel and fired.

Almost before the report, the angel disappeared, leaving behind a moderate turmoil of feathers that zigzagged like autumn leaves, except, of course, that they fell upward, gathering against the tent roof much as they had accumulated on Nancy's living-room ceiling.

Frustrated beyond rationality, Joe raised his arm higher and yanked off four more shots at that space where the feathers now congregated uneasily hoping for an exit hole to facilitate their return to heaven.

Nothing happened.

That is to say: Although loud gunshots brutalized his eardrums, no slugs tore through the fabric overhead, making the tent jerk and the feathers dance. And no tiny holes through which he could see the sky appeared in the slim cloth. In short, despite all the noise involved, no lead projectiles were leaving the gun barrel to cause havoc in the outside world.

The goddam pistol was loaded with blanks!

As soon as this information had properly sunk in, Joe sat up. Despite the dizzying rush of blood caused by the sudden elevation of his (ha ha) brain, Joe understood immediately that not only was he very hungry, but he had been bamboozled royally as well.

A few rabbit turds were nothing compared to the humiliation engendered by his swallowing—hook, line, and sinker—this unbelievable farce!

For a while Joe remained immobile, jaw agape, staring at the pistol. Then he patted himself all over, just to be sure, praying that, all evidence to the contrary, he might discover a bullet wound—but no such luck. This lad was hale and hearty, absolutely untouched by lethal lead. Old headlines paled beside new ones forming in his head:

MINIVER MANGLED BY IMAGINARY BULLET! IDIOT SPENDS 8
HOURS FLAT ON BACK FROM NONEXISTENT WOUND! GIRL
RIDDLES MONGOLOID BOYFRIEND WITH BLANKS!

His watch said 3:00 P.M. There was probably nothing he could salvage from this rapidly deteriorating situation except, perhaps, with luck, his life.

◦§

Joe grabbed Diana's little revolver and slipped it into his pocket. Very surreptitiously, he peeked out the tent flaps to see if anybody was waiting to hoot derisively as he emerged. But the coast was clear. So he exited into the midafternoon, cast about sheepishly, and scurried down the driveway.

A group of precious geeks, outfitted in beards, ribbon shirts, marijuana smoke, and hipster piety, labored in Eloy's front field, setting up the Hanuman unveiling. Ipu Miller and Egon Braithwhite decorated an aspen-branch gazebo with colorful crepe streamers; Nikita Smatterling and Baba Ram Bang

crouched on the U-Haul's roof, arranging more fruit and many
flowers; and down at the west end, Mimi McAllister and her
lesbian construction collective banged the finishing touches into
a line of flimsy public outhouses.

Spumoni Tatarsky stopped, leaning on the shovel with which
he had almost completed a cooking pit, and waved. Joe snorted
at the salutation, and focused on his bus.

Four notes, tucked under the wipers, fluttered against his
windshield. A fifth lay on the front seat. Blushing uncomfortably, Joe slowly perused each one.

Diana's was short, and to the point:

You son of a bitch! You scumbag! You heartless coward!
I wish I could have killed you! It would have been less cruel
of you to beat me up, violate me, and leave me lying like
a dog. I hope your conscience rapes you for the rest of your
life. You can have the tent and all my shit. I'm never coming
back!

It was unsigned, of course.
Nancy's approached him from a different angle:

Joe, what's the matter with you? I could give you so much,
and yet you seem incapable of accepting what I offer. I feel
so sad for you, because you are such a rich person. You
are sweet and gentle. You have a divine soul and a beautiful
passion. Yet all this is crippled by your fear. How I wish
I could discover a way to ease the tension that is debilitating
you and lead you to an understanding of love. Can you even
begin to comprehend what I'm talking about? Can you even
begin to understand that I don't want to take anything from
you, I don't want to control you in any way, I just want to
make you happy? And I know you can be happy, I can see
it in your eyes, I can feel it in your embraces. You are such
an intelligent and beautiful person. If only you would give
me a chance to help you see how easy it is to be loving,
and gentle, and easy. I have knowledge that could help you,
Joe. I know things that could open up your world and make
you sing like you never sang before. I can lead you to peace
of mind, I really can, if only you'll let me. I am waiting

for you always. Please come see me as soon as you can. Like the Beatles said, "Love is really all you need."

Nancy

P.S. Don't forget the Hanuman tomorrow. I hope we can go together. First there's a lunch; the unveiling is around two.

The death threat was witty, obscene, and—of course—anonymous:

Hello again, asshole.
Your minutes are numbered!

Heidi, of course, had read the other epistles before composing her own:

Hi, Loverboy,

I see the ever popular all-American hustler is really accumulating the sappy doggerel and bitter drivel: congratulations on a difficult job well done.

Michael cried all night, not so much from the pain in his nose, as from the pain of having the Marquis de Sade for a father.

Heather asks if you'll ever write us a letter, and I told her "Oh sure," you'd probably drop us a postcard or two every year.

I'm moving back to New York next Thursday. I can take neither the midnight phone calls from bloodthirsty gangsters, nor your humiliation of me. We should probably meet to discuss finances sometime before then, though it's no big

deal. We can iron out the details through my lawyer, Scott
Harrison.

Cheerio, pip pip, and all that sort of tommyrot—

Heidi

P.S. What's this I hear about you hijacking a helicopter?

Not to be an alarmist, but things had begun to look bleak.
And even before unfolding Iréné's note, he imagined exactly
what it would say:

Hey there, stud,
Thanks for the duh-vine lay. You sure know how to do
a girl up brown.

OOOOOOOOXXXXXXXXX,
Iréné

Instead, she surprised him.

Hi,
Don't forget the pre-Hanuman party tonight.

Iréné

Maybe he should thank God for small favors.

In the meantime, where to go? What to do? To say he had
lost the thread was a humongous understatement. How he had
lost it so totally, so vertiginously, defied comprehension. All
that remained to finalize his downfall now, should he miraculously escape the wrath of Ray Verboten, et al., were a few
fifty-five-gallon drums of cheap dago red, consumed in four-
quart quantities daily behind Rick Bomb's Liquor Store over
a fourteen-month period. If anything remained after that, then
the forces overseeing humanity's annihilation were even crueler
than he had surmised.

For the umpteen-billionth time, the car wouldn't start!

Joe leaped to the ground, spread his legs like Charlton Heston posing defiantly in front of the heroic craggy letters of *Ben-
Hur*, uplifted his arms to the glorious blue expanse crowning
his many moods, and howled: *"Why me, God?"*

A hundred tiny yellow warblers popped out of Eloy's fruit
trees. They joined momentarily, an airborne golden globe above

the orchard, then broke apart, scattering their lemony, tear-shaped bodies to the four winds.

Though enraged, Joe nevertheless doubled up laughing at the ludicrous figure he must have cut, gesturing at the sky, leading the droll life he led. Would it never end? Forgetting about his own drama, would there ever be Peace on Earth? Would there ever be a single day for just lolling around in the moss atop a plump pink maiden, listening to nightingales and guzzling Löwenbräu, while fauns grazed among lilies of the valley, and apples glittered like Christmas-tree baubles . . . ?

❧

On his way out the driveway, Joe almost banged head on against Tribby's battered Volvo skidding in. "Hey!" the lawyer cried jubilantly, leaping from his car into the cloud of dust that eddied around their two vehicles. "Where are you going in such a hurry, my good friend?"

"Crazy. You wanna come along?"

"Tut tut. Don't be bitter, now."

"What are you doing over here—you have jumped your keeper at feeding-time and escaped?"

Tribby assumed a kidding pontificating posture: "I've come, said the wise old man, to assess the situation."

"Well, there it is." Joe indicated the festival preparations with a sweep of his hand.

Tribby squinted, then slapped his thigh. "Hot dawg! Not only are they offering us a million free dollars, but to boot it's packaged to go. Look at that cable on the U-Haul."

Joe said, "Hey, man. Seriously, for a minute. I've been thinking. . . ."

Tribby turned on him. "No no, cut the shit. Nobody's paying you to think!"

"I'm *tired*," Joe whined. "I don't want to be rich. I've given up on the land. To hell with the dope. And especially screw your helicopter escapade. It's all fantasies. It's not worth it."

His chum's face fell. "I thought you wanted this land. You already risked your *life* for it."

"I did. I still do. But it's impossible. I can't compete. I don't want to compete, either. The game is too rough. I've already lost everything that was precious to me, and what have I received in return?"

"Passion," Tribby said excitedly, running his hand through his flowing white hair. "My God, doesn't the thought of buzzing down from the sky and snatching that thing get your thermometer rising?"

"It makes my bones clench and my asshole ache."

"There you go!"

"No. Those are horrendous feelings."

"It'll be . . . it'll be . . ." Tribby flapped his hands, searching for a hyperbole, a metaphor, an exclamation. "It'll be the crime of the century. We'll bamboozle the Hanumans, flimflam the Mafia, cheat all the nasty banks and all the corrupt lawyers!"

"You're not thinking ahead," Joe said meticulously. "We might get caught. They'll punish us worse than for the dope. And even if the authorities somehow can't follow the two billion clues we've given to their logical conclusions, the underworld will know who did it. And next time Bonatelli will squash my face instead of a grapefruit. Tribby, it's time to wake up. These monkey-and-gangster games are insane."

"Wait a minute. Before you knock it, listen to how simple the gig is gonna be. I mean seriously, it's like a plan sculpted by Michelangelo."

Joe shook his head. "No, no, no—you're not hearing me. The whole caper is like a bad movie. It has nothing to do with the real world, real life, real anything."

"Ralph is gonna remove the fly boxes from both the copters. So then if Ephraim Bonatelli and Ray Verboten try and beat us to the punch, they won't have a leg to stand on!"

Joe said, "My wife hates me, my kids hate me, and you've gone crazy! *It ain't worth it!*"

"Hey, calm down, bro." Tribby grabbed Joe's shoulders and rattled them. "Don't shout."

"I can't help it," Joe sobbed. "I'm not cut out for this line of work. All I ever wanted in life—"

"Hush, hush, calm down, easy boy. Listen, it's a piece of cake. Trust me, trust me." He pinched Joe's chin, forcing him to look into his eyes. "Trust me, partner. Just trust me. Okay? You got that now? Just trust *me*. I know what I'm doing."

Joe said, "There's a goddam *angel* walking around this town."

"What?"

"There's an angel walking around this town. I think it's the Angel of Death. He wants to kill me."

"Joe?" Tribby blanched. "Joe, for Christ's sake, look at me. What the hell are you on? What have you been taking?"

"I'm not kidding. There was a feather in the phone booth. Sanji Smatterling saw him there. Then I woke up this morning, and he was sitting in a chair, staring at me. We had a fight. Then I shot Diana's pistol at him."

"Oh shit," Tribby groaned. "You've flipped."

"I'm serious. He's six feet tall, maybe even bigger. He's got a beard. And wings. And a real halo."

Tribby let go his shoulders, backing up a step, aghast. "What are you on, man, psylocibin? LSD? Did somebody slip you a quiff of those cutworm moths soaked in PCP?"

"I don't even smoke dope. I'm telling you, he's real."

"Real?" Tribby banged his head. "I shoulda known you would crack. You frigging preppies can't stand the pressure. Christ man, we're so close, you can't fall apart. Please. I beg of you. I can hand you this land on a silver platter, if you'll only just keep it together."

"I can't anymore. I'm just a humble everyday working shmuck. All I ever wanted in life was—"

"No," Tribby said vehemently, "I'm not gonna let you do it. You set all of this in motion."

"Me and the guy who offed whatshisname, the Archduke Ferdinand at Sarajevo."

"But you're missing a very important point."

"Which is?"

"If you let them take it away from you, and away from your kids, and away from Eloy Irribarren, why then you're nothing better than just another patsy. You're the one who always used to lecture me on how important it was to seize the day. You're the one who always used to tell me that individuals can make a difference on historical scales. You're the one who's always telling me that we can affect our own destinies. You're the Communist Christer who always told me that each and every one of us has a moral imperative to halt progress, American-style. You're the son of a bitch who always claimed it was more important to die like a man on your feet than to live like a slave on your knees."

"But it's too difficult. They own all the horses. And anyway, what's the point of struggling for justice by selling dope or kidnapping granite monkeys? The means don't justify the end."

"Well, I refuse to let them do it to you," Tribby said quietly.

"You may want them to steamroller your marshmallow hide, but not me. I say enough is enough. They deserve a run for their money. I'm mad, José, and I aim to do something about it."

Morosely, Joe said, "Well all of us lose in the end. It can't succeed."

"Says you, Mr. Defeatist personified." He kicked at a pebble. "I never thought I'd see the day."

"Oh hell," Joe whimpered, "I'm sorry."

"Sorry? Don't hand me that liberal apologia trip."

Weakly, Joe tried to defend himself. "It's not liberal apologia. It's just that—"

"Say no more, I get the drift."

"But you don't understand. . . ."

"I understand, all right. They appeased Hitler, and look what happened." He retreated toward his Volvo.

"This has nothing to do with Hitler. . . ."

"Oh yeah? Who does Bonatelli represent? Who does Ray Verboten represent? Who does Nikita Smatterling represent?"

"I know, but—"

"No buts. I'm in this to the very end. And so is Ralph. We finally figured out a way to salvage your ass, and you come up with the screaming meemies. Some thanks."

Joe staggered over to the driverside of the automobile as Tribby slouched behind the wheel. "It's just that I've lost the thread," Joe pleaded. "I can't seem to do anything right. When I first spoke with Peter about scoring that crude dope, I thought it would be all so simple. But the situation keeps deteriorating. People attack me, they ridicule me, they want my body, they want my soul. I don't understand how everything could go so wrong. Can't you sympathize?"

"I got only a handful of hours to pull off one of the most daring heists in American history, and you want me to hold your hand?"

"Forget my hand. But you could make an attempt to understand my point of view."

"I understand," Tribby said quietly. "It's the point of view of a fifty-year-old, alcoholic, potbellied turkey who every day reads *The New York Times* on the five seventeen into Scarsdale, and has a bunch of clandestine *Playboy* magazines secreted in his den closet to beat off by while he dreams of diddling nubile starlets and writing letters of congratulations to Che Guevara."

"No. Wait a minute. I'm not like that. . . ."

Tribby slammed it into reverse, and peeled backward out of the driveway. His "Oh yes you are" ricocheting back among the pebbles stung Joe like a savage hornet.

"Wait!" he cried.

But his pal, a man of action in a world that moved too fast for the likes of Joe Miniver, was tearing off along the bumpy road, twisting a screeching Destiny by her slippery, sinuous tail.

And Joe ate the dust.

⌘

Nevertheless, later, tooling down the highway, his knees went weak with relief. "I'm no longer a player," he said aloud. "I'm tapped out of the game."

He had the distinct sensation—and he welcomed it—that his strange odyssey had almost ended. For one thing, he couldn't take the pace. For another, ultimately his priorities lay elsewhere. Lessons he had painfully learned these past few days he would never forget. What he and Heidi shared was precious almost to the point of being scared. During the last few years a sloppiness had wrangled into the marriage, but this traumatic upheaval would awaken them both, cementing the family more strongly together. First thing next week he planned to break out the tattered copy of *The Art of Loving* they both had read so long ago. And he could do it, Joe knew, because deep down he was a long-distance runner, with principles, morals, compassionate sensibilities. Neither he nor Heidi, nor the children, were lightweights. How absurd to flounder into the dope-and-guru-riddled carnival of middle-class anarchism in Chamisaville. None of them was even remotely that superficial.

Worn-out, pensive, and conciliatory, relaxing as he began to glow with benevolent feelings, Joe reread Heidi's note . . . and discovered that the vicious little epistle was hard to take with a grain of salt.

For starters, he had not been doing what she thought he was doing when she so snidely slipped it under his windshield wiper. Plus it was Heidi, essentially, who had driven him into exile after his initial slipup, thus forcing him to consolidate a sexual liaison he'd had no intention of consummating beyond that initial Saturday night. And what about the way she was now working overtime to poison the kids against him? Take for example the term *fornication sweepstakes*. Or: How nasty could you get, telling the kids their father might drop them "a postcard or two" every year?

Finally, where did that snotty bitch get off, threatening him with the legal expertise of a sexist creep like Scott Harrison? How could she pay the slick buzzard—by spreading her legs for bottlecaps? By paying his outrageous fees in pudendum, pussy, and pap? Or by lying that she'd destroyed the cocaine, and then unloading it on the side? If he got to Heidi before the Verboten-Bonatelli thugs, he'd do the coke kingpin's job on her for them!

Wow. Where did it come from, such a blithering, prejudiced, and yet alarmingly heartfelt, venom?

Barely sixty seconds ago, the Peace-Love-Groovy Kid had drawn his double six-guns and shot flowers into the cosmic domain of Tranquillity, Concern, and Caring. Now, suddenly, decked in black, he was firing dumdums at all those helpless, warm, and soft rabbits hopping about the greensward of Familial Experience.

Time to apply the brakes—to himself, not the bus—but in this he failed miserably. Completely disregarding his good intentions, totally ignoring the fact that he'd been a loyal husband and devoted father for a decade, his wife, Heidi Medea, would stop at nothing to poison the kids against their Daddy!

The accumulating fury soon boiled over. By the time he neared the Castle of Golden Fools, a wicked froth bubbled between his lips. After a fifth reading of Heidi's note, Joe concluded that the only way to handle her was with an ax. Or by kidnapping the kids.

He would abduct the only two human beings he truly loved before her poisonous fangs had sucked all their rational blood, transforming them into miniature hate-filled ogres greedy for dollars, property, and power!

ॐ§

As luck would have it, Heidi was gone when he entered the apartment in Tribby Gordon's infamous digs. Both kids were home, though, in the middle of a jigsaw derby.

Twice a year they hauled out every puzzle they owned, and initiated a marathon of jigsaw construction usually lasting the better part of a week. Or until the living-room floor became carpeted with the mosaics, and all family members had cramped calves from tiptoeing around the completed works of banal art. Some puzzles were so familiar they could do them in minutes. In fact, they often competed to see who could do a puzzle faster. Last Christmas Michael had received a stopwatch. Awed, Joe had watched them time each other doing a hundred-piece exercise in under five minutes. Their destinies, obviously, lay as genius physicists or inmate extras in the Titicut Follies. What else could you say about a little boy shrieking off stopwatch seconds as his kid sister raced to complete a puzzle faster than her brother had done it minutes earlier, with a quarter of her dollar allowance at stake?

Joe said, "All right, let's go, fetch the suitcases from the closet and pack all your clothes, we're getting out of here."

"No we're not," Heather said calmly. "We're doing puzzles."

"Screw the puzzles." Joe towered menacingly over them. "Where's Heidi?"

"We don't know."

"How can you not know? She didn't leave a note where she was going?"

"She was gone when we got home." Heather fitted a piece into Snoopy's nose.

"I can't believe she would split without giving you kids a number. I mean, suppose there was an emergency?"

"Aw, you don't have to make a federal case out of it." Heather added, "Come on, Daddy, be quiet. We hafta concentrate."

"Maybe you didn't hear me. I said find the suitcases and pack all your clothes, we're getting out of here."

Michael looked up. "Where are we going?"

"I don't know. But I've had it with this stupid town."

Heather asked, "Is Mommy coming?"

"No. I'm sick and tired of her, too."

"Then I'm not going."

Michael said, "Me neither."

"Wait a minute. I don't think you kids understand. I'm not *asking* you twerps if you want to go with me, I'm *ordering* you to pack your bags and tag along."

Heather said, "You can't make us if we don't want to."

"Heather, if you don't shut up and hop to it by the time I

count to three, I'll yank your pants down and give you a hundred whacks on a bare fanny."

"I don't care."

"This time I wouldn't be kidding around, I assure you. And believe me, it would hurt."

Michael looked uneasy. "If we go with you, does that mean I'll have to go to a different school?"

"Well, no . . . I mean, sure . . . uh, you know—I don't know. It depends on where we wind up. But probably—well, *sure*. I mean, I'm not going to hang around this town—"

"Then I'm not going. I don't want to leave my school."

"Whaddayou mean, you don't want to leave it? Yesterday a bunch of creeps hunted you down and busted your nose in cold blood."

"I don't care," he said defiantly, finishing off one of King Kong's ears, "I don't want to go to a different school right in the middle of the year."

"You got hardly any time left, Michael. Then you'll have all summer to adapt to a new neighborhood."

"Well, we're not going with you," Heather said, "and that's final."

"Heather, you stand up right this instant and go pack your suitcase or I'll really start kicking ass around here, and it won't be a damn bit funny."

To Michael, Heather said, "Gimme that piece over there, it goes on his leg."

At a loss for words, Joe hovered over them, capable of destroying their puzzles with one swift kick and of knocking their insolent little blocks off with one brutal haymaker, yet he could not act. Apparently, to them he was a small irritant, a mosquito buzzing on the outskirts of their action, and they had decided that, if they ignored him, he would soon buzz off.

Joe said, "I'm gonna start counting, dammit. You kids better pay attention."

"We still have a whole bunch of puzzles to do," Heather informed him.

Joe exploded: "I don't believe you monsters! You know what would have happened to me if I had defied my father like this? He would have slapped me unconscious, grabbed me by the ankles, and dropped me down the laundry chute. And you know what my mother would have done? She would have grabbed a chair and beaten me over the head with it. Then she would have snatched a log from beside the fireplace and chucked it at me."

"What's a laundry chute?" Heather asked.

Joe said, "If you guys won't do it, then I will."

"What?"

"I'll pack your goddam bags."

Heather exaggerated her typical obnoxious shrug: "It's all the same to me." And both kids sniggered. Michael set about finishing their work on the ape puzzle.

"Jesus, I don't know why I'm not killing you rats!" Joe stomped into the bedroom. "In my time, if somebody talked back to their folks like that they were boiled in oil!"

Many moons ago, he had very carefully stored the children's suitcases in the back of their closet. No longer were they very carefully stored where he had placed them.

"Where's the suitcases?" he growled . . . loudly.

"We don't know," they chimed back . . . in unison.

"Well, I put them in your closet. Now who moved them, dammit? I'm sick and tired of every time I try to find something around here, it's never where I put it!"

No response from the living room.

"Did you kids hear me?"

Vaguely: "Uh huh . . . yup . . ."

"Well, then answer me."

"Maybe somebody stole them."

"Who would steal such lousy bags? Come on, Heather, use your noodle."

"I already did in a bowl of chicken soup."

Joe said, "If you kids don't hop to it, I'm gonna flare. And then you'll be sorry."

Heather pantomimed an enormous yawn and spoke to Michael. "Give me that piece over there, the one with part of his finger on it—no, not that one, the other one . . . that's right. Thanks."

Joe warned, "I don't think you guys realize I'm serious."

The mouthpiece, Heather, future shyster for both the Mafia and some multinational corporate entity financing fascism around the globe, calmly replied: "We know you're serious, Daddy. That doesn't go over there, Michael, it goes right here. This piece belongs over there."

"I'm gonna count to three, and if you two little pricks aren't on your feet and hunting suitcases by then, the first thing I'll do is destroy all your puzzles. Then I'll break every toy in your room, especially your Baby Alive, Heather, and I'll burn all the *Mad* and *Cracked* magazines, Michael."

Michael looked uncomfortable and started to rise. Heather said, "You wouldn't dare."

With A Little Voice telling him this was no way to commence a kidnapping, Joe strode purposefully into their room, gathered the Baby Alive doll, three *Mad* magazines, and two models off the display shelf his kids had constructed and painted by themselves, and returned to the living room. "Watch this, you guys."

Michael stared. But Heather feigned intense interest in their puzzle. Onto the floor Joe dropped two fragile plastic airplanes that Michael had meticulously painted and decalled, and, in five quick stomps, reduced them to rubble.

Heather looked up.

One at a time, using swift no-nonsense rips, Joe reduced the *Mads* to smithereens and casually allowed the confetti to drift off his fingers.

Then, their beady, astonished eyes indicating rapt attention, Joe tore off the doll's head, arms, and legs: pathetic pink appendages clattered onto the floor.

"That's for starters," he said icily. "Now get your spoiled-brat butts in gear and find those suitcases before I actually get pissed off."

Hurriedly, they rose, circled Joe without letting their eyes off him for a second, and rushed to do his bidding. Michael found one suitcase behind a stack of games, a pile of filthy Jockey briefs, and a set of blocks and orange Hot Wheels tracks beneath his bed. The other turned up under an enormous dirty-clothes pile in the linen closet. Something rattled inside it—a half-dozen cat turds, hard as marble. But when the kids went to pack, they had no clothes in their bureau drawers.

"No *clothes*?"

Meekly, Michael said, "I guess they're all in the laundry."

"Doesn't your mother ever go to the laundromat?" Joe was a little frightened by the enormous anger causing his temple veins to stand out rigidly. "Can't she take even a tiny bit of responsibility when I'm not around?"

Michael asked, "Where are we going?"

"I don't know. We're just going."

"I still don't wanna leave," Michael whispered.

"You can't make us," Heather said. She was close to tears.

"I'm your father, and you'll do what I say whether you like it or not. Now, go gather some of your dirty clothes from the linen closet and fill those suitcases."

"But—"

"*Go!*"

They went.

Joe felt almost giddy with power. Never had he treated his children so insensitively. Always, even when he screamed, they had accepted his anger as a put-on, his ferocious epithets as a jest. Today was the first time he had ordered them about in a tone that absolutely meant business. Today was also the first time they had actually raced to do his bidding without arguing the semantics of his case until he retreated from their wizened little sophistical half-brains in total frustration.

Not such a bad feeling, this: a case could be made for fascism in the family! In fact, Joe experienced a downright sensual blast of heady well-being he'd rarely known. From now on, whenever he wanted a clean bathtub, the Kitty Litter divested of its fecal harvest, or the wastebaskets emptied, he would simply appear on the scene with a hammer in one hand and Heather's E-Z Bake Oven in the other hand, and start counting to ten.

"If you want to bring any toys or books, put them in too," he said gruffly.

Heather growled, "Boy, are you ever gonna be sorry." But she packed a Raggedy Ann doll, two Sesame Street coloring books, a box of forty crayons, and a miniature tea set. Michael threw in the chess set, a slingshot, and three Hardy Boys mysteries, and they were ready to haul ass.

"Take those suitcases down. I'll be there shortly."

Michael said, "I'm hungry."

"We'll eat on the road."

"But my stomach's about to explode."

"Okay, make yourself a sandwich. But hurry up."

"I'm hungry too," Heather said. Like condemned prisoners, seconds before the gallows, they would use any stalling tactic, hoping for the governor's last-second pardon. Which in this case would be Heidi's arrival and subsequent dramatic conniption, Joe surmised.

In the bathroom, he confirmed his worst premonitions. The tea box lay in the wastebasket. So she had done it—willfully, callously, insanely deprived him of a small fortune! Or was the empty box a ploy to throw him off the scent? Suppose she and Scott Harrison had plans to market the dope in secret, get married, and purchase Eloy Irribarren's land for themselves?

Using a bar of Dial soap, Joe scrawled a message on the medicine-cabinet mirror:

> I took the kids. Screw you
> and Scott Harrison!
>
>   J.
>
> PS   You owe me $100,000!

Sombre-and-fairly-silent characterized the children's mood as they loaded the bus. It was a little like leaving the chancellory bunkers during the final battle of Berlin in 1945. Pinched faces, compressed lips, weary and frightened eyes. Now that he was actually going to make the snatch, Joe felt self-conscious, and rather stupid. He wanted to cop out, call it all a big joke—ha ha. Instead, he slammed shut doors, initiated the crazy sequence necessary to fire up the engine, and, casting but a single backward glance, hit the road. Beside him, Michael and Heather stared through the windshield. Joe beeped nervously. The kids' heads swiveled; they fixed apprehensive, already-growing-adult eyes on their former home, saying au revoir to their childhoods, to all the cheerful unfettered times of youth. Only when the Castle had disappeared did they face forward again, their hard, mistrustful eyes peering into a future where beatings, street hustling, child pornography, and shoeshine kits waited to forge them as cynical little diablos long before their time.

Michael leaned over, whispering in Heather's ear. After he finished his spiel to her, she asked: "Daddy, are we gonna go through the capital?"

"I dunno. Maybe. I haven't exactly figured out . . ."

Like: Where now, brown cow? To a seaside retreat in a quaint Mexican village? To Dallas or Birmingham or New York City, and a return to the ad game? He would score a mint quick, then fly to Majorca one jump ahead of detectives Heidi had hired to track them down.

"Well, if we go through the capital, can we stop at the Baskin-Robbins?"

While he, the responsible parent, worried about detectives, escape, and earning a living, his children concerned themselves with the truly crucial issues in life—namely, ice cream!

"We'll see."

First off, Joe steered into the plaza, parking in front of Harbinger's Ski and Sport. Nick Danger happened at that moment to be darkly passing by, casting no furtive glances either to the left or right as he plowed along with his suitcase full of—money? dope? Dead Sea Scrolls?—to yet another mysterious assignation.

"What are we gonna do in here?" Michael asked.

"Stay in the car. I'll be back in a minute."

"But why are you stopping?" Heather demanded.

"None of your business."

"If you don't tell us, Daddy," Heather teased, "I'll shoot you right through the heart." She pointed Diana's revolver—the very weapon for which Joe planned to purchase ammunition in Harbinger's—at her father.

"Where did you find *that?*" Joe snatched it from her, too surprised even to castigate her for pointing a real gun at an alive person.

"It was on the floor when we got in the car."

And therefore must have fallen from his pocket. "Christ on a crutch," Joe moaned, slamming open a glass door into the sporting goods store: "I should be wearing diapers!"

Returning to the car, he tossed a box of .22 shells into the glove compartment, and they took off. Heather opened her mouth, but Joe beat her to the punch:

"Don't ask, kid. Like I said, it's none of your business."

A silent quarter-mile later, they hit their first roadblock. It consisted of all the usual amenities: two backhoes, a telephone-company truck, a generator, three ninety-thousand-pound prefab concrete four-way sewage pipe connectors, eleven worker-owned pickup trucks, twenty-one indolent hardhats drinking beer and scratching their bellies, and one large pit emitting noxious vapors.

Joe braked, fishtailed, turned around, and sought escape from the Chamisaville quagmire by another road. For six minutes they headed due south on the bumpy dirt artery until a fairly extensive puddle, of a fluid somewhat resembling water, blocked their path: yet one more faultily constructed and sloppily interred sewage main had sprung a leak. How bad were the potholes beneath the surface? Pinching his nose, Joe decided not to risk it. No point to bogging down in that hideously noisome pool of excrement, whose fumes, no doubt, would kill them long before a Highway Department helicopter arrived to whisk them away.

They traveled in reverse for a hundred yards, negotiated a turn in someone's driveway, and chose another route in another direction. Heading west, this time, they soon found their escape route blocked by a cable TV crew whose trencher had just chopped a ditch across the road prior to laying down cable.

Asked how long the delay might be, the foreman, one of Wilkerson Busbee's hippie capitalists, replied, "Aw hell, man. It's late, we're all quitting for supper in five minutes. Tomorrow we're all going to the Hanuman fiesta. So this won't be done until the weekend."

"But I can't drive across that trench like it is now."

The foreman assessed first the trench, then Joe: "I never said you could, man."

"Well, then how am I gonna get out of this crazy town?"

"Did you try Alta Mesa yet?"

"It's blocked off by another sewage-line break."

The amiable freak scratched his head. "Geez, whaddayou know? How about Route 240?"

"It's all messed up south of the S-turn by a convention of backhoes and monstrous prefabricated concrete culverts."

"Wow, that's too bad. Why don't you try Valverde? That'd get you a little bit south of all the construction down where they're excavating the underground cables for the high-school-and-hospital traffic light they just installed that doesn't work."

"Are you positive Valverde is clear? Last week, didn't they yank out an old culvert and forget to replace it?"

"That was last week. I heard they installed a new one this morning."

"I'll believe it when I see it." Again, Joe backed up, regained 240, and hung a louie on Valverde, another quaint dirt path teeming with rocks and potholes. As they jounced over mounds of ungraded gravel covering the new culvert, Joe gave a cheer:

"Free at last!" Ruffling Heather's hair, he added: "Cheer up kids, I think we made it."

But, as always, he was a fool, he'd spoken too soon. As they rounded a bend, an enormous felled cottonwood tree blocked the route. A guy wearing a black widebrimmed Mack hat with a leopardskin band, a red-velvet sheepskin-lined Afghanistan vest on which a monkey had been embroidered, and prefaded Gucci denims, and a girl in a silk granny dress and air-force flight boots, sat on top of the tree sharing a joint.

"What the hell happened here?" Joe asked.

The Afghanistan vest shrugged: "I dunno, man. I must of miscalculated."

"We thought it would fall the other way." The girl giggled. "But it didn't."

Joe said, "If it had fallen the other way it would have crushed your house."

"Naw, it wouldn't have hit it, man. That house has got powerful karma."

"Why did you cut it down in the first place?"

"Oh we asked it permission first," the girl explained. "It said it was okay. Like, you know, it granted us this really beautiful favor."

"But why?"

"Sunlight," the vest replied. "We got a ton of skylights, but the tree was still blocking out most of the light. Plus, of course, firewood." He extended his arm, offering the roach. "Want a toke? This is dynamite shit."

The transmission complained loudly as Joe jammed the shifting stick into reverse, and wheezed off to search for another of their rapidly diminishing escape hatches from Chamisaville.

Heather asked, "Are you and Mommy gonna get divorced?"

"That's what she implied in her note this afternoon. In any case, she hired Chamisaville's number-one gunslinger to do the job."

"Well, if you guys get divorced, which one are we gonna live with?"

"Neither. We'll probably send you to a military orphanage for juvenile delinquents."

"Come on, Daddy, be serious. Which one are we gonna live with?"

"I imagine we'll split the responsibility. On Mondays, Wednesdays, and Fridays, Michael will live with me and you'll live with Mommy—during the days, that is. But every night you'll switch: Michael will go to spend Monday, Wednesday, and Friday nights with Heidi, and you'll spend them with me. Tuesdays and Thursdays, we'll do it backwards. You'll spend the days with me and the nights with Heidi, while Michael does just the reverse. And every other weekend you'll spend together with me, except in February when you'll each spend two contiguous weekends together, first with Heidi, then with me. Got that?"

Heather said, "If you and Mommy get divorced will you marry Nancy Ryan?"

"Hey, Heather, you know sometimes you're really an obnoxious little girl."

"Well, will you?"

"I refuse to answer on the grounds that it may tend to degrade or incriminate me."

"I wouldn't mind that too much," Heather said brightly. "I think it'd be neat to have two mommies. Then, after you get divorced, maybe Mommy will get married again, and we'll have two fathers, too. I hope she marries somebody who isn't a garbage man, with a real car that starts up every time and has a heater."

"I like that. I paid your hospital bill when you were born, I changed your diapers for two solid years, I spent billions of dollars filling you full of the best food money could buy, I took you to the hospital when you had pneumonia and stood guard over you night and day until you got better, I gave you birthday parties and lavish Christmas mornings, I taught you how to bake cakes and cookies, I gave you kitties and puppies to make you happy, I held your hand on the first day of school . . . and you'd throw me over, just like that, for some creep in a late-model car and a cushy job."

"I only call 'em as I see 'em," Little Miss Wiseass rejoined.

"What about you, Michael? Don't you have any savage or ironic verbal daggers to thrust into the quivering belly of your defenseless father?"

"What's 'ironic'?" he asked.

"It's when they put machines inside your body to make you like Superman," Heather said before Joe could answer.

"That's 'bionic,' you nincompoop." Joe cuffed her head. "Ironic means, um, you know . . ." But he stalled. How did you explain it to a kid? "Ironic is kind of like when, well, suppose you were going to board an airplane for a flight to Denver. But at the last minute you couldn't get on it because your mother was sick. So the plane took off and crashed, killing everybody in it. You would really be counting your lucky stars your mother was sick, right? But then, say, that on your way over to see her, your car hit a patch of ice, you skidded off the road, turned over, and died. Well, it would be real ironic that, having escaped certain death in the airplane, you wound up being killed anyway in a stupid car accident on the way to see the mother who saved you from a horrible death in the first place. Is that clear?" he asked feebly, knowing damn well it was about as clear as mud.

Intellectual lazybones from the word go, both kids sagely nodded their heads. Their complaisance, their lack of curiosity, and above all their bland acceptance of such a piss-poor definition, angered Joe.

"All right, so go ahead, Heather, explain to me what 'ironic' means."

"But you just did, Daddy."

"Yeah, but I wanna hear it from your own lips. Just to be sure that you correctly grasp the concept."

"It's, you know, when a plane crashes and you have a car accident at the same time."

Through gritted teeth, Joe said, "What about you, Michael?"

"It's like Heather said." He averted his face from Joe's, obviously somewhat derailed by his father's emotional instability.

"No it is *not* like Heather said!" Joe roared belligerently. "It isn't even remotely like Heather said. In fact, it isn't even remotely like *I* said. That was a horrible definition! And you creeps just sit there, not even listening, nodding your heads like brainless automatons when it's over. Don't they encourage you to have any intellectual curiosity in school? If you don't understand something, then *raise your hands*, *dammit!*"

Heather said, "I have a question about something I don't understand."

"Okay, shoot."

Michael pointed his finger, pistol-style, at Joe: "Bang! Bang!"

Heather pushed her brother's hand away. "What I don't understand, Daddy, is how come you're kidnapping us?"

"Because you're such dear, sweet, adorable children I can't live a minute more without you."

"We don't want to be kidnapped," Michael said.

"Why—you hate my guts?"

"Well, where are we gonna *go*?" Heather asked shrilly. "What are we gonna *do*? Are we gonna live in motels? I hate motels. We won't have any friends. And anyway, Mommy promised to take us to the movies tomorrow night."

"Oh she did, did she? What's playing? *The Son of Flubber Meets Gidget*? *Honkies Versus Niggers in a Pornographic Race War*? The heartwarming story of how a woman with a clitoris in her throat learned to off corrupt cops by jabbing them with hypodermics full of battery acid when their attention was diverted by her singular talent?"

"Nuh-uh." Michael genuinely wished to placate his old man. "It's just about killer bees that take over America."

"Let's call it the United States of North America." Joe was really hitting his stride, here, as a carping SOB. "I don't know where we get the arrogance to call our country America. Mexico is also America, Central America and South America are also America. And so isn't Canada? It's absurd for us to call ourselves America, like we're the only country that exists in America."

That did it. They lapsed into stony silence.

A mile south of the plaza, Joe had to brake again. A small crane, a large unpiloted tar-laying machine, and a chauffeurless bulldozer blocked the route.

For almost a minute they remained stationary, confronting this latest blockade. Joe could feel his adrenaline dissolving. All the fight, all the anger, all the determination to heist his kids and blow this manic burg drained from his body, trickled down between his toes, left behind a mere shell of a man— weary, demoralized, defeated. He clung to the steering wheel as if to a life preserver. His head buzzed, his ears rang. Life was hopeless. Nothing would ever work out as he wanted it to. Why not sign up for a spiritual lobotomy, accepting enervation as a way of life? I'll eat nothing but taco chips and bean dip, I'll grow fat and lethargic and stupid. A rebel no more, I'll spend hours every day gooning at the boob tube: "Charlie's Angels," "The Gong Show," and "The Waltons." Ultimately, green leaves will sprout from my earlobes as I achieve a vegetal state, devoid of ambition and passion and intelligence and sexual desire. My only quality will be Placidity Personified.

Heather broke the silence. "Why are we just sitting here?"

Joe rubbed his aching eyes. "Because I'm tired."

"You're wasting gas letting it idle," Michael said.

"Tough beans. Let them arrest me, throw me in the hoose-gow, beat me insensate with rubber truncheons, I don't care, I've had it."

"Well, what are we gonna do now?"

"I don't know. I'm through making decisions."

"We wanna go home," Heather said.

"Fine. You get your wish. Tell me how to do it, and I'll drive you home."

"First you gotta turn the car around."

Robotlike, eyes so glazed he could barely see, Joe alternately mangled reverse and first gears until he had the car aimed in the opposite direction, and off they chugged at a crawl.

Michael said, "You mean we're not being kidnapped?"

"That's right. You win. I give up. The forces of Reaction and of the Right defeat the Forces of Conscience and of the Left once again."

After a minute, Heather said, "You're not a very good kidnapper."

Here it came, self-pity times infinity, pathos in a weak-kneed sniveling jellyfish: "I'm not a very good *any*thing, if you want to know the truth." Oh what had happened to that brash and brainy stud of yesteryear?

For all the usual arcane reasons, no barriers, highway blockades, construction boondoggles, malicious detours, or other assorted neanderthal, progress-oriented snafus punctuated the return trip. Arriving home before dark, Joe parked beside the strange-looking gray van with a bubble top, a cow skull on the front grille, and a Chicken River Funky Pie sign on the side. Desultorily he ordered the kids to take their luggage indoors. While they negotiated the ladder, he remained seated in an apathetic daze, grateful that he hadn't the guts to load the pistol in his pocket.

This hedonism was getting him nowhere!

In fact, he didn't want to move, ever again. He hadn't the energy, even, to raise one hand and scratch the tip of his nose. It had ended at long last—his life. I can will myself to die, Joe thought. I'll just blow a whistle in my brain, ordering everything in there to stop, lie down, go to sleep. It would be like absorbing a hit from one of those powerful ray guns in science-fiction thrillers—instant atrophy! Afterward, he would stay forever in his rusty machine. While autumn leaves ticked and scratched against the roof, and while snowflakes piled atop the vehicle and along the window ledges, he would remain immobile, a statue, a monument to the tragic end that selfishness, narcissism, greed, and a lack of historical focus could lead a person to. Eventually, mice would nest in the glove compartment; chipmunks would filch the stuffing from seat cushions; rattlesnakes would hibernate in the engine compartment. Little carnivores such as lizards and egg-eating skunks would mosey around; they'd take tiny bites of his toes and flaccid calves. He would be somehow awake, but inert, unfeeling yet able to see, and possibly even think. Having sniffed him out, an enterprising weasel would commence munching in earnest. Another summer would come and go; another autumn arrive. By the time the new snows flew, he'd be a skeleton, a mute conglomeration of white bones still seated behind the wheel, testimony to the aberrant lethargy of his comatose bourgeois sensibility.

What the hell does that mean, "*Aberrant lethargy of comatose bourgeois sensibility?*" Heidi shrieked.

That did it! He'd had it with her snotty iconoclasm. Joe grabbed a chair and broke it over her head. Then he knocked her down on the kitchen floor and tipped the refrigerator over on top of her.

Ay, such violent thoughts. "I'm getting to be as American as cherry pie."

Four rather curious-looking persons crept surreptitiously around the corner of the house. They wore frog feet and skin-tight black rubber outfits with white piping down the sides of the legs and arms, plus rubber hoods and glass-visored masks and snorkels. One carried a shotgun; another delicately held a small chemistry-set tray with a dozen rubber-corked test tubes sitting upright in it; a third toted a long lethal-looking pole with a sharp triple-snag on the end that must have been a grappling hook. In either hand, the fourth lugged a galvanized barnyard pail.

All of them were covered with shit.

Joe's fingers curled around Diana's little revolver in his pocket. Remembering he hadn't loaded the gun, Joe prayed he would not be called on to use it. How could he have been so stupid as to buy the bullets without inserting them where they belonged?

Hunched over slightly, casting furtive glances to the right
and left, their frog feet flopping up clouds of dust as they
progressed, the weirdly outfitted personages scurried to the
Chicken River Funky Pie van, opened its rear doors, and climbed
in. One frogman advanced up to the driver's seat, started the
motor, backed around in the Castle's driveway, and leisurely
drove away.

Joe let out a sigh and faced his own haggard visage in the
rearview mirror, telling his bewildered, demoralized self: "Now
I've seen it all."

But he hadn't, of course. Not yet. Not by a long shot.

Heather appeared on the porch overhead, shouting at
the top of her lungs: "Daddy! Telephone!"

"Who is it?"

"That's for me to know and you to find out."

Kids! How he admired their resiliency. Snatched from the
bosom of their family and dragged all over creation by a bushy-
eyed wild man threatening to destroy their sweet innocence,
they could nevertheless rebound in seconds to become their old
saucy selves. Swinging painfully out of the bus, Joe didn't
know whether to have his daughter cast in bronze or to yank
down her corduroy bell-bottoms and whack the living daylights
out of her!

On their knees in the living room, surrounded by jellied
breadcrusts and banana peels, they were back to poring over
jigsaw puzzles. On his way to the phone, Joe growled, "Pick
up the torn magazines, dismembered doll, and smashed airplanes, would you please?"

"But we didn't do it. It's not our responsibility."

Joe woke up. "I don't care if *God* did it, you pick it up!
Both of you! Jesus, sometimes I *hate* you kids!"

This syndrome, the one in which neither child would take
responsibility for any chore that hadn't gone through a CIA-
FBI check as to his or her absolute *personal* connection to it,
infuriated Joe. If, their room being an unholy mess, they were
ordered to clean it, each one would attack only that disarray
incontrovertibly attributable to him- or herself. For example:
Heather would approach a pile of records lying about outside
their jackets collecting dust, gobs of glop, and scratches, and

insert into their proper covers only those records which she had played. If asked to gather up filthy clothes for the hamper, Michael would select only vestments that he himself had worn. When Joe accused them of doing only half a job, they squealed like stuck pigs: "But I didn't *play* those other records, Michael did!" Or: "But I picked up all *my* dirty stuff. Tell Heather to pick up her *own* clothes!"

Capitalism!

Joe's incensed orations contesting such narrow-mindedness pretty much followed a formula: "I don't give a good goddam who played those records, or whose clothes those are! You kids are sick! What would happen if we all only took responsibility for ourselves? You kids would starve to death, because I'd never bother to buy or cook any food for you! You'd never get to any dance lessons because your mother and I would refuse to chauffeur you there! You'd never get to Little League baseball, either, unless you walked the six miles into town on your own! You'd never get to see a movie, because why should we waste *our* energy and *our* bread taking *you* nerds along? You'd never have any clean clothes or plates to eat off of, because Heidi and me would just do our own clothes and wash only enough dishes for ourselves! Now dammit, if you two selfish little shitheel capitalists don't start taking some kind of collective responsibility I'll sell you to a Korean orphanage, that's what I'll do! I'm sick and tired of your selfishness and narrow-mindedness! I'm sick and tired of your me-obsessed, private-property-oriented Fascist personalities! So you better start learning to show a little communal spirit and consideration for others and responsibility that goes beyond your own mean little egos, you unnerstand? And you better do it *fast*!"

On their own turf, confident that the snatch was off, Heather and Michael moved slouchily to do their father's bidding. And Joe picked up the phone.

Chamisaville's answer to the Noxzema siren said, "Hi . . ."

"Oh, hi."

"Goodness, that was quite a tirade. You don't really mean that you hate them, do you?"

"Nancy, please, get to the point."

"Did you read my note this morning?"

"Sure."

"Well . . . ?"

"Well what?"

"Well, what about the Hanuman unveiling tomorrow?"

"Uh, I don't know. I mean, I'd like to go, but I'm not sure yet. You know. Things are a little up in the air. How about if I call you around, say, maybe eleven in the morning, okay? I'll know better by then."

"It's not something I'd miss if I were you. I think it will be one of the most beautiful and intriguing events of the year."

"I'm sure it will. I'm not so sure I wanna be there, though. After all, I'm the father of the kid that shot your little simian gangster. Maybe my presence would blow the vibes."

"On the contrary. Everybody wants you to come. And your children, too. You see, there's no vindictiveness among spiritual people. . . ."

"You're kidding. Mahatma Gandhi gains independence for India, and five minutes later a million and a half Moslems and Hindus die in a holy war. When God doesn't like the way things are going, he wipes out humanity with a flood. In Northern Ireland the Protestants and the Catholics are machine-gunning each other on streetcorners in the name of a higher being. And Nikita Smatterling takes umbrage to Ephraim Bonatelli's advances on his son, so he pokes a loaded revolver into the dwarf's paunch and pulls the trigger. Whaddayou mean, there's no vindictiveness among spiritual people?"

No answer from the other end of the line.

Joe asked, "You still there?"

"Oh yes," she said pleasantly. "I'm just waiting for you to get hold of yourself."

"Nancy, I don't want to talk right now. I'm not in real good form today. I'll telephone tomorrow."

"All right." She continued brimming with cheerful equanimity. "I love you, Joe. . . ."

But the instant he cradled the instrument, it rang again.

Tribby said, "Where the hell were you? I've been calling your house for an hour!"

"Oh, you know—here and there. How's the helicopter business?"

"Listen—first things first. For starters, Natalie's frantic. Apparently you promised to deliver the coke before five?"

"I 'promised'? You're kidding. For twenty-four hours I haven't had any coke to deliver to anybody."

"Her version is that in Nancy Ryan's bathroom this morning, right after the healing ritual, you struck a bargain."

"No way! I told her I thought Heidi had flushed it down the toilet."

"Well, listen to this. When I returned to my office, it was turned upside down. My files are wrecked. My drawers were dumped upside down and smashed. Even my diplomas were slashed. They also knifed the couch apart: it looks like a cotton gin exploded in here."

"Oh dear."

"Where's the coke?" Tribby begged. "I want those particular monkeys off our backs. The whole caper business is getting congested. If we could locate the dope and either sell or give it to somebody, they'd figure we had played our hand and wouldn't look for any shenanigans from us at the Hanuman festivities. So where's Heidi? All day she hasn't answered the phone."

"Out. Gone. Who knows where?"

"Do you suppose somebody kidnapped her?"

Joe let that sink in. "But how could . . . but I mean . . ."

"She's playing games," Tribby said curtly. "She doesn't understand what people will do for that stuff. Natalie admitted she thinks either you and Heidi are in cahoots, trying to throw everybody off the scent with that toilet story, or else Heidi and Scott Harrison are bamboozling you. Heidi already hired him to be her lawyer in your divorce settlement. Today, the oily bastard refiled papers making a grab for Eloy's place in payment for legal services rendered. He's hoping to make the heist before the grace period expires and the bank initiates foreclosure proceedings."

Joe mumbled, "So what? For the record, you should know that four guys wearing rubber suits and frog feet just crawled out of your septic tank covered in shit."

Tribby said, "You honestly can't produce the coke?"

"Neither honestly nor dishonestly."

"And you truly got no idea where Heidi went?"

"Not even the faintest." Again, Joe slipped his fingers over Diana's pistol: fear chilled him thoroughly. Why had he still failed to load the weapon? It was happening at last—something evil, dark, irrevocably lethal. And no aspect of the charade would be funny ever again. His selfishness, amateur brain-power, amoral actions, and irresponsibility had forged a nightmare of Himalayan magnitude.

Tribby said, "I'll tell Natalie about the scuba divers."

"I bet she already knows. Those rubber zombies must be on Ray Verboten's payroll."

"Course, that's not all," Tribby said.

Joe thought: Oh no, what next?

"I heard a rumor that Cobey Dallas and Roger Petrie are planning to tip over the First State People's Jug in order to raise cash to outmuscle Skipper and Nikita and Ray for Eloy's land before the Bonatelli-Smatterling helicoptered insurance fraud goes down."

"Tribby, I'm beginning to have trouble fathoming this plot."

"You and me both. Well listen, if you find Heidi, tell her to call me quick. Meanwhile, I'm gonna overlook our driveway tête-à-tête. We're all in it too deep for second thoughts right now."

Joe mumbled, "What am I supposed to do?"

"Just don't blow it. Start a riot tomorrow when you hear us coming... if you can. If you can't, stay out of the way, at least. We'll cut you in for your piece of the action no matter what, seeing as how you launched this fantasy."

"That's big of you."

"Get hold of yourself, kid. Bye-bye...."

As soon as Joe hung up, the phone rang yet again.

"Joe, this is Ifené. Papadraxis."

"Oh, hi, hey, how you doing?" he said jovially. Thank God she couldn't see the look of horror and panic on his astonished features!

"Did you get my note?"

"Sure, yeah, gee, thanks a lot."

"I certainly hope you're coming to the party tonight."

"Well, I, uh, you know, I mean..."

"Listen, Joseph. I'm frightfully sorry about last night. I think I'd imbibed a little too heavily. It was awful of me to come on so strongly. I felt very sheepish this morning, I really did. I would love to see you again, and I promise not to be so overbearing. Strictly between us two, I must admit that I find you inordinately attractive. Is that a deal then?"

"Uh, well, I, um..."

All his life, lily-livered geek that he was despite his superficial athletic prowesses, Joe had allowed people to make him say yes when he wanted to say no, and today proved no exception. Hanging up after acquiescing to Irené's invitation, he knew he was doomed.

He also knew—will wonders never cease?—that despite
the morbid circumstances surrounding his life, his wife, their
future, he had somehow been sexually aroused by a woman he
thought had emasculated him forever only hours earlier. He
seemed to be like one of those incredibly robust villains in the
Dick Tracy comic strip who kept coming at you despite a
barrage of blood-spattered .357-Magnum slugs popping out of
their gunhands, thighs, and rib cages, their passion for survival
equaled only by Chester Gould's greedy love of graphic mayhem.

Impetuously, Joe stooped, hugging each of his kids hard,
until they groaned and squirmed. Then he kissed their lips—
"Yuucch, Daddy!"—and he would have fled in search of his
wife had not the door abruptly opened: Heidi said, "Hello."

"My God, you're alive!"

"Why would I be anything else?"

"Where the hell have you been?"

"I don't believe that's any of your business anymore."

"But I thought . . . but we thought maybe you had been kidnapped."

"Obviously," she said with pointed, sarcastic cheerfulness,
"you thought wrong. Sorry to disappoint. I guess I've failed
another test. Dearie me."

Joe said, "Wait a minute, let's not start."

"Did I begin it? I'm standing here perfectly calm, when
what to my wondering ears should I hear, but my devoted
husband chastising me because I haven't been kidnapped, raped,
or bumped off in some grisly manner."

Joe bit his tongue, crossed to the kitchenette and opened
the refrigerator, thirsty for a cold one. But they were out of
beer. In fact, the dearth of comestibles was depressing. "Hey,"
he announced petulantly, "this refrigerator is empty."

"Oh children oh children," Heidi cried in a breathless, mock-
ing voice, "our master is home and the refrigerator is empty.
Let's all run around tearing our hair. My God, what a tragedy!
In the next fifteen minutes we may all starve to death!"

Joe asked suspiciously, "Are you drunk?"

"Why do you ask—because I'm not acting like Joey's little
Kewpie doll?"

"Since when did you act like anybody's little Kewpie doll?"

"Well the answer is no, I'm not drunk. I'm a little pooped, though, and I had hoped to arrive at a peaceful home devoid of Joe Casanova and his boring, uptight maunderings."

"Heidi, I'm too tired myself to fight back; I'm sorry."

"All fucked out, is he, our Boy Wonder? Come back for a little Rest and Recuperation in the bosom of the family before he takes off on another tear, is that it?"

"I'm serious." Wearily, Joe plunked down at the kitchen table. "You win by default."

"What happened out there in the Cold Cruel? Did one of your paramours hit your ego with a deadly hickey?"

Deliberately, Joe closed his eyes, determined to give some kind of reconciliation a desperate shot. "Hey, I'm not here to bug you or attack you," he murmured nervously. "I'm here because I'm ashamed. I love you and Michael and Heather, and I wish this past week had never happened. I want to know if there's any way we could talk again, or at least try not to be enemies."

"I'm not exactly riddled with altrustic feelings for you, Joey, if the truth be known."

"I can accept that."

"I really don't give a damn if you accept it or not."

"I meant 'I understand.' You've got every right—"

"No, wait a sec," She gestured ludicrously with the arm in a half cast. "Don't *you* start investing *me* with the rights I have or I don't have. From here on in *I* decide my own rights. You have nothing to do with it anymore."

"Again . . . it was only a figure of speech."

"Our language is full of figures of speech guaranteed to promulgate an exploitative male-oriented world, and I'm sick of them."

"Okay," he said, thoroughly bruised, utterly helpless. "Maybe you could let me know where we stand, anyway."

"You're on my royal shit list. And you can't con me into some sickly sweet reconciliation by pulling a pathetic, downcast, pooped-little-boy routine. I'm wise to that shtik. Between you and me it's over."

"Well, what can I say, then?"

"Why not start by stating your purpose. You want more clothes?—go get 'em. You need a fresh checkbook?—be my guest, they're in the bedroom desk as always. If you'd like to trade the bus for the Green Gorilla, that's fine by me—they're both such a bargain. Other than that, what could you possibly desire. The kids for a movie? They're all yours. Or some of this wonderful furniture for your bachelor—"

"Stop."

"It's hard to stop, Joey. First I'd like to crucify you with words. Then I'd enjoy tying you up and burning you all over with cigarette butts. Finally, I'd like to buy a gun and blow your head off."

"I can't say that I blame you."

"'I can't say that I blame you,'" she mimicked ruthlessly. "What's the matter, don't you have any fight left? I liked you better when you were lying your ass off trying to salvage a homelife *and* your extracurricular scoring at the same time."

"It just happened," he said forlornly. "I didn't plan anything."

"So what is it called, then, this 'spontaneous fucking'? Adultery in the second or the third degree?"

"Go ahead. Keep it up. How many points must you score to win this particular game? Please, keep going until you hit the magic number and can stop."

Michael self-consciously feigned absorption in his soundless television program. Heather sat cross-legged in the middle of the living-room rug pretending to be fanatically spellbound by a Judy Blume novel.

After a long pause, Joe said, "Well, then, I guess there's no point in my being here."

"What do you want me to do?" she replied bitterly. "Forgive and forget? Now that they've chopped you up a bit and spat at you, now that you've discovered it isn't all glamour and white-hot *Playboy* pussy out there, I'm supposed to welcome you back with open arms? I'm supposed to stroke your poor sweet bruised little ego cooing 'Oh the poor little Joeytums?' I'm supposed to nurse you back to psychological health, and proceed along the Primrose Path of Life as if nothing had happened?"

"I think I have enough decency left not to suggest anything like that."

"Do you? I haven't really been impressed by your decency lately. As far as I can figure you out, you've had about as much sensitivity as a can of sardines."

"Actually," he joked lamely, "I think I've got as least as much sensitivity as a can of salmon."

"Help! Shecky Greene strikes again!"

Joe shrugged, playing the teary-eyed clown. "Laugh and the world laughs with you. Weep and you weep alone."

"I've done plenty of the latter this week. But I'm tired of it now. Time to move on."

"To what?"

"That's up for grabs, I guess. I spoke with Scott Harrison again this afternoon about our divorce."

"Why did you have to choose that scumbag?"

"Because he knows how to ream people."

"Do we *have* to get divorced?" His insides felt as if, little by little, they were being incapacitated by a creeping ice that was coating his vitals like some kind of poisonous Maalox.

"I'm bitter, Joey. Right up until it happened, I trusted you. I knew we might have troubles someday, but I always thought we were big enough to confront each other on the level, without going through all this stupid, banal deceit and clumsy fraudulent pain. Our struggle to make it as a family deserved better than that."

What could he say, except, "I can't defend myself. I'm guilty as charged."

Close to tears, Heidi said, "I always believed that come what may, our marriage had the emotional and ethical horses to sink or swim with honor."

"Divorce with 'honor'?"

"You're deliberately misinterpreting what I just said."

"No I'm not." He retreated. "I'm sorry."

"I feel like I'm covered with slime, Joey. I feel ashamed and humiliated, like our life together suddenly turned into an X-rated movie. We've been transformed into pornographic laughingstocks by your recent antics."

Joe nodded dismally. "You're right. I can't protest. Everything you say is the truth." And then, overwhelmed by frustration, he said, "I know to a woman this sounds stupid, but it's not easy being a man!"

With that, he burst into gut-wrenching, shoulder-wracking, back-spasming sobs. "*Oh shit!*" he cried. Immediately, the palms covering his face were lathered in tears. And he couldn't stop himself, no way. The humiliation was there for all to see. Heidi, the kids, the cat, even the blithering sea monkeys—

they would all understand just how incompetent and frail he was. Joe wailed, *"I'm sorry!"* and wondered if this debilitating soap opera would ever end.

Heidi started to rise, but Joe hollered, "You stay right where you are! I'm not crying to get your sympathy! I don't want it! I'm just crying because I can't help it, that's all!"

"Very well." Calmly, she sat back down. Both kids had quit pretending to book-read and tube-goon: they gawked openly, frightened and curious.

In a rage of tears, Joe sputtered at them: *"What's so goddam interesting? Michael, Heather, go to bed, will you? Beat it!"*

"Leave them alone," Heidi said.

"But I don't want them to see me like this!"

"It'll probably do them good. At least you're acting like a human being for a change."

"I'll kill you, Heidi!"

"Joey, the one good thing about you, I'll have to admit, is I don't believe you could kill a fly."

"You say!" In a senseless rage he grabbed the nearest weapon—a banana from the wooden salad bowl atop the fridge. Gripping the yellow fruit daggerlike in his hand, he lunged for his wife, stabbing her in the back as she scrambled for safety. Heidi shrieked, "Don't, you'll fracture my other arm!" They tumbled to the floor in a heap. Joe stabbed her repeatedly in rapid-fire fashion, right out of *Looking for Mr. Goodbar*—ten, twelve, fourteen times as she struggled to roll free. The banana disintegrated into a mushy pulp. *"I'll kill you!"* he continued to sob: *"I really will!"* And then suddenly he realized her shrieks were unmerciful laughter, and he stopped. The shredded limp concoction in his fist scarcely resembled a piece of fruit: Heidi was plastered with sticky goop.

"Oh God!" she giggled hysterically. "I'm gonna die from laughing!" And "Oh," she cried, crawling away from him, "my stomach *hurts!*"

MAD BANANA KILLER STRIKES AGAIN! "I KILLED HER BECAUSE
SHE APPEELED TO ME," SEZ MINIVER!

"It isn't funny!" he howled. *"Stop laughing!"*

"I can't! I don't believe you, Joey! You're unreal!"

"But it isn't funny," he blubbered. "What did you do with

the cocaine? They ransacked Tribby's office! Four freaks in rubber suits actually invaded the septic tank at the Castle! They'll slit throats if we don't cough up the goods and apologize. Everybody out there is crazy, and you don't know the half of it!"

Heidi quit laughing and stared at him. "Who'll slit throats?"

"Ray Verboten, Joe Bonatelli, Natalie Gandolf . . . or whoever else out there considers this their territory. For God's sake, what did you really do with it?"

Her eyes narrowed. "That's all you're interested in, isn't it? You came home solely because you want that cruddy cocaine."

"I don't want it, Heidi." Joe gasped, trying to catch his breath. "But unless you or me can deliver it to somebody, or prove that it's destroyed, they'll think we're pulling a double cross and cripple me, maim you, and terrorize the kids in hopes of making us cough it up!"

"Then that's simple. Tell everybody to forget it. The coke is gone."

"They won't believe me. Or you. You have to produce the shit, or its traces. Otherwise they'll think we're scamming to unload it in secret."

"I don't care what they think. I hope all of you kill each other for it. That'll serve you right."

"But you're involved. And they'll try to get at you through the kids."

"Tell them I'm not afraid anymore. I'm out of the stupid game. And that's final. I hope Tribby crashes that dumb helicopter tomorrow!"

"Oh my God—how did you hear about that?"

"How could I *not* hear about it? You wouldn't believe the rumors out there. Somebody told me today that Ephraim Bonatelli, on a contract from his own father, was going to snatch the Hanuman and hold it for ransom. *If* he can get up from his hospital bed."

"It so happens that your new boyfriend, Nikita Smatterling, is in cahoots with Mr. Bonatelli, to rob his own statue, both for the ransom and the publicity that they figure will make Iréné Papadraxis' hack job a best seller, and garner millions for the Simian Foundation."

"You lie! Nikita would never do anything like that!"

Weary beyond belief, Joe said, "Shoot, it doesn't matter. I

just want to resolve the coke scam and then flee to Timbuktu. So please tell me how you destroyed it," he begged. "Then I can relay the information to Tribby, and he can tell Ray Verboten—"

"Why don't you leave now?" Heidi interrupted. "We're getting nowhere."

"You refuse to tell me?"

"Oh Joey, you know I flushed it down the toilet!"

"No!"

"You knew I had all along."

"I don't believe you! You're lying! That stuff cost me twelve Gs! We could have sold it for a fortune! We could have—"

"You're the one who *told* me to do it."

"When? I'm not that crazy! You're nuts!"

"When you phoned from Tribby's office you said it wasn't worth it. You said, 'I would rather you flushed the shit down the toilet.' Those are your exact words."

"I never dreamed you'd take me seriously!"

"You were terrified they might harm Michael or Heather."

Joe sat there, benumbed, contemplating the hands in his lap. She had actually done it! He thought his hopes for the land had vanished long ago, but her statement now cut him apart with machete strokes. Finally, irrevocably, his family was destroyed; the children were scarred for the duration. Nothing to do but end it all. Joe giggled, reached into his pocket, removed the revolver, and pointed it at his right temple.

As he pulled the trigger, Heidi shrieked, *"Joey, don't!"*

Incredibly, though he had assumed it was empty, the gun went off: *blam!* Joe keeled over sideways in a great hullabaloo of flame and smoke.

"Oh no!" Heidi shrieked.

"Oh help I killed myself!" Joe wailed.

His eardrum must have burst; a fire engine clanged through his brain. A muscular maniac pounded an enormous Chinese gong. And yet his senses were reasonably intact: he could smell gunpowder, he could see Heidi, absolutely horrified, her knuckles pressed against her teeth. And he could even hear Michael crying, "What happened, Mom? What did Daddy do?" And he could feel the gun, still in his hand—cold, hard, and somehow not as deadly as guns are supposed to be when discharged at point-blank range.

Joe whispered hoarsely, "Heidi, I'm still alive. Can you see where it hit? Is there any blood?"

"I can't see a thing." When she bent over him, her plaster cast accidentally banged the back of his head—he cried "Ouch!" Heidi said, "There's just a little burnt area, nothing else. No hole. No blood..."

"I thought it was empty," Joe moaned weakly. "But there must have been one blank left."

"'Blank?'"

"It was loaded with blanks this morning. But I thought I had fired all of them. I guess I counted wrong. I feel sick, I'm gonna throw up."

"Blanks? Joey, what kind of monster are you? I thought you had actually *shot* yourself!"

"Nothing was supposed to discharge, believe me. I didn't mean—"

"Out! Get out of here!"

"It's cold out there."

"Out, buster, before I call the cops!"

"It was a stupid gesture. I'm sorry I scared you. I scared myself. I'm gonna vomit."

"Just get out, Joey, I'm warning you."

"But where will I go?"

"Go to hell. Now come on—adiós! If I have to look at you for ten more seconds—"

She slapped his face and tugged him into a sitting position.

"Hey, take it easy. Christ, I'm going."

"Not fast enough to suit me. On your feet—alley *ooop!*" She actually heaved him upright. He staggered, dropping the gun. Heidi stooped, picked it up, and handed it over. "Take this, let's go."

"I don't want it. I'm gonna upchuck."

"I don't want it either. You carry it for protection in your helicopter."

"Heidi, I'm really going to blow my lunch!"

"So barf already! Need I draw a map to the bathroom?"

Hands clapped over his mouth, Joe lumbered across the living room, plunged into the can, and sank whimpering to his knees, tears already galloping from his eyes as his stomach's contents lurched northward. Terror had always accompanied his throw-ups. Heidi barely flinched when nausea struck: at the first queasy pangs she stuck a finger down her throat and regurgitated the poison in a matter-of-fact manner. But Joe would suffer a rocky stomach for days in order to postpone, or even avoid entirely, the horrible moment of truth.

Currently, however, he had zero choice. In no uncertain terms he vomited, punctuating the painful heaves with agonized watery sobs. Inside a minute, having coughed up the very dregs of his guts, Joe rocked back, resting on his heels, bleary-eyed and thoroughly frazzled.

Heidi occupied the doorway. "That's it? You through? Because if you're entirely finished—"

"I'm done. Christ, woman, have a heart. I'll just take this for a souvenir." So saying, he reached into the wastebasket for that empty tea carton.

Empty? Joe gripped it lightly, thinking it weightless, but the carton slipped from his grasp, striking the tiles with a heavy *chunk*!

For a second, nothing registered. Then, befuddled, he grasped the box again. "Hey . . . this thing's heavy." Fumbling weakly, Joe pried open a flap, discovering what he should have known all along—the carton positively *groaned* with uncut cocaine!

"Holy mackerel. Heidi . . . ?"

But she had turned and commenced walking away.

"This box is *full*!" he called after her. "You didn't flush it down the toliet!"

"Fuck you, Joey. I've had it, I mean it."

"*You've* had it?" He jumped to his feet. "You lied to me, Heidi! You said you flushed it down the toilet!"

"You lied to me about Nancy Ryan. In the last five days you've become the most shiftless monster I ever met!"

"Oh no, hold on just a minute, here. This is different. We're talking about a hundred Gs, here." Joe advanced menacingly across the living room, shaking the box at her. "We're talking about Eloy's property, and his future well-being, and the future of ourselves and our children. We're talking about goods that people are prepared to kill to obtain, and you *lied* to me, Heidi!"

"Don't be self-righteous, Joey. Under the circumstances that would be very unbecoming."

"'Unbecoming'?" Instant apoplexy! Veins bulged, ears blazed, Joe's heart trumpeted against his sternum. "I don't *believe* you can stand there with that pinched, twitty smirk on your face putting *me* down, after trying to launch a caper like that! What were you gonna do, give it to Scott Harrison for reaming me? Abscond to New York and make a killing in secret? You son of a bitch!" His arms flailed, his hair stood on end. "You would double-cross me like that? What happened, you made a deal under the table with Ray Verboten? Did Nikita Smatterling seduce you into turning it over to Skipper Nuzum? I don't believe it! Everyone of those assholes tried to make me double-cross you and Eloy and Tribby and anybody else in the valley with even a smidgen of decency left, but I told them to walk! You scumbag! The junk in this little box could send our kids to college! It could pay all your hospital bills if you ever got cancer! It could give us a little bit of security in this goddam shark-infested country! It could . . . it could . . ."

All the while he ranted, she had stared at him frozenly, her arms folded, her eyes absolute slits, her face arctic. Now, as he sputtered off incoherently, she said, "My, my, would you look at the Fascist rising up out of the Communist rhetoric."

Joe hit her with all his might. A right-hand cross that bounced off her left temple. He screamed "*Ouch!*" as Heidi capsized sideways, tripping over the coffee table in a watery explosion of sea monkeys—her right arm, in the cast, swung into the TV set, smashing the picture tube with a scary hollow *pop!* Glass sprayed across her body as she bounced to earth.

Joe cried, "*Oh no!*"

Heather shrieked.

Michael stared disbelievingly, his mouth awkwardly open, palms cupped over his ears.

"My hand!" Joe howled. "*You broke my hand!*" He doubled over as pain leaped splinteringly, like haywire needles, up his arm and tried to break his neck. Through a screen of sputtering freckles before his eyes that forewarned fainting, Joe saw Heidi flop on all fours and start scrambling like a terrified crab through the carnage toward the telephone: a red haze seemed to spray off her shocked and stormy features. At the same instant, Heather flew through the air as if propelled by a mammoth slingshot: she crunched into his belly, fists flailing, and knocked him head over teakettle. Enraged, Joe flung her aside and hollered at Heidi as she fumbled with the phone: "*What are you doing?*"

"I'm calling the police! You better get out of here!"

"Call the police and I'll kill you!"

"No you won't, Daddy, *I'll kill you!*" Volume J-K of the World Book Encyclopedia thumped against Joe's cranium, catching his tongue directly between his teeth and driving his head halfway to China.

Joe elbowed his whirlwind daughter aside and bolted toward Heidi. "You call the cops and they'll find the cocaine! We'll *all* go to jail!"

She warded him off, viciously swinging the cast: it caught him in the shoulder, shunting his charge sideways. Her eyes bugged out of a face smeared in red. Rent across the chest, her blouse was ruined. Joe belly-flopped, clutching the coke box to his ribs like a good tailback. Immediately, he rolled, grasping for Heidi with his free hand. She kicked at his face, meaning to maim; at the same time her fingers scrabbled to register a single digit: "Operator! This is an emergency!"

Joe cried, "Wait a minute, I'm leaving!" Heather crashed into his back, grabbing hair, ears, shoulders; her knees frantically drubbed his kidneys. "This is crazy!" Joe dumped his daughter brusquely on her ass again. They looked like a scene from the cover of *Police Gazette*. Eighty percent of all American murders occurred within families, among lovers and estranged spouses.

"Operator, I want the police!"

"I'm *going*, Heidi! Shit, please don't—" Staggering erect, Joe stumbled toward freedom. The empty fishbowl, pitched by Heather, ricocheted off his rump, knocking him off-balance again: he pitched over the arm of the easy chair.

Michael remained paralyzed, hands covering his ears, mouth wide open.

"I didn't want this to happen!" Joel bawled, as Heather, a miniature wounded rhino, charged again.

"Hello, police? This is an emergency. I live on Ranchitos Road . . . Castle of Golden Fools . . . a big, dumb, two-story mansion by the S-curve. A man is going amok . . . he tried to kill me. . . ."

Next time around, Heather drove straight for his balls: one fist caught him there. Reacting to the pain, Joe boxed her ears—she cartwheeled into the bookcase: *crash*!

Joe stammered and gestured pathetically: if only he could retract this mayhem. Jumping up from the phone, Heidi grabbed the nearest weapon, an oversized red Wiffle Ball bat; even her teeth were soaked in blood.

"You're a lunatic, Joey! Be gone!"

"But I didn't mean . . ."

Here came Heather again, the Floyd Patterson of the kiddy pugilists, up off the floor for the umpteenth time.

"*Out*, you bastard!"

"Not like this—*oof*!" Tiny teeth sank into his forearm and held on, mongoose-fanatical: boneless and floppy, Heather twitched like a rag doll in a hurricane as Joe tried to shake her loose.

Wielding the Wiffle Ball bat like an expert, Heidi caught him broadside with a home-run swing. Stars appeared; Joe's ears popped and clanged; and he realized that if they prolonged this rumble, a death might truly be the outcome. Gasping, Joe located the doorknob and toppled over backward outside, landing on the deck.

"I'm going," he gurgled. "I give up!"

"Not fast enough!" Heidi croaked. The bat drummed against his forearms, head, and shoulders.

Using every last bit of strength, Joe humped onto the ladder, lost his footing, and clung one-handed to a rung. Heidi bounced a final blow off his head, placed her foot against the top rung, and kicked outward. Joe screeched, letting go, and experienced a briefly euphoric free fall before crunching to earth: the ladder jounced off his thighs, underscoring—emphatically—the fact that their marriage was over.

"I hate you, Daddy!" came from over the parapets above. "I hate you, I hate you, *I hate you*!"

"Come near us again and you're dead!" Heidi threatened. "I'll obtain an injunction! I'll have bodyguards from Women Against Rape!"

What next—boiling oil? *The cops!* She had called them, they must be on their way. Astonished, Joe found himself still clutching the tea box. Apparently, nothing except his spirit was broken. Frantically, then, he clawed free of the ladder.

"I love my children!" he sobbed.

"The police are coming!"

"Good-bye, Michael!" Joe wailed up at the blank apartment walls. "I love you, Heather! I'm sorry!" Would his son be catatonic from now until eternity, instantly transformed into an autistic zombie, forever captured in that sitting position, horrified eyes and mouth wide open, hands clapped over his ears to ward off the obscenity of his parents' final explosion?

Heather and Heidi disappeared: the door slammed: from here on in it was a whole new ball game.

❧

From his flotation tank, Ralph said, "What's all the commotion, Miniver? Your sexual chickens coming home to roost, you lecherous rascal you?"

"What would you know about sexual chickens coming home to roost?" Ralph was supine in his Sensu-Casket beside a female body.

"C'mere," the plump man said. "I need to talk to you."

"It's all over, Ralph," Joe whimpered. "Heidi lied to me about flushing the dope down the toilet. She tried to double-cross me. We had a fight. I almost killed her. We actually came to blows. Heather tried to kill me. Michael is up there struck dumb with shock. The cops are coming."

The woman beside Ralph had a hefty bosom. A gold star glittered against her forehead. She wore tiny, black-rimmed goggles, such as competitive swimmers use. Her hands were protected from the brine by rubber gloves. Ralph balanced a mauve jar, into which a burning incense stick was stabbed, atop his watermelon-sized belly.

"Forget about the dope," Ralph soothed pleasantly. He was obviously stoned. "Not to worry, old sport. The Hanuman caper will net ten times the score. I want you to meet Sahdreeni."

"Sahdreeni?"

"It's a derivation of a Sanskrit dialect meaning 'holy song-bird,'" the chipper girl explained. "I changed it to that last year after my car accident."

"Sahdreeni who?"

"Just Sahdreeni, that makes it pure."

"Where are you from?" he droned lifelessly.

"I'm a citizen of the conscious universe. Everyplace is my home."

"What was your name before you changed it?" Joe nattered stupidly, wishing to run, and yet held spellbound by this prosaic exchange.

"Laurie Feldencropper."

"Her grandparents were Lithuanian cabinetmakers," Ralph explained.

Joe said, "What do you do for a living?"

"I'm an astral cartographer."

"I don't know what that is."

"I make maps for people to follow when they travel."

"You mean like Triple-A? How to get to Boston from Cundy's Harbor, Maine?"

Sahdreeni giggled. "No, silly. I help guide people who are into soul travel."

"Ahhhh . . ." Joe nodded wisely. One ear twitched, listening for sirens.

Ralph said, "She's looking for a house to rent, if you hear of any good places cheap."

"Listen, Ralph, excuse me but I gotta go. I'm right in the middle of having a sort of nervous breakdown."

"We'll be out of the tank in about twenty minutes if you want to use it."

"No thanks. I'll see you. . . ."

"At the party later on, bro. You're going, of course? Ray Verboten won't dare kick ass in front of all those aristocratic honkies."

Joe's vision, as once again he aimed the decrepit bus out of the Castle's driveway, was so blurred from tears that he almost hit a tank truck entering the yard, and could barely read the logo on its rounded, rusty flanks: VALLEY SEPTIC—YOUR SHIT MAKES US RICH. In the front seat sat two men in those same rubber suits. The passenger wore a snorkel and a diving mask, and the driver was disguised in one of those ubiquitous and grotesque gorilla faces.

When had he last inserted something edible into his body? Suddenly ravenous, Joe decided to hit the Prince of Whales for a bite. If he ate something, maybe at least his body could survive. But then what—the Nuzums' party? He couldn't think. Now he was totally, hopelessly adrift. He squeezed the tea box in his crotch, between his thighs. What to do next? Pin it to his chest as a target for their high-powered rifle slugs? "I've lost the will to care anymore." They'd be doing him a favor to end his blithering existence. Beyond all else he intently desired a respite from his own ridiculous drama.

Yet by the time he parked on the plaza, Joe had sucked a last few drops of stubborn resistance from the pool of his ramshackle survival instincts: he took the box of cartridges from the glove compartment, and, after fitting six bullets into

Diana's gun, queasily returned the pistol to his pocket. Then, cradling his cocaine football in the crook of one arm, Joe crossed the relatively deserted plaza to the relatively empty café.

Relatively being a relative term, of course. As soon as he walked through the door, almost heady from anticipating a cup of hot coffee, Joe realized that the only person there besides Darlene was Diana.

At the corner table by the jukebox she sat, death warmed over. Bedraggled, scraggled, and lovelorn, she nursed a cup of caffeine as if it was the only thing between her and a messy suicide.

What to do—nonchalantly plunk himself elsewhere, ignoring her? No way. Their eyes met: immediately, she looked down and away. Joe inhaled deeply, shuddered, wiped a tear from his eye, approached her table, and, laying a tentatively proprietory hand on an empty chairback, he asked, "May I?"

"May you what?"

"Sit down here. I'm very tired."

"It's a free country."

"I won't if you don't want me to."

"I can't stop you, can I?"

"Listen, if you don't want to talk, I can understand."

"Oh yeah?" Her eyes flashed fire. "Then you'd be the first man I ever met who could understand anything beyond the parameters of his own cock."

"Look, I'm sorry. I came over because I figured it would be pretty insulting if I didn't." He wanted to add: *Please, Diana, don't hurt me, I feel so fragile. I'm tired of being at war. I'm scared stiff. I don't want to molest you. I'm so confused. I need somebody right at this crucial moment in my deteriorating existence.*

She was sublimely hostile: "Well, now you know."

"What?"

"That it's more insulting that you did."

"Hey, Diana—"

"Hay is for horses, straw is cheaper, you can get grass free."

Joe said, "Glurg," shrugged miserably, and placed his coke box on the table before him. Light-headed, ears buzzing, he swallowed hard: "I'm sorry."

"Take your sorrow and shove it."

"I . . . but . . . isn't there any way . . . ?" *Please*, Diana, lighten

up, tender at least a partial forgiveness. He needed to touch
her, be held, make a connection, feel some kind of—*any* kind
of—love.

"Look, Joe. You already got what you want from me, so
why not split? Go find another dummy with big tits and a tight
cunt. Christ, I hate men."

"It's not so bleeding easy being a man." Joe coughed painfully, fighting tears. How could he deal with her? How could
he convince her of his humanity? The urge arose to say "I love
you, I want to marry you." Anything to win even a brief respite.

"'Bleeding,'" she mimicked scornfully. "What is this, National British Day in the southern Rockies?"

"Oh Diana," he pleaded. "Gimme a break. I know I did
wrong, but I'm so confused. I'm blowing everything. I've lost
the thread. I came over because I wanted to apologize for this
morning, honest. I mean, life is tough enough without—"

"You're not kidding it's tough enough. I'll tell you one
thing, though. You're the last male macho son of a bitch that
ever gets inside my pants for free. And I'm not kidding. The
next motherfucker that pulls a sexual double cross on me, there
won't be blanks in the gun I'm carrying."

Joe sagged. No use . . . no use! If only he had a time machine
and could rewind his life back to yesterday. Or back to last
Saturday night, for that matter. An awful queasiness shook his
foundations. He couldn't bear being hated. Yet how could he
prove to her, in twenty-five words or less, that he was actually
a decent fellow? Show her his throbbing fist that ached from
smashing Heidi? Explain the bite marks on his forearm?

Dully, he said, "Did it ever occur to you, Diana, that the
reason you're always getting beat up is maybe your personal
actions with other people aren't exactly above reproach? I mean,
you talk about playing games, you're not exactly the straightest
shooter I ever met."

"The gun had blanks in it, idiot, in case you didn't notice."

How could she completely miss the point? "I didn't mean
that. I meant you really pull some pretty complex shit yourself
when it comes to relating with men."

"Don't give me a lecture. I think I actually like better the
guys who slug me than the assholes who lecture me on how
I'm supposed to be."

"Maybe you should listen to their lectures sometime."

"What for? Everybody wants me to be like *they* want me

to be, not like I am. I'm never supposed to have my own
personality. I'm just supposed to be this cute little extension
of their personalities. Well, I've had it. Never again."

"We didn't even have a chance to get started before you
jumped all over me. You're projecting onto me all these traits
you *think* I'm gonna have. So you wind up killing it before it
even has a chance to catch a second wind. How do you know
I'm gonna be like everybody else? You make me like everybody
else by treating me that way before I'm even halfway able to
start to show you who *I* am."

"I know," she said sullenly. "But I'm a professional at
reading the writing on the wall. You got to learn how to do
that, in advance. If you wait around until some jerk actually
proves he's like everybody else, it's too late. 'Too late' meaning
the son of a bitch is already squirting inside you, trying to
wreck your freedom and cripple your body by making you
pregnant so he can leave you the name of a good abortionist
and then take a powder."

"Not everybody's like that."

"Do you want to marry me, Joe?"

Fighting an urge to say yes, Joe stared at the tea box.

"I thought so. Do you want to have a child with me?"

Words struggled to escape his throat. If only he could release
them, accepting her offer, casting his lot with this strangled
woman in order to begin again. But suppose it went haywire?
He would never be able to rub out the sight of Michael's
terrified countenance barely an hour ago.

"So there you go, Joe. Now shuttup and get off my case.
I can't believe that only yesterday I actually thought you were
a human being."

That jarred a raw nerve. As if somehow all this sturm and
drang were *his* fault. As if he, Joe Miniver, a cross from birth
between Adolf Eichmann and Charley Starkweather, with a
little Fatty Arbuckle thrown in for good measure, had appren-
ticed under Jack the Ripper and the Boston Strangler in order
to become the human Jaws of Chamisaville. Joe stiffened. He
knew, beyond the shadow of a doubt, that at heart he was a
good person who had always tried to do right by everybody.
For so long he had struggled to forge a decent marriage, be an
understanding and loving daddy. Then of a sudden, inspired
by totally altruistic motives, he had stumbled out of his league,
fallen among sophisticated gangsters, and lost his bearings.

Not a true criminal bone existed in his simplistic body, yet somehow he had floundered into a corner where he resembled the reincarnation of a Kiplingesque cobra in an English colonial garden—it wasn't fair! Diana had no right to accuse him of dastardly motivations! Especially after intimately catering, for so long, to the sadistic ministrations of an unholy creep like Angel Guts!

He wanted to hit the supercilious little cocktease. He actually wanted to grab a saltcellar and clock her one atop the noggin. Or stab her in the shoulder with a fork. Where did they come from, these aggravating cripples? The cocaine tea box pulsed naughtily between his tightly clenched fists. Heidi's bloody face focused, but he quashed *that* vision immediately. And shut his eyes, attempting to regain control. *Stand up, say good-bye, walk off,* the voice of reason continued. *Pull her own gun, blast away, and cackle as she croaks,* the voice of vengeance and stupidity urged. Joe chose a middle road, remaining inert, forging a blank mind, becoming a useless blob.

They stalled. Joe fiddled with a knife. Quietly, Diana drew nonsensical patterns on the shiny table with a finger dipped in her cold coffee. Tears streamed down her cheeks, dropped off her chin, splashed onto the table. Joe's voice cracked as he finally broke the silence:

"Diana, I hate talking like this. I don't want to anymore. It's too cruel."

She didn't speak.

"Look. I don't understand you, I'll admit. I don't know what you've been through. I'm sorry I offended you so badly. Believe me, I didn't want to. I just can't seem to function correctly in this snakepit. Maybe I was married for too long."

"But you hadda get into my pants, didn't you? That's all anybody ever wants. Just once I'd like a relationship the driving force of which wasn't somebody's manic desire to nail my cunt."

Joe remained mute. What could he say—that he hadn't wanted to screw? That he wasn't guilty of the yearning she blamed him for? But why did he have to be so *wrong*? Or, at least, why did sex have to evolve into something unutterably complex and riddled with contradictions, making it impossible to enjoy? All the psychologists wrote books on how beautiful it could be. Erica Jong had had a ball balling. The *Playboy* adviser guided people through innumerable excursions of kinky

delights. Swinging swinglers extolled the phallic and cloacal
virtues of orgies galore and communal S and M. Even the
lesbians and the male homosexuals were united in joyous radical revolutions to win their hornball rights. But Joe Miniver,
nudnik supreme, not only couldn't get off in a strange babe,
but after five days on the liberated hustings he had managed
to co-opt every coherent sexual, spiritual, and political bone
in his blatantly immature body!

Sighing, Joe fashioned a helpless gesture.

"Well, what the hell." Diana dried her tears on the sleeve
of her blue work shirt. "The nice thing is you leave me feeling
neutral, Joe. I couldn't care less if you survive or drop dead.
Already, you're not even a memory in my heart."

Joe hung his hangdog head.

"I can't muster hatred for you, Joe. It doesn't even bug me
that while I assumed you were so conscientiously trying to start
your car last night, you were actually over in the Nuzums'
mansion doing a number on that middle-aged Bulgarian with
the phony accent who's going to write a best-selling book about
the Hanuman snatch tomorrow. So what? Tant pis. I feel nothing. I'm staring at you and I can't even remember your face."

He awoke slightly. "Where did you hear about the Hanuman
snatch?"

"On the street, in the dives—who knows?"

"*What* did you hear?"

"One version has it that your lawyer pal, Tribby Gordon,
and Ephraim Bonatelli, in the pay of Ephraim's pop and Nikita
Smatterling, are teaming up to fly in a Floresta helicopter to
grab the statue and dump it in a high-country lake, hoping the
sensationalism will give Iréné Papadraxis enough material to
write a best seller that'll keep the Simian Foundation, which
has a forty-percent interest in the book, on easy street for the
rest of its natural-born spiritual existence."

Joe groaned.

"Like I said, that's one version. I don't care if it's true or
false. You're just a pathetic little puddle of protoplasm in my
book, Joe. A nonentity. A vapid ghoul."

"Well, uh, I guess I'll be going. . . ." Would he faint when
he stood up?

She actually smiled, in control again. "Nobody's stopping
you."

"I'm really sorry you hate me." Gathering his cocaine, Joe

backed away from her, terrified that any second a devil-wrought impulse would cause him to shriek and leap at her, kung-fu fists flying.

Darlene had just arrived. "The grille's already shut off, José. All I can give you is a sandwich, or juice. And we got hot coffee, a Danish—you know, anything that doesn't need cooking."

"I'm leaving, Darlene."

"You going to that party tonight, or will you be busy polishing your flight goggles?"

Ignoring her last comment, Joe mumbled, "I dunno, yeah, maybe . . ."

"Do me a favor," Darlene said. "If you arrive before me, tell Spumoni it dragged on a little here and I decided to shower at home first, okay?"

"Sure, Darlene. You can count on me."

"From what I've been hearing lately, I wouldn't bet on it." Jauntily, she swung around the counter, heading into the kitchen.

"Why, what have you been hearing?" His voice hailed his own ears from across distant chasms.

"I heard you've got to walk it on a leash to revive it with fresh air at least four times a day because it's been getting such a workout," she giggled, disappearing into the smoky arena where all the Prince of Whales' synthetic grub was deep-fried, baked, or radiated.

Diana laughed.

Joe said, "That isn't funny."

"But it couldn't happen to a nicer guy."

Joe floated out the door on the bitterly redolent currents of her unadulterated disdain.

❧

       He had lost something precious forever. Nostalgia, as strong as the scent of popcorn, eddied about the plaza. A remarkable lull was in progress. Incredibly, the plaza was empty.

Joe hesitated, absentmindedly stroking the cocaine, wondering how to function. A mongrel trotted through the plaza's antitank structures and circled the South Seas bandstand gazebo: its toenails clicked against the bricks. A few lilac bushes boasted purple blossoms. Fluffy seed tufts from two cottonwoods parachuted dreamily earthward.

Nick Danger shuffled into the plaza, outfitted in the Tyrolean hat, vinyl trenchcoat, and black laceless dress shoes. Clutching his mysterious suitcase as always, he glanced neither to the right nor to the left as he navigated toward the Prince of Whales, on a collision course with Joe, who leaned against a portal post. As the secretive, Bogeyesque little gnome drew near, Joe suddenly had an urge to give it one more try. What a kick to be bounteous and friendly again, capable of vastly enriching the world by tossing it bouquets of sensitivity, love, commitment, and compassion . . . starting right now with Nick Danger.

"Hello, there," he said pleasantly. "Beautiful evening, isn't it?"

The little man stopped dead five feet away. His shoulders were hunched gloomily, his chapped and scabby hands clutched the battered suitcase almost defiantly, his lips were compressed in a grim grimace, his hat was pulled down over eyes trained on the ground directly in front of his toes.

"Are you talking to *me*, mister?"

"Sure, I just said hello. It's a lovely evening."

"Nobody ever simply *talks* to me," Nick said icily. "So what's your beef?"

"Beef? I'm sorry, I don't understand. All I said was hello."

"Nobody just says 'hello' in life," Nick threatened. "Everybody has an ulterior motive. So, you know, next time you see me coming, if you ain't got business to transact save your breath. I don't need a bunch of fucking people bugging me every day with pleasantries, y'unnerstand?"

"Okay, if you insist. I'm sorry."

"Well, watch it next time."

"Sure."

"I heard you had been marked for death anyway," Nick said offhandedly. Then the mysterious little man went into motion again, heading for the café.

Joe flared. "Hey, wait a minute, creep!"

Nick Danger froze in midstep, but did not turn around.

Emboldened by his ridiculous anger, Joe said, "Just what in hell do you keep in that stupid suitcase, anyway?"

His threatening back still to Joe, Nick snarled, "Who wants to know?"

"Me, dammit. What were you doing in that hospital room with Ray Verboten and Ephraim Bonatelli and Nikita Smatterling? What's in that moth-eaten bag anyway—dope? Guns? Money?"

Slowly... theatrically... menacingly, Nick turned around. His bruising eyes glinted in the shadow beneath the Tyrolean's brim. His mouth was so tight and malicious that a chill struck with the fury of a malignant stab between Joe's shoulder blades, and, too late, he realized what that singular suitcase contained: a tommy gun! Or, worse yet, the shrunken heads of dope-interloper morons, like Joe Miniver, that the grotesque Mafia hitman had severed, as proof of terminated contracts, for employers like Joseph Bonatelli and Ray Verboten.

"What I got in this suitcase is none of your business unless you want to do business," the gangster-derelict proclaimed. Like a disguised blackbelt karate expert, he seemed balanced on the balls of his feet, waiting for his enemy to make one false move so that he could press a spring latch on his guncase and mow Joe down in spades... In Self-Defense. Yet Joe quivered, enraged, allowing foolhardy adrenal spurts to mug his rational brain. Once too often had his good intentions had been misunderstood, his lust for a compassionate interaction deflected into a mucky territory where hysteria and assholeism reigned. Well, he'd had it: let the dangerous little fart do his worst. If he couldn't respond to a cheerful and heartfelt greeting, then by God Joe would jump the arrogant half-pint motherfucker, give him a mouthful of bloody Chiclets, and satisfy his curiosity as to what that decrepit valise concealed!

And, ignoring an inner wail that decreed this absurd hoax was about the least intelligent thing he'd ever promulgated, Joe dropped his cocaine and jumped Nick Danger: they both toppled earthward, emitted startled grunts. Nick's head, clopping against the cement gutter, sounded like the proverbial melon splitting. The tattered valise struck the sidewalk and flew open. From the corner of one eye, Joe saw something ecru-colored and rubbery, like an enormous mocking tongue, flap out of the dingy innards with a loud hiss. Right before his eyes, the thing twisted, boinged, and bloomed as compressed air, from a can whose nozzle was attached to the latex apparition, blew it up. A naked female leg appeared out of the tumultuous ether and ricocheted off his fending forearm: then a voluptuous belly and enormous lascivious tits surged into being. Finally, still within the blink of an eye, a head puffed out, decorated in platinum curls. Ruby-red lips, pursed around a penis-sized hole, flew into Joe's face, propelled by an arm springing into airy shape. The thing—a life-size Japanese fuck doll, Joe realized instantly!—hovered above them both for a second as final spurts of the accidentally triggered compressed oxygen filled out its hollow, fleshy skin, then it plopped weightlessly across Nick Danger's stomach and quivered, settling.

Kneeling (the doll's heels against his either shoulder), Joe found himself staring down between a long pair of slightly spread gams into a make-believe but deeply recessed vagina that appeared to have been molded into the lifelike rubbery crotch with fluorescent Play-Doh.

"Holy shit."

Nick Danger's Tyrolean headpiece lay beside a garbage can: the sinister little shtarker was bald. And out, apparently, for the duration. A tattoo of a rattlesnake coiled to strike blared off of his incongruously naked scalp. Beside his shoulder lay the open suitcase, stacked with large painted and layered rubber pancakes—more dolls. The one lying across Nick's chest must have been a demonstration model.

Hideously ashamed and also horrified, Joe gawked and balked. My God, what had he unleashed this time? How could he have been so cruel?

SEX-CRAZED GARBAGE MAN MUGS FUCK-DOLL SALESMAN! BERSERK S & MER KILLED BY EXPLODING LOLITA! COPS CORNER KINKY JOYBOY IN INFLATABLE-CUTIE HEIST!

A stir, a groan, a twitch—Nick Danger was still alive! Stuttering, Joe asked, "Are you all right?" An eye, Nick's left one, opened halfway and fastened tentatively on Joe. "What'd you do that for?" he whimpered. "You want a Daring Debbie, I woulda sold you one. I thought maybe you were a porno cop."

"'Daring Debbie'?"

"Sure." Nick opened his other eye, but remained immobile. "I sell a dozen of these rubber babes every week."

"For how much?"

"A hunnert bucks."

"But I never see anybody talk to you. I mean, I didn't even know you had a voice. Whoever approaches you . . . ?"

"Not while you're looking, no—I'm very discreet. But they give me high signs, and we meet later. Every Chamisaville male knows what Nick is selling. I'm the most popular sex therapist in town. You want one? I'll give you a discount— eighty bucks. A jar of Vaseline comes free."

Joe lifted shakily to his feet, and located the cocaine. "I don't . . . I mean . . . but . . . are you all right?"

"My head hurts."

"Can you move?" He bent over to extend a helping hand.

"Don't touch me, gonif. I can handle myself." Still not budging, Nick fumbled with the plastic figure across his chest, located a pressure-relief valve, and depressed it: air escaped in a noisy rush—the doll deflated completely within seconds.

Joe said, "I'm sorry . . . I didn't mean . . ."

"Apologize your head off." Nick suddenly scrambled erect, folding the empty girl back into a pancake; he relatched the battered suitcase. "But save your wind for my lawyer if your lawyer pal doesn't kill you in the helicopter tomorrow!"

"Who's your lawyer?" What did he plan to do now, this gnomish anomaly—sue?

"Scott Harrison, turkey," the lugubrious little charlatan said smugly, with one hand adjusting the Tyrolean hat on his head as he scuttled away. "The best shyster in the West!"

"You gotta be kidding!" Joe called plaintively.

"Sure," Nick chortled gleefully. "Me and Bob Hope!"

"But you're not even hurt!" Joe cried. "And I apologized. I'm truly sorry."

"Wait'll you see my whiplash in court!" the ugly profiteer trailed behind himself as he slithered into the Prince of Whales.

MILLIONAIRE PORNO GRIFTER STINGS
CHAMISAVILLE GARBAGE MAN!

And Joe could see it already: a miracle occurred, somehow he unloaded the coke for a hundred Gs, bought Eloy Irribarren's land, paid off Heidi, built a humble but wonderful house, and was about to live happily ever after when Nick Danger came out on top in Chamisaville's legal snake pit, and the scraggly hustlerito wound up as king of Joe's manor, while Joe himself inherited a suitcase jam-packed with sex dolls, and, outfitted in Tyrolean green, vinyl skin, and Depression-era black pumps, shuffled about this nasty burg, selling female-shaped balloons to lonely bourgeois monkey worshipers.

It wasn't easy being a humanist!

❧

Joe had just turned to leave when Jeff Orbison braked his dusty Trans-Am and called out the window: "Hey Joe, c'mere a sec."

"What for?"

"I got a deal for you."

Blindly, buffeted by the cruel winds of his crippled destiny, Joe staggered into the street. "I don't want what you're selling," he groused. "Leave me alone."

"Hear me out first, man. You're in trouble, big, but maybe I can save your ass."

"My ass is already grass."

"No, listen. Dig this deal. I hear on the grapevine that you and that old man, Eloy whatshisname, are gonna rob the First State People's Jug tomorrow."

"Who told you that?"

"Who tells anybody anything in this town? I got ears. But here's the scoop. If Tom Yard ain't on your side, you don't stand a chance. He'll mow you down like spring wheat. But I can protect you so you won't even get nicked."

"I have no plans to rob the bank, Jeff."

"Bullshit. Now listen: for a small cut of your take, I'll buy Tom off. He won't even quiver when you barrel in to do the job."

"I'm serious, Jeff. I'm not gonna rob the bank tomorrow. Honest."

"You better take my offer, man. If you don't, Tom will go nuts protecting his vaults when you and that senile old geezer try to tip 'em over. All I'm asking is ten percent—five for me, five for Tom. Just say okay, and I'll take your word—it's a deal. Tom's gun stays in its holster, and we all retire on easy street."

"You're crazy," Joe blubbered. "I'm telling you, we have no plans to rob that bank."

"Okay, bro. Don't say I didn't try. Good luck. And rest in peace."

With a roar, he departed. Once more, Joe choked on the fumes.

"You didn't try," Joe squeaked inaudibly. And when nothing deadly—like a machete or a sledgehammer—clobbered him from behind, he felt—smugly—as if he had gotten away with murder.

But thirty yards down the plaza, Jeff hit the brakes, slammed it into reverse, and squealed back to a hair-raising stop inches from Joe's toes.

"Hey," he chided belligerently. "What's in that tea box you're carrying?"

"Five pounds of uncut cocaine."

"That's what I thought!"

And he evaporated.

"I don't care," Joe muttered forlornly. "They'll be doing me a favor."

CHAMISAVILLE PARIAH COMMITS BIZARRE SUICIDE! LOCATED IN GUTTER TORN TO SHREDS BY HUMAN JACKALS!

Give up? *This* turkey?

Behind the wheel of his dilapidated wheels, Joe pried at the carton flaps. White powder sparkled insolently. Dipping in a pinkie, he scooped up a tiny mound. You snorted it into your nose—at least that's what he had always heard. Now, at last, he would learn what made this stuff so valuable. Lifting the laden pinkie to his right nostril, Joe hesitated for a last look around. The plaza shimmered uneventfully. A breeze had sprung up; tree leaves trembled soothingly. *Good-bye, cruel world!* Joe exhaled—waited a beat—pressed shut his left nostril, and gave a sharp toot. Tears sprang to his eyes.

And then the insides of his head went *boiing!*

❧

Oh Gatsby, oh Gatsby, wherefore art thou, Gatsby? Colored floodlights shone brilliantly from the rooftops, the gables, and from hidden platforms in the spruce and weeping willow trees. Though specifically a Christmas tradition, rows of luminarias lined the adobe mansion's fire wall ramparts; breezes caused the candles resting in sand inside paper bags to flicker romantically. Linen-draped tables on the lawn were laden with the best booze money could buy. Eats abounded on barge-long counters: deviled eggs, Romanoff caviar, swiss cheese, exotic meats, salamis, kielbasas, chicken legs coated with lemon-colored aspic—oh what a riot of culinary delights!

Cans of soda pop and beer crowded enormous ice-filled tubs.
Diaphanous crepe-paper streamers decorated the portal. Mist
curled off the heated swimming pool, wherein several nude
bathers of both sexes lazily frolicked. From branches of every
tree, from the corbels atop every portal post, attached to pieces
of colored yarn, dangled little stuffed monkeys similar to the
one Joe had seen at Nancy's healing. And right in the middle
of the yard, hanging from an improvised scaffold, was a wonderfully frilly, outrageous, comic, and lovable monkey piñata,
no doubt full of bonbons.

Slipping her arm through his, Iréné welcomed Joe to the
blast. "Have you ever seen anything so bizarre?"

"It's beautiful. Just like a fairy tale. What a crazy town this
is!"

"You know what they spent on this little shindig?"

"Who wants to hear? Don't talk about money."

"Two and a half fat ones."

$250 or $2,500? Joe asked for no clarification. Right now
he had suspended all his critical faculties. Maybe for once in
his life he could enjoy himself. Let the party be decadent
without his pathetically undisciplined Marxism-Leninism
creeping around on the fringes, casting portentous glances of
disapprobation at all the revel-makers. Fie on all his personal
guilt hang-ups. At dawn he would lead his self-righteous saviors
of humankind against the mansion, set fire to the building with
pine-pitch torches, and banish its occupants to Cleveland, Ohio,
or Detroit. But right now his advice to himself was: Keep a
low profile, don't blow your cover, cast a lean and critical eye,
observing (and even partaking in) these ghoulish remnants of
capitalist decadence, learning about the system from the inside
in order to fight it better later on.

Beautiful people everywhere were getting blasted, smoking
dope. In lieu of a band, Jeff Orbison handled a microphone
and an enormous stereo console beside the spacious outdoor
dance floor, doing a disco trip, introducing platters in a jargon-
riddled patter almost incomprehensible. On the dance floor,
Chamisavillains, whom Joe knew and yet hardly recognized,
engaged in wild psychedelic antics. Joe had mothballed his
rocker's gyrations somewhere back around the Mashed Potatoes and the Hully-Gully. These days, everybody resembled
John Travolta. Men wore hot-crotch double knits and maricón
boots; women wore snakeskin-tight nipple-revealers or trans-

parent chiffon, and erotic high heels. It was another world, another century, another class of people. Joe gaped, and kept his mouth shut. Like Alice, he had landed in a Wonderland.

He wandered, sipping on a vodka and tonic, nodding hello to Mimi McAllister, Tad Hooten and Meridel Carter, Wilkerson Busbee and Jane Zuckerman. Cuddled against him all the way, Iréné chattered.

"About last night, Joseph: I'm truly sorry." He hated it when people called him Joseph. "I don't know what got into me. It's so stupid to push all that frenetic macho crap, especially on the first try. Honestly, Joseph dear"—*dear?*—"when I awoke this morning I felt truly ashamed. It was so sad not to have you in my arms. I'll never forgive myself for driving you off into the night."

Moths had gathered around the floodlights: bats flickered ghostily, hunting them. Occasionally a wingèd thing dipped into a luminaria and emerged on fire. Joe watched the tiny frantic meteors spin dizzily above the crowd, falling like spent fireworks to earth, totally consumed by flames long before they hit. A moth torch, headed kamikaze-like toward Joe, burnt out quickly and arrived as a tiny spattering of warm ashes against the tip of his nose.

Over a dozen revelers cavorted in the swimming pool. Some tapped a large balloon with one hand while expertly guarding a drink in the other hand. Several women and two guys playfully wrestled in shallow water, cudgeling each other's privates. Ralph Kapansky sat on the poolside tiles, dangling his dungareed legs in the water. One hand held a quaking Rimpoche, who was terrified of the party. At his other side a naked lady— Sahdreeni—giggled every time he made a popeyed lascivious face and, his hands flopping spastically in the air, leaned over like a foaming rabid dog to make comically menacing tongue-flapping, tooth-clacking, drool-inducing gestures just millimeters away from her preposterous tits.

Used to the uproar, Siamese cats sauntered through the turbulence hunting tidbits of Virginia ham. A miniature poodle and a bloodhound vacuumed the lawn for similar goodies. Joe refurbished his drink, downed it, and poured another as he continued to circulate with Iréné on his arm.

"I think I acted abominably last night because I was nervous. Lord knows why, I've been with oodles of men, but sometimes, for no apparent reason, I become terribly ill at ease. I lose all my confidence. Then I find myself behaving atrociously, like last night."

Ray Verboten matriculated, offering a toke they couldn't refuse. His heavy-lidded expressionless eyes not even aimed at Joe, Ray removed a small automatic pistol from an armpit holster and shoved the snout under Joe's nose. Smiling cruelly, he said, "I want you to smell my gun."

Joe sniffed, grinning impishly.

"I'm not gonna kill you here, Joe. Too many people. I don't want to wreck Natalie's blast."

"It's all the same to me, Ray. Do your worst. Give me sixty Gs and you can have it. But I don't honestly care anymore."

"You could save your life by handing over the white stuff, kid. That septic-tank riff didn't check out."

"Up yours, mister."

Ray holstered his piece. "*If* you live until the unveiling tomorrow, you better not try any fast steps with your psycho buddies in the helicopter."

"Not me," Joe giggled stupidly. "From here on in, I'm just a happy little onlooker."

Somebody else proffered a joint—Joe inhaled it. His heart did a drum-roll, flip-flopped disconcertingly, palpitated in a hand-jive rhythm, then settled into a slightly accelerated, but still comfortable beat. The bush, mingling with the coke, gave a weird rush. Again he giggled, mystified and enthralled by existence.

"It's okay, really," Joe said repeatedly, not in the least irritated by Iréné's endless apologetic harangue. They drifted indoors, nodding to Pancho Nordica and Tim Eberhardt, Gil Forrester and Cobey Dallas. Angel Guts slunk toward them, surlier than ever. Lackadaisically, Joe checked his pocket to make sure Diana's pistol was still there. Yet Angel Guts merely grinned a gap-toothed grin, clicked his heels, gave the Nazi salute, and said "Sieg heil!" Joe fashioned a Communist fist. Rugs beneath his feet undulated like waterbeds. People had pulled the little monkeys off the trees and now had them tucked underneath their arms, or dangling from their wrists. One couple laughed uproariously while putting their stuffed simians through copulating motions. A few kibitzers laughed so hard they were in pain, rolling on the floor. Joe soon lost control himself; he gasped for air. My God those monkeys were hilarious!

"Let's retire someplace, Joseph, all right? I'm going to make it up to you tonight, you'll see. God, I feel almost faint from wanting you."

"I like all these people," Joe said happily. "I like watching everybody. It's crazy. I never went to a party like this. I never actually saw anybody inhale a line of coke except in a movie."

He felt like a beautiful and pampered butterfly imprisoned in a genteel cocoon of conspicuous consumption. The Playboy mansion West; the hedonistic black Naugahyde innards of the Big Bunny. He delighted in the trip like a little kid in Disneyland. What next? What iridescent far-out concoction of sex, indolence, and Xanadu would dance around the corner, giving him the Big Eye? It was such fun. "Look this way!" Rama Unfug called. "I'm making your movie." "Not *my* movie," Joe replied. "Whatever I do belongs to all of us," Rama insisted, "because we all belong to God." Iréné laughed, and they kissed, tonguing hungrily. Everybody had such shiny boots. Their costumes were estupendously original. Jewelry, purple velour, midnight velveteen. And oh them crazy bodices! Half the people Joe didn't know. He suspected they hailed from Los Angeles and Aspen. Their flagrant garments shone like hummingbirds, wood ducks, peacocks. Some men had shirts with ruffly, scalloped jabots—they also wore cowboy hats and turquoise necklaces. And oh those fancy foxy women with their diaphanous drapery: tits galore! A babel of breasts! Their slinky cigarettes resided in black ebony holders. Provocative skirts derived from a forties style. And platform heels. Others wore pants so tight at the buttocks their gluteals twitched even while standing still.

Iréné's voice throbbed. "Joseph, I don't know how much longer I can hold out. You're such a devil. You're making me suffer. You're an ogre, but such a beautiful ogre. Christ, feel those biceps. I get goosebumps. Oh God, excuse me, but I think I'm falling in love."

When she leaned very close to him, her breasts flanked his upper arm. She whispered: *"I'm positively sopping wet almost down to my knees."*

He smiled benevolently. His eyes emoted tenderness and compassion that surpassethed all understanding. Wilting under his beatific gaze, she tugged on his hand. "Please, Joe, let's go."

"S'plenny of time. . . ." Joe could travel from here to over there by a mere flick of his wings. Fresh from the swimming

pool, wrapped in a rich crimson towel, Paula Husky balleted
past them, chased by a bear. Joe tipped an imaginary Stetson
in greeting. Dr. Phil Horney, a red-lipped grinning imbecile,
tagged after a woman, not Gretchen: she had a gardenia in her
jet-black hair, an artificial beauty-mole just above her upper
lip. Scott Harrison clinked glasses, said "Prosit" and "You're
a goddam arrogant fool!," and aroused no animosity in Joe.
Cobey Dallas yelled and went after somebody. Jeff Orbison
played a heartrending lament Joe loved, although he couldn't
remember if it was sung by Emmylou Harris or Linda Ronstadt.
A bunch of children gallivanted through the bacchanal waving
sparklers.

"Oh Joe, don't make me suffer so."

"Okay," he murmured thickly, wondering idly if he would
pass out. "Let's go."

Yet it made him forlorn to leave the crowd. He had really
enjoyed spectating that scene. The Prado and the Louvre had
wonderful fourteenth-century paintings that reminded him of
this night. Meandering among all the ribald molecules had been
fun. It had also been incredibly hollow. Yet all the pain and
beauty of the faces and the costumes and the dope and sex and
alcoholic antics of his friends and sophisticated strangers had
seeded in Joe a benevolent ache of gigantic and satisfying
proportions. They were like butterflies on the brink of winter.
(Let's hear it for clichés!) Of course, he knew it wasn't glamorous. Cavalier and arrogant—maybe; scornful and vapid—
yes; lush and ludicrous—true; criminal and scatological—you
bet . . . garnets and rhinestones galore.

Sounds receded. Joe heard ice cubes clinking, but not voices.
He felt tears on his cheeks. Splashes carried from the pool,
but not laughter. Briefly, he panicked; all that noise and animation had kept him buoyed, strong, invulnerable. Now, as
she opened a door, he suffered a wave of jitters—call it stage
fright.

"Stage fright," Joe whispered drunkenly, and giggled.
Brother, was he ever ripped!

Gloom. "This is Natalie's holler haven." Iréné was panting.
"She's into Primal Screaming, you know." He couldn't see a
thing. His heart raced uncomfortably. The evening had traveled
so fast. Her hands reconnoitered his body like professional
spiders, unbuttoning, unbuckling, unzipping.

"God, Joey, I'm wet. It's like a *swamp* between my legs!"

She dropped to her knees; her lips rolled over him like a combine harvesting a wheat field. Joe teetered but balanced himself by digging fingers into her hair. The pitch-black darkness unnerved him. He wanted something, if only starlight, defining her skin. The blackness was suffocating and airless, like the devil's womb. Joe wavered slightly, listening to her crude sounds. Alcohol, cocaine, and marijuana had numbed him to the point where he wondered if he had a hard-on or not. He looked down, up, all around—but could see nothing. Darkness had even occupied the spaces between his teeth, making him wish for a toothpick. He kept his mouth shut, praying this feral blackness wouldn't surge down his throat, drowning him in thick velvet. It was stark and surreal. Joe said, "I can't see you."

"You don't need to see me." She gasped for air, then attached herself again, suckling to beat the band.

Iréné started chanting, moving in and out on him, her voice muffled and gargling: "Gmphf ill tummy . . . gumpf ill tummy. . . ."

After a while he realized she was saying, "Give it to me . . . give it to me. . . ."

But did he have it to give? Joe had no sensation down there. With his hand he touched her nose, her cheeks, her lips . . . yoiks! he was erect! He mixed his fingers in her foamy mouth and she moaned . . . fiddled with his balls . . . teased his anus . . . and mumbled her refrain again.

Then her voice was coming through loud and clear: "Joe, take me in the helicopter with you tomorrow."

"What?"

"Take me in the helicopter," she hissed, softly twisting his balls.

"I'm not going in a helicopter." He fumbled for her face, seeking to guide his penis back into her mouth.

She sucked him briefly, then tried again:

"I know all about it—don't worry. You can trust me. Give me a ride, and I'll tell you their plans."

"I don't know what you're talking about," he whimpered. "Let's make love."

"Oh yes . . . please . . . give me your pud. . . ." She sucked him in, all the way down her throat, gagged, but held him there.

Spooked by the dark, Joe floated earthward, needing more tactile reference points. She gave a protesting cry as he pulled clear of her mouth. Abruptly, he got his bearings, moved smoothly, thrust into her. Her lips slapped his face. Her mouth was as large as that of those strange, depth-dwelling fish they occasionally pulled from the ocean. Her body, in his grasp, under his weight, squirming against the midnight rug, seemed terribly fragile. Bursts of tortured sound escaping her throat made him feel sorry for her, for them both. "Oh love me!" she cried. "Fuck me to death. Don't ever stop! You can scream if you want, nobody can hear us! Don't ever leave me! I love you! Murder me with it! Fuck out my heart! Cripple me! Tomorrow we'll do it together in your helicopter! Shove it up my ass and pull the trigger!"

This last, in that frightening cloacal darkness, he did for her—but could not pull the trigger. She screamed, and her high-pitched noise reverberated in his eardrums, it threatened to crack open his skull. His balls swelled, and his penis strained, but still he could bring about no discharge to complement her howls.

"Oh, Joey," she cried, *"I adore you."*

"No, Iréné. Please. No love..."

"Let me turn over. I want you in my mouth."

"You shouldn't..."

"I want you in my mouth. I'll do anything you want, if only you'll take me along...."

Though small, like an ant she was unbelievably powerful. Iréné contorted herself—twisting—and grasped Joe, actually lifting him King Kong-like, and placing him on her heaving chest. "Ah," she said, guiding his cock between her teeth again. He smelled shit in the black air. It scared him. If only there were just a pinprick of light somewhere, anything to orient by. This was the most loveless thing he had ever done. And it was transforming his psyche, his heart, even the composition of his blood as surely as if he were committing murder. Her hands reached up, plucking at his lips. Then she forced him to ooze backward and out of her for a moment, whispering up at him with awe:

"My eyes are wide open, Joseph. They've been open all this time. I've never made it with *my eyes wide open* before!"

The music stopped with a crash.

෴

He was gone—him and the wind and the stars—long before she awoke.

The swashbuckler sun leaped over the mountains like an actor playing the lead role in a Zorro film, unleashed a dazzling "en garde!," and postured swordlike with its lucid golden rays: "Touché!"

The world, as seen from Joe Miniver's perspective, recoiled from such an abundance of cloudless joy. The acrylic-blue sky seemed unbelievably corny. And electrified. Invisible archangels flashing trumpet-shaped hair dryers had quartered the valley, fluffing and feathering all tree leaves, which appeared to be etched against a superelegant fourth dimension. Every ridge on every mountain seemed to pop out in a totally false but stunning clarity reminiscent of Edward Weston and Eliot Porter. He could not help but tingle from the effects of such a primal lucidity!

It was six o'clock on a serene spring morning. Joe drove through the vitreous ether of a town not yet aroused. Though he piloted a vehicle, he had the sensation of cruising through a dementedly gossamer atmosphere in a structure no more prepossessing or weighted or technological than a chiffon cloud. All night he had rested unhappily in the arms of a fitfully twitching woman who uttered frightened cries and clung tightly, robbing him of sleep. He had cooed and tried to soothe, afraid to wake her, desperately wanting to atone. His arms, torso, and neck were littered with small yellowish bruises from her anguished pinches. The backs of his thighs burned bitterly with fingernail welts. Fatigue had him worse than light-headed. Not only did he want to withdraw from the world, but hibernation until *all* his wounds had healed was the only answer. All night he had assured her: "Hush. It's gonna be okay."

Oh, for a long time in his life Joe had cultivated an erotic curiosity, but already, only moments after launching the quest, he had burned out, unable to take it. Curses on that sexual drive leading people into these arenas where they paid for their tits and ass in priceless emotional coin!

The sun was an enormous Smilie. The world seemed scrubbed up for visiting Grandma. Joe half expected a few sprites in

diaphanous veils to prance across the road. Flurries of cottonwood fluff swirled by. A magpie swoop-swoop-swooped ahead
of him like a pilot tugboat leading a liner into the harbor; then
it veered leftward. On such a glorious day as this he had never
felt worse. His head, his eyes, his entire body throbbed. His
brain was damaged—no doubt permanently. His soul was in
shreds. He had forged an irrevocable distance between himself
and his wife and children. A hundred thousand dollars worth
of cocaine lay on the seat beside him . . . but so what? Why
hadn't they killed him for it last night, ending his misery?
"What kind of joke is this anyway, God? Turn me into a pillar
of salt, you mother! Drown me! Drive nails through my heart!
Fill my car full of man-eating grasshoppers!"

LORD IGNORES MINIVER PLEAS! THUNDEROUS CACKLE, TEN
TIMES LOUDER THAN SONIC BOOM, STAGGERS CHAMISA
VALLEY!

His penis was raw and sore—had he shoved it into a mammoth electric pencil-sharpener last night? His blue balls, burst-
ing with unrequited semen, cried out in pain, "I'll never make
love again!" *Thank God!*
Then . . . *eureka!* A brainstorm!
Joe braked so abruptly he would have erased the windshield
had not the steering wheel slammed his chest. Why hadn't he
thought of this earlier? "I'll commit suicide by gobbling that
whole box of cocaine!" A teaspoon of pure garbage could kill
him—right? Sure. Hot dog! Eager fingers scrabbled to open
the carton. Dream powder winked at him in all its unadulterated
malevolent whiteness.

MINIVER AUTO, PLASTERED IN TINY PIECES OF FLESH, FOUND
PARKED ON SHOULDER! CORONER RULES DEATH FROM
HUMONGOUS COKE OD! LEGEND IS BORN! LOCAL GANGSTERS—
AWED—ATTEND FUNERAL!

Two fingers scooped out a heap and slapped it onto his
tongue. "So long, world!" Giggling, Joe dug in again and
sucked hungrily, chewed voraciously, swallowed. How sweet,
how sugary—he hadn't noticed that last night. Frenetically,
Joe gouged up another half-ounce and tossed it away. He must
rapidly ingest enough to do the job before the effects blew his

mind into gaga incapacity. Any second now, a horrible rainbow
would shatter his cerebellum, a psychedelic burst of jungle
erotica would crunch free of his dull skull, blooming with
beautiful brutality into the blood-soaked air while naked leering
chorus girls crowed Handel's *Messiah*. . . .

Joe gulped one, two, three more crunchy fistfuls, gagged,
chewed, and feverishly swallowed.

But nothing happened. What's this—you had to *snort* the
dope to make it work? Not in a year could he inhale all that
dry, grating goop! All the sweet granules had produced so far
was nausea. Sugary crystals had sponged up his saliva; swallowing was difficult. The coke tasted more like powdered
doughnuts than dope.

"Sugar . . . ?"

Joe enticed several sensory faculties back into his mouth,
activating taste buds, and ran a quick chemical analysis. Concentrating, he soon realized that only a real moron would fail
to reach the conclusion he finally stumbled upon.

It *was* sugar.

MINIVER DOUBLE-CROSSED AGAIN!

Burned by his Philadelphia pal! Twelve thousand dollars
for a two-bit mix of granulated and confectioners' sugar!

Joe spat out some crud against the dashboard, and wondered
what to do now except sputter hysterically at the horrendous
humor of it all.

"Curses, foiled again!"

At which point Joe glanced up: and here they all came,
girded for an epic battle. While he'd been busily catering to a
sweet tooth, their cars had quietly glided in, surrounding him.
Ray Verboten and Angel Guts, Jeff Orbison and the Chicken
River Funky Pie van chauffeur, Tom Yard from the First State
People's Jug, and a tall, rawboned geek, probably Algernon
from the Joe Bonatelli Phalange of Lisping Freaks. Guns drawn
purposefully, they had him surrounded.

"Give it here," Ray said quietly, sighting along the glistening blue barrel of his elephant pistol. "That coke belongs to
the people now, Joe. No more fun and games."

Meekly, Joe passed his carton through the open driverside
window. "It's all yours, Ray. I give up. But it ain't worth
much, believe me."

"That's a good boy." Gently, Ray relieved Joe of his burden. Instantly, the carton's weight, the look and texture and smell of its contents, tipped off the pusher. Tucking his mammoth betsy into an armpit, Ray licked a finger, dapped up a touch of powder, and tasted it. His wry face said it all. In unison with Joe, he cried:

"It's sugar!"

"Jinx, touch blue!" Joe lightly slapped Ray's shirt. "You owe me a Coke."

Lips contorted in a puzzled snarl, Ray glowered at Joe, then frowned into the tea box, then lifted a confounded countenance to question Joe again.

Face drenched in a wimpy smile, Joe shrugged. "I'm sorry. My East Coast buddy burned me in the deal. I just found out myself. What can I say?"

Ray dug into the box, scooping sugar off the top, splashing it onto the roadway. Every few seconds he ventured another taste, spitting it out disgustedly, and kept on digging. Fascinated, Joe watched the pusher analyze his way swiftly to the bottom—but no dice. Two thousand miles away, Peter Roth must have been yukking up a real storm. Twelve free Gs he had prestidigitated on a $2.98 box of Shurfine concoction!

Well, well, life sure had its little ups and downs.

Ray locked into Joe's bloodshot eyes, searching for telltale quivers, a glint of mendacity. Joe had nothing but the truth to give him, and, practiced in such arts, Ray could tell. All of them had taken a flying douche.

"You dumb motherfucker, Joe Miniver."

Ray pitched the empty box through Joe's window. Then, with a toss of his head, he summoned the troops: they retreated dispiritedly and, angrily spitting blue exhaust, departed for once and for all.

Sunshine cuddled Joe's ears, playfully tousled his hair, warmed the tip of his nose. Dazedly, he started the bus. Most desperately, he desired a drink of water.

᜕᠍

Joe yawned, though not from fatigue. Something was happening to the incredible tension inside his body. Molecules hummed and a crazy sensation attacked his blood. Light and floaty muscles seemed to have lost their tethers. Had he miraculously received an injection of zero gravity? His foot wanted to levitate off the gas pedal. If he released the steering wheel, he might float like an astronaut in a space capsule, weightless, euphoric. Squeezed sensations in his bowels felt like tentative orgasm embryos. An alien electricity, not exactly unpleasant, coursed through his nerves. Maybe, like a sky diver, he had been launched into a free fall, twenty thousand psychic feet above his own nebulous insanity. Plummeting at a disquieting rate, with no markers to measure, by, Joe could enjoy a brief, extravagant freedom beyond the pale of rational restrictions. Entranced in a soporific calm, he did seem—in short—to be losing his marbles.

A lone jogger up ahead, in a powder-pink warm-up suit with a Day-Glo monkey on the back, caught his attention. From the rear, she looked provocative. Her buttocks jounced enticingly against the tight material of her pants. Blond hair fluttered youthfully at each step. Joe snarled, whimpered, and accelerated a little to catch up and ogle her no-doubt pretty face, tormented by a lustful twinge—in him whom he had just thought might never lust again!

But as he drew ahead, eyes prepared to feast, he gasped. In place of that blue-eyed, luscious-lipped face he had counted on for yet another decadent pop to his twisted guts was an apparition of polished bone surrounding blank black eyeholes, and the grinning jagged teeth of a sardonic skull.

"Oh no!"

Joe swerved across the median line, then frantically swung the wheel in the other direction as a horn-tooting pickup narrowly swept by him inches from a head-on collision.

And when he dared glance back via the rearview mirror, the shoulder of the road, curiously hazy in the bright, early morning light, was deserted.

"You're hallucinating, bro," he told his trembling self. "It's time for a little shut-eye."

But where now? Who would have this scatological wreck? A powerful, sweet, deathlike sexual numbness gripped his brain and his loins. And so, as if connected to an automatic homing device, he turned into the Perry Kahn Subdivision #4.

Bradley sat on the front stoop in his pajamas, mainlining malnutrition and brain damage from a bowl of Cocoa Puffs. He waved. Joe cranked a handle, banging open the door. Emerging from the bus like a parachute unfolding, he cantered lopsidedly toward the house. Bradley barely looked up as Joe sailed past, a giddy grin pinned to his puffed and rosy features.

Cute and cool in a lime-green shorty nightgown, Nancy rounded a corner as he danced tipsily into her home. But Joe hardly noticed her outfit. He swished by, barely aware of fingers fluttering off one shoulder. Down the short, narrow hallway he plunged, bouncing softly off cardboard walls—and hung a left at Sasha's room.

The hospital-bound monkey was no doubt occupied elsewhere in tawdry deviltries, buggering nurses. Joe left his feet, crumpling luxuriously toward the glistening Daring Debbie. Her prominent pneumatic bosom rose in prolific greeting: he sank between tanned latex thighs. Her arms enclosed him in erotic chub as he shoved his penis into the ample, foam-rubber vagina. Joe gasped gratefully, running his tongue over slick rubber cheeks as soft as angel-pussy. And pumped, slipping greedy hands beneath her to squeeze plump buttocks. A sexy *whoosh*! escaped her perfectly pouted mouth as he frenched her. Thighs rolled and bounced against his jagged hips in airy delight. Joe groaned, and whispered, "I love you," as he repeatedly stabbed the carefully contoured recess between her legs. Oh how pornographically she joggled in his arms!

"I love you, I love you. . . ." he murmured as the semen reared from his balls with stallionesque enthusiasm. "I love you, god dammit," he croaked in erotic rage. "I want us to marry and live together forever!"

Thus released, jism galloped through his shaft, ignoring emotional Stop signs along the way, and burst from the tip of his cock with a real *éclat!*, splashing wonderful gobs of frustrated goo every whichway, filling up in a wink her cavernous hole, and overflowing against her swollen, perfectly textured belly. "Oh thank you!" Joe cried, knocked for a loop by such ecstasy and relief. *"Oh my God you're wonderful!"*

For long minutes afterward he ground his stomach against her slippery swells, and mooshed his tingle-happy skin against the gratifying wholeness of this abominably heavenly whore.

Until finally, as if coldcocked by a mallet, he blacked out.

6
Thursday

Shock comes—oh, oh!
Then follow laughing words—ha, ha!

Gently, but persistently, she shook his shoulder. Joe opened one eye, somewhat disappointed to be still alive. Sunlight glorified her bedroom. How had he arrived here?

"You walked," Nancy said. "Of course, I helped you a little."

"I walked in my sleep?" He remembered nothing: it was eerie.

"Let's just say I helped. Gosh, you look adorable when you sleep." Her hand ruffled his hair; goosebumps sprung up on his neck. He could picture it: telepathically she had lifted him from Sasha's mattress. Like a sleeping pasha on a bewitched Persian carpet, he had floated out the door, down the hallway, and into this room. The carpet had tilted slightly, dumping him onto the bed. Then her psychic powers snapped back into her head like a carpenter's metal tape measure: *brrrrrrrrrrrap!*

"What time is it?"

"Time to drive out for the Hanuman unveiling."

"I don't wanna go. They'll stone me to death."

"Don't be silly."

"I need a bath. I stink."

"Whatever you wish. Though I think you smell wonderful."

Like shit? Or Iréné Papadraxis? Imitating Rocky Marciano, guilt landed a combination to his conscience that rocked Joe back on his heels. Wearing black hats and cowboy boots, walking grim-lipped through Chamisaville streets fingering six-guns in leather holsters tied against their thighs, they were eager to gun him down: Heidi, Diana, Iréné.

Joe said, "How come *you* don't hate me?"

"Hate isn't my thing."

"What is?"

"Love."

He *hated* her for that!

"Remind me," Joe called from the bathtub a few minutes later, "to nominate the inventor of hot water for the Nobel Peace Prize, would you?" Then he slouched down: water sloshed

525

over his aching skin. Cut adrift, he was now a man without a country. His right-hand knuckles had swelled to double their size. An image of Heidi, swathed in blood on her knees at the telephone, gave his heart an uncomfortable moment. Quickly, he blocked out the scene before it could trigger the specter of horror-struck Michael, hands clasping his ears. Heather's bite marks on his arm pulsed angrily: Joe kissed the spot, trying to make it better. The skin flinched from his poison lips.

Bozo appeared, growled halfheartedly, stuck his head into the toilet, and thirstily lapped up water. Lathering himself good, Joe tried to hum a few bars of a Willie Nelson song—but the sounds were croaks and desultory gurgles. When next he glanced up, Joe almost shit a brick. Resembling a war veteran in his pink eyepatch and plaster-cast arm, Sasha stood in the doorway, morosely regarding Joe. Where the vet had shaved him to remove BBs, gobs of fur were missing.

"Oh no, *the monkey's back*!"

From the kitchen she called, "Yes, isn't it wonderful? I fetched him last night."

Sasha's malicious face lit up. He clicked his teeth at Joe, then about-faced and bent over, throwing a moon. A bright-orange carrot emerged from halfway up his rectum.

The Incredible Hulk versus Mighty Monsterito!—Joe hurled a wet sponge at the gross little creature. Sasha snagged in it midair with his good hand and proceeded to insolently devour it, tearing off large chunks with his yellow chiseling teeth. Then he burped and scampered off. Joe closed his eyes—*they deserved each other*.

Nancy arrived, wearing only panties, and stood before the medicine-cabinet mirror putting on eye shadow and lipgloss. Joe enjoyed the tranquil domesticity of the scene until Nancy said: "Whoever she was sure gave you a good butchering last night."

"Come again?"

"Your body looks like it really went through a sexual meat grinder."

"Well, uh, you know, I mean . . ."

"How was the party?"

"What party?" Why couldn't he stop himself? When they broke through the line and came running at him full tilt, his linebacker's instinct was to rush forward and tackle them with lies.

"Come on, Joe. You know what party."

"Oh, *that* party."

"Well, how was it?"

"I dunno. Okay I guess." He didn't want to remember. "Pretty boring, actually. You know, all the typical stuff: disco music, nude bathing, lots of dope, good eats, asinine conversation."

"You seem to have done all right for yourself with whats-hername."

"Me? Hey, wait a minute. What business is it of yours what I did last night?"

"Nobody said it was my business." Nancy smiled, obviously aware that she looked delectable. "I was just making idle conversation."

"Idle my eye. You're trying to slip ice picks into my jugular. Talk about devious . . ." No oomph characterized his protests. They sallied lacklusterly, by rote.

"You must learn to trust people someday." She squatted beside the tub, then leaned through the steam, making him heady by touching her lips lightly against his. "Only then can you begin to lead a gorgeous life. All that suspiciousness clouds the issues."

"But everybody's out to get you. Nobody ever does anything without an ulterior motive."

"If that's how you think, then you'll always be unhappy."

"But I'll survive to a ripe old age!" he muttered as she sauntered off for the bedroom.

Her pretty head reappeared in the doorway. "We all live forever, Joe."

◆§

Behind the wheel of her VW Beetle, heading west for Eloy Irribarren's place, Joe glimpsed himself in the rearview mirror: he looked almost human again. Beside him, Nancy was downright foxy in a sunny skirt, low-cut peasant blouse, and moderately high-heeled sandals. A daisy he had plucked from her coffee table vase was tucked in her hair. Behind them, Bradley squirmed uncomfortably in the old-fashioned splendor of a short-sleeved white shirt, gray flannel shorts, and Buster Brown oxfords. His official expression for the day was an Imperial Scowl mixed with a Spoiled-Brat Pout and a Snot-

Nosed Frown. You couldn't impress that kid with statues of simian hermaphrodites!

Beside Bradley, Sasha was methodically eating a small bouquet of daisies Nancy had fitted with a rubber band to his good wrist. For the occasion, she and Bradley had crayoned a rainbow and words like *peace* and *love* on his cast.

Heading west off the plaza, they entered a caravan of VWs, ancient bread trucks, renovated hearses, and old pickups driven by millionaires from Big Sur and Closter, New Jersey. Some had little toy monkeys attached to their radio and CB aerials. One bumper sticker said, "Monkeys, monkeys, rah rah rah!" Peace symbols, ecology flags, and antinuke slogans decorated their windows. Each dilapidated pickup bed harbored a dozen healthy, sunburned kids in colorful hippie regalia.

Joe could not help remarking yet again on the land flanking their route: not three years ago it had still been a semivast pasture and sagebrush expanse. But now a thousand cleverly obtuse little castles populated by artists, dope pushers, grade-school teachers, pipe smokers, and retired air-force colonels plundered the mauve plain. People splashed in pools, hopped around outdoor tennis courts, mowed lawns that resembled putting greens.

"This must have been a lovely valley," Joe said, surprised by his ability to summon outrage. A sense of loss, concerning something he had never known, nailed him in the heart. Sasha farted.

"It's still beautiful, Joe. It's all in the eye of the beholder. You're the one who makes or breaks any landscape, no one else."

Despite himself, defensive juices began percolating. After all, whatever could he hope to accomplish with this woman, in this cavalcade of American escapists, heading off to stuff his stomach and worship at the feet of a stone idol sculpted in the image of King Kong? That curiosity decreed he see for himself seemed but a feeble justification. Only a weak and malleable man would even passively support a ritual he knew ahead of time he'd find insulting to any semi-attuned intelligence. How could a person once pretending to hold a rabid scorn for every spiritual Mickey Mouse milking the American psyche for dollar-plunder and -power actually wind up complacently supporting this whole hokey operation by showing up in person to gawk, talk, nosh, and who knew what else? He was so tired of narcissism—theirs, his own.

Then all of a sudden he remembered. *Oh no!* Today was the day Tribby and Ralph battled Ephraim Bonatelli for supremacy of the Chamisaville skies! In his name, in honor of Eloy's land, they were going to grab the Hanuman! How had he managed to push *that* from his rapidly mushifying mind?

The answer, of course, was "What mind?" That limp lump of cerebral muck encased by a rusted tin-can cranium balanced awkwardly like a rotting Halloween pumpkin atop the shoulders of the cowardly jellyfish contraption he had the nerve to call his "body"?

Brake the car, Joe, pull over, get out, and run away! And in his head Joe did brake; he banged open his door, leapt out, and scrambled off, leaving Bradley and Nancy horrified . . . yet also secretly enamored of his courage, his refusal to cop out.

No sheep blood in the veins of this revolutionary, by gum!

In real life, Bradley said, "Mom, Sasha stepped on a frog— make him stop it." And Joe accelerated, giving up, carrying them ever closer to a signal event in the Chamisa Valley's spiritual history. He hadn't the guts to run; he'd lost the willpower to arbitrate his own destiny. He could almost feel his soul as it squeezed out his left ear, said "Ta-ta," and evaporated into thin air. He was so full of fatal flaws they hummed inside his body like a rickety old refrigerator. Somewhere along the way, demons had robbed him of a selfhood that might have had noble intentions. And all that remained was a feeble and lackluster stubbornness that said, "Well, at least I won't foment that riot they asked me to launch. . . ."

Oh jeepers creepers, what sort of demeaning catharsis lay in store for them all?

When their motorcade quit pavement for Upper Ranchitos Road, Joe's heart quickened. Dust enveloped them; he couldn't breathe. Fumbling in his shirt pocket for a pill, he realized they were all in the bus glove compartment . . . right beside the Alupent inhaler.

"Maybe you're being set up for a cure," Nancy said cheerfully.

"Meaning?"

"The Hanuman has powers."

"That'll be the day."

"If only you were open, Joe. Your life would be so much easier."

"I'm a street person," he wheezed, disliking himself already for the rap to come; his self-righteousness emerged from a dark hypocrisy hissing dangerously, like a cobra. "I like the action of real people, real struggles. I can't stand the effete cosmic bullshit of privileged dingbats with nothing better to do than lug a ten-thousand-pound, million-dollar statue all the way from India to the Rocky Mountains for the purpose of grooving on an idol when they get ripped on Moroccan kif and feel in need of a spiritual hit so they can float around in bare feet looking beautiful and transcending the hellish carnage of Life in the Trenches where nine-tenths of humanity, not blessed with trust funds or PhDs or a Westchester childhood, toils."

"My my. You certainly are touchy today."

"I hate India. I can't help it" Why couldn't he shut up, groveling through the upcoming charade with at least one small shred of dignity? "All those geeks in loincloths and turbans selling Zen this, Hanuman that, and Tibetan such-and-such to rich Americanos, while ninety percent of the people over there suffer hellish torments every day, and live in putrid sinkholes."

"Have you ever been to India?"

"No—have you?"

"Not in a way you'd understand."

"Try me."

"Well, I haven't actually been in, you know—in person. My corporeal body."

"What way have you been?"

"I don't want to discuss it with you. All you do is make fun."

"I won't make fun of you. Seriously, I'm really interested."

"Well, there are ways of traveling to a place other than buying a plane ticket, or taking a boat."

"Sure. You can get on a train."

"See what I mean? You can't resist."

"No, hey, please—I wasn't trying to be funny."

"Well, anyway—you know."

"Know what? What did you find over there?"

"Tranquillity. Peace. A beauty that is so radiant it's almost impossible to talk about, especially in this sort of situation."

"Where did you find it?" Somehow, he still had the chutzpah to flush angrily. But how hollow sounded his words! "Do the beggars, who deliberately maim themselves in order to earn a living, sell you three Tranquillities for a nickel on the streets of Calcutta? Do little baskets of Beauty float among the turds in the open sewers of Delhi? Can you get a real hit of Peace watching them burn—on the banks of the Ganges in Varanasi—the ten thousand bodies a day that expire from cholera? Or did some Nepalese sherpa with a life expectancy of thirty-eight, earning two dollars a day for risking death by leading you up to world fame and glory at the summit of Mount Everest, give to you the secret of Eternal Radiance?"

Quietly, she said, "Well, that settles *that* conversation. I hate to say it, but you're not being very fair."

"I'm talking about people *starving* to death." Tears dribbled from his eyes. "I'm talking about crippling parasites in every stomach, open running sores on every limb, millions of families who sleep in their own excrement on the sidewalks every night. I'm talking about one fucking doctor for every five hundred thousand people, where there's a fakir-guru on every street-corner, selling pie in the sky so that all that slavery just perpetuates itself!"

"I know what you're talking about, but . . ."

"But what?"

She parted her glistening lips a trifle and whispered, just a tad mockingly: "But, but, but."

He melted. His own ineffectual blood sabotaged the crying of these blues.

"You got no conscience," he complained meekly.

"I have so many things I could teach you, if only you would let me."

"I'm afraid of you. After today I want nothing more to do with you."

"I'm not afraid of you."

"So I noticed."

"After today what will you do?"

"I don't know. I've destroyed all my credibility. I'm badly damaged goods."

"You're not damaged goods, Joe. Not to me."

"What am I to you, then?"

"Oh, I don't know exactly. You're a large, vital bundle of raw material without any real guidelines, I suppose."

"And you just happen to have the correct guidelines, right?"

"You might say that."

"Tell me something," he asked, truly puzzled. "How do you get off being so calm and cocky?"

"I found an inner peace."

"Where?"

Nancy laughed, and declined to reply. Bradley said, "Mom, Sasha's making mean faces at me. Tell him to stop. I hate his guts."

"He's only an animal, darling. He doesn't know any better."

Their motorcade reached its destination. One shabby vehicle after another filed into the west end of Eloy's front fields, destroying the grass. Joe parked between a midnight-blue Dodge van decorated with Day-Glo characters from the "Fabulous Furry Freak Brothers" comic strip and a chartreuse 1952 Chevy pickup packed full of little children wearing calico granny dresses and yellow wisteria crowns.

"We're here." Nancy affixed a slim red-leather leash to Sasha's collar. "You can get out now."

"I'm scared."

"Of what?"

"Of all those vibes out there. I forgot to wear my tennis shoes. I'm not grounded. I'll be electrocuted."

"Very funny."

"They'll put acid in the punch—I'll have a horrible trip, I'll freak out. I wanna go back to my Lone Star and honky-tonk women."

Bradley said, "Mom, is he crazy?"

"Nope. He's just a little boy like you, dear. Now come on, everybody—alley oop!" She opened her door. Unbalanced by his pink eyepatch and arm cast, Sasha lost control in midleap, did a somersault, and hit the deck with a pained squeal.

Joe slouched as low as possible behind the wheel. "It's a trap," he groaned. "Half the revelers out there are narcs, just cruising around, looking to bust heavy political types like me."

"Joe, you're really absurd." She giggled over his antics.

"Oh yeah?" Joe sniffed the air. "Get a whiff of that. What are they doing, burning an entire marijuana field so that everybody inhaling the smoke in unison can get loaded at the same time?"

"All right, that does it—let's go, Bradley."

"Wait for me," Joe cried. "Do you want the car locked?"

"In this place?"

Catching up to her, Joe raised his collar, hunched his shoulders, scrunched down his neck, and, though honestly terrified, he pantomimed the acts of a comically paranoid man: "Hey," he whispered, "do you think anybody'll notice my karma?" His hand bumped into Diana's gun—why hadn't he left it in the car? It was burning a hole in his pocket. I'll shoot that helicopter out of the sky! I'll commit suicide! I'll go berserk and take a bunch of them with me! I'll assassinate Nikita Smatterling! I'll plug the Hanuman when they swing open those U-Haul doors!

Nancy laughed lightly, and touched her fist to his nose, a symbolic punch.

"Is my aura okay? If it isn't, will they notice and attack like a pack of jackals?"

"Absolutely."

"But I'm too young to be reincarnated!" Mayhaps he was on the verge of a nervous breakdown?

"In your last life," she joshed, "I bet you were a toad. In your next life, I hope you reappear as a gnat."

"Then por lo menos, in my next life, I'll be gnattily attired."

"Oh lord." Politely, she made a funny gesture that suggested barfing. "You know, you really don't have to feel so self-conscious, though. Nobody will stick their tongue out at you. And anyway, they've all had their rabies shots."

Nevertheless, Joe wished he could dart unnoticed behind a bush and speedily unload the revolver. *Stop me before I kill again!* Then he thought: The next time Sasha does something obscene, my final act in life will be to pull out the gun and tattoo my monogram across that monkey's scrawny chest!

A grove of silvertip poplar trees in cardboard buckets had grown up near the aspen gazebo, compliments of Ragtime Flowershop. Gray cooking-smoke seeped idly up through the new-leafed branches at the east end of the field, carrying delicious smells of exotic foods in preparation. Heading there, they passed the U-Haul: its side door was still locked to keep folks from prematurely viewing the Hanuman. The cable harness and the ring on top gleamed lazily, inviting grappling hooks. Surrounding the ring atop the trailer, among a cornucopia of colorful fruits and flowers, sat a gold-framed photograph of Baba Ram Bang. Other people ambled past the trailer, self-consciously ignoring it as they trickled toward the food. A little child, naked except for a beaded headband and cowboy boots, her face decorated by white paint, sat beneath the U-

Haul cradling a stuffed monkey in her arms. Sasha scampered out to the end of his leash, hissed and clattered his rotten teeth, and, with his good hand, lifted the pink eyepatch, exposing his gory wound. Nancy tugged him away gently, clucking her tongue, but not before the little girl started crying.

From off to one side, Egon Braithwhite called out to Joe: Shin hua mabuchi!"

Joe gritted his teeth, refusing to turn around: he continued advancing.

"Ma jhong! Ma jhong!"

Joe upped the pace as the U-Haul receded behind them.

"Hi ti rabba mogup!"

Nancy said, "Aren't you going to answer him?"

"I would, but I don't know whether to say 'Chop hee go dum dum' or 'Bee tachiwa!'"

And then Diana appeared, forlorn, mystifyingly beautiful. Though Joe's instincts said "Turn away," her dark eyes held him: they stared at each other briefly. Her anguish and agony, muted by a curiously serene tristesse that positively glowed from her bearing, floated through the air, caressed Joe, caused pain. She seemed sweetly superior and scornful . . . and pity-ing—*Are you one of them now, Joe? Do you cuddle monkeys in your sleep?* He wished desperately to explain, avow eternal love for her—Diana's soul intrigued him so much more than Nancy's.

A demure smile . . . then she quietly took her provocative darkness elsewhere.

Incense smoke mixed with the pungent vapor of five cook-fires. Half a dozen swarthy, turbaned east Indians scurried between large cauldrons, basting, tasting, prodding, and prob-ing their stews, brews, goulashes, and other concoctions. About thirty people already sat in a large circle near the campfires. Baba Ram Bang hunkered at the head of the circle, leading a song. Some people jangled cheerful little castanetlike contrap-tions affixed to their fingers. Rama Unfug was energetically filming the scene. Joe quickly canvassed the crowd, searching for the telltale bulges of burp guns and surreptitious hand gre-nades hidden under the clothing of the various troops involved in protecting the Hanuman or planning to pinch it. But nobody seemed even the least bit prepared for holocaust.

Anyone expecting a bunch of American freaks all decked out as swamis, gurus, and holy men and women would have been sorely disappointed. Costumes ranged from T-shirts and jeans, through everyday, run-of-the-mill, slighty shabby summer stuff. A few far-out costumes added flavor. Nikita himself wore a linen hospital gown whose enormous cuffs were elaborately embroidered with Far Eastern designs. His youngest kid, Siddhartha, was attired in a white Mowgli loincloth and sandals. Nearby another child checked in wearing a Hopalong Cassidy (or was that a Lash LaRue?) cowboy outfit. Dr. Phil Horney had chosen to appear in a tie and cord sportcoat, double-knit slacks, and oxblood cordovans. His wife preferred her spiritual events in a revealing black body shirt, old-fashioned pedal pushers, and a silver concho belt. Cowboy hats—perched atop Old West-moustachioed hippies—outnumbered turbans six to one. A gaggle of far-out dudes and outtasight chicks wore Hanuman T-shirts. Others' skimpy tops advertised the wearer's personality. Natalie Gandolf's T-shirt said "Nice Jugs"; Skipper Nuzum's ballyhooed "Go, Boomer Sooners!" A dozen kids' shirts displayed the Grease and Star Wars symbols. One Joe noticed in particular said "Any Man Who Eat Fried Chicken Bound to Get Greezy."

A hideous revelation shook Joe. His paranoia had *fantasized* the upcoming conflagration! Under pressure, his mind had floated off its moorings. He had dreamed up the helicopters, Joe Bonatelli's grapefruit, Jeff Orbison's offer to bribe Tom Yard. For days, Chamisaville's gathering surrealism had been but a figment of his schizophrenic imagination. He had projected a hysteria that didn't exist except in the morbid chambers of his own disintegrating brain!

As she approached him, Iréné Papadraxis's breasts jiggled tantalizingly behind the slogan "I'm a Real Softy." *Oh no*, Joe cried; *I'm a goner*! No doubt she would slip one hand behind her back, removing a silver, pearl-handled derringer, and plant an odd-caliber hollow-nosed slug in his sternum. As he fell, Diana would reappear, this time packing a loaded police .38, and commence blasting. Heidi, no doubt, would add her two cents with a sawed-off twelve-gauge shotgun spewing those good ol' double-ought buck loads. Then Ray Verboten would out with his reliable betsy, no doubt a .357 Mag, and deliver the coup de grace.

MINIVER MEETS MONSTROUS MAKER
AT MALEVOLENT MONKEY FETE!

Instead, Iréné did worse.

She mortified him mortally by extending an amiable hand and smiling cheerfully. "Hello, Joseph. I'm so glad you could make it." Her professional politeness chilled him to the bones. How could people experience the depravity they had suffered through last night, and be so detached and civilized next morning? It was like television: you blew each other's brains out, marched into exterminating ovens, and crippled your opponent for life on the same emotional level at which you bought a car or waxed your kitchen . . . and nothing truly mattered.

He heard his absurdly lighthearted reply: "Hi yourself. It's a great day for the party, isn't it?"

Ozzie and Harriet Visit Lobotomy Land with Mickey Mouse and Rod McKuen!

She betrayed no emotion indicating terror, excitement, or anticipation of the dramatic snatch to come.

But wait! Nancy felt compelled to join the banality orgy. "You're Iréné Papadraxis, aren't you? I'm so pleased to meet you. I've heard so much . . ."

Peter Pan in Circle-Jerk Heaven! How could they all be so *grown-up?* If they all exchanged one more sickly-sweet amenity Joe thought he'd go insane. Better they should leap at each other, tearing hair, gouging eyeballs, shredding tits with their feral teeth! Whatever had happened to passion? Jealousy? Or even Death by Embarrassment?

"I'm having a ball," Iréné said enthusiastically. "This is all too wonderful and original for words! My book is writing itself. Is that the famous Sasha?" She bent over to pet him. "What a darling little beast." Sasha snapped at her finger, but Iréné was quick: he missed. "Tut tut," the foxy lady scolded. "He seems a trifle hostile. Do crowds sour his stomach?"

"Not at all," Nancy blithely replied. "Isn't it as if God personally ordered up the day?"

A smooth little man in a pink turban tinkled a triangular gong.

"Chow time," Nancy chirruped.

"Let's all sit together," Iréné liltingly suggested.

They chose a spot in the outer circle. The singing was melodic, lyrical, happy. In spite of himself, Joe found it difficult to prolong his inner discomfort. He actually forgot about the women and the pending squall and felt himself relaxing. He had anticipated a more formal ritual. But everything so far had been casual and pretty. If anybody here had inklings of the trauma about to explode over their heads, they certainly weren't letting on. A shrine in the center of the circle contained another stuffed monkey and a photograph of Baba Ram Bang. Crammed down into the monkey's sawdust cranium was a peacefully smoking incense stick.

Nancy said, "Now this isn't so bad, is it?"

Joe giggled passively, realizing, at long last, that somehow Tribby's bizarre plan was a thing he had dreamed. He said, "I'm waiting for the moment when they put hooks in their breasts and tear their flesh apart."

"Honestly—you know something?"

"What?"

"You're a bona fide idiot."

"But," he leered, leaning close to whisper, "I got a great shlong."

"Let's put it this way: for a nonspiritual person, you're not a bad lover."

People meandered around the ersatz glen obviously ripped and feeling no pain. Sometimes they halted, jabbing fingers into various cauldrons for a preview taste of the upcoming feast. Others merely floated, hailing each other laconically. Everybody "ooh'd" and "ah'd" over Sasha, praising the Lord for his survival. Enthralled in dismembering a gooshy avocado, Sasha paid them little attention. A pretty girl scooped something out of a fruit bowl and tossed it to Joe: a strawberry.

He bit off half, and offered the rest to Nancy. While he held on to the green stem, her pretty white teeth nibbled at the fruit.

"Mmmm . . . delicious."

Joe leaned close, licking juice and a fleck of pulp off her lower lip. Relief had him positively euphoric. He would live to flounder another day. In this sort of atmosphere, nothing could go wrong.

Five tipis had been raised in the field near the Pacheco Ditch. People in various stages of undress drifted among the white cone structures. Their oiled torsos glistened. Several couples gave each other massages. Yellow-and-white butterflies zigzagged and flip-flopped through the meadow.

Somebody sat down close behind them; a friendly hand touched his shoulder; a familiar voice said, "Hello, Joey, how's by you today?"

Oh no, not *Heidi*!

So here it came: For Reals. They had set him up for her, the two devious and heartless women flanking him! He should have known. Heidi would slide the slim, eight-inch, razor-honed blade between his ribs with a mere flick of her powerful wrist, finding the heart, killing him instantly. Iréné and Nancy would grip his arms before he could fall over, holding him upright for a while, gradually allowing the body to settle backward as if peacefully reclining into sleep.

Again, his imagination had blown it.

"How was the party last night?" Her voice was peppy, noncommittal, neutral. "Did you have fun?"

Joe turned, squinting at her. She met his gaze with absolute blandness. A few red welts, from flying glass bits, marred her otherwise unblemished countenance. How had such tiny cuts released those terrifying scads of blood?

How carefree she seemed! On drugs? Her face was flushed with beauty, her tawny hair feathered as if she had just been running. Too late, he realized anew how much he loved her. At the same time, Joe judged from her creepily disinterested eyes that she could face him calmly today because she had surgically carved from her heart every last filament of emotional connection to him. He didn't know her anymore: they had never made love or reared kids together. Joe had rarely been left more aghast by an impersonal encounter.

Dimly, he answered her question about the party. "Sure, it was okay." *I sodomized this lady beside me in the Nuzums' Primal Scream room.* "There were lots of people there. And, you know . . . good eats, good music . . ."

"Yes, I heard it was a real blast. Aren't you excited to see the Hanuman?"

Heidi, he wanted to cry, *what's the matter with you?* Had a herd of devilish foreign pod-people enzombified everybody's lilting frames. *Only yesterday, at least we wanted to kill each other! We threatened suicide! The children were bawling! I've been diddling three other women!* "It's sort of curious so far," he said nicely. "Very friendly, though."

"Well, I've gotta run." She bestowed a cool good-bye tap. "There's Nikita." And off she bounded before Joe could ask, Where are the kids? The sight of her prancing away, no longer connected to his life, was worse than murder.

Yet presently, the singing, the finger bells jangling, the

tinkling wind chimes, the redolent cooking steam, the piñon
and cedar smell, the entire slowed-down, semidrugged and laid-
back motion of the event created an uneasy serenity in Joe:
what else could he do, anyway, except accept the sensuous
bovinity completely? A joint traveled down the line—he inhaled deeply more than once. In the far background, Joe saw
Eloy Irribarren exit from his house carrying a rifle, which he
placed inside his battered pickup: then he returned to his dwelling. Vapidly happy as a little ol' clam, Joe clamped his arm
around Nancy's shoulder and nuzzled in her hair. His lips
touched her ear. He whispered, "Nothing . . . nothing . . .
nothing . . ." She giggled. Iréné placed her hand on his thigh:
"Isn't this delightful?" Bradley had wandered off. Sasha gnawed
at his cast, biting off little plaster chunks: noisily, he spat them
at children gamboling past.

Ay, qué tranquillity! Sunlight enchanted their circle with
dappled patterns of brightness. Everybody grew fuzzy. Mel-
lifluized by friendly trembling leaf-shadows, people swayed to
their own rhythm, eyes closed. More arrived each minute. They
took places behind Joe, building a third, outer circle. They
smiled for Rama Unfug's camera. Eloy emerged from his house
again, gingerly carrying a little bag. He paused, staring down
through mammouth cottonwoods at the festival. Then he placed
the bag in his truck, and retreated slowly to his hovel. When
Rachel Parquielli came over to say hello, Joe asked, "Where's
Tribby?"

"He went trout fishing."

Eyes closed, Joe pictured Tribby alone on this glorious
bluebird day. Above his head, as he pumped his arm, line—
like a spider's silver thread—flashed as it uncoiled along the
graceful looping curve of its tether, then hissed forward, alighting with barely a ripple on the smooth incandescent surface of
a tear-shaped pool.

"Joe, we're eating. . . ."

He welcomed a plate, a Dixie cup, plastic spoons. He would
have accepted Jim Jonesian strychnine without a murmur, happily slurping up his doom. Various munificent angels supplied
him with ice-cold water, a vegetable pourri, little doughballs
called ladoo, papadums, a heaping spoonful of potato subji, a
yogurt-and-cucumber mix called raita, and some kir.

The plate of goodies Sasha accepted he immediately turned

upside down on his head. Everybody laughed tolerantly and lazily allowed as how he was an adorable monkey.

Tentatively at first, then with great gusto, Joe dug in. It was like decorating his gastric temple, known as the Taj Ma-stomach, with diamonds and rubies and curlicued inlays of ivory! Here, at least, some feeling survived. What a feast! A fleet of eight hummingbirds, their iridescent russet-green backs and ruby throats flashing perkily, zoomed through the fiesta and were gone, buzzing off into the sunny distance. Eloy's screen door banged faintly once more as the old man headed for his truck again, this time carting several large gunnysacks. He placed these in the bed, stood thoughtfully for a moment, and finally disappeared into his adobe shack once more.

Facing north now, Joe let his eyes wander up the Midnight foothills to mountain peaks barely a dozen miles away. Their snow-colored summits were almost spookily pristine against the absolutely pure blue sky.

It was enough to make anybody believe in magic!

Last vestiges of tension fell off him at the nudge of this sight. Joe sighed and wondered: "Oh dear—am I being born again?" Relaxation entered his flesh (the way smoke must enter a ham), curing him. His shoulders sagged, he half closed his eyes, ceased conversing, and shoveled in the subji, papadums, and raita.

Such bliss! With each mouthful, Joe's affection for Nancy multiplied. Fate had decreed her to be his rock in the Angry Sea. He would learn to love. If this was one of her scenes, so be it: no more, never again, would he knock it. An innocent passion at play here he found positively beguiling. A person could do worse than spend the rest of their life noshing these eats and laying around in the spring sunshine, glistening with unguents, while expert fingers manipulated sinews, tendons, and muscles until their body felt like a reincarnation of ethereal redemption. Saint Francis, blissfully chatting with warblers and hedgehogs, had nothing on these cats. While his intellect snoozed, and his high blood pressure dissipated, Joe would entertain dozens of cosmic teenyboppers and kundalini freaks lined up outside his tipi prepared to offer themselves up as human prasad. . . .

He had almost fallen asleep when something hot and wet anointed his right ankle—Sasha, it turned out . . . urinating.

Tch-tch. Nancy framed his face between her palms and further opened his eyes with a kiss. "We can see the Hanuman now."

"Huh? Isn't there gonna be a ceremony?"

"No, somebody opened the trailer while we were eating. Everybody can just go over and have a look at their leisure. They don't believe in confining things by making a self-conscious effort to invest them with importance."

Standing, Joe swayed dizzily. "Careful, now." She braced him. "Are you all right?"

"I'm wonderful," Joe said. "I'm actually groggy with serenity."

Arm in arm, dragging a reluctant jabbering Sasha, they sauntered across the trampled grass, joining a relaxed flow of people heading for the U-Haul. Its side doors had been opened, revealing the four-foot-high statue set against a blue-velvet altar. Joe stopped and gazed. He had never seen anything so disturbingly androgynous. The white marble figure was naked except for a skimpy red sash about its waist. Posed as if in flight, it had muscular legs and a powerful chest. Only the face and ears seemed monkeylike. One hand held a scepter leafed in gold and jewels—rubies? emeralds? Lord how they glittered! The other hand was limp, very effeminate. Atop the head sat a gold crown. And the expression on the peculiarly elongated monkey-face almost defied description.

Accented by painted orange eyelashes, the half-closed rich brown eyes were effete, sensual. The nostrils seemed prissily tensed, as if smelling a heavenly perfume. Exquisitely painted ruby lips pursed as if to plant a precious little kiss on the powdered cheek of a great-aunt. Overall, the effect was of puzzling power and lassitude, mingled with aesthetic snobbism and homosexuality. Joe did not understand this beautiful and vulgar decadence from another culture.

Out of the corner of an eye he saw Eloy emerge from his house yet again, a cowboy hat planted firmly on his head, a pistol in a leather holster on his hip. He climbed stiffly into the truck, started it up, backed around, and headed slowly down the driveway.

Beside Joe a blue-eyed California surfer, her long blond hair twisted into bedraggled Rastafarian dreadnoughts, murmured, "I'm in bliss," swooned, and prostrated herself, quivering enrapturedly.

Sasha strained at his leash, whirling around furiously un-

derneath the U-Haul, kicking apart a pile of prasad. Eloy turned
left out of the driveway onto Upper Ranchitos Road. Nikita
Smatterling approached Joe, puffing on a pipe. Amiably, he
asked, "Well, what do you think?"

"I don't know. Look at Sasha—he's smashing all the fruit."

"Oh, monkeys will be monkeys."

Nancy said, "It's gorgeous."

"When the U-Haul first arrived, before any of us even had
a look, the vibes emanating from it were incredible. We had
a heated debate over whether or not to display it in a public
way, for fear the power would be too strong for those not used
to dealing with it."

Rama Unfug was awed. "It's incredible." He aimed his
camera at Sasha's destructive antics and pulled the trigger.

Several people produced Instamatics. Iréné sidled up to Joe,
saying, "What do you think?"

"Hard to say." His only hit off it was ambiguity. He hadn't
expected anything so grotesque *and* lovely. But ultimately, it
left him cold. After their languorous scarfing time, Joe had
almost hoped the painted marble could thrill him into a better
life. Instead, the neutrality bored him. He lifted his eyes to the
clean mountain snowfields and the ultrasonic sky in which a
single black raven circled, glinting once—suddenly—like a
gunshot every 360 degrees at that point where its wings caught
the sunlight.

And then all of a sudden it came over him—a terribly dark
and menacing cloud, a burgeoning thunderhead, an urgent cry
of lamentation. Dizziness almost forced him to his knees, and
Diana's loaded pistol came alive in his grasp . . . he nearly
swooned from an attack of bellicosity. A sense of outrage (over
the swindle, the complacency around him) such as he had rarely
experienced compelled Joe to close his eyes quickly so nobody
could see the frightening devils aborning underneath his quivering shell. The wound, an enormous rent in the center of his
heart, left him breathless.

Joe opened his eyes. The statue's perverse and ominous
eyes regarded him haughtily. They stroked him with sensual,
more-superior-than-thou disdain. They rebuffed and mocked
and baffled; they were sinister and derisive, fraudulent and
farcical. Cancer was spreading across the land like a plague,
yet hundreds of insidious new chemicals reached the markets
every month. The ozone was about to perish. The earth itself

was becoming leached out, poisoned, useless. Though only six percent of the world's population, Americans consumed thirty-six percent of its resources. Millions of soldiers, laundered greenbacks, corrupt puppets, and CIA assassination squads kept those resources coming. In fact, they assured that Americans would have *eaten the entire earth* by the year 2000! Nuclear wastes, impossible to dispose of, waited to be disposed of. Priorities were technological instead of human. The system ate the soul first, in order to nourish the body—half the budget went for weaponry. Like a sick, vengeful moon, the Ku Klux Klan was rising. . . .

Where was the helicopter?

Nancy said, "Can you believe it?"

"Believe what?" he mumbled dimly from the heart of a tumultuous isolation.

"This. That. The Hanuman."

"Do you like it?" His voice reverberated oddly in his own ears.

"I love it."

"Why?"

She winked gently. "Because it's there."

Egon Braithwhite sneaked up behind them and hiss-whispered into Joe's left ear. "Oro goiboi! Cha chee kow uru bon-angie!"

"You son of a bitch!"

He'd had it. Never again! No more! Joe whirled and, screaming *"Speak English!,"* he uncranked a bolo punch that connected with Egon's temple. The bearded beanpole dropped, poleaxed, and Joe landed on his back, flailing away hysterically, punching, kneeing, even savagely biting Egon's whiskers! God damn if this retarded clown would ridicule him one minute longer! If he had to tear out the maniac's tongue and grind it beneath his heels, Joe could do it! Passionate angry words gurgled in his throat; they emerged nonsensically in sputtering blasts of incoherency! He pummeled the squeaking nudnik, who seemed incapable of fighting back. In fact, Egon curled into a protective tuck, and in very short order Joe found himself belaboring a human armadillo. Heaping insanity atop insanity, Egon pled for his life in his make-believe language. "Ho mangi noguchi! Ow ow ow! Choro me no go chabitsu! Oro gruduyakki! Ay ay ay!" Showing no mercy, Joe tried to bang him into silence. He hadn't been in a fight, in a real down-to-earth, playground-style, hit-'em-with-everything-you-got fracas since childhood days. And for a moment, he exulted. Hot dog, warm puppy, cold frank! Hit 'em with a left, hit 'em with a right, stand up, siddown, *fight fight fight*! A week of frustration catapulted from his body through his flying fists! Joe unleashed a triumphant cry—half bloodthirsty, a quarter Tarzanian, one-eighth triumphant, another eighth apologetic.

For some reason, in the midst of his vengeful fury, he looked up just in time to see something zooming toward his head. His brain even defined the object before it hit—one of those fuzzy toy monkeys, no doubt flung by somebody in a silly effort to end the slaughter. Afterward, Joe recalled very clearly scoffing at such a meek effort to halt his ferocious onslaught. He actually laughed during that split instant before the toy reached his forehead.

Worse yet, he had actually taken his eyes off it in order to guide a cattle-killing blow against the back of Egon's noodle.

The metaphors applying to the nature of the force with which that lightweight stuffed simian struck him were:

1) like a ten-ton truck.
2) like a runaway freight train.
3) like an elephant shot from a cannon.

It knocked him off Egon so hard he bounced head over heels in the dust as if tumbling from a speeding automobile. At the end of these acrobatics, Joe sprang to his feet, arms outstretched, lost his blanace, and careened through a crowd of people, leaning over at a steeper angle with each step until he crash-landed again, plowing a furrow with his nose. And he lay there, wide awake but paralyzed. In his ears police and fire sirens screamed. Bare feet planted themselves only inches from his nose, and heard a pontificating voice—vibrating hollowly as if amplified through an echo chamber: "*It's not nice to fight, Joe.*"

Stunned . . . immobile . . . helpless. Joe grew dizzy and blacked out, even though still wide awake. Many hands touched and gripped his body. Lifting gently, they carried him somewhere. He heard sobs. And singing. Melodic castanets jangled. He smelled incense and cedar smoke. A car engine started. Obviously, they planned to drive him westward, tie lead monkeys around his neck and ankles, and dump him into the Rio Grande. Wanting to struggle, Joe couldn't move. In motion, they bounced over potholed roads. He still heard weeping, but although his eyes were wide open, nothing made sense. No coherent light entered his brain. And he couldn't lift a finger, or wiggle a toe. A direct whack from a lightning bolt would not have rendered him more helpless. Vocal cords had been shocked right out of his throat; his glottis had been whomped.

Eventually, they quit bouncing, tires hummed, the weeping petered out. And all Joe could do was lie there helplessly (or stand there or crouch there—in what posture lay his body?), trapped in the spell of an east Asian monkey god, awaiting his total destruction . . . or deliverance.

Nancy's quiet, melancholic voice broke the spell.

"Well, you really did it this time, Joe."

He did not exactly open his eyes. Rather, he stretched them a little, while also shaping his mouth in a silent howl. With that, the dark magic membrane obstructing his vision burst and sunlight flooded his brain. At the same time he located his voice and muttered awkwardly, "Did what?"

"You blew it. Even in my eyes—and I'm a pretty tolerant person—you blew it."

The VW Bug was parked in Nancy's driveway. She sat in the front seat, Joe huddled in back. The engine had been cut, Bradley had flown the coop. His fur matted with pear, peach, and pomegranate gore, Sasha squatted on the front hood, fiddling with his dick as he peered in at them.

Joe said, "What happened?"

"You went crazy. You tried to kill Egon Braithwhite. You were like a mad dog. I've never seen anybody flip out like that, not even in football games on television."

"Something just snapped."

"I don't know, Joe. I really don't." From her tone he realized he was about to be bagged again, this time by the one person imbued with an aggravatingly saintly patience vis-à-vis his spontaneous transgressions. A new quality in her voice suggested that even her sponsorship was now being withdrawn. Nancy wanted no further part of his act.

Joe said, "I guess, once again, I owe you an apology."

"I don't believe in apologies."

"I was having a good time, you know. I thought it was lovely out there." Sasha grabbed hold of the aerial . . .

"So why suddenly go berserk?"

"He came up behind me and said something in that fake language."

. . . and slowly bent it over double.

"Is that any reason to attempt murder during the key moment of a spiritual festival put on by a lot of considerate and fairly aware and centered people?"

"In case you forgot, a few days ago the organizer of it tried to blow away Ephraim Bonatelli with a loaded pistol. By the way, whatever happened to the helicopters?"

"You mean the accident at the Forest Service helipad? How did you know about that?"

"They had an accident?"

"According to Jeff Orbison. He arrived late just as we left."

"Oh Jesus! What happened to Tribby? And to Ralph?"

"Tribby? I don't know. Was he supposed to be in a helicopter?"

"You don't know? Oh man—but there was an accident?"

"Apparently nobody was hurt." She draped her hands on the steering wheel. "Why talk about that?" Sasha hopped out of sight onto the roof.

"But . . . I mean . . . oh wow." Joe closed his eyes, shattered.

"Really—nobody was hurt. Apparently they both tried to take off at the same time: in a hurry, I suppose. And they forgot to release the tiedown cables."

"Say that again." Joe opened his eyes.

"According to Jeff, they started to lift off, but, because they were anchored, they tipped over into each other. The helicopters were more or less destroyed. But nobody inside suffered much damage."

"You're making all this up."

"That's Jeff's version. You know this town."

Joe giggled hysterically. Who was programming this farce— Heather's hermaphrodite karate god? Did any dignity remain in Chamisaville? He could picture it, all right. Tribby and Ralph and Rimpoche galloping for one bird, while Ephraim Bonatelli and—who else? Nick Danger with his suitcase full of Daring Debbies?—sprinted for the other bubblecopter. No doubt Ralph had fogotten to remove the—what were they called? The flight boxes? So a crazy lawyer in search of passion, and a dwarf in a chartreuse jumpsuit with a naked blonde in silver cowboy boots on the back, fired up their engines, popped their clutches imultaneously, and toppled into each other, rotor blades slamning together with a hellacious *twang*! like a thousand machtes shot from cannons into an armada of garbage cans . . . and hat was it. They all tumbled onto the helipad shouting vile urses at each other, then sprinted for the bushes before the authorities arrived, leaving behind that mangled hardware worth couple million dollars.

Somehow, miracles kept happening to save his bewildered ss. He should have been happier. Instead, the taste of defeat ay bitter on his tongue, and in his heart. If only, just once, omething *definitive* could happen.

Reaching forward, a satanic wish implicit in the move, Joe laced his fingers against her neck. He wanted to humiliate, hame, destroy her. At least he would take one of them down vith him: there had to be a victory *some*where. Nancy hunched ne shoulder, giving a slightly annoyed wrench of her head. Please don't touch me."

"I wasn't making a move. I just meant to be friendly."

"That may be, but I don't want you fondling me anymore."

"You don't understand," Joe said. "That Egon has been lriving me crazy for weeks. I can't make him talk English nymore. I think he actually believes we're communicating. I vouldn't mind so much, except every time I'm in a café, or a novie, or at a party, he starts yelling at me in that made-up ingo. It's embarrassing. I even believe he's insulting me half he time. I'm convinced the words are vulgar epithets. I mean, ow much ridicule am I supposed to take?"

"I hate to be this frank, but you seem impervious to ridicule. All Chamisaville is laughing behind your back."

"Why?"

"Because you've been making a spectacle of yourself."

"Me and Anton van Leeuwenhoek."

"Joe—"

"Nancy, this past week I haven't acted any different from nybody else in town. In fact, far as I can figure out, the second ve tumbled into the hay last Saturday night I started living this normous cliché that, God knows how, I had avoided for years."

"Not very many people around here have the distinction of omenting a brawl during the unveiling of a very sacred and neaningful statue. What you did was tantamount to comnencing a free-for-all in a cathedral."

"Nancy, I didn't intend to sabotage the event. But all of a

sudden it seemed so supercilious. Even criminal. Look what's happening in the *world*! And when that creep snuck up behind me and dropped a nonsense epithet in my ear, something snapped. He epitomizes everything. I lost control."

"It was awful." Joe realized she was crying. Overhead, Sasha blammed "shave and a haircut!" against the tin with his good fist. "I thought I would die. First Sasha, and then this."

"I'll admit we Minivers aren't building a very good reputation among the Hanuman set. Yet believe me, there's nothing deliberate . . ."

"You might not *think* it's deliberate. But subconsciously you really want to destroy everything I believe in."

"That's a lie," Joe lied, attempting conservative vehemence. "I don't want to hurt you, or put you down. Believe it or not, I respect you. Maybe I don't agree with your philosophy, but shoot, we're all different. That's what makes a horse race."

Bam baddle bam bam . . . bam *bam*!

"You don't mean what you're saying. At heart, Joe—and I don't blame you for this, understand, because blame isn't one of the games I play—but at heart you are a very prejudiced person."

"Not prejudiced, just skeptical."

"What makes it so sad is that you're very attractive, too. You put out a charismatic and loving energy . . . that is, when you're not being a total neanderthal. It's rare to meet somebody with your intensity. I'm going to miss you very much."

" 'Miss me'? What is this, the big kiss-off?" Their eyes met in the rearview mirror, hers red-rimmed and bloodshot, his fatigued and cruel-looking. "Only minutes ago, almost, I could do no wrong. You said that you loved me."

"I guess I finally realized that no matter what I did you wouldn't reciprocate. I made a mistake. I read you incorrectly."

Bam baddle bam bam . . . bam *bam*!

"But you knew I was flawed. You knew I was weak. You've already tolerated a slew of nonsensical shenanigans, asthma attacks, infidelity, and humiliating mockery. You can't just pull the rug out from underneath when the going gets tough. I thought one trait metaphysical people cultivated was a profound understanding of human nature."

"That's true. But you pulled a stunt out there worthy of a truly sadistic person. I have never been so shocked or humil iated. It's as if *I* deliberately transported you out there to ruin the ceremony."

"You can't believe that. It was an emotional accident. Nobody's gonna blame you."

"Blame isn't the point—I already said that. It's just that I feel so, so silly for having trusted you. . . ."

"Listen, Nancy, you're a lovely person, a staunch ally. I mean it. I've really enjoyed being with you this past week. Making love has been funky and wonderful. I'm amazed at your ability to uphold your own goodwill against such heavy odds. I don't want us to be enemies."

"Who said anything about enemies?"

Bam baddle bam bam . . . bam *bam*!

"But it sounds as if you're saying good-bye."

"I'm not saying good-bye in the larger sense. But I guess I am in the more intimate sense."

"The intimate sense being . . . ?"

Sasha's face, upside down, appeared in the center of the front windshield.

"I don't want to make love anymore. I don't want us to be connected in other than a, you know, a social acquaintanceship. I give up on trying to incorporate you into my life. I finally realized today that you don't want it, and I certainly can't make you want it. In a sense, I've been very selfish. I wanted so much for you to conform to this image I have of a valid set of priorities for governing one's existence—but my set isn't yours, and vice versa. Thus it's very egotistical and self-seeking of me to pursue the matter."

"You don't think that maybe, with patience, we could grow to understand and value each other?"

"I don't think I have enough patience for the task."

"What about me? I mean, you're not exactly a flawless human being, you know."

"That I'll admit. I'm riddled with flaws."

Sasha's face, upside down, appeared in the middle of the driverside window.

"So we're on similar terrain. Maybe we could really be good for each other."

"Mmm. Like—where else but in the sack?"

"Like today. I mean, the altercation with Egon was unfortunate, but aside from that, I learned something. It was gratifying."

"What did you learn?"

"All those people—well, they didn't seem threatening." Was he really saying this? How come she seemed not to peg his insincerity. "They seemed like okay folks. Some of my harsher prejudices were tempered radically, just from the mood, the brotherly atmosphere."

"I noticed that it really soaked in." Her sarcasm came as a surprise: she hadn't utilized it before.

"No, seriously. I apologize." Those infernal tingles grew stronger. Lust settled into the old gutbucket, bound and determined to give him a final shot at her. Again, Joe placed one hand against her neck; this time she did not flinch. "I wish you could just forget about Egon. What can I do or say to make it up to you?" Cautiously, his fingertips massaged her skin. Sasha's face, upside down, appeared in the middle of the passengerside front window.

"It's no good, Joe. There's too much real and psychic distance between us."

"I don't get it. You spend a whole week tolerating my every transgression in order to break down barriers between us, then all of a sudden the going gets a wee bit tough and you fold like a lily-livered coward. I thought you were strong."

"I'm not really as strong as I may occasionally appear to be. Granted, I've made progress over the years. But I'm still fragile, as anybody could see this afternoon during your karate demonstration. Ohh, that feels nice. Apply pressure a little higher. I've got a headache and that might help."

"Here?"

"Yes . . . that's wonderful. Oh Joe," she said unhappily, "when you touch me I melt."

"If we humans could only keep our mouths shut. . . ."

Sasha's head disappeared. A faint slithering occurred overhead.

"Mmm . . . gosh that's good." She twisted her neck, responding to his massage, and tilted back her head. Joe smoothed the fabulous skin of her throat.

"There . . . It's not all that bad, is it?"

"And how . . ." Then she stiffened a trifle, remembering. "Joe, will you do me a favor?"

"Sure. Of course. Anything you want, my love."

"Well, I really can't ever again go through something like

that scene at the Hanuman this afternoon. So if . . ." She failed to complete the thought.

"So if what?"

"Oh, it doesn't make sense. Forget it."

Joe slipped down his hand, cupping one breast. "Try me. 'So if' what?"

"Well, if, you know. If we were to try and be together some more, I just think, I just feel . . ."

"Go on," he prompted, ready to butcher, thoroughly aroused, and confident she was also.

"I mean, I really couldn't take another scene like that, Joe. I know I'm pretty strong, but you've caused me a lot of anguish in the past few days, and I'm honestly freaked out. It's as if, for some utterly preposterous reason, I've chosen to further my spiritual growth by hooking up with a Fascist."

"A Fascist? *Me*?"

She pouted. "Well, I'm not accustomed to being as manipulated in a relationship as I have been with you. I don't seem to have much of a say at all in how we are together, when we can be together, what we can share together."

"Uh, not to contradict, but fascism isn't exactly my bag."

"No . . . ?"

Nobody had ever called him a Fascist before. Or had they? The epithet hurt; it triggered a faint queasiness. Probably he deserved it. Then he accepted it. Of course he was a Fascist. And this thing he was about to do to her would be tantamount to rape.

"I'm sorry," he whispered contritely. "I guess I have been a shitheel. But you don't understand how truly I . . . I love you."

"Oh gee, Joe . . . do you really mean it?"

As Joe caressed her breasts, Sasha slid down the front windshield, then backed up against it, pressed his obscene little buttocks against the glass, and began to take a smeary shit. Joe watched, fascinated, while continuing to fondle Nancy. She unleashed a flutter of sweet, hiccoughing moans. When next she spoke, however, she seemed clearheaded and in control. "Let's suppose, just for the sake of argument, that we keep up our relationship."

"I hope we do," the weasel whispered insipidly into her ear. "I want us to love each other forever."

Wiggling his buttocks in a rotary fashion, Sasha smeared

all across the windshield the brown pancake that had emerged from his wiry body.

Nancy squirmed. "Well, before we make love again, I think you need to reach some very important decisions about how you feel about me."

Both his fraudulent hands were at work now. While his counterfeit lips nuzzled her neck, he tugged up her skirt, spreading her white thighs. He rubbed light circles around the silky crotch of her pink briefs. Hands raised over her head, Nancy caressed his ears. Joe murmured, "All right," and lifted his hands, crushing her breasts. "What sort of decisions did you have in mind?"

Nancy groaned and arched. Her eyes had shut. Joe probed her mouth with a couple of fingers. She sucked hungrily, then gasped. "Well, first of all you should decide who's more valuable to you—me, or your wife and family. As long as you're intimate with Heidi, I doubt it would work with us."

Slurring deliberately (huskily), the mealymouthed Janus said, "Come into the back seat. I have to make love with you. . . ."

Nancy swung one leg over the passengerside seatback. Joe scooped an arm under and around her waist, hoisting her into the back. Sasha turned around and began to fingerpaint in his windshield excrement. Their lips locked in a passionate kiss. The rest of their limbs were tangled in cramped quarters. Her knee landed painfully in his groin. Joe said, "Ouch, wait a sec. Can you shift over that way a little? This is awkward."

Her hot breath almost fogging his eyes, Nancy said, "I've always been a one-man woman, and I really believe that's the only way a relationship can work out. This past week, whenever you've been with Heidi, or Diana, or even whatshername— the Romanian fan dancer—I can always tell, because your relationship with them gets in the way of our time together. I can feel you reacting to me as if I were one of them, but I'm not. And so naturally I resent it."

Joe lurched—painfully—working to unzip his fly. Grunting, he tried to muscle her around so that they were not pinned tightly against each other. He strained, pushing and pulling. She said, "Wait a minute, my leg is wedged down there. Can you move a little that way?—there, that's better."

A cramp hit his twisted calf. "Ow! Nancy! Raise your ass a second, would you? My foot is pinned . . . listen, can you shift over to my other side . . . maybe if I could somehow work on top of you . . ."

"Okay. But there isn't much space in here . . . is that better?"

"It's not too bad." Passionately, their lips remet. Sasha was creating a Kandinskiesque work of art on the windshield. Though his arm was painfully bent at the elbow, Joe twisted a hand between her legs, applying a few more erotic softeners. Nancy pressed against him sideways, one leg caught pincerlike in a space between the two front seats. Her other leg was caught under his right leg: her thigh levered painfully up between his legs, squashing one testicle. Diana's gun jabbed into his groin. Joe shifted to ease the pain; she cried, "Ouch! Your elbow is killing me!"

"I'm sorry, but I can't move it. I'm trapped. Can you swivel your left arm over there? That'd give me room, maybe, to slip around on top of you."

"I can't. You've got my left leg pinned."

"Okay, wait a minute, we can figure this out." Joe kissed her, tasting salt: both of them were sweating profusely. He probed inside her with two fingers until she wriggled. Then he broke another lascivious kiss to suggest a variation on their contortions.

"Listen, do the front seats move at all? Let's tip them forward."

"Only the driver's side—but I can't reach the release lever."

"Maybe if I tug you around on top of me. That'd free my left arm and I could reach up there and grab it."

"Like this?"

"Yeah, uh-huh, easy does it . . . fine . . . no! Ow!"

"Oh God, what?"

"You're killing my knee! Back off! No, not that way, the other way! *The other way, dammit!* There! Oh Jesus, you almost killed me."

"Can you lift your rump?" she pleaded politely. "It's squashing my other hand."

"I can't. I got no leverage. You're crushing my chest . . . I can't breathe."

"There's no room to move around back here," she complained. "How did we ever get into such a fix?"

Another typical symbol of my life, Joe thought. No doubt, God had decided to end his adventure trapped in the back of a VW Beetle, inadvertently locked in a double-pretzel even the most agile contortionists would admire. Somehow, attempting to perpetrate a final sexual swindle in the confined space, Joe had managed to tie himself up, in a foolproof knot, with the object of his lust. These headlines would top them all:

CHAMISAVILLE GARBAGE MAN AND METAPHYSICIAN EXPIRE IN
BACK OF BEETLE! HUMAN PRETZEL PROVES FATAL TO
GUINNESS RECORD ASPIREES. SUICIDE IN A BUG: SENSUALISTS
MEET TWISTED FATE.

Pilgrims would travel thousands of miles to laugh on his grave. Mortified, his children would seek anonymity by exiling themselves to Lithuania. Their coffin—for of course he and Nancy would have to be buried together—would resemble a large cube with sputniklike extensions poking out all over to accommodate their haphazardly jutting limbs. Once rigor mortis set in, would the authorities even be able to dislodge them from the car? Or would they wind up painting the Beetle black, taping a rose and silver dollar to the front hood, and lowering the car into a large hole by means of an enormous construction crane?

Joe groaned, "I'm wedged in tight, I can't reach the knob."

"Well, you have to move, otherwise I can't free my leg and change positions."

"But if you don't move first, Heidi, I can't get any leverage to change positions."

"My name isn't Heidi."

"I mean Nancy." Sasha chattered excitedly: fevered and animated, he continued to expand his excremental masterpiece.

"What I was talking to you about," Nancy said resolutely, "is I think anybody else that you're having a simultaneous relationship with intrudes on all other relationships you have. Your energy becomes so dispersed, you really can't give any one person you're involved with the attention an honest relationship needs. So if we continue being together, you really have to at least stop screwing the other women you've been screwing."

"Nancy, we're stuck, we can't move."

"I know."

"I'm uncomfortable as hell. I can't breathe. I hate confined spaces. I feel dizzy. I think I'm gonna faint. Can't you shift a little?"

"Only like this . . ."

"No . . . *no!* Christ, you'll break my knee!"

"Then I don't know what to do."

"How the hell did this happen?"

"You wanted to make love."

"You did too."

"Yes, I did too. We both did."

"I want out," Joe hissed threateningly. "I'm beginning to get hysterical."

"Maybe if I bend myself backwards this way . . ."

"Ow . . . *stop!* That's my groin! Those are my family jewels!"

Peering up underneath her left armpit, Joe could see a patch of the rear window . . . against which Bradley pressed his nose and lips, staring in at them.

Joe said, "Don't look now, but your kid's getting a real eyeful."

"Bradley?" She tried to turn her head. "Bradley, darling, open the door, please, and trip the little lever that knocks forward the front seat, okay?"

The kid didn't want to make an unduly hasty move, however. Not before assessing the potential bribe, kickback, or payola that might come his way. "What are you guys doing, Mom?"

"We were hugging and somehow got tangled up back here and we're stuck."

"Sasha's playing in his own caca on the front windshield."

"I know, darling. Now help us like I asked you, please."

Bradley disappeared from the window. Seconds later Joe heard the driverside door open. The kid said, "I don't know which is the lever, Mom. Is this one it?"

"I can't see, darling, but you're probably right. Just give it a twist."

Bradley punched in a button on the emergency-brake handle and lowered it. Parked on a slight incline, the car immediately began to roll backward.

Too late, Joe hollered, *"No, that's the emergency brake!"* Terrified, Bradley bailed out. Slowly, the car glided down the driveway and out into the middle of the subdivision's main street, where it stopped dead, blocking the road. Sasha banged his cast angrily on the roof, then returned to his chef d'oeuvre.

Joe said, "I don't believe it!"

A car purred down the street, braked, and the driver honked.

Joe whispered, "As soon as we get out of this I'm going to catch the first flight from the capital for Ulan Bator."

Nancy said, "There's a reason for everything. This isn't just happening in a void."

"Thanks. I feel a lot better."

The horn-honking grew louder, more insistent. "What the hell is the matter with him?" Joe snarled. "People are insane. Can't he see something's wrong?"

Eventually, the honking stopped, a door opened, feet landed on the ground, footsteps approached their vehicle. Joe held his breath, closed his eyes, and concentrated on remembering these last few seconds of sweet life on earth. For no doubt the notoriety arising from the discovery of himself and Nancy Ryan in this buffoonish predicament would immediately commence hounding him—like screaming beasts and cawing jackdaws— into an early grave.

"Well, well," said a disdainful, slightly limp-wristed voice, "look what we have here. Peck's Bad Boy in an uncompromising position."

Even without twisting his head, Joe realized he was farther up a creek minus the proverbial paddle than he had thought possible. "I don't believe it," he muttered fatalistically. "You again."

"Oh, I'm a persistent fellow." The angel's chuckle withered Joe. "Occasionally, I may lose a few feathers, but in general I always get my man. You certainly did frighten me, last time out, with that noisy little gun. I've always hated firearms."

"He has a gun in his pocket," Nancy said. "You better watch out."

"Not to worry, my dear. Thanks to your marvelous preparation, I doubt he can contort enough to use it. This time I believe we've got him, how would you say it, properly 'swinetied'?"

"Hog-tied."

"'We'?" Joe muttered. What other gruesome twists and turns could occur in the ordinary, everyday life of an all-American boy?

Nancy said, "Yes—'we.'"

"You two are in cahoots?"

"Cahoots," said the angel. "What a colorful word."

"Then it's true?" Joe asked Nancy. "They really did hire you to wreck my marriage and throw that land into limbo?"

The angel explained, "She wasn't exactly hired, Joe. Let's just say that all of us are always open for assignments on whatever happens to be expedient."

"I don't believe it." More rueful and bemused than angry, he said, "Nancy, how could you be so unethical?"

"I never cheated, Joe. I merely made it possible for you to do what you wanted to do. You constructed all the traps and tumbled into them yourself."

"But I thought you loved me. I thought—"

Abruptly, he clammed up, ashamed of his outrage. After all, she had him dead to rights. His weaknesses, and not her wiles, had preordained his doom.

Time to be contrite. Though he would have welcomed a smithereen job at the hands of Ray Verboten and his teddy boys, Joe gagged at the image of a blissful annihilation engineered by this feathered creep and his psychic concubine.

"All right, you guys win. Now, help us out of this pretzel."

"Not so fast, Joe." The angel leered munificently. "We've decided to take you on a little trip." Obviously enjoying his adversary's helpless position, he flicked open the door, and, after carefully arranging his wing-feathers, slid behind the wheel. Enthralled by his cacophonous windshield painting, Sasha was still up there, proving that "even a monkey could paint like that."

"What kind of trip? Where are you taking me?"

"It's all right," Nancy said. "Nothing bad can happen."

"You're such a roughneck, Joe. We want to refine you a little."

"Thanks but no thanks. I'm perfect just the way I am. Come on, Nancy, twist your leg over to the left. Hey, you in the front seat! Lean forward or get out, screw your help, I'll untangle myself."

"My name is Lorin, by the way. Any danger he can untangle himself?" the angel asked Nancy, poking blindly about on the dash like one thoroughly unaccustomed to driving a car. "How do I start this thing?"

"There's a key stuck into the dash beside the steering wheel."

To Nancy, Joe said, "You mean all along you *meant* to entice me into this pickle?"

"You might say that."

"What are you, some kind of Mata Hari?"

"She's one of our best agents," Lorin said. "Aha, here they are. Now what do I do?"

"Twist them—I think it's to the left. Don't give it gas until the engine's ready to catch."

"What does that mean, 'to give it gas'?"

"Place the gearshift in neutral—it's that stick in the floor by your right hand."

"What's 'neutral'?"

Joe said, "Is this guy for real? Didn't you arrive in a car?"

"No gratuitous denigration, Miniver. I arrived in an auto in which I believe the expression is I had 'hitched' a ride. My wings were tired."

"There's five gears," Nancy explained. "Four forward and one reverse. In between all of them is a resting place called neutral, because it isn't any gear at all. If you play around a little you can feel it."

Joe bleated, *"Nancy, stop him, he's gonna kill us!"*

"Maybe I should drive," she suggested.

"No sir, lady!" Lorin's turn to panic. "Don't let him free, or he'll murder us both."

"Well, the gas pedal is that rubber-coated tin lever underneath your right foot. The brake is between that pedal and the pedal on your left, which is the clutch."

"'Brakes'? 'Clutch'?"

"Stop him!" Joe struggled to dislodge an arm, a leg, an anything. "If he starts the engine and finds a gear, we're goners!"

"I need only about three hundred feet, I think," Lorin said.

"What's that supposed to mean, 'three hundred feet'? Come on, Nancy, we've got to try. He's a guaranteed slaughter."

"My job, Joe, is to keep you hors de combat. I'm sorry."

"Three hundred feet is all I need to raise us off the ground," Lorin explained. "Good God, what's happening to the windscreen?"

"My monkey defecated," Nancy explained. "Now he thinks he's Picasso."

"'Off the ground'?" Joe wailed.

"Sure. It takes a certain speed to create an aerodynamically favorable situation for flight. But believe me, once we're in the air, I can handle everything."

"Did you hear that, Nancy? He's gonna *fly* this Bug. The bum is nuts!"

"He's not a bum, Joe. He's a celestial guide."

Lorin twisted the ignition keys. The engine turned over and the car gallumphed humpingly forward, bone-jarring them all.

"Stop!" Nancy cried. "You don't have the shifting stick in neutral."

Joe moaned, "I wanna go home...."

"It won't move," Lorin complained.

"Is the clutch depressed?"

"Which one is the clutch?"

"The pedal underneath your left foot. When it's pushed to the floor, you can move the gearshift lever into neutral."

Lorin stepped on the clutch and commenced wiggling the stick. "Is this neutral?"

"I can't see." Nancy tried twisting her head, but failed. "You'll have to judge from the feel. Generally, when there's some play in the stick, then it's in neutral. Try starting up again, and we'll see."

He tried, but the car jounced forward. Sasha banged his cast again and chattered angrily: full of hatred, his bloodshot eyes peered through a clearing in the windshield muck.

Joe barked sharply, "Forget about neutral. Just depress the clutch pedal, that'll disengage the gears! Nancy, this apparition is a maniac!"

"Hush, Joe, you'll only confuse him."

"More than already?"

Lorin properly stomped the clutch pedal, again turned the keys, and, with only minor grating, the engine caught. When he popped the clutch, however, they lunged forward and stalled. The emergency brake and seatbelt buzzer blared. Sasha stomped his little feet and tore off his pink eyepatch and threw it away.

"Oh shucks," Lorin groused. "I'm an abysmal learner." Flustered, he banged at the dashboard, trying to quell the warning buzzers. Instead, he whacked a button activating the windshield wipers. A rubber blade swept across Sasha's tail. Startled, the monkey did an inadvertent flip, trying to escape. A loop in his tail caught around his own neck and one leg bent upward unnaturally to head-height. Knocked awry, twisting as he fell, Sasha landed helplessly against the hood, snagged in a hangman's noose composed of his own tail, the top of which was knotted around the powerful wiper.

"Oh my gosh!" Lorin exclaimed. "Look at the monkey!"

Jerked back and forth with each wiper pass, and hopelessly off-balance thanks to the bizarre nature of his trussed condition, Sasha screeched.

Nancy had her back to the situation. She cried, "What's the matter?"

Sasha's next holler was cut short as the noose yanked tighter. "I can't stop it!" Lorin sobbed. *"Which lever do I push?"*

Tumbled to the right, then leftward, Sasha's eyes bulged horribly until a final yank mercifully snapped his fragile neck.

Joe had opened his mouth to say "hallelujah!" when a bomb exploded. That is, they were engulfed by a shocking metallic thunderclap that crumpled their little car the way a hairy fist collapses an aluminum beer can after its contents have been swigged in a single gulp. The windshield and other glass panes shattered outward in a trillion glittering bits as the Bug's exoskeleton buckled. They were airborne for a period of time Joe found difficult to judge because his limbs were being torn asunder by a gigantic invisible madman. Yet the savage whirlwind probably lasted hardly longer than a second. The Bug landed; Joe's teeth clacked, and tiny chips of ivory spewed from between his lips.

He was free! Tossed over the seats, Nancy lay in a painful heap on the front floor, dress wrenched up under her armpits, pink panties glossy as Salvation. Feathers clogged the air; Joe inhaled a bunch and sneezed. As usual, under duress, Lorin had evaporated. His remnant foliage swirled within the VW's interior. Batting feathers away, Joe could only surmise, bewilderedly, that they had either run over a land mine, or been nailed broadside by the Wrath of the Monkey God.

A figure materialized outside the Beetle. And a familiar, Spanish-accented voice asked, "Is anybody alive in there?"

"Eloy?"

"Is that you, Joe?"

"It's me, all right. What happened?"

"A miracle!" cried the old man, whose face Joe could not as yet make out—feathery turbulence created a wall between them. "An enormous bird jumped from your car and flapped off into the sky."

"But what happened?" Joe insisted. "Why are you here?"

"I wanted to rob the bank," Eloy said sheepishly. "I hated to do it alone, but I couldn't find you anywhere. I heard a rumor that you had kidnapped your children and gone to Alaska. Another rumor says your wife flushed all that cocaine down the toilet. So I knew you wouldn't have the money. And I figured I wouldn't be a man if I did not at least try."

"Did you get any money?"

"I was afraid. I parked outside for half an hour, staring at the First State People's Jug. Finally, I knew I couldn't do it alone. Then I decided to drive around town and pray that I might bump into you."

"Are you hurt?" Joe waved his arms frantically, warding off feathers that threatened to enter his mouth in droves each time he spoke.

"Not at all. Are you okay?"

"I think so. What the hell happened?"

"I hit you. I was preoccupied."

"With your truck?"

"Yup."

"Did you hear that, Nancy? Nancy . . . !"

"I'm here," she said calmly. "I'm all right."

"You sure you're not hurt."

"Joe," she said with soft chagrin, "am I *ever* hurt?"

"You double-crossed me," he said meekly. "How could you do such a thing? I trusted you. . . ."

Abruptly, she was sullen. "Don't feed me that garbage. You happen to be about as shallow, Joe Miniver, as any male I've had occasion to come across."

"I need you to help me rob the bank," Eloy rasped. "If you're all right, can we do it now, before they close?"

"I don't know . . . I'm a little groggy. . . ." Leaning over the driver's seat, Joe banged open the bent door, kneed the seat forward, and pulled himself into the cloudless munificent day.

"We must hurry." Eloy had disguised himself with one of those grotesque rubber gorilla masks. The front of his old pickup was totaled, the hood had erupted upward as it bent in two, almost blocking the windshield view. The left front tire, a mess of shredded rubber, had apparently burst upon impact. How fast had the son of a bitch been going?

Joe said, "I can't rob a bank looking like this."

"I brought another mask and a T-shirt."

"If we fail, we're goners," Joe said, abruptly realizing that—yes—Eloy was serious.

"Granted. But when I saw all those monkey people in my front field, I knew I had to try. I'm an old man, and sometimes my brain doesn't function so good. But I know right from wrong."

Nancy crawled clear of the Bug and wavered for a moment, brushing feathers off her shoulders, shaking them from her hair. Then, with a soft whimper, she reached for Sasha's limp body on the hood of the VW.

"Will you drive?" Eloy asked. "I'm tired. And I have the shakes."

"But . . . we're not prepared. We haven't cased the joint, or made any plans. . . ."

"It's our last chance," Eloy reasoned quietly. "If we don't have the money by Monday, everyone else gets to fight over my land."

Joe gripped his throbbing head. "What can I drive—that truck?"

"It's all I can offer."

"Well . . . shoot." Dazedly, Joe stared at the old pickup. His mind seemed unwilling to function. Eloy added up to the one beautiful person he knew. And Joe wished to help save his soul. But this surreal day had left him stymied. He seemed aimed on a collision course with disaster; no rational alternatives existed. Outlaw blood made his body tingle. Yet neither anarchy nor carelessly squandering humanity's most precious resource—life itself—turned him on. Never had he sympathized with the cavalier bravado martyrdom of handsome, bitter fools. If he died robbing a bank for obscure reasons, he died in a vacuum—apolitical, useless. Only Eloy would understand. Yet, as his head cleared, the urge grew inside. For too long mountainous frustrations had clobbered his aching psyche. Down with his bleeding heart and bourgeois antics!—he could use a hint of revolutionary action. If an old man and his prep-school sidekick managed to relieve the First State People's Jug of enough bread to salvage Eloy's land, the symbolism of that tiny farm in Chamisaville—the values underlying its vitality—would far outweigh and outlast the fragile body of its caretakers. *Should I agree to rob the bank,* Joe thought finally, *I'll be acting without equivocation, courageous at last.*

"All right," he said quietly. "Get in."

Eloy stumbled entering the passenger door and Joe caught him. It was like handling a body stuffed with silk handkerchiefs. Joe said, "Can you breathe okay? You should take off that mask."

"I got bursitis, I can't reach up with my right hand—could you help me?"

Gently, Joe tugged the rubber monstrosity off Eloy's red, dripping-wet face. The old man's eyes were pallid and drained, betraying fear, fatigue, desperation. In this absurd game, a real human being was hurt...maybe critically.

"Eloy," he said gingerly. "Are you all right?"

"I am resolved." He laid back his head, closed his eyes. "Take me where I want to go." Eloy gritted his teeth. "Otherwise, I'll know you're a sinvergüenza like all the rest of them." Then he murmured apologetically: "It breaks my heart even to *think* like a criminal."

"You know we could die."

Eloy opened one sad eye: "Who said I was afraid to die?"

Circling the badly wounded vehicle, Joe complained, "This truck ain't gonna work."

"It's been running since 1945."

Joe climbed in and fired it up. Sparks sailed skyward on either side of the jackknifed hood, but the engine caught and idled. So Joe killed it, hopped out, fetched the spare, a lug wrench, and a bumper jack from the rear bed, and changed tires.

Cradling Sasha in her arms, a bewildered Nancy said, "You two are really going to do it? They'll kill you."

Bitterly, Joe replied, "Why don't you wrap us in a pink cloud? Or protect us with a Sanskrit chant?"

"Joseph, you'll never understand." Turning, she walked away, entered her house, and slammed the door.

ॐ

Joe heaved tools and the shredded tire into the rear bed, fired up the truck again, and they headed for town. Stoically composed, hands folded in his lap, the old man jounced stiffly. Joe slowed to make the ride more comfortable, but worn-out springs sabotaged this consideration.

Quietly, they inched through Chamisaville. Joggers decorated in ebullient costumes waved cheerfully—Joe ignored them.

Bright shiny cars waited patiently in traffic jams, but Joe sought out a half-dozen winding side roads in order to avoid them. Eloy said, "Long ago, I realized it wouldn't work out. My time is over. I'm a fool to want more than my share. Now, for a while, it's the devil's turn. But for some reason, I can't go down without a fight. . . ."

The bank loomed. Joe felt silly, as if he were piloting Eloy's ridiculous truck through a melodramatic gangster film, a forties western, a TV soap opera. Any moment now a British-accented fink in silk ascot and Abercrombie tweed would holler "Cut!" and bawl them out for being so stilted in their roles. Yet nothing happened: no deus ex machina dropped out of the sky or bolted around the cardboard false front of the bank to halt these potentially deadly proceedings.

Joe pulled into the parking lot and killed the engine. Cars shimmered silently in the glorious spring sunshine; on the First State portal, a kid, waiting for her mom, no doubt, unwrapped a stick of gum, letting the paper flutter away as she bent the Juicy Fruit into her mouth.

"Well, here we are." Joe's voice sounded the way an Italian sausage might look, squeezed through the latex rollers of an old-fashioned wringer washing-machine.

Eloy fumbled at his holster, removed a long-barreled six-shot Colt, and handed it over. Joe accepted the gun, but couldn't believe it wasn't a toy. "How do you fire it?" he asked.

Eloy arranged Joe's hand correctly. "Don't put your finger on the trigger yet. You cock it by pulling the hammer all the way back, like this." He clicked it into lock position. "Then you simply touch the trigger." Carefully, keeping his thumb on the hammer, Eloy depressed the trigger, and slowly lowered the hammer back down.

"Or, since it's a double-action gun, you can just pull the trigger. But that's not a very accurate way of firing."

Joe said, "I don't know if I could actually shoot at somebody."

"I doubt that I could either."

"That makes us crazy."

Several pigeons fluttered clear of the azure sky, alighting along a false fire wall on the eastern parapet of the First State roof. Butterflies rampaged in Joe's stomach; he had a strong urge to defecate. The tips of his fingers tingled, growing numb; a faint ringing entered his ears. He anticipated a holocaust, and

the overall effect inside it was one of lightheadedness, along
with a curiously sensual laziness that he'd never before experienced, some metabolic alloy of real fear mixed with the
timid exaltation raised by action—irrevocable and dangerous—at last. As if zapped by cold water, his scrotum had
contracted into a tightly wrinkled pouch. His anus throbbed,
but not painfully—the effect was almost pleasurable. Goosebumps rippled across his shoulders, they dived down along his
spine.

"Are you scared?" Joe asked the old man.

Eloy was reaching into the wrinkled Safeway shopping bag
at his feet. He hesitated. "I don't know if what I feel is fear.
I'm an old man, I have lived a full life. If I die, nobody's
taking that much away from me. It's just that if I live, I want
to live on my own terms, as always."

From the sack he removed another rubber gorilla mask for
Joe.

"I think I'm afraid," Joe said. "I also have an urge to giggle.
Now that we're actually gonna do it, you know something
weird? It doesn't even seem criminal. It just feels like a natural
thing to do."

Eloy nodded and swung his rifle barrel sideways so that the
muzzle touched Joe's knee. He worked the lever, chambering
a cartridge. Joe had absolutely no fear of the pistol in his lap
or of the weapon in Eloy's hands. Miraculously, in just minutes,
the guns had become a natural extension of his emotional state,
the logical tools of his upcoming trade.

Dizziness, then sudden euphoria . . . Joe welcomed a powerful sense of well-being in which he believed incontrovertibly
that nothing could go wrong. Such an unexpected sensation
floored him. All at once shot through with immunity, his muscles, heart, blood vessels, and shining skin had been washed
in immortality. Though the brain knew he was on the brink of
treacherous steps, his emotions decreed them both home free.

And the danger, as he slowly tugged on his gorilla mask,
became luxurious.

Joe's mind cleared, he knew exactly what to do. "I was in
here last week. . . ." Or was it yesterday or Monday, or a month
ago? "And I sort of cased the joint a little. We'll have to keep
our eyes on a lot of people."

His memory conjured a photographic copy of the room they
were about to accost. The clarity of detail stunned Joe. The

exact location of every person, every desk, every table, every seeing-eye camera, even every wastebasket focused clearly. Features of tellers and loan officers leaped to the familiar fore-front, almost as if they belonged to dear friends instead of strangers. Five tellers held down the south side. If the vault was open, watch out for that lady who had gone inside. Don't forget the folks working the drive-in window beyond the south-ern alcove. Too, somebody might climb the west-end stairs. And, of course, one of them would have to cover the seven desks and various officers on the north side. Beyond that? The seeing-eye cameras, naturally. Shoot them out at the start of the robbery? . . . or were they bullet-proof?

Mox nix. Eloy said, "Well, are you ready?"

"Almost. I'm just thinking about some things. We'll have to disarm Tom Yard at the start."

"Who's Tom Yard?"

"The bank dick. The guard with the gun and the uniform inside. As soon as we enter we'll have to spot him, rush to his side, order him to freeze. You point the rifle at him while I grab his pistol. Then you swing north and intimidate anybody at a desk on this side of the bank. I'll ask a teller for money. We'll empty all five cash drawers on the south side. Then, if the vault's open, I'll order somebody in there while you keep the others covered. A customer enters the bank during the robbery?—order them to freeze immediately. Somebody makes a dumb move, fire a warning shot in their general vicinity. Did you bring bags?"

"In the bed of the truck. Gunnysacks."

"Good." Joe's heart raced: the exhilaration spreading through his body seemed almost sexual. He wanted to shout, laugh, perform arrogant pirouettes. For the first time in too long, he felt proud, domineering, invincible. This fierce and daring move would give him stature at last, a revolutionary act in the name of Eloy Irribarren—his spirit, his pastures.

Joe spoke calmly: "Can you think of anything we've over-looked?"

Frowning, Eloy ran a thumb along his rifle barrel. "I don't know. Who can say? I hadn't thought it out like you. I just want to grab the bull by the horns."

"Afterwards, we'll probably have to ditch the truck," Joe said carefully. *In control.* My God, was he ever In Control! Not even Kryptonite could hurt them. "If anybody asks, you

empty: *he'd left the fucking revolver on the seat of Eloy's truck*! Then his left leg kicked backward from underneath him, and, as he dropped, another explosion sounded.

With that, Joe woke up, terrified, scrambling for his life . . . on his knees . . . toward Eloy. The floor at his fingertips exploded into fragments that stung his arm and belly but didn't stop him. He grabbed Eloy's rifle, swung it around wildly, and fired a shot; Tom Yard dove over a partition for cover. Dropping the .30-.30, Joe grabbed Eloy, and, with superhuman strength, yanked him erect. In the same desperate fluid motion, he whirled, staggering for the door. Two more loud reports deafened them: another slug, hitting Eloy, knocked them both over: they crunched into the glass door. On his knees, Joe banged open the exit with his head, strugging frantically upright, and plummeted outside, Eloy more or less in his arms.

They were drenched in hot, gooey blood.

The gum-chewing kid saluted them again: "Hiyah, monkeys—what's funky?"

Blindly, getting there by sheer instincts alone, Joe lugged Eloy to the passenger side of his pickup. Enraged, he yanked open the door, almost tearing it off its hinges, and thrust Eloy inside. He slammed the door—it wouldn't close, bouncing off Eloy's ankle: Joe kicked the offending foot away, and banged the door shut for good, then leaped around the hood, achieved the driver's seat, fired up the vehicle, and took off, his open door ricocheting off a shiny Chrysler and bouncing shut as they leaped into their getaway. Tom Yard crouched in the First State doorway, gun held in both hands, arms extended straight in front of him, aiming. Joe saw no smoke, heard no blast, yet the entire windshield shattered. Then they escaped, rocketing into a freedom of squealing rubber, shattering tin and expectations, groans, terror, and vehicular mayhem.

If startled pedestrians didn't give ground he would kill them . . . so they stepped aside. They leaped into ditches, flattened against buildings, crashed through fences, and smacked into each other; they dived, packages flew from their arms . . . a dog yelped . . . curses trailed their flight. Farther down the road, a crew of orange hardhats scattered, a backhoe driver bailed out in terror, and only at the last moment did Joe swerve enough to avoid plunging into a sewer pit. At that, the right rear tire caught on the edge of the hole, swinging them sideways: a terrific thump ensued, their rear end dropped, then they bounced so high Joe's head bashed the crippled ceiling of Eloy's pickup, almost knocking him out.

Yet it also brought him to his senses—the blow. Joe braked, skidded onto a shoulder, stopped, and yanked off his mask. Then he pushed Eloy upright, and tenderly, removed the old man's gorilla disguise. Eloy gulped for air. His cheeks were soaked and crimson.

"We're not far from the hospital," Joe said.

"Take me *home*, boy. I have to clear up some things."

"You might not live if you do. . . ."

"I'll live long enough to complete my chores."

Astonishingly, they ran the rest of the maze unhindered: no construction snafus, fallen trees, steaming pits, or unsavory detours shackled their travel intentions. Perhaps Eloy's defiant will to arrive home—a power as strong as Nancy Ryan's amazing ability to blithely negotiate the Chamisaville snarl—led them there. In any case, the battered truck floated across town as if guided by an infallible laser homing-beam, and within minutes they had reached Eloy's driveway.

❦

Most Hanuman-niks had dispersed; grass was trampled flat, churned into dust. A few worshipers remained, sitting cross-legged near the open U-Haul, gazing at the monkey idol, meditating. A half-dozen others meandered dazedly among the temporary poplars and cook cauldrons, dreamily cleaning up paper plates and cups and plastic spoons.

Eloy said, "I wish I hadn't rented them the land for their stupid fiesta."

"Where's Geronimo?"

"I tethered him up by the house."

"Where's the geese? And all the little dogs? What about the chickens and turkeys?"

"All gone." Eloy coughed. "Maybe I knew this place was lost when I heard about your cocaine." Blood glistened on his lips. "So I drove them into the hills yesterday evening. They're on their own. Perhaps a stray coyote will get a good meal."

The engine died. "Oh shit," Joe murmured, "we blew it." A great rage wrestled with mind-boggling bewilderment inside him: he had no idea what to do or suggest, and despised his helplessness. Impotent—a sorrowful excuse for a human being—he awaited orders on how best to die.

"Now you can do me a big favor," Eloy said, as they both descended from the truck.

"I'll try. Whatever you say."

"Geronimo has to die. Also Duke, and Wolfie. But I can't kill them myself. I tried. I couldn't pull the trigger."

Joe was horrified. "You can't shoot them!"

"Where will they live? If I don't kill them, an impersonal executioner will do the job once I'm gone. Please, let's do it quickly. Then we'll clean the acequia and irrigate the back field. It's the only way I know to say good-bye."

Grasping at straws, Joe said, "But we lost our guns at the bank."

"You still have a pistol in your pocket."

Diana's gun! How *could* he have forgotten? His hand, disembodied from his heart, emerged from a front pocket clutching that little .22. He turned the gun over—it resembled a toy. Middle-class city child that he was, Joe had never killed an animal.

Eloy circled the truck, limping, and leaned on one fender. A dark stain drenched half his shirt; a soaked pantleg was plastered against one scrawny thigh.

"Do it quickly, please—shoot him."

"How do you kill a horse?"

"Poke the barrel between his eyes."

Joe raised his arm, bringing the barrel to within an inch of the fuzzy white patch between Geronimo's eyes. Unspooked, nostrils fluttering faintly, the horse gave a soft compassionate whinny, and did not move his head. Instead, he lifted his tail.

"Stop a minute," Eloy cautioned. "Let him shit."

Joe waited while enormous, light-yellow gobs of steaming dung fell heavily onto the dull earth. When the horse had finished, Eloy issued a command: "Thumb back the hammer."

Joe did.

"Now pull the trigger."

Out in the open like this, the report was no louder than a cap pistol. Geronimo's legs seemed to buckle even before the slug cleared the barrel; instantly dead, he dropped heavily. Not a single bloody droplet oozed out of the tiny hole. Joe shivered, unable to comprehend that he could render inert such an enor-

mous bulk of muscle, bone, and blood with that minuscule
piece of lead.

"Now the dog."

Duke knew it was coming. Yet he had not flinched when
the gun discharged, killing Geronimo. Instead, he lay as always
in front of Eloy's door, his massive scarred head lodged against
his awkward oversized paws. Avoiding Joe, his melancholy
eyes gazed sadly at Eloy.

"Point the barrel at the same place."

Joe obeyed. Duke uttered a barely audible sound, a sorrowful, remote whimper.

"Thumb back the hammer."

Duke died instantly. His head twitched and settled, his eyes
remained open, his body stiffened slightly, then relaxed, without altering its posture.

"Hell, this is no fun." Joe fought crying. Eloy was dry-eyed
as he said, "Now for the wolf."

Together, dazedly, they walked past the empty pens and
corrals to Wolfie's lair. Joe knew he was hit in the leg—his
left side, from the crotch down, burned numbly, without pain.
He was afraid to look down or touch himself; his foot made a
sloshing noise in his sneaker. Eloy staggered once, but when
Joe reached to steady him, the old rancher swatted the helping
hand away, leaving red goop on Joe's wrist. Immediately, he
apologized:

"Excuse me, Joe. You do me a great favor, but I'm angry
at you for being a killer. I'll be all right in a minute. Pay no
attention."

At the pen, Eloy lifted a wooden peg out of the lock-clasp
holding the door. Wolfie waited expectantly. Eloy said, "Hello,
Lobo. Here comes the Sebastiana."

The wolf faced away from them slightly, and stiffened, staring into the back field where grasses grew and killdeer fluttered
about hunting their meals, raising families. A meadowlark called.
Starlings twittered in the four chinese elms.

"Touch it to the back of his head, right behind the ear."

Again, Joe followed instructions.

"Adiós, Lobo."

The wolf never took his eyes off the green grass, the killdeer, the trees, and the starlings. Unlike the others, he did not
drop when the bullet took his life, but remained standing, feet
firmly planted, eyes still sucking in the springtime for almost

ten seconds before he settled apologetically to earth, landing in an almost composed posture, eyes closed, forever asleep.

"Now," said Eloy, "we will clean the acequia."

"Are you strong enough?"

"I'm all right. I have exactly enough strength left to do what I have to do."

Eloy handed the newer shovel to Joe, keeping the old one for himself. Together, they entered the back field. Removing his hat, Eloy said, "This is some day." He revolved slowly, committing the mood to memory before they began their chore.

How to describe this suddenly beautiful and innocent afternoon? Joe wondered. The sky enfolded the planet like a little girl cuddling a kitten. The air was pure enough to have been a contestant in the Miss Teen-age America Pageant. The lilt to birdsongs totally belied their claim to be territorial imperatives. Suddenly, all ornithological music was made for the sheer joy of it. Tree leaves shimmered like a priceless chlorophyll treasure. More noisy starlings had landed in the chinese elms. On fence posts, meadowlarks unleashed their sensationally lucid belltones. On every cattail in the valley, a redwing blackbird sang chinking melodies. And magpies cavorted in Eloy's orchard, arguing for the sheer exhilarating fun of it like big-city cornerboys. And Joe wondered: If I hold my shovel in front of me and let go, will it levitate, held up by the buoyancy of this marvelous unflawed weather?

Such peace, at the end of the line, was almost religious. Joe shook his head, closed his eyes, and breathed deeply, ears keyed for the sound of distant sirens.

Instead, a magpie scrawked. Eloy said, "Let's start."

They began at the upper fenceline, cleaning the small acequia, and headed slowly north. They trenched the bottom of the knee-deep ditch and chopped at the sides, widening it a little. All the excavated dirt went on the banks, building them up a little. It seemed like a tiny and insignificant artery: I'm working on a toy acequia, Joe thought. Yet the sunshine warmed his bones; his leg remained numb and without hurt. Incredibly, despite their sorrowful situation, he could feel tugs on his heart—it wished to warble. And beside him, all of a sudden,

Eloy began to whistle. Terrified by the amount of crusting blood on Eloy's clothes, Joe could only venture quick peeks at the indomitable octogenarian. In a cracked but defiant voice Eloy sang a Spanish song. Soon they were both sweating. Eloy said, "Doing this work has always made me feel happy. I refuse to let today be an exception."

When they encountered dry grasses along the ditch banks, Eloy struck a wooden kitchen match on his thumbnail and flicked it into the brown stalks, which caught fire instantly. Leaning on their shovel handles, they watched dreamily as flames raced along the ditch. The serenity seemed otherworldly. Eloy even gathered strength as they moved along. Apparently his wounds had quit bleeding. And when Joe briefly confronted his eyes, they were alive and bright and determined.

Nevertheless, he understood that Eloy was going to die. Death was bright and beautiful and intimate all around the man.

The acequia wandered through backyards, it almost touched the foundations of newly built homes. Where burrowing dogs had blocked it, they had to clear it out again. Where planks, over which cars traveled, had flattened the banks, they worked to build up those banks again.

Unable to reflect for long on their tragedy-in-the-making, Joe worked quietly, on the verge of tears, yet almost happy. Eloy remained dry-eyed. Obviously, some newcomers occasionally used the acequia water for their lawns and gardens. But basically, the agricultural area the ditch had once served was extinct. They cleared out no horse dung, they patched no muskrat excavations. Instead, they removed from the channel smashed tricycles, overturned doghouses, and bald car-tires. They lifted out a wrecked TV set, shifted a jungle gym thoughtlessly constructed atop the acequia, moved a woodpile completely blocking it, and pushed aside a dozen fifty-five-gallon oil drums, the refuse of a home builder who was into solar collectors.

Often people sunning themselves in their yards challenged Eloy and Joe: "Hey, what are you people doing on this property?"

"We're just cleaning the ditch." Eloy always answered without looking up as he methodically redug, rearchitected, and revitalized the ditch after its winter of disuse.

"But what's the point?" a Harvard-Law-grad-turned-cocaine-dealer asked. "Who uses it anymore?"

Eloy explained: "We have a field, and we plan to irrigate it once again. Our water rights are in order. So please don't interrupt the water flow while we're using it."

"I'm tired of having that trench in my backyard," a woman complained. "It's dangerous. I twisted my ankle in it last autumn."

Eloy apologized politely and ambled ahead, rhythmically scooping out dirt, repeating a ritual as old as the first Indian tribes that had entered the Chamisa Valley nine centuries ago. "This is a public thoroughfare," he told the woman, without once breaking his chopping rhythm.

"Well, I'm sick of it. Nobody ever uses it anymore."

"We use it," Eloy said.

"Why are you all bloody?" she asked.

"I fell on my shovel."

She stared after them, offended by their raggedy-ass, bloody clothes.

A few minutes later they climbed over a chain link fence into Vincent and Marion Bailey's yard and shoveled up to the back line of a badminton court while a spirited game was in progress.

"Hey, Joe," Vincent complained, "what's going on here?"

Eloy said, "You aren't allowed to block the acequia."

"What's an 'acequia'?"

Joe said, "It's the ditch that transports irrigation water to our field."

"But this is our badminton court. You can't just come in here and—"

Eloy removed a dirty old manila envelope from his dungaree pocket. "I got all the papers in here, if you want to look at them. This acequia is the Lovatos Ditch, and it has a legal priority date of 1790. It's still a valid artery, because we are using it. All the correct papers are on file down in the state engineer's office, if you don't believe me."

"Wait a second." Deftly, Vincent loaded and packed a pipe, and rather portentously lit it. "Now, first of all, the two of you are trespassing on private property."

"The acequia is public property," Eloy reiterated calmly. "It has a three-foot easement on either side."

"All right, let's have a look at those papers."

Eloy handed over the blood-soaked documents, and everybody else lolled around, impatiently cooling their heels, while

Vincent frowned, puffed, and prepared to wade through the papers. Now, finally, Joe heard sirens: across the valley, miles away, cop-car cherrytops were blinking.

"Hey," Vincent cried. "These are all in Spanish!"

"It's the law," Eloy explained. "For many years they had to be in both Spanish and English. You can get an English copy on file at the courthouse."

Vincent tried another tack. He smiled, shook his head, toed the earth. "Look, this is silly. I mean, nobody can tell me what to do with my own backyard. When I bought this land nobody said I had to leave this trench open so that water could go through. If I'd known that . . . listen, I mean, what's this water used for? None of my neighbors irrigates."

"I use it to grow grass and alfalfa," Eloy said.

"Aw, come on. Nobody grows alfalfa anymore. Hey, I've got an idea. You can sell your water rights, no? I mean, for cash on the barrelhead?"

Eloy nodded.

"Okay, then here's what we'll do. Since nobody except you uses it anymore, I'll buy it. Or anyway, me and my neighbors, we'll chip in and purchase the rights from you. Then we can fill in this hole, and everybody will be happy. How much are they worth, your water rights? A hundred dollars? Two hundred?"

"Two hundred thousand."

"What?"

While Vincent, Marion, and their perspiring guests looked on aghast, Eloy led Joe up through the center of the badminton court, restoring the trench to its original depth, and building ramparts on either side.

"Why are you two all bloody?" one of the guests called to Joe.

"We fell on our shovels."

Further along people glowered, chided, or made hostile jokes as Joe and Eloy progressed through one yard after another, clearing a channel for the trickle of Midnight River water that would irrigate the diminutive back field, perhaps for the final time.

Eventually, they reached the river and sat down to rest. The water was high and swift and a little cloudy from spring runoff. A band of dampness circled Eloy's hat; the armpits and back

of his workshirt were drenched with sweat as well as blood.
Joe too was soggy. And groggy. And unable to think.

"Well," he sighed, "we did it."

"I'm tired," Eloy scratched his nose. "It's stupid for just
two men to clean the acequia. We used to clean this little veina
with twenty men, and it only took half an hour."

"But we did it. The thing will function."

"I first cleaned this ditch when I was eleven. That would
have been what...?" He tilted his head back dreamily, calculating. "Around 1906, qué no?"

"Hace muchos años."

"Yes." Eloy nodded. Joe forced himself to check the old
man's eyes: queerly out of focus, they drifted. On his lips a
sad and compassionate smile. Joe's attention was drawn to
Eloy's hands: they seemed exquisite, tender, all-powerful. If
only they would touch him, embrace his shoulders, communicate safety ... courage ... well-being. But how to ask for that
succor?

Eloy made a simple gesture. "I am the last leaf upon this
tree, as the poet said. I never thought it would happen. Nobody
thought it *could* happen. Sometimes I have felt sad, I have
pitied myself, I have given myself headaches. Today I went a
little crazy. I thank you for helping me. We did not lose our
dignity...."

Joe said, "It's a beautiful day." The trees surrounding them
and the river literally shivered with silken tranquillity and the
condoling permanence of natural things. Way far away police
sirens continued faintly whining.

"Every day is so beautiful." Eloy smiled: playfulness leav-
ened his tired eyes. "I never woke up but what the day was
beautiful. Even if I cursed the rain or the winter ice, it was
okay. Weather is perfect, just like horses and sheep. Today is
perfect also. Right now I am calm. I have no regrets. My
sorrow is for you, and your future, and the future of your
family."

"It's all right. I'm responsible for everything I did."

Leaves rustled overhead as a breeze swept through the cottonwoods. Joe almost hallucinated; he could picture his daughter, with her pants rolled up, wading along, peering intently
into the magical depths. He could picture his son seated on a
nearby rock, mesmerized by the currents. An overwhelming
urge to protect the world hit Joe. Compassion flooded his heart;

his real connections were to human universals far more important than the petty brouhahas constituting his own little plight. Because he realized this, with luck one day he might actually have a legitimate shot at growing up to be something more than just another self-interested American consumer. He might learn to make contributions beyond his own bailiwick. If only—

Joe experienced a rare, disquieting thrill. Inside him stirred inklings of a new sense of responsibility, not just for his own offspring, but for things, ideas, human beings way beyond them. Was it too late to retrench his life in favor of society, humanity, the planet...?

Eloy murmured, "Even if we had succeeded in exchanging ownership of my property with each other, I could never have walked away from it on my own."

"Listen, please, I mean..."

"A bad thing is that you won't even get back your earnest money. The day after you paid it, I signed your check over to the hospital. If I had not done that, last Monday, their lawyer would have initiated proceedings to—I can't think of the word. To garnishee the land, is that it?"

"Close enough. But—"

"I thought perhaps a miracle would happen. You would earn the dollars with your drugs to pay me. After that, I hoped you would let me remain on your property. While you raised your new house, I thought perhaps I could stay, helping to build it. I feel ashamed, but I had those plans. Many times when you came over recently I deliberately avoided you by staying indoors or hiding in the outhouse so as not to face you. And every night I have lain awake desperately trying to think how, if somehow you managed to purchase the land, I could convince you to let me stay on."

"It's over," Joe said. "Neither of us wins."

"I was so torn apart," Eloy continued. "For months now my thoughts have been shady, desperate, criminal. I cannot tell you how much vergüenza I have felt. I prayed that Scott Harrison would die, that the bank would self-destruct. I thought of setting fire to the hospital. When I heard that you might be divorced, I was both happy and frightened. On the one hand I hoped that even if you bought my place, the legal snarls would allow me more time on it. On the other hand, it terrified me to think that then the land would be claimed by others. At which point my last hopes for staying on would have flown the coop. You understand, I held out for almost two years, waiting to unload it, stalling the hospital and other creditors, until I found you. I didn't want to give that land to just anybody."

"Why choose me? I'm hardly a paragon of working-class virtue."

"You had a look." Eloy chucked a pebble into the river. "I sensed a rapport. You did not seem as greedy as most others. I don't know. Your eyes appear gentle. . . ."

"I'm glad somebody sees something in me."

Eloy smiled thinly. "You were patient: for that I am grateful. Myself, I have been a sneak and a thief with you; for that I apologize. Yesterday afternoon, however, I reached a conclusion. I knew that my life here was almost over. That's why I loaded up the pickup and scattered my smaller animals. After that, I had plans to kill myself. First, however, I needed to kill Geronimo and Duke and Wolfie—but I couldn't pull the trigger. Then I realized I should clean the acequia and do a final irrigation before I died. And when I awoke this morning, all of a sudden I had a rage to live. That's when I mustered the absurd courage to rob the bank. It was stupid. We never had a chance."

Eloy paused. A kingfisher rattled by overhead. Joe threw a pebble into the water and kept silent.

"Last night I dreamed I irrigated my field. Then I took my old rifle, the .25-.35 I used to hunt deer with. Fitting a single bullet into the chamber, I blew out my old man's senile brains. I died with the smell of my land in my nose. With the cool wet smell of a newly irrigated field in my heart."

"You're not gonna die. Soon as we finish here, I'll drive us to the hospital. You're as strong as ten men."

"Let's put it this way. I realized, eventually, that I couldn't bump myself off. In fact, when I awoke this morning in puro sunshine, I realized all those suicide thoughts were just stupid prattlings inside a tired brain. I love this life too much to throw it away just like that because I am ashamed of acting like a fool. Nossir," he said, unable to look Joe in the eye, "while we have been cleaning this acequia, I realized that I never could commit suicide. In fact, I realized that if you had actually bought my land, in order to take possession of it for yourself, even though you paid for it, you would have had to kill me to claim it."

"I wouldn't have killed you."

"This life is too sweet," Eloy said fervently. "Also, I could tell you really don't know beans about land, or about animals. That one-point-seven acres needed me."

Joe was exhausted from the effort to withhold tears. "I know. I agree. And it's over."

"Yes, it's over...."

Joe turned away, ashamed to have Eloy see him weeping. "I'm sorry it came to this," he blubbered. "I wish it hadn't. I don't know what to say. I can't deal with all this calamity...."

Eloy tapped his back. "Calmate, primo. We're not finished yet. Are you hurt badly?"

"I can't tell. I'm afraid to touch myself. There's no hurt, only numbness."

"Bueno, let's go, then." Eloy coughed, wiped his nose, and hawked a bloody lunger into some weeds. "We must build a headgate fast in order to irrigate before dark."

First, they dug a passage through the riverbank, connecting the acequia with the fast-flowing river. Then they gathered large dead cottonwood branches, lodging them in the water at an upstream slant to the mouth of the vein, funneling water into the ditch. Blood swirled away from their legs as they waded in the water. After that, they canvassed the riverbank for stones and lugged large rocks over to the headgate, lodging them against branches to keep them in place. Finally, Eloy found some old tires which they filled with rocks and sank against the tree branches, weighting down the makeshift dam.

They followed the road home. In Eloy's back field, they gathered at the fence where the ditch entered the property, waiting for the water. It seemed to take forever. Eloy unzipped his fly and pissed into the ditch; the urine was red; Joe averted his eyes.

"For luck," Eloy explained, flicking the last drops off his penis and smiling wanly.

In due course, it appeared. Excitedly, Eloy exclaimed: "Ya lo veo!"

And it came—an onrushing rivulet of muddy water only a few inches deep, pushing before it an earthen foam full of dry grass-stalks. Eloy raised the guillotinelike wooden blade on one headgate, and water tumbled into the field, gathering momentum, spreading quickly.

"Now what do you do?" Joe asked.

The old man smiled. "I wait until this part of the field is soaked. Then I drop the headgate, and open another one farther across the field. After this half is done, I open the gate at that turn, over there, and flood the eastern half. It's easier there, the land is flat."

Eloy limped off, checking his headgates. The sun was behind him and sinking fast—it seemed as if the old man walked through liquid fire. As the sun lowered even further, the afternoon metamorphosed into a savage, golden time. Joe couldn't move. He was incapacitated by serenity, sadness, a sense of loss. Though he had no desire to sleep, his eyelids drooped sleepily. As birds landed in the widening puddle, their exclamations grew remote, reaching him like cries from a distant childhood. Joe savored the moment, afraid of it, and aware that if he survived he would be haunted by its memory. Eloy leaned on his shovel handle, his eyes absorbed by the fingers of water spreading into the short grass. Occasionally, when little ramparts of foam and dry grass-stems impeded the flow, he moved forward, applying his shovel with spare, certain strokes. Moving along the ditch banks, he flicked out an old beer can, chopped at a recalcitrant stalk, and occasionally wandered out into the field to check on progress.

Birds gathered in nearby trees, their sharp eyes hunting worms and bugs carried to the surface. A sparrow hawk landed on a dead cottonwood branch: head cocked, it searched the field for fleeing mice. Magpies swooped from the sky and waddled through inch-deep puddles, spearing tidbits. Redwing blackbirds, grackles, and starlings alighted in the water and began to gobble.

It was enough to make you weep for joy; it was enough to make you bawl in outrage. My God, Joe wondered frantically, how could anybody possibly protect this fragile earth, or the few people—like Eloy Irribarren—who truly cared for it? What would you have to do, sandbag the field, set up machine-gun nests, and do a national mailing each week soliciting funds for the legal fight to protect the Lovatos acequia, so that this tiny field would be allowed to produce what it had produced for a millennium?

"It sure looks pretty, and it sure is peaceful," Joe said.

"Yessir." Eloy took off his hat, drying his brow against the crook of an elbow. "It sure is."

It seemed to Joe as if his blood were slowing down. They perched on the ditch bank, their attention fixed hypnotically on the spreading water. Everything settled into place as if posing for a photograph—the birds, the leaves, shadows, the reflections of sky in the slowly spreading irrigation water. And the people did too: Joe saw the phantoms of his children in the scene again, robbed of the futures this sweet terrain could have given. Michael was half turned, looking backward expectantly at his father as if for permission to grow up; Heather, with her lips pursed, stared at a sparrow hawk on the dead cottonwood limb....

Eloy cried, "Dios! *Cabrón!*" Startled birds fluttered up, alighting in nearby trees as the old man dropped to his knees. Joe whirled, stumbling, and almost fell into the shallow flood. Eloy dug his right hand into the cool water, and splashed his face. Then, gasping, he made a plaintive, questioning gesture, and died.

Joe gathered up the old rancher. The body weighed next to nothing. Had the skin split, a diaphanous white fluff, such as that contained in a milkweed pod, would have floated out of the corpse. And Joe stood there, cradling Eloy's body in his arms, waiting for something to happen.

Birds sailed back down out of the trees, landed, and resumed searching for food. Transformed by the setting sun, the water glowed as in a burnished dream. Sirens wailed in a remote, molasses-thick way as if echoing from memory instead of real life. Everywhere, the air was absolutely stilled.

Joe closed his eyes, held on to Eloy tightly, and absorbed the tragic hush. Automobile tires crunched on driveway gravel; doors slammed; men called out orders. A voice, magnified through a bullhorn, issued an ultimatum. "Put the old guy down, Miniver, then place your hands on your head and walk toward us, slowly."

Joe kept his eyes shut tightly . . . and giggled, envisioning the headlines:

SPASTIC DUO FLUBS BANK HEIST: COPS NAIL "MAD DOG" MINIVER IN DAMP FIELD WITH DEAD GEEZER IN ARMS!

The sun warmed his eyes: he changed position slightly,

facing that radiant glow. Veins in the protective skin lay like pretty flower stalks across his blindness. Eloy seemed poised, ready to perish weightlessly from his arms. His children had apprehensive faces, so fragile. Heidi tried to cup his heart in her strong hands. They had missed the point, coveting wrong things, wasting precious energy. If only a person could protect the Dianas and Irénés and Eloys. Tears curled over his upper lip; his tongue moved, tasting salt. Joe Hill had called out his own finish: "Ready . . . aim . . . *fire!*" Gently, Joe bent over, eyes still closed, and relieved himself of the human burden, setting Eloy's feathery corpse on the ditch bank. Straightening, then, he faced them blindly, and, removing Diana's pistol from his pocket, he pointed it at where he surmised they had gathered.

Joe knew it was a foolhardy move. "I don't wanna die," he whispered. But it seemed absolutely important, at last in his slipshod existence, to make that gesture.

He never heard the gunshot: nor felt death when it hit him.

Then darkness rolled softly across the soaking field; it consumed the trees and, soon, the entire valley. Finally, it lapped up gently to cover the brooding mountains and declared itself in residence over everything for a while.

Epilogue

Fear not.
Departure toward the South
Brings good fortune.

A millions years ago during his college days, if he had no classes in the early spring afternoons, Joe would lie down on his bed, tune the radio to soft pop music, and open the window a bit, allowing lilac and daffodil breezes to drowsily ruffle his hair. Still as a mouse in mellifluous sunshine, he would lie, happily cupping his groin as he leisurely drifted into sleep. For maybe an hour, just beneath the surface, he would dream, floating through a delectably lazy time, free of all woes, saturated with a sense of voluptuous irresponsibility. Then slowly he would emerge into wakefulness again. Whatever guided those wonderful soporific sessions let nothing jar his indolent ascent back into the world. And for a while, even with his eyes open, his body seemed caught in the longest, sweetest orgasm ever. When finally he urged himself into a sitting position, gingerly settled his feet on the floor, and ran fingers through his matted hair, it felt almost like a crime not to prolong forever the woozy, syrup-laden mood.

It resembled that now, awakening. Lulled by a demure background drone and the swishing of a weightless fabric such as silk, Joe came to slowly, savoring the luscious mood. He thought at first, Perhaps I'm hospital-bound, morphined into rapture and protected from terrestrial noises by a sophisticated bubble-shaped plastic breathing apparatus enclosing my entire body. But why open his eyes, finding out? This was too peaceful.

A slow and thoughtful lurch occurred. Was he floating, lodged in Ralph's somehow airborne sensory isolation tank? Again he rocked gently, as if on a fuzzy vapor, this time to the other side. Joe smiled, listening to the easy, nostalgic music from his college days. Instead, he heard a vaguely familiar rustle. Flowers? Satin sheets? *Wings?* His body felt creamy, infinitely delicate, and clean, as if he had just been bathed in very hot water, patted dry with a soft white towel, and sprinkled with Johnson's Baby Powder. Ecstasy was the name of this game, and Joe lay quite still, hoping to prolong it indefinitely.

Again he tilted, this time semi-severely, in a way he associated only with airplanes. And that did it. Though the action was smooth, perfectly controlled, at the buzz word *airplane* his heart lurched, and a tremor danced from his toes to his eyelids, killing the peaceful fog nullifying his anxiety centers.

Nevertheless, Joe held his eyes shut, desperate to sustain this carefree state. Such passive, erotic drunkenness infused his slugabed body. Heaven had never felt better.

Heaven?

Airplanes?

Joe thought, Oh no, I'd better open at least *one* eye.

He lifted the lid carefully, as if hesitantly raising it with delicate tweezers. And at first, the exterior world made little sense. What was this, the inside of a cocoon from the caterpillar's perspective? About a foot above Joe's head the rounded inner wall of an enormous silken-fibered chrysalis emitted a nacreous glow. Behind closed eyes he had thought himself prone; however, now he beheld himself seated in a body-molded cottony armchair, his head resting on an invisible cushion.

Joe opened the other eye.

He was, in effect, imprisoned in a shiny, spun-glass tube that quivered faintly, being airborne. Through a circular rent in the enveloping fiber—a tear-shaped porthole—Joe could see a limpid crepuscular sky, a tilted horizon, and the merging tones of the Chamisa Valley far below sprinkled with salt-and-peppery lights.

Aloft, in a soundless flying machine, and rising!

Before him, in the pearly, glowing cocoon, sat another figure, huge and skulking, its back presented, obviously piloting the smooth-bored, instrumentless rocket. Even without tapping one shoulder and asking to see a face, Joe knew with whom he was dealing: those wings he'd have recognized anywhere.

Not so much bitterly as bewilderedly, Joe exclaimed, "*You* again!"

Without turning, Lorin said, "Yes. But this time, Joe, it's for reals. That sure was a dumb move you pulled down there."

Joe's recollection had a blank space. "What are you talking about?"

"You don't remember?"

"My head feels funny, like there's a hole in my memory."

"And well there should be."

"How so?"

"That's where the bullet entered."

"Bullet?"

"When you pointed the little gun at them, they killed you, Joe. With one shot. Right in the middle of your forehead."

"Who's they? And where am I?"

"The 'cops,' I believe you call them. They arrived shortly after you tried to rob the bank. I must say, the whole thing was very messy. As for your whereabouts, you're with me, and we're taking a trip. Your immortal soul, Joe, is all that remains, and we're off to train it a bit before selecting your next body."

"Oh Christ. You're kidding!"

"Not me. Honesty is our most important product."

"There's no such thing as an afterlife."

"Tut tut, my friend. The proof is in the custard."

" 'Pudding.' "

"Beg pardon?"

"The expression is 'The proof is in the pudding.' "

"Oh yes, of course."

Incredulously, Joe peered earthward. Spread out below him lay Chamisaville. Lights had blazed on at the Pueblo's dog-racing track; the green-and-white Tennis Heaven bubble glowed eerily. Most automobiles sluggishly negotiating the town's clogged arteries had turned on head lamps as the dusk thickened. An excruciatingly poignant sadness struck Joe's heart as he viewed the scene: My God, I don't want to leave! Goodbye, earth; good-bye, Michael and Heather, I love you; good-bye, Heidi, I'm sorry....

"I'm too young," he murmured aloud.

Lorin cocked his head knowingly, like a New York cabby: "That's what they all say. You should have listened to Nancy Ryan."

"Why? What would I have learned?"

"That a trip like this is more fun when you're still alive. Not only that, but you could have learned things enabling you to inhabit your earthbound body for a longer and more enjoyable spell than you seemed to have managed as a raving agnostic."

"I really dislike your superior airs." Joe spoke guardedly, wondering if he now had any leverage with the offensive feathered creep.

"Feeling is mutual, Joe, I assure you. This has been a positively stinko assignment. In fact, after the orientation period,

I hope they send you back as a newt or as an untouchable from Calcutta."

"I thought angels weren't supposed to be vindictive."

"Since when do you—an atheist, a Communist, and an adulterer—know anything about the rules governing angels?"

"Well, whatever happened to Christian charity?"

"Such as that which launched the crusades or tosses hand grenades into the streets of Belfast?"

Joe said, "I can't believe I'm sitting here, having a conversation with a frigging... It's not *real*! How long until we get where we're going?"

"Time? What's that, a human concept? We're no longer dealing with such phenomena."

"But it's growing dark down there; the world is turning; clocks keep ticking."

"Where we're headed there's no nighttime, Joe. A wonderful white light infuses everything always."

"Stop this whateveritis, I need to get off!"

"Sorry, fella. We're on a Direct Current to the Source."

"What's that supposed to mean?"

"In layman's terms? We'll soon lock on to a beam guiding us home. You might say we'll be on automatic pilot. I'm just here to keep you company. They call me a Guide, so to speak, but you haven't taken very well to guidance, lately. I thought your experience at the bank might forge some humility, but I can see I underestimated your ego. You sure got an ugly soul, Joe. What makes it so heinous is that you often fooled everybody with your patina of humanistic respectablity. Yet underneath your heart was *sooooo* black."

"Thanks for the pep talk. What is this preparation for, suicide?"

"Suicide occurs down there, friend—not up here. And anyway, you already committed it."

Joe said, "I want out of this predicament immediately."

"Tant pis. No dice. Against the rules, I'm afraid."

"Rules, shmools, I got rights."

"Rights, shmights." Lorin sighed heavily. "Sometimes I wish souls weren't immortal. I'm tired of fussing with ingrates."

They banked again; once more Joe studied the land below. In the gathering darkness, Chamisaville seemed like a city of hundreds of thousands of inhabitants. Bright bulbs and soft beacons, streetlamps and headlights. Aluminum TV-glares marked every house, fell across countless lawns. Spring tree leaves—of cottonwoods and chinese elms—caught the last metallic daylight echo and, from on high, resembled burnished pompoms, remote and reminiscent of innocence. Viewed objectively, it seemed like a harmless and pretty civilization. White, flea-sized bodies of bikinied women paddled through the turquoise water of illuminated swimming pools. North of town, colorful Christmas-tree baubles at the Dynamite Shrine's outdoor dance pavilion twinkled merrily—Japanese lanterns, Joe knew: there would be old-fashioned music to which geriatrics could fox-trot.

Ay, those safe and lackluster suburbs! Floodlit kids in Bermuda shorts played basketball on driveway cement slabs. Two hundred cars in the General Custer Drive-In Movie waited for the picture to roll. Traffic lights blinked green, yellow and red. Neon lights fitzed, sputtered, and bap-a-dapped on the plaza, along the strip. Little groups of crimson flares flickered at countless construction sites. And white tipi cones reflected faint seven o'clock glimmers. Christmas, twenty-four hours a day, three hundred and sixty-five days per annum.

Joe said, "Listen, wherever we're headed, count me out."

"You have no choice in the matter, Joe. It's all inevitable."

"Oh yeah?" Reaching forward, Joe slipped his right arm around Lorin's neck, and quickly locked his forearm against the angel's throat by grabbing the right wrist in his left hand.

Lorin squawked. "Hey! Ouch! What are you *doing*?"

"I'm gonna get violent," Joe hissed threateningly. "Unless you change our destination."

The second Lorin tried to struggle, Joe clamped down on his windpipe, hissing *"No tricks, featherbrain!"* Lorin sagged. Weakly, he cried, "Ease up a little, for pete's sake, you're choking me!"

"I'll kill you unless you do what I ask!"

"You can't 'kill' angels, Joe. And anyway, I've been 'dead' since 1723."

"I'll beat you up. I'll create absolute mayhem. I'll rip all the feathers from your wings."

"Not the wings!" Lorin pleaded. "You've already made me look horribly tatty. *Ouch! Don't press so hard!* You'll leave a mark."

"I'll do more than leave a mark," Joe growled menacingly.

"I'll crush your windpipe, I'll tear your ears off with my teeth, I'll crumble your feathers in my fist, I'll kick in your bloated tummy—"

"Stop!" Lorin squealed. "What do you want?"

"Fly me to Cuba."

The angel gasped. "Oh no. I can't do that!"

Joe jerked his forearm viciously against Lorin's throat. "I'll make it hell for you if you don't."

"But you misunderstand. I can't fly over a Communist country."

"Who says?"

"We'll disintegrate."

"Bullshit. Why?"

"They don't believe. Ouch, *you're hurting me*!"

"What has belief got to do with it?"

"For starters, I don't exist if you don't believe in me."

"Hogwash. I never believed in angels, but you're here."

"Correction. You *thought* you didn't believe in angels."

Joe said, "I don't feel like arguing the semantics of bourgeois philosophy right now. Just shuttup and steer toward Cuba."

"What do you plan to do when we get there?"

"Jump clear of this thing. Does it have a door? Are there any parachutes on board?"

"Not necessary, Joe—you'll float. But you'll never reach the jungle, I guarantee."

"How come?"

"You'll evaporate as soon as you float within their Cerebral Ionosphere."

"You're lying." Joe yanked back a little.

"Urgh! Stop!" Lorin twitched and gurgled; his ham hands fluttered uselessly at Joe's forearm.

"Take it back then, and steer us for Cuba—am I communicating?"

"Okay." Lorin coughed painfully and Joe released his pressure a little. "Whatever you say, just don't hurt me anymore, please. I'll get in dutch, but so what? You're the most recalcitrant case I've meddled with in a decade. When I return I'm putting in for rotation to a more civilized nation, like Nepal."

All through the long night they hummed across America in their pearly blue cocoon. To forestall any monkey business, Joe maintained a loose stranglehold on Lorin's throat. He expected to grow drowsy and fatigued, yet such weakness never

"We just hit the outer limits of their Cerebral Ionosphere. You better hang on to your hat. The Mental Propaganda Belt over Communist countries can buffet you like a hurricane. We'll be lucky if negative anti-Christ forces don't blow us apart!"

They rolled, pitched, dropped a hundred feet in atheist pockets, floundered through invisible shockwaves caused by the outer atmospheric aura of Socialism, and shivered and stewed as if under the onslaught of invisible lightning bolts.

Lorin pleaded with Joe: "If you're going to jump, for pete's sake, man, *go*! Have pity on me! I don't want to die!"

"Die?" Joe cocked his head curiously. "How can you die, you're immortal."

"Under some conditions, yes. Under others, no. Oh please, have a heart."

Joe had lost his fear. In fact, despite their topsy-turvy progress, an almost beatific calm had settled into his soul. With great consideration for his fellow traveler, he disengaged the throatlock. Lorin slumped forward, rubbing his neck. "My God," he whimpered petulantly, "you're such a brute."

"I'm going, now. Thanks for the ride." With that, Joe plucked a single cream-colored souvenir feather from Lorin's wing, then eased himself erect and leisurely propelled himself through the shiny fabric of the cocoon. Expecting to be clobbered by a blast, Joe doubled up into a tuck position, arms flung across his face. But he tumbled into blue sunny space as effortlessly as any astronaut indulging a zero-gravity walk, buoyed by the myraid tugs of opposing stars.

Through a crack in his arms, Joe caught sight of the silver, tear-shaped husk that had carried him this far. It whisked away, diminishing quickly, like a wind-borne autumn leaf, becoming invisible against the ultramarine-blue sky and the verdant, expansive sea.

Unfolding, Joe turned his rapt attention to Cuba, stretching his arms wide in a flying position as he had seen in sky-diver photographs . . . beneath him lay the entire island.

Oh how the sweetness of a fresh and real start infused his spectral protoplasm! Tiny serene cloud puffs polka-dotted that sliver of green set in the brilliant emerald ocean. The shadows of her forested sierras, the white ribbons of her unspoiled beaches made him ache for the Garden of Eden, Socialist style. Granted, he was floating toward a myth, completely ignorant of what might lie in store. Could Lorin possibly be correct? When he entered a concentrated Communist ionosphere, would the power of atheist ions cause him to crumble?

No matter. If the soul had an eternal power, then he would land upon the courageous territory below, locate the body of anything from a butterfly to an aged cane cutter in need of animation, and try to be more worthy this time around, aided by his proximity to a more compassionate historical reality.

And if it developed that his presence on the airwaves was at best a bourgeois hype . . . so what? If this sensitive phantom he seemed to be was nothing more than a brief, vital minute about to burn out, or a complex death dream taking place during those moments between the bullet's entry and his brain's total demise . . . well, not to worry.

For his reveries at this instant in time were so full of hope he wanted to shout "Hallelujah!"

A soaring albatross, its wings set, its beautiful eyes searching lazily, glided by.

In his fist, Lorin's wing-feather began to disintegrate. The barbs came apart slowly, sprinkling into the air like pepper, evaporating. Very shortly, all that remained in his fingers was a hollow quill. Then it too crumbled, became dust, and trickled away into eternity.

Yet Joe remained intact, and continued falling toward the green hills and succulent valleys of a Communist country.

About the Author

John Nichols lives in Taos, New Mexico. *The Milagro Beanfield War, The Magic Journey,* and *The Nirvana Blues* make up his New Mexico trilogy. His most recent novel is *Conjugal Bliss.*